D1431045

140

THE THREE CLERKS

Oxford University Press, Walton Street, Oxford OX2 6DP

OXFORD   LONDON   GLASGOW

NEW YORK   TORONTO   MELBOURNE   WELLINGTON

IBADAN   NAIROBI   DAR ES SALAAM   LUSAKA   CAPE TOWN

KUALA LUMPUR   SINGAPORE   JAKARTA   HONG KONG   TOKYO

DELHI   BOMBAY   CALCUTTA   MADRAS   KARACHI

THE THREE CLERKS

BY

ANTHONY TROLLOPE

WITH AN
INTRODUCTION BY

W. TEIGNMOUTH SHORE

OXFORD UNIVERSITY PRESS

ANTHONY TROLLOPE

Born, London   .   .   .   .   April 24, 1815
Died, London   .   .   .   .   December 6, 1882

'*The Three Clerks*' *was first published in* 1858. *In* '*The World's Classics*' *it was first published in* 1907, *and reprinted in* 1925, 1929, 1943, 1952, 1959, 1978

ISBN 0 19 250140 2

PRINTED IN GREAT BRITAIN
BY THOMSON LITHO LTD,
EAST KILBRIDE, SCOTLAND

INTRODUCTION

THERE is the proper mood and the just environment for the reading as well as for the writing of works of fiction, and there can be no better place for the enjoying of a novel by Anthony Trollope than under a tree in Kensington Gardens of a summer day. Under a tree in the avenue that reaches down from the Round Pond to the Long Water. There, perhaps more than anywhere else, lingers the early Victorian atmosphere. As we sit beneath our tree, we see in the distance the dun, red-brick walls of Kensington Palace, where one night Princess Victoria was awakened to hear that she was Queen; there in quaint, hideously ugly Victorian rooms are to be seen Victorian dolls and other playthings; the whole environment is early Victorian. Here to the mind's eye how easy it is to conjure up ghosts of men in baggy trousers and long flowing whiskers, of prim women in crinolines, in hats with long trailing feathers and with ridiculous little parasols, or with Grecian-bends and chignons—church-parading to and fro beneath the trees or by the water's edge—perchance, even the fascinating Lady Crinoline and the elegant Mr. Macassar Jones, whose history has been written by Clerk Charley in the pages we are introducing to the ' gentle reader '. As a poetaster of an earlier date has written :—

> Where Kensington high o'er the neighbouring lands
> 'Midst green and sweets, a royal fabric, stands,

> And sees each spring, luxuriant in her bowers,
> A snow of blossoms, and a wild of flowers,
> The dames of Britain oft in crowds repair
> To gravel walks, and unpolluted air.
> Here, while the town in damps and darkness lies,
> They breathe in sunshine, and see azure skies;
> Each walk, with robes of various dyes bespread,
> Seems from afar a moving tulip bed,
> Where rich brocades and glossy damasks glow,
> And chintz, the rival of the showery bow.

Indeed, the historian of social manners, when dealing with the Victorian period, will perforce have recourse to the early volumes of Punch and to the novels of Thackeray, Dickens, and Trollope.

There are certain authors of whom personally we know little, but of whose works we cannot ever know enough, such a one for example as Shakespeare; others of whose lives we know much, but for whose works we can have but scant affection: such is Doctor Johnson; others who are intimate friends in all their aspects, as Goldsmith and Charles Lamb; yet others, who do not quite come home to our bosoms, whose writings we cannot entirely approve, but for whom and for whose works we find a soft place somewhere in our hearts, and such a one is Anthony Trollope. His novels are not for every-day reading, any more than are those of Marryat and Borrow—to take two curious examples. There are times and moods and places in which it would be quite impossible to read *The Three Clerks*; others in which this story is almost wholly delightful. With those who are fond of bed-reading Trollope should ever be a favourite, and it is no small compliment to say this, for small is the noble army of authors who have given us books which can enchant in the witching hour between waking and slumber. It is probable that all lovers of letters have their favourite bed-

books. Thackeray has charmingly told us of his. Of
the few novels that can really be enjoyed when the reader
is settling down for slumber almost all have been set
forth by writers who—consciously or unconsciously—have
placed character before plot ; Thackeray himself, Miss
Austen, Borrow, Marryat, Sterne, Dickens, Goldsmith
and—Trollope.

Books are very human in their way, as what else should
they be, children of men and women as they are ? Just
as with human friends so with book friends, first impres-
sions are often misleading ; good literary coin sometimes
seems to ring untrue, but the untruth is in the ear of the
reader, not of the writer.   For instance, Trollope has many
odd and irritating tricks which are apt to scare off those
who lack perseverance and who fail to understand that
there must be something admirable in that which was
once much admired by the judicious.   He shares with
Thackeray the sinful habit of pulling up his readers with
a wrench by reminding them that what is set before them
is after all mere fiction and that the characters in whose
fates they are becoming interested are only marionettes.
With Dickens and others he shares the custom, so irritating
to us of to-day, of ticketing his personages with clumsy,
descriptive labels, such as, in *The Three Clerks*, Mr. Chaffanbrass, Sir Gregory Hardlines, Sir Warwick West End,
Mr. Neverbend, Mr. Whip Vigil, Mr. Nogo and Mr. Gitemthruet.   He must plead guilty, also, to some bad ways
peculiarly his own, or which he made so by the thorough-
ness with which he indulged in them.   He moralizes in
his own person in deplorable manner : is not this terrible :
—' Poor Katie !—dear, darling, bonnie Katie !—sweet,
sweetest, dearest child ! why, oh, why, has that mother
of thine, that tender-hearted loving mother, put thee

unguarded in the way of such perils as this ? Has she not sworn to herself that over thee at least she would watch as a hen over her young, so that no unfortunate love should quench thy young spirit, or blanch thy cheek's bloom ? ' Is this not sufficient to make the gentlest reader swear to himself ?

Fortunately this and some other appalling passages occur after the story is in full swing and after the three Clerks and those with whom they come into contact have proved themselves thoroughly interesting companions. Despite all his old-fashioned tricks Trollope does undoubtedly succeed in giving blood and life to most of his characters ; they are not as a rule people of any great eccentricity or of profound emotions ; but ordinary, every-day folk, such as all of us have met, and loved or endured. Trollope fills very adequately a space between Thackeray and Dickens, of whom the former deals for the most part with the upper ten, the latter with the lower ' ten ' ; Trollope with the suburban and country-town ' ten ' ; the three together giving us a very complete and detailed picture of the lives led by our grandmothers and grandfathers, whose hearts were in the same place as our own, but whose manners of speech, of behaviour and of dress have now entered into the vague region known as the ' days of yore '.

The Three Clerks is an excellent example of Trollope's handiwork. The development of the plot is sufficiently skilful to maintain the reader's interest, and the major part of the characters is lifelike, always well observed and sometimes depicted with singular skill and insight. Trollope himself liked the work well :—

' The plot is not so good as that of *The Macdermots* ; nor are any characters in the book equal to those of Mrs. Proudie and the Warden ; but the work has a more continued interest, and contains the first well-described love-scene that I ever wrote. The passage in which Kate Woodward, thinking she will die, tries to take leave of the lad she loves, still brings tears to my eyes when I read it. I had not the heart to kill her. I never could do that. And I do not doubt that they are living happily together to this day.

' The lawyer Chaffanbrass made his first appearance in this novel, and I do not think that I have cause to be ashamed of him. But this novel now is chiefly noticeable to me from the fact that in it I introduced a character under the name of Sir Gregory Hardlines, by which I intended to lean very heavily on that much loathed scheme of competitive examination, of which at that time Sir Charles Trevelyan was the great apostle. Sir Gregory Hardlines was intended for Sir Charles Trevelyan—as any one at the time would know who had taken an interest in the Civil Service. " We always call him Sir Gregory," Lady Trevelyan said to me afterwards when I came to know her husband. I never learned to love competitive examination; but I became, and am, very fond of Sir Charles Trevelyan. Sir Stafford Northcote, who is now Chancellor of the Exchequer, was then leagued with his friend Sir Charles, and he too appears in *The Three Clerks* under the feebly facetious name of Sir Warwick West End.

' But for all that *The Three Clerks* was a good novel.'

Which excerpt from Trollope's *Autobiography* serves to throw light not only upon the novel in question, but also upon the character of its author.

Trollope served honestly and efficiently for many a long year in the Post Office, achieving his entrance through a farce of an examination :—

'The story of that examination', he says, 'is given accurately in the opening chapters of a novel written by me, called *The Three Clerks*. If any reader of this memoir would refer to that chapter and see how Charley Tudor was supposed to have been admitted into the Internal Navigation Office, that reader will learn how Anthony Trollope was actually admitted into the Secretary's office of the General Post Office in 1834.'

Poe's description of the manner in which he wrote *The

Raven is incredible, being probably one of his solemn and sombre jokes; equally incredible is Trollope's confession of his humdrum, mechanical methods of work. Doubtless he believed he was telling the whole truth, but only here and there in his *Autobiography* does he permit to peep out touches of light, which complete the portrait of himself. It is impossible that for the reader any character in fiction should live which has not been alive to its creator; so is it with Trollope, who, speaking of his characters, says,

'I have wandered alone among the rocks and woods, crying at their grief, laughing at their absurdities, and thoroughly enjoying their joy. I have been impregnated with my own creations till it has been my only excitement to sit with the pen in my hand, and drive my team before me at as quick a pace as I could make them travel.'

There is a plain matter-of-factness about Trollope's narratives which is convincing, making it difficult for the reader to call himself back to fact and to remember that he has been wandering in a world of fiction. In *The Three Clerks*, the young men who give the tale its title are all well drawn. To accomplish this in the cases of Alaric and Charley Tudor was easy enough for a skilled writer, but to breathe life into Harry Norman was difficult. At first he appears to be a lay-figure, a priggish dummy of an immaculate hero, a failure in portraiture; but toward the end of the book it is borne in on us that our dislike had been aroused by the lifelike nature of the painting, dislike toward a real man, priggish indeed in many ways, but with a very human strain of obstinacy and obdurateness, which few writers would have permitted to have entered into the make-up of any of their heroes. Of the other men, Undy Scott may be named as among the very

best pieces of portraiture in Victorian fiction; touch after
touch of detail is added to the picture with really admirable skill, and Undy lives in the reader's memory as
vividly as he must have existed in the imagination of his
creator.   There are some strong and curious passages in
Chapter XLIV, in which the novelist contrasts the lives and
fates of Varney, Bill Sykes and Undy Scott; they stir the
blood, proving uncontestibly that Undy Scott was as real
to Trollope as he is to us: ' The figure of Undy swinging
from a gibbet at the broad end of Lombard Street would
have an effect.   Ah, my fingers itch to be at the rope.'

Trollope possessed the rare and beautiful gift of painting
the hearts and souls of young girls, and of this power he
has given an admirable example in Katie Woodward.
It would be foolish and cruel to attempt to epitomize, or
rather to draw in miniature, this portrait that Trollope has
drawn at full length; were it not for any other end, those
that are fond of all that is graceful and charming in young
womanhood should read *The Three Clerks*, so becoming
the friend, nay, the lover of Katie.   Her sisters are not
so attractive, simply because nature did not make them
so; a very fine, faithful woman, Gertrude; a dear thing,
Linda.   All three worthy of their mother, she who, as we
are told in a delicious phrase, ' though adverse to a fool '
' could sympathize with folly '.

These eight portraits are grouped in the foreground of
this ' conversation ' piece, the background being filled
with slighter but always live figures.

Particularly striking, as being somewhat unusual with
Trollope, is the depiction of the public-house, ' The Pig
and Whistle ', in Norfolk Street, the landlady, Mrs. Davis,
and the barmaid, Norah Geraghty.   We can almost
smell the gin, the effluvia of stale beer, the bad tobacco,

hear the simpers and see the sidlings of Norah, feel sick
with and at Charley :—he ' got up and took her hand ; and
as he did so, he saw that her nails were dirty.   He put
his arms round her waist and kissed her ; and as he
caressed her, his olfactory nerves perceived that the
pomatum in her hair was none of the best . . . and then
he felt very sick '.   But, oh, why ' olfactory nerves ' ?
Was it vulgar in early Victorian days to call a nose a nose ?

How far different would have been Dickens's treatment
of such characters and such a scene ; out of Mrs. Davis
and Norah he would have extracted fun, and it would
never have entered into his mind to have brought such
a man as Charley into contact with them in a manner
that must hurt that young hero's susceptibilities.
Thackeray would have followed a third way, judging by
his treatment of the Fotheringay and Captain Costigan,
partly humorous, partly satirical, partly serious.

Trollope was not endowed with any spark of wit, his
satire tends towards the obvious, and his humour is mild,
almost unconscious, as if he could depict for us what of
the humorous came under his observation without himself
seeing the fun in it.   Where he sets forth with intent to
be humorous he sometimes attains almost to the tragic ;
there are few things so sad as a joke that misses fire or
a jester without sense of humour.

Of the genius of a writer of fiction there is scarce any
other test so sure as this of the reality of his characters.
Few are the authors that have created for us figures of
fiction that are more alive to us than the historic shadows
of the past, whose dead bones historians do not seem to
be able to clothe with flesh and blood.   Trollope hovers
on the border line between genius and great talent, or
rather it would be more fair to say that with regard to

him opinions may justly differ. For our own part we hold that his was not talent streaked with genius, but rather a jog-trot genius alloyed with mediocrity. He lacked the supreme unconsciousness of supreme genius, for of genius as of talent there are degrees. There are characters in *The Three Clerks* that live ; those who have read the tale must now and again when passing Norfolk Street, Strand, regret that it would be waste of time to turn down that rebuilt thoroughfare in search of ' The Pig and Whistle ', which was ' one of these small tranquil shrines of Bacchus in which the god is worshipped witn as constant a devotion, though with less noisy demonstration of zeal than in his larger and more public temples '. Alas ; lovers of Victorian London must lament that such shrines grow fewer day by day ; the great thoroughfares know them no more ; they hide nervously in old-world corners, and in them you will meet old-world characters, who not seldom seem to have lost themselves on their way to the pages of Charles Dickens.

Despite the advent of electric tramways, Hampton would still be recognized by the three clerks, ' the little village of Hampton, with its old-fashioned country inn, and its bright, quiet, grassy river.' Hampton is now as it then was, the ' well-loved resort of cockneydom '.

So let us alight from the tramcar at Hampton, and look about on the outskirts of the village for ' a small old-fashioned brick house, abutting on the road, but looking from its front windows on to a lawn and garden, which stretched down to the river '. Surbiton Cottage it is called. Let us peep in at that merry, happy family party ; and laugh at Captain Cuttwater, waking from his placid sleep, rubbing his eyes in wonderment, and asking, ' What the devil is all the row about ? '

But it is only with our mind's eye that we can see Surbiton Cottage—a cottage in the air it is, but more substantial to some of us than many a real jerry-built villa of red brick and stucco.

Old-fashioned seem to us the folk who once dwelt there, old-fashioned in all save that their hearts were true and their outlook on life sane and clean; they live still, though their clothes be of a quaint fashion and their talk be of yesterday.

Who knows but that they will live long after we who love them shall be dead and turned to dust?

W. TEIGNMOUTH SHORE.

CONTENTS

THE THREE CLERKS

CHAPTER I

THE WEIGHTS AND MEASURES

ALL the English world knows, or knows of, that branch
of the Civil Service which is popularly called the Weights
and Measures. Every inhabitant of London, and every
casual visitor there, has admired the handsome edifice
which generally goes by that name, and which stands so
conspicuously confronting the Treasury Chambers. It
must be owned that we have but a slip-slop way of christen-
ing our public buildings. When a man tells us that he
called on a friend at the Horse Guards, or looked in at
the Navy Pay, or dropped a ticket at the Woods and
Forests, we put up with the accustomed sounds, though
they are in themselves, perhaps, indefensible. The
'Board of Commissioners for Regulating Weights and
Measures', and the 'Office of the Board of Commissioners
for Regulating Weights and Measures', are very long
phrases; and as, in the course of this tale, frequent
mention will be made of the public establishment in
question, the reader's comfort will be best consulted by
maintaining its popular though improper denomination.

It is generally admitted that the Weights and Measures
is a well-conducted public office; indeed, to such a degree
of efficiency has it been brought by its present very excellent secretary, the two very worthy assistant-secretaries,
and especially by its late most respectable chief clerk,
that it may be said to stand quite alone as a high model
for all other public offices whatever. It is exactly anti-
podistic of the Circumlocution Office, and as such is always

referred to in the House of Commons by the gentleman
representing the Government when any attack on the
Civil Service, generally, is being made.

And when it is remembered how great are the interests
entrusted to the care of this board, and of these secretaries
and of that chief clerk, it must be admitted that nothing
short of superlative excellence ought to suffice the nation.
All material intercourse between man and man must be
regulated, either justly or unjustly, by weights and
measures ; and as we of all people depend most on such
material intercourse, our weights and measures should to
us be a source of never-ending concern. And then that
question of the decimal coinage ! is it not in these days
of paramount importance ? Are we not disgraced by the
twelve pennies in our shilling, by the four farthings in our
penny ? One of the worthy assistant-secretaries, the
worthier probably of the two, has already grown pale
beneath the weight of this question. But he has sworn
within himself, with all the heroism of a Nelson, that he
will either do or die. He will destroy the shilling or the
shilling shall destroy him. In his more ardent moods he
thinks that he hears the noise of battle booming round
him, and talks to his wife of Westminster Abbey or
a peerage. Then what statistical work of the present age
has shown half the erudition contained in that essay lately
published by the secretary on *The Market Price of Coined
Metals* ? What other living man could have compiled
that chronological table which is appended to it, showing
the comparative value of the metallic currency for the
last three hundred years ? Compile it indeed ! What
other secretary or assistant-secretary belonging to any
public office of the present day, could even read it and
live ? It completely silenced Mr. Muntz for a session, and
even *The Times* was afraid to review it.

Such a state of official excellence has not, however,
been obtained without its drawbacks, at any rate in the
eyes of the unambitious tyros and unfledged novitiates
of the establishment. It is a very fine thing to be pointed
out by envying fathers as a promising clerk in the Weights
and Measures, and to receive civil speeches from mammas
with marriageable daughters. But a clerk in the Weights

and Measures is soon made to understand that it is not for him to—

> Sport with Amaryllis in the shade.

It behoves him that his life should be grave and his pursuits laborious, if he intends to live up to the tone of those around him. And as, sitting there at his early desk, his eyes already dim with figures, he sees a jaunty dandy saunter round the opposite corner to the Council Office at eleven o'clock, he cannot but yearn after the pleasures of idleness.

> Were it not better done, as others use ?

he says or sighs. But then comes Phoebus in the guise of the chief clerk, and touches his trembling ears—

> As he pronounces lastly on each deed,
> Of so much fame, in Downing Street—expect the meed.

And so the high tone of the office is maintained.

Such is the character of the Weights and Measures at this present period of which we are now treating. The exoteric crowd of the Civil Service, that is, the great body of clerks attached to other offices, regard their brethren of the Weights as prigs and pedants, and look on them much as a master's favourite is apt to be regarded by other boys at school. But this judgement is an unfair one. Prigs and pedants, and hypocrites too, there are among them, no doubt—but there are also among them many stirred by an honourable ambition to do well for their country and themselves, and to two such men the reader is now requested to permit himself to be introduced.

Henry Norman, the senior of the two, is the second son of a gentleman of small property in the north of England. He was educated at a public school, and thence sent to Oxford; but before he had finished his first year at Brasenose his father was obliged to withdraw him from it, finding himself unable to bear the expense of a university education for his two sons. His elder son at Cambridge was extravagant; and as, at the critical moment when decision became necessary, a nomination in the Weights and Measures was placed at his disposal, old Mr. Norman committed the not uncommon injustice of preferring the interests of his elder but faulty son to those of the younger with whom no fault had been found, and deprived his child of the chance of combining the glories and happiness of a double first, a fellow, a college tutor, and a don.

Whether Harry Norman gained or lost most by the change we need not now consider, but at the age of nineteen he left Oxford and entered on his new duties. It must not, however, be supposed that this was a step which he took without difficulty and without pause. It is true that the grand modern scheme for competitive examinations had not as yet been composed. Had this been done, and had it been carried out, how awful must have been the cramming necessary to get a lad into the Weights and Measures ! But, even as things were then, it was no easy matter for a young man to convince the chief clerk that he had all the acquirements necessary for the high position to which he aspired.

Indeed, that chief clerk was insatiable, and generally succeeded in making every candidate conceive the very lowest opinion of himself and his own capacities before the examination was over. Some, of course, were sent away at once with ignominy, as evidently incapable. Many retired in the middle of it with a conviction that they must seek their fortunes at the bar, or in medical pursuits, or some other comparatively easy walk of life. Others were rejected on the fifth or sixth day as being deficient in conic sections, or ignorant of the exact principles of hydraulic pressure. And even those who were retained were so retained, as it were, by an act of grace. The Weights and Measures was, and indeed is, like heaven —no man can deserve it. No candidate can claim as his right to be admitted to the fruition of the appointment which has been given to him. Henry Norman, however, was found, at the close of his examination, to be the least undeserving of the young men then under notice, and was duly installed in his clerkship.

It need hardly be explained, that to secure so high a level of information as that required at the Weights and Measures, a scale of salaries equally exalted has been found necessary. Young men consequently enter at £100 a year. We are speaking, of course, of that more respectable branch of the establishment called the Secretary's Department. At none other of our public offices do men commence with more than £90—except, of course, at those in which political confidence is required. Political confidence is indeed as expensive as hydraulic pressure, though generally found to be less difficult of attainment.

Henry Norman, therefore, entered on his labours under good auspices, having £10 per annum more for the business and pleasures of life in London than most of his young brethren of the Civil Service. Whether this would have sufficed of itself to enable him to live up to that tone of society to which he had been accustomed cannot now be surmised, as very shortly after his appointment an aunt died, from whom he inherited some £150 or £200 a year. He was, therefore, placed above all want, and soon became a shining light even in that bright gallery of spiritualized stars which formed the corps of clerks in the Secretary's Office at the Weights and Measures.

Young Norman was a good-looking lad when he entered the public service, and in a few years he grew up to be a handsome man. He was tall and thin and dark, muscular in his proportions, and athletic in his habits. From the date of his first enjoyment of his aunt's legacy he had a wherry on the Thames, and was soon known as a man whom it was hard for an amateur to beat. He had a racket in a racket-court at St. John's Wood Road, and as soon as fortune and merit increased his salary by another £100 a year, he usually had a nag for the season. This, however, was not attained till he was able to count five years' service in the Weights and Measures. He was, as a boy, somewhat shy and reserved in his manners, and as he became older he did not shake off the fault. He showed it, however, rather among men than with women, and, indeed, in spite of his love of exercise, he preferred the society of ladies to any of the bachelor gaieties of his unmarried acquaintance. He was, nevertheless, frank and confident in those he trusted, and true in his friendships, though, considering his age, too slow in making a friend. Such was Henry Norman at the time at which our tale begins. What were the faults in his character it must be the business of the tale to show.

The other young clerk in this office to whom we alluded is Alaric Tudor. He is a year older than Henry Norman, though he began his official career a year later, and therefore at the age of twenty-one. How it happened that he contrived to pass the scrutinizing instinct and deep powers of examination possessed by the chief clerk, was a great wonder to his friends, though apparently none at all to himself. He took the whole proceeding very easily; while another youth alongside of him, who for a year had been reading up for his promised nomination, was so awestruck by the severity of the proceedings as to lose his powers of memory and forget the very essence of the differential calculus.

Of hydraulic pressure and the differential calculus young Tudor knew nothing, and pretended to know nothing. He told the chief clerk that he was utterly ignorant of all such matters, that his only acquirements were a tolerably correct knowledge of English, French, and German, with a smattering of Latin and Greek, and such an intimacy with the ordinary rules of arithmetic and with the first books of Euclid, as he had been able to pick up while acting as a tutor, rather than a scholar, in a small German university.

The chief clerk raised his eyebrows and said he feared it would not do. A clerk, however, was wanting. It was very clear that the young gentleman who had only showed that he had forgotten his conic sections could not be supposed to have passed. The austerity of the last few years had deterred more young men from coming forward than the extra £10 had induced to do so. One unfortunate, on the failure of all his hopes, had thrown himself into the Thames from the neighbouring boat-stairs; and though he had been hooked out uninjured by the man who always attends there with two wooden legs, the effect on his parents' minds had been distressing. Shortly after this occurrence the chief clerk had been invited to attend the Board, and the Chairman of the Commissioners, who, on the occasion, was of course prompted by the Secretary, recommended Mr. Hardlines to be a *leetle* more lenient. In doing so the quantity of butter which he poured over Mr. Hardlines' head and shoulders with the view of alleviating the misery which such a communication would be sure to inflict, was very great. But, nevertheless, Mr. Hardlines came out from the Board a crestfallen and unhappy man. 'The service,' he said, ' would go to the dogs, and might do for anything he cared, and he did not mind how soon. If the Board chose to make the Weights and Measures a hospital for idiots, it might do so. He had done what little lay in his power to make the office respectable ; and now, because mammas complained when their cubs of sons were not allowed to come in there and rob the public and destroy the office books, he was to be thwarted and reprimanded ! He had been,' he said, ' eight-and-twenty years in office, and was still in his prime—but he should,' he thought, ' take advantage of the advice of his medical friends, and retire. He would never remain there to see the Weights and Measures become a hospital for incurables ! '

It was thus that Mr. Hardlines, the chief clerk, ex-pressed himself. He did not, however, send in a medical certificate, nor apply for a pension ; and the first apparent effect of the little lecture which he had received from the Chairman, was the admission into the service of Alaric Tudor. Mr. Hardlines was soon forced to admit that the appointment was not a bad one, as before his second year was over, young Tudor had produced a very smart paper on the merits—or demerits—of the strike bushel.

Alaric Tudor when he entered the office was by no means so handsome a youth as Harry Norman ; but yet there was that in his face which was more expressive, and perhaps more attractive. He was a much slighter man, though equally tall. He could boast no adventitious capillary graces, whereas young Norman had a pair of black curling whiskers, which almost surrounded his face, and had been the delight and wonder of the maidservants in his mother's house, when he returned home for his first official holiday. Tudor wore no whiskers, and his light-brown hair was usually cut so short as to give him some-thing of the appearance of a clean Puritan.

But in manners he was no Puritan ; nor yet in his mode of life. He was fond of society, and at an early period of his age strove hard to shine in it. He was ambitious ; and lived with the steady aim of making the most of such advantages as fate and fortune had put in his way. Tudor was perhaps not superior to Norman in point of intellect ; but he was infinitely his superior in having early acquired a knowledge how best to use such intellect as he had.

His education had been very miscellaneous, and disturbed by many causes, but yet not ineffective or deficient. His father had been an officer in a cavalry regiment, with a fair fortune, which he had nearly squandered in early life. He had taken Alaric when little more than an infant, and a daughter, his only other child, to reside in Brussels. Mrs. Tudor was then dead, and the remainder of the household had consisted of a French governess, a *bonne*, and a man-cook. Here Alaric remained till he had perfectly acquired the French pronunciation, and very nearly as perfectly forgotten the English. He was then sent to a private school in England, where he remained till he was sixteen, returning home to Brussels but once during those years, when he was invited to be present at his sister's marriage with a Belgian banker. At the age of sixteen he lost his father, who, on dying, did not leave behind him enough of the world's wealth to pay for his own burial. His half-pay of course died with him, and young Tudor was literally destitute.

His brother-in-law, the banker, paid for his half-year's schooling in England, and then removed him to a German academy, at which it was bargained that he should teach English without remuneration, and learn German without expense. Whether he taught much English may be doubtful, but he did learn German thoroughly ; and in that, as in most other transactions of his early life, certainly got the best of the bargain which had been made for him.

At the age of twenty he was taken to the Brussels bank as a clerk ; but here he soon gave visible signs of disliking the drudgery which was exacted from him. Not that he disliked banking. He would gladly have been a partner with ever so small a share, and would have trusted to himself to increase his stake. But there is a limit to the good-nature of brothers-in-law, even in Belgium ; and Alaric was quite aware that no such good luck as this could befall him, at any rate until he had gone through many years of servile labour. His sister also, though sisterly enough in her disposition to him, did not quite like having a brother employed as a clerk in her husband's office. They therefore put their heads together, and, as the Tudors had good family connexions in England, a nomination in the Weights and Measures was procured.

The nomination was procured ; but when it was ascertained how very short a way this went towards the attainment of the desired object, and how much more difficult it was to obtain Mr. Hardlines' approval than the Board's favour, young Tudor's friends despaired, and recommended him to abandon the idea, as, should he throw himself into the Thames, he might perhaps fall beyond the reach of the waterman's hook. Alaric himself, however, had no such fears. He could not bring himself to conceive that he could fail in being fit for a clerkship in a public office, and the result of his examination proved at any rate that he had been right to try.

The close of his first year's life in London found him living in lodgings with Henry Norman. At that time Norman's income was nearly three times as good as his own. To say that Tudor selected his companion because of his income would be to ascribe unjustly to him vile motives and a mean instinct. He had not done so. The two young men had been thrown together by circumstances. They worked at the same desk, liked each other's society, and each being alone in the world, thereby not unnaturally came together. But it may probably be said that had Norman been as poor as Tudor, Tudor might probably have shrunk from rowing in the same boat with him.

As it was they lived together and were fast allies ; not the less so that they did not agree as to many of their avocations. Tudor, at his friend's solicitation, had occasionally attempted to pull an oar from Searle's slip to Battersea bridge. But his failure in this line was so complete, and he had to encounter so much of Norman's raillery, which was endurable, and of his instruction,

which was unendurable, that he very soon gave up the
pursuit. He was not more successful with a racket ; and
keeping a horse was of course out of the question.

They had a bond of union in certain common friends
whom they much loved, and with whom they much
associated. At least these friends soon became common
to them. The acquaintance originally belonged to
Norman, and he had first cemented his friendship with
Tudor by introducing him at the house of Mrs. Woodward.
Since he had done so, the one young man was there nearly
as much as the other.

Who and what the Woodwards were shall be told in
a subsequent chapter. As they have to play as important
a part in the tale about to be told as our two friends of
the Weights and Measures, it would not be becoming to
introduce them at the end of this.

As regards Alaric Tudor it need only be further said, by
way of preface, of him as of Harry Norman, that the faults
of his character must be made to declare themselves in the
course of our narrative.

CHAPTER II

THE INTERNAL NAVIGATION

The London world, visitors as well as residents, are well
acquainted also with Somerset House ; and it is moreover
tolerably well known that Somerset House is a nest of
public offices, which are held to be of less fashionable
repute than those situated in the neighbourhood of
Downing Street, but are not so decidedly plebeian as the
Custom House, Excise, and Post Office.

But there is one branch of the Civil Service located in
Somerset House, which has little else to redeem it from
the lowest depths of official vulgarity than the ambiguous
respectability of its material position. This is the office
of the Commissioners of Internal Navigation. The duties
to be performed have reference to the preservation of canal

banks, the tolls to be levied at locks, and disputes with
the Admiralty as to points connected with tidal rivers.
The rooms are dull and dark, and saturated with the fog
which rises from the river, and their only ornament is
here and there some dusty model of an improved barge.
Bargees not unfrequently scuffle with hobnailed shoes
through the passages, and go in and out, leaving behind
them a smell of tobacco, to which the denizens of the
place are not unaccustomed.

Indeed, the whole office is apparently infected with
a leaven of bargedom. Not a few of the men are employed
from time to time in the somewhat lethargic work of
inspecting the banks and towing-paths of the canals
which intersect the country. This they generally do
seated on a load of hay, or perhaps of bricks, in one of
those long, ugly, shapeless boats, which are to be seen
congregating in the neighbourhood of Brentford. So
seated, they are carried along at the rate of a mile and
a half an hour, and usually while away the time in gentle
converse with the man at the rudder, or in silent abstrac-
tion over a pipe.

But the dullness of such a life as this is fully atoned
for by the excitement of that which follows it in London.
The men of the Internal Navigation are known to be
fast, nay, almost furious in their pace of living; not that
they are extravagant in any great degree, a fault which
their scale of salaries very generally forbids; but they
are one and all addicted to Coal Holes and Cider Cellars;
they dive at midnight hours into Shades, and know all
the back parlours of all the public-houses in the neighbourhood of the Strand. Here they leave messages for one
another, and call the girl at the bar by her Christian
name. They are a set of men endowed with sallow complexions, and they wear loud clothing, and spend more
money in gin-and-water than in gloves.

The establishment is not unusually denominated the
'Infernal Navigation', and the gentlemen employed are
not altogether displeased at having it so called. The
'Infernal Navvies', indeed, rather glory in the name.
The navvies of Somerset House are known all over London,
and there are those who believe that their business has

some connexion with the rivers or railroads of that bourne from whence no traveller returns. Looking, however, from their office windows into the Thames, one might be tempted to imagine that the infernal navigation with which they are connected is not situated so far distant from the place of their labours.

The spirit who guards the entrance into this elysium is by no means so difficult to deal with as Mr. Hardlines. And it was well that it was so some few years since for young Charley Tudor, a cousin of our friend Alaric; for Charley Tudor could never have passed muster at the Weights and Measures. Charles Tudor, the third of the three clerks alluded to in our title-page, is the son of a clergyman, who has a moderate living on the Welsh border, in Shropshire. Had he known to what sort of work he was sending his son, he might probably have hesitated before he accepted for him a situation in the Internal Navigation Office. He was, however, too happy in getting it to make many inquiries as to its nature. We none of us like to look a gift-horse in the mouth. Old Mr. Tudor knew that a clerkship in the Civil Service meant, or should mean, a respectable maintenance for life, and having many young Tudors to maintain himself, he was only too glad to find one of them provided for.

Charley Tudor was some few years younger than his cousin Alaric when he came up to town, and Alaric had at that time some three or four years' experience of London life. The examination at the Internal Navigation was certainly not to be so much dreaded as that at the Weights and Measures; but still there was an examination; and Charley, who had not been the most diligent of school-boys, approached it with great dread after a preparatory evening passed with the assistance of his cousin and Mr. Norman.

Exactly at ten in the morning he walked into the lobby of his future workshop, and found no one yet there but two aged seedy messengers. He was shown into a waiting-room, and there he remained for a couple of hours, during which every clerk in the establishment came to have a look at him. At last he was ushered into the Secretary's room.

' Ah ! ' said the Secretary, ' your name is Tudor, isn't it ? '

Charley confessed to the fact.

' Yes,' said the Secretary, ' I have heard about you from Sir Gilbert de Salop.' Now Sir Gilbert de Salop was the great family friend of this branch of the Tudors. But Charley, finding that no remark suggested itself to him at this moment concerning Sir Gilbert, merely said, ' Yes, sir.'

' And you wish to serve the Queen ? ' said the Secretary.

Charley, not quite knowing whether this was a joke or not, said that he did.

' Quite right—it is a very fair ambition,' continued the great official functionary—' quite right—but, mind you, Mr. Tudor, if you come to us you must come to work. I hope you like hard work ; you should do so, if you intend to remain with us.'

Charley said that he thought he did rather like hard work. Hereupon a senior clerk standing by, though a man not given to much laughter, smiled slightly, probably in pity at the unceasing labour to which the youth was about to devote himself.

' The Internal Navigation requires great steadiness, good natural abilities, considerable education, and—and—and no end of application. Come, Mr. Tudor, let us see what you can do.' And so saying, Mr. Oldeschole, the Secretary, motioned him to sit down at an office table opposite to himself.

Charley did as he was bid, and took from the hands of his future master an old, much-worn quill pen, with which the great man had been signing minutes.

' Now,' said the great man, ' just copy the few first sentences of that leading article—either one will do,' and he pushed over to him a huge newspaper.

To tell the truth, Charley did not know what a leading article was, and so he sat abashed, staring at the paper.

' Why don't you write ? ' asked the Secretary.

' Where shall I begin, sir ? ' stammered poor Charley, looking piteously into the examiner's face.

' God bless my soul ! there ; either of those leading

articles,' and leaning over the table, the Secretary pointed to a particular spot.

Hereupon Charley began his task in a large, ugly, round hand, neither that of a man nor of a boy, and set himself to copy the contents of the paper. 'The name of Pacifico stinks in the nostril of the British public. It is well known to all the world how sincerely we admire the versitility of Lord Palmerston's genius; how cordially we simpathize with his patriotic energies. But the admiration which even a Palmerston inspires must have a bound, and our simpathy may be called on too far. When we find ourselves asked to pay——'. By this time Charley had half covered the half-sheet of foolscap which had been put before him, and here at the word 'pay' he unfortunately suffered a large blot of ink to fall on the paper.

'That won't do, Mr. Tudor, that won't do—come, let us look,' and stretching over again, the Secretary took up the copy.

'Oh dear! oh dear! this is very bad; versatility with an "i!"—sympathy with an "i!" sympathize with an "i!" Why, Mr. Tudor, you must be very fond of "i's" down in Shropshire.'

Charley looked sheepish, but of course said nothing.

'And I never saw a viler hand in my life. Oh dear, oh dear, I must send you back to Sir Gilbert. Look here, Snape, this will never do—never do for the Internal Navigation, will it?'

Snape, the attendant senior clerk, said, as indeed he could not help saying, that the writing was very bad.

'I never saw worse in my life,' said the Secretary. 'And now, Mr. Tudor, what do you know of arithmetic?'

Charley said that he thought he knew arithmetic pretty well;—'at least some of it,' he modestly added.

'Some of it!' said the Secretary, slightly laughing. 'Well, I'll tell you what—this won't do at all;' and he took the unfortunate manuscript between his thumb and forefinger. 'You had better go home and endeavour to write something a little better than this. Mind, if it is not very much better it won't do. And look here; take care that you do it yourself. If you bring me the writing of any one else, I shall be sure to detect you. I have not any more time now; as to arithmetic, we'll examine you in " some of it " to-morrow.'

So Charley, with a faint heart, went back to his cousin's lodgings and waited till the two friends had arrived from the Weights and Measures. The men there made a point of staying up to five o'clock, as is the case with all model officials, and it was therefore late before he could get himself properly set to work. But when they did arrive, preparations for calligraphy were made on a great scale; a volume of Gibbon was taken down, new quill pens, large and small, and steel pens by various makers were procured; cream-laid paper was provided, and ruled lines were put beneath it. And when this was done, Charley was especially cautioned to copy the spelling as well as the wording.

He worked thus for an hour before dinner, and then for three hours in the evening, and produced a very legible copy of half a chapter of the ' Decline and Fall.'

' I didn't think they examined at all at the Navigation,' said Norman.

' Well, I believe it's quite a new thing,' said Alaric Tudor. 'The schoolmaster must be abroad with a vengeance, if he has got as far as that.'

And then they carefully examined Charley's work, crossed his t's, dotted his i's, saw that his spelling was right, and went to bed.

Again, punctually at ten o'clock, Charley presented himself at the Internal Navigation; and again saw the two seedy old messengers warming themselves at the lobby fire. On this occasion he was kept three hours in the waiting-room, and some of the younger clerks ventured to come and speak to him. At length Mr. Snape appeared, and desired the acolyte to follow him. Charley, supposing that he was again going to the awful Secretary, did so with a palpitating heart. But he was led in another direction into a large room, carrying his manuscript neatly rolled in his hand. Here Mr. Snape introduced him to five other occupants of the chamber; he, Mr. Snape himself, having a separate desk there, being, in official parlance, the head of the room. Charley was told to take a seat at a desk, and did so, still thinking that the dread hour of his examination was soon to come. His examination, however, was begun and over. No one ever asked for his calligraphic manuscript, and as to his arithmetic, it may be presumed that his assurance that he knew 'some of it,' was deemed to be adequate evidence of sufficient capacity. And in this manner, Charley Tudor became one of the Infernal Navvies.

He was a gay-hearted, thoughtless, rollicking young lad, when he came up to town ; and it may therefore be imagined that he easily fell into the peculiar ways and habits of the office. A short bargee's pilot-coat, and a pipe of tobacco, were soon familiar to him ; and he had not been six months in London before he had his house-of-call in a cross lane running between Essex Street and Norfolk Street. 'Mary, my dear, a screw of bird's-eye !' came quite habitually to his lips ; and before his first year was out, he had volunteered a song at the Buckingham Shades.

The assurance made to him on his first visit to the office by Mr. Secretary Oldeschole, that the Internal Navigation was a place of herculean labours, had long before this time become matter to him of delightful ridicule. He had found himself to be one of six young men, who habitually spent about five hours a day together in the same room, and whose chief employment was to render the life of the wretched Mr. Snape as unendurable as possible. There were copies to be written, and entries to be made, and books to be indexed. But these things were generally done by some extra hand, as to the necessity of whose attendance for such purpose Mr. Snape was forced to certify. But poor Snape knew that he had no alternative. He rule six unruly young navvies ! There was not one of them who did not well know how to make him tremble in his shoes.

Poor Mr. Snape had selected for his own peculiar walk in life a character for evangelical piety. Whether he was a hypocrite—as all the navvies averred—or a man sincere as far as one so weak could accomplish sincerity, it is hardly necessary for us to inquire. He was not by nature an ill-natured man, but he had become by education harsh to those below him, and timid and cringing with

those above. In the former category must by no means
be included the six young men who were nominally under
his guidance. They were all but acknowledged by him
as his superiors. Ignorant as they were, they could hardly
be more so than he. Useless as they were, they did as much
for the public service as he did. He sometimes complained
of them ; but it was only when their misconduct had been
so loud as to make it no longer possible that he should not
do so.

Mr. Snape being thus by character and predilection
a religious man, and having on various occasions in olden
days professed much horror at having his ears wounded
by conversation which was either immoral or profane,
it had of course become the habitual practice of the navvies
to give continual utterance to every description of ribaldry
and blasphemy for his especial edification. Doubtless it
may be concluded from the habits of the men, that even
without such provocation, their talk would have exceeded
the yea, yea, and nay, nay, to which young men should
confine themselves. But they especially concerted schemes
of blasphemy and dialogues of iniquity for Mr. Snape's
particular advantage ; and continued daily this disinterested amusement, till at last an idea got abroad among
them that Mr. Snape liked it. Then they changed their
tactics and canted through their noses in the manner
which they imagined to be peculiar to methodist preachers.
So on the whole, Mr. Snape had an uneasy life of it at the
Internal Navigation.

Into all these malpractices Charley Tudor plunged
headlong. And how should it have been otherwise ?
How can any youth of nineteen or twenty do other than
consort himself with the daily companions of his usual
avocations ? Once and again, in one case among ten
thousand, a lad may be found formed of such stuff, that
he receives neither the good nor the bad impulses of
those around him. But such a one is a *lapsus naturae*.
He has been born without the proper attributes of youth,
or at any rate, brought up so as to have got rid of them.

Such a one, at any rate, Charley Tudor was not. He
was a little shocked at first by the language he heard ; but
that feeling soon wore off. His kind heart, also, in the

first month of his novitiate, sympathized with the daily miseries of Mr. Snape; but he also soon learnt to believe that Mr. Snape was a counterfeit, and after the first half year could torture him with as much gusto as any of his brethren. Alas! no evil tendency communicates itself among young men more quickly than cruelty. Those infernal navvies were very cruel to Mr. Snape.

And yet young Tudor was a lad of a kindly heart, of a free, honest, open disposition, deficient in no proportion of mind necessary to make an estimable man. But he was easily malleable, and he took at once the full impression of the stamp to which he was subjected. Had he gone into the Weights and Measures, a hypothesis which of course presumes a total prostration of the intellects and energy of Mr. Hardlines, he would have worked without a groan from ten till five, and have become as good a model as the best of them. As it was, he can be hardly said to have worked at all, soon became *facile princeps* in the list of habitual idlers, and was usually threatened once a quarter with dismissal, even from that abode of idleness, in which the very nature of true work was unknown.

Some tidings of Charley's doings in London, and non-doings at the Internal Navigation, of course found their way to the Shropshire parsonage. His dissipation was not of a very costly kind; but £90 per annum will hardly suffice to afford an ample allowance of gin-and-water and bird's-eye tobacco, over and above the other wants of a man's life. Bills arrived there requiring payment; and worse than this, letters also came through Sir Gilbert de Salop from Mr. Oldeschole, the Secretary, saying that young Tudor was disgracing the office, and lowering the high character of the Internal Navigation; and that he must be removed, unless he could be induced to alter his line of life, &c.

Urgent austere letters came from the father, and fond heart-rending appeals from the mother. Charley's heart was rent. It was, at any rate, a sign in him that he was not past hope of grace, that he never laughed at these monitions, that he never showed such letters to his companions, never quizzed his 'governor's' lectures, or made merry over the grief of his mother. But if it be hard for

a young man to keep in the right path when he has not
as yet strayed out of it, how much harder is it to return
to it when he has long since lost the track ! It was well
for the father to write austere letters, well for the mother
to make tender appeals, but Charley could not rid himself
of his companions, nor of his debts, nor yet even of his
habits. He could not get up in the morning and say that
he would at once be as his cousin Alaric, or as his cousin's
friend, Mr. Norman. It is not by our virtues or our vices
that we are judged, even by those who know us best ; but
by such credit for virtues or for vices as we may have
acquired. Now young Tudor's credit for virtue was very
slight, and he did not know how to extend it.

At last papa and mamma Tudor came up to town to
make one last effort to save their son ; and also to save,
on his behalf, the valuable official appointment which he
held. He had now been three years in his office, and his
salary had risen to £110 per annum. £110 per annum
was worth saving if it could be saved. The plan adopted
by Mrs. Tudor was that of beseeching their cousin Alaric
to take Charley under his especial wing.

When Charley first arrived in town, the fact of Alaric
and Norman living together had given the former a good
excuse for not offering to share his lodgings with his cousin.
Alaric, with the advantage in age of three or four years—
at that period of life the advantage lies in that direction—
with his acquired experience of London life, and also with
all the wondrous éclat of the Weights and Measures
shining round him, had perhaps been a little too unwilling
to take by the hand a rustic cousin who was about to enter
life under the questionable auspices of the Internal
Navigation. He had helped Charley to transcribe the
chapter of Gibbon, and had, it must be owned, lent him
from time to time a few odd pounds in his direst necessi-
ties. But their course in life had hitherto been apart.
Of Norman, Charley had seen less even than of his cousin.

And now it became a difficult question with Alaric how
he was to answer the direct appeal made to him by
Mrs. Tudor ;—' Pray, pray let him live with you, if it be
only for a year, Alaric,' the mother had said, with the
tears running down her cheeks. ' You are so good, so

discreet, so clever—you can save him.' Alaric promised,
or was ready to promise, anything else, but hesitated as
to the joint lodgings. 'How could he manage it,' said he,
'living, as he was, with another man? He feared that
Mr. Norman would not accede to such an arrangement.
As for himself, he would do anything but leave his friend
Norman.'   To tell the truth, Alaric thought much,
perhaps too much, of the respectability of those with
whom he consorted. He had already begun to indulge
ambitious schemes, already had ideas stretching even
beyond the limits of the Weights and Measures, and fully
intended to make the very most of himself.

Mrs. Tudor, in her deep grief, then betook herself to
Mr. Norman, though with that gentleman she had not
even the slightest acquaintance. With a sinking heart,
with a consciousness of her unreasonableness, but with
the eloquence of maternal sorrow, she made her request.
Mr. Norman heard her out with all the calm propriety of
the Weights and Measures, begged to have a day to
consider, and then acceded to the request.

'I think we ought to do it,' said he to Alaric. The
mother's tears had touched his heart, and his sense of
duty had prevailed. Alaric, of course, could now make
no further objection, and thus Charley the Navvy became
domesticated with his cousin Alaric and Harry Norman.

The first great question to be settled, and it is a very
great question with a young man, was that of latch-key or
no latch-key. Mrs. Richards, the landlady, when she
made ready the third bedroom for the young gentleman,
would, as was her wont in such matters, have put a latch-
key on the toilet-table as a matter of course, had she not
had some little conversation with Mamma Tudor regard-
ing her son. Mamma Tudor had implored and coaxed,
and probably bribed Mrs. Richards to do something more
than 'take her son in and do for him'; and Mrs. Richards,
as her first compliance with these requests, had kept the
latch-key in her own pocket. So matters went on for
a week; but when Mrs. Richards found that her maid-
servant was never woken by Mr. Charley's raps after
midnight, and that she herself was obliged to descend in
her dressing-gown, she changed her mind, declared to

herself that it was useless to attempt to keep a grown gentleman in leading-strings, and put the key on the table on the second Monday morning.

As none of the three men ever dined at home, Alaric and Norman having clubs which they frequented, and Charley eating his dinner at some neighbouring dining-house, it may be imagined that this change of residence did our poor navvy but little good. It had, however, a salutary effect on him, at any rate at first. He became shamed into a quieter and perhaps cleaner mode of dressing himself; he constrained himself to sit down to breakfast with his monitors at half-past eight, and was at any rate so far regardful of Mrs. Richards as not to smoke in his bedroom, and to come home sober enough to walk upstairs without assistance every night for the first month.

But perhaps the most salutary effect made by this change on young Tudor was this, that he was taken by his cousin one Sunday to the Woodwards. Poor Charley had had but small opportunity of learning what are the pleasures of decent society. He had gone headlong among the infernal navvies too quickly to allow of that slow and gradual formation of decent alliances which is all in all to a young man entering life. A boy is turned loose into London, and desired to choose the good and eschew the bad. Boy as he is, he might probably do so if the opportunity came in his way. But no such chance is afforded him. To eschew the bad is certainly possible for him; but as to the good, he must wait till he be chosen. This it is, that is too much for him. He cannot live without society, and so he falls.

Society, an ample allowance of society, this is the first requisite which a mother should seek in sending her son to live alone in London; balls, routs, picnics, parties; women, pretty, well-dressed, witty, easy-mannered; good pictures, elegant drawing rooms, well got-up books, Majolica and Dresden china—these are the truest guards to protect a youth from dissipation and immorality.

> These are the books, the arts, the academes
> That show, contain, and nourish all the world,

if only a youth could have them at his disposal. Some
of these things, though by no means all, Charley Tudor
encountered at the Woodwards.

CHAPTER III

It is very difficult nowadays to say where the suburbs
of London come to an end, and where the country begins.
The railways, instead of enabling Londoners to live in the
country, have turned the country into a city. London
will soon assume the shape of a great starfish. The old
town, extending from Poplar to Hammersmith, will be
the nucleus, and the various railway lines will be the
projecting rays.

There are still, however, some few nooks within reach
of the metropolis which have not been be-villaed and
be-terraced out of all look of rural charm, and the little
village of Hampton, with its old-fashioned country inn,
and its bright, quiet, grassy river, is one of them, in spite
of the triple metropolitan waterworks on the one side,
and the close vicinity on the other of Hampton Court,
that well-loved resort of cockneydom.

It was here that the Woodwards lived. Just on the
outskirts of the village, on the side of it farthest from
town, they inhabited not a villa, but a small old-fashioned
brick house, abutting on to the road, but looking from its
front windows on to a lawn and garden, which stretched
down to the river.

The grounds were not extensive, being included, house
and all, in an area of an acre and a half: but the most
had been made of it; it sloped prettily to the river, and
was absolutely secluded from the road. Thus Surbiton
Cottage, as it was called, though it had no pretension to
the grandeur of a country-house, was a desirable residence
for a moderate family with a limited income.

Mrs. Woodward's family, for there was no Mr. Woodward in the case, consisted of herself and three daughters.
There was afterwards added to this an old gentleman, an

uncle of Mrs. Woodward's, but he had not arrived at the time at which we would wish first to introduce our readers to Hampton.

Mrs. Woodward was the widow of a clergyman who had held a living in London, and had resided there. He had, however, died when two of his children were very young, and while the third was still a baby. From that time Mrs. Woodward had lived at the cottage at Hampton, and had there maintained a good repute, paying her way from month to month as widows with limited incomes should do, and devoting herself to the amusements and education of her daughters.

It was not, probably, from any want of opportunity to cast them aside, that Mrs. Woodward had remained true to her weeds; for at the time of her husband's death she was a young and a very pretty woman; and an income of £400 a year, though moderate enough for all the wants of a gentleman's family, would no doubt have added sufficiently to her charms to have procured her a second alliance, had she been so minded.

Twelve years, however, had now elapsed since Mr. Woodward had been gathered to his fathers, and the neighbouring world of Hampton, who had all of them declared over and over again that the young widow would certainly marry again, were now becoming as unanimous in their expressed opinion that the old widow knew the value of her money too well to risk it in the keeping of the best he that ever wore boots.

At the date at which our story commences, she was a comely little woman, past forty, somewhat below the middle height, rather *embonpoint,* as widows of forty should be, with pretty fat feet, and pretty fat hands; wearing just a *soupçon* of a widow's cap on her head, with her hair, now slightly grey, parted in front, and brushed very smoothly, but not too carefully, in *bandeaux* over her forehead.

She was a quick little body, full of good-humour, slightly given to repartee, and perhaps rather too impatient of a fool. But though averse to a fool, she could sympathize with folly. A great poet has said that women are all rakes at heart; and there was something of the rake at heart about Mrs. Woodward. She never could be got to express adequate horror at fast young men, and was apt to have her own sly little joke at women who prided themselves on being punctilious. She could, perhaps, the more safely indulge in this, as scandal had never even whispered a word against herself.

With her daughters she lived on terms almost of equality. The two elder were now grown up; that is, they were respectively eighteen and seventeen years old. They were devotedly attached to their mother, looked on her as the only perfect woman in existence, and would willingly do nothing that could vex her; but they perhaps were not quite so systematically obedient to her as children should be to their only surviving parent. Mrs. Woodward, however, found nothing amiss, and no one else therefore could well have a right to complain.

They were both pretty—but Gertrude, the elder, was by far the more strikingly so. They were, nevertheless, much alike; they both had rich brown hair, which they, like their mother, wore simply parted over the forehead. They were both somewhat taller than her, and were nearly of a height. But in appearance, as in disposition, Gertrude carried by far the greater air of command. She was the handsomer of the two, and the cleverer. She could write French and nearly speak it, while her sister could only read it. She could play difficult pieces from sight, which it took her sister a morning's pains to practise. She could fill in and finish a drawing, while her sister was still struggling, and struggling in vain, with the first principles of the art.

But there was a softness about Linda, for such was the name of the second Miss Woodward, which in the eyes of many men made up both for the superior beauty and superior talent of Gertrude. Gertrude was, perhaps, hardly so soft as so young a girl should be. In her had been magnified that spirit of gentle raillery which made so attractive a part of her mother's character. She enjoyed and emulated her mother's quick sharp sayings, but she hardly did so with her mother's grace, and sometimes attempted it with much more than her mother's severity. She also detested fools; but in promulgating her opinion on this subject, she was too apt to declare who the fools were whom she detested.

It may be thought that under such circumstances there could be but little confidence between the sisters; but, nevertheless, in their early days, they lived together as sisters should do. Gertrude, when she spoke of fools, never intended to include Linda in the number; and Linda appreciated too truly, and admired too thoroughly, her sister's beauty and talent to be jealous of either.

Of the youngest girl, Katie, it is not necessary at present to say much. At this time she was but thirteen years of age, and was a happy, pretty, romping child. She gave fair promise to be at any rate equal to her sisters in beauty, and in mind was quick and intelligent. Her great taste was for boating, and the romance of her life consisted in laying out ideal pleasure-grounds, and building ideal castles in a little reedy island or ait which lay out in the Thames, a few perches from the drawing-room windows.

Such was the family of the Woodwards. Harry Norman's father and Mr. Woodward had been first cousins, and hence it had been quite natural that when Norman came up to reside in London he should be made welcome to Surbiton Cottage. He had so been made welcome, and had thus got into a habit of spending his Saturday evenings and Sundays at the home of his relatives. In summer he could row up in his own wherry, and land himself and carpet-bag direct on the Woodwards' lawn, and in the winter he came down by the Hampton Court five p.m. train—and in each case he returned on the Monday morning. Thus, as regards that portion of his time which was most his own, he may be said almost to have lived at Surbiton Cottage, and if on any Sunday he omitted to make his appearance, the omission was ascribed by the ladies of Hampton, in some half-serious sort of joke, to metropolitan allurements and temptations which he ought to have withstood.

When Tudor and Norman came to live together, it was natural enough that Tudor also should be taken down to Surbiton Cottage. Norman could not leave him on every Saturday without telling him much of his friends whom

he went to visit, and he could hardly say much of them
without offering to introduce his companion to them.
Tudor accordingly went there, and it soon came to pass
that he also very frequently spent his Sundays at Hampton.

It must be remembered that at this time, the time, that
is, of Norman and Tudor's first entrance on their London
life, the girls at Surbiton Cottage were mere girls—that is,
little more than children; they had not, as it were, got
their wings so as to be able to fly away when the provocation to do so might come; they were, in short, Gertrude
and Linda Woodward, and not the Miss Woodwards:
their drawers came down below their frocks, instead of
their frocks below their drawers; and in lieu of studying
the French language, as is done by grown-up ladies, they
did French lessons, as is the case with ladies who are not
grown-up.   Under these circumstances there was no
embarrassment as to what the young people should call
each other, and they soon became very intimate as Harry
and Alaric, Gertrude and Linda.

It is not, however, to be conceived that Alaric Tudor
at once took the same footing in the house as Norman.
This was far from being the case. In the first place he
never slept there, seeing that there was no bed for him;
and the most confidential intercourse in the household
took place as they sat cosy over the last embers of the
drawing-room fire, chatting about everything and nothing,
as girls always can do, after Tudor had gone away to his
bed at the inn, on the opposite side of the way. And then
Tudor did not come on every Saturday, and at first did
not do so without express invitation; and although the
girls soon habituated themselves to the familiarity of
their new friend's Christian name, it was some time before
Mrs. Woodward did so.

Two—three years soon flew by, and Linda and Gertrude
became the Miss Woodwards; their frocks were prolonged,
their drawers curtailed, and the lessons abandoned. But
still Alaric Tudor and Harry Norman came to Hampton
not less frequently than of yore, and the world resident
on that portion of the left bank of the Thames found out
that Harry Norman and Gertrude Woodward were to be
man and wife, and that Alaric Tudor and Linda Wood-

ward were to go through the same ceremony. They found this out, or said that they had done so. But, as usual, the world was wrong; at least in part, for at the time of which we are speaking no word of love-making had passed, at any rate, between the last-named couple.

And what was Mrs. Woodward about all this time? Was she match-making or match-marring; or was she negligently omitting the duties of a mother on so important an occasion? She was certainly neither match-making nor match-marring; but it was from no negligence that she was thus quiescent. She knew, or thought she knew, that the two young men were fit to be husbands to her daughters, and she felt that if the wish for such an alliance should spring up between either pair, there was no reason why she should interfere to prevent it. But she felt also that she should not interfere to bring any such matter to pass. These young people had by chance been thrown together. Should there be love-passages among them, as it was natural to suppose there might be, it would be well. Should there be none such, it would be well also. She thoroughly trusted her own children, and did not distrust her friends; and so as regards Mrs. Woodward the matter was allowed to rest.

We cannot say that on this matter we quite approve of her conduct, though we cannot but admire the feeling which engendered it. Her daughters were very young; though they had made such positive advances as have been above described towards the discretion of womanhood, they were of the age when they would have been regarded as mere boys had they belonged to the other sex. The assertion made by Clara Van Artevelde, that women ' grow upon the sunny side of the wall,' is doubtless true; but young ladies, gifted as they are with such advantages, may perhaps be thought to require some counsel, some advice, in those first tender years in which they so often have to make or mar their fortunes.

Not that Mrs. Woodward gave them no advice; not but that she advised them well and often—but she did so, perhaps, too much as an equal, too little as a parent.

But, be that as it may—and I trust my readers will not be inclined so early in our story to lean heavily on

Mrs. Woodward, whom I at once declare to be my own chief favourite in the tale—but, be that as it may, it so occurred that Gertrude, before she was nineteen, had listened to vows of love from Harry Norman, which she neither accepted nor repudiated; and that Linda had, before she was eighteen, perhaps unfortunately, taught herself to think it probable that she might have to listen to vows of love from Alaric Tudor.

There had been no concealment between the young men as to their feelings. Norman had told his friend scores of times that it was the first wish of his heart to marry Gertrude Woodward; and had told him, moreover, what were his grounds for hope, and what his reasons for despair.

'She is as proud as a queen,' he had once said as he was rowing from Hampton to Searle's Wharf, and lay on his oars as the falling tide carried his boat softly past the green banks of Richmond—'she is as proud as a queen, and yet as timid as a fawn. She lets me tell her that I love her, but she will not say a word to me in reply; as for touching her in the way of a caress, I should as soon think of putting my arm round a goddess.'

'And why not put your arms round a goddess?' said Alaric, who was perhaps a little bolder than his friend, and a little less romantic. To this Harry answered nothing, but, laying his back to his work, swept on past the gardens of Kew, and shot among the wooden dangers of Putney Bridge.

'I wish you could bring yourself to make up to Linda,' said he, resting again from his labours; 'that would make the matter so much easier.'

'Bring myself!' said Alaric; 'what you mean is, that you wish I could bring Linda to consent to be made up to.'

'I don't think you would have much difficulty,' said Harry, finding it much easier to answer for Linda than for her sister; 'but perhaps you don't admire her?'

'I think her by far the prettier of the two,' said Alaric.

'That's nonsense,' said Harry, getting rather red in the face, and feeling rather angry.

'Indeed I do; and so, I am convinced, would most men.

You need not murder me, man. You want me to make up to Linda, and surely it will be better that I should admire my own wife than yours.'

'Oh ! you may admire whom you like ; but to say that she is prettier than Gertrude—why, you know, it is non-sense.'

'Very well, my dear fellow ; then to oblige you, I'll fall in love with Gertrude.'

'I know you won't do that,' said Harry, 'for you are not so very fond of each other ; but, joking apart, I do wish so you would make up to Linda.'

'Well, I will when *my* aunt leaves *me* £200 a year.'

There was no answering this ; so the two men changed the conversation as they walked up together from the boat wharf to the office of the Weights and Measures.

It was just at this time that fortune and old Mr. Tudor, of the Shropshire parsonage, brought Charley Tudor to reside with our two heroes. For the first month, or six weeks, Charley was ruthlessly left by his companions to get through his Sundays as best he could. It is to be hoped that he spent them in divine worship ; but it may, we fear, be surmised with more probability, that he paid his devotions at the shrine of some very inferior public-house deity in the neighbourhood of Somerset House. As a matter of course, both Norman and Tudor spoke much of their new companion to the ladies at Surbiton Cottage, and as by degrees they reported somewhat favourably of his improved morals, Mrs. Woodward, with a woman's true kindness, begged that he might be brought down to Hampton.

'I am afraid you will find him very rough,' said his cousin Alaric.

'At any rate you will not find him a fool,' said Norman, who was always the more charitable of the two.

'Thank God for that !' said Mrs. Woodward, 'and if he will come next Saturday, let him by all means do so. Pray give my compliments to him, and tell him how glad I shall be to see him.'

And thus was this wild wolf to be led into the sheep-cote ; this infernal navvy to be introduced among the angels of Surbiton Cottage. Mrs. Woodward thought that

she had a taste for reclaiming reprobates, and was determined to try her hand on Charley Tudor.

Charley went, and his début was perfectly successful.
We have hitherto only looked on the worst side of his
character; but bad as his character was, it had a better
side. He was good-natured in the extreme, kind-hearted
and affectionate; and, though too apt to be noisy and
even boisterous when much encouraged, was not without
a certain innate genuine modesty, which the knowledge
of his own iniquities had rather increased than blunted;
and, as Norman had said of him, he was no fool. His
education had not been good, and he had done nothing by
subsequent reading to make up for this deficiency; but
he was well endowed with mother-wit, and owed none of
his deficiencies to nature's churlishness.

He came, and was well received. The girls thought he
would surely get drunk before he left the table, and
Mrs. Woodward feared the austere precision of her parlour-
maid might be offended by some unworthy familiarity;
but no accident of either kind seemed to occur. He came
to the tea-table perfectly sober, and, as far as Mrs. Woodward could tell, was unaware of the presence of the
parlour-maiden.

On the Sunday morning, Charley went to church, just
like a Christian. Now Mrs. Woodward certainly had
expected that he would have spent those two hours in
smoking and attacking the parlour-maid. He went to
church, however, and seemed in no whit astray there;
stood up when others stood up, and sat down when others
sat down. After all, the infernal navvies, bad as they
doubtless were, knew something of the recognized manners
of civilized life.

Thus Charley Tudor ingratiated himself at Surbiton
Cottage, and when he left, received a kind intimation
from its mistress that she would be glad to see him again.
No day was fixed, and so Charley could not accompany
his cousin and Harry Norman on the next Saturday;
but it was not long before he got another direct invitation,
and so he also became intimate at Hampton. There could
be no danger of any one falling in love with him, for Katie
was still a child.

Things stood thus at Surbiton Cottage when Mrs. Woodward received a proposition from a relative of her own, which surprised them all not a little. This was from a certain Captain Cuttwater, who was a maternal uncle to Mrs. Woodward, and consisted of nothing less than an offer to come and live with them for the remaining term of his natural life. Now Mrs. Woodward's girls had seen very little of their grand-uncle, and what little they had seen had only taught them to laugh at him. When his name was mentioned in the family conclave, he was always made the subject of some little feminine joke; and Mrs. Woodward, though she always took her uncle's part, did so in a manner that made them feel that he was fair game for their quizzing.

When the proposal was first enunciated to the girls, they one and all, for Katie was one of the council, suggested that it should be declined with many thanks.

'He'll take us all for midshipmen,' said Linda, 'and stop our rations, and mast-head us whenever we displease him.'

'I am sure he is a cross old hunks, though mamma says he's not,' said Katie, with all the impudence of spoilt fourteen.

'He'll interfere with every one of our pursuits,' said Gertrude, more thoughtfully, 'and be sure to quarrel with the young men.'

But Mrs. Woodward, though she had consulted her daughters, had arguments of her own in favour of Captain Cuttwater's proposition, which she had not yet made known to them. Good-humoured and happy as she always was, she had her cares in the world. Her income was only £400 a year, and that, now that the Income Tax had settled down on it, was barely sufficient for her modest wants. A moiety of this died with her, and the remainder would be but a poor support for her three daughters, if at the time of her death it should so chance that she should leave them in want of support. She had always regarded Captain Cuttwater as a probable source of future aid. He was childless and unmarried, and had not, as far as she was aware, another relative in the world. It would, therefore, under any circumstances, be bad policy to offend him. But the letter in which he had made his offer had been of a very peculiar kind. He had begun by saying that he was to be turned out of his present berth by a d—— Whig Government on account of his age, he being as young a man as ever he had been; that it behoved him to look out for a place of residence, in which he might live, and, if it should so please God, die also. He then said that he expected to pay £200 a year for his board and lodging, which he thought might as well go to his niece as to some shark, who would probably starve him. He also said that, poor as he was and always had been, he had contrived to scrape together a few hundred pounds; that he was well aware that if he lived among strangers he should be done out of every shilling of it; but that if his niece would receive him, he hoped to be able to keep it together for the benefit of his grand-nieces, &c.

Now Mrs. Woodward knew her uncle to be an honest-minded man; she knew also, that, in spite of his protestation as to being a very poor man, he had saved money enough to make him of some consequence wherever he went; and she therefore conceived that she could not with prudence send him to seek a home among chance strangers. She explained as much of this to the girls as she thought proper, and ended the matter by making them understand that Captain Cuttwater was to be received.

On the Saturday after this the three scions of the Civil Service were all at Surbiton Cottage, and it will show how far Charley had then made good his ground, to state that the coming of the captain was debated in his presence.

'And when is the great man to be here?' said Norman.

'At once, I believe,' said Mrs. Woodward; 'that is, perhaps, before the end of this week, and certainly before the end of next.'

'And what is he like?' said Alaric.

'Why, he has a tail hanging down behind, like a cat or a dog,' said Katie.

'Hold your tongue, miss,' said Gertrude. 'As he is to come he must be treated with respect; but it is a great bore. To me it will destroy all the pleasures of life.'

'Nonsense, Gertrude,' said Mrs. Woodward; 'it is almost wicked of you to say so. Destroy all the pleasure of life to have an old gentleman live in the same house with you!—you ought to be more moderate, my dear, in what you say.'

'That's all very well, mamma,' said Gertrude, ' but you know you don't like him yourself.'

'But is it true that Captain Cuttwater wears a pigtail?' asked Norman.

'I don't care what he wears,' said Gertrude; 'he may wear three if he likes.'

'Oh! I wish he would,' said Katie, laughing; 'that would be so delicious. Oh, Linda, fancy Captain Cuttwater with three pigtails!'

'I am sorry to disappoint you, Katie,' said Mrs. Woodward, ' but your uncle does not wear even one; he once did, but he cut it off long since.'

'I am so sorry,' said Katie.

'I suppose he'll want to dine early, and go to bed early?' said Linda.

'His going to bed early would be a great blessing,' said Gertrude, mindful of their midnight conclaves on Saturdays and Sundays.

'But his getting up early won't be a blessing at all,' said Linda, who had a weakness on that subject.

'Talking of bed, Harry, you'll have the worst of it,' said Katie, ' for the captain is to have your room.'

'Yes, indeed,' said Mrs. Woodward, sighing gently, ' we shall no longer have a bed for you, Harry; that *is* the worst of it.'

Harry of course assured her that if that was the worst of it there was nothing very bad in it. He could have a bed at the inn as well as Alaric and Charley. The amount of that evil would only be half-a-crown a night.

And thus the advent of Captain Cuttwater was discussed.

CHAPTER IV

CAPTAIN CUTTWATER

CAPTAIN CUTTWATER had not seen much service afloat; that is, he had not personally concerned in many of those sea-engagements which in and about the time of Nelson gave so great a halo of glory to the British Lion; nor had it even been permitted to him to take a prominent part in such minor affairs as have since occurred; he had not the opportunity of distinguishing himself either at the battle of Navarino or the bombarding of Acre; and, unfortunately for his ambition, the period of his retirement came before that great Baltic campaign, in which, had he been there, he would doubtless have distinguished himself as did so many others. His earliest years were spent in cruising among the West Indies; he then came home and spent some considerable portion of his life in idleness—if that time can be said to have been idly spent which he devoted to torturing the Admiralty with applications, remonstrances, and appeals. Then he was rated as third lieutenant on the books of some worm-eaten old man-of-war at Portsmouth, and gave up his time to looking after the stowage of anchors, and counting fathoms of rope. At last he was again sent afloat as senior lieutenant in a ten-gun brig, and cruised for some time off the coast of Africa, hunting for slavers; and returning after a while from this enterprising employment, he received a sort of amphibious appointment at Devonport. What his duties were here, the author, being in all points a landsman, is unable to describe. Those who were inclined to ridicule Captain Cuttwater declared that the most important of them consisted in seeing that the midshipmen in and about the dockyard washed their faces, and put on clean linen not less often than three times a week. According to his own account, he had many things of a higher nature to attend to; and, indeed, hardly a ship sank or swam in Hamoaze except by his special permission, for a space of twenty years, if his own view of his own career may be accepted as correct.

He had once declared to certain naval acquaintances, over his third glass of grog, that he regarded it as his birthright to be an Admiral; but at the age of seventy-two he had not yet acquired his birthright, and the probability of his ever attaining it was becoming very small indeed. He was still bothering Lords and Secretaries of the Admiralty for further promotion, when he was astounded by being informed by the Port-Admiral that he was to be made happy by half-pay and a pension. The Admiral, in communicating the intelligence, had pretended to think that he was giving the captain information which could not be otherwise than grateful to him, but he was not the less aware that the old man would be furious at being so treated. What, pension him! put him on half-pay— shelf him for life, while he was still anxiously expecting that promotion, that call to higher duties which had so long been his due, and to which, now that his powers were matured, could hardly be longer denied to him! And after all that he had done for his country—his ungrateful, thankless, ignorant country—was he thus to be treated? Was he to be turned adrift without any mark of honour, any special guerdon, any sign of his Sovereign's favour to testify as to his faithful servitude of sixty years' devotion? He, who had regarded it as his merest right to be an Admiral, and had long indulged the hope of being greeted in the streets of Devonport as Sir Bartholomew Cuttwater, K.C.B., was he to be thus thrown aside in his prime, with no other acknowledgement than the bare income to which he was entitled!

It is hardly too much to say, that no old officers who have lacked the means to distinguish themselves, retire from either of our military services, free from the bitter disappointment and sour feelings of neglected worth, which Captain Cuttwater felt so keenly. A clergyman, or a doctor, or a lawyer, feels himself no whit disgraced if he reaches the end of his worldly labours without special note or honour. But to a soldier or a sailor, such indifference to his merit is wormwood. It is the bane of the professions. Nine men out of ten who go into it must live discontented, and die disappointed.

Captain Cuttwater had no idea that he was an old man. He had lived for so many years among men of his own stamp, who had grown grey and bald, and rickety, and weak alongside of him, that he had no opportunity of seeing that he was more grey or more rickety than his neighbours. No children had become men and women at his feet ; no new race had gone out into the world and fought their battles under his notice. One set of midshipmen had succeeded to another, but his old comrades in the news-rooms and lounging-places at Devonport had remained the same ; and Captain Cuttwater had never learnt to think that he was not doing, and was not able to do good service for his country.

The very name of Captain Cuttwater was odious to every clerk at the Admiralty. He, like all naval officers, hated the Admiralty, and thought, that of all Englishmen, those five who had been selected to sit there in high places as joint lords were the most incapable. He pestered them with continued and almost continuous applications on subjects of all sorts. He was always asking for increased allowances, advanced rank, more assistance, less work, higher privileges, immunities which could not be granted, and advantages to which he had no claim. He never took answers, but made every request the subject of a prolonged correspondence ; till at last some energetic Assistant-Secretary declared that it should no longer be borne, and Captain Cuttwater was dismissed with pension and half-pay. During his service he had contrived to save some four or five thousand pounds, and now he was about to retire with an assured income adequate to all his wants. The public who had the paying of Captain Cuttwater may, perhaps, think that he was amply remunerated for what he had done ; but the captain himself entertained a very different opinion.

Such is the view which we are obliged to take of the professional side of Captain Cuttwater's character. But the professional side was by far the worst. Counting fathoms of rope and looking after unruly midshipmen on shore are not duties capable of bringing out in high relief the better traits of a man's character. Uncle Bat, as during the few last years of his life he was always called at Surbiton Cottage, was a gentleman and a man of honour, in spite of anything that might be said to the contrary at the Admiralty. He was a man with a soft heart, though the end of his nose was so large, so red, and so pimply ; and rough as was his usage to little midshipmen when his duty caused him to encounter them in a body, he had befriended many a one singly with kind words and an open hand. The young rogues would unmercifully quiz Old Nosey, for so Captain Cuttwater was generally called in Devonport, whenever they could safely do so ; but, nevertheless, in their young distresses they knew him for their friend, and were not slow to come to him.

In person Captain Cuttwater was a tall. heavy man, on whose iron constitution hogsheads of Hollands and water seemed to have had no very powerful effect. He was much given to profane oaths ; but knowing that manners required that he should refrain before ladies, and being unable to bring his tongue sufficiently under command to do so, he was in the habit of 'craving the ladies' pardon' after every slip.

All that was really remarkable in Uncle Bat's appearance was included in his nose. It had always been a generous, weighty, self-confident nose, inviting to itself more observation than any of its brother features demanded. But in latter years it had spread itself out in soft, porous, red excrescences, to such an extent as to make it really deserving of considerable attention. No stranger ever passed Captain Cuttwater in the streets of Devonport without asking who he was, or, at any rate, specially noticing him.

It must, of course, be admitted that a too strongly pronounced partiality for alcoholic drink had produced these defects in Captain Cuttwater's nasal organ ; and yet he was a most staunch friend of temperance. No man alive or dead had ever seen Captain Cuttwater the worse for liquor ; at least so boasted the captain himself, and there were none, at any rate in Devonport, to give him the lie. Woe betide the midshipman whom he should

see elated with too much wine; and even to the common
sailor who should be tipsy at the wrong time, he would
show no mercy. Most eloquent were the discourses which
he preached against drunkenness, and they always ended
with a reference to his own sobriety. The truth was, that
drink would hardly make Captain Cuttwater drunk. It
left his brain untouched, but punished his nose.

Mrs. Woodward had seen her uncle but once since she
had become a widow. He had then come up to London
to attack the Admiralty at close quarters, and had
sojourned for three or four days at Surbiton Cottage.
This was now some ten years since, and the girls had
forgotten even what he was like. Great preparations
were made for him. Though the summer had nearly
commenced, a large fire was kept burning in his bedroom
—his bed was newly hung with new curtains; two feather
beds were piled on each other, and everything was done
which five women could think desirable to relieve the
ailings of suffering age. The fact, however, was. that
Captain Cuttwater was accustomed to a small tent bed-
stead in a room without a carpet, that he usually slept
on a single mattress, and that he never had a fire in his
bedroom, even in the depth of winter.

Travelling from Devonport to London is now an easy
matter; and Captain Cuttwater, old as he was, found
himself able to get through to Hampton in one day.
Mrs. Woodward went to meet him at Hampton Court in
a fly, and conveyed him to his new home, together with
a carpet-bag, a cocked hat, a sword, and a very small
portmanteau. When she inquired after the remainder of
his luggage, he asked her what more lumber she supposed
he wanted. No more lumber at any rate made its appearance, then or afterwards; and the fly proceeded with an
easy load to Surbiton Cottage.

There was great anxiety on the part of the girls when
the wheels were heard to stop at the front door. Gertrude
kept her place steadily standing on the rug in the drawing-
room; Linda ran to the door and then back again; but
Katie bolted out and ensconced herself behind the parlour-
maid, who stood at the open door, looking eagerly forth to
get the first view of Uncle Bat.

'So here you are, Bessie, as snug as ever,' said the captain, as he let himself ponderously down from the fly. Katie had never before heard her mother called Bessie, and had never seen anything approaching in size or colour to such a nose, consequently she ran away frightened.

'That's Gertrude—is it?' said the captain.

'Gertrude, uncle! Why Gertrude is a grown-up woman now. That's Katie, whom you remember an infant.'

'God bless my soul!' said the captain, as though he thought that girls must grow twice quicker at Hampton than they did at Devonport or elsewhere, 'God bless my soul!'

He was then ushered into the drawing-room, and introduced in form to his grand-nieces. 'This is Gertrude, uncle, and this Linda; there is just enough difference for you to know them apart. And this Katie. Come here, Katie, and kiss your uncle.'

Katie came up, hesitated, looked horrified, but did manage to get her face somewhat close to the old man's without touching the tremendous nose, and then having gone through this peril she retreated again behind the sofa.

'Well; bless my stars, Bessie, you don't tell me those are your children?'

'Indeed, uncle, I believe they are. It's a sad tale for me to tell, is it not?' said the blooming mother with a laugh.

'Why, they'll be looking out for husbands next,' said Uncle Bat.

'Oh! they're doing that already, every day,' said Katie.

'Ha, ha, ha!' laughed Uncle Bat; 'I suppose so, I suppose so;—ha, ha, ha!'

Gertrude turned away to the window, disgusted and angry, and made up her mind to hate Uncle Bat for ever afterwards. Linda made a little attempt to smile, and felt somewhat glad in her heart that her uncle was a man who could indulge in a joke.

He was then taken upstairs to his bedroom, and here he greatly frightened Katie, and much scandalized the parlour-maid by declaring, immediately on his entering

the room, that it was 'd—— hot, d——ation hot ; craving
your pardon, ladies ! '

'We thought, uncle, you'd like a fire,' began Mrs.
Woodward, 'as—— '

'A fire in June, when I can hardly carry my coat on my
back ! '

'It's the last day of May now,' said Katie timidly,
from behind the bed-curtains.

This, however, did not satisfy the captain, and orders
were forthwith given that the fire should be taken away,
the curtains stripped off, the feather beds removed, and
everything reduced to pretty much the same state in which
it had usually been left for Harry Norman's accommodation. So much for all the feminine care which had been
thrown away upon the consideration of Uncle Bat's
infirmities.

'God bless my soul ! ' said he, wiping his brow with
a huge coloured handkerchief as big as a mainsail, 'one
night in such a furnace as that would have brought on
the gout.'

He had dined in town, and by the time that his chamber
had been stripped of its appendages, he was nearly ready
for bed. Before he did so, he was asked to take a glass
of sherry.

'Ah ! sherry,' said he, taking up the bottle and putting
it down again. 'Sherry, ah ! yes ; very good wine, I am
sure. You haven't a drop of rum in the house, have
you ? '

Mrs. Woodward declared with sorrow that she had not.

'Or Hollands ? ' said Uncle Bat. But the ladies of
Surbiton Cottage were unsupplied also with Hollands.

'Gin ? ' suggested the captain, almost in despair.

Mrs. Woodward had no gin, but she could send out and
get it ; and the first evening of Captain Cuttwater's visit
saw Mrs. Woodward's own parlour-maid standing at the
bar of the Green Dragon, while two gills of spirits were
being measured out for her.

'Only for the respect she owed to Missus,' as she afterwards declared, 'she never would have so demeaned
herself for all the captains in the Queen's battalions.'

The captain, however, got his grog ; and having en-

larged somewhat vehemently while he drank it on the
iniquities of those scoundrels at the Admiralty, took
himself off to bed ; and left his character and peculiarities
to the tender mercies of his nieces.

The following day was Friday, and on the Saturday
Norman and Tudor were to come down as a matter of
course. During the long days, they usually made their
appearance after dinner ; but they had now been specially
requested to appear in good early time, in honour of
the captain. Their advent had been of course spoken of,
and Mrs. Woodward had explained to Uncle Bat that her
cousin Harry usually spent his Sundays at Hampton,
and that he usually also brought with him a friend of
his, a Mr. Tudor. To all this, as a matter of course, Uncle
Bat had as yet no objection to make.

The young men came, and were introduced with due
ceremony. Surbiton Cottage, however, during dinner-
time, was very unlike what it had been before, in the
opinion of all the party there assembled. The girls felt
themselves called upon, they hardly knew why, to be
somewhat less intimate in their manner with the young
men than they customarily were ; and Harry and Alaric,
with quick instinct, reciprocated the feeling. Mrs. Woodward, even, assumed involuntarily somewhat of a company
air ; and Uncle Bat, who sat at the bottom of the table,
in the place usually assigned to Norman, was awkward in
doing the honours of the house to guests who were in fact
much more at home there than himself.

After dinner the young people strolled out into the
garden, and Katie, as was her wont, insisted on Harry
Norman rowing her over to her damp paradise in the
middle of the river. He attempted, vainly, to induce
Gertrude to accompany them. Gertrude was either coy
with her lover, or indifferent ; for very few were the
occasions on which she could be induced to gratify him
with the rapture of a *tête-à-tête* encounter. So that, in
fact, Harry Norman's Sunday visits were generally
moments of expected bliss of which the full fruition was
but seldom attained. So while Katie went off to the island,
Alaric and the two girls sat under a spreading elm tree
and watched the little boat as it shot across the water.

'And what do you think of Uncle Bat?' said Gertrude.

'Well, I am sure he's a good sort of fellow, and a very gallant officer, but——'

'But what?' said Linda.

'It's a thousand pities he should have ever been removed from Devonport, where I am sure he was both useful and ornamental.'

Both the girls laughed cheerily; and as the sound came across the water to Norman's ears, he repented himself of his good nature to Katie, and determined that her sojourn in the favourite island should, on this occasion, be very short.

'But he is to pay mamma a great deal of money,' said Linda, 'and his coming will be a great benefit to her in that way.'

'There ought to be something to compensate for the bore,' said Gertrude.

'We must only make the best of him,' said Alaric. 'For my part, I am rather fond of old gentlemen with long noses; but it seemed to me that he was not quite so fond of us. I thought he looked rather shy at Harry and me.'

Both the girls protested against this, and declared that there could be nothing in it.

'Well, now, I'll tell you what, Gertrude,' said Alaric, 'I am quite sure that he looks on me, especially, as an interloper; and yet I'll bet you a pair of gloves I am his favourite before a month is over.'

'Oh, no; Linda is to be his favourite,' said Gertrude.

'Indeed I am not,' said Linda. 'I liked him very well till he drank three huge glasses of gin-and-water last night, but I never can fancy him after that. You can't conceive, Alaric, what the drawing-room smelt like. I suppose he'll do the same every evening.'

'Well, what can you expect?' said Gertrude; 'if mamma will have an old sailor to live with her, of course he'll drink grog.'

While this was going on in the garden, Mrs. Woodward sat dutifully with her uncle while he sipped his obnoxious toddy, and answered his questions about their two friends.

'They were both in the Weights and Measures, by far the most respectable public office in London,' as she told him, ' and both doing extremely well there. They were, indeed, young men sure to distinguish themselves and get on in the world. Had this not been so, she might perhaps have hesitated to receive them so frequently, and on such intimate terms, at Surbiton Cottage.' This she said in a half-apologetic manner, and yet with a feeling of anger at herself that she should condescend to apologize to any one as to her own conduct in her own house.

' They are very nice young men, I am sure,' said Uncle Bat.

' Indeed they are,' said Mrs. Woodward.

' And very civil to the young ladies,' said Uncle Bat.

' They have known them since they were children, uncle ; and of course that makes them more intimate than young men generally are with young ladies ; ' and again Mrs. Woodward was angry with herself for making any excuses on the subject.

' Are they well off ? ' asked the prudent captain.

' Harry Norman is very well off ; he has a private fortune. Both of them have excellent situations.'

' To my way of thinking that other chap is the better fellow. At any rate he seems to have more gumption about him.'

' Why, uncle, you don't mean to tell me that you think Harry Norman a fool ? ' said Mrs. Woodward. Harry Norman was Mrs. Woodward's special friend, and she fondly indulged the hope of seeing him in time become the husband of her elder and favourite daughter ; if, indeed, she can be fairly said to have had a favourite child.

Captain Cuttwater poured out another glass of rum, and dropped the subject.

Soon afterwards the whole party came in from the lawn. Katie was all draggled and wet, for she had persisted in making her way right across the island to look out for a site for another palace. Norman was a little inclined to be sulky, for Katie had got the better of him ; when she had got out of the boat, he could not get her into it again ; and as he could not very well leave her in the island, he had been obliged to remain paddling about, while he heard the happy voices of Alaric and the two girls from the lawn. Alaric was in high good-humour, and entered the room intent on his threatened purpose of seducing Captain Cuttwater's affections. The two girls were both blooming with happy glee, and Gertrude was especially bright in spite of the somewhat sombre demeanour of her lover.

Tea was brought in, whereupon Captain Cuttwater, having taken a bit of toast and crammed it into his saucer, fell fast asleep in an arm-chair.

'You'll have very little opportunity to-night,' said Linda, almost in a whisper.

'Opportunity for what?' asked Mrs. Woodward.

'Hush,' said Gertrude, 'we'll tell you by and by, mamma. You'll wake Uncle Bat if you talk now.'

'I am so thirsty,' said Katie, bouncing into the room with dry shoes and stockings on. 'I am so thirsty. Oh, Linda, do give me some tea.'

'Hush,' said Alaric, pointing to the captain, who was thoroughly enjoying himself, and uttering sonorous snores at regular fixed intervals.

'Sit down, Katie, and don't make a noise,' said Mrs. Woodward, gently.

Katie slunk into a chair, opened wide her large bright eyes, applied herself diligently to her teacup, and then, after taking breath, said, in a very audible whisper to her sister, 'Are not we to talk at all, Linda? That will be very dull, I think.'

'Yes, my dear, you are to talk as much as you please, and as often as you please, and as loud as you please; that is to say, if your mamma will let you,' said Captain Cuttwater, without any apparent waking effort, and in a moment the snoring was going on again as regularly as before.

Katie looked round, and again opened her eyes and laughed. Mrs. Woodward said, 'You are very good-natured, uncle.' The girls exchanged looks with Alaric, and Norman, who had not yet recovered his good-humour, went on sipping his tea.

As soon as the tea-things were gone, Uncle Bat yawned and shook himself, and asked if it was not nearly time to go to bed.

'Whenever you like, Uncle Bat,' said Mrs. Woodward, who began to find that she agreed with Gertrude, that early habits on the part of her uncle would be a family blessing. 'But perhaps you'll take something before you go?'

'Well, I don't mind if I do take a thimbleful of rum-and-water.' So the odious spirit-bottle was again brought into the drawing-room.

'Did you call at the Admiralty, sir, as you came through town?' said Alaric.

'Call at the Admiralty, sir!' said the captain, turning sharply round at the questioner; 'what the deuce should I call at the Admiralty for? craving the ladies' pardon.'

'Well, indeed, I don't know,' said Alaric, not a bit abashed. 'But sailors always do call there, for the pleasure, I suppose, of kicking their heels in the lords' waiting-room.'

'I have done with that game,' said Captain Cuttwater, now wide awake; and in his energy he poured half a glass more rum into his beaker. 'I've done with that game, and I'll tell you what, Mr. Tudor, if I had a dozen sons to provide for to-morrow——'

'Oh, I do so wish you had,' said Katie; 'it would be such fun. Fancy Uncle Bat having twelve sons, Gertrude. What would you call them all, uncle?'

'Why, I tell you what, Miss Katie, I wouldn't call one of them a sailor. I'd sooner make tailors of them.'

'Tinker, tailor, soldier, sailor, gentleman, apothecary, ploughboy, thief,' said Katie. 'That would only be eight; what should the other four be, uncle?'

'You're quite right, Captain Cuttwater,' said Alaric, 'at least as far as the present moment goes; but the time is coming when things at the Admiralty will be managed very differently.'

'Then I'm d—— if that time can come too soon—craving the ladies' pardon!' said Uncle Bat.

'I don't know what you mean, Alaric,' said Harry Norman, who was just at present somewhat disposed to contradict his friend, and not ill-inclined to contradict the captain also; 'as far as I can judge, the Admiralty is the very last office the Government will think of touching.'

'The Government!' shouted Captain Cuttwater; 'oh!
if we are to wait for the Government, the navy may go to
the deuce, sir.'

'It's the pressure from without that must do the work,'
said Alaric.

'Pressure from without!' said Norman, scornfully;
'I hate to hear such trash.'

'We'll see, young gentleman, we'll see,' said the
captain; 'it may be trash, and it may be right that five
fellows who never did the Queen a day's service in their
life, should get fifteen hundred or two thousand a year,
and have the power of robbing an old sailor like me of
the reward due to me for sixty years' hard work. Reward!
no; but the very wages that I have actually earned.
Look at me now, d—— me, look at me! Here I am,
Captain Cuttwater—with sixty years' service—and I've
done more perhaps for the Queen's navy than—than——'

'It's too true, Captain Cuttwater,' said Alaric, speaking
with a sort of mock earnestness which completely took in
the captain, but stealing a glance at the same time at the
two girls, who sat over their work at the drawing-room
table, 'it's too true; and there's no doubt the whole
thing must be altered, and that soon. In the first place,
we must have a sailor at the head of the navy.'

'Yes,' said the captain, 'and one that knows something
about it too.'

'You'll never have a sailor sitting as first lord,' said
Norman, authoritatively; 'unless it be when some party
man, high in rank, may happen to have been in the navy
as a boy.'

'And why not?' said Captain Cuttwater quite angrily.

'Because the first lord must sit in the Cabinet, and to
do that he must be a thorough politician.'

'D—— politicians! craving the ladies' pardon,' said
Uncle Bat.

'Amen!' said Alaric.

Uncle Bat, thinking that he had thoroughly carried his
point, finished his grog, took up his candlestick, and
toddled off to bed.

'Well, I think I have done something towards carrying
my point,' said Alaric.

'I didn't think you were half so cunning,' said Linda, laughing.

'I cannot think how you can condescend to advocate opinions diametrically opposed to your own convictions,' said Norman, somewhat haughtily.

'Fee, fo, fum!' said Alaric.

'What is it all about?' said Mrs. Woodward.

'Alaric wants to do all he can to ingratiate himself with Uncle Bat,' said Gertrude; 'and I am sure he's going the right way to work.'

'It's very good-natured on his part,' said Mrs. Woodward.

'I don't know what you are talking about,' said Katie, yawning, 'and I think you are all very stupid; so I'll go to bed.'

The rest soon followed her. They did not sit up so late chatting over the fire this evening, as was their wont on Saturdays, though none of them knew what cause prevented it.

CHAPTER V

BUSHEY PARK

THE next day being Sunday, the whole party very properly went to church; but during the sermon Captain Cuttwater very improperly went to sleep, and snored ponderously the whole time. Katie was so thoroughly shocked that she did not know which way to look; Norman, who had recovered his good-humour, and Alaric, could not refrain from smiling as they caught the eyes of the two girls; and Mrs. Woodward made sundry little abortive efforts to wake her uncle with her foot. Altogether abortive they were not, for the captain would open his eyes and gaze at her for a moment in the most good-natured, lack-lustre manner conceivable; but then, in a moment, he would be again asleep and snoring, with all the regularity of a kitchen-clock. This was at first very dreadful to the Woodwards; but after a month or two they got used to it, and so apparently did the pastor and the people of Hampton.

After church there was a lunch of course; and then, according to their wont, they went out to walk. These Sunday walks in general were matters of some difficulty. The beautiful neighbourhood of Hampton Court, with its palace-gardens and lovely park, is so popular with Londoners that it is generally alive on that day with a thronged multitude of men, women, and children, and thus becomes not an eligible resort for lovers of privacy. Captain Cuttwater, however, on this occasion, insisted on seeing the chestnuts and the crowd, and consequently, they all went into Bushey Park.

Uncle Bat, who professed himself to be a philanthropist, and who was also a bit of a democrat, declared himself delighted with what he saw. It was a great thing for the London citizens to come down there with their wives and children, and eat their dinners in the open air under the spreading trees; and both Harry and Alaric agreed with him. Mrs. Woodward, however, averred that it would be much better if they would go to church first, and Gertrude and Linda were of opinion that the Park was spoilt by the dirty bits of greasy paper which were left about on all sides. Katie thought it very hard that, as all the Londoners were allowed to eat their dinners in the Park, she might not have hers there also. To which Captain Cuttwater rejoined that he should give them a picnic at Richmond before the summer was over.

All the world knows how such a party as that of our friends by degrees separates itself into twos and threes, when sauntering about in shady walks. It was seldom, indeed, that Norman could induce his Dulcinea to be so complaisant in his favour; but either accident or kindness on her part favoured him on this occasion, and as Katie went on eliciting from Uncle Bat fresh promises as to the picnic, Harry and Gertrude found themselves together under one avenue of trees, while Alaric and Linda were equally fortunate, or unfortunate, under another.

'I did so wish to speak a few words to you, Gertrude,' said Norman; 'but it seems as though, now that this captain has come among us, all our old habits and ways are to be upset.'

'I don't see that *you* need say that,' said she. '*We* may, perhaps, be put out a little—that is, mamma and Linda and I ; but I do not see that you need suffer.'

'Suffer—no, not suffer—and yet it is suffering.'

'What is suffering ?' said she.

'Why, to be as we were last night—not able to speak to each other.'

'Come, Harry, you should be a little reasonable,' said she, laughing. 'If you did not talk last night whose fault was it ?'

'I suppose you will say it was my own. Perhaps it was. But I could not feel comfortable while he was drinking gin-and-water—— '

'It was rum,' said Gertrude, rather gravely.

'Well, rum-and-water in your mother's drawing-room, and cursing and swearing before you and Linda, as though he were in the cockpit of a man-of-war.'

'Alaric you saw was able to make himself happy, and I am sure he is not more indifferent to us than you are.'

'Alaric seemed to me to be bent on making a fool of the old man ; and, to tell the truth, I cannot approve of his doing so.'

'It seems to me, Harry, that you do not approve of what any of us are doing,' said she ; 'I fear we are all in your black books—Captain Cuttwater, and mamma, and Alaric, and I, and all of us.'

'Well now, Gertrude, do you mean to say you think it right that Katie should sit by and hear a man talk as Captain Cuttwater talked last night ? Do you mean to say that the scene which passed, with the rum and the curses, and the absurd ridicule which was thrown on your mother's uncle, was such as should take place in your mother's drawing-room ?'

'I mean to say, Harry, that my mother is the best and only judge of what should, and what should not, take place there.'

Norman felt himself somewhat silenced by this, and walked on for a time without speaking. He was a little too apt to take upon himself the character of Mentor ;

and, strange to say, he was aware of his own fault in this particular. Thus, though the temptation to preach was very powerful, he refrained himself for a while. His present desire was to say soft things rather than sharp words; and though lecturing was at this moment much easier to him than love-making, he bethought himself of his object, and controlled the spirit of morality which was strong within him.

'But we were so happy before your uncle came,' he said, speaking with his sweetest voice, and looking at the beautiful girl beside him with all the love he was able to throw into his handsome face.

'And we are happy now that he has come—or at any rate ought to be,' said Gertrude, doing a little in the Mentor line herself, now that the occasion came in her way.

'Ah! Gertrude, you know very well there is only one thing can make me happy,' said Harry.

'Why, you unreasonable man! just now you said you were perfectly happy before Captain Cuttwater came. I suppose the one thing now necessary is to send him away again.'

'No, Gertrude, the thing necessary is to take you away.'

'What! out of the contamination of poor old Uncle Bat's bottle of rum? But, Harry, you see it would be cowardly in me to leave mamma and Linda to suffer the calamity alone.'

'I wonder, Gertrude, whether, in your heart of hearts, you really care a straw about me,' said Harry, who was now very sentimental and somewhat lachrymose.

'You know we all care very much about you, and it is very wrong in you to express such a doubt,' said Gertrude, with a duplicity that was almost wicked; as if she did not fully understand that the kind of 'caring' of which Norman spoke was of a very different nature from the general 'caring' which she, on his behalf, shared with the rest of her family.

'All of you—yes, but I am not speaking of all of you; I am speaking of you, Gertrude—you in particular. Can you ever love me well enough to be my wife?'

'Well, there is no knowing what I may be able to do in three or four years' time; but even that must depend very much on how you behave yourself in the mean time. If you get cross because Captain Cuttwater has come here, and snub Alaric and Linda, as you did last night, and scold at mamma because she chooses to let her own uncle live in her own house, why, to tell you the truth, I don't think I ever shall.'

All persons who have a propensity to lecture others have a strong constitutional dislike to being lectured themselves. Such was decidedly the case with Harry Norman. In spite of his strong love, and his anxious desire to make himself agreeable, his brow became somewhat darkened, and his lips somewhat compressed. He would not probably have been annoyed had he not been found fault with for snubbing his friend Tudor. Why should Gertrude, his Gertrude, put herself forward to defend his friend ? Let her say what she chose for her mother, or even for her profane, dram-drinking, vulgar old uncle, but it was too much that she should take up the cudgels for Alaric Tudor.

'Well,' said he, 'I was annoyed last night, and I must own it. It grieved me to hear Alaric turning your uncle into ridicule, and that before your mother's face ; and it grieved me to see you and Linda encourage him. In what Alaric said about the Admiralty he did not speak truthfully.'

'Do you mean to say that Alaric said what was false ? '

'Inasmuch as he was pretending to express his own opinion, he did say what was false.'

'Then I must and will say that I never yet knew Alaric say a word that was not true ; and, which is more, I am quite sure that he would not accuse you of falsehood behind your back in a fit of jealousy.'

'Jealousy ! ' said Norman, looking now as black as grim death itself.

'Yes, it is jealousy. It so turned out that Alaric got on better last night with Captain Cuttwater than you did, and that makes you jealous.'

'Pish ! ' said Norman, somewhat relieved, but still sufficiently disgusted that his lady-love should suppose that he could be otherwise than supremely indifferent to the opinion of Captain Cuttwater.

The love-scene, however, was fatally interrupted; and the pair were not long before they joined the captain, Mrs. Woodward, and Katie.

And how fared it with the other pair under the other avenue of chestnuts?

Alaric Tudor had certainly come out with no defined intention of making love as Harry Norman had done; but with such a companion it was very difficult for him to avoid it. Linda was much more open to attacks of this nature than her sister. Not that she was as a general rule willingly and wilfully inclined to give more encouragement to lovers than Gertrude; but she had less power of fence, less skill in protecting herself, and much less of that haughty self-esteem which makes some women fancy that all love-making to them is a liberty, and the want of which makes others feel that all love-making is to them a compliment.

Alaric Tudor had no defined intention of making love; but he had a sort of suspicion that he might, if he pleased, do so successfully; and he had no defined intention of letting it alone. He was a far-seeing, prudent man; for his age perhaps too prudent; but he was nevertheless fully susceptible of the pleasure of holding an affectionate, close intercourse with so sweet a girl as Linda Woodward; and though he knew that marriage with a girl without a dowry would for him be a death-blow to all his high hopes, he could hardly resist the temptation of conjugating the verb to love. Had he been able to choose from the two sisters, he would probably have selected Gertrude in spite of what he had said to Norman in the boat; but Gertrude was bespoken; and it therefore seemed all but unnatural that there should not be some love passages between him and Linda.

Ah! Mrs. Woodward, my friend, my friend, was it well that thou shouldst leave that sweet unguarded rosebud of thine to such perils as these?

They, also, commenced their wooing by talking over Captain Cuttwater; but they did not quarrel over him. Linda was quite content to be told by her friend what she ought to do, and how she ought to think about her uncle; and Alaric had a better way of laying down the law than

Norman. He could do so without offending his hearer's pride, and consequently was generally better listened to than his friend, though his law was probably not in effect so sound.

But they had soon done with Captain Cuttwater, and Alaric had to choose another subject. Gertrude and Norman were at some distance from them, but were in sight and somewhat in advance.

'Look at Harry,' said Alaric; 'I know from the motion of his shoulder that he is at this moment saying something very tender.'

'It is ten times more likely that they are quarrelling,' said Linda.

'Oh! the quarrels of lovers—we know all about that, don't we?'

'You must not call them lovers, Alaric; mamma would not like it, nor indeed would Gertrude, I am sure.'

'I would not for the world do anything that Mrs. Woodward would not like; but between ourselves, Linda, are they not lovers?'

'No; that is, not that I know of. I don't believe that they are a bit,' said Linda, blushing at her own fib.

'And why should they not be? How indeed is it possible that they should not be; that is—for I heartily beg Gertrude's pardon—how is it possible that Harry should not be in love with her?'

'Indeed, Gertrude is very, very beautiful,' said Linda, with the faintest possible sigh, occasioned by the remembrance of her own inferior charms.

'Indeed she is, very, very beautiful,' repeated Alaric, speaking with an absent air as though his mind were fully engaged in thinking of the beauty of which he spoke.

It was not in Linda's nature to be angry because her sister was admired, and because she was not. But yet there was something in Alaric's warm tone of admiration which gave her a feeling of unhappiness which she would have been quite unable to define, even had she attempted it. She saw her sister and Harry Norman before her, and she knew in her heart that they were lovers, in spite of her little weak declaration to the contrary. She saw how earnestly her sister was loved, and she in her kindly loving nature could not but envy her fancied happiness. Envy —no—it certainly was not envy. She would not for worlds have robbed her sister of her admirer ; but it was so natural for her to feel that it must be delicious to be admired !

She did not begrudge Gertrude Norman's superior beauty, nor his greater wealth ; she knew that Gertrude was entitled to more, much more, than herself. But seeing that Norman was Gertrude's lover, was it not natural that Alaric should be hers ? And then, though Harry was the handsomer and the richer, she liked Alaric so much the better of the two. But now that Alaric was alone with her, the only subject he could think to talk of was Gertrude's beauty !

It must not be supposed that these thoughts in their plainly-developed form passed through Linda's mind. It was not that she thought all this, but that she felt it. Such feelings are quite involuntary, whereas one's thoughts are more or less under command. Linda would not have allowed herself to think in this way for worlds ; but she could not control her feelings.

They walked on side by side, perfectly silent for a minute or two, and an ill-natured tear was gathering itself in the corner of Linda's eye : she was afraid even to raise her hand to brush it away, for fear Alaric should see her, and thus it went on gathering till it was like to fall.

'How singular it is,' said Alaric—'how very singular, the way in which I find myself living with you all ! such a perfect stranger as I am.'

'A perfect stranger !' said Linda, who, having remembered Alaric since the days of her short frocks and lessons, looked on him as a very old friend indeed.

'Yes, a perfect stranger, if you think of it. What do any of you know about me ? Your mother never saw my mother ; your father knew nothing of my father ; there is no kindred blood common to us. Harry Norman, there, is your near cousin ; but what am I that I should be thus allowed to live with you, and walk with you, and have a common interest in all your doings ? '

'Why, you are a dear friend of mamma's, are you not ? '

'A dear friend of mamma's! said he, 'well, indeed, I hope I am ; for your mother is at any rate a dear friend to me. But, Linda, one cannot be so much without longing to be more. Look at Harry, how happy he is ! '

'But, Alaric, surely you would not interfere with Harry,' said Linda, whose humble, innocent heart thought still of nothing but the merits of her sister ; and then, remembering that it was necessary that she should admit nothing on Gertrude's behalf, she entered her little protest against the assumption that her sister acknowledged Norman for her lover. 'That is, you would not do so, if there were anything in it.'

'I interfere with Harry ! ' said Alaric, switching the heads off the bits of fern with the cane he carried. 'No, indeed. I have no wish at all to do that. It is not that of which I was thinking. Harry is welcome to all his happiness ; that is, if Gertrude can be brought to make him happy.'

Linda made no answer now ; but the tear came running down her face, and her eyes became dim, and her heart beat very quick, and she didn't quite remember where she was. Up to this moment no man had spoken a word of love to Linda Woodward, and to some girls the first word is very trying.

'Interfere with Harry ! ' Alaric repeated again, and renewed his attack on the ferns. 'Well, Linda, what an opinion you must have of me ! '

Linda was past answering ; she could not protest—nor would it have been expedient to do so—that her opinion of her companion was not unfavourable.

'Gertrude is beautiful, very beautiful,' he continued, still beating about the bush as modest lovers do, and should do ; 'but she is not the only beautiful girl in Surbiton Cottage, nor to my eyes is she the most so.'

Linda was now quite beside herself. She knew that decorum required that she should say something stiff and stately to repress such language, but if all her future character for propriety had depended on it, she could not bring herself to say a word. She knew that Gertrude, when so addressed, would have maintained her dignity, and have concealed her secret, even if she allowed herself to have a secret to conceal. She knew that it behoved her to be repellent and antagonistic to the first vows of a first lover. But, alas! she had no power of antagonism, no energy for repulse left in her. Her knees seemed to be weak beneath her, and all she could do was to pluck to pieces the few flowers that she carried at her waist.

Alaric saw his advantage, but was too generous to push it closely; nor indeed did he choose to commit himself to all the assured intentions of a positive declaration. He wished to raise an interest in Linda's heart, and having done so, to leave the matter to chance. Something, however, it was necessary that he should say. He walked a while by her in silence, decapitating the ferns, and then coming close to her, he said—

'Linda, dear Linda! you are not angry with me?' Linda, however, answered nothing. 'Linda, dearest Linda! speak one word to me.'

'Don't!' said Linda through her tears. 'Pray don't, Alaric; pray don't.'

'Well, Linda, I will not say another word to you now. Let us walk gently; we shall catch them up quite in time before they leave the park.'

And so they sauntered on, exchanging no further words. Linda by degrees recovered her calmness, and as she did so, she found herself to be, oh! so happy. She had never, never envied Gertrude her lover; but it was so sweet, so very sweet, to be able to share her sister's happiness. And Alaric, was he also happy? At the moment he doubtless enjoyed the triumph of his success. But still he had a feeling of sad care at his heart. How was he to marry a girl without a shilling? Were all his high hopes, was all his soaring ambition, to be thrown over for a dream of love?

Ah! Mrs. Woodward, my friend, my friend, thou who wouldst have fed thy young ones, like the pelican, with blood from thine own breast, had such feeding been of avail; thou who art the kindest of mothers; has it been well for thee to subject to such perils this poor weak young dove of thine?

Uncle Bat had become tired with his walk, and crawled home so slowly that Alaric and Linda caught the party just as they reached the small wicket which leads out of the park on the side nearest to Hampton. Nothing was said or thought of their absence, and they all entered the house together. Four of them, however, were conscious that that Sunday's walk beneath the chestnuts of Bushey Park would long be remembered.

Nothing else occurred to make the day memorable. In the evening, after dinner, Mrs. Woodward and her daughters went to church, leaving her younger guests to entertain the elder one. The elder one soon took the matter in his own hand by going to sleep ; and Harry and Alaric being thus at liberty, sauntered out down the river side. They both made a forced attempt at good-humour, each speaking cheerily to the other ; but there was no confidence between them as there had been on that morning when Harry rowed his friend up to London. Ah me ! what had occurred between them to break the bonds of their mutual trust—to quench the ardour of their firm friendship ? But so it was between them now. It was fated that they never again should place full confidence in each other.

There was no such breach between the sisters, at least not as yet ; but even between them there was no free and full interchange of their hopes and fears. Gertrude and Linda shared the same room, and were accustomed —as what girls are not ?—to talk half through the night of all their wishes, thoughts, and feelings. And Gertrude was generally prone enough to talk of Harry Norman. Sometimes she would say she loved him a little, just a little ; at others she would declare that she loved him not at all—that is, not as heroines love in novels, not as she thought she could love, and would do, should it ever be her lot to be wooed by such a lover as her young fancy pictured to her. Then she would describe her beau idéal, and the description certainly gave no counterpart of Harry Norman. To tell the truth, however, Gertrude was as yet heart whole ; and when she talked of love and Harry Norman, she did not know what love was.

On this special Sunday evening she was disinclined to speak of him at all. Not that she loved him more than usual, but that she was beginning to think that she could

not ever really love him at all. She had taught herself to
think that he might probably be her husband, and had
hitherto felt no such repugnance to her destiny as caused
her to shun the subject. But now she was beginning to
think of the matter seriously; and as she did so, she felt
that life might have for her a lot more blessed than that
of sharing the world with her cousin Harry.

When, therefore, Linda began to question her about her
lover, and to make little hints of her desire to tell what
Alaric had said of her and Norman, Gertrude gave her no
encouragement. She would speak of Captain Cuttwater,
of Katie's lessons, of the new dress they were to make for
their mother, of Mr. Everscreech's long sermon, of anything in fact but of Harry Norman.

Now this was very hard on poor Linda. Her heart was
bursting within her to tell her sister that she also was
beloved; but she could not do so without some little
encouragement.

In all their conferences she took the cue of the conversation from her sister; and though she could have
talked about Alaric by the hour, if Gertrude would have
consented to talk about Harry, she did not know how to
start the subject of her own lover, while Gertrude was so
cold and uncommunicative as to hers. She struggled very
hard to obtain the privilege for which she so anxiously
longed; but in doing so she only met with a sad and sore
rebuff.

'Gertrude,' at last said Linda, when Gertrude thought
that the subject had been put to rest at any rate for
that night, 'don't you think mamma would be pleased
if she knew that you had engaged yourself to Harry
Norman?'

'No,' said Gertrude, evincing her strong mind by the
tone in which she spoke; 'I do not. If mamma wished
it, she would have told me; for she never has any secrets.
I should be as wrong to engage myself with Harry as you
would be with Alaric. For though Harry has property
of his own, while poor Alaric has none, he has a very
insufficient income for a married man, and I have no
fortune with which to help him. If nothing else prevented
it, I should consider it wicked in me to make myself

a burden to a man while he is yet so young and comparatively so poor.'

Prudent, sensible, high-minded, well-disciplined Gertrude ! But had her heart really felt a spark of love for
the man of whom she spoke, how much would prudent,
sensible, high-minded considerations have weighed with
her ? Alas ! not a feather.

Having made her prudent, high-minded speech, she
turned round and slept ; and poor Linda also turned
round and bedewed her pillow. She no longer panted to
tell her sister of Alaric's love.

On the next morning the two young men returned to
town, and the customary dullness of the week began.

CHAPTER VI

SIR GREGORY HARDLINES

GREAT changes had been going on at the Weights and
Measures ; or rather it might be more proper to say that
great changes were now in progress. From that moment
in which it had been hinted to Mr. Hardlines that he
must relax the rigour of his examinations, he had pon-
dered deeply over the matter. Hitherto he had confined
his efforts to his own office, and, so far from feeling
personally anxious for the amelioration of the Civil
Service generally, had derived no inconsiderable share of
his happiness from the knowledge that there were such
sinks of iniquity as the Internal Navigation. To be widely
different from others was Mr. Hardlines' glory. He was,
perhaps, something of a Civil Service Pharisee, and wore
on his forehead a broad phylactery, stamped with the
mark of Crown property. He thanked God that he was
not as those publicans at Somerset House, and took glory
to himself in paying tithes of official cumin.

But now he was driven to a wider range. Those higher
Pharisees who were above him in his own pharisaical
establishment, had interfered with the austerity of his

worship. He could not turn against them there, on their own ground. He, of all men, could not be disobedient to official orders. But if he could promote a movement beyond the walls of the Weights and Measures; if he could make Pharisees of those benighted publicans in the Strand; if he could introduce conic sections into the Custom House, and political economy into the Post Office; if, by any effort of his, the Foreign Office clerks could be forced to attend punctually at ten; and that wretched saunterer, whom five days a week he saw lounging into the Council Office—if he could be made to mend his pace, what a wide field for his ambition would Mr. Hardlines then have found!

Great ideas opened themselves to his mind as he walked to and from his office daily. What if he could become the parent of a totally different order of things! What if the Civil Service, through his instrumentality, should become the nucleus of the best intellectual diligence in the country, instead of being a byword for sloth and ignorance! Mr. Hardlines meditated deeply on this, and, as he did so, it became observed on all sides that he was an altered man as regarded his solicitude for the Weights and Measures. One or two lads crept in, by no means conspicuous for their attainments in abstract science; young men, too, were observed to leave not much after four o'clock, without calling down on themselves Mr. Hardlines' usual sarcasm. Some said he was growing old, others that he was broken-hearted. But Mr. Hardlines was not old, nor broken in heart or body. He was thinking of higher things than the Weights and Measures, and at last he published a pamphlet.

Mr. Hardlines had many enemies, all in the Civil Service, one of the warmest of whom was Mr. Oldeschole, of the Navigation, and at first they rejoiced greatly that Job's wish had been accomplished on their behalf, and that their enemy had written a book. They were down on Mr. Hardlines with reviews, counter pamphlets, official statements, and indignant contradiction; but Mr. Hardlines lived through this storm of missiles, and got his book to be fêted and made much of by some Government pundits, who were very bigwigs indeed. And at last he was invited over to the building on the other side, to discuss the matter with a President, a Secretary of State, a Lord Commissioner, two joint Secretaries, and three Chairmen.

And then, for a period of six months, the light of Mr. Hardlines' face ceased to shine on the children of the Weights and Measures, and they felt, one and all, that the glory had in a certain measure departed from their house. Now and again Mr. Hardlines would look in, but he did so rather as an enemy than as a friend. There was always a gleam of antagonistic triumph in his eye, which showed that he had not forgotten the day when he was called in question for his zeal. He was felt to be in opposition to his own Board, rather than in co-operation with it. The Secretary and the Assistant-Secretaries would say little caustic things about him to the senior clerks, and seemed somewhat to begrudge him his new honours. But for all this Mr. Hardlines cared little. The President and the Secretary of State, the joint Secretaries and the Chairmen, all allowed themselves to be led by him in this matter. His ambition was about to be gratified. It was his destiny that he should remodel the Civil Service. What was it to him whether or no one insignificant office would listen to his charming ? Let the Secretary at the Weights and Measures sneer as he would ; he would make that hero of the metallic currency know that he, Mr. Hardlines, was his master.

At the end of six months his budding glory broke out into splendid, full-blown, many-coloured flowers. He resigned his situation at the Weights and Measures, and was appointed Chief Commissioner of the Board of Civil Service Examination, with a salary of £2,000 a year; he was made a K.C.B., and shone forth to the world as Sir Gregory Hardlines ; and he received a present of £1,000, that happy *ne plus ultra* of Governmental liberality. Sir Gregory Hardlines was forced to acknowledge to himself that he was born to a great destiny.

When Sir Gregory, as we must now call him, was first invited to give his attendance at another office, he found it expedient to take with him one of the young men from the Weights and Measures, and he selected Alaric

Tudor. Now this was surprising to many, for Tudor had been brought into the office not quite in accordance with Sir Gregory's views. But during his four years of service Alaric had contrived to smooth down any acerbity which had existed on this score ; either the paper on the strike-bushel, or his own general intelligence, or perhaps a certain amount of flattery which he threw into his daily inter-course with the chief clerk, had been efficacious, and when Sir Gregory was called upon to select a man to take with him to his new temporary office, he selected Alaric Tudor.

The main effect which such selection had upon our story rises from the circumstance that it led to an introduc-tion between Tudor and the Honourable Undecimus Scott, and that this introduction brought about a close alliance.

We will postpone for a short while such description of the character and position of this gentleman as it may be indispensable to give, and will in this place merely say that the Honourable Undecimus Scott had been chosen to act as secretary to the temporary commission that was now making inquiry as to the proposed Civil Service examinations, and that in this capacity he was necessarily thrown into communication with Tudor. He was a man who had known much of officialities, had filled many situations, was acquainted with nearly all the secretaries, assistant-secretaries, and private secretaries in London, had been in Parliament, and was still hand-and-glove with all young members who supported Government. Tudor, therefore, thought it a privilege to know him, and allowed himself to become, in a certain degree, subject to his influence.

When it was declared to the world of Downing Street that Sir Gregory Hardlines was to be a great man, to have an office of his own, and to reign over assistant-commis-sioners and subject secretaries, there was great commotion at the Weights and Measures ; and when his letter of resignation was absolutely there, visible to the eyes of clerks, properly docketed and duly minuted, routine business was, for a day, nearly suspended. Gentlemen walked in and out from each other's rooms, asking this momentous question—Who was to fill the chair which had so long been honoured by the great Hardlines? Who was to be thought worthy to wear that divine mantle?

But even this was not the question of the greatest moment which at that period disturbed the peace of the office. It was well known that the chief clerk must be chosen from one of the three senior clerks, and that he would be so chosen by the voice of the Commissioners. There were only three men who were deeply interested in this question. But who would then be the new senior clerk, and how would he be chosen? A strange rumour began to be afloat that the new scheme of competitive examination was about to be tried in filling up this vacancy, occasioned by the withdrawal of Sir Gregory Hardlines. From hour to hour the rumour gained ground, and men's minds began to be much disturbed.

It was no wonder that men's minds should be disturbed. Competitive examinations at eighteen, twenty, and twenty-two may be very well, and give an interesting stimulus to young men at college. But it is a fearful thing for a married man with a family, who has long looked forward to rise to a certain income by the worth of his general conduct and by the value of his seniority—it is a fearful thing for such a one to learn that he has again to go through his school tricks, and fill up examination papers, with all his juniors round him using their stoutest efforts to take his promised bread from out of his mouth. *Detur digno* is a maxim which will make men do their best to merit rewards; every man can find courage within his heart to be worthy; but *detur digniori* is a fearful law for such a profession as the Civil Service. What worth can make a man safe against the possible greater worth which will come treading on his heels? The spirit of the age raises, from year to year, to a higher level the standard of education. The prodigy of 1857, who is now destroying all the hopes of the man who was well enough in 1855, will be a dunce to the tyro of 1860.

There were three or four in the Weights and Measures who felt all this with the keenest anxiety. The fact of their being there, and of their having passed the scrutiny of Mr. Hardlines, was proof enough that they were men of high attainments; but then the question arose to

them and others whether they were men exactly of those
attainments which were *now* most required. Who is to
say what shall constitute the merits of the *dignior*? It
may one day be conic sections, another Greek iambics,
and a third German philosophy. Rumour began to say
that foreign languages were now very desirable. The
three excellent married gentlemen who stood first in
succession for the coveted promotion were great only in
their vernacular.

Within a week from the secession of Sir Gregory, his
immediate successor had been chosen, and it had been
officially declared that the vacant situation in the senior
class was to be thrown open as a prize for the best man in
the office. Here was a brilliant chance for young merit!
The place was worth £600 a-year, and might be gained by
any one who now received no more than £100. Each
person desirous of competing was to send in his name to
the Secretary, on or before that day fortnight; and on
that day month, the candidates were to present themselves
before Sir Gregory Hardlines and his board of Commissioners.

And yet the joy of the office was by no means great.
The senior of those who might become competitors, was
of course a miserable, disgusted man. He went about
fruitlessly endeavouring to instigate rebellion against Sir
Gregory, that very Sir Gregory whom he had for many
years all but worshipped. Poor Jones was, to tell the
truth, in a piteous case. He told the Secretary flatly that
he would not compete with a lot of boys fresh from school,
and his friends began to think of removing his razors.
Nor were Brown and Robinson in much better plight.
They both, it is true, hated Jones ruthlessly, and desired
nothing better than an opportunity of supplanting him.
They were, moreover, fast friends themselves; but not
the less on that account had Brown a mortal fear of
Robinson, as also had Robinson a mortal fear of Brown.

Then came the bachelors. First there was Uppinall,
who, when he entered the office, was supposed to know
everything which a young man had ever known. Those
who looked most to dead knowledge were inclined to back
him as first favourite. It had, however, been remarked,

that his utility as a clerk had not been equal to the profundity of his acquirements. Of all the candidates he was the most self-confident.

The next to him was Mr. A. Minusex, a wondrous arithmetician. He was one who could do as many sums without pen and paper as a learned pig; who was so given to figures that he knew the number of stairs in every flight he had gone up and down in the metropolis; one who, whatever the subject before him might be, never thought but always counted. Many who knew the peculiar propensities of Sir Gregory's earlier days thought that Mr. Minusex was not an unlikely candidate.

The sixth in order was our friend Norman. The Secretary and the two Assistant-Secretaries, when they first put their heads together on the matter, declared that he was the most useful man in the office.

There was a seventh, named Alphabet Precis. Mr. Precis' peculiar forte was a singular happiness in official phraseology. Much that he wrote would doubtless have been considered in the purlieus of Paternoster Row as ungrammatical, if not unintelligible; but according to the syntax of Downing Street, it was equal to Macaulay, and superior to Gibbon. He had frequently said to his intimate friends, that in official writing, style was everything; and of his writing it certainly did form a very prominent part. He knew well, none perhaps so well, when to beg leave to lay before the Board—and when simply to submit to the Commissioners. He understood exactly to whom it behoved the secretary ' to have the honour of being a very humble servant,' and to whom the more simple ' I am, sir,' was a sufficiently civil declaration. These are qualifications great in official life, but were not quite so much esteemed at the time of which we are speaking as they had been some few years previously.

There was but one other named as likely to stand with any probability of success, and he was Alaric Tudor. Among the very juniors of the office he was regarded as the great star of the office. There was a dash about him and a quick readiness for any work that came to hand in which, perhaps, he was not equalled by any of his compeers. Then, too, he was the special friend of Sir Gregory.

But no one had yet heard Tudor say that he intended to compete with his seven seniors—none yet knew whether he would put himself forward as an adversary to his own especial friend, Norman. That Norman would be a candidate had been prominently stated. For some few days not a word was spoken, even between the friends themselves, as to Tudor's intention.

On the Sunday they were as usual at Hampton, and then the subject was mooted by no less a person than Captain Cuttwater.

'So you young gentlemen up in London are all going to be examined, are you?' said he; 'what is it to be about? Who's to be first lieutenant of the ship, is that it?'

'Oh no,' said Alaric, 'nothing half so high as that. Boatswain's mate would be nearer the mark.'

'And who is to be the successful man?'

'Oh, Harry Norman, here. He was far the first favourite in yesterday's betting.'

'And how do you stand yourself?' said Uncle Bat.

'Oh! I'm only an outsider,' said Alaric. 'They put my name down just to swell the number, but I shall be scratched before the running begins.'

'Indeed he won't,' said Harry. 'He'll run and distance us all. There is no one who has a chance with him. Why, he is Sir Gregory's own pet.'

There was nothing more said on the subject at Surbiton Cottage. The ladies seemed instinctively to perceive that it was a matter which they had better leave alone. Not only were the two young men to be pitted against each other, but Gertrude and Linda were as divided in their wishes on the subject as the two candidates could be themselves.

On the following morning, however, Norman introduced the subject. 'I suppose you were only jesting yesterday,' said he, 'when you told the captain that you were not going to be a candidate?'

'Indeed I can hardly say that I was in jest or in earnest,' said Alaric. 'I simply meant to decline to discuss the subject with Uncle Bat.'

'But of course you do mean to stand?' said Harry. Alaric made no answer.

' Perhaps you would rather decline to discuss the matter with me also ? ' said Harry.

' Not at all ; I would much prefer discussing it openly and honestly. My own impression is, that I had better leave it alone.'

' And why so ? ' said Harry.

' Why so ? ' repeated Alaric. ' Well, there are so many reasons. In the first place, there would be seven to one against me ; and I must confess that if I did stand I should not like to be beaten.'

' The same argument might keep us all back,' said Norman.

' That's true ; but one man will be more sensitive, more cowardly, if you will, than another ; and then I think no one should stand who does not believe himself to have a fair chance. His doing so might probably mar his future prospects. How can I put myself in competition with such men as Uppinall and Minusex ? '

Harry laughed slightly, for he knew it had been asked by many how such men as Uppinall and Minusex could think of putting themselves in competition with Alaric Tudor.

' That is something like mock-modesty, is it not, Alaric ? '

' No, by heaven, it is not ! I know well what those men are made of ; and I know, or think I know, my own abilities. I will own that I rank myself as a human creature much higher than I rank them. But they have that which I have not, and that which they have is that which these examiners will chiefly require.'

' If you have no other reason,' said Norman, ' I would strongly advise you to send in your name.'

' Well, Harry, I have another reason ; and, though last, it is by no means the least. You will be a candidate, and probably the successful one. To tell you the truth, I have no inclination to stand against you.'

Norman turned very red, and then answered somewhat gravely : ' I would advise you to lay aside that objection. I fairly tell you that I consider your chance better than my own.'

' And suppose it be so, which I am sure it is not—but suppose it be so, what then ? '

'Why, you will do right to take advantage of it.'

'Yes, and so gain a step and lose a friend!' said Alaric. 'No; there can be no heartburn to me in your being selected, for though I am older than you, you are my senior in the office. But were I to be put over your head, it would in the course of nature make a division between us; and if it were possible that you should forgive it, it would be quite impossible that Gertrude should do so. I value your friendship and that of the Woodwards too highly to risk it.'

Norman instantly fired up with true generous energy. 'I should be wretched,' said he, 'if I thought that such a consideration weighed with you; I would rather withdraw myself than allow such a feeling to interfere with your prospects. Indeed, after what you have said, I shall not send in my own name unless you also send in yours.'

'I shall only be creating fuel for a feud,' said Alaric. 'To put you out of the question, no promotion could compensate to me for what I should lose at Hampton.'

'Nonsense, man; you would lose nothing. Faith, I don't know whether it is not I that should lose, if I were successful at your expense.'

'How would Gertrude receive me?' said Alaric, pushing the matter further than he perhaps should have done.

'We won't mind Gertrude,' said Norman, with a little shade of black upon his brow. 'You are an older man than I, and therefore promotion is to you of more importance than to me. You are also a poorer man. I have some means besides that drawn from my office, which, if I marry, I can settle on my wife; you have none such. I should consider myself to be worse than wicked if I allowed any consideration of such a nature to stand in the way of your best interests. Believe me, Alaric, that though I shall, as others, be anxious for success myself, I should, in failing, be much consoled by knowing that you had succeeded.' And as he finished speaking he grasped his friend's hand warmly in token of the truth of his assertion.

Alaric brushed a tear from his eye, and ended by promising to be guided by his friend's advice. Harry Norman, as he walked into the office, felt a glow of triumph as he reflected that he had done his duty by his friend with true disinterested honesty. And Alaric, he also felt a glow of triumph as he reflected that, come what might, there would be now no necessity for him to break with Norman or with the Woodwards. Norman must now always remember that it was at his own instigation that he, Alaric, had consented to be a candidate.

As regarded the real fact of the candidature, the prize was too great to allow of his throwing away such a chance. Alaric's present income was £200; that which he hoped to gain was £600 !

CHAPTER VII

MR. FIDUS NEVERBEND

IMMEDIATELY on entering the office, Tudor gave it to be understood that he intended to give in his name as a candidate; but he had hardly done so when his attention was called off from the coming examinations by another circumstance, which was ultimately of great importance to him. One of the Assistant-Secretaries sent for him, and told him that his services having been required by Sir Gregory Hardlines for a week or so, he was at once to go over to that gentleman's office; and Alaric could perceive that, as Sir Gregory's name was mentioned, the Assistant-Secretary smiled on him with no aspect of benign solicitude.

He went over accordingly, and found that Sir Gregory, having been desired to select a man for a special service in the country, had named him. He was to go down to Tavistock with another gentleman from the Woods and Forests, for the purpose of settling some disputed point as to the boundaries and privileges of certain mines situated there on Crown property.

' You know nothing about mining, I presume ? ' said Sir Gregory.

' Nothing whatever,' said Alaric.

' I thought not ; that was one reason why I selected you. What is wanted is a man of sharp intelligence and plain common sense, and one also who can write English ; for it will fall to your lot to draw up the report on the matter. Mr. Neverbend, who is to be your colleague, cannot put two words together.'

' Mr. Neverbend ! ' said Alaric.

' Yes, Fidus Neverbend, of the Woods and Forests, a very excellent public servant, and one in whom the fullest confidence can be placed. But between you and me, he will never set the Thames on fire.'

' Does he understand mining ? ' asked Alaric.

' He understands Government properties, and will take care that the Crown be not wronged ; but, Tudor, the Government will look to you to get the true common-sense view of the case. I trust—I mean that I really do trust, that you will not disgrace my choice.'

Alaric of course promised that he would do his best, expressed the deepest gratitude to his patron, and went off to put himself into communication with Mr. Neverbend at the Woods and Forests, having received an assurance that the examination in his own office should not take place till after his return from Tavistock. He was not slow to perceive that if he could manage to come back with all the *éclat* of a successful mission, the prestige of such a journey would go far to assist him on his coming trial.

Mr. Fidus Neverbend was an absolute dragon of honesty. His integrity was of such an all-pervading nature, that he bristled with it as a porcupine does with its quills. He had theories and axioms as to a man's conduct, and the conduct especially of a man in the Queen's Civil Service, up to which no man but himself could live. Consequently no one but himself appeared to himself to be true and just in all his dealings.

A quarter of an hour spent over a newspaper was in his eyes a downright robbery. If he saw a man so employed, he would divide out the total of salary into hourly portions, and tell him to a fraction of how much he was defrauding the public. If he ate a biscuit in the middle of the day, he did so with his eyes firmly fixed on some document, and he had never been known to be absent from his office after ten or before four.

When Sir Gregory Hardlines declared that Mr. Fidus Neverbend would never set the Thames on fire, he meant to express his opinion that that gentleman was a fool ; and that those persons who were responsible for sending Mr. Neverbend on the mission now about to be undertaken, were little better than fools themselves for so sending him. But Mr. Neverbend was no fool. He was not a disciple of Sir Gregory's school. He had never sat in that philosopher's porch, or listened to the high doctrines prevalent at the Weights and Measures. He could not write with all Mr. Precis' conventional correctness, or dispose of any subject at a moment's notice as would Mr. Uppinall ; but, nevertheless, he was no fool. Sir Gregory, like many other wise men, thought that there were no swans but of his own hatching, and would ask, with all the pompous conceit of Pharisees in another age, whether good could come out of the Woods and Forests ?

Sir Gregory, however, perfectly succeeded in his object of imbuing Tudor with a very indifferent opinion of his new colleague's abilities. It was his object that Tudor should altogether take the upper hand in the piece of work which was to be done between them, and that it should be clearly proved how very incapable the Woods and Forests were of doing their own business.

Mr. Fidus Neverbend, however, whatever others in the outer world might think of him, had a high character in his own office, and did not under-estimate himself. He, when he was told that a young clerk named Tudor was to accompany him, conceived that he might look on his companion rather in the light of a temporary private secretary than an equal partner, and imagined that new glory was added to him by his being so treated. The two men therefore met each other with very different views.

But though Mr. Neverbend was no fool, he was not an equal either in tact or ability to Alaric Tudor. Alaric had his interview with him, and was not slow to perceive the sort of man with whom he had to act. Of course, on this occasion, little more than grimaces and civility passed between them ; but Mr. Neverbend, even in his grimaces and civility, managed to show that he regarded himself as decidedly No. 1 upon the occasion.

'Well, Mr. Tudor,' said he, 'I think of starting on Tuesday. Tuesday will not, I suppose, be inconvenient to you ?'

'Sir Gregory has already told me that we are expected to be at Tavistock on Tuesday evening.'

'Ah! I don't know about that,' said Neverbend; 'that may be all very well for Sir Gregory, but I rather think I shall stay the night at Plymouth.'

'It will be the same to me,' said Tudor; 'I haven't looked at the papers yet, so I can hardly say what may be necessary.'

'No, no ; of course not. As to the papers, I don't know that there is much with which you need trouble yourself. I believe I am pretty well up in the case. But, Mr. Tudor, there will be a good deal of writing to do when we are there.'

'We are both used to that, I fancy,' said Tudor, 'so it won't kill us.'

'No, of course not. I understand that there will be a good many people for me to see, a great many conflicting interests for me to reconcile ; and probably I may find myself obliged to go down two or three of these mines.'

'Well, that will be good fun,' said Alaric.

Neverbend drew himself up. The idea of having fun at the cost of Government was painful to him ; however, he spared the stranger his reproaches, and merely remarked that the work he surmised would be heavy enough both for the man who went below ground, and for the one who remained above.

The only point settled between them was that of their starting by an early train on the Tuesday named ; and then Alaric returned to Sir Gregory's office, there to read through and digest an immense bulk of papers all bearing on the question at issue. There had, it appeared, been lately opened between the Tamar and the Tavy a new mine, which had become exceedingly prosperous—outrageously prosperous, as shareholders and directors of neighbouring mines taught themselves to believe. Some question had arisen as to the limits to which the happy possessors of this new tin El Dorado were entitled to go; squabbles, of course, had been the result, and miners and masters had fought and bled, each side in defence of its own rights. As a portion of these mines were on Crown property it became necessary that the matter should be looked to, and as the local inspector was accused of having been bribed and bought, and of being, in fact, an absolute official Judas, it became necessary to send some one to inspect the inspector. Hence had come Alaric's mission. The name of the mine in question was Wheal Mary Jane, and Alaric had read the denomination half a score of times before he learnt that there was no real female in the case.

The Sunday before he went was of course passed at Hampton, and there he received the full glory of his special appointment. He received glory, and Norman in an equal degree fell into the background. Mrs. Woodward stuck kindly to Harry, and endeavoured, in her gentle way, to quiz the projected trip to Devonshire. But the other party was too strong, and her raillery failed to have the intended effect. Gertrude especially expressed her opinion that it was a great thing for so young a man to have been selected for such employment by such a person; and Linda, though she said less, could not prevent her tell-tale face from saying more. Katie predicted that Alaric would certainly marry Mary Jane Wheal, and bring her to Surbiton Cottage, and Captain Cuttwater offered to the hero introductions to all the old naval officers at Devonport.

'By jingo! I should like to go with you,' said the captain.

'I fear the pleasure would not repay the trouble,' said Alaric, laughing.

'Upon my word I think I'll do it,' said the captain. 'It would be of the greatest possible service to you as an officer of the Crown. It would give you so much weight there. I could make you known, you know——'

'I could not hear of such a thing,' said Alaric, trembling at the idea which Uncle Bat had conjured up.

'There is Admiral Starbod, and Captain Focassel, and old Hardaport, and Sir Jib Boom—why, d—n me, they would all do anything for me—craving the ladies' pardon.'

Alaric, in his own defence, was obliged to declare that the rules of the service especially required that he should hold no friendly communication with any one during the time that he was employed on this special service. Poor Captain Cuttwater, grieved to have his good nature checked, was obliged to put up with this excuse, and consoled himself with abusing the Government which could condescend to give so absurd an order.

This was on the Saturday. On the Sunday, going to church, the captain suggested that Alaric might, at any rate, just call upon Sir Jib on the sly. 'It would be a great thing for you,' said Uncle Bat. 'I'll write a note to-night, and you can take it with you. Sir Jib is a rising man, and you'll regret it for ever if you miss the opportunity.' Now Sir Jib Boom was between seventy and eighty, and he and Captain Cuttwater had met each other nearly every day for the last twenty years, and had never met without a squabble.

After church they had their usual walk, and Linda's heart palpitated as she thought that she might have to undergo another *tête-à-tête* with her lover. But it palpitated in vain. It so turned out that Alaric either avoided, or, at any rate, did not use the privilege, and Linda returned home with an undefined feeling of gentle disappointment. She had fully made up her mind to be very staid, very discreet, and very collected ; to take a leaf out of her sister's book, and give him no encouragement whatever ; she would not absolutely swear to him that she did not now, and never could, return his passion ; but she would point out how very imprudent any engagement between two young persons, situated as they were, must be—how foolish it would be for them to bind themselves, for any number of years, to a marriage which must be postponed ; she would tell Alaric all this, and make him understand that he was not to regard himself as affianced to her ; but she with a woman's faith would nevertheless remain true to him. This was Linda's great resolve, and the strong hope, that in a very few weeks, Alaric would be promoted to a marrying income of £600 per annum, made the prospect of the task not so painful as it might otherwise have been. Fate, however, robbed her of the pleasure, if it would have been a pleasure, of sacrificing her love to her duty ; and 'dear Linda, dearest Linda,' was not again whispered into her ear.

'And what on earth is it that you are to do down in the mines ?' asked Mrs. Woodward as they sat together in the evening.

'Nothing on the earth, Mrs. Woodward—it is to be all below the surface, forty fathom deep,' said Alaric.

'Take care that you ever come up again,' said she.

'They say the mine is exceedingly rich—perhaps I may be tempted to stay down there.'

'Then you'll be like the gloomy gnome, that lives in dark, cold mines,' said Katie.

'Isn't it very dangerous, going down into those places ?' asked Linda.

'Men go down and come up again every day of their lives, and what other men can do, I can, I suppose.'

'That doesn't follow at all,' said Captain Cuttwater, 'What sort of a figure would you make on a yard-arm, reefing a sail in a gale of wind ?'

'Pray do take care of yourself,' said Gertrude.

Norman's brow grew black. 'I thought that it was settled that Mr. Neverbend was to go down, and that you were to stay above ground,' said he.

'So Mr. Neverbend settled it ; but that arrangement may, perhaps, be unsettled again,' said Alaric, with a certain feeling of confidence in his own strong will.

'I don't at all doubt,' said Mrs. Woodward, 'that if we were to get a sly peep at you, we should find you both sitting comfortably at your inn all the time, and that neither of you will go a foot below the ground.'

'Very likely. All I mean to say is, that if Neverbend goes down I'll go too.'

'But mind, you gloomy gnome, mind you bring up a bit of gold for me,' said Katie.

On the Monday morning he started with the often-expressed good wishes of all the party, and with a note for Sir Jib Boom, which the captain made him promise that he would deliver, and which Alaric fully determined to lose long before he got to Plymouth.

That evening he and Norman passed together. As soon as their office hours were over, they went into the London Exhibition, which was then open ; and there, walking up and down the long centre aisle, they talked with something like mutual confidence of their future prospects. This was a favourite resort with Norman, who had schooled himself to feel an interest in works of art. Alaric's mind was of a different cast ; he panted rather for the great than the beautiful ; and was inclined to ridicule the growing taste of the day for torsos, Palissy ware, and Assyrian monsters.

There was then some mutual confidence between the two young men. Norman, who was apt to examine himself and his own motives more strictly than Alaric ever did, had felt that something like suspicion as to his friend had crept over him ; and he had felt also that there was no ground for such suspicion. He had determined to throw it off, and to be again cordial with his companion. He had resolved so to do before his last visit at Hampton ; but it was at Hampton that the suspicion had been engendered, and there he found himself unable to be genial, kindly, and contented. Surbiton Cottage was becoming to him anything but the abode of happiness that it had once been. A year ago he had been the hero of the Hampton Sundays ; he could not but now feel that Alaric had, as it were, supplanted him with his own friends. The arrival even of so insignificant a person as Captain Cuttwater—and Captain Cuttwater was very insignificant in Norman's mind—had done much to produce this state of things. He had been turned out of his bedroom at the cottage, and had therefore lost those last, loving, lingering words, sometimes protracted to so late an hour, which had been customary after Alaric's departure to his inn—those last lingering words which had been so sweet because their sweetness had not been shared with his friend.

He could not be genial and happy at Surbiton Cottage ; but he was by no means satisfied with himself that he should not have been so. When he found that he had been surly with Alaric, he was much more angry with himself than Alaric was with him. Alaric, indeed, was indifferent about it. He had no wish to triumph over Harry, but he had an object to pursue, and he was not the man to allow himself to be diverted from it by any one's caprice.

'This trip is a great thing for you,' said Harry.

'Well, I really don't know. Of course I could not decline it; but on the whole I should be just as well pleased to have been spared. If I get through it well, why it will be well. But even that cannot help me at this examination.'

'I don't know that.'

'Why—a week passed in the slush of a Cornish mine won't teach a man algebra.'

'It will give you *prestige*.'

'Then you mean to say the examiners won't examine fairly; well, perhaps so. But what will be the effect on me if I fail? I know nothing of mines. I have a colleague with me of whom I can only learn that he is not weak enough to be led, or wise enough to lead; who is so self-opinionated that he thinks he is to do the whole work himself, and yet so jealous that he fears I shall take the very bread out of his mouth. What am I to do with such a man?'

'You must manage him,' said Harry.

'That is much easier said than done,' replied Alaric. 'I wish you had the task instead of me.'

'So do not I. Sir Gregory, when he chose you, knew what he was about.'

'Upon my word, Harry, you are full of compliments to-day. I really ought to take my hat off.'

'No, I am not; I am in no mood for compliments. I know very well what stuff you are made of. I know your superiority to myself. I know you will be selected to go up over all our heads. I feel all this; and Alaric, you must not be surprised that, to a certain degree, it is painful to me to feel it. But, by God's help I will get over it; and if you succeed it shall go hard with me, but I will teach myself to rejoice at it. Look at that fawn there,' said he, turning away his face to hide the tear in his eye, 'did you ever see more perfect motion?'

Alaric was touched; but there was more triumph than sympathy in his heart. It was sweet, much too sweet, to him to hear his superiority thus acknowledged. He *was* superior to the men who worked round him in his office. He was made of a more plastic clay than they, and despite the inferiority of his education, he knew himself to be fit for higher work than they could do. As the acknowledgement was made to him by the man whom, of those around him, he certainly ranked second to himself, he could not but feel that his heart's blood ran warm within him, he could not but tread with an elastic step.

But it behoved him to answer Harry, and to answer him in other spirit than this.

'Oh, Harry,' said he, 'you have some plot to ruin me by my own conceit; to make me blow myself out and destroy myself, poor frog that I am, in trying to loom as largely as that great cow, Fidus Neverbend. You know I am fully conscious how much inferior my education has been to yours.'

'Education is nothing,' said Harry.

Education *is* nothing! Alaric triumphantly re-echoed the words in his heart—'Education is nothing—mind, mind is everything; mind and the will.' So he expressed himself to his own inner self; but out loud he spoke much more courteously.

'It is the innate modesty of your own heart, Harry, that makes you think so highly of me and so meanly of yourself. But the proof of what we each can do is yet to be seen. Years alone can decide that. That your career will be honourable and happy, of that I feel fully sure! I wish I were as confident of mine.'

'But, Alaric,' said Norman, going on rather with the thread of his own thoughts, than answering or intending to answer what the other said, 'in following up your high ambition—and I know you have a high ambition—do not allow yourself to believe that the end justifies the means, because you see that men around you act as though they believed so.'

'Do I do so—do I seem to do so?' said Alaric, turning sharply round.

'Don't be angry with me, Alaric; don't think that I want to preach; but sometimes I fancy, not that you do so, but that your mind is turning that way; that in your eager desire for honourable success you won't scrutinize the steps you will have to take.'

'That I would get to the top of the hill, in short, even though the hillside be miry. Well, I own I wish to get to the top of the hill.'

'But not to defile yourself in doing so.'

'When a man comes home from a successful chase, with his bag well stuffed with game, the women do not quarrel with him because there is mud on his gaiters.'

'Alaric, that which is evil is evil. Lies are evil——'

'And am I a liar ?'

'Heaven forbid that I should say so : heaven forbid that I should have to think so ! but it is by such doctrines as that that men become liars.'

'What ! by having muddy gaiters ?'

'By disregarding the means in looking to the end.'

'And I will tell you how men become mere vegetables, by filling their minds with useless—needless scruples—by straining at gnats——'

'Well, finish your quotation,' said Harry.

'I have finished it ; in speaking to you I would not for the world go on, and seem to insinuate that you would swallow a camel. No insinuation could be more base or unjust. But, nevertheless, I think you may be too over-scrupulous. What great man ever rose to greatness,' continued Alaric, after they had walked nearly the length of the building in silence, ' who thought it necessary to pick his steps in the manner you have described ?'

'Then I would not be great,' said Harry.

'But, surely, God intends that there shall be great men on the earth ?'

'He certainly wishes that there should be good men,' said Harry.

'And cannot a man be good and great ?'

'That is the problem for a man to solve. Do you try that. Good you certainly can be, if you look to Him for assistance. Let that come first ; and then the greatness, if that be possible.'

'It is all a quibble about a word,' said Alaric. 'What is good ? David was a man after God's own heart, and a great man too, and yet he did things which, were I to

do, I should be too base to live. Look at Jacob—how
did he achieve the tremendous rights of patriarchal
primogeniture ? But, come, the policemen are trying to
get rid of us ; it is time for us to go,' and so they left the
building, and passed the remainder of the evening in
concord together—in concord so soon to be dissolved, and,
ah ! perhaps never to be renewed.

On the next morning Alaric and his new companion
met each other at an early hour at the Paddington station.
Neverbend was rather fussy with his dispatch-box, and
a large official packet, which an office messenger, dashing
up in a cab, brought to him at the moment of his departure.
Neverbend's enemies were wont to declare that a messenger, a cab, and a big packet always rushed up at the
moment of his starting on any of his official trips. Then
he had his ticket to get and his *Times* to buy, and he
really had not leisure to do more than nod at Alaric till
he had folded his rug around him, tried that the cushion
was soft enough, and completed his arrangements for the
journey.

'Well, Mr. Tudor,' at last he said, as soon as the train
was in motion, ' and how are you this morning—ready for
work, I hope ? '

'Well, not exactly at this moment,' said Alaric. ' One
has to get up so early for these morning trains.'

' Early, Mr. Tudor ! my idea is that no hour should be
considered either early or late when the Crown requires
our services.'

' Just at present the Crown requires nothing else of us,
I suppose, but that we should go along at the rate of forty
miles an hour.'

' There is nothing like saving time,' said Neverbend.
' I know you have, as yet, had no experience in these
sort of cases, so I have brought you the papers which
refer to a somewhat similar matter that occurred in the
Forest of Dean. I was sent down there, and that is the
report which I then wrote. I propose to take it for the
model of that which we shall have to draw up when we
return from Tavistock ; ' and as he spoke he produced
a voluminous document, or treatise, in which he had
contrived to render more obscure some matter that he

had been sent to clear up, on the Crown property in the
Forest of Dean.

Now Alaric had been told of this very report, and was
aware that he was going to Tavistock in order that the
joint result of his and Mr. Neverbend's labours might be
communicated to the Crown officers in intelligible language.

The monster report before him contained twenty-six
pages of close folio writing, and he felt that he really
could not oblige Mr. Neverbend by reading it.

'Forest of Dean! ah, that's coal, is it not?' said Alaric.
'Mary Jane seems to be exclusively in the tin line. I fear
there will be no analogy.'

'The cases are in many respects similar,' said Neverbend, 'and the method of treating them——'

'Then I really cannot concur with you as to the propriety of my reading it. I should feel myself absolutely
wrong to read a word of such a report, for fear I might be
prejudiced by your view of the case. It would, in my
mind, be positively dishonest in me to encourage any bias
in my own feelings either on one side or the other.'

'But really, Mr. Tudor——'

'I need not say how much personal advantage it would
be to me to have the benefit of your experience, but my
conscience tells me that I should not do it—so I think
I'll go to sleep.'

Mr. Neverbend did not know what to make of his
companion; whether to admire the high tone of his official
honesty, or to reprobate his idleness in refusing to make
himself master of the report. While he was settling the
question in his own mind, Tudor went to sleep, and did
not wake till he was invited to partake of ten minutes'
refreshment at Swindon.

'I rather think,' said Mr. Neverbend, 'that I shall go
on to Tavistock to-night.'

'Oh! of course,' said Alaric. 'I never for a moment
thought of stopping short of it;' and, taking out a book,
he showed himself disinclined for further conversation.

'Of course, it's open to me to do as I please in such
a matter,' said Neverbend, continuing his subject as soon
as they reached the Bristol station, 'but on the whole
I rather think we had better go on to Tavistock to-night.'

' No, I will not stop at Plymouth,' he said, as he passed by Taunton ; and on reaching Exeter he declared that he had fully made up his mind on the subject.

' We'll get a chaise at Plymouth,' said Alaric.

' I think there will be a public conveyance,' said Neverbend.

' But a chaise will be the quickest,' said the one.

' And much the dearest,' said the other.

' That won't signify much to us,' said Alaric ; ' we shan't pay the bill.'

' It will signify a great deal to me,' said Neverbend, with a look of ferocious honesty ; and so they reached Plymouth.

On getting out of the railway carriage, Alaric at once hired a carriage with a pair of horses ; the luggage was strapped on, and Mr. Neverbend, before his time for expostulation had fairly come, found himself posting down the road to Tavistock, followed at a respectful distance by two coaches and an omnibus.

They were soon drinking tea together at the Bedford Hotel, and I beg to assure any travelling readers that they might have drunk tea in a much worse place. Mr. Neverbend, though he made a great struggle to protect his dignity, and maintain the superiority of his higher rank, felt the ground sinking from beneath his feet from hour to hour. He could not at all understand how it was, but even the servants at the hotel seemed to pay more deference to Tudor than to him ; and before the evening was over he absolutely found himself drinking port wine negus, because his colleague had ordered it for him.

' And now,' said Neverbend, who was tired with his long journey, ' I think I'll go to bed.'

' Do,' said Alaric, who was not at all tired, ' and I'll go through this infernal mass of papers. I have hardly looked at them yet. Now that I am in the neighbourhood I shall better understand the strange names.'

So Alaric went to work, and studied the dry subject that was before him. It will luckily not be necessary for us to do so also. It will be sufficient for us to know that Wheal Mary Jane was at that moment the richest of all the rich mines that had then been opened in that district ;

that the, or its, or her shares (which is the proper way of speaking of them I am shamefully ignorant) were at an enormous premium ; that these two Commissioners would have to see and talk to some scores of loud and angry men, deeply interested in their success or failure, and that that success or failure might probably in part depend on the view which these two Commissioners might take.

CHAPTER VIII

THE HON. UNDECIMUS SCOTT

THE HON. UNDECIMUS SCOTT was the eleventh son of the Lord Gaberlunzie. Lord Gaberlunzie was the representative of a very old and very noble race, more conspicuous, however, at the present time for its age and nobility than for its wealth. The Hon. Undecimus, therefore, learnt, on arriving at manhood, that he was heir only to the common lot of mortality, and that he had to earn his own bread. This, however, could not have surprised him much, as nine of his brethren had previously found themselves in the same condition.

Lord Gaberlunzie certainly was not one of those wealthy peers who are able to make two or three elder sons, and after that to establish any others that may come with comfortable younger children's portions. The family was somewhat accustomed to the *res angusta domi ;* but they were fully alive to the fact, that a noble brood, such as their own, ought always to be able to achieve comfort and splendour in the world's broad field, by due use of those privileges which spring from a noble name. Cauldkail Castle, in Aberdeenshire, was the family residence ; but few of the eleven young Scotts were ever to be found there after arriving at that age at which they had been able to fly from the paternal hall.

It is a terrible task, that of having to provide for eleven sons. With two or three a man may hope, with some reasonable chance of seeing his hope fulfilled, that things will go well with him, and that he may descend to his grave without that worst of wretchedness, that gnawing grief which comes from bad children. But who can hope that eleven sons will all walk in the narrow path ?

Had Lord Gaberlunzie, however, been himself a patriarch, and ruled the pastoral plains of Palestine, instead of the bleak mountains which surround Cauldkail Castle, he could not have been more indifferent as to the number of his sons. They flew away, each as his time came, with the early confidence of young birds, and as seldom returned to disturb the family nest.

They were a cannie, comely, sensible brood. Their father and mother, if they gave them nothing else, gave them strong bodies and sharp brains. They were very like each other, though always with a difference. Red hair, bright as burnished gold ; high, but not very high, cheek bones ; and small, sharp, twinkling eyes, were the Gaberlunzie personal characteristics. There were three in the army, two in the navy, and one at a foreign embassy; one was at the diggings, another was chairman of a railway company, and our own more particular friend, Undecimus, was picking up crumbs about the world in a manner that satisfied the paternal mind that he was quite able to fly alone.

There is a privilege common to the sons of all noble lords, the full value of which the young Scotts learnt very early in life—that of making any woman with a tocher an honourable lady. ' Ye maun be a puir chiel, gin ye'll be worth less than ten thoosand pound in the market o' marriage ; and ten thoosand pound is a gawcey grand heritage ! ' Such had been the fatherly precept which Lord Gaberlunzie had striven to instil into each of his noble sons ; and it had not been thrown away upon them. One after the other they had gone forth into the market-place alluded to, and had sold themselves with great ease and admirable discretion. There had been but one Moses in the lot : the Hon. Gordon Hamilton Scott had certainly brought home a bundle of shagreen spectacle cases in the guise of a widow with an exceedingly doubtful jointure ; doubtful indeed at first, but very soon found to admit of no doubt whatever. He was the one who, with true Scotch enterprise, was prosecuting his fortunes at the

Bendigo diggings, while his wife consoled herself at home with her title.

Undecimus, with filial piety, had taken his father exactly at his word, and swapped himself for £10,000. He had, however, found himself imbued with much too high an ambition to rest content with the income arising from his matrimonial speculation. He had first contrived to turn his real £10,000 into a fabulous £50,000, and had got himself returned to Parliament for the Tillietudlem district burghs on the credit of his great wealth; he then set himself studiously to work to make a second market by placing his vote at the disposal of the Government.

Nor had he failed of success in his attempt, though he had hitherto been able to acquire no high or permanent post. He had soon been appointed private secretary to the First Lord of the Stannaries, and he found that his duty in this capacity required him to assist the Government whip in making and keeping houses. This occupation was congenial to his spirit, and he worked hard and well at it; but the greatest of men are open to the tainting breath of suspicion, and the Honourable Undecimus Scott, or Undy Scott, as he was generally now called, did not escape. Ill-natured persons whispered that he was not on all occasions true to his party; and once when his master, the whip-in-chief, overborne with too much work, had been tempted to put himself to bed comfortably in his own house, instead of on his usual uneasy couch behind the Speaker's chair, Undy had greatly failed. The leader of a party whose struggles for the religion of his country had hitherto met but small success, saw at a glance the opportunity which fortune had placed in his way; he spied with eagle eye the nakedness of that land of promise which is compressed in the district round the Treasury benches; the barren field before him was all his own, and he put and carried his motion for closing the parks on Sundays.

He became a hero; but Undy was all but undone. The highest hope of the Sabbatarian had been to address an almost empty house for an hour and a half on this his favourite subject. But the chance was too good to be lost; he sacrificed his oratorical longings on the altar of

party purpose, and limited his speech to a mere statement
of his motion. Off flew on the wings of Hansom a youthful
member, more trusty than the trusted Undy, to the
abode of the now couchant Treasury Argus. Morpheus
had claimed him all for his own. He was lying in true
enjoyment, with his tired limbs stretched between the
unaccustomed sheets, and snoring with free and sonorous
nose, restrained by the contiguity of no Speaker's elbow.
But even in his deepest slumber the quick wheels of the
bounding cab struck upon the tympanum of his anxious
ear. He roused himself as does a noble watch-dog when
the 'suspicious tread of theft' approaches. The hurry of
the jaded horse, the sudden stop, the maddened furious
knock, all told a tale which his well-trained ear only knew
too well. He sat up for a moment, listening in his bed,
stretched himself with one involuntary yawn, and then
stood upright on the floor. It should not at any rate be
boasted by any one that he had been found in bed.

With elastic step, three stairs at a time, up rushed that
young and eager member. It was well for the nerves of
Mrs. Whip Vigil that the calls of society still held her
bound in some distant brilliant throng; for no consideration would have stopped the patriotic energy of that
sucking statesman. Mr. Vigil had already performed the
most important act of a speedy toilet, when his door was
opened, and as his young friend appeared was already
buttoning his first brace.

'Pumpkin is up!' said the eager juvenile, 'and we have
only five men in the house.'

'And where the devil is Undy Scott?' said the Right
Hon. Mr. Vigil.

'The devil only knows,' said the other.

'I deserve it for trusting him,' said the conscience-
stricken but worthy public servant. By this time he had
on his neckcloth and boots; in his eager haste to serve
his country he had forgotten his stockings. 'I deserve it
for trusting him—and how many men have they?'

'Forty-one when I left.'

'Then they'll divide, of course?'

'Of course they will,' said the promising young dove of
the Treasury.

And now Mr. Whip Vigil had buttoned on that well-made frock with which the Parliamentary world is so conversant, and as he descended the stairs, arranged with pocket-comb his now grizzling locks. His well-brushed hat stood ready to his touch below, and when he entered the cab he was apparently as well dressed a gentleman as when about three hours after noon he may be seen with slow and easy step entering the halls of the Treasury chambers.

But ah! alas, he was all too late. He came but to see the ruin which Undy's defection had brought about. He might have taken his rest, and had a quiet mind till the next morning's *Times* revealed to him the fact of Mr. Pumpkin's grand success. When he arrived, the numbers were being taken, and he, even he, Mr. Whip Vigil, he the great arch-numberer, was excluded from the number of the counted. When the doors were again open the Commons of England had decided by a majority of forty-one to seven that the parks of London should, one and all, be closed on Sundays; and Mr. Pumpkin had achieved among his own set a week's immortality.

'We mustn't have this again, Vigil,' said a very great man the next morning, with a good-humoured smile on his face, however, as he uttered the reprimand. 'It will take us a whole night, and God knows how much talking, to undo what those fools did yesterday.'

Mr. Vigil resolved to leave nothing again to the unassisted industry or honesty of Undy Scott, and consequently that gentleman's claims on his party did not stand so highly as they might have done but for this accident. Parliament was soon afterwards dissolved, and either through the lukewarm support of his Government friends, or else in consequence of his great fortune having been found to be ambiguous, the independent electors of the Tillietudlem burghs took it into their heads to unseat Mr. Scott. Unseated for Tillietudlem, he had no means of putting himself forward elsewhere, and he had to repent, in the sackcloth and ashes of private life, the fault which had cost him the friendship of Mr. Vigil.

His life, however, was not strictly private. He had used the Honourable before his name, and the M.P. which for a time had followed after it, to acquire for himself a seat as director at a bank board. He was a Vice-President of the Caledonian, English, Irish, and General European and American Fire and Life Assurance Society; such, at least, had been the name of the joint-stock company in question when he joined it; but he had obtained much credit by adding the word 'Oriental,' and inserting it after the allusion to Europe; he had tried hard to include the fourth quarter of the globe; but, as he explained to some of his friends, it would have made the name too cumbrous for the advertisements. He was a director also of one or two minor railways, dabbled in mining shares, and, altogether, did a good deal of business in the private stock-jobbing line.

In spite of his former delinquencies, his political friends did not altogether throw him over. In the first place, the time might come when he would be again useful, and then he had managed to acquire that air and tact which make one official man agreeable to another. He was always good-humoured; when in earnest, there was a dash of drollery about him; in his most comic moods he ever had some serious purpose in view; he thoroughly understood the esoteric and exoteric bearings of modern politics, and knew well that though he should be a model of purity before the public, it did not behove him to be very strait-laced with his own party. He took everything in good part, was not over-talkative, over-pushing, or presumptuous; he felt no strong bias of his own; had at his fingers' ends the cant phraseology of ministerial subordinates, and knew how to make himself useful. He knew also—a knowledge much more difficult to acquire —how to live among men so as never to make himself disagreeable.

But then he could not be trusted! True. But how many men in his walk of life can be trusted? And those who can—at how terribly high a price do they rate their own fidelity! How often must a minister be forced to confess to himself that he cannot afford to employ good faith! Undy Scott, therefore, from time to time, received some ministerial bone, some Civil Service scrap of victuals thrown to him from the Government table, which, if it did not suffice to maintain him in all the comforts of a Treasury career, still preserved for him a connexion with the Elysium of public life ; gave him, as it were, a link by which he could hang on round the outer corners of the State's temple, and there watch with advantage till the doors of Paradise should be re-opened to him. He was no Lucifer, who, having wilfully rebelled against the high majesty of Heaven, was doomed to suffer for ever in unavailing, but still proud misery, the penalties of his asserted independence ; but a poor Peri, who had made a lapse and thus forfeited, for a while, celestial joys, and was now seeking for some welcome offering, striving to perform some useful service, by which he might regain his lost glory.

The last of the good things thus tendered to him was not yet all consumed. When Mr. Hardlines, now Sir Gregory, was summoned to assist at, or rather preside over, the deliberations of the committee which was to organize a system of examination for the Civil Service, the Hon. U. Scott had been appointed secretary to that committee. This, to be sure, afforded but a fleeting moment of halcyon bliss ; but a man like Mr. Scott knew how to prolong such a moment to its uttermost stretch. The committee had ceased to sit, and the fruits of their labour were already apparent in the establishment of a new public office, presided over by Sir Gregory ; but still the clever Undy continued to draw his salary.

Undy was one of those men who, though married and the fathers of families, are always seen and known ' en garçon.' No one had a larger circle of acquaintance than Undy Scott ; no one, apparently, a smaller circle than Mrs. Undy Scott. So small, indeed, was it, that its *locale* was utterly unknown in the fashionable world. At the time of which we are now speaking Undy was the happy possessor of a bedroom in Waterloo Place, and rejoiced in all the comforts of a first-rate club. But the sacred spot, in which at few and happy intervals he received the caresses of the wife of his bosom and the children of his loins, is unknown to the author.

In age, Mr. Scott, at the time of the Tavistock mining inquiry, was about thirty-five. Having sat in Parliament for five years, he had now been out for four, and was anxiously looking for the day when the universal scramble of a general election might give him another chance. In person he was, as we have said, stalwart and comely, hirsute with copious red locks, not only over his head, but under his chin and round his mouth. He was well made, six feet high, neither fat nor thin, and he looked like a gentleman. He was careful in his dress, but not so as to betray the care that he took ; he was imperturbable in temper, though restless in spirit ; and the one strong passion of his life was the desire of a good income at the cost of the public.

He had an easy way of getting intimate with young men when it suited him, and as easy a way of dropping them afterwards when that suited him. He had no idea of wasting his time or opportunities in friendships. Not that he was indifferent as to his companions, or did not appreciate the pleasure of living with pleasant men ; but that life was too short, and with him the race too much up hill, to allow of his indulging in such luxuries. He looked on friendship as one of those costly delights with which none but the rich should presume to gratify themselves. He could not afford to associate with his fellow-men on any other terms than those of making capital of them. It was not for him to walk and talk and eat and drink with a man because he liked him. How could the eleventh son of a needy Scotch peer, who had to maintain his rank and position by the force of his own wit, how could such a one live, if he did not turn to some profit even the convivialities of existence ?

Acting in accordance with his fixed and conscientious rule in this respect, Undy Scott had struck up an acquaintance with Alaric Tudor. He saw that Alaric was no ordinary clerk, that Sir Gregory was likely to have the Civil Service under his thumb, and that Alaric was a great favourite with the great man. It would but little have availed Undy to have striven to be intimate with Sir Gregory himself. The Knight Commander of the Bath would have been deaf to his blandishments ; but it seemed probable that the ears of Alaric might be tickled.

And thus Alaric and Undy Scott had become fast

friends ; that is, as fast as such friends generally are.
Alaric was no more blind to his own interest than was
his new ally. But there was this difference between them ;
Undy lived altogether in the utilitarian world which he
had formed around himself, whereas Alaric lived in two
worlds. When with Undy his pursuits and motives were
much such as those of Undy himself ; but at Surbiton
Cottage, and with Harry Norman, he was still susceptible
of a higher feeling. He had been very cool to poor Linda
on his last visit to Hampton ; but it was not that his
heart was too hard for love. He had begun to discern
that Gertrude would never attach herself to Norman ; and
if Gertrude were free, why should she not be his ?

Poor Linda !

Scott had early heard—and of what official event did
he not obtain early intelligence ?—that Neverbend was to
go down to Tavistock about the Mary Jane tin mine, and
that a smart colleague was required for him. He would
fain, for reasons of his own, have been that smart colleague
himself ; but that he knew was impossible. He and
Neverbend were the Alpha and Omega of official virtues
and vices. But he took an opportunity of mentioning
before Sir Gregory, in a passing unpremeditated way, how
excellently adapted Tudor was for the work. It so turned
out that his effort was successful, and that Tudor was
sent.

The whole of their first day at Tavistock was passed by
Neverbend and Alaric in hearing interminable statements
from the various mining combatants, and when at seven
o'clock Alaric shut up for the evening he was heartily
sick of the job. The next morning before breakfast he
sauntered out to air himself in front of the hotel, and who
should come whistling up the street, with a cigar in his
mouth, but his new friend Undy Scott.

CHAPTER IX

MR. MANYLODES

ALARIC TUDOR was very much surprised. Had he seen Sir Gregory himself, or Captain Cuttwater, walking up the street of Tavistock, he could not have been more startled. It first occurred to him that Scott must have been sent down as a third Commissioner to assist at the investigation; and he would have been right glad to have known that this was the case, for he found that the management of Mr. Neverbend was no pastime. But he soon learnt that such relief was not at hand for him.

'Well, Tudor, my boy,' said he, 'and how do you like the clotted cream and the thick ankles of the stout Devon-shire lasses?'

'I have neither tasted the one, nor seen the other,' said Alaric. 'As yet I have encountered nothing but the not very civil tongues, and not very clear brains of Cornish roughs.'

'A Boeotian crew! but, nevertheless, they know on which side their bread is buttered—and in general it goes hard with them but they butter it on both sides. And how does the faithful Neverbend conduct himself? Talk of Boeotians, if any man ever was born in a foggy air, it must have been my friend Fidus.'

Alaric merely shrugged his shoulders, and laughed slightly. 'But what on earth brings you down to Tavistock?' said he.

'Oh! I am a denizen of the place, naturalized, and all but settled; have vast interests here, and a future constituency. Let the Russells look well to themselves. The time is quickly coming when you will address me in the House with bitter sarcasm as the honourable but inconsistent member for Tavistock; egad, who knows but you may have to say Right Honourable?'

'Oh! I did not know the wind blew in that quarter,' said Alaric, not ill-pleased at the suggestion that he also, on some future day, might have a seat among the faithful Commons.

'The wind blows from all quarters with me,' said Undy; 'but in the meantime I am looking out for shares.'

'Will you come in and breakfast?' asked the other.

'What, with friend Fidus? no, thank'ee; I am not, by many degrees, honest enough to suit his book. He would be down on some little public peccadillo of mine before I had swallowed my first egg. Besides, I would not for worlds break the pleasure of your *tête-à-tête*.'

'Will you come down after dinner?'

'No; neither after dinner, nor before breakfast; not all the coffee, nor all the claret of the Bedford shall tempt me. Remember, my friend, you are paid for it; I am not.'

'Well, then, good morning,' said Alaric. 'I must go in and face my fate, like a Briton.'

Undy went on for a few steps, and then returned, as though a sudden thought had struck him. 'But, Tudor, I have bowels of compassion within me, though no pluck. I am willing to rescue you from your misery, though I will not partake it. Come up to me this evening, and I will give you a glass of brandy-punch. Your true miners never drink less generous tipple.'

'How on earth am I to shake off this incubus of the Woods and Works?'

'Shake him off? Why, make him drunk and put him to bed; or tell him at once that the natural iniquity of your disposition makes it necessary that you should spend a few hours of the day in the company of a sinner like myself. Tell him that his virtue is too heavy for the digestive organs of your unpractised stomach. Tell him what you will, but come. I myself am getting sick of those mining Vandals, though I am so used to dealing with them.'

Alaric promised that he would come, and then went in to breakfast. Undy also returned to his breakfast, well pleased with this first success in the little scheme which at present occupied his mind. The innocent young Commissioner little dreamt that the Honourable Mr. Scott had come all the way to Tavistock on purpose to ask him to drink brandy-punch at the Blue Dragon !

Another day went wearily and slowly on with Alaric and Mr. Neverbend. Tedious, never-ending statements had to be taken down in writing ; the same things were repeated over and over again, and were as often contradicted ; men who might have said in five words all that they had to say, would not be constrained to say it in less than five thousand, and each one seemed to think, or pretended to seem to think, that all the outer world and the Government were leagued together to defraud the interest to which he himself was specially attached. But this was not the worst of it. There were points which were as clear as daylight ; but Tudor could not declare them to be so, as by doing so he was sure to elicit a different opinion from Mr. Neverbend.

'I am not quite so clear on that point, Mr. Tudor,' he would say.

Alaric, till experience made him wise, would attempt to argue it.

'That is all very well, but I am not quite so sure of it. We will reserve the point, if you please,' and so affairs went on darkly, no ray of light being permitted to shine in on the matter in dispute.

It was settled, however, before dinner, that they should both go down the Wheal Mary Jane on the following day. Neverbend had done what he could to keep this crowning honour of the inquiry altogether in his own hands, but he had found that in this respect Tudor was much too much for him.

Immediately after dinner Alaric announced that he was going to spend the evening with a friend.

'A friend ! ' said Neverbend, somewhat startled ; 'I did not know that you had any friends in Tavistock.'

'Not a great many ; but it so happened that I did meet a man I know, this morning, and promised to go to him in the evening. I hope you'll excuse my leaving you ? '

'Oh ! I don't mind for myself,' said Neverbend, 'though, when men are together, it's as well for them to keep together. But, Mr. Tudor —— '

'Well ? ' said Alaric, who felt growing within him a

determination to put down at once anything like interference with his private hours.

'Perhaps I ought not to mention it,' said Neverbend, ' but I do hope you'll not get among mining people. Only think what our position here is.'

'What on earth do you mean ? ' said Alaric. ' Do you think I shall be bribed over by either side because I choose to drink a glass of wine with a friend at another hotel ? '

'Bribed ! No, I don't think you'll be bribed ; but I think we should both keep ourselves absolutely free from all chance of being talked to on the subject, except before each other and before witnesses. I would not drink brandy-and-water at the Blue Dragon, before this report be written, even if my brother were there.'

'Well, Mr. Neverbend, I am not so much afraid of myself. But wherever there are two men, there will be two opinions. So good night, if it so chance that you are in bed before my return.'

So Tudor went out, and Neverbend prepared himself to sit up for him. He would sooner have remained up all night than have gone to bed before his colleague came back.

Three days Alaric Tudor had now passed with Mr. Neverbend, and not only three days but three evenings also ! A man may endure to be bored in the course of business through the day, but it becomes dreadful when the infliction is extended to post-prandial hours. It does not often occur that one is doomed to bear the same bore both by day and night ; any change gives some ease ; but poor Alaric for three days had had no change. He felt like a liberated convict as he stepped freely forth into the sweet evening air, and made his way through the town to the opposition inn.

Here he found Undy on the door-steps with a cigar in his mouth. ' Here I am, waiting for you,' said he. ' You are fagged to death, I know, and we'll get a mouthful of fresh air before we go upstairs,'—and so saying he put his arm through Alaric's, and they strolled off through the suburbs of the town.

'You don't smoke,' said Undy, with his cigar-case in his hand. ' Well—I believe you are right—cigars cost a great deal of money, and can't well do a man any real good. God Almighty could never have intended us to make chimneys of our mouths and noses. Does Fidus ever indulge in a weed ? '

' He never indulges in anything,' said Alaric.

' Except honesty,' said the other, ' and in that he is a beastly glutton. He gorges himself with it till all his faculties are overpowered and his mind becomes torpid. It's twice worse than drinking. I wonder whether he'll do a bit of speculation before he goes back to town.'

' Who, Neverbend ?—he never speculates ! '

' Why not ? Ah, my fine fellow, you don't know the world yet. Those sort of men, dull drones like Neverbend, are just the fellows who go the deepest. I'll be bound he will not return without a few Mary Janes in his pocket-book. He'll be a fool if he does, I know.'

' Why, that's the very mine we are down here about.'

' And that 's the very reason why he'll purchase Mary Janes. He has an opportunity of knowing their value. Oh, let Neverbend alone. He is not so young as you are, my dear fellow.'

' Young or old, I think you mistake his character.'

' Why, Tudor, what would you think now if he not only bought for himself, but was commissioned to buy by the very men who sent him down here ? '

' It would be hard to make me believe it.'

' Ah ! faith is a beautiful thing ; what a pity that it never survives the thirtieth year ;—except with women and fools.'

' And have you no faith, Scott ? '

' Yes—much in myself—some little in Lord Palmerston, that is, in his luck ; and a good deal in a bank-note. But I have none at all in Fidus Neverbend. What ! have faith in a man merely because he tells me to have it ! His method of obtaining it is far too easy.'

' I trust neither his wit nor his judgement ; but I don't believe him to be a thief.'

' Thief ! I said nothing of thieves. He may, for aught I know, be just as good as the rest of the world ; all I say is, that I believe him to be no better. But come, we must go back to the inn ; there is an ally of mine coming to me ; a perfect specimen of a sharp Cornish mining stock-jobber—as vulgar a fellow as you ever met, and as shrewd. He won't stay very long, so you need not be afraid of him.'

Alaric began to feel uneasy, and to think that there might by possibility be something in what Neverbend had said to him. He did not like the idea of meeting a Cornish stock-jobber in a familiar way over his brandy-punch, while engaged, as he now was, on the part of Government ; he felt that there might be impropriety in it, and he would have been glad to get off if he could. But he felt ashamed to break his engagement, and thus followed Undy into the hotel.

'Has Mr. Manylodes been here ?' said Scott, as he walked upstairs.

'He's in the bar now, sir,' said the waiter.

'Beg him to come up, then. In the bar ! why, that man must have a bar within himself—the alcohol he consumes every day would be a tidy sale for a small public-house.'

Up they went, and Mr. Manylodes was not long in following them. He was a small man, more like an American in appearance than an Englishman. He had on a common black hat, a black coat, black waistcoat, and black trousers, thick boots, a coloured shirt, and very dirty hands. Though every article he wore was good, and most of them such as gentlemen wear, no man alive could have mistaken him for a gentleman. No man, conversant with the species to which he belonged, could have taken him for anything but what he was. As he entered the room, a faint, sickly, second-hand smell of alcohol pervaded the atmosphere.

'Well, Manylodes,' said Scott, 'I'm glad to see you again. This is my friend, Mr. Tudor.'

'Your servant, sir,' said Manylodes, just touching his hat, without moving it from his head. 'And how are you, Mr. Scott ? I am glad to see you again in these parts, sir.'

'And how's trade ? Come, Tudor, what will you drink ? Manylodes, I know, takes brandy ; their sherry is vile, and their claret worse ; maybe they may have a fairish glass of port. And how is trade, **Many-lodes** ? '

' We're all as brisk as bees at present. I never knew things sharper. If you've brought a little money with you, now 's your time. But I tell you this, you'll find it sharp work for the eyesight.'

' Quick 's the word, I suppose.'

' Lord love you ! Quick ! Why, a fellow must shave himself before he goes to bed if he wants to be up in time these days.'

' I suppose so.'

' Lord love you ! why there was old Sam Weazle ; never caught napping yet—why at Truro, last Monday, he bought up to 450 New Friendships, and before he was a-bed they weren't worth, not this bottle of brandy. Well, old Sam was just bit by those Cambourne lads.'

' And how did that happen ? '

' Why, the New Friendships certainly was very good while they lasted ; just for three months they was the thing certainly. Why, it came up, sir, as if there weren't no end of it, and just as clean as that half-crown—but I know'd there was an end coming.'

' Water, I suppose,' said Undy, sipping his toddy.

' Them clean takes, Mr. Scott, they never lasts. There was water, but that weren't the worst. Old Weazle knew of that ; he calculated he'd back the metal agin the water, and so he bought all up he could lay his finger on. But the stuff was run out. Them Cambourne boys—what did they do ? Why, they let the water in on purpose. By Monday night old Weazle knew it all, and then you may say it was as good as a play.'

' And how did you do in the matter ? '

' Oh, I sold. I did very well—bought at £7 2s. 3d. and sold at £6 19s. 10½d., and got my seven per cent. for the four months. But, Lord love you, them clean takes never lasts. I won't going to hang on. Here's your health, Mr. Scott. Yours, Mr. ——, I didn't just catch the gen'leman's name ; ' and without waiting for further information on the point, he finished his brandy-and-water.

' So it 's all up with the New Friendships, is it ? ' said Undy.

'Up and down, Mr. Scott; every dog has his day; these Mary Janes will be going the same way some of them days. We're all mortal;' and with this moral comparison between the uncertainty of human life and the vicissitudes of the shares in which he trafficked, Mr. Manylodes proceeded to put some more sugar and brandy into his tumbler.

'True, true—we are all mortal—Manylodes and Mary Janes; old friendships and New Friendships: while they last we must make the most we can of them; buy them cheap and sell them dear; and above all things get a good percentage.'

'That's the game, Mr. Scott; and I will say no man understands it better than yourself—keep the ball a-running—that's your maxim. Are you going it deep in Mary Jane, Mr. Scott?'

'Who? I! O no—she's a cut above me now, I fear. The shares are worth any money now, I suppose.'

'Worth any money! I think they are, Mr. Scott, but I believe——' and then bringing his chair close up to that of his aristocratic friend, resting his hands, one on Mr. Scott's knee, and the other on his elbow, and breathing brandy into his ear, he whispered to him words of great significance.

'I'll leave you, Scott,' said Alaric, who did not enjoy the society of Mr. Manylodes, and to whom the nature of the conversation was, in his present position, extremely irksome; 'I must be back at the Bedford early.'

'Early—why early? surely our honest friend can get himself to bed without your interference. Come, you don't like the brandy toddy, nor I either. We'll see what sort of a hand they are at making a bowl of bishop.'

'Not for me, Scott.'

'Yes, for you, man; surely you are not tied to that fellow's apron-strings,' he said, removing himself from the close contiguity of Mr. Manylodes, and speaking under his voice; 'take my advice; if you once let that man think you fear him, you'll never get the better of him.'

Alaric allowed himself to be persuaded and stayed.

'I have just ten words of business to say to this fellow,' continued Scott, 'and then we will be alone.'

It was a lovely autumn evening, early in September, and Alaric sat himself at an open window, looking out from the back of the hotel on to the Brentor, with its singular parish church, built on its highest apex, while Undy held deep council with his friend of the mines. But from time to time, some word of moment found its way to Alaric's ears, and made him also unconsciously fix his mind on the *irritamenta malorum*, which are dug from the bowels of the earth in those western regions.

'Minting money, sir; it's just minting money. There's been no chance like it in my days. £4 12s. 6d. paid up; and they'll be at £25 in Truro before sun sets on Saturday, Lord love you, Mr. Scott, now's your time. If, as I hear, they——' and then there was a very low whisper, and Alaric, who could not keep his eye altogether from Mr. Manylodes' countenance, saw plainly that that worthy gentleman was talking of himself; and in spite of his better instincts, a desire came over him to know more of what they were discussing, and he could not keep from thinking that shares bought at £4 12s. 6d., and realizing £25, must be very nice property.

'Well, I'll manage it,' said Scott, still in a sort of whisper, but audibly enough for Alaric to hear. 'Forty, you say? I'll take them at £5 1s. 1d.—very well;' and he took out his pocket-book and made a memorandum. 'Come, Tudor, here's the bishop. We have done our business, so now we'll enjoy ourselves. What, Manylodes, are you off?'

'Lord love you, Mr. Scott, I've a deal to do before I get to my downy; and I don't like those doctored tipples. Good night, Mr. Scott. I wishes you good night, sir;' and making another slight reference to his hat, which had not been removed from his head during the whole interview, Mr. Manylodes took himself off.

'There, now, is a specimen of a species of the *genus homo*, class Englishman, which is, I believe, known nowhere but in Cornwall.'

'Cornwall and Devonshire, I suppose,' said Alaric.

'No; he is out of his true element here. If you want to see him in all the glory of his native county you should go west of Truro. From Truro to Hayle is the land of

the Manylodes. And a singular species it is. But, Tudor,
you'll be surprised, I suppose, if I tell you that I have
made a purchase for you.'

'A purchase for me!'

'Yes; I could not very well consult you before that
fellow, and yet as the chance came in my way, I did not
like to lose it. Come, the bishop ain't so bad, is it, though
it is doctored tipple?' and he refilled Alaric's glass.

'But what have you purchased for me, Scott?'

'Forty shares in the Mary Jane.'

'Then you may undo the bargain again, for I don't
want them, and shall not take them.'

'You need not be a bit uneasy, my dear fellow. I've
bought them at a little over £5, and they'll be saleable
to-morrow at double the money—or at any rate to-morrow
week. But what's your objection to them?'

'In the first place, I've got no money to buy shares.'

'That's just the reason why you should buy them;
having no money, you can't but want some; and here's
your way to make it. You can have no difficulty in raising
£200.'

'And in the next place, I should not think of buying
mining shares, and more especially these, while I am
engaged as I now am.'

'Fal de ral, de ral, de ral! That's all very fine, Mr.
Commissioner; only you mistake your man; you think
you are talking to Mr. Neverbend.'

'Well, Scott, I shan't have them.'

'Just as you please, my dear fellow; there's no com-
pulsion. Only mark this; the ball is at your foot now,
but it won't remain there. "There is a tide in the affairs
of men"—you know the rest; and you know also that
"tide and time wait for no man." If you are contented
with your two or three hundred a year in the Weights
and Measures, God forbid that I should tempt you to
higher thoughts—only in that case I have mistaken my
man.'

'I must be contented with it, if I can get nothing better,'
said Tudor, weakly.

'Exactly; you must be contented—or rather you must
put up with it—if you can get nothing better. That's the

meaning of contentment all the world over. You argue in a circle. You must be a mere clerk if you cannot do better than other mere clerks. But the fact of your having such an offer as that I now make you, is proof that you can do better than others; proves, in fact, that you need not be a mere clerk, unless you choose to remain so.'

' Buying these shares might lose me all that I have got, and could not do more than put a hundred pounds or so in my pocket.'

' Gammon—— '

' Could I go back and tell Sir Gregory openly that I had bought them ? '

' Why, Tudor, you are the youngest fish I ever met, sent out to swim alone in this wicked world of ours. Who the deuce talks openly of his speculations ? Will Sir Gregory tell you what shares he buys ? Is not every member of the House, every man in the Government, every barrister, parson, and doctor, that can collect a hundred pounds, are not all of them at the work ? And do they talk openly of the matter ? Does the bishop put it into his charge, or the parson into his sermon ? '

' But they would not be ashamed to tell their friends.'

' Would not they ? Oh ! the Rev. Mr. Pickabit, of St. Judas Without, would not be ashamed to tell his bishop ! But the long and the short of the thing is this ; most men circumstanced as you are have no chance of doing anything good till they are forty or fifty, and then their energies are worn out. You have had tact enough to push yourself up early, and yet it seems you have not pluck enough to take the goods the gods provide you.'

' The gods !—you mean the devils rather,' said Alaric, who sat listening and drinking, almost unconsciously, his doctored tipple.

' Call them what you will for me. Fortune has generally been esteemed a goddess, but misfortune a very devil. But, Tudor, you don't know the world. Here is a chance in your way. Of course that keg of brandy who went out just now understands very well who you are. He wants to be civil to me, and he thinks it wise to be civil to you also. He has a hat full of these shares, and he tells me that, knowing my weakness, and presuming that you have

the same, he bought a few extra this morning, thinking
we might like them. Now, I have no hesitation in saying
there is not a single man whom the Government could
send down here, from Sir Gregory downwards, who could
refuse the chance.'

'I am quite sure that Neverbend——'

'Oh! for Heaven's sake don't choke me with Neverbend; the fools are fools, and will be so; they are used
for their folly. I speak of men with brains. How do you
think that such men as Hardlines, Vigil, and Mr. Estimate
have got up in the world? Would they be where they are
now, had they been contented with their salaries?'

'They had private fortunes.'

'Very private they must have been—I never heard of
them. No; what fortunes they have they made. Two
of them are in Parliament, and the other has a Government
situation of £2,000 a year, with little or nothing to do.
But they began life early, and never lost a chance.'

'It is quite clear that that blackguard who was here just
now thinks that he can influence my opinion by inducing
me to have an interest in the matter.'

'He had no such idea—nor have I. Do you think
I would persuade you to such villainy? Do you think
I do not know you too well? Of course the possession
of these shares can have no possible effect on your report,
and is not expected to have any. But when men like you
and me become of any note in the world, others, such as
Manylodes, like to know that we are embarked in the
same speculation with themselves. Why are members of
Parliament asked to be directors, and vice-governors, and
presidents, and guardians, of all the joint-stock societies
that are now set agoing? Not because of their capital,
for they generally have none; not for their votes, because
one vote can be but of little use in any emergency. It is
because the names of men of note are worth money.
Men of note understand this, and enjoy the fat of the land
accordingly. I want to see you among the number.'

'Twas thus the devil pleaded for the soul of Alaric Tudor;
and, alas! he did not plead in vain. Let him but have
a fair hearing, and he seldom does. 'Tis in this way that
the truth of that awful mystery, the fall of man, comes

home to us ; that we cannot hear the devil plead, and
resist the charm of his eloquence. To listen is to be lost.
' Lead us not into temptation, but deliver us from evil ! '
Let that petition come forth from a man's heart, a true
and earnest prayer, and he will be so led that he shall not
hear the charmer, let him charm ever so wisely.

'Twas but a thin veil that the Hon. Undecimus Scott
threw over the bait with which he fished for the honesty
of Alaric Tudor, and yet it sufficed. One would say that
a young man, fortified with such aspirations as those
which glowed in Alaric's breast, should have stood a
longer siege ; should have been able to look with clearer
eyesight on the landmarks which divide honour from
dishonour, integrity from fraud, and truth from falsehood.
But he had never prayed to be delivered from evil. His
desire had rather been that he might be led into temptation.

He had never so prayed—yet had he daily said his
prayers at fitting intervals. On every returning Sunday
had he gone through, with all the fitting forms, the ordinary worship of a Christian. Nor had he done this as
a hypocrite. With due attention and a full belief he had
weekly knelt at God's temple, and given, if not his mind,
at least his heart, to the service of his church. But the
inner truth of the prayer which he repeated so often had
not come home to him. Alas ! how many of us from
week to week call ourselves worms and dust and miserable
sinners, describe ourselves as chaff for the winds, grass
for the burning, stubble for the plough, as dirt and filth
fit only to be trodden under foot, and yet in all our doings
before the world cannot bring home to ourselves the
conviction that we require other guidance than our own !

Alaric Tudor had sighed for permission to go forth
among worldlings and there fight the world's battle.
Power, station, rank, wealth, all the good things which
men earn by tact, diligence, and fortune combined, and
which were so far from him at his outset in life, became
daily more dear to his heart. And now his honourable
friend twitted him with being a mere clerk ! No, he was
not, never had been, never would be such. Had he not
already, in five or six short years, distanced his competitors,

and made himself the favourite and friend of men infinitely above him in station ? Was he not now here in Tavistock on a mission which proved that he was no mere clerk ? Was not the fact of his drinking bishop in the familiar society of a lord's son, and an ex-M.P., a proof of it ?

It would be calumny on him to say that he had allowed Scott to make him tipsy on this occasion. He was far from being tipsy ; but yet the mixture which he had been drinking had told upon his brain.

'But, Undy,' said he—he had never before called his honourable friend by his Christian name—' but, Undy, if I take these shares, where am I to get the money to pay for them ? '

'The chances are you may part with them before you leave Tavistock. If so, you will not have to pay for them. You will only have to pocket the difference.'

'Or pay the loss.'

'Or pay the loss. But there's no chance of that. I'll guarantee you against that.'

'But I shan't like to sell them. I shan't choose to be trafficking in shares. Buying a few as an investment may, perhaps, be a different thing.'

Oh, Alaric, Alaric, to what a pass had your conscience come, when it could be so silenced !

'Well, I suppose you can raise a couple of hundred— £205 will cover the whole thing, commission and all ; but, mind, I don't advise you to keep them long—I shall take two months' dividends, and then sell.'

'Two hundred and five pounds,' said Tudor, to whom the sum seemed anything but trifling ; ' and when must it be paid ? '

'Well, I can give Manylodes a cheque for the whole, dated this day week. You'll be back in town before that. We must allow him £5 for the accommodation. I suppose you can pay the money in at my banker's by that day ? '

Alaric had some portion of the amount himself, and he knew that Norman had money by him ; he felt also a half-drunken conviction that if Norman failed him, Captain Cuttwater would not let him want such a sum ; and so he said that he could, and the bargain was completed.

As he went downstairs whistling with an affected ease,

and a gaiety which he by no means felt, Undy Scott leant
back in his chair, and began to speculate whether his new
purchase was worth the purchase-money. ' He's a sharp
fellow, certainly, in some things, and may do well yet ;
but he's uncommonly green. That, however, will wear
off. I should not be surprised if he told Neverbend the
whole transaction before this time to-morrow.' And then
Mr. Scott finished his cigar and went to bed.

When Alaric entered the sitting-room at the Bedford,
he found Neverbend still seated at a table covered with
official books and huge bundles of official papers. An
enormous report was open before him, from which he was
culling the latent sweets, and extracting them with a
pencil. He glowered at Alaric with a severe suspicious
eye, which seemed to accuse him at once of the deed
which he had done.

' You are very late,' said Neverbend, ' but I have not
been sorry to be alone. I believe I have been able to
embody in a rough draft the various points which we
have hitherto discussed. I have just been five hours and
a half at it ; ' and Fidus looked at his watch ; ' five hours
and forty minutes. To-morrow, perhaps, that is, if you
are not going to your friend again, you'll not object to
make a fair copy——— '

' Copy ! ' shouted Alaric, in whose brain the open air
had not diminished the effect of the bishop, and who
remembered, with all the energy of pot valour, that he
was not a mere clerk ; ' copy—bother ; I'm going to bed,
old fellow ; and I advise you to do the same.'

And then, taking up a candlestick and stumbling somewhat awkwardly against a chair, Tudor went off to his
room, waiting no further reply from his colleague.

Mr. Neverbend slowly put up his papers and followed
him. ' He is decidedly the worse for drink—decidedly
so,' said he to himself, as he pulled off his clothes. ' What
a disgrace to the Woods and Works—what a disgrace ! '

And he resolved in his mind that he would be very early
at the pit's mouth. He would not be kept from his duty
while a dissipated colleague collected his senses by the
aid of soda-water.

CHAPTER X

WHEAL MARY JANE

MR. MANYLODES was, at any rate, right in this, that that beverage, which men call bishop, is a doctored tipple ; and Alaric Tudor, when he woke in the morning, owned the truth. It had been arranged that certain denizens of the mine should meet the two Commissioners at the pit-mouth at eight o'clock, and it had been settled at dinner-time that breakfast should be on the table at seven, sharp. Half an hour's quick driving would take them to the spot.

At seven Mr. Fidus Neverbend, who had never yet been known to be untrue to an appointment by the fraction of a second, was standing over the breakfast-table alone. He was alone, but not on that account unhappy. He could hardly disguise the pleasure with which he asked the waiter whether Mr. Tudor was yet dressed, or the triumph which he felt when he heard that his colleague was not *quite ready*.

'Bring the tea and the eggs at once,' said Neverbend, very briskly.

'Won't you wait for Mr. Tudor ?' asked the waiter, with an air of surprise. Now the landlord, waiter, boots, and chambermaid, the chambermaid especially, had all, in Mr. Neverbend's estimation, paid Tudor by far too much consideration ; and he was determined to show that he himself was first fiddle.

'Wait ! no ; quite out of the question—bring the hot water immediately—and tell the ostler to have the fly at the door at half-past seven exact.'

'Yes, sir,' said the man, and disappeared.

Neverbend waited five minutes, and then rang the bell impetuously. 'If you don't bring me my tea immediately, I shall send for Mr. Boteldale.' Now Mr. Boteldale was the landlord.

'Mr. Tudor will be down in ten minutes,' was the waiter's false reply; for up to that moment poor Alaric had not yet succeeded in lifting his throbbing head from his pillow. The boots was now with him administering soda-water and brandy, and he was pondering in his sickened mind whether, by a manful effort, he could rise and dress himself; or whether he would not throw himself backwards on his coveted bed, and allow Neverbend the triumph of descending alone to the nether world.

Neverbend nearly threw the loaf at the waiter's head. Wait ten minutes longer! what right had that vile Devonshire napkin-twirler to make to him so base a proposition? 'Bring me my breakfast, sir,' shouted Neverbend, in a voice that made the unfortunate sinner jump out of the room, as though he had been moved by a galvanic battery.

In five minutes, tea made with lukewarm water, and eggs that were not half boiled were brought to the impatient Commissioner. As a rule Mr. Neverbend, when travelling on the public service, made a practice of enjoying his meals. It was the only solace which he allowed himself; the only distraction from the cares of office which he permitted either to his body or his mind. But on this great occasion his country required that he should forget his comforts; and he drank his tasteless tea, and ate his uncooked eggs, threatening the waiter as he did so with sundry pains and penalties, in the form of sixpences withheld.

'Is the fly there?' said he, as he bolted a last morsel of cold roast beef.

'Coming, sir,' said the waiter, as he disappeared round a corner.

In the meantime Alaric sat lackadaisical on his bedside, all undressed, leaning his head upon his hand, and feeling that his struggle to dress himself was all but useless. The sympathetic boots stood by with a cup of tea—well-drawn comfortable tea—in his hand, and a small bit of dry toast lay near on an adjacent plate.

'Try a bit o' toast, sir,' said boots.

'Ugh!' ejaculated poor Alaric.

'Have a leetle drop o' rum in the tea, sir, and it'll set you all to rights in two minutes.'

The proposal made Alaric very sick, and nearly completed the catastrophe. ' Ugh ! ' he said.

' There 's the trap, sir, for Mr. Neverbend,' said the boots, whose ears caught the well-known sound.

' The devil it is ! ' said Alaric, who was now stirred up to instant action. ' Take my compliments to Mr. Neverbend, and tell him I'll thank him to wait ten minutes.'

Boots, descending with the message, found Mr. Neverbend ready coated and gloved, standing at the hotel door. The fly was there, and the lame ostler holding the horse ; but the provoking driver had gone back for his coat.

' Please, sir, Mr. Tudor says as how you're not to go just at present, but to wait ten minutes till he be ready.'

Neverbend looked at the man, but he would not trust himself to speak. Wait ten minutes, and it now wanted five-and-twenty minutes to eight !—no—not for all the Tudors that ever sat upon the throne of England.

There he stood with his watch in his hand as the returning Jehu hurried round from the stable yard. ' You are now seven minutes late,' said he, ' and if you are not at the place by eight o'clock, I shall not give you one farthing ! '

' All right,' said Jehu. ' We'll be at Mary Jane in less than no time ; ' and off they went, not at the quickest pace. But Neverbend's heart beat high with triumph, as he reflected that he had carried the point on which he had been so intent.

Alaric, when he heard the wheels roll off, shook from him his lethargy. It was not only that Neverbend would boast that he alone had gone through the perils of their subterranean duty, but that doubtless he would explain in London how his colleague had been deterred from following him. It was a grievous task, that of dressing himself, as youthful sinners know but too well. Every now and then a qualm would come over him, and make the work seem all but impossible. Boots, however, stuck to him like a man, poured cold water over his head, renewed his tea-cup, comforted him with assurances of the bracing air, and put a paper full of sandwiches in his pocket.

' For heaven's sake put them away,' said Alaric, to whom the very idea of food was repulsive.

' You'll want 'em, sir, afore you are half way to Mary
Jane ; and it a'n't no joke going down and up again.
I know what's what, sir.'

The boots stuck to him like a man. He did not only
get him sandwiches, but he procured for him also Mr.
Boteldale's own fast-trotting pony, and just as Neverbend
was rolling up to the pit's mouth fifteen minutes after his
time, greatly resolving in his own mind to button his
breeches-pocket firmly against the recreant driver, Alaric
started on the chase after him.

Mr. Neverbend had a presentiment that, sick as his
friend might be, nauseous as doubtless were the qualms
arising from yesterday's intemperance, he would make an
attempt to recover his lost ground. He of the Woods
and Works had begun to recognize the energy of him of
the Weights and Measures, and felt that there was in it
a force that would not easily be overcome, even by the
fumes of bishop. But yet it would be a great thing for
the Woods and Works if he, Neverbend, could descend in
this perilous journey to the deep bowels of the earth,
leaving the Weights and Measures stranded in the upper
air. This descent among the hidden riches of a lower
world, this visit to the provocations of evils not yet dug
out from their durable confinement, was the keystone, as
it were, of the whole mission. Let Neverbend descend
alone, alone inspect the wonders of that dirty deep, and
Tudor might then talk and write as he pleased. In such
case all the world of the two public offices in question,
and of some others cognate to them, would adjudge
that he, Neverbend, had made himself master of the
situation.

Actuated by these correct calculations, Mr. Neverbend
was rather fussy to begin an immediate descent when he
found himself on the spot. Two native gentlemen, who
were to accompany the Commissioners, or the Commissioner, as appeared likely to be the case, were already
there, as were also the men who were to attend upon
them.

It was an ugly uninviting place to look at, with but few
visible signs of wealth. The earth, which had been
burrowed out by these human rabbits in their search after

tin, lay around in huge ungainly heaps; the overground buildings of the establishment consisted of a few ill-arranged sheds, already apparently in a state of decadence; dirt and slush, and pools of water confined by muddy dams, abounded on every side; muddy men, with muddy carts and muddy horses, slowly crawled hither and thither, apparently with no object, and evidently indifferent as to whom they might overset in their course. The inferior men seemed to show no respect to those above them, and the superiors to exercise no authority over those below them. There was a sullen equality among them all. On the ground around was no vegetation; nothing green met the eye, some few stunted bushes appeared here and there, nearly smothered by heaped-up mud, but they had about them none of the attractiveness of foliage. The whole scene, though consisting of earth alone, was un-earthly, and looked as though the devil had walked over the place with hot hoofs, and then raked it with a huge rake.

'I am afraid I am very late,' said Neverbend, getting out of his fly in all the haste he could muster, and looking at his watch the moment his foot touched the ground, 'very late indeed, gentlemen; I really must apologize, but it was the driver; I was punctual to the minute, I was indeed. But come, gentlemen, we won't lose another moment,' and Mr. Neverbend stepped out as though he were ready at an instant's notice to plunge head foremost down the deepest shaft in all that region of mines.

'Oh, sir, there a'n't no cause of hurry whatsomever,' said one of the mining authorities; 'the day is long enough.'

'Oh, but there is cause of hurry, Mr. Undershot,' said Neverbend, angrily, 'great cause of hurry; we must do this work very thoroughly; and I positively have not time to get through all that I have before me.'

'But a'n't the other gen'leman a-coming?' said Mr. Undershot.

'Surely Mr. Tooder isn't a-going to cry off?' said the other. 'Why, he was so hot about it yesterday.'

'Mr. Tudor is not very well this morning,' said Mr. Neverbend. 'As his going down is not necessary for the inquiry, and is merely a matter of taste on his part, he has not joined me this morning. Come, gentlemen, are we ready ? '

It was then for the first time explained to Mr. Neverbend that he had to go through a rather complicated adjustment of his toilet before he would be considered fit to meet the infernal gods. He must, he was informed, envelop himself from head to foot in miner's habiliments, if he wished to save every stitch he had on him from dirt and destruction. He must also cover up his head with a linen cap, so constituted as to carry a lump of mud with a candle stuck in it, if he wished to save either his head from filth or his feet from falling. Now Mr. Neverbend, like most clerks in public offices, was somewhat particular about his wardrobe ; it behoved him, as a gentleman frequenting the West End, to dress well, and it also behoved him to dress cheaply ; he was, moreover, careful both as to his head and feet ; he could not, therefore, reject the recommended precautions, but yet the time !— the time thus lost might destroy all.

He hurried into the shed where his toilet was to be made, and suffered himself to be prepared in the usual way. He took off his own great-coat, and put on a muddy coarse linen jacket that covered the upper portion of his body completely ; he then dragged on a pair of equally muddy overalls ; and, lastly, submitted to a most uninviting cap, which came down over his ears, and nearly over his eyes, and on the brow of which a lump of mud was then affixed, bearing a short tallow candle.

But though dressed thus in miner's garb, Mr. Neverbend could not be said to look the part he filled. He was a stout, reddish-faced gentleman, with round shoulders and huge whiskers, he was nearly bald, and wore spectacles, and in the costume in which he now appeared he did not seem to be at his ease. Indeed, all his air of command, all his personal dignity and dictatorial tone, left him as soon as he found himself metamorphosed into a fat pseudo-miner. He was like a cock whose feathers had been trailed through the mud, and who could no longer crow aloud, or claim the dunghill as his own. His appearance was somewhat that of a dirty dissipated cook who, having

been turned out of one of the clubs for drunkenness, had
been wandering about the streets all night. He began to
wish that he was once more in the well-known neighbourhood of Charing Cross.

The adventure, however, must now be carried through.
There was still enough of manhood in his heart to make
him feel that he could not return to his colleague at
Tavistock without visiting the wonders which he had
come so far to see. When he reached the head of the
shaft, however, the affair did appear to him to be more
terrible than he had before conceived. He was invited
to get into a rough square bucket, in which there was
just room for himself and another to stand; he was
specially cautioned to keep his head straight, and his
hands and elbows from protruding, and then the windlass
began to turn, and the upper world, the sunlight, and all
humanity receded from his view.

The world receded from his view, but hardly soon
enough; for as the windlass turned and the bucket
descended, his last terrestrial glance, looking out among
the heaps of mud, descried Alaric Tudor galloping on Mr.
Boteldale's pony up to the very mouth of the mine.

'*Facilis descensus Averni.*' The bucket went down
easy enough, and all too quick. The manner in which it
grounded itself on the first landing grated discordantly
on Mr. Neverbend's finer perceptibilities. But when he
learnt, after the interchange of various hoarse and to
him unintelligible bellowings, that he was to wait in that
narrow damp lobby for the coming of his fellow-Commis-
sioner, the grating on his feelings was even more discordant.
He had not pluck enough left to grumble: but he grunted
his displeasure. He grunted, however, in vain; for in
about a quarter of an hour Alaric was close to him,
shoulder to shoulder. He also wore a white jacket, &c.,
with a nightcap of mud and candle on his head; but
somehow he looked as though he had worn them all his
life. The fast gallop, and the excitement of the masquerade,
which for him had charms the sterner Neverbend could
not feel, had dissipated his sickness; and he was once
more all himself.

'So I've caught you at the first stage,' said he, good-

humouredly; for though he knew how badly he had
been treated, he was much too wise to show his knowledge. 'It shall go hard but I'll distance you before we
have done,' he said to himself. Poor Neverbend only
grunted.

And then they all went down a second stage in another
bucket; and then a third in a third bucket; and then
the business commenced. As far as this point passive
courage alone had been required; to stand upright in
a wooden tub and go down, and down, and down, was in
itself easy enough, so long as the heart did not utterly
faint. Mr. Neverbend's heart had grown faintish, but
still he had persevered, and now stood on a third lobby,
listening with dull, unintelligent ears to eager questions
asked by his colleague, and to the rapid answers of their
mining guides. Tudor was absolutely at work with paper
and pencil, taking down notes in that wretched Pande-
monium.

'There now, sir,' said the guide; 'no more of them
ugly buckets, Mr. Neverbend; we can trust to our own
arms and legs for the rest of it,' and so saying, he pointed
out to Mr. Neverbend's horror-stricken eyes a perpendicular iron ladder fixed firmly against the upright side of
a shaft, and leading—for aught Mr. Neverbend could see—
direct to hell itself.

'Down here, is it?' said Alaric, peeping over.

'I'll go first,' said the guide; and down he went, down,
down, down, till Neverbend looking over, could barely
see the glimmer of his disappearing head light. Was it
absolutely intended that he should disappear in the same
way? Had he bound himself to go down that fiendish
upright ladder? And were he to go down it, what then?
Would it be possible that a man of his weight should ever
come up again?

'Shall it be you or I next?' said Alaric, very civilly.
Neverbend could only pant and grunt, and Alaric, with
a courteous nod, placed himself on the ladder, and went
down, down, down, till of him also nothing was left but
the faintest glimmer. Mr. Neverbend remained above
with one of the mining authorities; one attendant miner
also remained with them.

'Now, sir,' said the authority, 'if you are ready, the ladder is quite free.'

Free ! What would not Neverbend have given to be free also himself ! He looked down the free ladder, and the very look made him sink. It seemed to him as though nothing but a spider could creep down that perpendicular abyss. And then a sound, slow, sharp, and continuous, as of drops falling through infinite space on to deep water, came upon his ear ; and he saw that the sides of the abyss were covered with slime ; and the damp air made him cough, and the cap had got over his spectacles and nearly blinded him ; and he was perspiring with a cold, clammy sweat.

'Well, sir, shall we be going on ? ' said the authority. 'Mr. Tooder 'll be at the foot of the next set before this.'

Mr. Neverbend wished that Mr. Tudor's journey might still be down, and down, and down, till he reached the globe's centre, in which conflicting attractions might keep him for ever fixed. In his despair he essayed to put one foot upon the ladder, and then looked piteously up to the guide's face. Even in that dark, dingy atmosphere the light of the farthing candle on his head revealed the agony of his heart. His companions, though they were miners, were still men. They saw his misery, and relented.

'Maybe thee be afeared ? ' said the working miner, 'and if so be thee bee'st, thee'd better bide.'

'I am sure I should never come up again,' said Neverbend, with a voice pleading for mercy, but with all the submission of one prepared to suffer without resistance if mercy should not be forthcoming.

'Thee bee'st for sartan too thick and weazy like for them stairs,' said the miner.

'I am, I am,' said Neverbend, turning on the man a look of the warmest affection, and shoving the horrid, heavy, encumbered cap from off his spectacles ; 'yes, I am too fat.' How would he have answered, with what aspect would he have annihilated the sinner, had such a man dared to call him weazy up above, on *terra firma*, under the canopy of heaven ?

His troubles, however, or at any rate his dangers, were brought to an end. As soon as it became plainly

manifest that his zeal in the public service would carry
him no lower, and would hardly suffice to keep life throbbing in his bosom much longer, even in his present level,
preparations were made for his ascent. A bell was rung ;
hoarse voices were again heard speaking and answering
in sounds quite unintelligible to a Cockney's ears ; chains
rattled, the windlass whirled, and the huge bucket came
tumbling down, nearly on their heads. Poor Neverbend
was all but lifted into it. Where now was all the pride
of the morn that had seen him go forth the great dictator
of the mines ? Where was that towering spirit with which
he had ordered his tea and toast, and rebuked the slowness
of his charioteer ? Where the ambition that had soared
so high over the pet of the Weights and Measures ? Alas,
alas ! how few of us there are who have within us the
courage to be great in adversity. '*Aequam memento*'
—&c., &c. !—if thou couldst but have thought of it,
O Neverbend, who need'st must some day die.

But Neverbend did not think of it. How few of us do
remember such lessons at those moments in which they
ought to be of use to us ! He was all but lifted into the
tub, and then out of it, and then again into another, till
he reached the upper world, a sight piteous to behold.
His spectacles had gone from him, his cap covered his
eyes, his lamp had reversed itself, and soft globules of
grease had fallen on his nose, he was bathed in perspiration, and was nevertheless chilled through to his very
bones, his whiskers were fringed with mud, and his black
cravat had been pulled from his neck and lost in some
infernal struggle. Nevertheless, the moment in which he
seated himself on a hard stool in that rough shed was
perhaps the happiest in his life ; some Christian brought
him beer ; had it been nectar from the brewery of the gods,
he could not have drunk it with greater avidity.

By slow degrees he made such toilet as circumstances
allowed, and then had himself driven back to Tavistock,
being no more willing to wait for Tudor now than he had
been in the early morning. But Jehu found him much
more reasonable on his return ; and as that respectable
functionary pocketed his half-crown, he fully understood
the spirit in which it was given. Poor Neverbend had

not now enough pluck left in him to combat the hostility of a postboy.

Alaric, who of course contrived to see all that was to be seen, and learn all that was to be learnt, in the dark passages of the tin mine, was careful on his return to use his triumph with the greatest moderation. His conscience was, alas, burdened with the guilty knowledge of Undy's shares. When he came to think of the transaction as he rode leisurely back to Tavistock, he knew how wrong he had been, and yet he felt a kind of triumph at the spoil which he held ; for he had heard among the miners that the shares of Mary Jane were already going up to some incredible standard of value. In this manner, so said he to himself, had all the great minds of the present day made their money, and kept themselves afloat. 'Twas thus he tried to comfort himself ; but not as yet successfully.

There were no more squabbles between Mr. Neverbend and Mr. Tudor ; each knew that of himself, which made him bear and forbear ; and so the two Commissioners returned to town on good terms with each other, and Alaric wrote a report, which delighted the heart of Sir Gregory Hardlines, ruined the opponents of the great tin mine, and sent the Mary Jane shares up, and up, and up, till speculating men thought that they could not give too high a price to secure them.

Alaric returned to town on Friday. It had been arranged that he, and Charley, and Norman, should all go down to Hampton on the Saturday ; and then, on the following week, the competitive examination was to take place. But Alaric's first anxiety after his return was to procure the £205, which he had to pay for the shares which he held in his pocket-book. He all but regretted, as he journeyed up to town, with the now tame Fidus seated opposite to him, that he had not disposed of them at Tavistock even at half their present value, so that he might have saved himself the necessity of being a borrower, and have wiped his hands of the whole affair.

He and Norman dined together at their club in Waterloo Place, the Pythagorean, a much humbler establishment than that patronized by Scott, and one that was dignified by no politics. After dinner, as they sat over their pint of sherry, Alaric made his request.

'Harry,' said he, suddenly, 'you are always full of money—I want you to lend me £150.'

Norman was much less quick in his mode of speaking than his friend, and at the present moment was inclined to be somewhat slower than usual. This affair of the examination pressed upon his spirits, and made him dull and unhappy. During the whole of dinner he had said little or nothing, and had since been sitting listlessly gazing at vacancy, and balancing himself on the hind-legs of his chair.

'O yes—certainly,' said he; but he said it without the eagerness with which Alaric thought that he should have answered his request.

'If it's inconvenient, or if you don't like it,' said Alaric, the blood mounting to his forehead, 'it does not signify. I can do without it.'

'I can lend it you without any inconvenience,' said Harry. 'When do you want it—not to-night, I suppose?'

'No—not to-night—I should like to have it early to-morrow morning; but I see you don't like it, so I'll manage it some other way.'

'I don't know what you mean by not liking it. I have not the slightest objection to lending you any money I can spare. I don't think you'll find any other of your friends who will like it better. You can have it by eleven o'clock to-morrow.'

Intimate as the two men were, there had hitherto been very little borrowing or lending between them; and now Alaric felt as though he owed it to his intimacy with his friend to explain to him why he wanted so large a sum in so short a time. He felt, moreover, that he would not himself be so much ashamed of what he had done if he could confess it to some one else. He could then solace himself with the reflection that he had done nothing secret. Norman, he supposed, would be displeased; but then Norman's displeasure could not injure him, and with Norman there would be no danger that the affair would go any further.

'You must think it very strange,' said he, 'that

I should want such a sum ; but the truth is I have bought some shares.'

' Railway shares ? ' said Norman, in a tone that certainly did not signify approval. He disliked speculation altogether, and had an old-fashioned idea that men who do speculate, should have money wherewith to do it.

' No—not railway shares exactly.'

' Canal ? ' suggested Norman.

' No—not canal.'

' Gas ? '

' Mines,' said Alaric, bringing out the dread truth at last.

Harry Norman's brow grew very black. ' Not that mine that you've been down about, I hope,' said he.

' Yes—that very identical Mary Jane that I went down, and down about,' said Alaric, trying to joke on the subject. ' Don't look so very black, my dear fellow. I know all that you have to say upon the matter. I did what was very foolish, I dare say ; but the idea never occurred to me till it was too late, that I might be suspected of making a false report on the subject, because I had embarked a hundred pounds in it.'

' Alaric, if it were known—— '

' Then it mustn't be known,' said Tudor. ' I am sorry for it ; but, as I told you, the idea didn't occur to me till it was too late. The shares are bought now, and must be paid for to-morrow. I shall sell them the moment I can, and you shall have the money in three or four days.'

' I don't care one straw about the money,' said Norman, now quick enough, but still in great displeasure ; ' I would give double the amount that you had not done this.'

' Don't be so suspicious, Harry,' said the other—' don't try to think the worst of your friend. By others, by Sir Gregory Hardlines, Neverbend, and such men, I might expect to be judged harshly in such a matter. But I have a right to expect that you will believe me. I tell you that I did this inadvertently, and am sorry for it ; surely that ought to be sufficient.'

Norman said nothing more ; but he felt that Tudor had done that which, if known, would disgrace him for ever. It might, however, very probably never be known ; and it might also be that Tudor would never act so dishonestly again. On the following morning the money was paid; and in the course of the next week the shares were resold, and the money repaid, and Alaric Tudor, for the first time in his life, found himself to be the possessor of over three hundred pounds.

Such was the price which Scott, Manylodes, & Co., had found it worth their while to pay him for his good report on Mary Jane.

CHAPTER XI

THE THREE KINGS

AND now came the all-important week. On the Saturday the three young men went down to Hampton. Charley had lately been leading a very mixed sort of life. One week he would consort mainly with the houri of the Norfolk Street beer-shop, and the next he would be on his good behaviour, and live as respectably as circumstances permitted him to do. His scope in this respect was not large. The greatest respectability which his unassisted efforts could possibly achieve was to dine at a cheap eating-house, and spend his evenings at a cigar divan. He belonged to no club, and his circle of friends, except in the houri and navvy line, was very limited. Who could expect that a young man from the Internal Navigation would sit for hours and hours alone in a dull London lodging, over his book and tea-cup? Who should expect that any young man will do so? And yet mothers, and aunts, and anxious friends, do expect it—very much in vain.

During Alaric's absence at Tavistock, Norman had taken Charley by the hand and been with him a good deal. He had therefore spent an uncommonly respectable week, and the Norfolk Street houri would have been au désespoir, but that she had other Charleys to her bow. When he found himself getting into a first-class carriage at the

Waterloo-bridge station with his two comrades, he began
to appreciate the comfort of decency, and almost wished
that he also had been brought up among the stern morals
and hard work of the Weights and Measures.

Nothing special occurred at Surbiton Cottage. It might
have been evident to a watchful bystander that Alaric was
growing in favour with all the party, excepting Mrs. Woodward, and that, as he did so, Harry was more and more
cherished by her.

This was specially shown in one little scene. Alaric
had brought down with him to Hampton the documents
necessary to enable him to draw out his report on Mary
Jane. Indeed, it was all but necessary that he should do
so, as his coming examination would leave him but little
time for other business during the week. On Saturday
night he sat up at his inn over the papers, and on Sunday
morning, when Mrs. Woodward and the girls came down,
ready bonneted, for church, he signified his intention of
remaining at his work.

'I certainly think he might have gone to church,' said
Mrs. Woodward, when the hall-door closed behind the
party, as they started to their place of worship.

'Oh! mamma, think how much he has to do,' said
Gertrude.

'Nonsense,' said Mrs. Woodward; 'it's all affectation,
and he ought to go to church. Government clerks are not
worked so hard as all that; are they, Harry?'

'Alaric is certainly very busy, but I think he should go
to church all the same,' said Harry, who himself never
omitted divine worship.

'But surely this is a work of necessity?' said Linda.

'Fiddle-de-de,' said Mrs. Woodward; 'I hate affectation, my dear. It's very grand, I dare say, for a young
man's services to be in such request that he cannot find
time to say his prayers. He'll find plenty of time for
gossiping by and by, I don't doubt.'

Linda could say nothing further, for an unbidden tear
moistened her eyelid as she heard her mother speak so
harshly of her lover. Gertrude, however, took up the
cudgels for him, and so did Captain Cuttwater.

'I think you are a little hard upon him, mamma,' said

Gertrude, 'particularly when you know that, as a rule, he always goes to church. I have heard you say yourself what an excellent churchman he is.'

'Young men change sometimes,' said Mrs. Woodward.

'Upon my word, Bessy, I think you are very uncharitable this fine Sunday morning,' said the captain. 'I wonder how you'll feel if we have that chapter about the beam and the mote.'

Mrs. Woodward did not quite like being scolded by her uncle before her daughters, but she said nothing further. Katie, however, looked daggers at the old man from out her big bright eyes. What right had any man, were he ever so old, ever so much an uncle, to scold her mamma ? Katie was inclined to join her mother and take Harry Norman's side, for it was Harry Norman who owned the boat.

They were now at the church door, and they entered without saying anything further. Let us hope that charity, which surpasseth all other virtues, guided their prayers while they were there, and filled their hearts. In the meantime Alaric, unconscious how he had been attacked and how defended, worked hard at his Tavistock notes.

Mrs. Woodward was quite right in this, that the Commissioner of the Mines, though he was unable to find time to go to church, did find time to saunter about with the girls before dinner. Was it to be expected that he should not do so ? for what other purpose was he there at Hampton ?

They were all very serious this Sunday afternoon, and Katie could make nothing of them. She and Charley, indeed, went off by themselves to a desert island, or a place that would have been a desert island had the water run round it, and there built stupendous palaces and laid out glorious gardens. Charley was the most good-natured of men, and could he have only brought a boat with him, as Harry so often did, he would soon have been first favourite with Katie.

'It shan't be at all like Hampton Court,' said Katie, speaking of the new abode which Charley was to build for her.

'Not at all,' said Charley.

'Nor yet Buckingham Palace.'

'No,' said Charley, 'I think we'll have it Gothic.'

'Gothic!' said Katie, looking up at him with all her eyes. 'Will Gothic be most grand? What's Gothic?'

Charley began to consider. 'Westminster Abbey,' said he at last.

'Oh—but Charley, I don't want a church. Is the Alhambra Gothic?'

Charley was not quite sure, but thought it probably was. They decided, therefore, that the new palace should be built after the model of the Alhambra.

The afternoon was but dull and lugubrious to the remainder of the party. The girls seemed to feel that there was something solemn about the coming competition between two such dear friends, which prevented and should prevent them all from being merry. Harry perfectly sympathized in the feeling; and even Alaric, though depressed himself by no melancholy forebodings, was at any rate conscious that he should refrain from any apparent anticipation of a triumph. They all went to church in the evening; but even this amendment in Alaric's conduct hardly reconciled him to Mrs. Woodward.

'I suppose we shall all be very clever before long,' said she, after tea; 'but really I don't know that we shall be any the better for it. Now in this office of yours, by the end of next week, there will be three or four men with broken hearts, and there will be one triumphant jackanapes, so conceited and proud, that he'll never bring himself to do another good ordinary day's work as long as he lives. Nothing will persuade me but that it is not only very bad, but very unjust also.'

'The jackanapes must learn to put up with ordinary work,' said Alaric, 'or he'll soon find himself reduced to his former insignificance.'

'And the men with the broken hearts; they, I suppose, must put up with their wretchedness too,' said Mrs. Woodward; 'and their wives, also, and children, who have been looking forward for years to this vacancy as the period of their lives at which they are to begin to be comfortable.

I hate such heartlessness. I hate the very name of Sir Gregory Hardlines.'

'But, mamma, won't the general effect be to produce a much higher class of education among the men?' said Gertrude.

'In the army and navy the best men get on the best,' said Linda.

'Do they, by jingo!' said Uncle Bat. 'It's very little you know about the navy, Miss Linda.'

'Well, then, at any rate they ought,' said Linda.

'I would have a competitive examination in every service,' said Gertrude. 'It would make young men ambitious. They would not be so idle and empty as they now are, if they had to contend in this way for every step upwards in the world.'

'The world,' said Mrs. Woodward, 'will soon be like a fishpond, very full of fish, but with very little food for them. Every one is scrambling for the others' prey, and they will end at last by eating one another. If Harry gets this situation, will not that unfortunate Jones, who for years has been waiting for it, always regard him as a robber?'

'My maxim is this,' said Uncle Bat; 'if a youngster goes into any service, say the navy, and does his duty by his country like a man, why, he shouldn't be passed over. Now look at me; I was on the books of the *Catamaran*, one of the old seventy-fours, in '96; I did my duty then and always; was never in the black book or laid up sick; was always rough and ready for any work that came to hand; and when I went into the *Mudlark* as lieutenant in year '9, little Bobby Howard had just joined the old *Cat.* as a young middy. And where am I now? and where is Bobby Howard? Why, d—e, I'm on the shelf, craving the ladies' pardon; and he's a Lord of the Admiralty, if you please, and a Member of Parliament. Now I say Cuttwater's as good a name as Howard for going to sea with any day; and if there'd been a competitive examination for Admiralty Lords five years ago, Bobby Howard would never have been where he is now, and somebody else who knows more about his profession than all the Howards put together, might perhaps have been in his place. And so, my lads, here's to you, and I hope the best man will win.'

Whether Uncle Bat agreed with his niece or with his grandnieces was not very apparent from the line of his argument; but they all laughed at his eagerness, and nothing more was said that evening about the matter.

Alaric, Harry, and Charley, of course returned to town on the following day. Breakfast on Monday morning at Surbiton Cottage was an early affair when the young men were there; so early, that Captain Cuttwater did not make his appearance. Since his arrival at the cottage, Mrs. Woodward had found an excuse for a later breakfast in the necessity of taking it with her uncle; so that the young people were generally left alone. Linda was the family tea-maker, and was, therefore, earliest down; and Alaric being the first on this morning to leave the hotel, found her alone in the dining-room.

He had never renewed the disclosure of his passion; but Linda had thought that whenever he shook hands with her since that memorable walk, she had always felt a more than ordinary pressure. This she had been careful not to return, but she had not the heart to rebuke it. Now, when he bade her good morning, he certainly held her hand in his longer than he need have done. He looked at her too, as though his looks meant something more than ordinary looking; at least so Linda thought; but yet he said nothing, and so Linda, slightly trembling, went on with the adjustment of her tea-tray.

'It will be all over, Linda, when we meet again,' said Alaric. His mind she found was intent on his examination, not on his love. But this was natural, was as it should be. If—and she was certain in her heart that it would be so—if he should be successful, then he might speak of love without having to speak in the same breath of poverty as well. 'It will be all over when we meet again,' he said.

'I suppose it will,' said Linda.

'I don't at all like it; it seems so unnatural having to contend against one's friend. And yet one cannot help it; one cannot allow one's self to go to the wall.'

'I'm sure Harry doesn't mind it,' said Linda.

'I'm sure I do,' said he. 'If I fail I shall be unhappy, and if I succeed I shall be equally so. I shall set all the world against me. I know what your mother meant when she talked of a jackanapes yesterday. If I get the promotion I may wish good-bye to Surbiton Cottage.'

'Oh, Alaric!'

'Harry would forgive me; but Harry's friends would never do so.'

'How can you say so? I am sure mamma has no such feeling, nor yet even Gertrude; I mean that none of us have.'

'It is very natural all of you should, for he is your cousin.'

'You are just the same as our cousin. I am sure we think quite as much of you as of Harry. Even Gertrude said she hoped that you would get it.'

'Dear Gertrude!'

'Because, you know, Harry does not want it so much as you do. I am sure I wish you success with all my heart. Perhaps it's wicked to wish for either of you over the other; but you can't both get it at once, you know.'

At this moment Katie came in, and soon afterwards Gertrude and the two other young men, and so nothing further was said on the subject.

Charley parted with the competitors at the corner of Waterloo Bridge. He turned into Somerset House, being there regarded on these Monday mornings as a prodigy of punctuality; and Alaric and Harry walked back along the Strand, arm-in-arm, toward their own office.

'Well, lads, I hope you'll both win,' said Charley. 'And whichever wins most, why of course he'll stand an uncommon good dinner.'

'Oh! that's of course,' said Alaric. 'We'll have it at the Trafalgar.'

And so the two walked on together, arm-in-arm, to the Weights and Measures.

The ceremony which was now about to take place at the Weights and Measures was ordained to be the first of those examinations which, under the auspices of Sir Gregory Hardlines, were destined to revivify, clarify, and render perfect the Civil Service of the country. It was a great triumph to Sir Gregory to see the darling object of his heart thus commencing its existence in the very cradle in which he, as an infant Hercules, had made his first exertions in the cause. It was to be his future fortune to superintend these intellectual contests, in a stately office of his own, duly set apart and appointed for the purpose. But the throne on which he was to sit had not yet been prepared for him, and he was at present constrained to content himself with exercising his power, now here and now there, according as his services might be required, carrying the appurtenances of his royalty about with him.

But Sir Gregory was not a solitary monarch. In days long gone by there were, as we all know, three kings at Cologne, and again three kings at Brentford. So also were there three kings at the Civil Service Examination Board. But of these three Sir Gregory was by far the greatest king. He sat in the middle, had two thousand jewels to his crown, whereas the others had only twelve hundred each, and his name ran first in all the royal warrants. Nevertheless, Sir Gregory, could he have had it so, would, like most other kings, have preferred an undivided sceptre.

Of his co-mates on the throne the elder in rank was a west country baronet, who, not content with fatting beeves and brewing beer like his sires, aspired to do something for his country. Sir Warwick Westend was an excellent man, full of the best intentions, and not more than decently anxious to get the good things of Government into his hand. He was, perhaps, rather too much inclined to think that he could see further through a millstone than another, and had a way of looking as though he were always making the attempt. He was a man born to grace, if not his country, at any rate his county; and his conduct was uniformly such as to afford the liveliest satisfaction to his uncles, aunts, and relations in general. If as a king he had a fault, it was this, that he allowed that other king, Sir Gregory, to carry him in his pocket.

But Sir Gregory could not at all get the third king into his pocket. This gentleman was a worthy clergyman from Cambridge, one Mr. Jobbles by name. Mr. Jobbles-had for many years been examining undergraduates for little goes and great goes, and had passed his life in putting posing questions, in detecting ignorance by viva voce scrutiny, and eliciting learning by printed papers. He, by a stupendous effort of his mathematical mind, had divided the adult British male world into classes and sub-classes, and could tell at a moment's notice how long it would take him to examine them all. His soul panted for the work. Every man should, he thought, be made to pass through some ' go.' The greengrocer's boy should not carry out cabbages unless his fitness for cabbage-carrying had been ascertained, and till it had also been ascertained that no other boy, ambitious of the prefer-ment, would carry them better. Difficulty! There was no difficulty. Could not he, Jobbles, get through 5,000 viva voces in every five hours—that is, with due assistance ? and would not 55,000 printed papers, containing 555,000 questions, be getting themselves answered at the same time, with more or less precision ?

So now Mr. Jobbles was about to try his huge plan by a small commencement.

On the present occasion the examination was actually to be carried on by two of the kings in person. Sir Gregory had declared that as so large a portion of his heart and affections was bound up with the gentlemen of the Weights and Measures, he could not bring himself actually to ask questions of them, and then to listen to or read their answers. Should any of his loved ones make some fatal *faux pas*, his tears, like those of the recording angel, would blot out the error. His eyes would refuse to see faults, if there should be faults, in those whom he himself had nurtured. Therefore, though he came with his colleagues to the Weights and Measures, he did not himself take part in the examination.

At eleven o'clock the Board-room was opened, and the candidates walked in and seated themselves. Fear of Sir Gregory, and other causes, had thinned the number. Poor Jones, who by right of seniority should have had the prize, declined to put himself in competition with his juniors, and in lieu thereof sent up to the Lords of the Treasury an awful memorial spread over fifteen folio pages—very uselessly. The Lords of the Treasury referred it to the three kings, whose secretary put a minute upon it. Sir Gregory signed the minute, and some gentleman at the Treasury wrote a short letter to Mr. Jones, apprising that unhappy gentleman that my Lords had taken the matter into their fullest consideration, and that nothing could be done to help him. Had Jones been consulted by any other disappointed Civil Service Werter as to the expediency of complaining to the Treasury Lords, Jones would have told him exactly what would be the result. The disappointed one, however, always thinks that all the Treasury Lords will give all their ears to him, though they are deafer than Icarus to the world beside.

Robinson stood his ground like a man ; but Brown found out, a day or two before the struggle came, that he could not bring himself to stand against his friend. Jones, he said, he knew was incompetent, but Robinson ought to get it ; so he, for one, would not stand in Robinson's way.

Uppinall was there, as confident as a bantam cock ; and so was Alphabet Precis, who had declared to all his friends that if the pure well of official English undefiled was to count for anything, he ought to be pretty safe. But poor Minusex was ill, and sent a certificate. He had so crammed himself with unknown quantities, that his mind —like a gourmand's stomach—had broken down under the effort, and he was now sobbing out algebraic positions under his counterpane.

Norman and Alaric made up the five who still had health, strength, and pluck to face the stern justice of the new kings ; and they accordingly took their seats on five chairs, equally distant, placing themselves in due order of seniority.

And then, first of all, Sir Gregory made a little speech, standing up at the head of the Board-room table, with an attendant king on either hand, and the Secretary, and two Assistant-Secretaries, standing near him. Was not this a proud moment for Sir Gregory ?

' It had now become his duty,' he said, ' to take his position in that room, that well-known, well-loved room, under circumstances of which he had little dreamt when he first entered it with awe-struck steps, in the days of his early youth. But, nevertheless, even then ambition had warmed him. That ambition had been to devote every energy of his mind, every muscle of his body, every hour of his life, to the Civil Service of his country. It was not much, perhaps, that he had been able to do; he could not boast of those acute powers of mind, of that gigantic grasp of intellect, of which they saw in those days so wonderful an example in a high place.' Sir Gregory here gratefully alluded to that statesman who had given him his present appointment. ' But still he had devoted all his mind, such as it was, and every hour of his life, to the service; and now he had his reward. If he might be allowed to give advice to the gentlemen before him, gentlemen of whose admirable qualifications for the Civil Service of the country he himself was so well aware, his advice should be this—That they should look on none of their energies as applicable to private purposes, regard none of their hours as their own. They were devoted in a peculiar way to the Civil Service, and they should feel that such was their lot in life. They should know that their intellects were a sacred pledge intrusted to them for the good of that service, and should use them accordingly. This should be their highest ambition. And what higher ambition,' asked Sir Gregory, ' could they have ? They all, alas ! knew that the service had been disgraced in other quarters by idleness, incompetency, and, he feared he must say, dishonesty; till incompetency and dishonesty had become, not the exception, but the rule. It was too notorious that the Civil Service was filled by the family fools of the aristocracy and middle classes, and that any family who had no fool to send, sent in lieu thereof some invalid past hope. Thus the service had become a hospital for incurables and idiots. It was,' said Sir Gregory, ' for him and them to cure all that. He would not,' he said, ' at that moment, say anything with reference to salaries. It was, as they were all aware, a very difficult subject, and did not seem to be necessarily connected with the few remarks which the present opportunity had seemed to him to call for.' He then told them they were all his beloved children; that they were a credit to the establishment; that he handed them over without a blush to his excellent colleagues, Sir Warwick Westend and Mr. Jobbles, and that he wished in his heart that each of them could be successful. And having so spoken, Sir Gregory went his way.

It was beautiful then to see how Mr. Jobbles swam down the long room and handed out his examination papers to the different candidates as he passed them. 'Twas a pity there should have been but five; the man did it so well, so quickly, with such a gusto! He should have been allowed to try his hand upon five hundred instead of five. His step was so rapid and his hand and arm moved so dexterously, that no conceivable number would have been too many for him. But, even with five, he showed at once that the right man was in the right place. Mr. Jobbles was created for the conducting of examinations.

And then the five candidates, who had hitherto been all ears, of a sudden became all eyes, and devoted themselves in a manner which would have been delightful to Sir Gregory, to the papers before them. Sir Warwick, in the meantime, was seated in his chair, hard at work looking through his millstone.

It is a dreadful task that of answering examination papers—only to be exceeded in dreadfulness by the horrors of Mr. Jobbles' viva voce torments. A man has before him a string of questions, and he looks painfully down them, from question to question, searching for some allusion to that special knowledge which he has within him. He too often finds that no such allusion is made. It appears that the Jobbles of the occasion has exactly known the blank spots of his mind and fitted them all. He has perhaps crammed himself with the winds and tides, and there is no more reference to those stormy subjects than if Luna were extinct; but he has, unfortunately, been loose about his botany, and question after question would appear to him to have been dictated by Sir Joseph Paxton or the head-gardener at Kew. And then to his own blank face and puzzled look is opposed the fast scribbling of some botanic candidate, fast as though reams of folio could hardly contain all the knowledge which he is able to pour forth.

And so, with a mixture of fast-scribbling pens and blank

faces, our five friends went to work. The examination lasted for four days, and it was arranged that on each of the four days each of the five candidates should be called up to undergo a certain quantum of Mr. Jobbles' viva voce. This part of his duty Mr. Jobbles performed with a mildness of manner that was beyond all praise. A mother training her first-born to say 'papa,' could not do so with a softer voice, or more affectionate demeanour.

'The planet Jupiter,' said he to Mr. Precis; 'I have no doubt you know accurately the computed distance of that planet from the sun, and also that of our own planet. Could you tell me now, how would you calculate the distance in inches, say from London Bridge to the nearest portion of Jupiter's disc, at twelve o'clock on the first of April?' Mr. Jobbles, as he put his little question, smiled the sweetest of smiles, and spoke in a tone conciliating and gentle, as though he were asking Mr. Precis to dine with him and take part of a bottle of claret at half-past six.

But, nevertheless, Mr. Precis looked very blank.

'I am not asking the distance, you know,' said Mr. Jobbles, smiling sweeter than ever; 'I am only asking how you would compute it.'

But still Mr. Precis looked exceedingly blank.

'Never mind,' said Mr. Jobbles, with all the encouragement which his voice could give, 'never mind. Now, suppose that a be a milestone; b a turnpike-gate——,' and so on.

But Mr. Jobbles, in spite of his smiles, so awed the hearts of some of his candidates, that two of them retired at the end of the second day. Poor Robinson, thinking, and not without sufficient ground, that he had not a ghost of a chance, determined to save himself from further annoyance; and then Norman, put utterly out of conceit with himself by what he deemed the insufficiency of his answers, did the same. He had become low in spirits, unhappy in temperament, and self-diffident to a painful degree. Alaric, to give him his due, did everything in his power to persuade him to see the task out to the last. But the assurance and composure of Alaric's manner did more than anything else to provoke and increase Norman's

discomfiture.   He had been schooling himself to bear
a beating with a good grace, and he began to find that he
could only bear it as a disgrace.   On the morning of the
third day, instead of taking his place in the Board-room,
he sent in a note to Mr. Jobbles, declaring that he withdrew
from the trial.   Mr. Jobbles read the note, and smiled with
satisfaction as he put it into his pocket.   It was an acknowledgement of his own unrivalled powers as an Examiner.

Mr. Precis, still trusting to his pure well, went on to the
end, and at the end declared that so ignorant was Mr.
Jobbles of his duty that he had given them no opportunity
of showing what they could do in English composition.
Why had he not put before them the papers in some
memorable official case, and desired them to make an
abstract ; those, for instance, on the much-vexed question
of penny *versus* pound, as touching the new standard for
the decimal coinage ?   Mr. Jobbles an Examiner indeed !
And so Mr. Precis bethought himself that he also, if
unsuccessful, would go to the Lords of the Treasury.

And Mr. Uppinall and Alaric Tudor also went on.
Those who knew anything of the matter, when they saw
how the running horses were reduced in number, and
what horses were left on the course—when they observed
also how each steed came to the post on each succeeding
morning, had no doubt whatever of the result.   So that
when Alaric was declared on the Saturday morning to
have gained the prize, there was very little astonishment
either felt or expressed at the Weights and Measures.

Alaric's juniors wished him joy with some show of
reality in their manner ; but the congratulations of his
seniors, including the Secretary and Assistant-Secretaries,
the new Chief Clerk and the men in the class to which
he was now promoted, were very cold indeed.   But to
this he was indifferent.   It was the nature of Tudor's
disposition, that he never for a moment rested satisfied
with the round of the ladder on which he had contrived
to place himself.   He had no sooner gained a step than he
looked upwards to see how the next step was to be achieved.
His motto might well have been ' Excelsior ! ' if only he
could have taught himself to look to heights that were
really high.   When he found that the august Secretary

received him on his promotion without much *empressement*, he comforted himself by calculating how long it would be before he should fill that Secretary's chair—if indeed it should ever be worth his while to fill it.

The Secretary at the Weights and Measures had, after all, but a dull time of it, and was precluded by the routine of his office from parliamentary ambition and the joys of government. Alaric was already beginning to think that this Weights and Measures should only be a stepping-stone to him; and that when Sir Gregory, with his stern dogma of devotion to the service, had been of sufficient use to him, he also might with advantage be thrown over. In the meantime an income of £600 a year brought with it to the young bachelor some very comfortable influence. But the warmest and the pleasantest of all the congratulations which he received was from his dear friend Undy Scott.

'Ah, my boy,' said Undy, pressing his hand, 'you'll soon be one of us. By the by, I want to put you up for the Downing; you should leave that Pythagorean: there's nothing to be got by it.'

Now, the Downing was a political club, in which, however, politics had latterly become a good deal mixed. But the Government of the day generally found there a liberal support, and recognized and acknowledged its claim to consideration.

CHAPTER XII

CONSOLATION

ON the following Sunday neither Tudor nor Norman was at Hampton. They had both felt that they could not comfortably meet each other there, and each had declined to go. They had promised to write; and now that the matter was decided, how were they or either of them to keep the promise?

It may be thought that the bitterness of the moment was over with Norman as soon as he gave up; but such was not the case. Let him struggle as he would with himself he could not rally, nor bring himself to feel happy on what had occurred. He would have been better satisfied if Alaric would have triumphed; but Alaric seemed to take it all as a matter of course, and never spoke of his own promotion unless he did so in answer to some remark of his companion; then he could speak easily enough; otherwise he was willing to let the matter go by as one settled and at rest. He had consulted Norman about the purchase of a horse, but he hitherto had shown no other sign that he was a richer man than formerly.

It was a very bitter time for Norman. He could not divest his mind of the subject. What was he to do? Where was he to go? How was he to get away, even for a time, from Alaric Tudor? And then, was he right in wishing to get away from him? Had he not told himself, over and over again, that it behoved him as a man and a friend and a Christian to conquer the bitter feeling of envy which preyed on his spirits? Had he not himself counselled Alaric to stand this examination? and had he not promised that his doing so should make no difference in their friendship? Had he not pledged himself to rejoice in the success of his friend? and now was he to break his word both to that friend and to himself?

Schooling himself, or trying to school himself in this way, he made no attempt at escaping from his unhappiness. They passed the Wednesday, Thursday, and Friday evenings together. It was now nearly the end of September, and London was empty; that is, empty as regards those friends and acquaintances with whom Norman might have found some resource. On the Saturday they left their office early; for all office routine had, during this week, been broken through by the immense importance of the ceremony which was going on; and then it became necessary to write to Mrs. Woodward.

'Will you write to Hampton or shall I?' said Alaric, as they walked arm-in-arm under the windows of Whitehall.

'Oh! you, of course,' said Norman; 'you have much to tell them; I have nothing.'

'Just as you please,' said the other. 'That is, of course,

I will if you like it. But I think it would come better from you. You are nearer to them than I am ; and it will have less a look of triumph on my part, and less also of disappointment on yours, if you write. If you tell them that you literally threw away your chance, you will only tell them the truth.'

Norman assented, but he said nothing further. What business had Alaric to utter such words as triumph and disappointment ? He could not keep his arm, on which Alaric was leaning, from spasmodically shrinking from the touch. He had been beaten by a man, nay worse, had yielded to a man, who had not the common honesty to refuse a bribe ; and yet he was bound to love this man. He could not help asking himself the question which he would do. Would he love him or hate him ?

But while he was so questioning himself, he got home, and had to sit down and write his letter—this he did at once, but not without difficulty. It ran as follows :—

'My dear Mrs. Woodward,—

'I write a line to tell you of my discomfiture and Alaric's success. I gave up at the end of the second day. Of course I will tell you all about it when we meet. No one seemed to doubt that Alaric would get it, as a matter of course. I shall be with you on next Saturday. Alaric says he will not go down till the Saturday after, when I shall be at Normansgrove. My best love to the girls. Tell Katie I shan't drown either myself or the boat.

'Yours ever affectionately,

'H. N.

'Saturday, September, 185-.

'Pray write me a kind letter to comfort me.'

Mrs. Woodward did write him a very kind letter, and it did comfort him. And she wrote also, as she was bound to do, a letter of congratulation to Alaric. This letter, though it expressed in the usual terms the satisfaction which one friend has in another's welfare, was not written in the same warm affectionate tone as that to Norman. Alaric perceived instantly that it was not cordial. He

loved Mrs. Woodward dearly, and greatly desired her love
and sympathy. But what then? He could not have
everything. He determined, therefore, not to trouble his
mind. If Mrs. Woodward did not sympathize with him,
others of the family would do so; and success would
ultimately bring her round. What woman ever yet refused
to sympathize with successful ambition?

Alaric also received a letter from Captain Cuttwater,
in which that gallant veteran expressed his great joy at
the result of the examination—'Let the best man win
all the world over,' said he, 'whatever his name is.
And they'll have to make the same rule at the Admiralty
too. The days of the Howards are gone by; that is,
unless they can prove themselves able seamen, which very
few of them ever did yet. Let the best man win; that's
what I say; and let every man get his fair share of
promotion.' Alaric did not despise the sympathy of
Captain Cuttwater. It might turn out that even Captain
Cuttwater could be made of use.

Mrs. Woodward's letter to Harry was full of the tenderest affection. It was a flattering, soothing, loving
letter, such as no man ever could have written. It was
like oil poured into his wounds, and made him feel that
the world was not all harsh to him. He had determined
not to go to Hampton that Saturday; but Mrs. Woodward's letter almost made him rush there at once that he
might throw himself into her arms—into her arms, and
at her daughter's feet. The time had now come to him
when he wanted to be comforted by the knowledge that
his love was returned. He resolved that during his next
visit he would formally propose to Gertrude.

The determination to do this, and a strong hope that
he might do it successfully, kept him up during the
interval. On the following week he was to go to his father's
place to shoot, having obtained leave of absence for
a month; and he felt that he could still enjoy himself if
he could take with him the conviction that all was right
at Surbiton Cottage. Mrs. Woodward, in her letter, though
she had spoken much of the girls, had said nothing special
about Gertrude. Nevertheless, Norman gathered from it
that she intended that he should go thither to look for

comfort, and that he would find there the comfort that he required.

And Mrs. Woodward had intended that such should be the effect of her letter. It was at present the dearest wish of her heart to see Norman and Gertrude married. That Norman had often declared his love to her eldest daughter she knew very well, and she knew also that Gertrude had never rejected him. Having perfect confidence in her child, she had purposely abstained from saying anything that could bias her opinion. She had determined to leave the matter in the hands of the young people themselves, judging that it might be best arranged as a true love-match between them, without interference from her; she had therefore said nothing to Gertrude on the subject.

Mrs. Woodward, however, discovered that she was in error, when it was too late for her to retrieve her mistake; and, indeed, had she discovered it before that letter was written, what could she have done? She could not have forbidden Harry to come to her house—she could not have warned him not to throw himself at her daughter's feet. The cup was prepared for his lips, and it was necessary that he should drink of it. There was nothing for which she could blame him; nothing for which she could blame herself; nothing for which she did blame her daughter. It was sorrowful, pitiful, to be lamented, wept for, aye, and groaned for; many inward groans it cost her; but it was at any rate well that she could attribute her sorrow to the spite of circumstances rather than to the ill-conduct of those she loved.

Nor would it have been fair to blame Gertrude in the matter. While she was yet a child, this friend of her mother's had been thrown with her, and when she was little more than a child, she found that this friend had become a lover. She liked him, in one sense loved him, and was accustomed to regard him as one whom it would be almost wrong in her not to like and love. What wonder then that when he first spoke to her warm words of adoration, she had not been able at once to know her own heart, and tell him that his hopes would be in vain?

She perceived by instinct, rather than by spoken words,

that her mother was favourable to this young lover, that if she accepted him she would please her mother, that the course of true love might in their case run smooth. What wonder then that she should have hesitated before she found it necessary to say that she could not, would not, be Harry Norman's wife?

On the Saturday morning, the morning of that night which was, as he hoped, to see him go to bed a happy lover, so happy in his love as to be able to forget his other sorrows, she was sitting alone with her mother. It was natural that their conversation should turn to Alaric and Harry. Alaric, with his happy prospects, was soon dismissed; but Mrs. Woodward continued to sing the praises of him who, had she been potent with the magi of the Civil Service, would now be the lion of the Weights and Measures.

'I must say I think it was weak of him to retire,' said Gertrude. 'Alaric says in his letter to Uncle Bat, that had he persevered he would in all probability have been successful.'

'I should rather say that it was generous,' said her mother.

'Well, I don't know, mamma; that of course depends on his motives; but wouldn't generosity of that sort between two young men in such a position be absurd?'

'You mean that such regard for his friend would be Quixotic.'

'Yes, mamma.'

'Perhaps it would. All true generosity, all noble feeling, is now called Quixotic. But surely, Gertrude, you and I should not quarrel with Harry on that account.'

'I think he got frightened, mamma, and had not nerve to go through with it.'

Mrs. Woodward looked vexed; but she made no immediate reply, and for some time the mother and daughter went on working without further conversation. At last Gertrude said:—

'I think every man is bound to do the best he can for himself—that is, honestly; there is something spoony in one man allowing another to get before him, as long as he can manage to be first himself.'

Mrs. Woodward did not like the tone in which her daughter spoke. She felt that it boded ill for Harry's welfare; and she tried, but tried in vain, to elicit from her daughter the expression of a kinder feeling.

'Well, my dear, I must say I think you are hard on him. But, probably, just at present you have the spirit of contradiction in you. If I were to begin to abuse him, perhaps I should get you to praise him.'

'Oh, mamma, I did not abuse him.'

'Something like it, my dear, when you said he was spoony.'

'Oh, mamma, I would not abuse him for worlds—I know how good he is, I know how you love him, but, but——' and Gertrude, though very little given to sobbing moods, burst into tears.

'Come here, Gertrude; come here, my child,' said Mrs. Woodward, now moved more for her daughter than for her favourite; 'what is it? what makes you cry? I did not really mean that you abused poor Harry.'

Gertrude got up from her chair, knelt at her mother's feet, and hid her face in her mother's lap. 'Oh, mamma,' she said, with a half-smothered voice, 'I know what you mean; I know what you wish; but—but—but, oh, mamma, you must not—must not, must not think of it any more.'

'Then may God help him!' said Mrs. Woodward, gently caressing her daughter, who was still sobbing with her face buried in her mother's lap. 'May God Almighty lighten the blow to him! But oh, Gertrude, I had hoped, I had so hoped——'

'Oh, mamma, don't, pray don't,' and Gertrude sobbed as though she were going into hysterics.

'No, my child, I will not say another word. Dear as he is to me, you are and must be ten times dearer. There, Gertrude, it is over now; over at least between us. We know each other's hearts now. It is my fault that we did not do so sooner.' They did understand each other at last, and the mother made no further attempt to engage her daughter's love for the man she would have chosen as her daughter's husband.

But still the worst was to come, as Mrs. Woodward

well knew—and as Gertrude knew also; to come, too, on this very day. Mrs. Woodward, with a woman's keen perception, felt assured that Harry Norman, when he found himself at the Cottage, freed from the presence of the successful candidate, surrounded by the affectionate faces of all her circle, would melt at once and look to his love for consolation. She understood the feelings of his heart as well as though she had read them in a book; and yet she could do nothing to save him from his fresh sorrows. The cup was prepared for him, and it was necessary that he should drink it. She could not tell him, could not tell even him, that her daughter had rejected him, when as yet he had made no offer.

And so Harry Norman hurried down to his fate. When he reached the Cottage, Mrs. Woodward and Linda and Katie were in the drawing-room.

'Harry, my dear Harry,' said Mrs. Woodward, rushing to him, throwing her arms round him, and kissing him; 'we know it all, we understand it all—my fine, dear, good Harry.'

Harry was melted in a moment, and in the softness of his mood kissed Katie too, and Linda also. Katie he had often kissed, but never Linda, cousins though they were. Linda merely laughed, but Norman blushed; for he remembered that had it so chanced that Gertrude had been there, he would not have dared to kiss her.

'Oh, Harry,' said Katie, 'we are so sorry—that is, not sorry about Alaric, but sorry about you. Why were there not two prizes?'

'It's all right as it is, Katie,' said he; 'we need none of us be sorry at all. Alaric is a clever fellow; everybody gave him credit for it before, and now he has proved that everybody is right.'

'He is older than you, you know, and therefore he ought to be cleverer,' said Katie, trying to make things pleasant.

And then they went out into the garden. But where was Gertrude all this time? She had been in the drawing-room a moment before his arrival. They walked out into the lawn, but nothing was said about her absence. Norman could not bring himself to ask for her, and Mrs. Woodward could not trust herself to talk of her.

' Where is the captain ? ' said Harry.

' He's at Hampton Court,' said Linda ; ' he has found another navy captain there, and he goes over every day to play backgammon.' As they were speaking, however, the captain walked through the house on to the lawn.

' Well, Norman, how are you, how are you ? sorry you couldn't all win. But you're a man of fortune, you know, so it doesn't signify.'

' Not a great deal of fortune,' said Harry, looking sheepish.

' Well, I only hope the best man got it. Now, at the Admiralty the worst man gets it always.'

' The worst man didn't get it here,' said Harry.

' No, no,' said Uncle Bat, ' I'm sure he did not ; nor he won't long at the Admiralty either, I can tell them that. But where's Gertrude ? '

' She's in her bedroom, dressing for dinner,' said Katie.

' Hoity toity,' said Uncle Bat, ' she's going to make herself very grand to-day. That's all for you, Master Norman. Well, I suppose we may all go in and get ready ; but mind, I have got no sweetheart, and so I shan't make myself grand at all ; ' and so they all went in to dress for dinner.

When Norman came down, Gertrude was in the drawing-room alone. But he knew that they would be alone but for a minute, and that a minute would not serve for his purpose. She said one soft gentle word of condolence to him, some little sentence that she had been studying to pronounce. All her study was thrown away ; for Norman, in his confusion, did not understand a word that she spoke. Her tone, however, was kind and affectionate ; and she shook hands with him apparently with cordiality. He, however, ventured no kiss with her. He did not even press her hand, when for a moment he held it within his own.

Dinner was soon over, and the autumn evening still admitted of their going out. Norman was not sorry to urge the fact that the ladies had done so, as an excuse to Captain Cuttwater for not sitting with him over his wine. He heard their voices in the garden, and went out to join them, prepared to ascertain his fate if fortune would give him an opportunity of doing so. He found the party to consist of Mrs. Woodward, Linda, and Katie; Gertrude was not there.

' I think the evenings get warmer as the winter gets nearer,' said Harry.

' Yes,' said Mrs. Woodward, ' but they are so dangerous. The night comes on all at once, and then the air is so damp and cold.'

And so they went on talking about the weather.

' Your boat is up in London, I know, Harry,' said Katie, with a voice of reproach, but at the same time with a look of entreaty.

' Yes, it's at Searle's,' said Norman.

' But the punt is here,' said Katie.

' Not this evening, Katie,' said he.

' Katie, how can you be such a tease ? ' said Mrs. Woodward ; ' you'll make Harry hate the island, and you too. I wonder you can be so selfish.'

Poor Katie's eyes became suffused with tears.

' My dear Katie, it's very bad of me, isn't it ? ' said Norman, ' and the fine weather so nearly over too ; I ought to take you, oughtn't I ? come, we will go.'

' No, we won't,' said Katie, taking his big hand in both her little ones, ' indeed we won't. It was very wrong of me to bother you ; and you with—with—with so much to think of. Dear Harry, I don't want to go at all, indeed I don't,' and she turned away from the little path which led to the place where the punt was moored.

They sauntered on for a while together, and then Norman left them. He said nothing, but merely stole away from the lawn towards the drawing-room window. Mrs. Woodward well knew with what object he went, and would have spared him from his immediate sorrow by following him ; but she judged that it would be better both for him and for her daughter that he should learn the truth.

He went in through the open drawing-room window, and found Gertrude alone. She was on the sofa with a book in her hand ; and had he been able to watch her closely he would have seen that the book trembled as he entered the room. But he was unable to watch anything

closely. His own heart beat so fast, his own confusion
was so great, that he could hardly see the girl whom he
now hoped to gain as his wife. Had Alaric been coming
to his wooing, he would have had every faculty at his
call. But then Alaric could not have loved as Norman
loved.

And so we will leave them. In about half an hour,
when the short twilight was becoming dusk, Mrs. Woodward returned, and found Norman standing alone on the
hearthrug before the fireplace. Gertrude was away, and
he was leaning against the mantelpiece, with his hands
behind his back, staring at vacancy ; but oh ! with such
an aspect of dull, speechless agony in his face.

Mrs. Woodward looked up at him, and would have
burst into tears, had she not remembered that they would
not be long alone ; she therefore restrained herself, but
gave one involuntary sigh ; and then, taking off her
bonnet, placed herself where she might sit without staring
at him in his sorrow.

Katie came in next. 'Oh ! Harry, it's so lucky we
didn't start in the punt,' said she, 'for it's going to pour,
and we never should have been back from the island in
that slow thing.'

Norman looked at her and tried to smile, but the attempt
was a ghastly failure. Katie, gazing up into his face, saw
that he was unhappy, and slunk away, without further
speech, to her distant chair. There, from time to time,
she would look up at him, and her little heart melted
with ruth to see the depth of his misery. 'Why, oh
why,' thought she, 'should that greedy Alaric have taken
away the only prize ?'

And then Linda came running in with her bonnet ribbons
all moist with the big raindrops. 'You are a nice squire
of dames,' said she, 'to leave us all out to get wet through
by ourselves ;' and then she also, looking up, saw that
jesting was at present ill-timed, and so sat herself down
quietly at the tea-table.

But Norman never moved. He saw them come in one
after another. He saw the pity expressed in Mrs. Woodward's face ; he heard the light-hearted voices of the two
girls, and observed how, when they saw him, their light-

heartedness was abashed; but still he neither spoke nor moved. He had been stricken with a fearful stroke, and for a while was powerless.

Captain Cuttwater, having shaken off his dining-room nap, came for his tea; and then, at last, Gertrude also, descending from her own chamber, glided quietly into the room. When she did so, Norman, with a struggle, roused himself, and took a chair next to Mrs. Woodward, and opposite to her eldest daughter.

Who could describe the intense discomfiture of that tea-party, or paint in fitting colours the different misery of each one there assembled? Even Captain Cuttwater at once knew that something was wrong, and munched his bread-and-butter and drank his tea in silence. Linda surmised what had taken place; though she was surprised, she was left without any doubt. Poor Katie was still in the dark, but she also knew that there was cause for sorrow, and crept more and more into her little self. Mrs. Woodward sat with averted face, and ever and anon she put her handkerchief to her eyes. Gertrude was very pale, and all but motionless, but she had schooled herself, and managed to drink her tea with more apparent indifference than any of the others. Norman sat as he had before been standing, with that dreadful look of agony upon his brow.

Immediately after tea Mrs. Woodward got up and went to her dressing-room. Her dressing-room, though perhaps not improperly so called, was not an exclusive closet devoted to combs, petticoats, and soap and water. It was a comfortable snug room, nicely furnished, with sofa and easy chairs, and often open to others besides her handmaidens. Thither she betook herself, that she might weep unseen; but in about twenty minutes her tears were disturbed by a gentle knock at the door.

Very soon after she went, Gertrude also left the room, and then Katie crept off.

'I have got a headache to-night,' said Norman, after the remaining three had sat silent for a minute or two; 'I think I'll go across and go to bed.'

'A headache!' said Linda. 'Oh, I am so sorry that you have got to go to that horrid inn.'

'Oh! I shall do very well there,' said Norman, trying to smile.

'Will you have my room?' said the captain good-naturedly; 'any sofa does for me.'

Norman assured them as well as he could that his present headache was of such a nature that a bed at the inn would be the best thing for him; and then, shaking hands with them, he moved to the door.

'Stop a moment, Harry,' said Linda, 'and let me tell mamma. She'll give you something for your head.' He made a sign to her, however, to let him pass, and then, creeping gently upstairs, he knocked at Mrs. Woodward's door.

'Come in,' said Mrs. Woodward, and Harry Norman, with all his sorrows still written on his face, stood before her.

'Oh! Harry,' said she, 'come in; I am so glad that you have come to me. Oh! Harry, dear Harry, what shall I say to comfort you? What can I say—what can I do?'

Norman, forgetting his manhood, burst into tears, and throwing himself on a sofa, buried his face on the arm and sobbed like a young girl. But the tears of a man bring with them no comfort as do those of the softer sex. He was a strong tall man, and it was dreadful to see him thus convulsed.

Mrs. Woodward stood by him, and put her hand caressingly on his shoulder. She saw he had striven to speak, and had found himself unable to do so. 'I know how it is,' said she, 'you need not tell me; I know it all. Would that she could have seen you with my eyes; would that she could have judged you with my mind!'

'Oh, Mrs. Woodward!'

'To me, Harry, you should have been the dearest, the most welcome son. But you are so still. No son could be dearer. Oh, that she could have seen you as I see you!'

'There is no hope,' said he. He did not put it as a question; but Mrs. Woodward saw that it was intended that she should take it as such if she pleased. What could she say to him? She knew that there was no hope. Had it been Linda, Linda might have been moulded to

her will. But with Gertrude there could now be no hope.
What could she say ? She knelt down and kissed his
brow, and mingled her tears with his.

'Oh, Harry—oh, Harry ! my dearest, dearest son !'

'Oh, Mrs. Woodward, I have loved her so truly.'

What could Mrs. Woodward do but cry also ? what but
that, and throw such blame as she could upon her own
shoulders ? She was bound to defend her daughter.

'It has been my fault, Harry,' she said ; 'it is I whom
you must blame, not poor Gertrude.'

'I blame no one,' said he.

'I know you do not ; but it is I whom you should
blame. I should have learnt how her heart stood, and
have prevented this—but I thought, I thought it would
have been otherwise.'

Norman looked up at her, and took her hand, and
pressed it. 'I will go now,' he said, 'and don't expect me
here to-morrow. I could not come in. Say that I thought
it best to go to town because I am unwell. Good-bye,
Mrs. Woodward ; pray write to me. I can't come to the
Cottage now for a while, but pray write to me : do not you
forget me, Mrs. Woodward.'

Mrs. Woodward fell upon his breast and wept, and bade
God bless him, and called him her son and her dearest
friend, and sobbed till her heart was nigh to break.
'What,' she thought, 'what could her daughter wish for,
when she repulsed from her feet such a suitor as Harry
Norman ?'

He then went quietly down the stairs, quietly out of the
house, and having packed up his bag at the inn, started
off through the pouring rain, and walked away through
the dark stormy night, through the dirt and mud and wet,
to his London lodgings ; nor was he again seen at Surbiton
Cottage for some months after this adventure.

CHAPTER XIII

A COMMUNICATION OF IMPORTANCE

NORMAN's dark wet walk did him physically no harm, and morally some good. He started on it in that frame of mind which induces a man to look with indifference on all coming evils under the impression that the evils already come are too heavy to admit of any increase. But by the time that he was thoroughly wet through, well splashed with mud, and considerably fatigued by his first five or six miles' walk, he began to reflect that life was not over with him, and that he must think of future things as well as those that were past.

He got home about two o'clock, and having knocked up his landlady, Mrs. Richards, betook himself to bed. Alaric had been in his room for the last two hours, but of Charley and his latch-key Mrs. Richards knew nothing. She stated her belief, however, that two a.m. seldom saw that erratic gentleman in his bed.

On the following morning, Alaric, when he got his hot water, heard that Norman returned during the night from Hampton, and he immediately guessed what had brought him back. He knew that nothing short of some great trouble would have induced Harry to leave the Cottage so abruptly, and that that trouble must have been of such a nature as to make his remaining with the Woodwards an aggravation of it. No such trouble could have come on him but the one.

As Charley seldom made his appearance at the breakfast table on Sunday mornings, Alaric foresaw that he must undergo a *tête-à-tête* which would not be agreeable to himself, and which must be much more disagreeable to his companion ; but for this there was no help. Harry had, however, prepared himself for what he had to go through, and immediately that the two were alone, he told his tale in a very few words.

' Alaric,' said he, ' I proposed to Gertrude last night, and she refused me.'

Alaric Tudor was deeply grieved for his friend. There was something in the rejected suitor's countenance—something in the tone of voice, which would have touched any heart softer than stone ; and Alaric's heart had not as yet been so hardened by the world as to render him callous to the sight of such grief as this.

'Take my word for it, Harry, she'll think better of it in a month or two,' he said.

'Never—never ; I am sure of it. Not only from her own manner, but from her mother's,' said Harry. And yet, during half his walk home, he had been trying to console himself with the reflection that most young ladies reject their husbands once or twice before they accept them.

There is no offering a man comfort in such a sorrow as this ; unless, indeed, he be one to whom the worship of Bacchus may be made a fitting substitute for that of the Paphian goddess.

There is a sort of disgrace often felt, if never acknowledged, which attaches itself to a man for having put himself into Norman's present position, and this generally prevents him from confessing his defeat in such matters. The misfortune in question is one which doubtless occurs not unfrequently to mankind ; but as mankind generally bear their special disappointments in silence, and as the vanity of women is generally exceeded by their good-nature, the secret, we believe, in most cases remains a secret.

> Shall I, wasting in despair,
> Die because a woman's fair ?
> If she be not fair for me,
> What care I how fair she be ?

This was the upshot of the consideration which Withers, the poet, gave to the matter, and Withers was doubtless right. 'Tis thus that rejected lovers should think, thus that they should demean themselves ; but they seldom come to this philosophy till a few days have passed by, and talking of their grievance does not assist them in doing so.

When, therefore, Harry had declared what had happened

to him, and had declared also that he had no further hope, he did not at first find himself much the better for what he had confessed. He was lackadaisical and piteous, and Alaric, though he had endeavoured to be friendly, soon found that he had no power of imparting any comfort. Early in the day they parted, and did not see each other again till the following morning.

'I was going down to Normansgrove on Thursday,' said Harry.

'Yes, I know,' said Alaric.

'I think I shall ask leave to go to-day. It can't make much difference, and the sooner I get away the better.'

And so it was settled. Norman left town the same afternoon, and Alaric, with his blushing honours thick upon him, was left alone.

London was now very empty, and he was constrained to enjoy his glory very much by himself. He had never associated much with the Minusexes and Uppinalls, nor yet with the Joneses and Robinsons of his own office, and it could not be expected that there should be any specially confidential intercourse between them just at the present moment. Undy was of course out of town with the rest of the fashionable world, and Alaric, during the next week, was left very much on his own hands.

'And so,' said he to himself, as he walked solitary along the lone paths of Rotten Row, and across the huge desert to the Marble Arch, 'and so poor Harry's hopes have been all in vain; he has lost his promotion, and now he has lost his bride—poor Harry!'—and then it occurred to him that as he had acquired the promotion it might be his destiny to win the bride also. He had never told himself that he loved Gertrude; he had looked on her as Norman's own, and he, at any rate, was not the man to sigh in despair after anything that was out of his reach. But now, now that Harry's chance was over, and that no bond of friendship could interfere with such a passion, why should he not tell himself that he loved Gertrude? 'If, as Harry had himself said, there was no longer any hope for him, why,' said Alaric to himself, 'why should not I try my chance?' Of Linda, of 'dear, dearest Linda,' at this moment he thought very little, or, perhaps, not at all. Of what Mrs. Woodward might say, of that he did think a good deal.

The week was melancholy and dull, and it passed very slowly at Hampton. On the Sunday morning it became known to them all that Norman was gone, but the subject, by tacit consent, was allowed to pass all but unnoticed. Even Katie, even Uncle Bat, were aware that something had occurred which ought to prevent them from inquiring too particularly why Harry had started back to town in so sudden a manner; and so they said nothing. To Linda, Gertrude had told what had happened; and Linda, as she heard it, asked herself whether she was prepared to be equally obdurate with her lover. He had now the means of supporting a wife, and why should she be obdurate?

Nothing was said on the subject between Gertrude and her mother. What more could Mrs. Woodward say? It would have been totally opposed to the whole principle of her life to endeavour, by any means, to persuade her daughter to the match, or to have used her maternal influence in Norman's favour. And she was well aware that it would have been impossible to do so successfully. Gertrude was not a girl to be talked into a marriage by any parent, and certainly not by such a parent as her mother. There was, therefore, nothing further to be said about it.

On Saturday Alaric went down, but his arrival hardly made things more pleasant. Mrs. Woodward could not bring herself to be cordial with him, and the girls were restrained by a certain feeling that it would not be right to show too much outward joy at Alaric's success. Linda said one little word of affectionate encouragement, but it produced no apparent return from Alaric. His immediate object was to recover Mrs. Woodward's good graces; and he thought before he went that he had reason to hope that he might do so.

Of all the household, Captain Cuttwater was the most emphatic in his congratulations. 'He had no doubt,' he said, 'that the best man had won. He had always hoped that the best man might win. He had not had the same luck when he was young, but he was very glad to see such an excellent rule brought into the service. It would soon work great changes, he was quite sure, at the Board of Admiralty.'

On the Sunday afternoon Captain Cuttwater asked him into his own bedroom, and told him with a solemn, serious manner that he had a communication of importance to make to him. Alaric followed the captain into the well-known room in which Norman used to sleep, wondering what could be the nature of Uncle Bat's important communication. It might, probably, be some tidings of Sir Jib Boom.

' Mr. Alaric,' said the old man, as soon as they were both seated on opposite sides of a little Pembroke table that stood in the middle of the room, ' I was heartily glad to hear of your success at the Weights and Measures ; not that I ever doubted it if they made a fair sailing match of it.'

' I am sure I am much obliged to you, Captain Cuttwater.'

' That is as may be, by and by. But the fact is, I have taken a fancy to you. I like fellows that know how to push themselves.'

Alaric had nothing for it but to repeat again that he felt himself grateful for Captain Cuttwater's good opinion.

' Not that I have anything to say against Mr. Norman —a very nice young man, indeed, he is, very nice, though perhaps not quite so cheerful in his manners as he might be.'

Alaric began to take his friend's part, and declared what a very worthy fellow Harry was.

' I am sure of it—I am sure of it,' said Uncle Bat ; ' but everybody can't be A 1 ; and a man can't make everybody his heir.'

Alaric pricked up his ears. So after all Captain Cuttwater was right in calling his communication important. But what business had Captain Cuttwater to talk of making new heirs ?—had he not declared that the Woodwards were his heirs ?

' I have got a little money, Mr. Alaric,' he went on saying in a low modest tone, very different from that he ordinarily used ; ' I have got a little money—not much—and it will of course go to my niece here.'

' Of course,' said Alaric.

' That is to say—it will go to her children, which is all the same thing.'

' Quite the same thing,' said Alaric.

' But my idea is this : if a man has saved a few pounds himself, I think he has a right to give it to those he loves best. Now I have no children of my own.'

Alaric declared himself aware of the fact.

' And I suppose I shan't have any now.'

' Not if you don't marry,' said Alaric, who felt rather at a loss for a proper answer. He could not, however, have made a better one.

' No; that's what I mean ; but I don't think I shall marry. I am very well contented here, and I like Surbiton Cottage amazingly.'

' It's a charming place,' said Alaric.

' No, I don't suppose I shall ever have any children of my own,'—and then Uncle Bat sighed gently—' and so I have been considering whom I should like to adopt.'

' Quite right, Captain Cuttwater.'

' Whom I should like to adopt. I should like to have one whom I could call in a special manner my own. Now, Mr. Alaric, I have made up my mind, and who do you think it is ? '

' Oh ! Captain Cuttwater, I couldn't guess on such a matter. I shouldn't like to guess wrong.'

' Perhaps not—no ; that's right ;—well then, I'll tell you ; it's Gertrude.'

Alaric was well aware that it was Gertrude before her name had been pronounced.

' Yes, it's Gertrude ; of course I couldn't go out of Bessie's family—of course it must be either Gertrude, or Linda, or Katie. Now Linda and Katie are very well, but they haven't half the gumption that Gertrude has.'

' No, they have not,' said Alaric.

' I like gumption,' said Captain Cuttwater. ' You've a great deal of gumption—that's why I like you.'

Alaric laughed, and muttered something.

' Now I have been thinking of something ; ' and Uncle Bat looked strangely mysterious—' I wonder what you think of Gertrude ? '

'Who—I?' said Alaric.

'I can see through a millstone as well as another,' said the captain; 'and I used to think that Norman and Gertrude meant to hit it off together.'

Alaric said nothing. He did not feel inclined to tell Norman's secret, and yet he could not belie Gertrude by contradicting the justice of Captain Cuttwater's opinion.

'I used to think so—but now I find there's nothing in it. I am sure Gertrude wouldn't have him, and I think she's right. He hasn't gumption enough.'

'Harry Norman is no fool.'

'I dare say not,' said the captain; 'but take my word, she'll never have him—Lord bless you, Norman knows that as well as I do.'

Alaric knew it very well himself also; but he did not say so.

'Now, the long and the short of it is this—why don't you make up to her? If you'll make up to her and carry the day, all I can say is, I will do all I can to keep the pot a-boiling; and if you think it will help you, you may tell Gertrude that I say so.'

This was certainly an important communication, and one to which Alaric found it very difficult to give any immediate answer. He said a great deal about his affection for Mrs. Woodward, of his admiration for Miss Woodward, of his strong sense of Captain Cuttwater's kindness, and of his own unworthiness; but he left the captain with an impression that he was not prepared at the present moment to put himself forward as a candidate for Gertrude's hand.

'I don't know what the deuce he would have,' said the captain to himself. 'She's as fine a girl as he's likely to find; and two or three thousand pounds isn't so easily got every day by a fellow that hasn't a shilling of his own.'

When Alaric took his departure the next morning, he thought he perceived, from Mrs. Woodward's manner, that there was less than her usual cordiality in the tone in which she said that of course he would return at the end of the week.

'I will if possible,' he said, 'and I need not say that I hope to do so; but I fear I may be kept in town—at any

rate I'll write.' When the end of the week came he wrote
to say that unfortunately he was kept in town.   He
thoroughly understood that people are most valued when
they make themselves scarce.   He got in reply a note
from Gertrude, saying that her mother begged that on the
following Saturday he would come and bring Charley with
him.

On his return to town, Alaric, by appointment, called on
Sir Gregory.   He had not seen his patron yet since his
great report on Wheal Mary Jane had been sent in.   That
report had been written exclusively by himself, and poor
Neverbend had been obliged to content himself with putting all his voluminous notes into Tudor's hands.   He
afterwards obediently signed the report, and received his
reward for doing so.   Alaric never divulged to official ears
how Neverbend had halted in the course of his descent to
the infernal gods.

'I thoroughly congratulate you,' said Sir Gregory.
'You have justified my choice, and done your duty with
credit to yourself and benefit to the public.   I hope you
may go on and prosper.   As long as you remember that
your own interests should always be kept in subservience
to those of the public service, you will not fail to receive
the praise which such conduct deserves.'

Alaric thanked Sir Gregory for his good opinion, and
as he did so, he thought of his new banker's account, and
of the £300 which was lying there.   After all, which of
them was right, Sir Gregory Hardlines or Undy Scott?
Or was it that Sir Gregory's opinions were such as should
control the outward conduct, and Undy's those which
should rule the inner man?

CHAPTER XIV

VERY SAD

NORMAN prolonged his visit to his father considerably beyond the month. At first he applied for and received permission to stay away another fortnight, and at the end of that fortnight he sent up a medical certificate in which the doctor alleged that he would be unable to attend to business for some considerable additional period. It was not till after Christmas Day that he reappeared at the Weights and Measures.

Alaric kept his appointment at Hampton, and took Charley with him. And on the two following Saturdays he also went there, and on both occasions Charley accompanied him. During these visits, he devoted himself, as closely as he could, to Mrs. Woodward. He talked to her of Norman, and of Norman's prospects in the office; he told her how he had intended to abstain from offering himself as a competitor, till he had, as it were, been forced by Norman to do so; he declared over and over again that Norman would have been victorious had he stood his ground to the end, and assured her that such was the general opinion through the whole establishment. And this he did without talking much about himself, or praising himself in any way when he did so. His speech was wholly of his friend, and of the sorrow that he felt that his friend should have been disappointed in his hopes.

All this had its effects. Of Norman's rejected love they neither of them spoke. Each knew that the other must be aware of it, but the subject was far too tender to be touched, at any rate as yet. And so matters went on, and Alaric regained the footing of favour which he had for a while lost with the mistress of the house.

But there was one inmate of Surbiton Cottage who saw that though Alaric spent so much of his time with Mrs. Woodward, he found opportunity also for other private conversation; and this was Linda. Why was it that in

the moments before they dressed for dinner Alaric was
whispering with Gertrude, and not with her ? Why was
it that Alaric had felt it necessary to stay from church
that Sunday evening when Gertrude also had been prevented from going by a headache ? He had remained,
he said, in order that Captain Cuttwater might have
company ; but Linda was not slow to learn that Uncle
Bat had been left to doze away the time by himself. Why,
on the following Monday, had Gertrude been down so
early, and why had Alaric been over from the inn full half
an hour before his usual time ? Linda saw and knew all
this, and was disgusted. But even then she did not, could
not think that Alaric could be untrue to her ; that her
own sister would rob her of her lover. It could not be that
there should be such baseness in human nature !

Poor Linda !

And yet, though she did not believe that such falseness
could exist in this world of hers at Surbiton Cottage, she
could not restrain herself from complaining rather petu-
lantly to her sister, as they were going to bed on that
Sunday evening.

'I hope your headache is better,' she said, in a tone of
voice as near to irony as her soft nature could produce.

'Yes, it is quite well now,' said Gertrude, disdaining to
notice the irony.

'I dare say Alaric had a headache too. I suppose one
was about as bad as the other.'

'Linda,' said Gertrude, answering rather with dignity
than with anger, 'you ought to know by this time that it
is not likely that I should plead false excuses. Alaric
never said he had a headache.'

'He said he stayed from church to be with Uncle Bat ;
but when we came back we found him with you.'

'Uncle Bat went to sleep, and then he came into the
drawing-room.'

The two girls said nothing more about it. Linda should
have remembered that she had never breathed a word to
her sister of Alaric's passion for herself. Gertrude's
solemn propriety had deterred her, just as she was about
to do so. How very little of that passion had Alaric
breathed himself ! and yet, alas ! enough to fill the fond

girl's heart with dreams of love, which occupied all her waking, all her sleeping thoughts. Oh! ye ruthless swains, from whose unhallowed lips fall words full of poisoned honey, do ye never think of the bitter agony of many months, of the dull misery of many years, of the cold monotony of an uncheered life, which follow so often as the consequence of your short hour of pastime ?

On the Monday morning, as soon as Alaric and Charley had started for town—it was the morning on which Linda had been provoked to find that both Gertrude and Alaric had been up half an hour before they should have been— Gertrude followed her mother to her dressing-room, and with palpitating heart closed the door behind her.

Linda remained downstairs, putting away her tea and sugar, not in the best of humours ; but Katie, according to her wont, ran up after her mother.

'Katie,' said Gertrude, as Katie bounced into the room, 'dearest Katie, I want to speak a word to mamma—alone. Will you mind going down just for a few minutes ?' and she put her arm round her sister, and kissed her with almost unwonted tenderness.

'Go, Katie, dear,' said Mrs. Woodward ; and Katie, speechless, retired.

'Gertrude has got something particular to tell mamma ; something that I may not hear. I wonder what it is about,' said Katie to her second sister.

Linda's heart sank within her. 'Could it be ? No, it could not, could not be, that the sweet voice which had whispered in her ears those well-remembered words, could have again whispered the same into other ears— that the very Gertrude who had warned her not to listen to such words from such lips, should have listened to them herself, and have adopted them and made them her own ! It could not, could not be !' and yet Linda's heart sank low within her.

. . . .

'If you really love him,' said the mother, again caressing her eldest daughter as she acknowledged her love, but hardly with such tenderness as when that daughter had repudiated that other love—'if you really love him, dearest, of course I do not, of course I cannot, object.'

'I do, mamma; I do.'

'Well, then, Gertrude, so be it. I have not a word to say against your choice. Had I not believed him to be an excellent young man, I should not have allowed him to be here with you so much as he has been. We cannot all see with the same eyes, dearest, can we?'

'No, mamma; but pray don't think I dislike poor Harry; and, oh! mamma, pray don't set him against Alaric because of this——'

'Set him against Alaric! No, Gertrude. I certainly shall not do that. But whether I can reconcile Harry to it, that is another thing.'

'At any rate he has no right to be angry at it,' said Gertrude, assuming her air of dignity.

'Certainly not with you, Gertrude.'

'No, nor with Alaric,' said she, almost with indignation.

'That depends on what has passed between them. It is very hard to say how men so situated regard each other.'

'I know everything that has passed between them,' said Gertrude. 'I never gave Harry any encouragement. As soon as I understood my own feelings I endeavoured to make him understand them also.'

'But, my dearest, no one is blaming you.'

'But you are blaming Alaric.'

'Indeed I am not, Gertrude.'

'No man could have behaved more honourably to his friend,' said Gertrude; 'no man more nobly; and if Harry does not feel it so, he has not the good heart for which I always gave him credit.'

'Poor fellow! his friendship for Alaric will be greatly tried.'

'And, mamma, has not Alaric's friendship been tried? and has it not borne the trial nobly? Harry told him of—of—of his intentions; Harry told him long, long, long ago——'

'Ah me!—poor Harry!' sighed Mrs. Woodward.

'But you think nothing of Alaric!'

'Alaric is successful, my dear, and can——' Think sufficiently of himself, Mrs. Woodward was going to say, but she stopped herself.

'Harry told him all,' continued Gertrude, 'and Alaric

—Alaric said nothing of his own feelings. Alaric never said a word to me that he might not have said before his friend—till—till—— You must own, mamma, that no one can have behaved more nobly than Alaric has done.'

Mrs. Woodward, nevertheless, had her own sentiments on the matter, which were not quite in unison with those of her daughter. But then she was not in love with Alaric, and her daughter was. She thought that Alaric's love was a passion that had but lately come to the birth, and that had he been true to his friend—nobly true as Gertrude had described him—it would never have been born at all, or at any rate not till Harry had had a more prolonged chance of being successful with his suit. Mrs. Woodward understood human nature better than her daughter, or, at least, flattered herself that she did so, and she felt well assured that Alaric had not been dying for love during the period of Harry's unsuccessful courtship. He might, she thought, have waited a little longer before he chose for his wife the girl whom his friend had loved, seeing that he had been made the confidant of that love.

Such were the feelings which Mrs. Woodward felt herself unable to repress; but she could not refuse her consent to the marriage. After all, she had some slight twinge of conscience, some inward conviction that she was prejudiced in Harry's favour, as her daughter was in Alaric's. Then she had lost all right to object to Alaric, by allowing him to be so constantly at the Cottage; and then again, there was nothing to which in reason she could object. In point of immediate income, Alaric was now the better match of the two. She kissed her daughter, therefore, and promised that she would do her best to take Alaric to her heart as her son-in-law.

'You will tell Uncle Bat, mamma?' said Gertrude.

'O yes—certainly, my dear; of course he'll be told. But I suppose it does not make much matter, immediately?'

'I think he should be told, mamma; I should not like him to think that he was treated with anything like disrespect.'

'Very well, my dear, I'll tell him,' said Mrs. Woodward,

who was somewhat surprised at her daughter's punctilious feelings about Uncle Bat. However, it was all very proper ; and she was glad to think that her children were inclined to treat their grand-uncle with respect, in spite of his long nose.

And then Gertrude was preparing to leave the room, but her mother stopped her. 'Gertrude, dear,' said she.

'Yes, mamma.'

'Come here, dearest ; shut the door. Gertrude, have you told Linda yet ?'

'No, mamma, not yet.'

As Mrs. Woodward asked the question, there was an indescribable look of painful emotion on her brow. It did not escape Gertrude's eye, and was not to her perfectly unintelligible. She had conceived an idea—why, she did not know—that these recent tidings of hers would not be altogether agreeable to her sister.

'No, mamma, I have not told her ; of course I told you first. But now I shall do so immediately.'

'Let me tell her,' said Mrs. Woodward, 'will you, Gertrude ?'

'Oh ! certainly, mamma, if you wish it.'

Things were going wrong with Mrs. Woodward. She had perceived, with a mother's anxious eye, that her second daughter was not indifferent to Alaric Tudor. While she yet thought that Norman and Gertrude would have suited each other, this had caused her no disquietude. She herself had entertained none of those grand ideas to which Gertrude had given utterance with so much sententiousness, when she silenced Linda's tale of love before the telling of it had been commenced. Mrs. Woodward had always felt sufficiently confident that Alaric would push himself in the world, and she would have made no objection to him as a son-in-law had he been contented to take the second instead of the first of her flock.

She had never spoken to Linda on the matter, and Linda had offered to her no confidence ; but she felt all but sure that her second child would not have entertained the affection which she had been unable altogether to conceal, had no lover's plea been poured into her ears. Mrs. Woodward questioned her daughters but little, but she understood well the nature of each, and could nearly read their thoughts. Linda's thoughts it was not difficult to read.

'Linda, pet,' she said, as soon as she could get Linda into her room without absolutely sending for her, 'you have not yet heard Gertrude's news ? '

'No,' said Linda, turning very pale, and feeling that her heart was like to burst.

'I would let no one tell you but myself, Linda. Come here, dearest; don't stand there away from me. Can you guess what it is ? '

Linda, for a moment, could not speak. 'No, mamma,' she said at last, 'I don't know what it is.'

Mrs. Woodward twined her arm round her daughter's waist, as they sat on the sofa close to each other. Linda tried to compose herself, but she felt that she was trembling in her mother's arms. She would have given anything to be calm; anything to hide her secret. She little guessed then how well her mother knew it. Her eyes were turned down, and she found that she could not raise them to her mother's face.

'No, mamma,' she said. 'I don't know—what is it ? '

'Gertrude is to be married, Linda. She is engaged.'

'I thought she refused Harry,' said Linda, through whose mind a faint idea was passing of the cruelty of nature's arrangements, which gave all the lovers to her sister.

'Yes, dearest, she did; and now another has made an offer—she has accepted him.' Mrs. Woodward could hardly bring herself to speak out that which she had to say, and yet she felt that she was only prolonging the torture for which she was so anxious to find a remedy.

'Has she ? ' said Linda, on whom the full certainty of her misery had now all but come.

'She has accepted our dear Alaric.'

Our dear Alaric! what words for Linda's ears! They did reach her ears, but they did not dwell there—her soft gentle nature sank beneath the sound. Her mother, when she looked to her for a reply, found that she was sinking through her arms. Linda had fainted.

Mrs. Woodward neither screamed, nor rang for assistance, nor emptied the water-jug over her daughter, nor did anything else which would have the effect of revealing to the whole household the fact that Linda had fainted. She had seen girls faint before, and was not frightened. But how, when Linda recovered, was she to be comforted?

Mrs. Woodward laid her gently on the sofa, undid her dress, loosened her stays, and then sat by her chafing her hands, and moistening her lips and temples, till gradually the poor girl's eyes reopened. The recovery from a fainting fit, a real fainting fit I beg young ladies to understand, brings with it a most unpleasant sensation, and for some minutes Linda's sorrow was quelled by her sufferings; but as she recovered her strength she remembered where she was and what had happened, and sobbing violently she burst into an hysterical storm of tears.

Her most poignant feeling now was one of fear lest her mother should have guessed her secret; and this Mrs. Woodward well understood. She could do nothing towards comforting her child till there was perfect confidence between them. It was easy to arrive at this with Linda, nor would it afterwards be difficult to persuade her as to the course she ought to take. The two girls were so essentially different; the one so eager to stand alone and guide herself, the other so prone to lean on the nearest support that came to her hand.

It was not long before Linda had told her mother everything. Either by words, or tears, or little signs of mute confession, she made her mother understand, with all but exactness, what had passed between Alaric and herself, and quite exactly what had been the state of her own heart. She sobbed, and wept, and looked up to her mother for forgiveness as though she had been guilty of a great sin; and when her mother caressed her with all a mother's tenderness, and told her that she was absolved from all fault, free of all blame, she was to a certain degree comforted. Whatever might now happen, her mother would be on her side. But Mrs. Woodward, when she looked into the matter, found that it was she that should have demanded pardon of her daughter, not her daughter of her! Why had this tender lamb been allowed to wander out of the fold, while a wolf in sheep's clothing was invited into the pasture-ground?

Gertrude, with her talent, her beauty, and dignity of demeanour, had hitherto been, perhaps, the closest to the mother's heart—had been, if not the most cherished, yet the most valued ; Gertrude had been the apple of her eye. This should be altered now. If a mother's love could atone for a mother's negligence, Mrs. Woodward would atone to her child for this hour of misery ! And Katie—her sweet bonny Katie—she, at least, should be protected from the wolves. Those were the thoughts that passed through Mrs. Woodward's heart as she sat there caressing Linda.

But how were things to be managed now at the present moment ? It was quite clear that the wolf in sheep's clothing must be admitted into the pastoral family ; either that, or the fairest lamb of the flock must be turned out altogether, to take upon herself lupine nature, and roam the woods a beast of prey. As matters stood it behoved them to make such a sheep of Alaric as might be found practicable.

And so Mrs. Woodward set to work to teach her daughter how best she might conduct herself in her present state of wretchedness. She had to bear with her sister's success, to listen to her sister's joy, to enter into all her future plans, to assist at her toilet, to prepare her wedding garments, to hear the congratulations of friends, and take a sister's share in a sister's triumph, and to do this without once giving vent to a reproach. And she had worse than this to do ; she had to encounter Alaric, and to wish him joy of his bride ; she had to protect her female pride from the disgrace which a hopeless but acknowledged love would throw on it ; she had to live in the house with Alaric as though he were her brother, and as though she had never thought to live with him in any nearer tie. She would have to stand at the altar as her sister's bridesmaid, and see them married, and she would have to smile and be cheerful as she did so.

This was the lesson which Mrs. Woodward had now to teach her daughter ; and she so taught it that Linda did all that circumstances and her mother required of her. Late on that afternoon she went to Gertrude, and, kissing her, wished her joy. At that moment Gertrude was the more embarrassed of the two.

'Linda, dear Linda,' she said, embracing her sister convulsively.

'I hope you will be happy, Gertrude, with all my heart,' said Linda ; and so she relinquished her lover.

We talk about the weakness of women—and Linda Woodward was, in many a way, weak enough—but what man, what giant, has strength equal to this ? It was not that her love was feeble. Her heart was capable of truest love, and she had loved Alaric truly. But she had that within her which enabled her to overcome herself, and put her own heart, and hopes, and happiness—all but her maiden pride—into the background, when the hopes and happiness of another required it.

She still shared the same room with her sister ; and those who know how completely absorbed a girl is by her first acknowledged love, may imagine how many questions she had to answer, to how many propositions she was called to assent, for how many schemes she had to vouch-safe a sister's interest, while her heart was telling her that she should have been the questioner, that she should have been the proposer, that the schemes should all have been her own.

But she bore it bravely. When Alaric first came down, which he did in the middle of the week, she was, as she told her mother, too weak to stand in his presence. Her mother strongly advised her not to absent herself ; so she sat gently by, while he kissed Mrs. Woodward and Katie. She sat and trembled, for her turn she knew must come. It did come ; Alaric, with an assurance which told more for his courage than for his heart, came up to her, and with a smiling face offered her his hand. She rose up and muttered some words which she had prepared for the occasion, and he, still holding her by the hand, stooped down and kissed her cheek. Mrs. Woodward looked on with an angry flush on her brow, and hated him for his cold-hearted propriety of de-meanour.

Linda went up to her mother's room, and, sitting on her mother's bed, sobbed herself into tranquillity.

It was very grievous to Mrs. Woodward to have to welcome Alaric to her house. For Alaric's own sake she would no longer have troubled herself to do so; but Gertrude was still her daughter, her dear child. Gertrude had done nothing to disentitle her to a child's part, and a child's protection; and even had she done so, Mrs. Woodward was not a woman to be unforgiving to her child. For Gertrude's sake she had to make Alaric welcome; she forced herself to smile on him and call him her son; to make him more at home in her house even than Harry had ever been; to give him privileges which he, wolf as he was, had so little deserved.

But Captain Cuttwater made up by the warmth of his congratulations for any involuntary coolness which Alaric might have detected in those of Mrs. Woodward. It had become a strong wish of the old man's heart that he might make Alaric, at any rate in part, his heir, without doing an injustice to his niece or her family. He had soon seen and appreciated what he had called the 'gumption' both of Gertrude and Alaric. Had Harry married Gertrude, and Alaric Linda, he would have regarded either of those matches with disfavour. But now he was quite satisfied—now he could look on Alaric as his son and Gertrude as his daughter, and use his money according to his fancy, without incurring the reproaches of his conscience.

'Quite right, my boy,' he said to Alaric, slapping him on the back at the same time with pretty nearly all his power—'quite right. Didn't I know you were the winning horse?—didn't I tell you how it would be? Do you think I don't know what gumption means? If I had not had my own weather-eye open, aye, and d—— wide open, the most of my time, I shouldn't have two or three thousand pounds to give away now to any young fellow that I take a fancy to.'

Alaric was, of course, all smiles and good humour, and Gertrude not less so. The day after he heard of the engagement Uncle Bat went to town, and, on his return, he gave Gertrude £100 to buy her wedding-clothes, and half that sum to her mother, in order that the thing might go off, as he expressed himself, 'slip-slap, and no mistake.' To Linda he gave nothing, but promised her that he would not forget her when her time came.

All this time Norman was at Normansgrove ; but there were three of the party who felt that it behoved them to let him know what was going on. Mrs. Woodward wrote first, and on the following day both Gertrude and Alaric wrote to him, the former from Hampton, and the latter from his office in London.

All these letters were much laboured, but, with all this labour, not one of them contained within it a grain of comfort. That from Mrs. Woodward came first and told the tale. Strange to say, though Harry had studiously rejected from his mind all idea of hope as regarded Gertrude, nevertheless the first tidings of her betrothal with Alaric struck him as though he had still fancied himself a favoured lover. He felt as though, in his absence, he had been robbed of a prize which was all his own, as though a chattel had been taken from him to which he had a full right ; as though all the Hampton party, Mrs. Woodward included, were in a conspiracy to defraud him the moment his back was turned.

The blow was so severe that it laid him prostrate at once. He could not sob away his sorrow on his mother's bosom ; no one could teach him how to bear his grief with meek resignation. He had never spoken of his love to his friends at Normansgrove. They had all been witnesses to his deep disappointment, but that had been attributed to his failure at his office. He was not a man to seek for sympathy in the sorrows of his heart. He had told Alaric of his rejection, because he had already told him of his love, but he had whispered no word of it to anyone besides. On the day on which he received Mrs. Woodward's letter, he appeared at dinner ghastly pale, and evidently so ill as to be all but unable to sit at table ; but he would say nothing to anybody ; he sat brooding over his grief till he was unable to sit any longer.

And yet Mrs. Woodward had written with all her skill, with all her heart striving to pluck the sting away from the tidings which she had to communicate. She had felt, however, that she owed as much, at least, to her daughter as she did to him, and she failed to call Alaric perjured, false, dishonoured, unjust, disgraced, and treacherous. Nothing short of her doing so would have been deemed by Norman fitting mention of Tudor's sin; nothing else would have satisfied the fury of his wrath.

On the next morning he received Gertrude's letter and Alaric's. The latter he never read—he opened it, saw that it began as usual, 'My dear Harry,' and then crammed it into his pocket. By return of post it went back under a blank cover, addressed to Alaric at the Weights and Measures. The days of duelling were gone by—unfortunately, as Norman now thought, but nothing, he determined, should ever induce him again to hold friendly intercourse with the traitor. He abstained from making any such oath as to the Woodwards; but determined that his conduct in that respect should be governed by the manner in which Alaric was received by them.

But Gertrude's letter he read over and over again, and each time he did so he indulged in a fresh burst of hatred against the man who had deceived him. 'A dishonest villain!' he said to himself over and over again; 'what right had I to suppose he would be true to me when I found that he had been so false to others?'

'Dearest Harry,' the letter began. Dearest Harry!—Why should she begin with a lie? He was not dearest! 'You must not, must not, must not be angry with Alaric,' she went on to say, as soon as she had told her tale. Oh, must he not? Not be angry with Alaric! Not angry with the man who had forgotten every law of honour, every principle of honesty, every tie of friendship! Not angry with the man whom he had trusted with the key of his treasure, and who had then robbed him; who had stolen from him all his contentment, all his joy, his very heart's blood; not angry with him!

'Our happiness will never be perfect unless you will consent to share it.' Thus simply, in the affection of her heart, had Gertrude concluded the letter by which she intended to pour balm into the wounds of her rejected lover, and pave the way for the smoothing of such difficulties as might still lie in the way of her love.

'Their happiness would not be perfect unless he would consent to share it.' Every word in the sentence was

gall to him. It must have been written with the object
of lacerating his wounds, and torturing his spirit; so at
least said Norman to himself. He read the letter over
and over again. At one time he resolved to keep it till
he could thrust it back into her hand, and prove to her
of what cruelty she had been guilty. Then he thought
of sending it to Mrs. Woodward, and asking her how,
after that, could she think that he should ever again enter
her doors at Hampton. Finally he tore it into a thousand
bits, and threw them behind the fire.

'Share their happiness!' and as he repeated the words
he gave the last tear to the fragments of paper which he
still held in his hand. Could he at that moment as easily
have torn to shreds all hope of earthly joys for those two
lovers, he would then have done it, and cast the ruins to
the flames.

Oh! what a lesson he might have learnt from Linda!
And yet what were his injuries to hers? He in fact had
not been injured, at least not by him against whom the
strength of his wrath most fiercely raged. The two men
had both admired Gertrude, but Norman had started on
the race first. Before Alaric had had time to know his
own mind, he had learnt that Norman claimed the beauty
as his own. He had acknowledged to himself that
Norman had a right to do so, and had scrupulously abstained from interfering with him. Why should Norman,
like a dog in the manger, begrudge to his friend the
fodder which he himself could not enjoy? To him, at
any rate, Alaric had in this been no traitor. 'Twas thus
at least that Gertrude argued in her heart, and 'twas thus
that Mrs. Woodward tried to argue also.

But who could excuse Alaric's falseness to Linda? And
yet Linda had forgiven him.

CHAPTER XV

NORMAN RETURNS TO TOWN

HARRY NORMAN made no answer to either of his three letters beyond that of sending Alaric's back unread; but this, without other reply, was sufficient to let them all guess, nearly with accuracy, what was the state of his mind. Alaric told Gertrude how his missive had been treated, and Gertrude, of course, told her mother.

There was very little of that joy at Surbiton Cottage which should have been the forerunner of a wedding. None of the Woodward circle were content thus to lose their friend. And then their unhappiness on this score was augmented by hearing that Harry had sent up a medical certificate, instead of returning to his duties when his prolonged leave of absence was expired.

To Alaric this, at the moment, was a relief. He had dreaded the return of Norman to London. There were so many things to cause infinite pain to them both. All Norman's things, his books and clothes, his desks and papers and pictures, his whips and sticks, and all those sundry belongings which even a bachelor collects around him—were strewing the rooms in which Alaric still lived. He had of course felt that it was impossible that they should ever again reside together. Not only must they quarrel, but all the men at their office must know that they had quarrelled. And yet some intercourse must be maintained between them; they must daily meet in the rooms at the Weights and Measures; and it would now in their altered position become necessary that in some things Norman should receive instructions from Alaric as his superior officer. But if Alaric thought of this often, so did Norman; and before the last fortnight had expired, the thinking of it had made him so ill that his immediate return to London was out of the question.

Mrs. Woodward's heart melted within her when she heard that Harry was really ill. She had gone on waiting day after day for an answer to her letter, but no answer came. No answer came, but in lieu thereof she heard that Harry was laid up at Normansgrove. She heard it, and Gertrude heard it, and in spite of the coming wedding there was very little joy at Surbiton Cottage.

And then Mrs. Woodward wrote again; and a man must have had a heart of stone not to be moved by such a letter. She had 'heard,' she said, 'that he was ill, and the tidings had made her wretched—the more so inasmuch as he had sent no answer to her last letter. Was he very ill? was he dangerously ill? She hoped, she would fain hope, that his illness had not arisen from any mental grief. If he did not reply to this, or get some of his family to do so, there would be nothing for her but to go, herself, to Normansgrove. She could not remain quiet while she was left in such painful doubt about her dearest, well-loved Harry Norman.' How to speak of Gertrude, or how not to speak of her, Mrs. Woodward knew not—at last she added : 'The three girls send their kindest love; they are all as wretchedly anxious as I am. I know you are too good to wish that poor Gertrude should suffer, but, if you did, you might have your wish. The tidings of your illness, together with your silence, have robbed her of all her happiness ;' and it ended thus :—' Dearest Harry! do not be cruel to us ; our hearts are all with you.'

This was too much for Norman's sternness ; and he relented, at least as far as Mrs. Woodward was concerned. He wrote to say that though he was still weak, he was not dangerously ill ; and that he intended, if nothing occurred amiss, to be in town about the end of the year. He hoped he might then see her to thank her for all her kindness. She would understand that he could not go down to Surbiton Cottage ; but as she would doubtless have some occasion for coming up to town, they might thus contrive to meet. He then sent his love to Linda and Katie, and ended by saying that he had written to Charley Tudor to take lodgings for him. Not the slightest allusion was made either to Gertrude or Alaric, except that which might seem to be conveyed in the intimation that he could make no more visits to Hampton.

This letter was very cold. It just permitted Mrs.
Woodward to know that Norman did not regard them
all as strangers; and that was all. Linda said it was
very sad; and Gertrude said, not to her mother but to
Alaric, that it was heartless. Captain Cuttwater predicted that he would soon come round, and be as sound
as a roach again in six months' time. Alaric said nothing;
but he went on with his wooing, and this he did so successfully, as to make Gertrude painfully alive to what would
have been, in her eyes, the inferiority of her lot, had she
unfortunately allowed herself to become the victim of
Norman's love.

Alaric went on with his wooing, and he also went on
with his share-buying. Undy Scott had returned to town
for a week or two to wind up the affairs of his expiring
secretaryship, and he made Alaric understand that a nice
thing might yet be done in Mary Janes. Alaric had been
very foolish to sell so quickly; so at least said Undy. To
this Alaric replied that he had bought the shares thought-
lessly, and had felt a desire to get rid of them as quickly
as he could. Those were scruples at which Undy laughed
pleasantly, and Alaric soon laughed with him.

'At any rate,' said Undy, 'your report is written,
and off your hands now: so you may do what you
please in the matter, like a free man, with a safe conscience.'

Alaric supposed that he might.

'I am as fond of the Civil Service as any man,' said
Undy; 'just as fond of it as Sir Gregory himself. I have
been in it, and may be in it again. If I do, I shall do my
duty. But I have no idea of having my hands tied. My
purse is my own, to do what I like with it. Whether
I buy beef or mutton, or shares in Cornwall, is nothing
to anyone. I give the Crown what it pays for, my
five or six hours a day, and nothing more. When I was
appointed private secretary to the First Lord of the
Stannaries, I told my friend Whip Vigil that those were
the terms on which I accepted office; and Vigil agreed
with me.' Alaric, pupil as he was to the great Sir Gregory,
declared that he also agreed with him. 'That is not
Sir Gregory's doctrine, but it's mine,' said Undy; 'and

though it 's my own, I think it by far the honester doctrine
of the two.'

Alaric did not sift the matter very deeply, nor did he
ask Undy, or himself either, whether in using the contents
of his purse in the purchase of shares he would be justified
in turning to his own purpose any information which he
might obtain in his official career. Nor did he again
offer to put that broad test to himself which he had
before proposed, and ask himself whether he would
dare to talk of what he was doing in the face of day, in
his own office, before Sir Gregory, or before the Neverbends
of the Service. He had already learnt the absurdity of
such tests. Did other men talk of such doings ? Was it
not notorious that the world speculated, and that the
world was generally silent in the matter ? Why should
he attempt to be wiser than those around him ? Was it
not sufficient for him to be wise in his generation ? What
man had ever become great, who allowed himself to be
impeded by small scruples ? If the sportsman returned
from the field laden with game, who would scrutinize the
mud on his gaiters ? 'Excelsior !' said Alaric to himself with a proud ambition ; and so he attempted to rise
by the purchase and sale of mining shares.

When he was fairly engaged in the sport, his style of
play so fascinated Undy that they embarked in a sort of
partnership, *pro hac vice*, good to the last during the ups
and downs of Wheal Mary Jane. Mary Jane, no doubt,
would soon run dry, or else be drowned, as had happened
to New Friendship. But in the meantime something
might be done.

'Of course you'll be consulted about those other papers,'
said Undy. 'It might be as well they should be kept
back for a week or two.'

'Well, I'll see,' said Alaric ; and as he said it, he felt
that his face was tinged with a blush of shame. But what
then ? Who would look at the dirt on his gaiters, if he
filled his bag with game ?

Mrs. Woodward was no whit angered by the coldness of
Norman's letter. She wished that he could have brought
himself to write in a different style, but she remembered
his grief, and knew that as time should work its cure

upon it, he would come round and again be gentle and affectionate, at any rate with her.

She misdoubted Charley's judgement in the choice of lodgings, and therefore she talked over the matter with Alaric. It was at last decided that he, Alaric, should move instead of driving Norman away. His final movement would soon take place; that movement which would rob him of the freedom of lodginghood, and invest him with all the ponderous responsibility and close restraint of a householder. He and Gertrude were to be married in February, and after spending a cold honeymoon in Paris and Brussels, were to begin their married life amidst the sharp winds of a London March. But love, gratified love, will, we believe, keep out even an English east wind. If so, it is certainly the only thing that will.

Charley, therefore, wrote to Norman, telling him that he could remain in his old home, and humbly asking permission to remain there with him. To this request he received a kind rejoinder in the affirmative. Though Charley was related to Alaric, there had always apparently been a closer friendship between him and Norman than between the two cousins; and now, in his fierce unbridled quarrel with Alaric, and in his present coolness with the Woodwards, he seemed to turn to Charley with more than ordinary affection.

Norman made his appearance at the office on the first Monday of the new year. He had hitherto sat at the same desk with Alaric, each of them occupying one side of it; on his return he found himself opposite to a stranger. Alaric had, of course, been promoted to a room of his own.

The Weights and Measures had never been a noisy office; but now it became more silent than ever. Men there talked but little at any time, and now they seemed to cease from talking altogether. It was known to all that the Damon and Pythias of the establishment were Damon and Pythias no longer; that war waged between them, and that if all accounts were true, they were ready to fly each at the other's throat. Some attributed this to the competitive examination; others said it was love; others declared that it was money, the root of evil; and one rash young gentleman stated his positive knowledge

that it was all three.   At any rate something dreadful was
expected ; and men sat anxious at their desks, fearing the
coming evil.

On the Monday the two men did not meet, nor on the
Tuesday.   On the next morning, Alaric, having acknowledged to himself the necessity of breaking the ice, walked
into the room where Norman sat with three or four others.
It was absolutely necessary that he should make some
arrangement with him as to a certain branch of office-
work ; and though it was competent for him, as the
superior, to have sent for Norman as the inferior, he
thought it best to abstain from doing so, even though he
were thereby obliged to face his enemy, for the first time,
in the presence of others.

'Well, Mr. Embryo,' said he, speaking to the new
junior, and standing with his back to the fire in an easy
way, as though there was nothing wrong under the sun,
or at least nothing at the Weights and Measures, 'well,
Mr. Embryo, how do you get on with those calculations ? '

'Pretty well, I believe, sir ; I think I begin to understand them now,' said the tyro, producing for Alaric's
gratification five or six folio-sheets covered with intricate
masses of figures.

'Ah ! yes ; that will do very well,' said Alaric, taking
up one of the sheets, and looking at it with an assumed air
of great interest.   Though he acted his part pretty well,
his mind was very far removed from Mr. Embryo's efforts.

Norman sat at his desk, as black as a thunder-cloud,
with his eyes turned intently at the paper before him ;
but so agitated that he could not even pretend to write.

'By the by, Norman,' said Alaric, 'when will it suit you
to look through those Scotch papers with me ? '

'My name, sir, is Mr. Norman,' said Harry, getting up
and standing by his chair with all the firmness of a Paladin
of old.

'With all my heart,' said Alaric.   'In speaking to you
I can have but one wish, and that is to do so in any way
that may best please you.'

'Any instructions you may have to give I will attend
to, as far as my duty goes,' said Norman.

And then Alaric, pushing Mr. Embryo from his chair

without much ceremony, sat down opposite to his former friend, and said and did what he had to say and do with an easy unaffected air, in which there was, at any rate, none of the usual superciliousness of a neophyte's authority. Norman was too agitated to speak reasonably, or to listen calmly, but Alaric knew that though he might not do so to-day, he would to-morrow, or if not to-morrow, then the next day; and so from day to day he came into Norman's room and transacted his business. Mr. Embryo got accustomed to looking through the window at the Council Office for the ten minutes that he remained there, and Norman also became reconciled to the custom. And thus, though they never met in any other way, they daily had a kind of intercourse with each other, which, at last, contrived to get itself arranged into a certain amount of civility on both sides.

Immediately that Norman's arrival was heard of at Surbiton Cottage, Mrs. Woodward hastened up to town to see him. She wrote to him to say that she would be at his lodgings at a certain hour, and begged him to come thither to her. Of course he did not refuse, and so they met. Mrs. Woodward had much doubted whether or no she would take Linda or Katie with her, but at last she resolved to go alone. Harry, she thought, would be more willing to speak freely to her, to open his heart to her, if there were nobody by but herself.

Their meeting was very touching, and characteristic of the two persons. Mrs. Woodward was sad enough, but her sadness was accompanied by a strength of affection that carried before it every obstacle. Norman was also sad; but he was at first stern and cold, and would have remained so to the last, had not his manly anger been overpowered by her feminine tenderness.

It was singular, but not the less true, that at this period Norman appeared to have forgotten altogether that he had ever proposed to Gertrude, and been rejected by her. All that he said and all that he thought was exactly what he might have said and thought had Alaric taken from him his affianced bride. No suitor had ever felt his suit to be more hopeless than he had done; and yet he now regarded himself as one whose high hopes of happy love had all been destroyed by the treachery of a friend and the fickleness of a woman.

This made the task of appeasing him very difficult to Mrs. Woodward. She could not in plain language remind him that he had been plainly rejected; nor could she, on the other hand, permit her daughter to be branded with a fault of which she had never been guilty.

Mrs. Woodward had wished, though she had hardly hoped, so to mollify Norman as to induce him to promise to be at the wedding; but she soon found that this was out of the question. There was no mitigating his anger against Alaric.

'Mrs. Woodward,' said he, standing very upright, and looking very stiff, 'I will never again willingly put myself in any position where I must meet him.'

'Oh! Harry, don't say so—think of your close friendship, think of your long friendship.'

'Why did he not think of it?'

'But, Harry—if not for his sake, if not for your own, at any rate do so for ours; for my sake, for Katie's and Linda's, for Gertrude's sake.'

'I had rather not speak of Gertrude, Mrs. Woodward.'

'Ah! Harry, Gertrude has done you no injury; why should you thus turn your heart against her? You should not blame her; if you have anyone to blame, it is me.'

'No; you have been true to me.'

'And has she been false? Oh! Harry, think how we have loved you! You should be more just to us.'

'Tush!' he said. 'I do not believe in justice; there is no justice left. I would have given everything I had for him. I would have made any sacrifice. His happiness was as much my thought as my own. And now—and yet you talk to me of justice.'

'And if he had injured you, Harry, would you not forgive him? Do you repeat your prayers without thinking of them? Do you not wish to forgive them that trespass against you?' Norman groaned inwardly in the spirit. 'Do you not think of this when you kneel every night before your God?'

'There are injuries which a man cannot forgive, is not expected to forgive.'

'Are there, Harry ? Oh ! that is a dangerous doctrine. In that way every man might nurse his own wrath till anger would make devils of us all. Our Saviour has made no exceptions.'

'In one sense, I do forgive him, Mrs. Woodward. I wish him no evil. But it is impossible that I should call a man who has so injured me my friend. I look upon him as disgraced for ever.'

She then endeavoured to persuade him to see Gertrude, or at any rate to send his love to her. But in this also he was obdurate. 'It could,' he said, 'do no good.' He could not answer for himself that his feelings would not betray him. A message would be of no use ; if true, it would not be gracious ; if false, it had better be avoided. He was quite sure Gertrude would be indifferent as to any message from him. The best thing for them both would be that they should forget each other.

He promised, however, that he would go down to Hampton immediately after the marriage, and he sent his kindest love to Linda and Katie. 'And, dear Mrs. Woodward,' said he, 'I know you think me very harsh, I know you think me vindictive—but pray, pray believe that I understand all your love, and acknowledge all your goodness. The time will, perhaps, come when we shall be as happy together as we once were.'

Mrs. Woodward, trying to smile through her tears, could only say that she would pray that that time might soon come ; and so, bidding God bless him, as a mother might bless her child, she left him and returned to Hampton, not with a light heart.

CHAPTER XVI

THE FIRST WEDDING

In spite, however, of Norman and his anger, on a cold snowy morning in the month of February, Gertrude stood at the altar in Hampton Church, a happy trusting bride, and Linda stood smiling behind her, the lovely leader of the nuptial train. Nor were Linda's smiles false or forced, much less treacherous. She had taught herself to look on Alaric as her sister's husband, and though in doing so she had suffered, and did still suffer, she now thought of her own lost lover in no other guise.

A housemaid, not long since, who was known in the family in which she lived to be affianced to a neighbouring gardener, came weeping to her mistress.

'Oh, ma'am!'

'Why, Susan, what ails you?'

'Oh, ma'am!'

'Well, Susan—what is it?—why are you crying?'

'Oh, ma'am—John!'

'Well—what of John? I hope he is not misbehaving.'

'Indeed, ma'am, he is then; the worst of misbehaviour; for he's gone and got hisself married.' And poor Susan gave vent to a flood of tears.

Her mistress tried to comfort her, and not in vain. She told her that probably she might be better as she was; that John, seeing what he had done, must be a false creature, who would undoubtedly have used her ill; and she ended her good counsel by trying to make Susan understand that there were still as good fish in the sea as had ever yet been caught out of it.

'And that's true too, ma'am,' said Susan, with her apron to her eyes.

'Then you should not be downhearted, you know.'

'Nor I han't down'arted, ma'am, for thank God I could love any man, but it's the looks on it, ma'am; it's that I mind.'

How many of us are there, women and men too, who

think most of the 'looks of it' under such circumstances; and who, were we as honest as poor Susan, ought to thank God, as she did, that we can love anyone; anyone, that is, of the other sex. We are not all of us susceptible of being torn to tatters by an unhappy passion; not even all those of us who may be susceptible of a true and honest love. And it is well that it is so. It is one of God's mercies; and if we were as wise as Susan, we should thank God for it.

Linda was, perhaps, one of those. She was good, affectionate, tender, and true. But she was made of that stuff which can bend to the north wind. The world was not all over with her because a man had been untrue to her. She had had her grief, and had been told to meet it like a Christian; she had been obedient to the telling, and now felt the good result. So when Gertrude was married she stood smiling behind her; and when her new brother-in-law kissed her in the vestry-room she smiled again, and honestly wished them happiness.

And Katie was there, very pretty and bonny, still childish, with her short dress and long trousers, but looking as though she, too, would soon feel the strength of her own wings, and be able to fly away from her mother's nest. Dear Katie! Her story has yet to be told. To her belongs neither the soft easiness of her sister Linda nor the sterner dignity of Gertrude. But she has a character of her own, which contains, perhaps, higher qualities than those given to either of her sisters.

And there were other bridesmaids there; how many it boots not now to say. We must have the spaces round our altars greatly widened if this passion for bevies of attendant nymphs be allowed to go on increasing—and if crinolines increase also. If every bride is to have twelve maidens, and each maiden to stand on no less than a twelve-yard circle, what modest temple will ever suffice for a sacrifice to Hymen?

And Mrs. Woodward was there, of course; as pretty to my thinking as either of her daughters, or any of the bridesmaids. She was very pretty and smiling and quiet. But when Gertrude said 'I will,' she was thinking of Harry Norman, and grieving that he was not there.

And Captain Cuttwater was there, radiant in a new blue coat, made specially for the occasion, and elastic with true joy. He had been very generous. He had given £1,000 to Alaric, and settled £150 a year on Gertrude, payable, of course, after his death. This, indeed, was the bulk of what he had to give, and Mrs. Woodward had seen with regret his exuberant munificence to one of her children. But Gertrude was her child, and of course she could not complain.

And Charley was there, acting as best man. It was just the place and just the work for Charley. He forgot all his difficulties, all his duns, and also all his town delights. Without a sigh he left his lady in Norfolk Street to mix gin-sling for other admirers, and felt no regret though four brother navvies were going to make a stunning night of it at the 'Salon de Seville dansant,' at the bottom of Holborn Hill. However, he had his hopes that he might be back in time for some of that fun.

And Undy Scott was there. He and Alaric had fraternized so greatly of late that the latter had, as a matter of course, asked him to his wedding, and Mrs. Woodward had of course expressed her delight at receiving Alaric's friend. Undy also was a pleasant fellow for a wedding party; he was full of talk, fond of ladies, being no whit abashed in his attendance on them by the remembrance of his bosom's mistress, whom he had left, let us hope, happy in her far domestic retirement. Undy Scott was a good man at a wedding, and made himself specially agreeable on this occasion.

But the great glory of the day was the presence of Sir Gregory Hardlines. It was a high honour, considering all that rested on Sir Gregory's shoulders, for so great a man to come all the way down to Hampton to see a clerk in the Weights and Measures married.

Cum tot sustineas, et tanta negotia solus,

—for we may call it 'solus,' Sir Warwick and Mr. Jobbles being sources of more plague than profit in carrying out your noble schemes—while so many things are on your shoulders, Sir Gregory; while you are defending the Civil Service by your pen [?], adorning it by your conduct, perfecting it by new rules, how could any man have had the face to ask you to a wedding ?

Nevertheless Sir Gregory was there, and did not lose the excellent opportunity which a speech at the breakfast-table afforded him for expressing his opinion on the Civil Service of his country.

And so Gertrude Woodward became Gertrude Tudor, and she and Alaric were whirled away by a post-chaise and post-boy, done out with white bows, to the Hampton Court station ; from thence they whisked up to London, and then down to Dover ; and there we will leave them.

They were whisked away, having first duly gone through the amount of badgering which the bride and bridegroom have to suffer at the wedding breakfast-table. They drank their own health in champagne. Alaric made a speech, in which he said he was quite unworthy of his present happiness, and Gertrude picked up all the bijoux, gold pencil-cases, and silver cream-jugs, which were thrown at her from all sides. All the men made speeches, and all the women laughed, but the speech of the day was that celebrated one made by Sir Gregory, in which he gave a sketch of Alaric Tudor as the beau ideal of a clerk in the Civil Service. ' His heart,' said he, energetically, ' is at the Weights and Measures ; ' but Gertrude looked at him as though she did not believe a word of it.

And so Alaric and Gertrude were whisked away, and the wedding guests were left to look sheepish at each other, and take themselves off as best they might. Sir Gregory, of course, had important public business which precluded him from having the gratification of prolonging his stay at Hampton. Charley got away in perfect time to enjoy whatever there might be to be enjoyed at the dancing saloon of Seville, and Undy Scott returned to his club.

Then all was again quiet at Surbiton Cottage. Captain Cuttwater, who had perhaps drunk the bride's health once too often, went to sleep ; Katie, having taken off her fine clothes, roamed about the house disconsolate, and Mrs. Woodward and Linda betook themselves to their needles.

The Tudors went to Brussels, and were made welcome

by the Belgian banker, whose counters he had deserted so much to his own benefit, and from thence to Paris, and, having been there long enough to buy a French bonnet and wonder at the enormity of French prices, they returned to a small but comfortable house they had prepared for themselves in the neighbourhood of West-bourne Terrace.

Previous to this Norman had been once, and but once, at Hampton, and, when there, he had failed in being comfortable himself, or in making the Woodwards so ; he could not revert to his old habits, or sit, or move, or walk, as though nothing special had happened since he had been last there.   He could not talk about Gertrude, and he could not help talking of her.   By some closer packing among the ladies a room had now been prepared for him in the house ; even this upset him, and brought to his mind all those unpleasant thoughts which he should have endeavoured to avoid.

He did not repeat his visit before the Tudors returned ; and then for some time he was prevented from doing so by the movements of the Woodwards themselves.   Mrs. Woodward paid a visit to her married daughter, and, when she returned, Linda did the same.   And so for a while Norman was, as it were, divided from his old friends, whereas Tudor, as a matter of course, was one of themselves.

It was only natural that Mrs. Woodward should forgive Alaric and receive him to her bosom, now that he was her son-in-law.   After all, such ties as these avail more than any predilections, more than any effort of judge-ment in the choice of the objects of our affections.   We associate with those with whom the tenor of life has thrown us, and from habit we learn to love those with whom we are brought to associate.

CHAPTER XVII

THE HONOURABLE MRS. VAL AND MISS GOLIGHTLY

THE first eighteen months of Gertrude's married life
were not unhappy, though, like all persons entering on
the realities of the world, she found much to disappoint
her. At first her husband's society was sufficient for
her; and to give him his due, he was not at first an
inattentive husband. Then came the baby, bringing
with him, as first babies always should do, a sort of second
honeymoon of love, and a renewal of those services which
women so delight to receive from their bosoms' lord.

She had of course made acquaintances since she had
settled herself in London, and had, in her modest way,
done her little part in adding to the gaiety of the great
metropolis. In this respect indeed Alaric's commencement of life had somewhat frightened Mrs. Woodward,
and the more prudent of his friends. Grand as his official
promotion had been, his official income at the time of
his marriage did not exceed £600 a year, and though
this was to be augmented occasionally till it reached
£800, yet even with this advantage it could hardly suffice
for a man and his wife and a coming family to live in an
expensive part of London, and enable him to 'see his
friends' occasionally, as the act of feeding one's acquaintance is now generally called.

Gertrude, like most English girls of her age, was at
first so ignorant about money that she hardly knew
whether £600 was or was not a sufficient income to justify
their present mode of living; but she soon found reason
to suspect that her husband at any rate endeavoured to
increase it by other means. We say to suspect, because
he never spoke to her on the subject; he never told her
of Mary Janes and New Friendships; or hinted that
he had extensive money dealings in connexion with
Undy Scott.

But it can be taken for granted that no husband can

carry on such dealings long without some sort of cognizance on his wife's part as to what he is doing; a woman who is not trusted by her lord may choose to remain in apparent darkness, may abstain from questions, and may consider it either her duty or her interest to assume an ignorance as to her husband's affairs; but the partner of one's bed and board, the minister who soothes one's headaches, and makes one's tea, and looks after one's linen, can't but have the means of guessing the thoughts which occupy her companion's mind and occasionally darken his brow.

Much of Gertrude's society had consisted of that into which Alaric was thrown by his friendship with Undy Scott. There was a brother of Undy's living in town, one Valentine Scott—a captain in a cavalry regiment, and whose wife was by no means of that delightfully retiring disposition evinced by Undy's better half. The Hon. Mrs. Valentine, or Mrs. Val Scott as she was commonly called, was a very pushing woman, and pushed herself into a prominent place among Gertrude's friends. She had been the widow of Jonathan Golightly, Esq., umquhile sheriff of the city of London, and stockbroker, and when she gave herself and her jointure up to Captain Val, she also brought with her, to enliven the house, a daughter Clementina, the only remaining pledge of her love for the stockbroker.

When Val Scott entered the world, his father's precepts as to the purposes of matrimony were deeply graven on his heart. He was the best looking of the family, and, except Undy, the youngest. He had not Undy's sharpness, his talent for public matters, or his aptitude for the higher branches of the Civil Service; but he had wit to wear his sash and epaulets with an easy grace, and to captivate the heart, person, and some portion of the purse, of the Widow Golightly. The lady was ten years older than the gentleman; but then she had a thousand a year, and, to make matters more pleasant, the beauteous Clementina had a fortune of her own.

Under these circumstances the marriage had been contracted without any deceit, or attempt at deceit, by either party. Val wanted an income, and the sheriff's widow wanted the utmost amount of social consideration which her not very extensive means would purchase for her. On the whole, the two parties to the transaction were contented with their bargain. Mrs. Val, it is true, kept her income very much in her own hands; but still she consented to pay Val's tailors' bills, and it is something for a man to have bed and board found him for nothing. It is true, again, the lady did not find that the noble blood of her husband gave her an immediate right of entry into the best houses in London; but it did bring her into some sort of contact with some few people of rank and fame; and being a sensible woman, she had not been unreasonable in her expectations.

When she had got what she could from her husband in this particular, she did not trouble him much further. He delighted in the Rag, and there spent the most of his time; happily, she delighted in what she called the charms of society, and as society expanded itself before her, she was also, we must suppose, happy. She soon perceived that more in her immediate line was to be obtained from Undy than from her own member of the Gaberlunzie family, and hence had sprung up her intimacy with Mrs. Tudor.

It cannot be said that Gertrude was very fond of the Honourable Mrs. Val, nor even of her daughter, Clementina Golightly, who was more of her own age. These people had become her friends from the force of circumstances, and not from predilection. To tell the truth, Mrs. Val, who had in her day encountered, with much patience, a good deal of snubbing, and who had had to be thankful when she was patronized, now felt that her day for being a great lady had come, and that it behoved her to patronize others. She tried her hand upon Gertrude, and found the practice so congenial to her spirits, so pleasantly stimulating, so well adapted to afford a gratifying compensation for her former humility, that she continued to give up a good deal of her time to No. 5, Albany Row, Westbourne Terrace, at which house the Tudors resided.

The young bride was not exactly the woman to submit quietly to patronage from any Mrs. Val, however honourable she might be; but for a while Gertrude hardly knew what it meant; and at her first outset the natural modesty of youth, and her inexperience in her new position, made her unwilling to take offence and unequal to rebellion. By degrees, however, this feeling of humility wore off; she began to be aware of the assumed superiority of Mrs. Val's friendship, and by the time that their mutual affection was of a year's standing, Gertrude had determined, in a quiet way, without saying anything to anybody, to put herself on a footing of more perfect equality with the Honourable Mrs. Val.

Clementina Golightly was, in the common parlance of a large portion of mankind, a 'doosed fine gal.' She stood five feet six, and stood very well, on very good legs, but with rather large feet. She was as straight as a grenadier, and had it been her fate to carry a milk-pail, she would have carried it to perfection. Instead of this, however, she was permitted to expend an equal amount of energy in every variation of waltz and polka that the ingenuity of the dancing professors of the age has been able to produce. Waltzes and polkas suited her admirably; for she was gifted with excellent lungs and perfect powers of breathing, and she had not much delight in prolonged conversation. Her fault, if she had one, was a predilection for flirting; but she did her flirtations in a silent sort of way, much as we may suppose the fishes do theirs, whose amours we may presume to consist in swimming through their cool element in close contiguity with each other. 'A feast of reason and a flow of soul' were not the charms by which Clementina Golightly essayed to keep her admirers spell-bound at her feet. To whirl rapidly round a room at the rate of ten miles an hour, with her right hand outstretched in the grasp of her partner's, and to know that she was tightly buoyed up, like a horse by a bearing-rein, by his other hand behind her back, was for her sufficient. To do this, as she did do it, without ever crying for mercy, with no slackness of breath, and apparently without distress, must have taken as much training as a horse gets for a race. But the training had in nowise injured her; and now, having gone through her gallops and run all her heats for three successive seasons, she was still sound of wind and limb, and fit to run at any moment when called upon.

We have said nothing about the face of the beauteous Clementina, and indeed nothing can be said about it. There was no feature in it with which a man could have any right to find fault; that she was a 'doosed fine girl' was a fact generally admitted; but nevertheless you might look at her for four hours consecutively on a Monday evening, and yet on Tuesday you would not know her. She had hair which was brownish and sufficiently silky— and which she wore, as all other such girls do, propped out on each side of her face by thick round velvet pads, which, when the waltzing pace became exhilarating, occasionally showed themselves, looking greasy. She had a pair of eyes set straight in her head, faultless in form, and perfectly inexpressive. She had a nose equally straight, but perhaps a little too coarse in dimensions. She had a mouth not over large, with two thin lips and small whitish teeth; and she had a chin equal in contour to the rest of her face, but on which Venus had not deigned to set a dimple. Nature might have defied a French passport officer to give a description of her, by which even her own mother or a detective policeman might have recognized her.

When to the above list of attractions it is added that Clementina Golightly had £20,000 of her own, and a reversionary interest in her mother's jointure, it may be imagined that she did not want for good-winded cavaliers to bear her up behind, and whirl around with her with outstretched hands.

'I am not going to stay a moment, my dear,' said Mrs. Val, seating herself on Gertrude's sofa, having rushed up almost unannounced into the drawing-room, followed by Clementina; 'indeed, Lady Howlaway is waiting for me this moment; but I must settle with you about the June flower-show.'

'Oh! thank you, Mrs. Scott, don't trouble yourself about me,' said Gertrude; 'I don't think I shall go.'

'Oh! nonsense, my dear; of course you'll go; it's the show of the year, and the Grand duke is to be there—

baby is all right now, you know; I must not hear of your not going.'

'All the same—I fear I must decline,' said Gertrude; 'I think I shall be at Hampton.'

'Oh! nonsense, my dear; of course you must show yourself. People will say all manner of things else. Clementina has promised to meet Victoire Jaquêtanápes there and a party of French people, people of the very highest ton. You'll be delighted, my dear.'

'M. Jaquêtanápes is the most delicious polkist you ever met,' said Clementina. 'He has got a new back step that will quite amaze you.' As Gertrude in her present condition was not much given to polkas, this temptation did not have great effect.

'Oh, you must come, of course, my dear—and pray let me recommend you to go to Madame Bosconi for your bonnet; she has such darling little ducks, and as cheap as dirt. But I want you to arrange about the carriage; you can do that with Mr. Tudor, and I can settle with you afterwards. Captain Scott won't go, of course; but I have no doubt Undecimus and Mr. Tudor will come later and bring us home; we can manage very well with the one carriage.'

In spite of her thousand a year the Honourable Mrs. Val was not ashamed to look after the pounds, shillings, and pence. And so, having made her arrangements, Mrs. Val took herself off, hurrying to appease the anger of Lady Howlaway, and followed by Clementina, who since her little outburst as to the new back step of M. Jaquêta-nápes had not taken much part in the conversation.

Flower-shows are a great resource for the Mrs. Scotts of London life. They are open to ladies who cannot quite penetrate the inner sancta of fashionable life, and yet they are frequented by those to whom those sancta are everyday household walks. There at least the Mrs. Scotts of the outer world can show themselves in close contiguity, and on equal terms, with the Mrs. Scotts of the inner world. And then, who is to know the difference? If also one is an Honourable Mrs. Scott, and can contrive to appear as such in the next day's *Morning Post*, may not one fairly boast that the ends of society have been attained ? Where is the citadel ? How is one to know when one has taken it ?

Gertrude could not be quite so defiant with her friends as she would have wished to have been, as they were borne with and encouraged by her husband. Of Undy's wife Alaric saw nothing and heard little, but it suited Undy to make use of his sister-in-law's house, and it suited Alaric to be intimate with Undy's sister-in-law. Moreover, had not Clementina Golightly £20,000, and was she not a ' doosed fine girl ? ' This was nothing to Alaric now, and might not be considered to be much to Undy. But that far-seeing, acute financier knew that there were other means of handling a lady's money than that of marrying her. He could not at present acquire a second fortune in that way ; but he might perhaps acquire the management of this £20,000 if he could provide the lady with a husband of the proper temperament. Undy Scott did not want to appropriate Miss Golightly's fortune, he only wanted to have the management of it.

Looking round among his acquaintance for a fitting *parti* for the sweet Clementina, his mind, after much consideration, settled upon Charley Tudor. There were many young men much nearer and dearer to Undy than Charley, who might be equally desirous of so great a prize ; but he could think of none over whom he might probably exercise so direct a control. Charley was a handsome gay fellow, and waltzed *au ravir ;* he might, therefore, without difficulty, make his way with the fair Clementina. He was distressingly poor, and would therefore certainly jump at an heiress—he was delightfully thoughtless and easy of leading, and therefore the money, when in his hands, might probably be manageable. He was also Alaric's cousin, and therefore acceptable.

Undy did not exactly open his mind to Alaric Tudor in this matter. Alaric's education was going on rapidly ; but his mind had not yet received with sufficient tenacity those principles of philosophy which would enable him to look at this scheme in its proper light. He had already learnt the great utility, one may almost say the necessity, of having a command of money ; he was beginning also to perceive that money was a thing not to be judged of by the ordinary rules which govern a man's conduct. In other matters it behoves a gentleman to be open, above-board, liberal, and true; good-natured, generous, confiding, self-denying, doing unto others as he would wish that others should do unto him; but in the acquirement and use of money—that is, its use with the object of acquiring more, its use in the usurer's sense—his practice should be exactly the reverse; he should be close, secret, exacting, given to concealment, not over troubled by scruples; suspicious, without sympathies, self-devoted, and always doing unto others exactly that which he is on his guard to prevent others from doing unto him— viz., making money by them. So much Alaric had learnt, and had been no inapt scholar. But he had not yet appreciated the full value of the latitude allowed by the genius of the present age to men who deal successfully in money. He had, as we have seen, acknowledged to himself that a sportsman may return from the field with his legs and feet a little muddy; but he did not yet know how deep a man may wallow in the mire, how thoroughly he may besmear himself from head to foot in the blackest, foulest mud, and yet be received an honoured guest by ladies gay and noble lords, if only his bag be sufficiently full.

> Rem . . ., quocunque modo rem!

The remainder of the passage was doubtless applicable to former times, but now is hardly worth repeating.

As Alaric's stomach was not yet quite suited for strong food, Undy fitted this matter to his friend's still juvenile capacities. There was an heiress, a 'doosed fine girl' as Undy insisted, laying peculiar strength on the word of emphasis, with £20,000, and there was Charley Tudor, a devilish decent fellow, without a rap. Why not bring them together? This would only be a mark of true friendship on the part of Undy; and on Alaric's part, it would be no more than one cousin would be bound to do for another. Looking at it in this light, Alaric saw nothing in the matter which could interfere with his quiet conscience.

'I'll do what I can,' said Undy. 'Mrs. Val is inclined

to have a way of her own in most things; but if anybody can lead her, I can. Charley must take care that Val himself doesn't take his part, that's all. If he interferes, it would be all up with us.'

And thus Alaric, intent mainly on the interest of his cousin, and actuated perhaps a little by the feeling that a rich cousin would be more serviceable than a poor one, set himself to work, in connexion with Undy Scott, to make prey of Clementina Golightly's £20,000.

But if Undy had no difficulty in securing the co-operation of Alaric in this matter, Alaric by no means found it equally easy to secure the co-operation of Charley. Charley Tudor had not yet learnt to look upon himself as a marketable animal, worth a certain sum of money, in consequence of such property in good appearance, address, &c., as God had been good enough to endow him withal.

He daily felt the depth and disagreeable results of his own poverty, and not unfrequently, when specially short of the Queen's medium, sighed for some of those thousands and tens of thousands with which men's mouths are so glibly full. He had often tried to calculate what would be his feelings if some eccentric, good-natured old stranger should leave him, say, five thousand a year; he had often walked about the street, with his hands in his empty pockets, building delicious castles in the air, and doing the most munificent actions imaginable with his newly-acquired wealth, as all men in such circumstances do; relieving distress, rewarding virtue, and making handsome presents to all his friends, and especially to Mrs. Woodward. So far Charley was not guiltless of coveting wealth; but he had never for a moment thought of realizing his dreams by means of his personal attractions. It had never occurred to him that any girl having money could think it worth her while to marry him. He, navvy as he was, with his infernal friends and pot-house love, with his debts and idleness and low associations, with his saloons of Seville, his Elysium in Fleet Street, and his Paradise near the Surrey Gardens, had hitherto thought little enough of his own attractions. No kind father had taught him that he was worth £10,000 in any market in the world. When he had dreamt of money, he had never dreamt of it as accruing to him in return for any value or worth which he had inherent in himself. Even in his lighter moments he had no such conceit; and at those periods, few and far between, in which he did think seriously of the world at large, this special method of escaping from his difficulties never once presented itself to his mind.

When, therefore, Alaric first spoke to him of marrying £20,000 and Clementina Golightly, his surprise was unbounded.

'£20,000!' said Alaric, 'and a doosed fine girl, you know;' and he also laid great stress on the latter part of the offer, knowing how inflammable was Charley's heart, and at the same time how little mercenary was his mind.

But Charley was not only surprised at the proposed arrangement, but apparently also unwilling to enter into it. He argued that in the first place no girl in her senses would accept him. To this Alaric replied that as Clementina had not much sense to speak of, that objection might fall to the ground. Then Charley expressed an idea that Miss Golightly's friends might probably object when they learnt what were the exact pecuniary resources of the expectant husband; to which Alaric argued that the circumstances of the case were very lucky, inasmuch as some of Clementina's natural friends were already prepossessed in favour of such an arrangement.

Driven thus from two of his strongholds, Charley, in the most modest of voices, in a voice one may say quite shamefaced and conscious of its master's weakness— suggested that he was not quite sure that at the present moment he was very much in love with the lady in question.

Alaric had married for love, and was not two years married, yet had his education so far progressed in that short period as to enable him to laugh at such an objection.

'Then, my dear fellow, what the deuce do you mean to do with yourself? You'll certainly go to the dogs.'

Charley had an idea that he certainly should; and also had an idea that Miss Clementina and her £20,000 might not improbably go in the same direction, if he had anything to do with them.

'And as for loving her,' continued Alaric, 'that's all my eye. Love is a luxury which none but the rich or the poor can afford. We middle-class paupers, who are born with good coats on our backs, but empty purses, can have nothing to do with it.'

'But you married for love, Alaric?'

'My marriage was not a very prudent one, and should not be taken as an example. And then I did get some fortune with my wife; and what is more, I was not so fearfully in want of it as you are.'

Charley acknowledged the truth of this, said that he would think of the matrimonial project, and promised, at any rate, to call on Clementina on an early occasion. He had already made her acquaintance, had already danced with her, and certainly could not take upon himself to deny that she was a 'doosed fine girl.'

But Charley had reasons of his own, reasons which he could not make known to Alaric, for not thinking much of, or trusting much to, Miss Golightly's fortune. In the first place, he regarded marriage on such a grand scale as that now suggested, as a ceremony which must take a long time to adjust; the wooing of a lady with so many charms could not be carried on as might be the wooing of a chambermaid or a farmer's daughter. It must take months at least to conciliate the friends of so rich an heiress, and months at the end of them to prepare the wedding gala. But Charley could not wait for months; before one month was over he would probably be laid up in some vile limbo, an unfortunate poor prisoner at the suit of an iron-hearted tailor.

At this very moment of Alaric's proposition, at this instant when he found himself talking with so much coolness of the expedience or inexpedience of appropriating to his own purpose a slight trifle of £20,000, he was in dire strait as to money difficulties.

He had lately, that is, within the last twelve months, made acquaintance with an interesting gentleman named Jabesh M'Ruen. Mr. Jabesh M'Ruen was in the habit of relieving the distresses of such impoverished young gentlemen as Charley Tudor; and though he did this with every assurance of philanthropic regard, though in doing so he only made one stipulation, ' Pray be punctual, Mr. Tudor, now pray do be punctual, sir, and you may always count on me,' nevertheless, in spite of all his goodness, Mr. M'Ruen's young friends seldom continued to hold their heads well up over the world's waters.

On the morning after this conversation with Alaric, Charley intended to call on his esteemed old friend. Many were the morning calls he did make; many were the weary, useless, aimless walks which he took to that little street at the back of Mecklenburg Square, with the fond hope of getting some relief from Mr. M'Ruen; and many also were the calls, the return visits, as it were, which Mr. M'Ruen made at the Internal Navigation, and numerous were the whispers which he would there whisper into the ears of the young clerk, Mr. Snape the while sitting by, with a sweet unconscious look, as though he firmly believed Mr. M'Ruen to be Charley's maternal uncle.

And then, too, Charley had other difficulties, which in his mind presented great obstacles to the Golightly scheme, though Alaric would have thought little of them, and Undy nothing. What was he to do with his Norfolk Street lady, his barmaid houri, his Norah Geraghty, to whom he had sworn all manner of undying love, and for whom in some sort of fashion he really had an affection? And Norah was not a light-of-love whom it was as easy to lay down as to pick up. Charley had sworn to love her, and she had sworn to love Charley; and to give her her due, she had kept her word to him. Though her life rendered necessary a sort of daily or rather nightly flirtation with various male comers—as indeed, for the matter of that, did also the life of Miss Clementina Golightly—yet she had in her way been true to her lover. She had been true to him, and Charley did not doubt her, and in a sort of low way respected her; though it was but a dissipated and debauched respect. There had even been talk between them of marriage, and who can say what in his softer moments, when his brain had been too weak or the toddy too strong, Charley may not have promised?

And there was yet another objection to Miss Golightly;
one even more difficult of mention, one on which Charley
felt himself more absolutely constrained to silence than
even either of the other two. He was sufficiently disinclined to speak to his cousin Alaric as to the merits
either of Mr. Jabesh M'Ruen or of Miss Geraghty, but
he could have been eloquent on either rather than whisper
a word as to the third person who stood between him and
the £20,000.

The school in which Charley now lived, that of the
infernal navvies, had taught him to laugh at romance;
but it had not been so successful in quelling the early
feelings of his youth, in drying up the fountains of poetry
within him, as had been the case with his cousin, in that
other school in which he had been a scholar. Charley
was a dissipated, dissolute rake, and in some sense had
degraded himself; but he had still this chance of safety
on his side, that he himself reprobated his own sins. He
dreamt of other things and a better life. He made
visions to himself of a sweet home, and a sweeter, sweetest,
lovely wife; a love whose hair should not be redolent of
smoke, nor her hands reeking with gin, nor her services
at the demand of every libertine who wanted a screw of
tobacco, or a glass of 'cold without.'

He had made such a vision to himself, and the angel
with which he had filled it was not a creature of his
imagination. She who was to reign in this ethereal
paradise, this happy home, far as the poles away from
Norfolk Street, was a living being in the sublunar globe,
present sometimes to Charley's eyes, and now so often
present to his thoughts; and yet she was but a child,
and as ignorant that she had ever touched a lover's
heart by her childish charms as though she had been
a baby.

After all, even on Charley's part, it was but a vision.
He never really thought that his young inamorata would
or could be to him a real true heart's companion, returning
his love with the double love of a woman, watching his
health, curing his vices, and making the sweet things of
the world a living reality around him. This love of his
was but a vision, but not the less on that account did it

interfere with his cousin Alaric's proposition in reference to Miss Clementina Golightly.

That other love also, that squalid love of his, was in truth no vision—was a stern, palpable reality, very difficult to get rid of, and one which he often thought to himself would very probably swallow up that other love, and drive his sweet dream far away into utter darkness and dim chaotic space.

But at any rate it was clear that there was no room in his heart for the beauteous Clementina, ' doosed fine girl' as she undoubtedly was, and serviceable as the £20,000 most certainly would have been.

CHAPTER XVIII

A DAY WITH ONE OF THE NAVVIES.—MORNING

ON the morning after this conversation with Alaric, Charley left his lodgings with a heavy heart, and wended his way towards Mecklenburg Square. At the corner of Davies Street he got an omnibus, which for fourpence took him to one of the little alleys near Gray's Inn, and there he got down, and threading the well-known locality, through Bedford Place and across Theobald's Road, soon found himself at the door of his generous patron. Oh ! how he hated the house ; how he hated the blear-eyed, cross-grained, dirty, impudent fish-fag of an old woman who opened the door for him ; how he hated Mr. Jabesh M'Ruen, to whom he now came a supplicant for assistance, and how, above all, he hated himself for being there.

He was shown into Mr. M'Ruen's little front parlour, where he had to wait for fifteen minutes, while his patron made such a breakfast as generally falls to the lot of such men. We can imagine the rancid butter, the stale be-fingered bread, the ha'porth of sky-blue milk, the tea innocent of China's wrongs, and the soiled cloth. Mr. M'Ruen always did keep Charley waiting fifteen minutes,

and so he was no whit surprised ; the doing so was a part
of the tremendous interest which the wretched old usurer
received for his driblets of money.

There was not a bit of furniture in the room on which
Charley had not speculated till speculation could go no
further ; the old escritoir or secrétaire which Mr. M'Ruen
always opened the moment he came into the room ;
the rickety Pembroke table, covered with dirty papers
which stood in the middle of it ; the horsehair-bottomed
chairs, on which Charley declined to sit down, unless he had
on his thickest winter trousers, so perpendicular had
become some atoms on the surface, which, when new,
had no doubt been horizontal ; the ornaments (!) on the
chimney, broken bits of filthy crockery, full of wisps
of paper, with a china duck without a tail, and a dog to
correspond without a head ; the pictures against the
wall, with their tarnished dingy frames and cracked
glasses, representing three of the Seasons ; how the
fourth had gone before its time to its final bourne by an
unhappy chance, Mr. M'Ruen had once explained to
Charley, while endeavouring to make his young customer
take the other three as a good value for £7 10s. in arranging
a little transaction, the total amount of which did not
exceed £15.

In that instance, however, Charley, who had already
dabbled somewhat deeply in dressing-cases, utterly refused
to trade in the articles produced.

Charley stood with his back to the dog and duck,
facing Winter, with Spring on his right and Autumn on
his left ; it was well that Summer was gone, no summer
could have shed light on that miserable chamber. He
knew that he would have to wait, and was not therefore
impatient, and at the end of fifteen minutes Mr. M'Ruen
shuffled into the room in his slippers.

He was a little man, with thin grey hair, which stood
upright from his narrow head—what his age might have
been it was impossible to guess ; he was wizened, and dry,
and grey, but still active enough on his legs when he had
exchanged his slippers for his shoes ; and as keen in all
his senses as though years could never tell upon him.

He always wore round his neck a stiff-starched deep

white handkerchief, not fastened with a bow in front,
the ends being tucked in so as to be invisible. This
cravat not only covered his throat but his chin also, so
that his head seemed to grow forth from it without the
aid of any neck ; and he had a trick of turning his face
round within it, an inch or two to the right or to the left,
in a manner which seemed to indicate that his cranium
was loose and might be removed at pleasure.

He shuffled into the room where Charley was standing
with little short quick steps, and putting out his hand,
just touched that of his customer, by way of going through
the usual process of greeting.

Some short statement must be made of Charley's money
dealings with Mr. M'Ruen up to this period. About
two years back a tailor had an over-due bill of his for
£20, of which he was unable to obtain payment, and
being unwilling to go to law, or perhaps being himself
in Mr. M'Ruen's power, he passed this bill to that worthy
gentleman—what amount of consideration he got for it,
it matters not now to inquire ; Mr. M'Ruen very shortly
afterwards presented himself at the Internal Navigation,
and introduced himself to our hero. He did this with
none of the overbearing harshness of the ordinary dun,
or the short caustic decision of a creditor determined to
resort to the utmost severity of the law. He turned his
head about and smiled, and just showed the end of the
bill peeping out from among a parcel of others, begged
Mr. Tudor to be punctual, he would only ask him to be
punctual, and would in such case do anything for him,
and ended his visit by making an appointment to meet
Charley in the little street behind Mecklenburg Square.
Charley kept his appointment, and came away from Mr.
M'Ruen's with a well-contented mind. He had, it is
true, left £5 behind him, and had also left the bill, still
entire ; but he had obtained a promise of unlimited
assistance from the good-natured gentleman, and had
also received instructions how he was to get a brother
clerk to draw a bill, how he was to accept it himself,
and how his patron was to discount it for him, paying
him real gold out of the Bank of England in exchange
for his worthless signature.

Charley stepped lighter on the ground as he left Mr. M'Ruen's house on that eventful morning than he had done for many a day. There was something delightful in the feeling that he could make money of his name in this way, as great bankers do of theirs, by putting it at the bottom of a scrap of paper. He experienced a sort of pride too in having achieved so respectable a position in the race of ruin which he was running, as to have dealings with a bill-discounter. He felt that he was putting himself on a par with great men, and rising above the low level of the infernal navvies. Mr. M'Ruen had pulled the bill out of a heap of bills which he always carried in his huge pocket-book, and showed to Charley the name of an impoverished Irish peer on the back of it ; and the sight of that name had made Charley quite in love with ruin. He already felt that he was almost hand-and-glove with Lord Mount-Coffeehouse ; for it was a descendant of the nobleman so celebrated in song. 'Only be punctual, Mr. Tudor ; only be punctual, and I will do anything for you,' Mr. M'Ruen had said, as Charley left the house. Charley, however, never had been punctual, and yet his dealings with Mr. M'Ruen had gone on from that day to this. What absolute money he had ever received into his hand he could not now have said, but it was very little, probably not amounting in all to £50. Yet he had already paid during the two years more than double that sum to this sharp-clawed vulture, and still owed him the amounts of more bills than he could number. Indeed he had kept no account of these double-fanged little documents ; he had signed them whenever told to do so, and had even been so preposterously foolish as to sign them in blank. All he knew was that at the beginning of every quarter Mr. M'Ruen got nearly the half of his little modicum of salary, and that towards the middle of it he usually contrived to obtain an advance of some small, some very small sum, and that when doing so he always put his hand to a fresh bit of paper.

He was beginning to be heartily sick of the bill-discounter. His intimacy with the lord had not yet commenced, nor had he experienced any of the delights which he had expected to accrue to him from the higher tone

of extravagance in which he entered when he made Mr.
M'Ruen's acquaintance. And then the horrid fatal waste
of time which he incurred in pursuit of the few pounds
which he occasionally obtained, filled even his heart with
a sort of despair. Morning after morning he would wait
in that hated room; and then day after day, at two
o'clock, he would attend the usurer's city haunt—and
generally all in vain. The patience of Mr. Snape was
giving way, and the discipline even of the Internal Navigation felt itself outraged.

And now Charley stood once more in that dingy little
front parlour in which he had never yet seen a fire, and
once more Mr. Jabesh M'Ruen shuffled into the room in
his big cravat and dirty loose slippers.

'How d'ye do, Mr. Tudor, how d'ye do? I hope you
have brought a little of this with you;' and Jabesh
opened out his left hand, and tapped the palm of it with
the middle finger of his right, by way of showing that
he expected some money: not that he did expect any,
cormorant that he was; this was not the period of the
quarter in which he ever got money from his customer.

'Indeed I have not, Mr. M'Ruen; but I positively
must get some.'

'Oh—oh—oh—oh—Mr. Tudor—Mr. Tudor! How can
we go on if you are so unpunctual? Now I would do
anything for you if you would only be punctual.'

'Oh! bother about that—you know your own game
well enough.'

'Be punctual, Mr. Tudor, only be punctual, and we
shall be all right—and so you have not got any of this?'
and Jabesh went through the tapping again.

'Not a doit,' said Charley; 'but I shall be up the spout
altogether if you don't do something to help me.'

'But you are so unpunctual, Mr. Tudor.'

'Oh, d—— it; you'll make me sick if you say that again.
What else do you live by but that? But I positively
must have some money from you to-day. If not I am
done for.'

'I don't think I can, Mr. Tudor; not to-day, Mr.
Tudor—some other day, say this day month; that is, if
you'll be punctual.'

'This day month! no, but this very day, Mr. M'Ruen —why, you got £18 from me when I received my last salary, and I have not had a shilling back since.'

'But you are so unpunctual, Mr. Tudor,' and Jabesh twisted his head backwards and forwards within his cravat, rubbing his chin with the interior starch.

'Well, then, I'll tell you what it is,' said Charley, 'I'll be shot if you get a shilling from me on the 1st of October, and you may sell me up as quick as you please. If I don't give a history of your business that will surprise some people, my name isn't Tudor.'

'Ha, ha, ha!' laughed Mr. M'Ruen, with a soft quiet laugh.

'Well, really, Mr. Tudor, I would do more for you than any other young man that I know, if you were only a little more punctual. How much is it you want now?'

'£15—or £10—£10 will do.'

'Ten pounds!' said Jabesh, as though Charley had asked for ten thousand—'ten pounds!—if two or three would do——'

'But two or three won't do.'

'And whose name will you bring?'

'Whose name! why Scatterall's, to be sure.' Now Scatterall was one of the navvies; and from him Mr. M'Ruen had not yet succeeded in extracting one farthing, though he had his name on a volume of Charley's bills.

'Scatterall—I don't like Mr. Scatterall,' said Jabesh; 'he is very dissipated, and the most unpunctual young man I ever met—you really must get some one else, Mr. Tudor; you really must.'

'Oh, that's nonsense—Scatterall is as good as anybody —I couldn't ask any of the other fellows—they are such a low set.'

'But Mr. Scatterall is so unpunctual. There's your cousin, Mr. Alaric Tudor.'

'My cousin Alaric! Oh, nonsense! you don't suppose I'd ask him to do such a thing? You might as well tell me to go to my father.'

'Or that other gentleman you live with; Mr. Norman. He is a most punctual gentleman. Bring me his name, and I'll let you have £10 or £8—I'll let you have £8 at once.'

'I dare say you will, Mr. M'Ruen, or £80; and be only too happy to give it me. But you know that is out of the question. Now I won't wait any longer; just give me an answer to this: if I come to you in the city will you let me have some money to-day? If you won't, why I must go elsewhere—that's all.'

The interview ended by an appointment being made for another meeting to come off at two p.m. that day, at the 'Banks of Jordan,' a public-house in Sweeting's Alley, as well known to Charley as the little front parlour of Mr. M'Ruen's house. 'Bring the bill-stamp with you, Mr. Tudor,' said Jabesh, by way of a last parting word of counsel; 'and let Mr. Scatterall sign it—that is, if it must be Mr. Scatterall; but I wish you would bring your cousin's name.'

'Nonsense!'

'Well, then, bring it signed—but I'll fill it; you young fellows understand nothing of filling in a bill properly.'

And then taking his leave the infernal navvy hurried off, and reached his office in Somerset House at a quarter past eleven o'clock. As he walked along he bought the bit of stamped paper on which his friend Scatterall was to write his name.

When he reached the office he found that a great commotion was going on. Mr. Snape was standing up at his desk, and the first word which greeted Charley's ears was an intimation from that gentleman that Mr. Oldeschole had desired that Mr. Tudor, when he arrived, should be instructed to attend in the board-room.

'Very well,' said Charley, in a tone of great indifference, 'with all my heart; I rather like seeing Oldeschole now and then. But he mustn't keep me long, for I have to meet my grandmother at Islington at two o'clock;' and Charley, having hung up his hat, prepared to walk off to the Secretary's room.

'You'll be good enough to wait a few minutes, Mr. Tudor,' said Snape. 'Another gentleman is with Mr. Oldeschole at present. You will be good enough to sit down and go on with the Kennett and Avon lock entries, till Mr. Oldeschole is ready to see you.'

Charley sat down at his desk opposite to his friend Scatterall. 'I hope, Mr. Snape, you had a pleasant meeting at evening prayers yesterday,' said he, with a tone of extreme interest.

'You had better mind the lock entries at present, Mr. Tudor ; they are greatly in arrear.'

'And the evening meetings are docketed up as close as wax, I suppose. What the deuce is in the wind, Dick ? ' Mr. Scatterall's Christian name was Richard. 'Where 's Corkscrew ? ' Mr. Corkscrew was also a navvy, and was one of those to whom Charley had specially alluded when he spoke of the low set.

'Oh, here 's a regular go,' said Scatterall. 'It 's all up with Corkscrew, I believe.'

'Why, what 's the cheese now ? '

'Oh ! it 's all about some pork chops, which Screwy had for supper last night.' Screwy was a name of love which among his brother navvies was given to Mr. Corkscrew. 'Mr. Snape seems to think they did not agree with him.'

'Pork chops in July ! ' exclaimed Charley.

'Poor Screwy forgot the time of year,' said another navvy ; 'he ought to have called it lamb and grass.'

And then the story was told. On the preceding afternoon, Mr. Corkscrew had been subjected to the dire temptation of a boating party to the Eel-pie Island for the following day, and a dinner thereon. There were to be at the feast no less than four-and-twenty jolly souls, and it was intimated to Mr. Corkscrew that as no soul was esteemed to be more jolly than his own, the party would be considered as very imperfect unless he could join it. Asking for a day's leave Mr. Corkscrew knew to be out of the question ; he had already taken too many without asking. He was therefore driven to take another in the same way, and had to look about for some excuse which might support him in his difficulty. An excuse it must be, not only new, but very valid ; one so strong that it could not be overset ; one so well avouched that it could not be doubted. Accordingly, after mature consideration, he sat down after leaving his office, and wrote the following letter, before he started on an evening cruising expedition with some others of the party to prepare for the next day's festivities.

'Thursday morning,—July, 185-.
'My dear Sir,

'I write from my bed where I am suffering a most tremendous indiggestion, last night I eat a stunning supper off pork chopps and never remembered that pork chopps always does disagree with me, but I was very indiscrete and am now teetotally unable to rise my throbing head from off my pillar, I have took four blu pills and some salts and sena, plenty of that, and shall be the thing to-morrow morning no doubt, just at present I feel just as if I had a mill stone inside my stomac— Pray be so kind as to make it all right with Mr. Oldeschole and believe me to remain,

'Your faithful and obedient servant,
'Verax Corkscrew.

'Thomas Snape, Esq., &c.,
'Internal Navigation Office, Somerset House.'

Having composed this letter of excuse, and not intending to return to his lodgings that evening, he had to make provision for its safely reaching the hands of Mr. Snape in due time on the following morning. This he did, by giving it to the boy who came to clean the lodging-house boots, with sundry injunctions that if he did not deliver it at the office by ten o'clock on the following morning, the sixpence accruing to him would never be paid. Mr. Corkscrew, however, said nothing as to the letter not being delivered before ten the next morning, and as other business took the boy along the Strand the same evening, he saw no reason why he should not then execute his commission. He accordingly did so, and duly delivered the letter into the hands of a servant girl, who was cleaning the passages of the office.

Fortune on this occasion was blind to the merits of Mr. Corkscrew, and threw him over most unmercifully. It so happened that Mr. Snape had been summoned to an evening conference with Mr. Oldeschole and the other pundits of the office, to discuss with them, or rather to hear discussed, some measure which they began to think it necessary to introduce, for amending the discipline of the department.

'We are getting a bad name, whether we deserve it or not,' said Mr. Oldeschole. 'That fellow Hardlines has put us into his blue-book, and now there's an article in the *Times !*'

Just at this moment, a messenger brought in to Mr. Snape the unfortunate letter of which we have given a copy.

'What's that?' said Mr. Oldeschole.

'A note from Mr. Corkscrew, sir,' said Snape.

'He's the worst of the whole lot,' said Mr. Oldeschole.

'He is very bad,' said Snape; 'but I rather think that perhaps, sir, Mr. Tudor is the worst of all.'

'Well, I don't know,' said the Secretary, muttering *sotto voce* to the Under-Secretary, while Mr. Snape read the letter—'Tudor, at any rate, is a gentleman.'

Mr. Snape read the letter, and his face grew very long. There was a sort of sneaking civility about Corkscrew, not prevalent indeed at all times, but which chiefly showed itself when he and Mr. Snape were alone together, which somewhat endeared him to the elder clerk. He would have screened the sinner had he had either the necessary presence of mind or the necessary pluck. But he had neither. He did not know how to account for the letter but by the truth, and he feared to conceal so flagrant a breach of discipline at the moment of the present discussion.

Things at any rate so turned out that Mr. Corkscrew's letter was read in full conclave in the board-room of the office, just as he was describing the excellence of his manœuvre with great glee to four or five other jolly souls at the 'Magpie and Stump.'

At first it was impossible to prevent a fit of laughter, in which even Mr. Snape joined; but very shortly the laughter gave way to the serious considerations to which such an epistle was sure to give rise at such a moment. What if Sir Gregory Hardlines should get hold of it and put it into his blue-book! What if the *Times* should print it and send it over the whole world, accompanied by a few of its most venomous touches, to the eternal disgrace of the Internal Navigation, and probably utter annihilation of Mr. Oldeschole's official career! An example must be made!

Yes, an example must be made. Messengers were sent off scouring the town for Mr. Corkscrew, and about midnight he was found, still true to the 'Magpie and Stump,' but hardly in condition to understand the misfortune which had befallen him. So much as this, however, did make itself manifest to him, that he must by no means join his jolly-souled brethren at the Eel-pie Island, and that he must be at his office punctually at ten o'clock the next morning if he had any intention of saving himself from dismissal. When Charley arrived at his office, Mr. Corkscrew was still with the authorities, and Charley's turn was to come next.

Charley was rather a favourite with Mr. Oldeschole, having been appointed by himself at the instance of Mr. Oldeschole's great friend, Sir Gilbert de Salop; and he was, moreover, the best-looking of the whole lot of navvies; but he was no favourite with Mr. Snape.

'Poor Screwy—it will be all up with him,' said Charley. 'He might just as well have gone on with his party and had his fun out.'

'It will, I imagine, be necessary to make more than one example, Mr. Tudor,' said Mr. Snape, with a voice of utmost severity.

'A-a-a-men,' said Charley. 'If everything else fails, I think I'll go into the green line. You couldn't give me a helping hand, could you, Mr. Snape?' There was a rumour afloat in the office that Mr. Snape's wife held some little interest in a small greengrocer's establishment.

'Mr. Tudor to attend in the board-room, immediately,' said a fat messenger, who opened the door wide with a start, and then stood with it in his hand while he delivered the message.

'All right,' said Charley; 'I'll tumble up and be with them in ten seconds;' and then collecting together a large bundle of the arrears of the Kennett and Avon lock

entries, being just as much as he could carry, he took the
disordered papers and placed them on Mr. Snape's desk,
exactly over the paper on which he was writing, and
immediately under his nose.

'Mr. Tudor—Mr. Tudor!' said Snape.

'As I am to tear myself away from you, Mr. Snape,
it is better that I should hand over these valuable documents to your safe keeping. There they are, Mr. Snape;
pray see that you have got them all;' and so saying,
he left the room to attend to the high behests of Mr.
Oldeschole.

As he went along the passages he met Verax Corkscrew
returning from his interview. 'Well, Screwy,' said he,
'and how fares it with you? Pork chops are bad things
in summer, ain't they?'

'It's all U-P,' said Corkscrew, almost crying. 'I'm to
go down to the bottom, and I'm to stay at the office till
seven o'clock every day for a month; and old Foolscap
says he'll ship me the next time I'm absent half-an-hour
without leave.'

'Oh! is that all?' said Charley. 'If that's all you
get for pork chops and senna, I'm all right. I shouldn't
wonder if I did not get promoted;' and so he went in to
his interview.

What was the nature of the advice given him, what
amount of caution he was called on to endure, need not
here be exactly specified. We all know with how light
a rod a father chastises the son he loves, let Solomon have
given what counsel he may to the contrary. Charley, in
spite of his manifold sins, was a favourite, and he came
forth from the board-room an unscathed man. In fact, he
had been promoted as he had surmised, seeing that Corkscrew who had been his senior was now his junior. He
came forth unscathed, and walking with an easy air into
his room, put his hat on his head and told his brother
clerks that he should be there to-morrow morning at ten,
or at any rate soon after.

'And where are you going now, Mr. Tudor?' said
Snape.

'To meet my grandmother at Islington, if you please,
sir,' said Charley. 'I have permission from Mr. Olde-

schole to attend upon her for the rest of the day—perhaps you would like to ask him.' And so saying he went off to his appointment with Mr. M'Ruen at the 'Banks of Jordan.'

CHAPTER XIX

A DAY WITH ONE OF THE NAVVIES.—AFTERNOON

THE 'Banks of Jordan' was a public-house in the city, which from its appearance did not seem to do a very thriving trade; but as it was carried on from year to year in the same dull, monotonous, dead-alive sort of fashion, it must be surmised that some one found an interest in keeping it open.

Charley, when he entered the door punctually at two o'clock, saw that it was as usual nearly deserted. One long, lanky, middle-aged man, seedy as to his outward vestments, and melancholy in countenance, sat at one of the tables. But he was doing very little good for the establishment: he had no refreshment of any kind before him, and was intent only on a dingy pocket-book in which he was making entries with a pencil.

You enter the 'Banks of Jordan' by two folding doors in a corner of a very narrow alley behind the Exchange. As you go in, you observe on your left a little glass partition, something like a large cage, inside which, in a bar, are four or five untempting-looking bottles; and also inside the cage, on a chair, is to be seen a quiet-looking female, who is invariably engaged in the manufacture of some white article of inward clothing. Anything less like the flashy-dressed bar-maidens of the western gin palaces it would be difficult to imagine. To this encaged sempstress no one ever speaks unless it be to give a rare order for a mutton chop or pint of stout. And even for this she hardly stays her sewing for a moment, but touches a small bell, and the ancient waiter, who never shows himself but when called for, and who is the only other inhabitant of the place ever visible, receives the order from her through an open pane in the cage as quietly as she received it from her customer.

The floor of the single square room of the establishment is sanded, and the tables are ranged round the walls, each table being fixed to the floor, and placed within wooden partitions, by which the occupier is screened from any inquiring eyes on either side.

Such was Mr. Jabesh M'Ruen's house-of-call in the city, and of many a mutton chop and many a pint of stout had Charley partaken there while waiting for the man of money. To him it seemed to be inexcusable to sit down in a public inn and call for nothing; he perceived, however, that the large majority of the frequenters of the 'Banks of Jordan' so conducted themselves.

He was sufficiently accustomed to the place to know how to give his orders without troubling that diligent barmaid, and had done so about ten minutes when Jabesh, more punctual than usual, entered the place. This Charley regarded as a promising sign of forthcoming cash. It very frequently happened that he waited there an hour, and that after all Jabesh would not come; and then the morning visit to Mecklenburg Square had to be made again; and so poor Charley's time, or rather the time of his poor office, was cut up, wasted, and destroyed.

'A mutton chop!' said Mr. M'Ruen, looking at Charley's banquet. 'A very nice thing indeed in the middle of the day. I don't mind if I have one myself,' and so Charley had to order another chop and more stout.

'They have very nice sherry here, excellent sherry,' said M'Ruen. 'The best, I think, in the city—that's why I come here.'

'Upon my honour, Mr. M'Ruen, I shan't have money to pay for it until I get some from you,' said Charley, as he called for a pint of sherry.

'Never mind, John, never mind the sherry to-day,' said M'Ruen. 'Mr. Tudor is very kind, but I'll take beer;' and the little man gave a laugh and twisted his head, and ate his chop and drank his stout, as though he found that both were very good indeed. When he had finished, Charley paid the bill and discovered that he was left with ninepence in his pocket.

And then he produced the bill stamp. 'Waiter,' said he, 'pen and ink,' and the waiter brought pen and ink.

'Not to-day,' said Jabesh, wiping his mouth with the table-cloth. 'Not to-day, Mr. Tudor—I really haven't time to go into it to-day—and I haven't brought the other bills with me; I quite forgot to bring the other bills with me, and I can do nothing without them,' and Mr. M'Ruen got up to go.

But this was too much for Charley. He had often before bought bill stamps in vain, and in vain had paid for mutton chops and beer for Mr. M'Ruen's dinner; but he had never before, when doing so, been so hard pushed for money as he was now. He was determined to make a great attempt to gain his object.

'Nonsense,' said he, getting up and standing so as to prevent M'Ruen from leaving the box; 'that's d—— nonsense.'

'Oh! don't swear,' said M'Ruen—'pray don't take God's name in vain; I don't like it.'

'I shall swear, and to some purpose too, if that's your game. Now look here——'

'Let me get up, and we'll talk of it as we go to the bank—you are so unpunctual, you know.'

'D— your punctuality.'

'Oh! don't swear, Mr. Tudor.'

'Look here—if you don't let me have this money to-day, by all that is holy I will never pay you a farthing again—not one farthing; I'll go into the court, and you may get your money as you can.'

'But, Mr. Tudor, let me get up, and we'll talk about it in the street, as we go along.'

'There's the stamp,' said Charley. 'Fill it up, and then I'll go with you to the bank.'

M'Ruen took the bit of paper, and twisted it over and over again in his hand, considering the while whether he had yet squeezed out of the young man all that could be squeezed with safety, or whether by an additional turn, by giving him another small advancement, he might yet get something more. He knew that Tudor was in a very bad state, that he was tottering on the outside edge of the precipice; but he also knew that he had friends. Would

his friends when they came forward to assist their young
Pickle out of the mire, would they pay such bills as these
or would they leave poor Jabesh to get his remedy at
law ? That was the question which Mr. M'Ruen had to
ask and to answer. He was not one of those noble vultures
who fly at large game, and who are willing to run considerable risk in pursuit of their prey. Mr. M'Ruen
avoided courts of law as much as he could, and preferred
a small safe trade ; one in which the fall of a single customer
could never be ruinous to him ; in which he need run no
risk of being transported for forgery, incarcerated for
perjury, or even, if possibly it might be avoided, gibbeted
by some lawyer or judge for his malpractices.

'But you are so unpunctual,' he said, having at last
made up his mind that he had made a very good thing of
Charley, and that probably he might go a *little* further
without much danger. 'I wish to oblige you, Mr. Tudor ;
but pray do be punctual ; ' and so saying he slowly spread
the little document before him, across which Scatterall had
already scrawled his name, and slowly began to write in
the date. Slowly, with his head low down over the table,
and continually twisting it inside his cravat, he filled up
the paper, and then looking at it with the air of a con-
noisseur in such matters, he gave it to Charley to
sign.

'But you haven't put in the amount,' said Charley.

Mr. M'Ruen twisted his head and laughed. He delighted in playing with his game as a fisherman does with
a salmon. 'Well—no—I haven't put in the amount yet.
Do you sign it, and I'll do that at once.'

'I'll do it,' said Charley ; 'I'll say £15, and you'll give
me £10 on that.'

'No, no, no !' said Jabesh, covering the paper over
with his hands ; 'you young men know nothing of filling
bills ; just sign it, Mr. Tudor, and I'll do the rest.' And
so Charley signed it, and then M'Ruen, again taking the
pen, wrote in 'fifteen pounds' as the recognized amount
of the value of the document. He also took out his
pocket-book and filled a cheque, but he was very careful
that Charley should not see the amount there written.
'And now,' said he, 'we will go to the bank.'

As they made their way to the house in Lombard Street which Mr. M'Ruen honoured by his account, Charley insisted on knowing how much he was to have for the bill. Jabesh suggested £3 10s.; Charley swore he would take nothing less than £8; but by the time they had arrived at the bank, it had been settled that £5 was to be paid in cash, and that Charley was to have the three Seasons for the balance whenever he chose to send for them. When Charley, as he did at first, positively refused to accede to these terms, Mr. M'Ruen tendered him back the bill, and reminded him with a plaintive voice that he was so unpunctual, so extremely unpunctual.

Having reached the bank, which the money-lender insisted on Charley entering with him, Mr. M'Ruen gave the cheque across the counter, and wrote on the back of it the form in which he would take the money, whereupon a note and five sovereigns were handed to him. The cheque was for £15, and was payable to C. Tudor, Esq., so that proof might be forthcoming at a future time, if necessary, that he had given to his customer full value for the bill. Then in the outer hall of the bank, unseen by the clerks, he put, one after another, slowly and unwillingly, four sovereigns into Charley's hand.

'The other—where's the other?' said Charley.

Jabesh smiled sweetly and twisted his head.

'Come, give me the other,' said Charley roughly.

'Four is quite enough, quite enough for what you want; and remember my time, Mr. Tudor; you should remember my time.'

'Give me the other sovereign,' said Charley, taking hold of the front of his coat.

'Well, well, you shall have ten shillings; but I want the rest for a purpose.'

'Give me the sovereign,' said Charley, 'or I'll drag you in before them all in the bank and expose you; give me the other sovereign, I say.'

'Ha, ha, ha!' laughed Mr. M'Ruen; 'I thought you liked a joke, Mr. Tudor. Well, here it is. And now do be punctual, pray do be punctual, and I'll do anything I can for you.'

And then they parted, Charley going westward towards

his own haunts, and M'Ruen following his daily pursuits
in the city.

Charley had engaged to pull up to Avis's at Putney
with Harry Norman, to dine there, take a country walk,
and row back in the cool of the evening; and he had
promised to call at the Weights and Measures with that
object punctually at five.

'You can get away in time for that, I suppose,' said
Harry.

'Well, I'll try and manage it,' said Charley, laughing.

Nothing could be kinder, nay, more affectionate, than
Norman had been to his fellow-lodger during the last year
and a half. It seemed as though he had transferred to
Alaric's cousin all the friendship which he had once felt
for Alaric; and the deeper were Charley's sins of idleness
and extravagance, the wider grew Norman's forgiveness,
and the more sincere his efforts to befriend him. As one
result of this, Charley was already deep in his debt. Not
that Norman had lent him money, or even paid bills for
him; but the lodgings in which they lived had been taken
by Norman, and when the end of the quarter came he
punctually paid his landlady.

Charley had once, a few weeks before the period of
which we are now writing, told Norman that he had no
money to pay his long arrear, and that he would leave the
lodgings and shift for himself as best he could. He had
said the same thing to Mrs. Richards, the landlady, and
had gone so far as to pack up all his clothes; but his back
was no sooner turned than Mrs. Richards, under Norman's
orders, unpacked them all, and hid away the portmanteau.
It was well for him that this was done. He had bespoken
for himself a bedroom at the public-house in Norfolk
Street, and had he once taken up his residence there he
would have been ruined for ever.

He was still living with Norman, and ever increasing
his debt. In his misery at this state of affairs, he had
talked over with Harry all manner of schemes for increasing his income, but he had never told him a word
about Mr. M'Ruen. Why his salary, which was now £150
per annum, should not be able to support him, Norman
never asked. Charley the while was very miserable, and

the more miserable he was, the less he found himself able
to rescue himself from his dissipation. What moments of
ease he had were nearly all spent in Norfolk Street; and
such being the case how could he abstain from going there?

'Well, Charley, and how do "Crinoline and Macassar"
go on?' said Norman, as they sauntered away together
up the towing-path above Putney. Now there were those
who had found out that Charley Tudor, in spite of his
wretched, idle, vagabond mode of life, was no fool; indeed,
that there was that talent within him which, if turned to
good account, might perhaps redeem him from ruin and
set him on his legs again; at least so thought some of
his friends, among whom Mrs. Woodward was the most
prominent. She insisted that if he would make use of his
genius he might employ his spare time to great profit by
writing for magazines or periodicals; and, inspirited by
so flattering a proposition, Charley had got himself introduced to the editor of a newly-projected publication.
At his instance he was to write a tale for approval, and
'Crinoline and Macassar' was the name selected for his
first attempt.

The affair had been fully talked over at Hampton, and
it had been arranged that the young author should submit
his story, when completed, to the friendly criticism of
the party assembled at Surbiton Cottage, before he sent
it to the editor. He had undertaken to have 'Crinoline
and Macassar' ready for perusal on the next Saturday,
and in spite of Mr. M'Ruen and Norah Geraghty, he had
really been at work.

'Will it be finished by Saturday, Charley?' said
Norman.

'Yes—at least I hope so; but if that's not done, I
have another all complete.'

'Another! and what is that called?'

'Oh, that's a very short one,' said Charley, modestly.

'But, short as it is, it must have a name, I suppose.
What's the name of the short one?'

'Why, the name is long enough; it's the longest part
about it. The editor gave me the name, you know, and
then I had to write the story. It's to be called "Sir
Anthony Allan-a-dale and the Baron of Ballyporeen."'

'Oh! two rival knights in love with the same lady, of course,' and Harry gave a gentle sigh as he thought of his own still unhealed grief. 'The scene is laid in Ireland, I presume?'

'No, not in Ireland; at least not exactly. I don't think the scene is laid anywhere in particular; it's up in a mountain, near a castle. There isn't any lady in it—at least, not alive.'

'Heavens, Charley! I hope you are not dealing with dead women.'

'No—that is, I have to bring them to life again. I'll tell you how it is. In the first paragraph, Sir Anthony Allan-a-dale is lying dead, and the Baron of Ballyporeen is standing over him with a bloody sword. You must always begin with an incident now, and then hark back for your explanation and description; that's what the editor says is the great secret of the present day, and where we beat all the old fellows that wrote twenty years ago.'

'Oh!—yes—I see. They used to begin at the beginning; that was very humdrum.'

'A devilish bore, you know, for a fellow who takes up a novel because he's dull. Of course he wants his fun at once. If you begin with a long history of who's who and all that, why he won't read three pages; but if you touch him up with a startling incident or two at the first go off, then give him a chapter of horrors, then another of fun, then a little love or a little slang, or something of that sort, why, you know, about the end of the first volume, you may describe as much as you like, and tell everything about everybody's father and mother for just as many pages as you want to fill. At least that's what the editor says.'

'*Meleager ab ovo* may be introduced with safety when you get as far as that,' suggested Norman.

'Yes, you may bring him in too, if you like,' said Charley, who was somewhat oblivious of his classicalities. 'Well, Sir Anthony is lying dead and the Baron is standing over him, when out come Sir Anthony's retainers——'

'Out—out of what?'

'Out of the castle: that's all explained afterwards. Out come the retainers, and pitch into the Baron till they make mincemeat of him.'

'They don't kill him, too?'

'Don't they though? I rather think they do, and no mistake.'

'And so both your heroes are dead in the first chapter.'

'First chapter! why that's only the second paragraph. I'm only to be allowed ten paragraphs for each number, and I am expected to have an incident for every other paragraph for the first four days.'

'That's twenty incidents.'

'Yes—it's a great bother finding so many.—I'm obliged to make the retainers come by all manner of accidents; and I should never have finished the job if I hadn't thought of setting the castle on fire. "And now forked tongues of liquid fire, and greedy lambent flames burst forth from every window of the devoted edifice. The devouring element——." That's the best passage in the whole affair.'

'This is for the *Daily Delight*, isn't it?'

'Yes, for the *Daily Delight*. It is to begin on the 1st of September with the partridges. We expect a most tremendous sale. It will be the first halfpenny publication in the market, and as the retailers will get them for sixpence a score—twenty-four to the score—they'll go off like wildfire.'

'Well, Charley, and what do you do with the dead bodies of your two heroes?'

'Of course I needn't tell you that it was not the Baron who killed Sir Anthony at all.'

'Oh! wasn't it? O dear—that was a dreadful mistake on the part of the retainers.'

'But as natural as life. You see these two grandees were next-door neighbours, and there had been a feud between the families for seven centuries—a sort of Capulet and Montague affair. One Adelgitha, the daughter of the Thane of Allan-a-dale—there were Thanes in those days, you know—was betrothed to the eldest son of Sir Waldemar de Ballyporeen. This gives me an opportunity of bringing in a succinct little account of the Conquest, which will be beneficial to the lower classes. The editor peremptorily insists upon that kind of thing.'

'*Omne tulit punctum*,' said Norman.

'Yes, I dare say,' said Charley, who was now too intent on his own new profession to attend much to his friend's quotation. 'Well, where was I?—Oh! the eldest son of Sir Waldemar went off with another lady and so the feud began. There is a very pretty scene between Adelgitha and her lady's-maid.'

'What, seven centuries before the story begins?'

'Why not? The editor says that the unities are altogether thrown over now, and that they are regular bosh—our game is to stick in a good bit whenever we can get it—I got to be so fond of Adelgitha that I rather think she's the heroine.'

'But doesn't that take off the interest from your dead grandees?'

'Not a bit; I take it chapter and chapter about. Well, you see, the retainers had no sooner made mincemeat of the Baron—a very elegant young man was the Baron, just returned from the Continent, where he had learnt to throw aside all prejudices about family feuds and everything else, and he had just come over in a friendly way, to say as much to Sir Anthony, when, as he crossed the drawbridge, he stumbled over the corpse of his ancient enemy—well, the retainers had no sooner made mincemeat of him, than they perceived that Sir Anthony was lying with an open bottle in his hand, and that he had taken poison.'

'Having committed suicide?' asked Norman.

'No, not at all. The editor says that we must always have a slap at some of the iniquities of the times. He gave me three or four to choose from; there was the adulteration of food, and the want of education for the poor, and street music, and the miscellaneous sale of poisons.'

'And so you chose poisons and killed the knight?'

'Exactly; at least I didn't kill him, for he comes all right again after a bit. He had gone out to get something to do him good after a hard night, a Seidlitz powder, or something of that sort, and an apothecary's apprentice had given him prussic acid in mistake.'

'And how is it possible he should have come to life after taking prussic acid ? '

'Why, there I have a double rap at the trade. The prussic acid is so bad of its kind, that it only puts him into a kind of torpor for a week. Then we have the trial of the apothecary's boy ; that is an excellent episode, and gives me a grand hit at the absurdity of our criminal code.'

'Why, Charley, it seems to me that you are hitting at everything.'

'Oh ! ah ! right and left, that 's the game for us authors. The press is the only *censor morum* going now— and who so fit ? Set a thief to catch a thief, you know. Well, I have my hit at the criminal code, and then Sir Anthony comes out of his torpor.'

'But how did it come to pass that the Baron's sword was all bloody ? '

'Ah, there was the difficulty ; I saw that at once. It was necessary to bring in something to be killed, you know. I thought of a stray tiger out of Wombwell's menagerie ; but the editor says that we must not trespass against the probabilities ; so I have introduced a big dog. The Baron had come across a big dog, and seeing that the brute had a wooden log tied to his throat, thought he must be mad, and so he killed him.'

'And what 's the end of it, Charley ? '

'Why, the end is rather melancholy. Sir Anthony reforms, leaves off drinking, and takes to going to church everyday. He becomes a Puseyite, puts up a memorial window to the Baron, and reads the Tracts. At last he goes over to the Pope, walks about in nasty dirty clothes all full of vermin, and gives over his estate to Cardinal Wiseman. Then there are the retainers ; they all come to grief, some one way and some another. I do that for the sake of the Nemesis.'

'I would not have condescended to notice them, I think,' said Norman.

'Oh ! I must ; there must be a Nemesis. The editor specially insists on a Nemesis.'

The conclusion of Charley's novel brought them back to the boat. Norman, when he started, had intended to employ the evening in giving good counsel to his friend, and in endeavouring to arrange some scheme by which he might rescue the brand from the burning; but he had not the heart to be severe and sententious while Charley was full of his fun. It was so much pleasanter to talk to him on the easy terms of equal friendship than turn Mentor and preach a sermon.

'Well, Charley,' said he, as they were walking up from the boat wharf—Norman to his club, and Charley towards his lodgings—from which route, however, he meant to deviate as soon as ever he might be left alone— 'well, Charley, I wish you success with all my heart; I wish you could do something—I won't say to keep you out of mischief.'

'I wish I could, Harry,' said Charley, thoroughly abashed; 'I wish I could—indeed I wish I could—but it is so hard to go right when one has begun to go wrong.'

'It is hard; I know it is.'

'But you never can know how hard, Harry, for you have never tried,' and then they went on walking for a while in silence, side by side.

'You don't know the sort of place that office of mine is,' continued Charley. 'You don't know the sort of fellows the men are. I hate the place; I hate the men I live with. It is all so dirty, so disreputable, so false. I cannot conceive that any fellow put in there as young as I was should ever do well afterwards.'

'But at any rate you might try your best, Charley.'

'Yes, I might do that still; and I know I don't; and where should I have been now, if it hadn't been for you?'

'Never mind about that; I sometimes think we might have done more for each other if we had been more together. But remember the motto you said you'd choose, Charley—Excelsior! We can none of us mount the hill without hard labour. Remember that word, Charley— Excelsior! Remember it now—now, to-night; remember how you dream of higher things, and begin to think of them in your waking moments also;' and so they parted.

CHAPTER XX

A DAY WITH ONE OF THE NAVVIES.—EVENING

'EXCELSIOR!' said Charley to himself, as he walked on a few steps towards his lodgings, having left Norman at the door of his club. 'Remember it now—now, to-night.'

Yes—now is the time to remember it, if it is ever to be remembered to any advantage. He went on with stoic resolution to the end of the street, determined to press home and put the last touch to 'Crinoline and Macassar;' but as he went he thought of his interview with Mr. M'Ruen and of the five sovereigns still in his pocket, and altered his course.

Charley had not been so resolute with the usurer, so determined to get £5 from him on this special day, without a special object in view. His credit was at stake in a more than ordinary manner; he had about a week since borrowed money from the woman who kept the public-house in Norfolk Street, and having borrowed it for a week only, felt that this was a debt of honour which it was incumbent on him to pay. Therefore, when he had walked the length of one street on his road towards his lodgings, he retraced his steps and made his way back to his old haunts.

The house which he frequented was hardly more like a modern London gin-palace than was that other house in the city which Mr. M'Ruen honoured with his custom. It was one of those small tranquil shrines of Bacchus in which the god is worshipped perhaps with as constant a devotion, though with less noisy demonstrations of zeal than in his larger and more public temples. None absolutely of the lower orders were encouraged to come thither for oblivion. It had about it nothing inviting to the general eye. No gas illuminations proclaimed its midnight grandeur. No huge folding doors, one set here and another there, gave ingress and egress to a wretched

crowd of poverty-stricken midnight revellers. No reiterated assertions in gaudy letters, each a foot long, as to
the peculiar merits of the old tom or Hodge's cream of
the valley, seduced the thirsty traveller. The panelling
over the window bore the simple announcement, in modest
letters, of the name of the landlady, Mrs. Davis; and
the same name appeared with equal modesty on the one
gas lamp opposite the door.

Mrs. Davis was a widow, and her customers were
chiefly people who knew her and frequented her house
regularly. Lawyers' clerks, who were either unmarried,
or whose married homes were perhaps not so comfortable
as the widow's front parlour; tradesmen, not of the best
sort, glad to get away from the noise of their children;
young men who had begun the cares of life in ambiguous
positions, just on the confines of respectability, and who,
finding themselves too weak in flesh to cling on to the
round of the ladder above them, were sinking from year
to year to lower steps, and depths even below the level of
Mrs. Davis's public-house. To these might be added some
few of a somewhat higher rank in life, though perhaps
of a lower rank of respectability; young men who, like
Charley Tudor and his comrades, liked their ease and
self-indulgence, and were too indifferent as to the class
of companions against whom they might rub their
shoulders while seeking it.

The 'Cat and Whistle,' for such was the name of
Mrs. Davis's establishment, had been a house of call for
the young men of the Internal Navigation long before
Charley's time. What first gave rise to the connexion
it is not now easy to say; but Charley had found it,
and had fostered it into a close alliance, which greatly
exceeded any amount of intimacy which existed previously
to his day.

It must not be presumed that he, in an ordinary way,
took his place among the lawyers' clerks, and general run
of customers in the front parlour; occasionally he condescended to preside there over the quiet revels, to sing
a song for the guests, which was sure to be applauded
to the echo, and to engage in a little skirmish of politics
with a retired lamp-maker and a silversmith's foreman

from the Strand, who always called him ' Sir,' and received
what he said with the greatest respect ; but, as a rule, he
quaffed his Falernian in a little secluded parlour behind
the bar, in which sat the widow Davis, auditing her
accounts in the morning, and giving out orders in the
evening to Norah Geraghty, her barmaid, and to an
attendant sylph, who ministered to the front parlour,
taking in goes of gin and screws of tobacco, and bringing
out the price thereof with praiseworthy punctuality.

Latterly, indeed, Charley had utterly deserted the front
parlour ; for there had come there a pestilent fellow,
highly connected with the Press, as the lamp-maker
declared, but employed as an assistant shorthand-writer
somewhere about the Houses of Parliament, according to
the silversmith, who greatly interfered with our navvy's
authority. He would not at all allow that what Charley
said was law, entertained fearfully democratic principles
of his own, and was not at all the gentleman. So Charley
drew himself up, declined to converse any further on
politics with a man who seemed to know more about
them than himself, and confined himself exclusively to the
inner room.

On arriving at this elysium, on the night in question,
he found Mrs. Davis usefully engaged in darning a stock-
ing, while Scatterall sat opposite with a cigar in his mouth,
his hat over his nose, and a glass of gin and water before
him.

' I began to think you weren't coming,' said Scatterall,
' and I was getting so deuced dull that I was positively
thinking of going home.'

' That 's very civil of you, Mr. Scatterall,' said the widow.

' Well, you've been sitting there for the last half-hour
without saying a word to me ; and it is dull. Looking at
a woman mending stockings is dull, ain't it, Charley ? '

' That depends,' said Charley, ' partly on whom the
woman may be, and partly on whom the man may be.
Where 's Norah, Mrs. Davis ? '

' She 's not very well to-night ; she has got a headache ;
there ain't many of them here to-night, so she 's lying
down.'

' A little seedy, I suppose,' said Scatterall.

Charley felt rather angry with his friend for applying such an epithet to his lady-love; however, he did not resent it, but sitting down, lighted his pipe and sipped his gin and water.

And so they sat for the next quarter of an hour, saying very little to each other. What was the nature of the attraction which induced two such men as Charley Tudor and Dick Scatterall to give Mrs. Davis the benefit of their society, while she was mending her stockings, it might be difficult to explain. They could have smoked in their own rooms as well, and have drunk gin and water there, if they had any real predilection for that mixture. Mrs. Davis was neither young nor beautiful, nor more than ordinarily witty. Charley, it is true, had an allurement to entice him thither, but this could not be said of Scatterall, to whom the lovely Norah was never more than decently civil. Had they been desired, in their own paternal halls, to sit and see their mother's housekeeper darn the family stockings, they would, probably, both of them have rebelled, even though the supply of tobacco and gin and water should be gratuitous and unlimited.

It must be presumed that the only charm of the pursuit was in its acknowledged impropriety. They both understood that there was something fast in frequenting Mrs. Davis's inner parlour, something slow in remaining at home; and so they both sat there, and Mrs. Davis went on with her darning-needle, nothing abashed.

'Well, I think I shall go,' said Scatterall, shaking off the last ash from the end of his third cigar.

'Do,' said Charley; 'you should be careful, you know; late hours will hurt your complexion.'

'It's so deuced dull,' said Scatterall.

'Why don't you go into the parlour, and have a chat with the gentlemen?' suggested Mrs. Davis; 'there's Mr. Peppermint there now, lecturing about the war; upon my word he talks very well.'

'He's so deuced low,' said Scatterall.

'He's a bumptious noisy blackguard too,' said Charley; 'he doesn't know how to speak to a gentleman, when he meets one.'

Scatterall gave a great yawn. 'I suppose you're not going, Charley?' said he.

'Oh yes, I am,' said Charley, 'in about two hours.'

'Two hours! well, good night, old fellow, for I'm off. Three cigars, Mrs. Davis, and two goes of gin and water, the last cold.' Then, having made this little commercial communication to the landlady, he gave another yawn, and took himself away. Mrs. Davis opened her little book, jotted down the items, and then, having folded up her stockings, and put them into a basket, prepared herself for conversation.

But, though Mrs. Davis prepared herself for conversation, she did not immediately commence it. Having something special to say, she probably thought that she might improve her opportunity of saying it by allowing Charley to begin. She got up and pottered about the room, went to a cupboard, and wiped a couple of glasses, and then out into the bar and arranged the jugs and pots. This done, she returned to the little room, and again sat herself down in her chair.

'Here's your five pounds, Mrs. Davis,' said Charley; 'I wish you knew the trouble I have had to get it for you.'

To give Mrs. Davis her due, this was not the subject on which she was anxious to speak. She would have been at present well inclined that Charley should remain her debtor. 'Indeed, Mr. Tudor, I am very sorry you should have taken any trouble on such a trifle. If you're short of money, it will do for me just as well in October.'

Charley looked at the sovereigns, and bethought himself how very short of cash he was. Then he thought of the fight he had had to get them, in order that he might pay the money which he had felt so ashamed of having borrowed, and he determined to resist the temptation.

'Did you ever know me flush of cash? You had better take them while you can get them,' and as he pushed them across the table with his stick, he remembered that all he had left was ninepence.

'I don't want the money at present, Mr. Tudor,' said the widow. 'We're such old friends that there ought not to be a word between us about such a trifle—now don't leave yourself bare ; take what you want and settle with me at quarter-day.'

'Well, I'll take a sovereign,' said he, 'for to tell you the truth, I have only the ghost of a shilling in my pocket.' And so it was settled ; Mrs. Davis reluctantly pocketed four of Mr. M'Ruen's sovereigns, and Charley kept in his own possession the fifth, as to which he had had so hard a combat in the lobby of the bank.

He then sat silent for a while and smoked, and Mrs. Davis again waited for him to begin the subject on which she wished to speak. 'And what's the matter with Norah all this time ? ' he said at last.

'What's the matter with her ? ' repeated Mrs. Davis. 'Well, I think you might know what's the matter with her. You don't suppose she's made of stone, do you ? '

Charley saw that he was in for it. It was in vain that Norman's last word was still ringing in his ears. 'Excelsior !' What had he to do with 'Excelsior ?' What miserable reptile on God's earth was more prone to crawl downwards than he had shown himself to be ? And then again a vision floated across his mind's eye of a young sweet angel face with large bright eyes, with soft delicate skin, and all the exquisite charms of gentle birth and gentle nurture. A single soft touch seemed to press his arm, a touch that he had so often felt, and had never felt without acknowledging to himself that there was something in it almost divine. All this passed rapidly through his mind, as he was preparing to answer Mrs. Davis's question touching Norah Geraghty.

'You don't think she's made of stone, do you ? ' said the widow, repeating her words.

'Indeed I don't think she's made of anything but what's suitable to a very nice young woman,' said Charley.

'A nice young woman ! Is that all you can say for her ? I call her a very fine girl.' Miss Golightly's friends could not say anything more, even for that young lady. 'I don't know where you'll pick up a handsomer, or a better-conducted one either, for the matter of that.'

'Indeed she is,' said Charley.

'Oh ! for the matter of that, no one knows it better than yourself, Mr. Tudor ; and she's as well able to

keep a man's house over his head as some others that
take a deal of pride in themselves.'

'I'm quite sure of it,' said Charley.

'Well, the long and the short of it is this, Mr. Tudor.'
And as she spoke the widow got a little red in the face:
she had, as Charley thought, an unpleasant look of resolution about her— a roundness about her mouth, and a sort
of fierceness in her eyes.   'The long and the short of it
is this, Mr. Tudor, what do you mean to do about the
girl ?'

'Do about her ?' said Charley, almost bewildered in
his misery.

'Yes, do about her.   Do you mean to make her your
wife ?   That's plain English.   Because I'll tell you what:
I'll not see her put upon any longer.   It must be one
thing or the other; and that at once.   And if you've
a grain of honour in you, Mr. Tudor—and I think you
are honourable—you won't back from your word with
the girl now.'

'Back from my word ?' said Charley.

'Yes, back from your word,' said Mrs. Davis, the
flood-gates of whose eloquence were now fairly opened.
'I'm sure you're too much of the gentleman to deny
your own words, and them repeated more than once in
my presence——Cheroots—yes, are there none there,
child ?—Oh, they are in the cupboard.'   These last words
were not part of her address to Charley, but were given
in reply to a requisition from the attendant nymph outside.   'You're too much of a gentleman to do that,
I know.   And so, as I'm her natural friend—and indeed
she's my cousin, not that far off—I think it's right that
we should all understand one another.'

'Oh, quite right,' said Charley.

'You can't expect that she should go and sacrifice herself for you, you know,' said Mrs. Davis, who now that
she had begun hardly knew how to stop herself.   'A girl's
time is her money.   She's at her best now, and a girl
like her must make her hay while the sun shines.   She
can't go on fal-lalling with you, and then nothing to come
of it.   You mustn't suppose she's to lose her market
that way.'

'God knows I should be sorry to injure her, Mrs. Davis.'

'I believe you would, because I take you for an honourable gentleman as will be as good as your word. Now, there's Peppermint there.'

'What! that fellow in the parlour?'

'And an honourable gentleman he is. Not that I mean to compare him to you, Mr. Tudor, nor yet doesn't Norah; not by no means. But there he is. Well, he comes with the most honourablest proposals, and will make her Mrs. Peppermint to-morrow, if so be that she'll have it.'

'You don't mean to say that there has been anything between them?' said Charley, who in spite of the intense desire which he had felt a few minutes since to get the lovely Norah altogether off his hands, now felt an acute pang of jealousy. 'You don't mean to say that there has been anything between them?'

'Nothing as you have any right to object to, Mr. Tudor. You may be sure I wouldn't allow of that, nor yet wouldn't Norah demean herself to it.'

'Then how did she get talking to him?'

'She didn't get talking to him. But he has eyes in his head, and you don't suppose but what he can see with them. If a girl is in the public line, of course any man is free to speak to her. If you don't like it, it is for you to take her out of it. Not but what, for a girl that is in the public line, Norah Geraghty keeps herself to herself as much as any girl you ever set eyes on.'

'What the d— has she to do with this fellow then?'

'Why, he's a widower, and has three young children; and he's looking out for a mother for them; and he thinks Norah will suit. There, now you have the truth, and the whole truth.'

'D— his impudence!' said Charley.

'Well, I don't see that there's any impudence. He has a house of his own and the means to keep it. Now I'll tell you what it is. Norah can't abide him——'

Charley looked a little better satisfied when he heard this declaration.

'Norah can't abide the sight of him; nor won't of any

man as long as you are hanging after her. She 's as true as steel, and proud you ought to be of her.' Proud, thought Charley, as he again muttered to himself, ' Excelsior ! '—' But, Mr. Tudor, I won't see her put upon ; that 's the long and the short of it. If you like to take her, there she is. I don't say she 's just your equal as to breeding, though she 's come of decent people too ; but she 's good as gold. She'll make a shilling go as far as any young woman I know ; and if £100 or £150 are wanting for furniture or the like of that, why, I've that regard for her, that that shan't stand in the way. Now, Mr. Tudor, I've spoke honest ; and if you're the gentleman as I takes you to be, you'll do the same.'

To do Mrs. Davis justice, it must be acknowledged that in her way she had spoken honestly. Of course she knew that such a marriage would be a dreadful misalliance for young Tudor ; of course she knew that all his friends would be heart-broken when they heard of it. But what had she to do with his friends ? Her sympathies, her good wishes, were for her friend. Had Norah fallen a victim to Charley's admiration, and then been cast off to eat the bitterest bread to which any human being is ever doomed, what then would Charley's friends have cared for her ? There was a fair fight between them. If Norah Geraghty, as a reward for her prudence, could get a husband in a rank of life above her, instead of falling into utter destruction as might so easily have been the case, who could do other than praise her— praise her and her clever friend who had so assisted her in her struggle ?

Dolus an virtus—

Had Mrs. Davis ever studied the classics she would have thus expressed herself.

Poor Charley was altogether thrown on his beam-ends. He had altogether played Mrs. Davis's game in evincing jealousy at Mr. Peppermint's attentions. He knew this, and yet for the life of him he could not help being jealous. He wanted to get rid of Miss Geraghty, and yet he could not endure that anyone else should lay claim to her favour. He was very weak. He knew how much depended on the way in which he might answer this woman at the present moment; he knew that he ought now to make it plain to her, that however foolish he might have been, however false he might have been, it was quite out of the question that he should marry her barmaid. But he did not do so. He was worse than weak. It was not only the disinclination to give pain, or even the dread of the storm that would ensue, which deterred him; but an absurd dislike to think that Mr. Peppermint should be graciously received there as the barmaid's acknowledged admirer.

'Is she really ill now?' said he.

'She's not so ill but what she shall make herself well enough to welcome you, if you'll say the word that you ought to say. The most that ails her is fretting at the long delay.—Bolt the door, child, and go to bed; there will be no one else here now. Go up, and tell Miss Geraghty to come down; she hasn't got her clothes off yet, I know.'

Mrs. Davis was too good a general to press Charley for an absolute, immediate, fixed answer to her question. She knew that she had already gained much, by talking thus of the proposed marriage, by setting it thus plainly before Charley, without rebuke or denial from him. He had not objected to receiving a visit from Norah, on the implied understanding that she was to come down to him as his affianced bride. He had not agreed to this in words; but silence gives consent, and Mrs. Davis felt that should it ever hereafter become necessary to prove anything, what had passed would enable her to prove a good deal.

Charley puffed at his cigar and sipped his gin and water. It was now twelve o'clock, and he thoroughly wished himself at home and in bed. The longer he thought of it the more impossible it appeared that he should get out of the house without the scene which he dreaded. The girl had bolted the door, put away her cups and mugs, and her step upstairs had struck heavily on his ears. The house was not large or high, and he fancied that he heard mutterings on the landing-place. Indeed he did not doubt but that Miss Geraghty had listened to most of the conversation which had taken place.

'Excuse me a minute, Mr. Tudor,' said Mrs. Davis, who was now smiling and civil enough; 'I will go up-stairs myself; the silly girl is shamefaced, and does not like to come down;' and up went Mrs. Davis to see that her barmaid's curls and dress were nice and jaunty. It would not do now, at this moment, for Norah to offend her lover by any untidiness. Charley for a moment thought of the front door. The enemy had allowed him an opportunity for retreating. He might slip out before either of the women came down, and then never more be heard of in Norfolk Street again. He had his hand in his waistcoat pocket, with the intent of leaving the sovereign on the table; but when the moment came he felt ashamed of the pusillanimity of such an escape, and therefore stood, or rather sat his ground, with a courage worthy of a better purpose.

Down the two women came, and Charley felt his heart beating against his ribs. As the steps came nearer the door, he began to wish that Mr. Peppermint had been successful. The widow entered the room first, and at her heels the expectant beauty. We can hardly say that she was blushing; but she did look rather shamefaced, and hung back a little at the door, as though she still had half a mind to think better of it, and go off to her bed.

'Come in, you little fool,' said Mrs. Davis. 'You needn't be ashamed of coming down to see him; you have done that often enough before now.'

Norah simpered and sidled. 'Well, I'm sure now!' said she. 'Here's a start, Mr. Tudor; to be brought downstairs at this time of night; and I'm sure I don't know what it's about;' and then she shook her curls, and twitched her dress, and made as though she were going to pass through the room to her accustomed place at the bar.

Norah Geraghty was a fine girl. Putting her in com-parison with Miss Golightly, we are inclined to say that she was the finer girl of the two; and that, barring position, money, and fashion, she was qualified to make the better wife. In point of education, that is, the effects of education, there was not perhaps much to choose between them. Norah could make an excellent pudding, and was willing enough to exercise her industry and art in doing so; Miss Golightly could copy music, but she did not like the trouble; and could play a waltz badly. Neither of them had ever read anything beyond a few novels. In this respect, as to the amount of labour done, Miss Golightly had certainly far surpassed her rival competitor for Charley's affections.

Charley got up and took her hand; and as he did so, he saw that her nails were dirty. He put his arms round her waist and kissed her; and as he caressed her, his olfactory nerves perceived that the pomatum in her hair was none of the best. He thought of those young lustrous eyes that would look up so wondrously into his face; he thought of the gentle touch, which would send a thrill through all his nerves; and then he felt very sick.

'Well, upon my word, Mr. Tudor,' said Miss Geraghty, 'you're making very free to-night.' She did not, however, refuse to sit down on his knee, though while sitting there she struggled and tossed herself, and shook her long ringlets in Charley's face, till he wished her—safe at home in Mr. Peppermint's nursery.

'And is that what you brought me down for, Mrs. Davis?' said Norah. 'Well, upon my word, I hope the door's locked; we shall have all the world in here else.'

'If you hadn't come down to him, he'd have come up to you,' said Mrs. Davis.

'Would he though?' said Norah; 'I think he knows a trick worth two of that;' and she looked as though she knew well how to defend herself, if any over-zeal on the part of her lover should ever induce him to violate the sanctum of her feminine retirement.

There was no over-zeal now about Charley. He ought to have been happy enough, for he had his charmer in his arms; but he showed very little of the ecstatic joy of a favoured lover. There he sat with Norah in his arms, and as we have said, Norah was a handsome girl; but he would much sooner have been copying the Kennett and Avon canal lock entries in Mr. Snape's room at the Internal Navigation.

'Lawks, Mr. Tudor, you needn't hold me so tight,' said Norah.

'He means to hold you tight enough now,' said Mrs. Davis. 'He's very angry because I mentioned another gentleman's name.'

'Well, now you didn't?' said Norah, pretending to look very angry.

'Well, I just did; and if you'd only seen him! You must be very careful what you say to that gentleman, or there'll be a row in the house.'

'I!' said Norah. 'What I say to him! It's very little I have to say to the man. But I shall tell him this; he'd better take himself somewhere else, if he's going to make himself troublesome.'

All this time Charley had said nothing, but was sitting with his hat on his head, and his cigar in his mouth. The latter appendage he had laid down for a moment when he saluted Miss Geraghty; but he had resumed it, having at the moment no intention of repeating the compliment.

'And so you were jealous, were you?' said she, turning round and looking at him. 'Well now, some people might have more respect for other people than to mix up their names that way, with the names of any men that choose to put themselves forward. What would you say if I was to talk to you about Miss——'

Charley stopped her mouth. It was not to be borne that she should be allowed to pronounce the name that was about to fall from her lips.

'So you were jealous, were you?' said she, when she was again able to speak. 'Well, my!'

'Mrs. Davis told me flatly that you were going to marry the man,' said Charley; 'so what was I to think?'

'It doesn't matter what you think now,' said Mrs. Davis; 'for you must be off from this. Do you know what o'clock it is? Do you want the house to get a bad name? Come, you two understand each other now, so you may as well give over billing and cooing for this time. It's all settled now, isn't it, Mr. Tudor?'

'Oh yes, I suppose so,' said Charley.

'Well, and what do you say, Norah?'

'Oh, I'm sure I'm agreeable if he is. Ha! ha! ha!
I only hope he won't think me too forward—he! he! he!'

And then with another kiss, and very few more words of
any sort, Charley took himself off.

'I'll have nothing more to do with him,' said Norah,
bursting into tears, as soon as the door was well bolted
after Charley's exit. 'I'm only losing myself with him.
He don't mean anything, and I said he didn't all along.
He'd have pitched me to Old Scratch, while I was sitting
there on his knee, if he'd have had his own way—so he
would;' and poor Norah cried heartily, as she went to
her work in her usual way among the bottles and taps.

'Why, you fool you, what do you expect? You don't
think he's to jump down your throat, do you? You can
but try it on; and then if it don't do, why there's the
other one to fall back on; only, if I had the choice, I'd
rather have young Tudor, too.'

'So would I,' said Norah; 'I can't abide that other
fellow.'

'Well, there, that's how it is, you know—beggars can't
be choosers. But come, make us a drop of something
hot; a little drop will do yourself good; but it's better
not to take it before him, unless when he presses you.'

So the two ladies sat down to console themselves, as
best they might, for the reverses which trade and love so
often bring with them.

Charley walked off a miserable man. He was thoroughly
ashamed of himself, thoroughly acknowledged his own
weakness; and yet as he went out from the 'Cat and
Whistle,' he felt sure that he should return there again
to renew the degradation from which he had suffered
this night. Indeed, what else could he do now? He
had, as it were, solemnly plighted his troth to the girl
before a third person who had brought them together,
with the acknowledged purpose of witnessing that ceremony. He had, before Mrs. Davis, and before the girl
herself, heard her spoken of as his wife, and had agreed
to the understanding that such an arrangement was a
settled thing. What else had he to do now but to return
and complete his part of the bargain? What else but
that, and be a wretched, miserable, degraded man for

the rest of his days; lower, viler, more contemptible,
infinitely lower, even than his brother clerks at the office,
whom in his pride he had so much despised?

He walked from Norfolk Street into the Strand, and
there the world was still alive, though it was now nearly
one o'clock. The debauched misery, the wretched out-
door midnight revelry of the world was there, streaming
in and out from gin-palaces, and bawling itself hoarse
with horrid, discordant, screech-owl slang. But he went
his way unheeding and uncontaminated. Now, now that
it was useless, he was thinking of the better things of
the world; nothing now seemed worth his grasp, nothing
now seemed pleasurable, nothing capable of giving joy,
but what was decent, good, reputable, cleanly, and
polished. How he hated now that lower world with
which he had for the last three years condescended to
pass so much of his time! how he hated himself for his
own vileness! He thought of what Alaric was, of what
Norman was, of what he himself might have been—he
that was praised by Mrs. Woodward for his talent, he
that was encouraged to place himself among the authors
of the day! He thought of all this, and then he
thought of what he was—the affianced husband of Norah
Geraghty!

He went along the Strand, over the crossing under the
statue of Charles on horseback, and up Pall Mall East till
he came to the opening into the park under the Duke of
York's column. The London night world was all alive
as he made his way. From the Opera Colonnade shrill
voices shrieked out at him as he passed, and drunken men
coming down from the night supper-houses in the Hay-
market saluted him with affectionate cordiality. The
hoarse waterman from the cabstand, whose voice had
perished in the night air, croaked out at him the offer
of a vehicle; and one of the night beggar-women who
cling like burrs to those who roam the street at these
unhallowed hours still stuck to him, as she had done ever
since he had entered the Strand.

'Get away with you,' said Charley, turning at the
wretched creature in his fierce anger; 'get away, or I'll
give you in charge.'

'That you may never know what it is to be in misery yourself!' said the miserable Irishwoman.

'If you follow me a step farther I'll have you locked up,' said Charley.

'Oh, then, it 's you that have the hard heart,' said she; 'and it 's you that will suffer yet.'

Charley looked round, threw her the odd halfpence which he had in his pocket, and then turned down towards the column. The woman picked up her prize, and, with a speedy blessing, took herself off in search of other prey. His way home would have taken him up Waterloo Place, but the space round the column was now deserted and quiet, and sauntering there, without thinking of what he did, he paced up and down between the Clubs and the steps leading into the park. There, walking to and fro slowly, he thought of his past career, of all the circumstances of his life since his life had been left to his own control, and of the absence of all hope for the future.

What was he to do? He was deeply, inextricably in debt. That wretch, M'Ruen, had his name on bills which it was impossible that he should ever pay. Tradesmen held other bills of his which were either now over-due, or would very shortly become so. He was threatened with numerous writs, any one of which would suffice to put him into gaol. From his poor father, burdened as he was with other children, he knew that he had no right to expect further assistance. He was in debt to Norman, his best, he would have said his only friend, had it not been that in all his misery he could not help still thinking of Mrs. Woodward as his friend.

And yet how could he venture to think longer of her, contaminated as he now was with the horrid degradation of his acknowledged love at the 'Cat and Whistle!' No; he must think no more of the Woodwards; he must dream no more of those angel eyes which in his waking moments had so often peered at him out of heaven, teaching him to think of higher things, giving him higher hopes than those which had come to him from the working of his own unaided spirit. Ah! lessons taught in vain! vain hopes! lessons that had come all too late! hopes that had been cherished only to be deceived! It was all over now! He had made his bed, and he must lie on it; he had sown his seed, and he must reap his produce; there was now no 'Excelsior' left for him within the bounds of human probability.

He had promised to go to Hampton with Harry Norman on Saturday, and he would go there for the last time. He would go there and tell Mrs. Woodward so much of the truth as he could bring himself to utter; he would say farewell to that blest abode; he would take Linda's soft hand in his for the last time; for the last time he would hear the young, silver-ringing, happy voice of his darling Katie; for the last time look into her bright face; for the last time play with her as with a child of heaven—and then he would return to the 'Cat and Whistle.'

And having made this resolve he went home to his lodgings. It was singular that in all his misery the idea hardly once occurred to him of setting himself right in the world by accepting his cousin's offer of Miss Golightly's hand and fortune.

CHAPTER XXI

HAMPTON COURT BRIDGE

BEFORE the following Saturday afternoon Charley's spirits had somewhat recovered their natural tone. Not that he was in a happy frame of mind; the united energies of Mr. M'Ruen and Mrs. Davis had been too powerful to allow of that; not that he had given over his projected plan of saying a long farewell to Mrs. Woodward, or at any rate of telling her something of his position; he still felt that he could not continue to live on terms of close intimacy both with her daughters and with Norah Geraghty. But the spirits of youth are ever buoyant, and the spirits of no one could be endowed with more natural buoyancy than those of the young navvy. Charley, therefore, in spite of his misfortunes, was ready with his manuscript when Saturday afternoon arrived, and, according to agreement, met Norman at the railway station.

Only one evening had intervened since the night in which he had ratified his matrimonial engagement, and in spite of the delicate nature of his position he had for that evening allowed Mr. Peppermint to exercise his eloquence on the heart of the fair Norah without interruption. He the while had been engaged in completing the memoirs of ' Crinoline and Macassar.'

' Well, Charley,' they asked, one and all, as soon as he reached the Cottage, ' have you got the story ? Have you brought the manuscript ? Is it all finished and ready for that dreadful editor ? '

Charley produced a roll, and Linda and Katie instantly pounced upon it.

' Oh ! it begins with poetry,' said Linda.

' I am so glad,' said Katie. ' Is there much poetry in it, Charley ? I do so hope there is.'

' Not a word of it,' said Charley ; ' that which Linda sees is a song that the heroine is singing, and it isn't supposed to be written by the author at all.'

' I'm so sorry that there's no poetry,' said Katie. ' Can't you write poetry, Charley ? '

' At any rate there's lots of love in it,' said Linda, who was turning over the pages.

' Is there ? ' said Katie. ' Well, that's next best ; but they should go together. You should have put all your love into verse, Charley, and then your prose would have done for the funny parts.'

' Perhaps it's all fun,' said Mrs. Woodward. ' But come, girls, this is not fair ; I won't let you look at the story till it's read in full committee.' And so saying, Mrs. Woodward took the papers from her daughters, and tying them up, deposited them safe in custody. ' We'll have it out when the tea-things are gone.'

But before the tea-things had come, an accident happened, which had been like to dismiss ' Crinoline and Macassar ' altogether from the minds of the whole of the Woodward family. The young men had, as usual, dined in town, and therefore they were all able to spend the long summer evening out of doors. Norman's boat was down at Hampton, and it was therefore determined that they should row down as far as Hampton Court Park and back. Charley and Norman were to row; and Mrs. Woodward agreed to accompany her daughters. Uncle Bat was left at home, to his nap and rum and water.

Norman was so expert a Thames waterman, that he was quite able to manage the boat without a steersman, and Charley was nearly his equal. But there is some amusement in steering, and Katie was allowed to sit between the tiller-ropes.

'I can steer very well, mamma: can't I, Harry? I always steer when we go to the island, and we run the boat straight into the little creek, only just broad enough to hold it.' Katie's visits to the island, however, were not so frequent as they had heretofore been, for she was approaching to sixteen years of age, and wet feet and draggled petticoats had lost some of their charms. Mrs. Woodward, trusting more to the experience of her two knights than to the skill of the lady at the helm, took her seat, and they went off merrily down the stream.

All the world knows that it is but a very little distance from Hampton Church to Hampton Court Bridge, especially when one has the stream with one. They were very soon near to the bridge, and as they approached it, they had to pass a huge barge, that was lazily making its way down to Brentford.

'There's lots of time for the big arch,' said Charley.

'Pull away then,' said Harry.

They both pulled hard, and shot alongside and past the barge. But the stream was strong, and the great ugly mass of black timber moved behind them quicker than it seemed to do.

'It will be safer to take the one to the left,' said Harry.

'Oh! there's lots of time,' said Charley.

'No,' said Harry, 'do as I tell you and go to the left.— Pull your left hand a little, Katie.'

Charley did as he was bid, and Katie intended to do the same; but unfortunately she pulled the wrong hand. They were now very near the bridge, and the barge was so close to them as to show that there might have been danger in attempting to get through the same arch with her.

'Your left hand, Katie, your left,' shouted Norman; 'your left string.' Katie was confused, and gave first a pull with her right, and then a pull with her left, and then a strong pull with her right. The two men backed water as hard as they could, but the effect of Katie's steering was to drive the nose of the boat right into one of the wooden piers of the bridge.

The barge went on its way, and luckily made its entry under the arch before the little craft had swung round into the stream before it; as it was, the boat, still clinging by its nose, came round with its stern against the side of the barge, and as the latter went on, the timbers of Norman's wherry cracked and crumpled in the rude encounter.

The ladies should all have kept their seats. Mrs. Woodward did do so. Linda jumped up, and being next to the barge, was pulled up into it by one of the men. Katie stood bolt upright, with the tiller-ropes still in her hand, awe-struck at the misfortune she had caused; but while she was so standing, the stern of the boat was lifted nearly out of the water by the weight of the barge, and Katie was pitched, behind her mother's back, head foremost into the water.

Norman, at the moment, was endeavouring to steady the boat, and shove it off from the barge, and had also lent a hand to assist Linda in her escape. Charley was on the other side, standing up and holding on by the piers of the bridge, keeping his eyes on the ladies, so as to be of assistance to them when assistance might be needed.

And now assistance was sorely needed, and luckily had not to be long waited for. Charley, with a light and quick step, passed over the thwarts, and, disregarding Mrs. Woodward's scream, let himself down, over the gunwale behind her seat into the water. Katie can hardly be said to have sunk at all. She had, at least, never been so much under the water as to be out of sight. Her clothes kept up her light body; and when Charley got close to her, she had been carried up to the piers of the bridge, and was panting with her head above water, and beating the stream with her little hands.

She was soon again in comparative safety. Charley had her by one arm as he held on with the other to the boat, and kept himself afloat with his legs. Mrs. Woodward leaned over and caught her daughter's clothes; while Linda, who had seen what had happened, stood shrieking on the barge, as it made its way on, heedless of the ruin it left behind.

Another boat soon came to their assistance from the shore, and Mrs. Woodward and Katie were got safely into it. Charley returned to the battered wherry, and assisted Norman in extricating it from its position; and a third boat went to Linda's rescue, who would otherwise have found herself in rather an uncomfortable position the next morning at Brentford.

The hugging and kissing to which Katie was subjected when she was carried up to the inn, near the boat-slip on the Surrey side of the river, may be imagined; as may also the faces she made at the wineglassful of stiff brandy and water which she was desired to drink. She was carried home in a fly, and by the time she arrived there, had so completely recovered her life and spirits as to put a vehement negative on her mother's proposition that she should at once go to bed.

'And not hear dear Charley's story?' said she, with tears in her eyes. 'And, mamma, I can't and won't go to bed without seeing Charley. I didn't say one word yet to thank him for jumping into the water after me.'

It was in vain that her mother told her that Charley's story would amuse her twice as much when she should read it printed; it was in vain that Mrs. Woodward assured her that Charley should come up to her room door, and hear her thanks as he stood in the passage, with the door ajar. Katie was determined to hear the story read. It must be read, if read at all, that Saturday night, as it was to be sent to the editor in the course of the week; and reading 'Crinoline and Macassar' out loud on a Sunday was not to be thought of at Surbiton Cottage. Katie was determined to hear the story read, and to sit very near the author too during the reading; to sit near him, and to give him such praise as even in her young mind she felt that an author would like to hear. Charley had pulled her out of the river, and no one, as far as her efforts could prevent it, should be allowed to throw cold water on him.

Norman and Charley, wet as the latter was, contrived to bring the shattered boat back to Hampton. When they reached the lawn at Surbiton Cottage they were both in high spirits. An accident, if it does no material harm, is always an inspiriting thing, unless one feels that it has been attributable to one's own fault. Neither of them could in this instance attach any blame to himself, and each felt that he had done what in him lay to prevent the possible ill effect of the mischance. As for the boat, Harry was too happy to think that none of his friends were hurt to care much about that.

As they walked across the lawn Mrs. Woodward ran out to them. 'My dear, dear Charley,' she said, 'what am I to say to thank you?' It was the first time Mrs. Woodward had ever called him by his Christian name. It had hitherto made him in a certain degree unhappy that she never did so, and now the sound was very pleasant to him.

'Oh, Mrs. Woodward,' said he, laughing, 'you mustn't touch me, for I'm all mud.'

'My dear, dear Charley, what can I say to you? and dear Harry, I fear we've spoilt your beautiful new boat.'

'I fear we've spoilt Katie's beautiful new hat,' said Norman.

Mrs. Woodward had taken and pressed a hand of each of them, in spite of Charley's protestations about the mud.

'Oh! you're in a dreadful state,' said she; 'you had better take something at once; you'll catch your death of cold.'

'I'd better take myself off to the inn,' said Charley, 'and get some clean clothes; that's all I want. But how is Katie—and how is Linda?'

And so, after a multitude of such inquiries on both sides, and of all manner of affectionate greetings, Charley went off to make himself dry, preparatory to the reading of the manuscript.

During his absence, Linda and Katie came down to the drawing-room. Linda was full of fun as to her journey with the bargeman; but Katie was a little paler than usual, and somewhat more serious and quiet than she was wont to be.

Norman was the first in the drawing-room, and received the thanks of the ladies for his prowess in assisting them; and Charley was not slow to follow him, for he was never very long at his toilet. He came in with a jaunty laughing air, as though nothing particular had happened, and as if he had not a care in the world. And yet while he had been dressing he had been thinking almost more than ever of Norah Geraghty. O that she, and Mrs. Davis with her, and Jabesh M'Ruen with both of them, could be buried ten fathom deep out of his sight, and out of his mind!

When he entered the room, Katie felt her heart beat so strongly that she hardly knew how to thank him for saving her life. A year ago she would have got up and kissed him innocently; but a year makes a great difference. She could not do that now, so she gave him her little hand, and held his till he came and sat down at his place at the table.

'Oh, Charley, I don't know what to say to you,' said she; and he could see and feel that her whole body was shaking with emotion.

'Then I'll tell you what to say: "Charley, here is your tea, and some bread, and some butter, and some jam, and some muffin," for I'll tell you what, my evening bath has made me as hungry as a hunter. I hope it has done the same to you.'

Katie, still holding his hand, looked up into his face, and he saw that her eyes were suffused with tears. She then left his side, and, running round the room, filled a plate with all the things he had asked for, and, bringing them to him, again took her place beside him. 'I wish I knew how to do more than that,' said she.

'I suppose, Charley, you'll have to make an entry about that barge on Monday morning, won't you?' said Linda. 'Mind you put in it how beautiful I looked sailing through the arch.'

'Yes, and how very gallant the bargeman was,' said Norman.

'Yes, and how much you enjoyed the idea of going down the river with him, while we came back to the Cottage,' said Charley. 'We'll put it all down at the Navigation, and old Snape shall make a special minute about it.'

Katie drank her tea in silence, and tried to eat, though without much success. When chatting voices and jokes were to be heard at the Cottage, the sound of her voice was usually the foremost; but now she sat demure and quiet. She was realizing the danger from which she had escaped, and, as is so often the case, was beginning to fear it now that it was over.

'Ah, Katie, my bonny bird,' said her mother, seeing that she was not herself, and knowing that the excitement and overpowering feelings of gratitude were too much for her—'come here; you should be in bed, my foolish little puss, should you not?'

'Indeed, she should,' said Uncle Bat, who was somewhat hard-hearted about the affair of the accident, and had been cruel enough, after hearing an account of it, to declare that it was all Katie's fault. 'Indeed, she should; and if she had gone to bed a little earlier in the evening it would have been all the better for Master Norman's boat.'

'Oh! mamma, don't send me to bed,' said she, with tears in her eyes. 'Pray don't send me to bed now; I'm quite well, only I can't talk because I'm thinking of what Charley did for me;' and so saying she got up, and, hiding her face on her mother's shoulder, burst into tears.

'My dearest child,' said Mrs. Woodward, 'I'm afraid you'll make yourself ill. We'll put off the reading, won't we, Charley? We have done enough for one evening.'

'Of course we will,' said he. 'Reading a stupid story will be very slow work after all we've gone through to-day.'

'No, no, no,' said Katie; 'it shan't be put off; there won't be any other time for hearing it. And, mamma, it must be read; and I know it won't be stupid. Oh,

mamma, dear mamma, do let us hear it read; I'm quite
well now.'

Mrs. Woodward found herself obliged to give way.
She had not the heart to bid her daughter go away to
bed, nor, had she done so, would it have been of any
avail. Katie would only have lain and sobbed in her own
room, and very probably have gone into hysterics. The
best thing for her was to try to turn the current of her
thoughts, and thus by degrees tame down her excited
feelings.

'Well, darling, then we will have the story, if Charley
will let us. Go and fetch it, dearest.' Katie raised herself from her mother's bosom, and, going across the room,
fetched the roll of papers to Charley. As he prepared to
take it she took his hand in hers, and, bending her head
over it, tenderly kissed it. 'You mustn't think,' said
she, 'that because I say nothing, I don't know what it
is that you've done for me; but I don't know how to
say it.'

Charley was at any rate as ignorant what he ought to
say as Katie was. He felt the pressure of her warm lips
on his hand, and hardly knew where he was. He felt that
he blushed and looked abashed, and dreaded, fearfully
dreaded, lest Mrs. Woodward should surmise that he
estimated at other than its intended worth, her daughter's
show of affection for him.

'I shouldn't mind doing it every night,' said he, 'in
such weather as this. I think it rather good fun going
into the water with my clothes on.' Katie looked up at
him through her tears, as though she would say that she
well understood what that meant.

Mrs. Woodward saw that if the story was to be read,
the sooner they began it the better.

'Come, Charley,' said she, 'now for the romance.
Katie, come and sit by me.' But Katie had already taken
her seat, a little behind Charley, quite in the shade, and
she was not to be moved.

'But I won't read it myself,' said Charley; 'you must
read it, Mrs. Woodward.'

'O yes, Mrs. Woodward, you are to read it,' said
Norman.

'O yes, do read it, mamma,' said Linda. Katie said nothing, but she would have preferred that Charley should have read it himself.

'Well, if I can,' said Mrs. Woodward.

'Snape says I write the worst hand in all Somerset House,' said Charley; 'but still I think you'll be able to manage it.'

'I hate that Mr. Snape,' said Katie, *sotto voce*. And then Mrs. Woodward unrolled the manuscript and began her task.

CHAPTER XXII

CRINOLINE AND MACASSAR; OR, MY AUNT'S WILL

'WELL, Linda was right,' said Mrs. Woodward, 'it does begin with poetry.'

'It's only a song,' said Charley, apologetically—'and after all there is only one verse of that'—and then Mrs. Woodward began

"CRINOLINE AND MACASSAR."

'Ladies and gentlemen, that is the name of Mr. Charles Tudor's new novel.'

'Crinoline and Macassar!' said Uncle Bat. 'Are they intended for human beings' names?'

'They are the heroine and the hero, as I take it,' said Mrs. Woodward, 'and I presume them to be human, unless they turn out to be celestial.'

'I never heard such names in my life,' said the captain.

'At any rate, uncle, they are as good as Sir Jib Boom and Captain Hardaport,' said Katie, pertly.

'We won't mind about that,' said Mrs. Woodward; 'I'm going to begin, and I beg I may not be interrupted.'

"CRINOLINE AND MACASSAR.

"The lovely Crinoline was sitting alone at a lattice window on a summer morning, and as she sat she sang with melancholy cadence the first part of the now cele-

brated song which had then lately appeared, from the distinguished pen of Sir G— H—.'

'Who is Sir G— H—, Charley?'

'Oh, it wouldn't do for me to tell that,' said Charley. 'That must be left to the tact and intelligence of my readers.'

'Oh, very well,' said Mrs. Woodward, 'we will abstain from all impertinent questions'——" from the distinguished pen of Sir G— H—. The ditty which she sang ran as follows :—

My heart's at my office, my heart is always there—
My heart's at my office, docketing with care;
Docketing the papers, and copying all day,
My heart's at my office, though I be far away.

"' Ah me!' said the Lady Crinoline——"

'What—is she a peer's daughter?' said Uncle Bat.

'Not exactly,' said Charley, 'it's only a sort of semi-poetic way one has of speaking of one's heroine.'

"' Ah me!' said the Lady Crinoline—'his heart! his heart!—I wonder whether he has got a heart;' and then she sang again in low plaintive voice the first line of the song, suiting the cadence to her own case :—

His heart is at his office, his heart is *always* there.

" It was evident that the Lady Crinoline did not repeat the words in the feeling of their great author, who when he wrote them had intended to excite to high deeds of exalted merit that portion of the British youth which is employed in the Civil Service of the country.

" Crinoline laid down her lute—it was in fact an accordion—and gazing listlessly over the rails of the balcony, looked out at the green foliage which adorned the enclosure of the square below.

" It was Tavistock Square. The winds of March and the showers of April had been successful in producing the buds of May."

'Ah, Charley, that's taken from the old song,' said Katie, ' only you've put buds instead of flowers.'

'That's quite allowable,' said Mrs. Woodward——

" successful in producing the buds of May. The sparrows chirped sweetly on the house-top, and the coming summer gladdened the hearts of all—of all except poor Crinoline.

" ' I wonder whether he has a heart,' said she ; ' and if he has, I wonder whether it *is* at his office.'

" As she thus soliloquized, the door was opened by a youthful page, on whose well-formed breast, buttons seemed to grow like mushrooms in the meadows in August.

" ' Mr. Macassar Jones,' said the page ; and having so said, he discreetly disappeared. He was in his line of life a valuable member of society. He had brought from his last place a twelvemonth's character that was creditable alike to his head and heart ; he was now found to be a trustworthy assistant in the household of the Lady Crinoline's mother, and was the delight of his aged parents, to whom he regularly remitted no inconsiderable portion of his wages. Let it always be remembered that the life even of a page may be glorious. All honour to the true and brave ! "

' Goodness, Charley—how very moral you are ! ' said Linda.

' Yes,' said he ; ' that 's indispensable. It 's the intention of the *Daily Delight* always to hold up a career of virtue to the lower orders as the thing that pays. Honesty, high wages, and hot dinners. Those are our principles.'

' You'll have a deal to do before you'll bring the lower orders to agree with you,' said Uncle Bat.

' We have a deal to do,' said Charley, ' and we'll do it. The power of the cheap press is unbounded.'

" As the page closed the door, a light, low, melancholy step was heard to make its way across the drawing-room. Crinoline's heart had given one start when she had heard the announcement of the well-known name. She had once glanced with eager inquiring eye towards the door. But not in vain to her had an excellent mother taught the proprieties of elegant life. Long before Macassar Jones was present in the chamber she had snatched up the tambour-frame that lay beside her, and when she entered she was zealously engaged on the fox's head that was to ornament the toe of a left-foot slipper. Who shall dare to say that those slippers were intended to grace the feet of Macassar Jones ? ' "

' But I suppose they were,' said Katie.

' You must wait and see,' said her mother ; ' for my part I am not at all so sure of that.'

' Oh, but I know they must be ; for she 's in love with him,' said Katie.

" ' Oh, Mr. Macassar,' said the Lady Crinoline, when he had drawn nigh to her, ' and how are you to-day ? ' This mention of his Christian name betrayed no undue familiarity, as the two families were intimate, and Macassar had four elder brothers. ' I am so sorry mamma is not at home ; she will regret not seeing you amazingly.'

" Macassar had his hat in his hand, and he stood a while gazing at the fox in the pattern. ' Won't you sit down ? ' said Crinoline.

" ' Is it very dusty in the street to-day ? ' asked Crinoline ; and as she spoke she turned upon him a face wreathed in the sweetest smiles, radiant with elegant courtesy, and altogether expressive of extreme gentility, unsullied propriety, and a very high tone of female education. ' Is it very dusty in the street to-day ? '

" Charmed by the involuntary grace of her action, Macassar essayed to turn his head towards her as he replied ; he could not turn it much, for he wore an all-rounder ; but still he was enabled by a side glance to see more of that finished elegance than was perhaps good for his peace of mind.

" ' Yes,' said he, ' it is dusty ;—it certainly is dusty, rather ;—but not very—and then in most streets they've got the water-carts.'

" ' Ah, I love those water-carts ! ' said Crinoline ; ' the dust, you know, is so trying.'

" ' To the complexion ? ' suggested Macassar, again looking round as best he might over the bulwark of his collar.

" Crinoline laughed slightly ; it was perhaps hardly more than a simper, and turning her lovely eyes from her work, she said, ' Well, to the complexion, if you will. What would you gentlemen say if we ladies were to be careless of our complexions ? '

"Macassar merely sighed gently—perhaps he had no fitting answer; perhaps his heart was too full for him to answer. He sat with his eye fixed on his hat, which still dangled in his hand; but his mind's eye was far away.

"'Is it in his office?' thought Crinoline to herself; 'or is it here? Is it anywhere?'

"'Have you learnt the song I sent you?' said he at last, waking, as it were, from a trance.

"'Not yet,' said she—'that is, not quite; that is, I could not sing it before strangers yet.'

"'Strangers!' said Macassar; and he looked at her again with an energy that produced results not beneficial either to his neck or his collar.

"Crinoline was delighted at this expression of feeling. 'At any rate it is somewhere,' said she to herself; 'and it can hardly be all at his office.'

"'Well, I will not say strangers,' she said out loud; 'it sounds—it sounds—I don't know how it sounds. But what I mean is, that as yet I've only sung it before mamma!'"

'I declare I don't know which is the biggest fool of the two,' said Uncle Bat, very rudely. 'As for him, if I had him on the forecastle of a man-of-war for a day or two, I'd soon teach him to speak out.'

'You forget, sir,' said Charley, 'he's not a sailor, he's only in the Civil Service; we're all very bashful in the Civil Service.'

'I think he is rather spooney, I must say,' said Katie; whereupon Mrs. Woodward went on reading.

"'It's a sweet thing, isn't it?' said Macassar.

"'Oh, very!' said Crinoline, with a rapturous expression which pervaded her whole head and shoulders as well as her face and bust—'very sweet, and so new.'

"'It quite comes home to me,' said Macassar, and he sighed deeply.

"'Then it is at his office,' said Crinoline to herself; and she sighed also.

"They both sat silent for a while, looking into the square—Crinoline was at one window, and Macassar at the other: 'I must go now,' said he: 'I promised to be back at three.'

" ' Back where ? ' said she.

" ' At my office,' said he.

" Crinoline sighed. After all, it was at his office ; it was too evident that it was there, and nowhere else. Well, and why should it not be there ? why should not Macassar Jones be true to his duty and to his country ? What had she to do with his heart ? Why should she wish it elsewhere ? 'Twas thus she tried to console herself, but in vain. Had she had an office of her own it might perhaps have been different ; but Crinoline was only a woman ; and often she sighed over the degradation of her lot.

" ' Good morning, Miss Crinoline,' said he.

" ' Good morning, Mr. Macassar,' said she ; ' mamma will so regret that she has lost the pleasure of seeing you.'

" And then she rung the bell. Macassar went downstairs perhaps somewhat slower, with perhaps more of melancholy than when he entered. The page opened the hall-door with alacrity, and shut it behind him with a slam.

" All honour to the true and brave !

" Crinoline again took up the note of her sorrow, and with her lute in her hand, she warbled forth the line which stuck like a thorn in her sweet bosom :—

His heart is in his office—his heart IS ALWAYS *there*."

' There,' said Mrs. Woodward, ' that's the end of the first chapter.'

' Well, I like the page the best,' said Linda, ' because he seems to know what he is about.'

' Oh, so does the lady,' said Charley ; ' but it wouldn't at all do if we made the hero and heroine go about their work like humdrum people. You'll see that the Lady Crinoline knows very well what's what.'

' Oh, Charley, pray don't tell us,' said Katie ; ' I do so like Mr. Macassar, he is so spooney ; pray go on, mamma.'

' I'm ready,' said Mrs. Woodward, again taking up the manuscript.

" CHAPTER II

" The lovely Crinoline was the only daughter of fond parents ; and though they were not what might be called extremely wealthy, considering the vast incomes of some residents in the metropolis, and were not perhaps wont to mix in the highest circles of the Belgravian aristocracy, yet she was enabled to dress in all the elegance of fashion, and contrived to see a good deal of that society which moves in the highly respectable neighbourhood of Russell Square and Gower Street.

" Her dresses were made at the distinguished establishment of Madame Mantalini, in Hanover Square; at least she was in the habit of getting one dress there every other season, and this was quite sufficient among her friends to give her a reputation for dealing in the proper quarter. Once she had got a bonnet direct from Paris, which gave her ample opportunity of expressing a frequent opinion not favourable to the fabricators of a British article. She always took care that her shoes had within them the name of a French *cordonnier ;* and her gloves were made to order in the Rue Du Bac, though usually bought and paid for in Tottenham Court Road."

' What a false creature ! ' said Linda.

' False ! ' said Charley ; ' and how is a girl to get along if she be not false ? What girl could live for a moment before the world if she were to tell the whole truth about the get-up of her wardrobe—the patchings and make-believes, the chipped ribbons and turned silks, the little bills here, and the little bills there ? How else is an allowance of £20 a year to be made compatible with an appearance of unlimited income ? How else are young men to be taught to think that in an affair of dress money is a matter of no moment whatsoever ? '

' Oh, Charley, Charley, don't be slanderous,' said Mrs. Woodward.

' I only repeat what the editor says to me—I know nothing about it myself. Only we are requested " to hold the mirror up to nature,"—and to art too, I believe. We are to set these things right, you know.'

' We—who are we ? ' said Katie.

'Why, the *Daily Delight*,' said Charley.

'But I hope there's nothing false in patching and turning,' said Mrs. Woodward; 'for if there be, I'm the falsest woman alive.

To gar the auld claes look amaist as weel's the new is, I thought, one of the most legitimate objects of a woman's diligence.'

'It all depends on the spirit of the stitches,' said Charley the censor.

'Well, I must say I don't like mending up old clothes a bit better than Charley does,' said Katie; 'but pray go on, mamma;' so Mrs. Woodward continued to read.

"On the day of Macassar's visit in Tavistock Square, Crinoline was dressed in a most elegant morning costume. It was a very light barege muslin, extremely full; and which, as she had assured her friend, Miss Manasseh, of Keppel Street, had been sent home from the establishment in Hanover Square only the day before. I am aware that Miss Manasseh instantly propagated an ill-natured report that she had seen the identical dress in a milliner's room up two pairs back in Store Street; but then Miss Manasseh was known to be envious; and had moreover seen twelve seasons out in those localities, whereas the fair Crinoline, young thing, had graced Tavistock Square only for two years; and her mother was ready to swear that she had never passed the nursery door till she came there. The ground of the dress was a light pea-green, and the pattern was ivy wreaths entwined with pansies and tulips—each flounce showed a separate wreath—and there were nine flounces, the highest of which fairy circles was about three inches below the smallest waist that ever was tightly girded in steel and whalebone.

"Macassar had once declared, in a moment of ecstatic energy, that a small waist was the chiefest grace in woman. How often had the Lady Crinoline's maid, when in the extreme agony of her labour, put a malediction on his name on account of this speech!

"It is unnecessary to speak of the drapery of the arms, which showed the elaborate lace of the sleeve beneath, and sometimes also the pearly whiteness of that rounded arm. This was a sight which would almost drive Macassar to distraction. At such moments as that the hopes of the patriotic poet for the good of the Civil Service were not strictly fulfilled in the heart of Macassar Jones. Oh, if the Lady Crinoline could but have known!

"It is unnecessary also to describe the strange and hidden mechanism of that mysterious petticoat which gave such full dimensions, such ample sweeping proportions to the *tout ensemble* of the lady's appearance. It is unnecessary, and would perhaps be improper, and as far as I am concerned, is certainly impossible."

Here Charley blushed, as Mrs. Woodward looked at him from over the top of the paper.

"Let it suffice to say that she could envelop a sofa without the slightest effort, throw her draperies a yard and a half from her on either side without any appearance of stretching, completely fill a carriage; or, which was more frequently her fate, entangle herself all but inextricably in a cab.

"A word, however, must be said of those little feet that peeped out now and again so beautifully from beneath the artistic constructions above alluded to—of the feet, or perhaps rather of the shoes. But yet, what can be said of them successfully? That French name so correctly spelt, so elaborately accented, so beautifully finished in gold letters, which from their form, however, one would say that the *cordonnier* must have imported from England, was only visible to those favoured knights who were occasionally permitted to carry the shoes home in their pockets.

"But a word must be said about the hair dressed *à l'impératrice*, redolent of the sweetest patchouli, disclosing all the glories of that ingenuous, but perhaps too open brow. A word must be said; but, alas! how inefficacious to do justice to the ingenuity so wonderfully displayed! The hair of the Lady Crinoline was perhaps more lovely than abundant: to produce that glorious effect, that effect which has now symbolized among English lasses the head-dress *à l'impératrice* as the one idea of feminine beauty, every hair was called on to give its separate aid. As is the case with so many of us who are anxious to put our best foot foremost, everything was abstracted from the rear in order to create a show in the front. Then to complete the garniture of the head, to make all perfect, to leave no point of escape for the susceptible admirer of modern beauty, some dorsal appendage was necessary of mornings as well as in the more fully bedizened period of evening society.

"Everything about the sweet Crinoline was wont to be green. It is the sweetest and most innocent of colours; but, alas! a colour dangerous for the heart's ease of youthful beauty. Hanging from the back of her head were to be seen moss and fennel, and various grasses—rye grass and timothy, trefoil and cinquefoil, vetches, and clover, and here and there young fern. A story was told, but doubtless false, as it was traced to the mouth of Miss Manasseh, that once while Crinoline was reclining in a paddock at Richmond, having escaped with the young Macassar from the heat of a neighbouring drawing-room, a cow had attempted to feed from her head."

'Oh, Charley, a cow!' said Katie.

'Well, but you see I don't give it as true,' said Charley.

'I shall never get it done if Katie won't hold her tongue,' said Mrs. Woodward.

"But perhaps it was when at the seaside in September, at Broadstairs, Herne Bay, or Dover, Crinoline and her mamma invigorated themselves with the sea-breezes of the ocean—perhaps it was there that she was enabled to assume that covering for her head in which her soul most delighted. It was a Tom and Jerry hat turned up at the sides, with a short but knowing feather, velvet trimmings, and a steel buckle blinking brightly in the noonday sun. Had Macassar seen her in this he would have yielded himself her captive at once, quarter or no quarter. It was the most marked, and perhaps the most attractive peculiarity of the Lady Crinoline's face, that the end of her nose was a little turned up. This charm, in unison with the upturned edges of her cruel-hearted hat, was found by many men to be invincible.

"We all know how dreadful is the spectacle of a Saracen's head, as it appears, or did appear, painted on a huge board at the top of Snow Hill. From that we are left to surmise with what tremendous audacity of

countenance, with what terror-striking preparations of
the outward man, an Eastern army is led to battle. Can
any men so fearfully bold in appearance ever turn their
backs and fly ? They look as though they could destroy
by the glance of their ferocious eyes. Who could withstand the hirsute horrors of those fiery faces ?

"There is just such audacity, a courage of a similar
description, perhaps we may say an equal invincibility,
in the charms of those Tom and Jerry hats when duly
put on, over a face of the proper description—over such
a face as that of the Lady Crinoline. They give to the
wearer an appearance of concentration of pluck. But as
the Eastern array does quail before the quiet valour of
Europe, so, we may perhaps say, does the open, quick
audacity of the Tom and Jerry tend to less powerful
results than the modest enduring patience of the bonnet."

'So ends the second chapter—bravo, Charley,' said
Mrs. Woodward. 'In the name of the British female
public, I beg to thank you for your exertions.'

'The editor said I was to write down turned-up hats,'
said Charley. 'I rather like them myself.'

'I hope my new slouch is not an audacious Saracen's
head,' said Linda.

'Or mine,' said Katie. 'But you may say what you
like about them now ; for mine is drowned.'

'Come, girls, there are four more chapters, I see. Let
me finish it, and then we can discuss it afterwards.'

"   CHAPTER III

"Having thus described the Lady Crinoline——"

'You haven't described her at all,' said Linda ; 'you
haven't got beyond her clothes yet.'

'There is nothing beyond them,' said Charley.

'You haven't even described her face,' said Katie ;
'you have only said that she had a turned-up nose.'

'There is nothing further that one can say about it,'
said Charley.

"Having thus described the Lady Crinoline," continued Mrs. Woodward, "it now becomes our duty, as
impartial historians, to give some account of Mr. Macassar
Jones.

" We are not prepared to give the exact name of the artist by whom Mr. Macassar Jones was turned out to the world so perfectly dressed a man. Were we to do so, the signal service done to one establishment by such an advertisement would draw down on us the anger of the trade at large, and the tailors of London would be in league against the *Daily Delight*. It is sufficient to remark that the artist's offices are not a hundred miles from Pall Mall. Nor need we expressly name the boot-maker to whom is confided the task of making those feet ' small by degrees and beautifully less.' The process, we understand, has been painful, but the effect is no doubt remunerative.

" In three especial walks of dress has Macassar Jones been more than ordinarily careful to create a sensation ; and we believe we may assert that he has been successful in all. We have already alluded to his feet. Ascending from them, and ascending not far, we come to his coat. It is needless to say that it is a frock ; needless to say that it is a long frock—long as those usually worn by younger infants, and apparently made so for the same purpose. But look at the exquisitely small proportions of the collar ; look at the grace of the long sleeves, the length of back, the propriety, the innate respectability, the perfect decorum—we had almost said the high moral worth—of the whole. Who would not willingly sacrifice any individual existence that he might become the exponent of such a coat ? Macassar Jones was proud to do so.

" But he had bestowed perhaps the greatest amount of personal attention on his collar. It was a matter more within his own grasp than those great and important articles to which attention has been already drawn ; but one, nevertheless, on which he was able to expend the whole amount of his energy and genius. Some people may think that an all-rounder is an all-rounder, and that if one is careful to get an all-rounder one has done all that is necessary. But so thought not Macassar Jones. Some men wear collars of two plies of linen, some men of three ; but Macassar Jones wore collars of four plies. Some men—some sensual, self-indulgent men—appear to

think that the collar should be made for the neck; but
Macassar Jones knew better. He, who never spared himself when the cause was good, he knew that the neck had
been made for the collar—it was at any rate evident that
such was the case with his own. Little can be said of
his head, except that it was small, narrow, and genteel;
but his hat might be spoken of, and perhaps with advantage. Of the loose but studied tie of his inch-wide cravat
a paragraph might be made; but we would fain not be
tedious.

"We will only further remark that he always carried
with him a wonderful representation of himself, like to
him to a miracle, only smaller in its dimensions, like as
a duodecimo is to a folio—a babe, as it were, of his own
begetting—a little *alter ego* in which he took much delight.
It was his umbrella. Look at the delicate finish of its
lower extremity; look at the long, narrow, and well-made
coat in which it is enveloped from its neck downwards,
without speck, or blemish, or wrinkle; look at the little
wooden head, nicely polished, with the effigy of a human
face on one side of it—little eyes it has, and a sort of
nose; look closer at it, and you will perceive a mouth,
not expressive indeed, but still it is there—a mouth and
chin; and is it, or is it not, an attempt at a pair of
whiskers? It certainly has a moustache.

"Such were Mr. Macassar Jones and his umbrella.
He was an excellent clerk, and did great credit to the
important office to which he was attached—namely, that
of the Episcopal Audit Board. He was much beloved
by the other gentlemen who were closely connected with
him in that establishment; and may be said, for the first
year or two of his service, to have been, not exactly
the life and soul, but, we may perhaps say with more
propriety, the pervading genius of the room in which
he sat.

"But, alas! at length a cloud came over his brow.
At first it was but a changing shadow; but it settled
into a dark veil of sorrow which obscured all his virtues,
and made the worthy senior of his room shake his thin
grey locks once and again. He shook them more in
sorrow than in anger; for he knew that Macassar was in

love, and he remembered the days of his youth. Yes; Macassar was in love. He had seen the lovely Crinoline. To see was to admire; to admire was to love; to love—that is, to love her, to love Crinoline, the exalted, the sought-after, the one so much in demand, as he had once expressed himself to one of his bosom friends—to love her was to despair. He did despair; and despairing sighed, and sighing was idle.

"But he was not all idle. The genius of the man had that within it which did not permit itself to evaporate in mere sighs. Sighs, with the high-minded, force themselves into the guise of poetry, and so it had been with him. He got leave of absence for a week, and shut himself up alone in his lodgings; for a week in his lodgings, during the long evenings of winter, did he remain unseen and unheard of. His landlady thought that he was in debt, and his friends whispered abroad that he had caught scarlatina. But at the end of the seven days he came forth, pale indeed, but with his countenance lighted up by ecstatic fire, and as he started for his office, he carefully folded and put into his pocket the elegantly written poem on which he had been so intently engaged."

'I'm so glad we are to have more poetry,' said Katie. 'Is it another song?'

'You'll see,' said Mrs. Woodward.

"Macassar had many bosom friends at his office, to all of whom, one by one, he had confided the tale of his love. For a while he doubted to which of them he should confide the secret of his inspiration; but genius will not hide its head under a bushel; and thus, before long, did Macassar's song become the common property of the Episcopal Audit Board. Even the Bishops sang it, so Macassar was assured by one of his brother clerks who was made of a coarser clay than his colleague—even the Bishops sang it when they met in council together on their own peculiar bench.

"It would be useless to give the whole of it here; for it contained ten verses. The last two were those which Macassar was wont to sing to himself, as he wandered lonely under the elms of Kensington Gardens.

" ' Oh, how she walks,
    And how she talks,
And sings like a bird serene ;
    But of this be sure
    While the world shall endure,
The loveliest lady that'll ever be seen
Will still be the Lady Crinoline,
    The lovely Lady Crinoline.

    With her hair done all *à l'impératrice*,
    Sweetly done with the best of grease,
She looks like a Goddess or Queen,—
    And so I declare,
    And solemnly swear,
That the loveliest lady that ever was seen
Is still the Lady Crinoline,
    The lovely Lady Crinoline.' "

' And so ends the third chapter,' said Mrs. Woodward.
Both Katie and Linda were beginning to criticize, but
Mrs. Woodward repressed them sternly, and went on with

" CHAPTER IV

" It was a lovely day towards the end of May that
Macassar Jones, presenting himself before the desk of the
senior clerk at one o'clock, begged for permission to be
absent for two hours. The request was preferred with
meek and hesitating voice, and with downcast eyes.

" The senior clerk shook his grey locks sadly ! sadly
he shook his thin grey locks, for he grieved at the sight
which he saw. 'Twas sad to see the energies of this
young man thus sapped in his early youth by the all-
absorbing strength of a hopeless passion. Crinoline was
now, as it were, a household word at the Episcopal Audit
Board. The senior clerk believed her to be cruel, and
as he knew for what object these two hours of idleness
were requested, he shook his thin grey locks in sorrow.

" ' I'll be back at three, sir, punctual,' said Macassar.

" ' But, Mr. Jones, you are absent nearly every day for
the same period.'

" ' To-day shall be the last ; to-day shall end it all,'
said Macassar, with a look of wretched desperation.

" ' What—what would Sir Gregory say ? ' said the senior clerk.

" Macassar Jones sighed deeply. Nature had not made the senior clerk a cruel man ; but yet this allusion *was* cruel. The young Macassar had drunk deeply of the waters that welled from the fountain of Sir Gregory's philosophy. He had been proud to sit humbly at the feet of such a Gamaliel ; and now it rent his young heart to be thus twitted with the displeasure of the great master whom he so loved and so admired.

" ' Well, go, Mr. Jones,' said the senior clerk, ' go, but as you go, resolve that to-morrow you will remain at your desk. Now go, and may prosperity attend you ! '

" ' All shall be decided to-day,' said Macassar, and as he spoke an unusual spark gleamed in his eye. He went, and as he went the senior clerk shook his thin grey hairs. He was a bachelor, and he distrusted the charms of the sex.

" Macassar, returning to his desk, took up his hat and his umbrella, and went forth. His indeed was a plight at which that old senior clerk might well shake his thin grey hairs in sorrow, for Macassar was the victim of mysterious circumstances, which, from his youth upwards, had marked him out for a fate of no ordinary nature. The tale must now be told."

' O dear ! ' said Linda ; ' is it something horrid ? '

' I hope it is,' said Katie ; ' perhaps he 's already married to some old hag or witch.'

' You don't say who his father and mother are ; but I suppose he'll turn out to be somebody else's son,' said Linda.

' He 's a very nice young man for a small tea-party, at any rate,' said Uncle Bat.

" The tale must now be told," continued Mrs. Woodward. " In his early years Macassar Jones had had a maiden aunt. This lady died——"

' Oh, mamma, if you read it in that way I shall certainly cry,' said Katie.

' Well, my dear, if your heart is so susceptible you had better indulge it.' " This lady died and left behind her——"

' What ? ' said Linda.

' A diamond ring ? ' said Katie.

' A sealed manuscript, which was found in a secret drawer ? ' suggested Linda.

' Perhaps a baby,' said Uncle Bat.

" And left behind her a will——"

' Did she leave anything else ? ' asked Norman.

' Ladies and gentlemen, if I am to be interrupted in this way, I really must resign my task,' said Mrs. Woodward ; ' we shall never get to bed.'

' I won't say another word,' said Katie.

" In his early years Macassar had had a maiden aunt. This lady died and left behind her a will, in which, with many expressions of the warmest affection and fullest confidence, she left £3,000 in the three per cents.——"

' What are the three per cents. ? ' said Katie.

' The three per cents. is a way in which people get some of their money to spend regularly, when they have got a large sum locked up somewhere,' said Linda.

' Oh ! ' said Katie.

' Will you hold your tongue, miss ? ' said Mrs. Woodward.

" Left £3,000 in the three per cents. to her nephew. But she left it on these conditions, that he should be married before he was twenty-five, and that he should have a child lawfully born in the bonds of wedlock before he was twenty-six. And then the will went on to state that the interest of the money should accumulate till Macassar had attained the latter age ; and that in the event of his having failed to comply with the conditions and stipulations above named, the whole money, principal and interest, should be set aside, and by no means given up to the said Macassar, but applied to the uses, purposes, and convenience of that excellent charitable institution, denominated the Princess Charlotte's Lying-in Hospital.

" Now the nature of this will had been told in confidence by Macassar to some of his brother clerks, and was consequently well known at the Episcopal Audit Board. It had given rise there to a spirit of speculation against which the senior clerk had protested in vain. Bets were made, some in favour of Macassar, and some in that of the hospital ; but of late the odds were going much against our hero. It was well known that in three short months he would attain that disastrous age, which, if it found him a bachelor, would find him also denuded of his legacy. And then how short a margin remained for the second event! The odds were daily rising against Macassar, and as he heard the bets offered and taken at the surrounding desks, his heart quailed within him.

"And the lovely Crinoline, she also had heard of this eccentric will; she and her mother. £3,000 with interest arising for some half score of years would make a settlement by no means despicable in Tavistock Square, and would enable Macassar to maintain a house over which even Crinoline need not be ashamed to preside. But what if the legacy should be lost! She also knew to a day what was the age of her swain; she knew how close upon her was that day, which, if she passed it unwedded, would see her resolved to be deaf for ever to the vows of Macassar. Still, if she managed well, there might be time—at any rate for the marriage.

"But, alas! Macassar made no vows; none at least which the most attentive ear could consider to be audible. Crinoline's ear was attentive, but hitherto in vain. He would come there daily to Tavistock Square; daily would that true and valiant page lay open the path to his mistress's feet; daily would Macassar sit there for a while and sigh. But the envious hour would pass away, while the wished-for word was still unsaid; and he would hurry back, and complete with figures, too often erroneous, the audit of some diocesan balance.

"'You must help him, my dear,' said Crinoline's mamma.

"'But he says nothing, mamma,' said Crinoline in tears.

"'You must encourage him to speak, my dear.'

"'I do encourage him; but by that time it is always three o'clock, and then he has to go away.'

"'You should be quicker, my dear. You should encourage him more at once. Now try to-day; if you can't do anything to-day I really must get your papa to interfere.'

"Crinoline had ever been an obedient child, and now, as ever, she determined to obey. But it was a hard task for her. In three months he would be twenty-five—

in fifteen months twenty-six. She, however, would do her best ; and then, if her efforts were unavailing, she could only trust to Providence and her papa.

"With sad and anxious heart did Macassar that day take up his new silk hat, take up also his darling umbrella, and descend the sombre steps of the Episcopal Audit Office. 'Seven to one on the Lying-in,' were the last words which reached his ears as the door of his room closed behind him. His was a dreadful position. What if that sweet girl, that angel whom he so worshipped, what if she, melted by his tale of sorrow—that is, if he could prevail on himself to tell it—should take pity, and consent to be hurried prematurely to the altar of Hymen ; and then if, after all, the legacy should be forfeited ! Poverty for himself he could endure ; at least he thought so ; but poverty for her ! could he bear that ? What if he should live to see her deprived of that green head-dress, robbed of those copious draperies, reduced to English shoes, compelled to desert that shrine in Hanover Square, and all through him ! His brain reeled round, his head swam, his temples throbbed, his knees knocked against each other, his blood stagnated, his heart collapsed, a cold clammy perspiration covered him from head to foot ; he could hardly reach the courtyard, and there obtain the support of a pillar. Dreadful thoughts filled his mind ; the Thames, the friendly Thames, was running close to him ; should he not put a speedy end to all his misery ? Those horrid words, that 'seven to one on the Lying-in,' still rang in his ears ; were the chances really seven to one against his getting his legacy ? ' Oh ! ' said he, ' my aunt, my aunt, my aunt, my aunt, my aunt ! '

"But at last he roused the spirit of the man within him. ' Faint heart never won fair lady,' seemed to be whispered to him from every stone in Somerset House. The cool air blowing through the passages revived him, and he walked forth through the wide portals, resolving that he would return a happy, thriving lover, or that he would return no more—that night. What would he care for Sir Gregory, what for the thin locks of the senior clerk, if Crinoline should reject him ?

"It was his custom, as he walked towards Tavistock

Square, to stop at a friendly pastry-cook's in Covent Garden, and revive his spirits for the coming interview with Banbury tarts and cherry-brandy. In the moments of his misery something about the pastry-cook's girl, something that reminded him of Crinoline, it was probably her nose, had tempted him to confide to her his love. He had told her everything; the kind young creature pitied him, and as she ministered to his wants, was wont to ask sweetly as to his passion.

" ' And how was the lovely Lady Crinoline yesterday ? ' asked she. He had entrusted to her a copy of his poem.

" ' More beauteous than ever,' he said, but somewhat indistinctly, for his mouth was clogged with the Banbury tart.

" ' And good-natured, I hope. Indeed, I don't know how she can resist,' said the girl; 'I'm sure you'll make it all right to-day, for I see you've got your winning way with you.'

" Winning way, with seven to one against him ! Macassar sighed, and spilt some of his cherry-brandy over his shirt front. The kind-hearted girl came and wiped it for him. 'I think I'll have another glass,' said he, with a deep voice. He did take another glass—and also another tart.

" ' He'll pop to-day as sure as eggs, now he's taken them two glasses of popping powder,' said the girl, as he went out of the shop. 'Well, it's astonishing to me what the men find to be afraid of.'

" And so Macassar hastened towards Tavistock Square, all too quickly; for, as he made his way across Great Russell Street, he found that he was very hot. He leant against the rail, and, taking off his hat and gloves, began to cool himself, and wipe away the dust with his pocket-handkerchief. 'I wouldn't have minded the expense of a cab,' said he to himself, 'only the chances are so much against me: seven to one !'

" But he had no time to lose. He had had but two precious hours at his disposal, and thirty minutes were already gone. He hurried on to Tavistock Square, and soon found that well-known door open before him.

" ' The Lady Crinoline sits upstairs alone,' said the

page, 'and is a-thinking of you.' Then he added in a whisper, 'Do you go at her straight, Mr. Macassar; slip-slap, and no mistake.'

" All honour to the true and brave !

" CHAPTER V

" As Macassar walked across the drawing-room, Crinoline failed to perceive his presence, although his boots did creak rather loudly. Such at least must be presumed to have been the case, for she made no immediate sign of having noticed him. She was sitting at the open window, with her lute in hand, gazing into the vacancy of the square below; and as Macassar walked across the room, a deep sigh escaped from her bosom. The page closed the door, and at the same moment Crinoline touched her lute, or rather pulled it at the top and bottom, and threw one wild witch note to the wind. As she did so, a line of a song escaped from her lips with a low, melancholy, but still rapturous cadence—

'His heart is *at* his office, *his* heart is *always* there.'

" ' Oh, Mr. Macassar, is that you ? ' she exclaimed. She struggled to rise, but, finding herself unequal to the effort, she sank back again on a chair, dropped her lute on a soft footstool, and then buried her face in her hands. It was dreadful for Macassar to witness such agony.

" ' Is anything the matter ? ' said he.

" ' The matter ! ' said she. 'Ah ! ah ! '

" ' I hope you are not sick ? ' said he.

" ' Sick ! ' said she. 'Well, I fear I am very sick.'

" ' What is it ? ' said he. 'Perhaps only bilious,' he suggested.

" ' Oh ! oh ! oh ! ' said she.

" ' I see I'm in the way ; and I think I had better go,' and so he prepared to depart.

" ' No ! no ! no ! ' said she, jumping up from her chair. ' Oh ! Mr. Macassar, don't be so cruel. Do you wish to see me sink on the carpet before your feet ? '

" Macassar denied the existence of any such wish ; and said that he humbly begged her pardon if he gave any offence.

" ' Offence ! ' said she, smiling sweetly on him ; sweetly, but yet sadly. ' Offence ! no—no offence. Indeed, I don't know how you could—but never mind—I am such a silly thing. One's feelings will sometimes get the better of one ; don't you often find it so ? '

" ' O yes ! quite so,' said Macassar. ' I think it 's the heat.'

" ' He 's a downright noodle,' said Crinoline's mamma to her sister-in-law, who lived with them. The two were standing behind a chink in the door, which separated the drawing-room from a chamber behind it.

" ' Won't you sit down, Mr. Macassar ? ' Macassar sat down. ' Mamma will be so sorry to miss you again. She 's calling somewhere in Grosvenor Square, I believe. She wanted me to go with her ; but I could not bring myself to go with her to-day. It 's useless for the body to go out, when the heart still remains at home. Don't you find it so ? '

" ' Oh, quite so,' said Macassar. The cherry-brandy had already evaporated before the blaze of all that beauty, and he was bethinking himself how he might best take himself off. Let the hospital have the filthy lucre ! He would let the money go, and would show the world that he loved for the sake of love alone ! He looked at his watch, and found that it was already past two.

" Crinoline, when she saw that watch, knew that something must be done at once. She appreciated more fully than her lover did the value of this world's goods ; and much as she doubtless sympathized with the wants of the hospital in question, she felt that charity should begin at home. So she fairly burst out into a flood of tears.

" Macassar was quite beside himself. He had seen her weep before, but never with such frightful violence. She rushed up from her chair, and passing so close to him as nearly to upset him by the waft of her petticoats, threw herself on to an ottoman, and hiding her face on the stump in the middle of it, sobbed and screeched, till Macassar feared that the buttons behind her dress would crack and fly off.

" ' Oh ! oh ! oh ! ' sobbed Crinoline.

" ' It must be the heat,' said Macassar, knocking down

a flower-pot in his attempt to open the window a little wider. 'O dear, what have I done?' said he. 'I think I'd better go.'

"'Never mind the flower-pot,' said Crinoline, looking up through her tears. 'Oh! oh! oh! oh! me. Oh! my heart.'

"Macassar looked at his watch. He had only forty-five minutes left for everything. The expense of a cab would, to be sure, be nothing if he were successful; but then, what chance was there of that?

"'Can I do anything for you in the Strand?' said he. 'I must be at my office at three.'

"'In the Strand!' she screeched. 'What could he do for me in the Strand? Heartless—heartless—heartless! Well, go—go—go to your office, Mr. Macassar; your heart is there, I know. It is always there. Go—don't let me stand between you and your duties—between you and Sir Gregory. Oh! how I hate that man! Go! why should I wish to prevent you? Of course I have no such wish. To me it is quite indifferent; only mamma will be so sorry to miss you. You don't know how mamma loves you. She loves you almost as a son. But go—go; pray go!'

"And then Crinoline looked at him. Oh! how she looked at him! It was as though all the goddesses of heaven were inviting him to come and eat ambrosia with them on a rosy-tinted cloud. All the goddesses, did we say? No, but one goddess, the most beautiful of them all. His heart beat violently against his ribs, and he felt that he was almost man enough for anything. Instinctively his hand went again to his waistcoat pocket.

"'You shan't look at your watch so often,' said she, putting up her delicate hand and stopping his. 'There I'll look at it for you. It's only just two, and you needn't go to your office for this hour;' and as she squeezed it back into his pocket, he felt her fingers pressing against his heart, and felt her hair—done all *à l'impératrice*—in sweet contact with his cheek. 'There, I shall hold it there,' said she, 'so that you shan't look at it again.'

"'Will you stay till I bid you go?' said Crinoline.

" Macassar declared that he did not care a straw for the
senior clerk, or for Sir Gregory either. He would stay
there for ever, he said.

" ' What! for ever in mamma's drawing-room ? ' said
Crinoline, opening wide her lovely eyes with surprise.

" ' For ever near to you,' said Macassar.

" ' Oh, Mr. Macassar,' said Crinoline, drópping her
hand from his waistcoat, and looking bashfully towards
the ground, ' what can you mean ? '

" Down went Macassar on his knees, and down went
Crinoline into her chair. There was perhaps rather too
much distance between them, but that did not much
matter now. There he was on both knees, with his
hands clasped together as they were wont to be when he
said his prayers, with his umbrella beside him on one
side, and his hat on the other, making his declaration in
full and unmistakable terms. A yard or two of floor,
more or less, between them, was neither here nor there.
At first the bashful Crinoline could not bring herself to
utter a distinct consent, and Macassar was very nearly
up and away, in a returning fit of despair. But her
good-nature came to his aid ; and as she quickly said,
' I will, I will, I will,' he returned to his posture in somewhat nearer quarters, and was transported into the
seventh heaven by the bliss of kissing her hand.

" ' Oh, Macassar ! ' said she.

" ' Oh, Crinoline ! ' said he.

" ' You must come and tell papa to-morrow,' said she.

" He readily promised to do so.

" ' You had better come to breakfast ; before he goes
into the city,' said she.

" And so the matter was arranged, and the lovely
Lady Crinoline became the affianced bride of the happy
Macassar.

. " It was past three when he left the house, but what
did he care for that ? He was so mad with joy that he
did not even know whither he was going. He went on
straight ahead, and came to no check, till he found himself waving his hat over his head in the New Road. He
then began to conceive that his conduct must have
been rather wild, for he was brought to a stand-still in a

crossing by four or five cabmen, who were rival candidates for his custom.

" 'Somerset House, old brick !' he shouted out, as he jumped into a hansom, and as he did so he poked one of the other cabbies playfully in the ribs with his umbrella.

" ' 'Is mamma don't know as 'ow 'e 's hout, I shouldn't vonder,' said the cabman—and away went Macassar, singing at the top of his voice as he sat in the cab—

> 'The loveliest lady that ever was seen
> Is the lovely Lady Crinoline.'

" The cab passed through Covent Garden on its way. 'Stop at the pastry-cook's at the corner,' said Macassar up through the little trap-door. The cab drew up suddenly. 'She 's mine, she 's mine !' shouted Macassar, rushing into the shop, and disregarding in the ecstasy of the moment the various customers who were quietly eating their ices. 'She 's mine, she 's mine !

> With her hair done all *à l'impératrice*,
> Sweetly done with the best of grease.

And now for Somerset House.'

" Arrived at those ancient portals, he recklessly threw eighteenpence to the cabman, and ran up the stone stairs which led to his office. As he did so the clock, with iron tongue, tolled four. But what recked he what it tolled ? He rushed into his room, where his colleagues were now locking their desks, and waving abroad his hat and his umbrella, repeated the chorus of his song. 'She 's mine, she 's mine—

> The loveliest lady that ever was seen
> Is the lovely Lady Crinoline ;

and she 's mine, she 's mine !'

" Exhausted nature could no more. He sank into a chair, and his brother clerks stood in a circle around him. Soon a spirit of triumph seemed to actuate them all ; they joined hands in that friendly circle, and dancing with joyful glee, took up with one voice the burden of the song—

'Oh how she walks,
    And how she talks,
And sings like a bird serene,
    But of this be sure,
    While the world shall endure,
The loveliest lady that ever was seen
    Is still the Lady Crinoline—
    The lovely Lady Crinoline.'

"And that old senior clerk with the thin grey hair—was he angry at this general ebullition of joy ? O no! The just severity of his discipline was always tempered with genial mercy. Not a word did he say of that broken promise, not a word of the unchecked diocesan balance, not a word of Sir Gregory's anger. He shook his thin grey locks ; but he shook them neither in sorrow nor in anger. 'God bless you, Macassar Jones,' said he, 'God bless you !'

"He too had once been young, had once loved, had once hoped and feared, and hoped again, and had once knelt at the feet of beauty. But alas! he had knelt in vain.

"'May God be with you, Macassar Jones,' said he, as he walked out of the office door with his coloured bandana pressed to his eyes. 'May God be with you, and make your bed fruitful !'

"'For the loveliest lady that ever was seen
    Is the lovely Lady Crinoline,'

shouted the junior clerks, still dancing in mad glee round the happy lover.

"We have said that they all joined in this kindly congratulation to their young friend. But no. There was one spirit there whom envy had soured, one whom the happiness of another had made miserable, one whose heart beat in no unison with these jocund sounds. As Macassar's joy was at its height, in the proud moment of his triumph, a hated voice struck his ears, and filled his soul with dismay once more.

"'There 's two to one still on the Lying-in,' said this hateful Lucifer.

"And so Macassar was not all happy even yet, as he walked home to his lodgings.

" CHAPTER VI

" We have but one other scene to record, but one
short scene, and then our tale will be told and our task
will be done. And this last scene shall not, after the
usual manner of novelists, be that of the wedding, but
rather one which in our eyes is of a much more enduring
interest. Crinoline and Macassar were duly married in
Bloomsbury Church. The dresses are said to have come
from the house in Hanover Square. Crinoline behaved
herself with perfect propriety, and Macassar went through
his work like a man. When we have said that, we have
said all that need be said on that subject.

" But we must beg our readers to pass over the space
of the next twelve months, and to be present with us in
that front sitting-room of the elegant private lodgings,
which the married couple now prudently occupied in
Alfred Place. Lodgings ! yes, they were only lodgings ;
for not as yet did they know what might be the extent
of their income.

" In this room during the whole of a long autumn day
sat Macassar in a frame of mind not altogether to be
envied. During the greater portion of it he was alone ;
but ever and anon some bustling woman would enter and
depart without even deigning to notice the questions
which he asked. And then after a while he found himself
in company with a very respectable gentleman in black,
who belonged to the medical profession.

" ' Is it coming ? ' asked Macassar. ' Is it, is it
coming ? '

" ' Well, we hope so—we hope so,' said the medical
gentleman. ' If not to-day, it will be to-morrow. If I
should happen to be absent, Mrs. Gamp is all that you
could desire. If not to-day, it will certainly be to-morrow,'
—and so the medical gentleman went his way.

" Now the coming morrow would be Macassar's birthday. On that morrow he would be twenty-six.

" All alone he sat there till the autumn sun gave way
to the shades of evening. Some one brought him a
mutton chop, but it was raw and he could not eat ; he
went to the sideboard and prepared to make himself

a glass of negus, but the water was all cold. His water at least was cold, though Mrs. Gamp's was hot enough. It was a sad and mournful evening. He thought he would go out, for he found that he was not wanted; but a low drizzling rain prevented him. Had he got wet he could not have changed his clothes, for they were all in the wardrobe in his wife's room. All alone he sat till the shades of evening were hidden by the veil of night.

"But what sudden noise is that he hears within the house? Why do those heavy steps press so rapidly against the stairs? What feet are they which are so busy in the room above him? He opens the sitting-room door, but he can see nothing. He has been left there without a candle. He peers up the stairs, but a faint glimmer of light shining through the keyhole of his wife's door is all that meets his eye. 'Oh, my aunt! my aunt!' he says as he leans against the banisters. 'My aunt, my aunt, my aunt!'

"What a birthday will this be for him on the morrow! He already hears the sound of the hospital bells as they ring with joy at the acquisition of their new wealth; he must dash from his lips, tear from his heart, banish for ever from his eyes, that vision of a sweet little cottage at Brompton, with a charming dressing-room for himself, and gas laid on all over the house.

"'Lodgings! I hate, I detest lodgings!' he said to himself. 'Connubial bliss and furnished lodgings are not compatible. My aunt, my aunt, for what misery hast thou not to answer! Oh, Mrs. Gamp, could you be so obliging as to tell me what o'clock it is?' The last question was asked as Mrs. Gamp suddenly entered the room with a candle. Macassar's watch had been required for the use of one of the servants.

"'It's just half-past heleven, this wery moment as is,' said Mrs. Gamp; 'and the finest boy babby as my heyes, which has seen a many, has ever sat upon.'

"Up, up to the ceiling went the horsehair cushion of the lodging-house sofa—up went the footstool after it, and its four wooden legs in falling made a terrible clatter on the mahogany loo-table. Macassar in his joy got hold of Mrs. Gamp, and kissed her heartily, forgetful of the fumes of gin. 'Hurrah!' shouted he, 'hurrah, hurrah, hurrah! Oh, Mrs. Gamp, I feel so—so—so—I really don't know how I feel.'

"He danced round the room with noisy joy, till Mrs. Gamp made him understand how very unsuited were such riotous ebullitions to the weak state of his lady-love upstairs. He then gave over, not the dancing but the noise, and went on capering round the room with suppressed steps, ever and anon singing to himself in a whisper,

'The loveliest lady that ever was seen
Is still the Lady Crinoline.'

"A few minutes afterwards a knock at the door was heard, and the monthly nurse entered. She held something in her embrace; but he could not see what. He looked down pryingly into her arms, and at the first glance thought that it was his umbrella. But then he heard a little pipe, and he knew that it was his child.

"We will not intrude further on the first interview between Macassar and his heir."

'And so ends the romantic history of "Crinoline and Macassar",' said Mrs. Woodward; 'and I am sure, Charley, we are all very much obliged to you for the excellent moral lessons you have given us.'

'I'm so delighted with it,' said Katie; 'I do so like that Macassar.'

'So do I,' said Linda, yawning; 'and the old man with the thin grey hair.'

'Come, girls, it's nearly one o'clock, and we'll go to bed,' said the mother. 'Uncle Bat has been asleep these two hours.'

And so they went off to their respective chambers.

CHAPTER XXIII

SURBITON COLLOQUIES

ALL further conversation in the drawing-room was forbidden for that night. Mrs. Woodward would have willingly postponed the reading of Charley's story so as to enable Katie to go to bed after the accident, had she been able to do so. But she was not able to do so without an exercise of a species of authority which was distasteful to her, and which was very seldom heard, seen, or felt within the limits of Surbiton Cottage. It would moreover have been very ungracious to snub Charley's manuscript, just when Charley had made himself such a hero; and she had, therefore, been obliged to read it. But now that it was done, she hurried Katie off to bed, not without many admonitions.

'Good night,' she said to Charley; 'and God bless you, and make you always as happy as we are now. What a household we should have had to-night, had it not been for you!'

Charley rubbed his eyes with his hand, and muttered something about there not having been the slightest danger in the world.

'And remember, Charley,' she said, paying no attention to his mutterings, 'we always liked you—liked you very much; but liking and loving are very different things. Now you are a dear, dear friend—one of the dearest.'

In answer to this, Charley was not even able to mutter; so he went his way to the inn, and lay awake half the night thinking how Katie had kissed his hand: during the other half he dreamt, first that Katie was drowned, and then that Norah was his bride.

Linda and Katie had been so hurried off, that they had only been just able to shake hands with Harry and Charley. There is, however, an old proverb, that though one man may lead a horse to water, a thousand cannot make him drink. It was easy to send Katie to bed, but very difficult to prevent her talking when she was there.

'Oh, Linda,' she said, 'what can I do for him ?'

'Do for him ?' said Linda; 'I don't know that you can do anything for him. I don't suppose he wants you to do anything.' Linda still looked on her sister as a child; but Katie was beginning to put away childish things.

'Couldn't I make something for him, Linda—something for him to keep as a present, you know ? I would work so hard to get it done.'

'Work a pair of slippers, as Crinoline did,' said Linda.

Katie was brushing her hair at the moment, and then she sat still with the brush in her hand, thinking. 'No,' said she, after a while, 'not a pair of slippers—I shouldn't like a pair of slippers.'

'Why not ?' said Linda.

'Oh—I don't know—but I shouldn't.' Katie had said that Crinoline was working slippers for Macassar because she was in love with him; and having said so, she could not now work slippers for Charley. Poor Katie! she was no longer a child when she thought thus.

'Then make him a purse,' said Linda.

'A purse is such a little thing.'

'Then work him the cover for a sofa, like what mamma and I are doing for Gertrude.'

'But he hasn't got a house,' said Katie.

'He'll have a house by the time you've done the sofa, and a wife to sit on it too.'

'Oh, Linda, you are so ill-natured.'

'Why, child, what do you want me to say ? If you were to give him one of those grand long tobacco pipes they have in the shop windows, that's what he'd like the best; or something of that sort. I don't think he cares much for girls' presents, such as purses and slippers.'

'Doesn't he ?' said Katie, mournfully.

'No; not a bit. You know he's such a rake.'

'Oh! Linda; I don't think he's so very bad, indeed I don't; and mamma doesn't think so; and you know Harry said on Easter Sunday that he was much better than he used to be.'

'I know Harry is very good-natured to him.'

'And isn't Charley just as good-natured to Harry? I am quite sure he is. Harry has only to ask the least thing, and Charley always does it. Do you remember how Charley went up to town for him the Sunday before last?'

'And so he ought,' said Linda. 'He ought to do whatever Harry tells him.'

'Well, Linda, I don't know why he ought,' said Katie. 'They are not brothers, you know, nor yet even cousins.'

'But Harry is very—so very—so very superior, you know,' said Linda.

'I don't know any such thing,' said Katie.

'Oh! Katie, don't you know that Charley is such a rake?'

'But rakes are just the people who don't do whatever they are told; so that's no reason. And I am quite sure that Charley is much the cleverer.'

'And I am quite sure he is not—nor half so clever; nor nearly so well educated. Why, don't you know the navvies are the most ignorant young men in London? Charley says so himself.'

'That's his fun,' said Katie: 'besides, he always makes little of himself. I am quite sure Harry could never have made all that about Macassar and Crinoline out of his own head.'

'No! because he doesn't think of such nonsensical things. I declare, Miss Katie, I think you are in love with Master Charley.'

Katie, who was still sitting at the dressing-table, blushed up to her forehead; and at the same time her eyes were suffused with tears. But there was no one to see either of those tell-tale symptoms, for Linda was in bed.

'I know he saved my life,' said Katie, as soon as she could trust herself to speak without betraying her emotion —'I know he jumped into the river after me, and very, very nearly drowned himself; and I don't think any other man in the world would have done so much for me besides him.'

'Oh, Katie! Harry would in a moment.'

'Not for me; perhaps he might for you—though I'm

not quite sure that he would.' It was thus that Katie
took her revenge on her sister.

'I'm quite sure he would for anybody, even for Sally.'
Sally was an assistant in the back kitchen. 'But I don't
mean to say, Katie, that you shouldn't feel grateful to
Charley; of course you should.'

'And so I do,' said Katie, now bursting out into tears,
overdone by her emotion and fatigue; 'and so I do—and
I do love him, and will love him, if he's ever so much
a rake! But you know, Linda, that is very different
from being in love; and it was very ill-natured of you to
say so, very.'

Linda was out of bed in a trice, and sitting with her
arm round her sister's neck.

'Why, you darling little foolish child, you! I was
only quizzing,' said she. 'Don't you know that I love
Charley too?'

'But you shouldn't quiz about such a thing as that.
If you'd fallen into the river, and Harry had pulled you
out, then you'd know what I mean; but I'm not
at all sure that he could have done it.'

Katie's perverse wickedness on this point was very
nearly giving rise to another contest between the sisters.
Linda's common sense, however, prevailed, and giving
up the point of Harry's prowess, she succeeded at last in
getting Katie into bed. 'You know mamma will be so
angry if she hears us,' said Linda, 'and I am sure you will
be ill to-morrow.'

'I don't care a bit about being ill to-morrow; and
yet I do too,' she added, after a pause, 'for it's Sunday.
It would be so stupid not to be able to go out to-morrow.'

'Well, then, try to go to sleep at once'—and Linda
carefully tucked the clothes around her sister.

'I think it shall be a purse,' said Katie.

'A purse will certainly be the best; that is, if you
don't like the slippers,' and Linda rolled herself up comfortably in the bed.

'No—I don't like the slippers at all. It shall be a
purse. I can do that the quickest, you know. It's so
stupid to give a thing when everything about it is forgotten, isn't it?'

'Very stupid,' said Linda, nearly asleep.

'And when it's worn out I can make another, can't I?'

'H'm 'm 'm,' said Linda, quite asleep.

And then Katie went asleep also, in her sister's arms.

Early in the morning—that is to say, not very early, perhaps between seven and eight—Mrs. Woodward came into their room, and having inspected her charges, desired that Katie should not get up for morning church, but lie in bed till the middle of the day.

'Oh, mamma, it will be so stupid not going to church after tumbling into the river; people will say that all my clothes are wet.'

'People will about tell the truth as to some of them,' said Mrs. Woodward; 'but don't you mind about people, but lie still and go to sleep if you can. Linda, do you come and dress in my room.'

'And is Charley to lie in bed too?' said Katie. 'He was in the river longer than I was.'

'It's too late to keep Charley in bed,' said Linda, 'for I see him coming along the road now with a towel; he's been bathing.'

'Oh, I do so wish I could go and bathe,' said Katie.

Poor Katie was kept in bed till the afternoon. Charley and Harry, however, were allowed to come up to her bedroom door, and hear her pronounce herself quite well.

'How d'ye do, Mr. Macassar?' said she.

'And how d'ye do, my Lady Crinoline?' said Harry. After that Katie never called Charley Mr. Macassar again.

They all went to church, and Katie was left to sleep or read, or think of the new purse that she was to make, as best she might.

And then they dined, and then they walked out; but still without Katie. She was to get up and dress while they were out, so as to receive them in state in the drawing-room on their return. Four of them walked together; for Uncle Bat now usually took himself off to his friend at Hampton Court on Sunday afternoon. Mrs. Woodward walked with Charley, and Harry and Linda paired together.

'Now,' said Charley to himself, 'now would have been the time to have told Mrs. Woodward everything, but for that accident of yesterday. Now I can tell her nothing; to do so now would be to demand her sympathy and to ask for assistance;' and so he determined to tell her nothing.

But the very cause which made Charley dumb on the subject of his own distresses made Mrs. Woodward inquisitive about them. She knew that his life was not like that of Harry—steady, sober, and discreet; but she felt that she did not like him, or even love him the less on this account. Nay, it was not clear to her that these failings of his did not give him additional claims on her sympathies. What could she do for him? how could she relieve him? how could she bring him back to the right way? She spoke to him of his London life, praised his talents, encouraged him to exertion, besought him to have some solicitude, and, above all, some respect for himself. And then, with that delicacy which such a woman, and none but such a woman, can use in such a matter, she asked him whether he was still in debt.

Charley, with shame we must own it, had on this subject been false to all his friends. He had been false to his father and his mother, and had never owned to them the half of what he owed; he had been false to Alaric, and false to Harry; but now, now, at such a moment as this, he would not allow himself to be false to Mrs. Woodward.

'Yes,' he said, 'he was in debt—rather.'

Mrs. Woodward pressed him to say whether his debts were heavy—whether he owed much.

'It's no use thinking of it, Mrs. Woodward,' said he; 'not the least. I know I ought not to come down here; and I don't think I will any more.'

'Not come down here!' said Mrs. Woodward. 'Why not? There's very little expense in that. I dare say you'd spend quite as much in London.'

'Oh—of course—three times as much, perhaps; that is, if I had it—but I don't mean that.'

'What do you mean?' said she.

Charley walked on in silence, with melancholy look, very crestfallen, his thumbs stuck into his waistcoat pockets.

'Upon my word I don't know what you mean,' said Mrs. Woodward. 'I should have thought coming to Hampton might perhaps—perhaps have kept you—I don't exactly mean out of mischief.' That, however, in spite of her denial, was exactly what Mrs. Woodward did mean.

'So it does—but——' said Charley, now thoroughly ashamed of himself.

'But what ?' said she.

'I am not fit to be here,' said Charley ; and as he spoke his manly self-control all gave way, and big tears rolled down his cheeks.

Mrs. Woodward, in her woman's heart, resolved, that if it might in any way be possible, she would make him fit, fit not only to be there, but to hold his head up with the best in any company in which he might find himself.

She questioned him no further then. Her wish now was not to torment him further, but to comfort him. She determined that she would consult with Harry and with her uncle, and take counsel from them as to what steps might be taken to save the brand from the burning. She talked to him as a mother might have done, leaning on his arm, as she returned ; leaning on him as a woman never leans on a man whom she deems unfit for her society. All this Charley's heart and instinct fully understood, and he was not ungrateful.

But yet he had but little to comfort him. He must return to town on Monday ; return to Mr. Snape and the lock entries, to Mr. M'Ruen and the three Seasons—to Mrs. Davis, Norah Geraghty, and that horrid Mr. Peppermint. He never once thought of Clementina Golightly, to whom at that moment he was being married by the joint energies of Undy Scott and his cousin Alaric.

And what had Linda and Norman been doing all this time ? Had they been placing mutual confidence in each other ? No ; they had not come to that yet. Linda still remembered the pang with which she had first heard of Gertrude's engagement, and Harry Norman had not yet been able to open his seared heart to a second love.

In the course of the evening a letter was brought to Captain Cuttwater, which did not seem to raise his spirits.

' Whom is your letter from, uncle ? ' said Mrs. Woodward.

' From Alaric,' said he, gruffly, crumpling it up and putting it into his pocket. And then he turned to his rum and water in a manner that showed his determination to say nothing more on the matter.

In the morning Harry and Charley returned to town. Captain Cuttwater went up with them ; and all was again quiet at Surbiton Cottage.

CHAPTER XXIV

MR. M'BUFFER ACCEPTS THE CHILTERN HUNDREDS

IT was an anxious hour for the Honourable Undecimus Scott when he first learnt that Mr. M'Buffer had accepted the Stewardship of the Chiltern Hundreds. The Stewardship of the Chiltern Hundreds ! Does it never occur to anyone how many persons are appointed to that valuable situation ? Or does anyone ever reflect why a Member of Parliament, when he wishes to resign his post of honour, should not be simply gazetted in the newspapers as having done so, instead of being named as the new Steward of the Chiltern Hundreds ? No one ever does think of it ; resigning and becoming a steward are one and the same thing, with this difference, however, that one of the grand bulwarks of the British constitution is thus preserved.

Well, Mr. M'Buffer, who, having been elected by the independent electors of the Tillietudlem burghs to serve them in Parliament, could not, in accordance with the laws of the constitution, have got himself out of that honourable but difficult position by any scheme of his own, found himself on a sudden a free man, the Queen having selected him to be her steward for the district in question. We have no doubt but that the deed of appointment set forth that her Majesty had been moved to this step by the firm trust she had in the skill and fidelity of the said Mr. M'Buffer ; but if so her Majesty's trust would seem to have been somewhat misplaced, as Mr. M'Buffer, having been a managing director of a bankrupt swindle, from which he had contrived to pillage some thirty or forty thousand pounds, was now unable to show his face at Tillietudlem, or in the House of Commons; and in thus retreating from his membership had no object but to save himself from the expulsion which he feared. It was, however, a consolation for him to think that in what he had done the bulwarks of the British constitution had been preserved.

It was an anxious moment for Undy. The existing Parliament had still a year and a half, or possibly two years and a half, to run. He had already been withdrawn from the public eye longer than he thought was suitable to the success of his career. He particularly disliked obscurity for he had found that in his case obscurity had meant comparative poverty. An obscure man, as he observed early in life, had nothing to sell. Now, Undy had once had something to sell, and a very good market he had made of it. He was of course anxious that those halcyon days should return. Fond of him as the electors of Tillietudlem no doubt were, devoted as they might be in a general way to his interests still, still it was possible that they might forget him, if he remained too long away from their embraces. 'Out of sight out of mind' is a proverb which opens to us the worst side of human nature. But even at Tillietudlem nature's worst side might sometimes show itself.

Actuated by such feelings as these, Undy heard with joy the tidings of M'Buffer's stewardship, and determined to rush to the battle at once. Battle he knew there must be. To be brought in for the district of Tillietudlem was a prize which had never yet fallen to any man's lot without a contest. Tillietudlem was no poor pocket borough to be disposed of, this way or that way, according to the caprice or venal call of some aristocrat. The men of Tillietudlem knew the value of their votes, and would only give them according to their consciences. The way to win these consciences, to overcome the sensitive doubts of a free and independent Tillietudlem elector, Undy knew to his cost.

It was almost a question, as he once told Alaric, whether all that he could sell was worth all that he was compelled to buy. But having put his neck to the collar in this line of life, he was not now going to withdraw. Tillietudlem was once more vacant, and Undy determined to try it again, undaunted by former outlays. To make an outlay, however, at any rate in electioneering matters, it is necessary that a man should have in hand some ready cash ; at the present moment Undy had very little, and therefore the news of Mr. M'Buffer's retirement to the German baths for his health was not heard with unalloyed delight.

He first went into the city, as men always do when they want money ; though in what portion of the city they find it, has never come to the author's knowledge. Charley Tudor, to be sure, did get £5 by going to the ' Banks of Jordan ; ' but the supply likely to be derived from such a fountain as that would hardly be sufficient for Undy's wants. Having done what he could in the city, he came to Alaric, and prayed for the assistance of all his friend's energies in the matter. Alaric would not have been, and was not unwilling to assist him to the extent of his own immediate means ; but his own immediate means were limited, and Undy's desire for ready cash was almost unlimited.

There was a certain railway or proposed railway in Ireland, in which Undy had ventured very deeply, more so indeed than he had deemed it quite prudent to divulge to his friend ; and in order to gain certain ends he had induced Alaric to become a director of this line. The line in question was the Great West Cork, which was to run from Skibbereen to Bantry, and the momentous question now hotly debated before the Railway Board was on the moot point of a branch to Ballydehob. If Undy could carry the West Cork and Ballydehob branch entire, he would make a pretty thing of it ; but if, as there was too much reason to fear, his Irish foes should prevail, and leave—as Undy had once said in an eloquent speech at a very influential meeting of shareholders—and leave the unfortunate agricultural and commercial interest of Ballydehob steeped in Cimmerian darkness, the

chances were that poor Undy would be wellnigh
ruined.

Such being the case, he had striven, not unsuccessfully,
to draw Alaric into the concern. Alaric had bought very
cheaply a good many shares, which many people said were
worth nothing, and had, by dint of Undy's machinations,
been chosen a director on the board. Undy himself
meanwhile lay by, hoping that fortune might restore him
to Parliament, and haply put him on that committee
which must finally adjudicate as to the great question of
the Ballydehob branch.

Such were the circumstances under which he came to
Alaric with the view of raising such a sum of money as
might enable him to overcome the scruples of the Tillietudlem electors, and place himself in the shoes lately
vacated by Mr. M'Buffer.

They were sitting together after dinner when he commenced the subject. He and Mrs. Val and Clementina
had done the Tudors the honour of dining with them;
and the ladies had now gone up into the drawing-room,
and were busy talking over the Chiswick affair, which
was to come off in the next week, and after which Mrs.
Val intended to give a small evening party to the most
élite of her acquaintance.

'We won't have all the world, my dear,' she had said
to Gertrude, ' but just a few of our own set that are really
nice. Clementina is dying to try that new back step
with M. Jaquêtanàpe, so we won't crowd the room.'
Such were the immediate arrangements of the Tudor and
Scott party.

' So M'Buffer is off at last,' said Scott, as he seated
himself and filled his glass, after closing the dining-
room door. ' He brought his pigs to a bad market
after all.'

' He was an infernal rogue,' said Alaric.

' Well, I suppose he was,' said Undy ; ' and a fool into
the bargain to be found out.'

' He was a downright swindler,' said Alaric.

' After all,' said the other, not paying much attention
to Alaric's indignation, ' he did not do so very badly.
Why, M'Buffer has been at it now for thirteen years. He

began with nothing ; he had neither blood nor money ; and God-knows he had no social merits to recommend him.   He is as vulgar as a hog, as awkward as an elephant, and as ugly as an ape.   I believe he never had a friend, and was known at his club to be the greatest bore that ever came out of Scotland ; and yet for thirteen years he has lived on the fat of the land ; for five years he has been in Parliament, his wife has gone about in her carriage, and every man in the city has been willing to shake hands with him.'

' And what has it all come to ? ' said Alaric, whom the question of M'Buffer's temporary prosperity made rather thoughtful.

' Well, not so bad either ; he has had his fling for thirteen years, and that's something.   Thirteen good years out of a man's life is more than falls to the lot of every one.   And then, I suppose, he has saved something.'

' And he is spoken of everywhere as a monster for whom hanging is too good.'

' Pshaw ! that won't hang him.   Yesterday he was a god ; to-day he is a devil ; to-morrow he 'll be a man again ; that's all.'

' But you don't mean to tell me, Undy, that the consciousness of such crimes as those which M'Buffer has committed must not make a man wretched in this world, and probably in the next also ? '

' " Judge not, and ye shall not be judged," ' said Undy, quoting Scripture as the devil did before him ;   ' and as for consciousness of crime, I suppose M'Buffer has none at all.   I have no doubt he thinks himself quite as honest as the rest of the world.   He firmly believes that all of us are playing the same game, and using the same means, and has no idea whatever that dishonesty is objectionable.'

' And you, what do you think about it yourself ? '

' I think the greatest rogues are they who talk most of their honesty ; and, therefore, as I wish to be thought honest myself, I never talk of my own.'

They both sat silent for a while, Undy bethinking himself what arguments would be most efficacious towards inducing Alaric to strip himself of every available shilling that he had ; and Alaric debating in his own mind that great question which he so often debated, as to whether men, men of the world, the great and best men whom he saw around him, really endeavoured to be honest, or endeavoured only to seem so. Honesty was preached to him on every side; but did he, in his intercourse with the world, find men to be honest? Or did it behove him, a practical man like him, a man so determined to battle with the world as he had determined, did it behove such a one as he to be more honest than his neighbours?

He also encouraged himself by that mystic word, 'Excelsior!' To him it was a watchword of battle, repeated morning, noon, and night. It was the prevailing idea of his life. 'Excelsior'! Yes; how great, how grand, how all-absorbing is the idea! But what if a man may be going down, down to Tophet, and yet think the while that he is scaling the walls of heaven?

'But you wish to think yourself honest,' he said, disturbing Undy just as that hero had determined on the way in which he would play his present hand of cards.

'I have not the slightest difficulty about that,' said Undy; 'and I dare say you have none either. But as to M'Buffer, his going will be a great thing for us, if, as I don't doubt, I can get his seat.'

'It will be a great thing for you,' said Alaric, who, as well as Undy, had his Parliamentary ambition.

'And for you too, my boy. We should carry the Ballydehob branch to a dead certainty; and even if we did not do that, we'd bring it so near it that the expectation of it would send the shares up like mercury in fine weather. They are at £2 12s. 6d. now, and, if I am in the House next Session, they'll be up to £7 10s. before Easter; and what's more, my dear fellow, if we can't help ourselves in that way, they'll be worth nothing in a very few months.'

Alaric looked rather blank; for he had invested deeply in this line, of which he was now a director, of a week's standing, or perhaps we should say sitting. He had sold out all his golden hopes in the Wheal Mary Jane for the sake of embarking his money and becoming a director in this Irish Railway, and in one other speculation nearer home, of which Undy had a great opinion, viz.: the

Limehouse Thames Bridge Company. Such being the case, he did not like to hear the West Cork with the Ballydehob branch spoken of so slightingly.

'The fact is, a man can do anything if he is in the House, and he can do nothing if he is not,' said Undy. 'You know our old Aberdeen saying, "You scratch me and I'll scratch you." It is not only what a man may do himself for himself, but it is what others will do for him when he is in a position to help them. Now, there are those fellows ; I am hand-and-glove with all of them ; but there is not one of them would lift a finger to help me as I am now ; but let me get my seat again, and they'll do for me just anything I ask them. Vigil moves the new writ to-night ; I got a line from him asking me whether I was ready. There was no good to be got by waiting, so I told him to fire away.'

'I suppose you'll go down at once ?' said Alaric.

'Well, that's as may be—at least, yes ; that's my intention. But there's one thing needful—and that is the needful.'

'Money ?' suggested Alaric.

'Yes, money—cash—rhino—tin—ready—or by what other name the goddess would be pleased to have herself worshipped ; money, sir ; there's the difficulty, now as ever. Even at Tillietudlem money will have its weight.'

'Can't your father assist you ?' said Alaric.

'My father ! I wonder how he'd look if he got a letter from me asking for money. You might as well expect a goose to feed her young with blood out of her own breast, like a pelican, as expect that a Scotch lord should give money to his younger sons like an English duke. What would my father get by my being member for Tillietudlem ? No ; I must look nearer home than my father. What can you do for me ?'

'I ?'

'Yes, you,' said Undy ; 'I am sure you don't mean to say you'll refuse to lend me a helping hand if you can. I *must* realize by the Ballydehobs, if I am once in the House ; and then you'd have your money back at once.'

'It is not that,' said Alaric ; 'but I haven't got it.'

'I am sure you could let me have a thousand or so,' said

Undy. ' I think a couple of thousand would carry it, and I could make out the other myself.'

' Every shilling I have,' said Alaric, ' is either in the Ballydehobs or in the Limehouse Bridge. Why don't you sell yourself ? '

' So I have,' said Undy ; ' everything that I can without utter ruin. The Ballydehobs are not saleable, as you know.'

' What can I do for you, then ? '

Undy set himself again to think. ' I have no doubt I could get a thousand on our joint names. That blackguard, M'Ruen, would do it.'

' Who is M'Ruen ? ' asked Alaric.

' A low blackguard of a discounting Jew Christian. He would do it ; but then, heaven knows what he would charge, and he'd make so many difficulties that I shouldn't have the money for the next fortnight.'

' I wouldn't have my name on a bill in such a man's hands on any account,' said Alaric.

' Well, I don't like it myself,' said Undy ; ' but what the deuce am I to do ? I might as well go to Tillietudlem without my head as without money.'

' I thought you'd kept a lot of the Mary Janes,' said Alaric.

' So I had, but they're gone now. I tell you I've managed £1,000 myself. It would murder me now if the seat were to go into other hands. I'd get the Committee on the Limehouse Bridge, and we should treble our money. Vigil told me he would not refuse the Committee, though of course the Government won't consent to a grant if they can help it.'

' Well, Undy, I can let you have £250, and that is every shilling I have at my banker's.'

' They would not let you overdraw a few hundreds ? ' suggested Undy.

' I certainly shall not try them,' said Alaric.

' You are so full of scruple, so green, so young,' said Undy, almost in an enthusiasm of remonstrance. ' What can be the harm of trying them ? '

' My credit.'

' Fal lal. What's the meaning of credit ? How are

you to know whether you have got any credit if you don't try? Come, I'll tell you how you can do it. Old Cuttwater would lend it you for the asking.'

To this proposition Alaric at first turned a deaf ear; but by degrees he allowed Undy to talk him over. Undy showed him that if he lost the Tillietudlem burghs on this occasion it would be useless for him to attempt to stand for them again. In such case, he would have no alternative at the next general election but to stand for the borough of Strathbogy in Aberdeenshire; whereas, if he could secure Tillietudlem as a seat for himself, all the Gaberlunzie interest in the borough of Strathbogy, which was supposed to be by no means small, should be transferred to Alaric himself. Indeed, Sandie Scott, the eldest hope of the Gaberlunzie family, would, in such case, himself propose Alaric to the electors. Ca'stalk Cottage, in which the Hon. Sandie lived, and which was on the outskirts of the Gaberlunzie property, was absolutely within the boundary of the borough.

Overcome by these and other arguments, Alaric at last consented to ask from Captain Cuttwater the loan of £700. That sum Undy had agreed to accept as a sufficient contribution to that desirable public object, the re-seating himself for the Tillietudlem borough, and as Alaric on reflection thought that it would be uncomfortable to be left penniless himself, and as it was just as likely that Uncle Bat would lend him £700 as £500, he determined to ask for a loan of the entire sum. He accordingly did so, and the letter, as we have seen, reached the captain while Harry and Charley were at Surbiton Cottage. The old gentleman was anything but pleased. In the first place he liked his money, though not with any over-weening affection; in the next place, he had done a great deal for Alaric, and did not like being asked to do more; and lastly, he feared that there must be some evil cause for the necessity of such a loan so soon after Alaric's marriage.

Alaric in making his application had not done so actually without making any explanation on the subject. He wrote a long letter, worded very cleverly, which only served to mystify the captain, as Alaric had intended that

it should do. Captain Cuttwater was most anxious that
Alaric, whom he looked on as his adopted son, should rise
in the world; he would have been delighted to think that
he might possibly live to see him in Parliament; would
probably have made considerable pecuniary sacrifice for
such an object. With the design, therefore, of softening
Captain Cuttwater's heart, Alaric in his letter had spoken
about great changes that were coming, of the necessity
that there was of his stirring himself, of the great pecuniary results to be expected from a small present expenditure; and ended by declaring that the money was to be
used in forwarding the election of his friend Scott for the
Tillietudlem district burghs.

Now, the fact was, that Uncle Bat, though he cared
a great deal for Alaric, did not care a rope's end for Undy
Scott, and could enjoy his rum-punch just as keenly if
Mr. Scott was in obscurity as he could possibly hope to
do even if that gentleman should be promoted to be a
Lord of the Treasury. He was not at all pleased to think
that his hard-earned moidores should run down the gullies
of the Tillietudlem boroughs in the shape of muddy ale
or vitriolic whisky; and yet this was the first request
that Alaric had ever made to him, and he did not like to
refuse Alaric's first request. So he came up to town himself on the following morning with Harry and Charley,
determined to reconcile all these difficulties by the light
of his own wisdom.

In the evening he returned to Surbiton Cottage, having
been into the city, sold out stock for £700, and handed
over the money to Alaric Tudor.

On the following morning Undy Scott set out for Scotland, properly freighted, Mr. Whip Vigil having in due
course moved for a new writ for the Tillietudlem borough
in the place of Mr. M'Buffer, who had accepted the
situation of Steward of the Chiltern Hundreds.

CHAPTER XXV

CHISWICK GARDENS

The following Thursday was as fine as a Chiswick
flower-show-day ought to be, and so very seldom is.
The party who had agreed to congregate there—the party,
that is, whom we are to meet—was very select. Linda
and Katie had come up to spend a few days with their
sister. Mrs. Val, Clementina, Gertrude, and Linda were
to go in a carriage, for which Alaric was destined to pay,
and which Mrs. Val had hired, having selected it regard-
less of expense, as one which, by its decent exterior and
polished outward graces, conferred on its temporary
occupiers an agreeable appearance of proprietorship. The
two Miss Neverbends, sisters of Fidus, were also to be
with them, and they with Katie followed humbly, as
became their station, in a cab, which was not only hired,
but which very vulgarly told the fact to all the world.

Slight as had been the intimacy between Fidus Neverbend and Alaric at Tavistock, nevertheless a sort of
friendship had since grown up between them. Alaric had
ascertained that Fidus might in a certain degree be useful
to him, that the good word of the Aristides of the Works
and Buildings might be serviceable, and that, in short,
Neverbend was worth cultivating. Neverbend, on the
other hand, when he perceived that Tudor was likely to
become a Civil Service hero, a man to be named with
glowing eulogy at all the Government Boards in London,
felt unconsciously a desire to pay him some of that reverence which a mortal always feels for a god. And thus
there was formed between them a sort of alliance, which
included also the ladies of the family.

Not that Mrs. Val, or even Mrs. A. Tudor, encountered
Lactimel and Ugolina Neverbend on equal terms. There
is a distressing habitual humility in many unmarried
ladies of an uncertain age, which at the first blush tells
the tale against them which they are so painfully anxious

to leave untold. In order to maintain their places but
yet a little longer in that delicious world of love, sighs,
and dancing partners, from which it must be so hard for
a maiden, with all her youthful tastes about her, to tear
herself for ever away, they smile and say pretty things,
put up with the caprices of married women, and play
second fiddle, though the doing so in no whit assists
them in their task. Nay, the doing so does but stamp
them the more plainly with that horrid name from which
they would so fain escape. Their plea is for mercy—
'Have pity on me, have pity on me; put up with me
but for one other short twelve months; and then, if
then I shall still have failed, I will be content to vanish
from the world for ever.' When did such plea for pity
from one woman ever find real entrance into the heart
of another?

On such terms, however, the Misses Neverbend were
content to follow Mrs. Val to the Chiswick flower-show,
and to feed on the crumbs which might chance to fall
from the rich table of Miss Golightly; to partake of broken
meat in the shape of cast-off adorers, and regale themselves with lukewarm civility from the outsiders in the
throng which followed that adorable heiress.

And yet the Misses Neverbend were quite as estimable
as the divine Clementina, and had once been, perhaps, as
attractive as she is now. They had never waltzed, it is
true, as Miss Golightly waltzes. It may be doubted,
indeed, whether any lady ever did. In the pursuit of
that amusement Ugolina was apt to be stiff and ungainly,
and to turn herself, or allow herself to be turned, as
though she were made of wood; she was somewhat flat in
her figure, looking as though she had been uncomfortably
pressed into an unbecoming thinness of substance, and
a corresponding breadth of surface, and this conformation
did not assist her in acquiring a graceful flowing style of
motion. The elder sister, Lactimel, was of a different
form, but yet hardly more fit to shine in the mazes of the
dance than her sister. She had her charms, nevertheless,
which consisted of a somewhat stumpy dumpy comeliness.
She was altogether short in stature, and very short below
the knee. She had fair hair and a fair skin, small bones

and copious soft flesh. She had a trick of sighing gently in the evolutions of the waltz, which young men attributed to her softness of heart, and old ladies to her shortness of breath. They both loved dancing dearly, and were content to enjoy it whenever the chance might be given to them by the aid of Miss Golightly's crumbs.

The two sisters were as unlike in their inward lights as in their outward appearance. Lactimel walked ever on the earth, but Ugolina never deserted the clouds. Lactimel talked prose and professed to read it; Ugolina read poetry and professed to write it. Lactimel was utilitarian. *Cui bono?*—though probably in less classic phrase—was the question she asked as to everything. Ugolina was transcendental, and denied that there could be real good in anything. Lactimel would have clothed and fed the hungry and naked, so that all mankind might be comfortable. Ugolina would have brought mankind back to their original nakedness, and have taught them to feed on the grasses of the field, so that the claims of the body, which so vitally oppose those of the mind, might remain unheeded and despised. They were both a little nebulous in their doctrines, and apt to be somewhat unintelligible in their discourse, when indulged in the delights of unrestrained conversation. Lactimel had a theory that every poor brother might eat of the fat and drink of the sweet, might lie softly, and wear fine linen, if only some body or bodies could be induced to do their duties; and Ugolina was equally strong in a belief that if the mind were properly looked to, all appreciation of human ill would cease. But they delighted in generalizing rather than in detailed propositions; and had not probably, even in their own minds, realized any exact idea as to the means by which the results they desired were to be brought about.

They toadied Mrs. Val—poor young women, how little should they be blamed for this fault, which came so naturally to them in their forlorn position!—they toadied Mrs. Val, and therefore Mrs. Val bore with them; they bored Gertrude, and Gertrude, for her husband's sake, bore with them also; they were confidential with Clementina, and Clementina, of course, snubbed them. They

called Clementina ' the sweetest creature.' Lactimel
declared that she was born to grace the position of a wife
and mother, and Ugolina swore that her face was perfect
poetry. Whereupon Clementina laughed aloud, and
elegantly made a grimace with her nose and mouth, as
she turned the ' perfect poetry ' to her mother. Such
were the ladies of the party who went to the Chiswick
flower-show, and who afterwards were to figure at Mrs.
Val's little evening ' the dansant,' at which nobody was
to be admitted who was not nice.

They were met at the gate of the Gardens by a party
of young men, of whom Victoire Jaquêtanàpe was foremost. Alaric and Charley were to come down there when
their office work was done. Undy was by this time on
his road to Tillietudlem ; and Captain Val was playing
billiards at his club. The latter had given a promise that
he would make his appearance—a promise, however,
which no one expected, or wished him to keep.

The happy Victoire was dressed up to his eyes. That,
perhaps, is not saying much, for he was only a few feet
high ; but what he wanted in quantity he fully made
up in quality. He was a well-made, shining, jaunty little
Frenchman, who seemed to be perfectly at ease with
himself and all the world. He had the smallest little
pair of moustaches imaginable, the smallest little imperial,
the smallest possible pair of boots, and the smallest
possible pair of gloves. Nothing on earth could be
nicer, or sweeter, or finer, than he was. But he did not
carry his finery like a hog in armour, as an Englishman
so often does when an Englishman stoops to be fine.
It sat as naturally on Victoire as though he had been
born in it. He jumped about in his best patent leather
boots, apparently quite heedless whether he spoilt them
or not ; and when he picked up Miss Golightly's parasol
from the gravel, he seemed to suffer no anxiety about
his gloves.

He handed out the ladies one after another, as though
his life had been passed in handing out ladies, as, indeed,
it probably had—in handing them out and handing them
in ; and when Mrs. Val's ' private ' carriage passed on, he
was just as courteous to the Misses Neverbend and Katie

in their cab, as he had been to the greater ladies who had descended from the more ambitious vehicle. As Katie said afterwards to Linda, when she found the free use of her voice in their own bedroom, 'he was a darling little duck of a man, only he smelt so strongly of tobacco.'

But when they were once in the garden, Victoire had no time for anyone but Mrs. Val and Clementina. He had done his duty by the Misses Neverbend and those other two insipid young English girls, and now he had his own affairs to look after. He also knew that Miss Golightly had £20,000 of her own !

He was one of those butterfly beings who seem to have been created that they may flutter about from flower to flower in the summer hours of such gala times as those now going on at Chiswick, just as other butterflies do. What the butterflies were last winter, or what will become of them next winter, no one but the naturalist thinks of inquiring. How they may feed themselves on flower-juice, or on insects small enough to be their prey, is matter of no moment to the general world. It is sufficient that they flit about in the sunbeams, and add bright glancing spangles to the beauty of the summer day.

And so it was with Victoire Jaquêtanàpe. He did no work. He made no honey. He appeared to no one in the more serious moments of life. He was the reverse of Shylock ; he would neither buy with you nor sell with you, but he would eat with you and drink with you ; as for praying, he did little of that either with or without company. He was clothed in purple and fine linen, as butterflies should be clothed, and fared sumptuously everyday ; but whence came his gay colours, or why people fed him with *pâté* and champagne, nobody knew and nobody asked.

Like most Frenchmen of his class, he never talked about himself. He understood life, and the art of pleasing, and the necessity that he should please, too well to do so. All that his companions knew of him was that he came from France, and that when the gloomy months came on in England, the months so unfitted for a French butterfly, he packed up his azure wings and sought some more genial climate, certain to return and be seen again when the world of London became habitable.

If he had means of living no one knew it ; if he was in debt no one ever heard of it ; if he had a care in the world he concealed it. He abounded in acquaintances who were always glad to see him, and would have regarded it as quite *de trop* to have a friend. Nevertheless time was flying on with him as with others ; and, butterfly as he was, the idea of Miss Golightly's £20,000 struck him with delightful amazement—500,000 francs ! 500,000 francs ! and so he resolved to dance his very best, warm as the weather undoubtedly was at the present moment.

' Ah, he was charmed to see madame and mademoiselle look so charmingly,' he said, walking between mother and daughter, but paying apparently much the greater share of attention to the elder lady. In this respect we Englishmen might certainly learn much from the manners of our dear allies. We know well enough how to behave ourselves to our fair young countrywomen ; we can be civil enough to young women—nature teaches us that ; but it is so seldom that we are sufficiently complaisant to be civil to old women. And yet that, after all, is the soul of gallantry. It is to the sex that we profess to do homage. Our theory is, that feminine weakness shall receive from man's strength humble and respectful service. But where is the chivalry, where the gallantry, if we only do service in expectation of receiving such guerdon as rosy cheeks and laughing eyes can bestow ?

It may be said that Victoire had an object in being civil to Mrs. Val. But the truth is, all French Victoires are courteous to old ladies. An Englishman may probably be as forward as a Frenchman in rushing into a flaming building to save an old woman's life ; but then it so rarely happens that occasion offers itself for gallantry such as that. A man, however, may with ease be civil to a dozen old women in one day.

And so they went on, walking through parterres and glass-houses, talking of theatres, balls, dinner-parties, picnics, concerts, operas, of ladies married and single, of single gentlemen who should be married, and of married gentlemen who should be single, of everything, indeed, except the flowers, of which neither Victoire nor his companions took the slightest notice.

'And madame really has a dance to-night in her own house ? '

'O yes,' said Mrs. Val ; 'that is, just a few quadrilles and waltzes for Clementina. I really hardly know whether the people will take the carpet up or no.' The people, consisting of the cook and housemaid—for the page had, of course, come with the carriage—were at this moment hard at work wrenching up the nails, as Mrs. Val was very well aware.

'It will be delightful, charming,' said Victoire.

'Just a few people of our own set, you know,' said Mrs. Val : 'no crowd, or fuss, or anything of that sort ; just a few people that we know are nice, in a quiet homely way.'

'Ah, that is so pleasing,' said M. Victoire : 'that is just what I like ; and is mademoiselle engaged for—— ? '

No. Mademoiselle was not engaged either for—or for —or for—&c., &c., &c. ; and then out came the little tablets, under the dome of a huge greenhouse filled with the most costly exotics, and Clementina and her fellow-labourer in the cause of Terpsichore went to work to make their arrangements for the evening.

And the rest of the party followed them. Gertrude was accompanied by an Englishman just as idle and quite as useless as M. Victoire, of the butterfly tribe also, but not so graceful, and without colour.

And then came the Misses Neverbend walking together, and with them, one on each side, two tall Frenchmen, whose faces had been remodelled in that mould into which so large a proportion of Parisians of the present day force their heads, in order that they may come out with some look of the Emperor about them. Were there not some such machine as this in operation, it would be impossible that so many Frenchmen should appear with elongated, angular, hard faces, all as like each other as though they were brothers ! The cut of the beard, the long prickly-ended, clotted moustache, which looks as though it were being continually rolled up in saliva, the sallow, half-bronzed, apparently unwashed colour—these may all,

perhaps, be assumed by any man after a certain amount
of labour and culture. But how it has come to pass that
every Parisian has been able to obtain for himself a pair
of the Emperor's long, hard, bony, cruel-looking cheeks,
no Englishman has yet been able to guess. That having
the power they should have the wish to wear this mask
is almost equally remarkable. Can it be that a political
phase, when stamped on a people with an iron hand of
sufficient power of pressure, will leave its impress on the
outward body as well as on the inward soul ? If so,
a Frenchman may, perhaps, be thought to have gained in
the apparent stubborn wilfulness of his countenance some
recompense for his compelled loss of all political wilfulness whatever.

Be this as it may, the two Misses Neverbend walked on,
each with a stubborn long-faced Frenchman at her side,
looking altogether not ill pleased at this instance of the
excellence of French manners. After them came Linda,
talking to some acquaintance of her own, and then poor
dear little Katie with another Frenchman, sterner, more
stubborn-looking, more long-faced, more like the pattern
after whom he and they had been remodelled, than any
of them.

Poor little Katie ! This was her first day in public.
With many imploring caresses, with many half-formed
tears in her bright eyes, with many assurances of her
perfect health, she had induced her mother to allow her
to come to the flower-show ; to allow her also to go to
Mrs. Val's dance, at which there were to be none but
such very nice people. Katie was to commence her life,
to open her ball with this flower-show. In her imagination it was all to be one long bright flower-show, in which,
however, the sweet sorrowing of the sensitive plant would
ever and anon invite her to pity and tears. When she
entered that narrow portal she entered the world, and
there she found herself walking on the well-mown grass
with this huge, stern, bearded Frenchman by her side !
As to talking to him, that was quite out of the question.
At the gate some slight ceremony of introduction had
been gone through, which had consisted in all the Frenchmen taking off their hats and bowing to the two married

ladies, and in the Englishmen standing behind and poking
the gravel with their canes.   But in this no special notice
had of course been taken of Katie; and she had a kind
of idea, whence derived she knew not, that it would be
improper for her to talk to this man, unless she were
actually and *bona fide* introduced to him.   And then,
again, poor Katie was not very confident in her French,
and then her companion was not very intelligible in his
English; so when the gentleman asked, 'Is it that
mademoiselle lofe de fleurs?' poor little Katie felt herself tremble, and tried in vain to mutter something;
and when, again essaying to do his duty, he suggested
that 'all de beauté of Londres did delight to valk itself
at Chisveek,' she was equally dumb, merely turning on him
her large eyes for one moment, to show that she knew
that he addressed her.   After that he walked on as silent
as herself, still keeping close to her side; and other ladies,
who had not the good fortune to have male companions,
envied her happiness in being so attended.

But Alaric and Charley were coming, she knew; Alaric
was her brother-in-law now, and therefore she would be
delighted to meet him; and Charley, dear Charley! she
had not seen him since he went away that morning, now
four days since; and four days was a long time, considering that he had saved her life.   Her busy little fingers
had been hard at work the while, and now she had in her
pocket the purse which she had been so eager to make,
and which she was almost afraid to bestow.

'Oh, Linda,' she had said, 'I don't think I will, after
all; it is such a little thing.'

'Nonsense, child, you wouldn't give him a worked
counterpane; little things are best for presents.'

'But it isn't good enough,' she said, looking at her
handiwork in despair.   But, nevertheless, she persevered,
working in the golden beads with constant diligence, so
that she might be able to give it to Charley among the
Chiswick flowers.   Oh! what a place it was in which
to bestow a present, with all the eyes of all the world
upon her!

And then this dance to which she was going!   The
thought of what she would do there troubled her.   Would

anyone ask her to dance ? Would Charley think of her
when he had so many grown-up girls, girls quite grown
up, all around him ? It would be very sad if at this
London party it should be her fate to sit down the whole
evening and see others dance. It would suffice for her,
she thought, if she could stand up with Linda, but she
had an idea that this would not be allowed at a London
party ; and then Linda, perhaps, might not like it.
Altogether she had much upon her mind, and was beginning to think that, perhaps, she might have been happier
to have stayed at home with her mamma. She had not
quite recovered from the effect of her toss into the water,
or the consequent excitement, and a very little misery
would upset her. And so she walked on with her Napo-
leonic companion, from whom she did not know how to
free herself, through one glass-house after another, across
lawns and along paths, attempting every now and then
to get a word with Linda, and not at all so happy as she
had hoped to have been.

At last Gertrude came to her rescue. They were all
congregated for a while in one great flower-house, and
Gertrude, finding herself near her sister, asked her how
she liked it all.

'Oh ! it is very beautiful,' said Katie, 'only——'

'Only what, dear ? '

'Would you let me come with you a little while ?
look here '—and she crept softly around to the other side
of her sister, sidling with little steps away from the Frenchman, at whom, however, she kept furtively looking, as
though she feared that he would detect her in the act.
Look here, Gertrude,' she said, twitching her sister's
arm ; ' that gentleman there—you see him, don't you ?
he 's a Frenchman, and I don't know *how* to get away
from him.'

'How to get away from him ? ' said Gertrude. ' That 's
M. Delabarbe de l'Empereur, a great friend of Mrs. Val's,
and a very quiet sort of man, I believe ; he won't eat you.'

'No, he won't eat me, I know ; but I can't look at
anything, because he will walk so close to me ! Mayn't
I come with you ? '

Gertrude told her she might, and so Katie made good

her escape, hiding herself from her enemy as well as she
could behind her sister's petticoats. He, poor man, was
perhaps as rejoiced at the arrangement as Katie herself;
at any rate he made no attempt to regain his prey, but
went on by himself, looking as placidly stern as ever, till
he was absorbed by Mrs. Val's more immediate party, and
then he devoted himself to her, while M. Jaquêtanàpe
settled with Clementina the properest arrangement for
the waltzes of the evening.

Katie was beginning to be tranquilly happy, and was
listening to the enthusiasm of Ugolina Neverbend, who
declared that flowers were the female poet's fitting food—
it may be doubted whether she had ever tried it—when
her heart leaped within her on hearing a sharp, clear,
well-known voice, almost close behind her. It was Charley
Tudor. After her silent promenade with M. Delabarbe
de l'Empereur, Katie had been well pleased to put up
with the obscure but yet endurable volubility of Ugolina;
but now she felt almost as anxious to get quit of Ugolina
as she had before been to shake off the Frenchman.

'Flowers are Nature's chef-d'œuvre,' said Ugolina;
'they convey to me the purest and most direct essence of
that heavenly power of production which is the sweetest
evidence which Jehovah gives us of His presence.'

'Do they?' said Katie, looking over her shoulder to
watch what Charley was doing, and to see whether he was
coming to notice her.

'They are the bright stars of His immediate handiwork,'
said Ugolina; 'and if our dim eyes could read them
aright, they would whisper to us the secret of His
love.'

'Yes, I dare say they would,' said Katie, who felt,
perhaps, a little disappointed because Charley lingered
a while shaking hands with Mrs. Val and Clementina
Golightly.

It was, however, but for a moment. There was much
shaking of hands to be done, and a considerable taking
off of hats to be gone through; and as Alaric and Charley
encountered the head of the column first, it was only
natural that they should work their way through it
gradually. Katie, however, never guessed—how could

she ?—that Charley had calculated that by reaching her last he would be able to remain with her.

She was still listening to Ugolina, who was mounting higher and higher up to heaven, when she found her hand in Charley's. Ugolina might now mount up, and get down again as best she could, for Katie could no longer listen to her.

Alaric had not seen her yet since her ducking. She had to listen to and to answer his congratulations, Charley standing by and making his comments.

'Charley says you took to the water quite naturally, and swam like a duck,' said Alaric.

'Only she went in head foremost,' said Charley.

'All bathers ought to do that,' said Alaric; 'and tell me, Katie, did you feel comfortable when you were in the water?'

'Indeed I don't recollect anything about it,' said she, 'only that I saw Charley coming to me, just when I was going to sink for the last time.'

'Sink! Why, I'm told that you floated like a deal board.'

'The big hat and the crinoline kept her up,' said Charley; 'she had no idea of sinking.'

'Oh! Charley, you know I was under the water for a long time; and that if you had not come, just at that very moment, I should never have come up again.'

And then Alaric went on, and Charley and Katie were left together.

How was she to give him the purse? It was burning a hole in her pocket till she could do so; and yet how was she to get it out of her possession into his, and make her little speech, here in the public garden? She could have done it easily enough at home in the drawing-room at Surbiton Cottage.

'And how do you like the gardens?' asked Charley.

'Oh! they are beautiful; but I have hardly been able to see anything yet. I have been going about with a great big Frenchman—there, that man there—he has such a queer name.'

'Did his name prevent your seeing?'

'No, not his name; I didn't know his name then.

But it seemed so odd to be walking about with such a man as that. But I want to go back, and look at the black and yellow roses in that house, there. Would you go with me? that is, if we may. I wonder whether we may!'

Charley was clearly of opinion that they might, and should, and would; and so away they sallied back to the roses, and Katie began to enjoy the first instalment of the happiness which she had anticipated. In the temple of the roses the crowd at first was great, and she could not get the purse out of her pocket, nor make her speech; but after a while the people passed on, and there was a lull before others filled their places, and Katie found herself opposite to a beautiful black rose, with no one close to her but Charley.

'I have got something for you,' she said; and as she spoke she felt herself to be almost hot with blushing.

'Something for me!' said Charley; and he also felt himself abashed, he did not know why.

'It's only a very little thing,' said Katie, feeling in her pocket, 'and I am almost ashamed to ask you to take it. But I made it all myself; no one else put a stitch in it,' and so saying, and looking round to see that she was not observed, she handed her gift to Charley.

'Oh! Katie, dearest Katie,' said he, 'I am so much obliged to you—I'll keep it till I die.'

'I didn't know what to make that was better,' said she.

'Nothing on earth could possibly be better,' said he.

'A plate of bread and butter and a purse are a very poor return for saving one's life,' said she, half laughing, half crying.

He looked at her with his eyes full of love; and as he looked, he swore within himself that come what might, he would never see Norah Geraghty again, but would devote his life to an endeavour to make himself worthy of the angel that was now with him. Katie the while was looking up anxiously into his face. She was thinking of no other love than that which it became her to feel for the man who had saved her life. She was thinking of no other love; but her young heart was opening itself to a very different feeling. She was sinking deep, deep, in waters which were to go near to drown her warm heart; much nearer than those other waters which she fancied had all but closed for ever over her life.

She looked into his face and saw that he was pleased; and that, for the present, was enough for her. She was at any rate happy now. So they passed on through the roses, and then lost themselves among the geraniums, and wondered at the gigantic rhododendrons, and beautiful azaleas, and so went on from house to house, and from flower-bed to flower-bed, Katie talking and Charley listening, till she began to wonder at her former supineness, and to say both to herself and out loud to her companion, how very, very, very glad she was that her mother had let her come.

Poor Katie!—dear, darling, bonny Katie!—sweet sweetest, dearest child! why, oh why, has that mother of thine, that tender-hearted loving mother, put thee unguarded in the way of such peril as this? Has she not sworn to herself that over thee at least she would watch as a hen does over her young, so that no unfortunate love should quench thy young spirit, or blanch thy cheek's bloom? Has she not trembled at the thought of what would have befallen thee, had thy fate been such as Linda's? Has she not often—oh, how often!—on her knees thanked the Almighty God that Linda's spirit was not as thine; that this evil had happened to the lamb whose temper had been fitted by Him to endure it? And yet—here thou art—all unguarded, all unaided, left by thyself to drink of the cup of sweet poison, and none near to warn thee that the draught is deadly.

Alas!—'twould be useless to warn thee now. The false god has been placed upon the altar, the temple all shining with gems and gold has been built around him, the incense-cup is already swinging; nothing will now turn the idolater from her worship, nothing short of a miracle.

Our Katie's childish days are now all gone. A woman's passion glows within her breast, though as yet she has not scanned it with a woman's intelligence. Her mother, listening to a child's entreaty, had suffered her darling to go forth for a child's amusement. It was doomed that the child should return no more ; but in lieu of her, a fair, heart-laden maiden, whose every fondest thought must henceforth be of a stranger's welfare and a stranger's fate.

But it must not be thought that Charley abused the friendship of Mrs. Woodward, and made love to Katie, as love is usually made—with warm words, assurances of affection, with squeezing of the hand, with sighs, and all a lover's ordinary catalogue of resources. Though we have said that he was a false god, yet he was hardly to be blamed for the temple, and gems, and gold, with which he was endowed ; not more so, perhaps, than the unconscious bird which is made so sacred on the banks of the Egyptian river. He loved too, perhaps as warmly, though not so fatally as Katie did ; but he spoke no word of his love. He walked among the flowers with her, laughing and listening to her in his usual light-hearted, easy manner ; every now and again his arm would thrill with pleasure, as he felt on it the touch of her little fingers, and his heart would leap within him as he gazed on the speaking beauty of her face ; but he was too honest-hearted to talk to the young girl, to Mrs. Woodward's child, of love. He talked to her as to a child—but she listened to him and loved him as a woman.

And so they rambled on till the hour appointed for quitting this Elysium had arrived. Every now and again they had a glimpse of some one of their party, which had satisfied Katie that they were not lost. At first Clementina was seen tracing with her parasol on the turf the plan of a new dance. Then Ugolina passed by them describing the poetry of the motion of the spheres in a full flow of impassioned eloquence to M. Delabarbe de l'Empereur : ' *C'est toujours vrai ; ce que mademoiselle dit est toujours vrai,*' was the Frenchman's answer, which they heard thrice repeated. And then Lactimel and Captain Val were seen together, the latter having disappointed the prophecies which had been made respecting him. Lactimel had an idea that as the Scotts were great people, they were all in Parliament, and she was endeavouring to persuade Captain Val that something ought to be done for the poor.

'Think,' said she, 'only think, Captain Scott, of all the money that this *fête* must cost.'

'A doosed sight,' said the captain, hardly articulating from under his thick, sandy-coloured moustache, which, growing downwards from his nose, looked like a heavy thatch put on to protect his mouth from the inclemency of the clouds above. 'A doosed sight,' said the captain.

'Now suppose, Captain Scott, that all this money could be collected. The tickets, you know, and the dresses, and——'

'I wish I knew how to do it,' said the captain.

Lactimel went on with her little scheme for expending the cost of the flower-show in bread and bacon for the poor Irish of Saffron Hill; but Charley and Katie heard no more, for the mild philosopher passed out of hearing and out of sight.

At last Katie got a poke in her back from a parasol, just as Charley had expended half a crown, one of Mr. M'Ruen's last, in purchasing for her one simple beautiful flower, to put into her hair that night.

'You naughty puss!' said Gertrude, 'we have been looking for you all over the gardens. Mrs. Val and the Miss Neverbends have been waiting this half-hour.' Katie looked terribly frightened. 'Come along, and don't keep them waiting any longer. They are all in the passage. This was your fault, Master Charley.'

'O no, it was not,' said Katie; 'but we thought——'

'Never mind thinking,' said Gertrude, 'but come along.' And so they hurried on, and were soon replaced in their respective vehicles, and then went back to town.

'Well, I do think the Chiswick Gardens is the nicest place in all the world,' said Katie, leaning back in the cab, and meditating on her past enjoyment.

'They are very pretty—very,' said Lactimel Neverbend. 'I only wish every cottar had such a garden behind his cottage. I am sure we might manage it, if we set about it in the right way.'

'What! as big as Chiswick?' said Katie.

'No; not so big,' said Lactimel; 'but quite as nicely kept.'

'I think the pigs would get in,' said Katie.

'It would be much easier, and more important too, to keep their minds nicely,' said Ugolina; 'and there the pigs could never get in.'

'No; I suppose not,' said Katie.

'I don't know that,' said Lactimel.

CHAPTER XXVI

KATIE'S FIRST BALL

IN spite of Mrs. Val's oft-repeated assurance that they would have none but nice people, she had done her best to fill her rooms, and not unsuccessfully. She had, it is true, eschewed the Golightly party, who resided some north of Oxford Street, in the purlieus of Fitzroy Square, and some even to the east of Tottenham Court Road. She had eschewed the Golightlys, and confined herself to the Scott connexion; but so great had been her success in life, that, even under these circumstances, she had found herself able to fill her rooms respectably. If, indeed, there was no absolute crowding, if some space was left in the front drawing-room sufficient for the operations of dancers, she could still attribute this apparent want of fashionable popularity to the selections of the few nice people whom she had asked. The Hon. Mrs. Val was no ordinary woman, and understood well how to make the most of the goods with which the gods provided her.

The Miss Neverbends were to dine with the Tudors, and go with them to the dance in the evening, and their brother Fidus was to meet them there. Charley was, of course, one of the party at dinner; and as there was no other gentleman there, Alaric had an excellent opportunity, when the ladies went up to their toilets, to impress on his cousin the expediency of his losing no time in securing to himself Miss Golightly's twenty thousand pounds. The conversation, as will be seen, at last became rather animated.

'Well, Charley, what do you think of the beautiful Clementina?' said Alaric, pushing over the bottle to his

cousin, as soon as they found themselves alone. 'A
"doosed" fine girl, as Captain Val says, isn't she?'

'A "doosed" fine girl, of course,' said Charley, laughing. 'She has too much go in her for me, I'm afraid.'

'Marriage and children will soon pull that down. She'd
make an excellent wife for such a man as you; and to
tell you the truth, Charley, if you'll take my advice,
you'll lose no time in making up to her. She has got
that d—— French fellow at her heels, and though I don't
suppose she cares one straw about him, it may be well
to make sure.'

'But you don't mean in earnest that you think that
Miss Golightly would have me?'

'Indeed I do—you are just the man to get on with
girls; and, as far as I can see, you are just the man that
will never get on in any other way under the sun.'

Charley sighed as he thought of his many debts, his
poor prospects, and his passionate love. There seemed,
indeed, to be little chance that he ever would get on at all
in the ordinary sense of the word. 'I'm sure she'd refuse
me,' said he, still wishing to back out of the difficulty.
'I'm sure she would—I've not got a penny in the world,
you know.'

'That's just the reason—she has got lots of money,
and you have got none.'

'Just the reason why she should refuse me, you should
say.'

'Well—what if she does? There's no harm done.
"Faint heart never won fair lady." You've everything
to back you—Mrs. Val is led by Undy Scott, and Undy
is all on your side.'

'But she has got guardians, hasn't she?'

'Yes—her father's first cousin, old Sam Golightly.
He is dying; or dead probably by this time; only
Mrs. Val won't have the news brought to her, because
of this party. He had a fit of apoplexy yesterday. Then
there's her father's brother-in-law, Figgs; he's bed-
ridden. When old Golightly is off the hooks altogether,
another will be chosen, and Undy talks of putting in my
name as that of a family friend; so you'll have everything to assist you.'

Charley looked very grave. He had not been in the habit of discussing such matters, but it seemed to him, that if Alaric was about to become in any legal manner the guardian of Miss Golightly's fortune, that that in itself was reason enough why he, Alaric, should not propose such a match as this. Needy men, to be sure, did often marry rich ladies, and the world looked on and regarded it only as a matter of course ; but surely it would be the duty of a guardian to protect his ward from such a fate, if it were in his power to do so.

Alaric, who saw something of what was going on in his cousin's mind, essayed to remove the impression which was thus made. ' Besides, you know, Clementina is no chicken. Her fortune is at her own disposal. All the guardians on earth cannot prevent her marrying you if she makes up her mind to do so.'

Charley gulped down his glass of wine, and then sat staring at the fire, saying nothing further. It was true enough that he was very poor—true enough that Miss Golightly's fortune would set him on his legs, and make a man of him—true enough, perhaps, that no other expedient of which he could think would do so. But then there were so many arguments that were ' strong against the deed.' In the first place, he thought it impossible that he should be successful in such a suit, and then again it would hardly be honest to obtain such success, if it were possible ; then, thirdly, he had no sort of affection whatsoever for Miss Golightly ; and fourthly, lastly, and chiefly, he loved so dearly, tenderly, loved poor Katie Woodward.

As he thought of this, he felt horror-stricken with himself at allowing the idea of his becoming a suitor to another to dwell for an instant on his mind, and looking up with all the resolution which he was able to summon, he said —' It 's impossible, Alaric, quite impossible ! I couldn't do it.'

' Then what do you mean to do ? ' said Alaric, who was angry at having his scheme thus thwarted ; ' do you mean to be a beggar ?—or if not, how do you intend to get out of your difficulties ? '

' I trust not a beggar,' said Charley, sadly.

'What other hope have you ? what rational hope of setting yourself right ?'

'Perhaps I may do something by writing,' said Charley, very bashfully.

'By writing ! ha, ha, ha,' and Alaric laughed somewhat cruelly at the poor navvy—'do something by writing ! what will you do by writing ? will you make £20,000—or 20,000 pence ? Of all trades going, that, I should say, is likely to be the poorest for a poor man—the poorest and the most heart-breaking. What have you made already to encourage you ?'

'The editor says that "Crinoline and Macassar" will come to £4 10s.'

'And when will you get it ?'

'The editor says that the rule is to pay six months after the date of publication. The *Daily Delight* is only a new thing, you know. The editor says that, if the sale comes up to his expectations, he will increase the scale of pay.'

'A prospect of £4 10s. for a fortnight's hard work ! That's a bad look-out, my boy ; you had better take the heiress.'

'It may be a bad look-out,' said Charley, whose spirit was raised by his cousin's sneers—'but at any rate it's honest. And I'll tell you what, Alaric, I'd sooner earn £50 by writing for the press, than get £1,000 in any other way you can think of. It may be a poor trade in one way ; and authors, I believe, are poor ; but I am sure it has its consolations.'

'Well, Charley, I hope with all my heart that you may find them. For my own part, seeing what a place the world is, seeing what are the general aspirations of other men, seeing what, as it appears to me, the Creator has intended for the goal of our labours, I look for advancement, prosperity, and such rank and station as I may be able to win for myself. The labourer is worthy of his hire, and I do not mean to refuse such wages as may come in my way.'

'Yes,' said Charley, who, now that his spirit was roused, determined to fight his battle manfully, 'yes, the labourer is worthy of his hire ; but were I to get Miss

Golightly's fortune I should be taking the hire without labour.'

'Bah!' said Alaric.

'It would be dishonest in every way, for I do not love her, and should not love her at the moment that I married her.'

'Honesty!' said Alaric, still sneering; 'there is no sign of the dishonesty of the age so strong as the continual talk which one hears about honesty!' It was quite manifest that Alaric had not sat at the feet of Undy Scott without profiting by the lessons which he had heard. 'With what face,' continued he, 'can you pretend to be more honest than your neighbours?'

'I know that it is wrong, and unmanly too, to hunt a girl down merely for what she has got.'

'There are a great many wrong and unmanly men about, then,' said Alaric. 'Look through the Houses of Parliament, and see how many men there have married for money; aye, and made excellent husbands afterwards. I'll tell you what it is, Charley, it is all humbug in you to pretend to be better than others; you are not a bit better;—mind, I do not say you are worse. We have none of us too much of this honesty of which we are so fond of prating. Where was your honesty when you ordered the coat for which you know you cannot pay? or when you swore to the bootmaker that he should have the amount of his little bill after next quarter-day, knowing in your heart at the time that he wouldn't get a farthing of it? If you are so honest, why did you waste your money to-day in going to Chiswick, instead of paying some portion of your debts? Honest! you are, I dare say, indifferently honest as the world goes, like the rest of us. But I think you might put the burden of Clementina's fortune on your conscience without feeling much the worse for it after what you have already gone through.'

Charley became very red in the face as he sat silent, listening to Alaric's address—nor did he speak at once at the first pause, so Alaric went on. 'The truth, I take it, is, that at the present moment you have no personal fancy for this girl.'

'No, I have not,' said Charley.

' And you are so incredibly careless as to all prudential considerations as to prefer your immediate personal fancies to the future welfare of your whole life. I can say no more. If you will think well of my proposition, I will do all I can to assist you. I have no doubt you would make a good husband to Miss Golightly, and that she would be very happy with you. If you think otherwise there is an end of it ; but pray do not talk so much about your honesty—your tailor would arrest you to-morrow if he heard you.'

' There are two kinds of honesty, I take it,' said Charley, speaking with suppressed anger and sorrow visible in his face, ' that which the world sees and that which it does not see. For myself, I have nothing to say in my own defence. I have made my bed badly, and must lie on it as it is. I certainly will not mend it by marrying a girl that I can never love. And as for you, Alaric, all who know you and love you watch your career with the greatest hope. We know your ambition, and all look to see you rise in the world. But in rising, as you will do, you should remember this—that nothing that is wrong can become right because other people do it.'

' Well, Charley,' said the other, ' thank you for the lecture. I did not certainly expect it from you ; but it is not on that account the less welcome. And now, suppose we go upstairs and dress for Mrs. Val ; ' and so they went upstairs.

Katie's heart beat high as she got out of the carriage—Mrs. Val's private carriage had been kept on for the occasion—and saw before and above her on the stairs a crowd of muslin crushing its way on towards the room prepared for dancing. Katie had never been to a ball before. We hope that the word ball may not bring down on us the adverse criticism of the *Morning Post*. It was probably not a ball in the strictly fashionable sense of the word, but it was so to Katie to all intents and purposes. Her dancing had hitherto been done either at children's parties, or as a sort of supplemental amusement to the evening tea-gatherings at Hampton or Hampton Court. She had never yet seen the muse worshipped with the premeditated ceremony of banished carpets, chalked

floors, and hired musicians. Her heart consequently beat
high as she made her way upstairs, linked arm-in-arm
with Ugolina Neverbend.

'Shall you dance much?' said Ugolina.

'Oh, I hope so,' said Katie.

'I shall not. It is an amusement of which I am peculiarly fond, and for which my active habits suit me.'
This was probably said with some allusion to her sister,
who was apt to be short of breath. 'But in the dances of
the present day conversation is impossible, and I look
upon any pursuit as barbaric which stops the "feast of
reason and the flow of soul."'

Katie did not quite understand this, but she thought
in her heart that she would not at all mind giving up
talking for the whole evening if she could only get dancing
enough. But on this matter her heart misgave her. To
be sure, she was engaged to Charley for the first quadrille
and second waltz; but there her engagements stopped,
whereas Clementina, as she was aware, had a whole book
full of them. What if she should get no more dancing
when Charley's good nature should have been expended?
She had an idea that no one would care to dance with her
when older partners were to be had. Ah, Katie, you do
not yet know the extent of your riches, or half the wealth
of your own attractions!

And then they all heard another little speech from
Mrs. Val. 'She was really quite ashamed—she really
was—to see so many people; she could not wish any of
her guests away, that would be impossible—though
perhaps one or two might be spared,' she said in a confidential whisper to Gertrude. Who the one or two
might be it would be difficult to decide, as she had made
the same whisper to every one; 'but she really was
ashamed; there was almost a crowd, and she had quite
intended that the house should be nearly empty. The
fact was, everybody asked had come, and as she could
not, of course, have counted on that, why, she had got,
you see, twice as many people as she had expected.'
And then she went on, and made the same speech to the
next arrival.

Katie, who wanted to begin the play at the beginning,

kept her eye anxiously on Charley, who was still standing with Lactimel Neverbend on his arm. 'Oh, now,' said she to herself, 'if he should forget me and begin dancing with Miss Neverbend!' But then she remembered how he had jumped into the water, and determined that, even with such provocation as that, she must not be angry with him.

But there was no danger of Charley's forgetting. 'Come,' said he, 'we must not lose any more time, if we mean to dance the first set. Alaric will be our *vis-à-vis* — he is going to dance with Miss Neverbend,' and so they stood up. Katie tightened her gloves, gave her dress a little shake, looked at her shoes, and then the work of the evening began.

'I shouldn't have liked to have sat down for the first dance,' she said confidentially to Charley, 'because it's my first ball.'

'Sit down! I don't suppose you'll be let to sit down the whole evening. You'll be crying out for mercy about three or four o'clock in the morning.'

'It's you to go on now,' said Katie, whose eyes were intent on the figure, and who would not have gone wrong herself, or allowed her partner to do so, on any consideration. And so the dance went on right merrily.

'I've got to dance the first polka with Miss Golightly,' said Charley.

'And the next with me,' said Katie.

'You may be sure I shan't forget that.'

'You lucky man to get Miss Golightly for a partner. I am told she is the most beautiful dancer in the world.'

'O no—Mademoiselle —— is much better,' said Charley, naming the principal stage performer of the day. 'If one is to go the whole hog, one had better do it thoroughly.'

Katie did not quite understand then what he meant, and merely replied that she would look at the performance. In this, however, she was destined to be disappointed, for Charley had hardly left her before Miss Golightly brought up to her the identical M. Delabarbe de l'Empereur who had so terribly put her out in the gardens. This was done so suddenly, that Katie's presence of mind was quite insufficient to provide her

with any means of escape. The Frenchman bowed very
low and said nothing. Katie made a little curtsy, and
was equally silent. Then she felt her own arm gathered
up and put within his, and she stood up to take her share
in the awful performance. She felt herself to be in such
a nervous fright that she would willingly have been home
again at Hampton if she could ; but as this was utterly
impossible, she had only to bethink herself of her steps,
and get through the work as best she might.

Away went Charley and Clementina leading the throng ;
away went M. Jaquêtanàpe and Linda ; away went another
Frenchman, clasping in his arms the happy Ugolina.
Away went Lactimel with a young Weights and Measures
—and then came Katie's turn. She pressed her lips
together, shut her eyes, and felt the tall Frenchman's
arms behind her back, and made a start. 'Twas like
plunging into cold water on the first bathing day of the
season—' ce n'est que le premier pas que coute.' When
once off Katie did not find it so bad. The Frenchman
danced well, and Katie herself was a wicked little adept.
At home, at Surbiton, dancing with another girl, she had
with great triumph tired out the fingers both of her
mother and sister, and forced them to own that it was
impossible to put her down. M. de l'Empereur, therefore,
had his work before him, and he did it like a man—as
long as he could.

Katie, who had not yet assumed the airs or will of
a grown-up young lady, thought that she was bound to go
on as long as her grand partner chose to go with her. He,
on the other hand, accustomed in his gallantry to obey
all ladies' wishes, considered himself bound to leave it to
her to stop when she pleased. And so they went on with
apparently interminable gyrations. Charley and the
heiress had twice been in motion, and had twice stopped,
and still they were going on ; Ugolina had refreshed
herself with many delicious observations, and Lactimel
had thrice paused to advocate dancing for the million,
and still they went on ; the circle was gradually left to
themselves, and still they went on ; people stood round,
some admiring and others pitying ; and still they went
on. Katie, thinking of her steps and her business, did

not perceive that she and her partner were alone; and ever and anon, others of course joined in—and so they went on—and on—and on.

M. Delabarbe de l'Empereur was a strong and active man, but he began to perceive that the lady was too much for him. He was already melting away with his exertions, while his partner was as cool as a cucumber. She, with her active young legs, her lightly filled veins, and small agile frame, could have gone on almost for ever; but M. de l'Empereur was more encumbered. Gallantry was at last beat by nature, his overtasked muscles would do no more for him, and he was fain to stop, dropping his partner into a chair, and throwing himself in a state of utter exhaustion against the wall.

Katie was hardly out of breath as she received the congratulations of her friends; but at the moment she could not understand why they were quizzing her. In after times, however, she was often reproached with having danced a Frenchman to death in the evening, in revenge for his having bored her in the morning. It was observed that M. Delabarbe de l'Empereur danced no more that evening. Indeed, he very soon left the house.

Katie had not been able to see Miss Golightly's performance, but it had been well worth seeing. She was certainly no ordinary performer, and if she did not quite come up to the remarkable movements which one sees on the stage under the name of dancing, the fault was neither in her will nor her ability, but only in her education. Charley also was peculiarly well suited to give her 'ample verge and room enough' to show off all her perfections. Her most peculiar merit consisted, perhaps, in her power of stopping herself suddenly, while going on at the rate of a hunt one way, and without any pause or apparent difficulty going just as fast the other way. This was done by a jerk which must, one would be inclined to think, have dislocated all her bones and entirely upset her internal arrangements. But no; it was done without injury, or any disagreeable result either to her brain or elsewhere. We all know how a steamer is manœuvred when she has to change her course, how we stop her and ease her and back her; but Miss Golightly stopped and

eased and backed all at once, and that without collision
with any other craft. It was truly very wonderful, and
Katie ought to have looked at her.

Katie soon found occasion to cast off her fear that her
evening's happiness would be destroyed by a dearth of
partners. Her troubles began to be of an exactly opposite
description. She had almost envied Miss Golightly her
little book full of engagements, and now she found herself
dreadfully bewildered by a book of her own. Some one
had given her a card and a pencil, and every moment she
could get to herself was taken up in endeavouring to
guard herself from perfidy on her own part. All down the
card, at intervals which were not very far apart, there were
great C's, which stood for Charley, and her firmest feeling
was that no earthly consideration should be allowed to
interfere with those landmarks. And then there were all
manner of hieroglyphics—sometimes, unfortunately, illegi-
ble to Katie herself—French names and English names
mixed together in a manner most vexatious; and to make
matters worse, she found that she had put down both
Victoire Jaquêtanàpe and Mr. Johnson of the Weights, by
a great I, and she could not remember with whom she was
bound to dance the lancers, and to which she had promised
the last polka before supper. One thing, however, was
quite fixed: when supper should arrive she was to go
downstairs with Charley.

'What dreadful news, Linda!' said Charley; 'did you
hear it?' Linda was standing up with Mr. Neverbend
for a sober quadrille, and Katie also was close by with her
partner. 'Dreadful news indeed!'

'What is it?' said Linda.

'A man can die but once, to be sure; but to be killed
in such a manner as that, is certainly very sad.'

'Killed! who has been killed?' said Neverbend.

'Well, perhaps I shouldn't say killed. He only died
in the cab as he went home.'

'Died in a cab! how dreadful!' said Neverbend.
'Who? who was it, Mr. Tudor?'

'Didn't you hear? How very odd! Why M. de
l'Empereur, to be sure. I wonder what the coroner will
bring it in.'

'How can you talk such nonsense, Charley?' said Linda.

'Very well, Master Charley,' said Katie. 'All that comes of being a writer of romances. I suppose that's to be the next contribution to the *Daily Delight*.'

Neverbend went off on his quadrille not at all pleased with the joke. Indeed, he was never pleased with a joke, and in this instance he ventured to suggest to his partner that the idea of a gentleman expiring in a cab was much too horrid to be laughed at.

'Oh, we never mind Charley Tudor,' said Linda; 'he always goes on in that way. We all like him so much.'

Mr. Neverbend, who, though not very young, still had a susceptible heart within his bosom, had been much taken by Linda's charms. He already began to entertain an idea that as a Mrs. Neverbend would be a desirable adjunct to his establishment at some future period, he could not do better than offer himself and his worldly goods to the acceptance of Miss Woodward; he therefore said nothing further in disparagement of the family friend; but he resolved that no such alliance should ever induce him to make Mr. Charles Tudor welcome at his house. But what could he have expected? The Internal Navigation had ever been a low place, and he was surprised that the Hon. Mrs. Val should have admitted one of the navvies inside her drawing-room.

And so the ball went on. Mr. Johnson came duly for the lancers, and M. Jaquêtanàpe for the polka. Johnson was great at the lancers, knowing every turn and vagary in that most intricate and exclusive of dances; and it need hardly be said that the polka with M. Jaquêtanàpe was successful. The last honour, however, was not without evil results, for it excited the envy of Ugolina, who, proud of her own performance, had longed, but hitherto in vain, to be whirled round the room by that wondrously expert foreigner.

'Well, my dear,' said Ugolina, with an air that plainly said that Katie was to be treated as a child, 'I hope you have had dancing enough.'

'Oh, indeed I have not,' said Katie, fully appreciating the purport and cause of her companion's remark; 'not near enough.'

'Ah—but, my dear—you should remember,' said Ugolina; 'your mamma will be displeased if you fatigue yourself.'

'My mamma is never displeased because we amuse ourselves, and I am not a bit fatigued;' and so saying Katie walked off, and took refuge with her sister Gertrude. What business had any Ugolina Neverbend to interfere between her and her mamma?

Then came the supper. There was a great rush to get downstairs, but Charley was so clever that even this did not put him out. Of course there was no sitting down; which means that the bashful, retiring, and obedient guests were to stand on their legs; while those who were forward, and impudent, and disobedient, found seats for themselves wherever they could. Charley was certainly among the latter class, and he did not rest therefore till he had got Katie into an old arm-chair in one corner of the room, in such a position as to enable himself to eat his own supper leaning against the chimney-piece.

'I say, Johnson,' said he, 'do bring me some ham and chicken—it's for a lady—I'm wedged up here and can't get out—and, Johnson, some sherry.'

The good-natured young Weights obeyed, and brought the desired provisions.

'And Johnson—upon my word I'm sorry to be so troublesome—but one more plateful if you please—for another lady—a good deal, if you please, for this lady, for she's very hungry; and some more sherry.'

Johnson again obeyed—the Weights are always obedient—and Charley of course appropriated the second portion to his own purposes.

'Oh, Charley, that was a fib—now wasn't it? You shouldn't have said it was for a lady.'

'But then I shouldn't have got it.'

'Oh, but that's no reason; according to that everybody might tell a fib whenever they wanted anything.'

'Well, everybody does—everybody except you, Katie.'

'O no,' said Katie—'no they don't—mamma, and Linda, and Gertrude never do; nor Harry Norman, he never does, nor Alaric.'

'No, Harry Norman never does,' said Charley, with

something like vexation in his tone. He made no exception to Katie's list of truth-tellers, but he was thinking within himself whether Alaric had a juster right to be in the catalogue than himself. ' Harry Norman never does, certainly. You must not compare me with them, Katie. They are patterns of excellence. I am all the other way, as everybody knows.' He was half laughing as he spoke, but Katie's sharp ear knew that he was more than half in earnest, and she felt she had pained him by what she had said.

' Oh, Charley, I didn't mean that ; indeed I did not. I know that in all serious things you are as truthful as they are—and quite as good—that is, in many ways.' Poor Katie ! she wanted to console him, she wanted to be kind, and yet she could not be dishonest.

' Quite as good ! no, you know I am not.'

' You are as good-hearted, if not better ; and you will be as steady, won't you, Charley ? I am sure you will ; and I know you are more clever, really more clever than either of them.'

' Oh ! Katie.'

' I am quite sure you are. I have always said so ; don't be angry with me for what I said.'

' Angry with you ! I couldn't be angry with you.'

' I wouldn't, for the world, say anything to vex you. I like you better than either of them, though Alaric is my brother-in-law. Of course I do ; how could I help it, when you saved my life ?'

' Saved your life ! Pooh ! I didn't save your life. Any boy could have done the same, or any waterman about the place. When you fell in, the person who was nearest you pulled you out, that was all.'

There was something almost approaching to ferocity in his voice as he said this ; and yet when Katie timidly looked up she saw that he had turned his back to the room, and that his eyes were full of tears. He had felt that he was loved by this child, but that he was loved from a feeling of uncalled-for gratitude. He could not stop to analyse this, to separate the sweet from the bitter ; but he knew that the latter prevailed. It is so little flattering to be loved when such love is the offspring of gratitude. And then when that gratitude is unnecessary, when it has been given in mistake for supposed favours, the acceptance of such love is little better than a cheat!

'That was not all,' said Katie, very decidedly. 'It never shall be all in my mind. If you had not been with us I should now have been drowned, and cold, and dead; and mamma! where would she have been? Oh! Charley, I shall think myself so wicked if I have said anything to vex you.'

Charley did not analyse his feelings, nor did Katie analyse hers. It would have been impossible for her to do so. But could she have done it, and had she done it, she would have found that her gratitude was but the excuse which she made to herself for a passionate love which she could not have excused, even to herself, in any other way.

He said everything he could to reassure her and make her happy, and she soon smiled and laughed again.

'Now, that's what my editor would call a Nemesis,' said Charley.

'Oh, that's a Nemesis, is it?'

'Johnson was cheated into doing my work, and getting me my supper; and then you scolded me, and took away my appetite, so that I couldn't eat it; that's a Nemesis. Johnson is avenged, only, unluckily, he doesn't know it, and wickedness is punished.'

'Well, mind you put it into the *Daily Delight*. But all the girls are going upstairs; pray let me get out,' and so Katie went upstairs again.

It was then past one. About two hours afterwards, Gertrude, looking for her sister that she might take her home, found her seated on a bench, with her feet tucked under her dress. She was very much fatigued, and she looked to be so; but there was still a bright laughing sparkle in her eye, which showed that her spirits were not even yet weary.

'Well, Katie, have you had enough dancing?'

'Nearly,' said Katie, yawning.

'You look as if you couldn't stand.'

'Yes, I *am* too tired to stand; but still I think I could dance a little more, only——'

' Only what ? '

' Whisper,' said Katie ; and Gertrude put down her ear near to her sister's lips. ' Both my shoes are quite worn out, and my toes are all out on the floor.'

It was clearly time for them to go home, so away they all went.

CHAPTER XXVII

EXCELSIOR

THE last words that Katie spoke as she walked down Mrs. Val's hall, leaning on Charley's arm, as he led her to the carriage, were these—

' You will be steady, Charley, won't you ? you will try to be steady, won't you, dear Charley ? ' and as she spoke she almost imperceptibly squeezed the arm on which she was leaning. Charley pressed her little hand as he parted from her, but he said nothing. What could he say, in that moment of time, in answer to such a request ? Had he made the reply which would have come most readily to his lips, it would have been this : ' It is too late, Katie—too late for me to profit by a caution, even from you—no steadiness now will save me.' Katie, however, wanted no other answer than the warm pressure which she felt on her hand.

And then, leaning back in the carriage, and shutting her eyes, she tried to think quietly over the events of the night. But it was, alas ! a dream, and yet so like reality that she could not divest herself of the feeling that the ball was still going on. She still seemed to see the lights and hear the music, to feel herself whirled round the room, and to see others whirling, whirling, whirling on every side of her. She thought over all the names on her card, and the little contests that had taken place for her hand, and all Charley's jokes, and M. de l'Empereur's great disaster ; and then as she remembered how long she had gone on twisting round with the poor unfortunate ill-used Frenchman, she involuntarily burst out into a fit of laughter.

' Good gracious, Katie, what is the matter ? I thought you were asleep,' said Gertrude.

' So did I,' said Linda. ' What on earth can you be laughing at now ? '

' I was laughing at myself,' said Katie, still going on with her half-suppressed chuckle, ' and thinking what a fool I was to go on dancing so long with that M. de l'Empereur. Oh dear, Gertrude, I am so tired : shall we be home soon ? ' and then she burst out crying.

The excitement and fatigue of the day had been too much for her, and she was now completely overcome. Ugolina Neverbend's advice, though not quite given in the kindest way, had in itself been good. Mrs. Woodward would, in truth, have been unhappy could she have seen her child at this moment. Katie made an attempt to laugh off her tears, but she failed, and her sobs then became hysterical, and she lay with her head on her married sister's shoulder, almost choking herself in her attempts to repress them.

' Dear Katie, don't sob so,' said Linda—' don't cry, pray don't cry, dear Katie.'

' She had better let it have its way,' said Gertrude ; ' she will be better directly, won't you, Katie ? '

In a little time she was better, and then she burst out laughing again. ' I wonder why the man went on when he was so tired. What a stupid man he must be ! '

Gertrude and Linda both laughed in order to comfort her and bring her round.

' Do you know, I think it was because he didn't know how to say " stop " in English ; ' and then she burst out laughing again, and that led to another fit of hysterical tears.

When they reached home Gertrude and Linda soon got her into bed. Linda was to sleep with her, and she also was not very long in laying her head on her pillow. But before she did so Katie was fast asleep, and twice in her sleep she cried out, ' Oh, Charley ! Oh, Charley ! ' Then Linda guessed how it was with her sister, and in the depths of her loving heart she sorrowed for the coming grief which she foresaw.

When the morning came Katie was feverish, and had

a headache. It was thought better that she should remain in town, and Alaric took Linda down to Hampton. The next day Mrs. Woodward came up, and as the invalid was better she took her home. But still she was an invalid. The doctor declared that she had never quite recovered from her fall into the river, and prescribed quiet and cod-liver oil. All the truth about the Chiswick fête and the five hours' dancing, and the worn-out shoes, was not told to him, or he might, perhaps, have acquitted the water-gods of the injury. Nor was it all, perhaps, told to Mrs. Woodward.

'I'm afraid she tired herself at the ball,' said Mrs. Woodward.

'I think she did a little,' said Linda.

'Did she dance much?' said Mrs. Woodward, looking anxiously.

'She did dance a good deal,' said Linda.

Mrs. Woodward was too wise to ask any further questions.

As it was a fine night Alaric had declared his intention of walking home from Mrs. Val's party, and he and Charley started together. They soon parted on their roads, but not before Alaric had had time to notice Charley's perverse stupidity as to Miss Golightly.

'So you wouldn't take my advice about Clementina?' said he.

'It was quite impossible, Alaric,' said Charley, in an apologetic voice. 'I couldn't do it, and, what is more, I am sure I never shall.'

'No, not now; you certainly can't do it now. If I am not very much mistaken, the chance is gone. I think you'll find she engaged herself to that Frenchman to-night.'

'Very likely,' said Charley.

'Well—I did the best I could for you. Good night, old fellow.'

'I'm sure I'm much obliged to you. Good night,' said Charley.

Alaric's suggestion with reference to the heiress was quite correct: M. Jaquêtanàpe had that night proposed, and been duly accepted. He was to present himself to his loved one's honourable mother on the following morning as her future son-in-law, comforted and supported in his task of doing so by an assurance from the lady that if her mother would not give her consent the marriage should go on all the same without it. How delightful to have such a dancer for her lover! thought Clementina. That was her 'Excelsior.'

Charley walked home with a sad heart. He had that day given a pledge that he would on the morrow go to the 'Cat and Whistle,' and visit his lady-love. Since the night when he sat there with Norah Geraghty on his knee, now nearly a fortnight since, he had spent but little of his time there. He had, indeed, gone there once or twice with his friend Scatterall, but had contrived to avoid any confidential intercourse with either the landlady or the barmaid, alleging, as an excuse for his extraordinary absence, that his time was wholly occupied by the demands made on it by the editor of the *Daily Delight*. Mrs. Davis, however, was much too sharp, and so also we may say was Miss Geraghty, to be deceived. They well knew that such a young man as Charley would go wherever his inclination led him. Till lately it had been all but impossible to get him out of the little back parlour at the 'Cat and Whistle'; now it was nearly as difficult to get him into it. They both understood what this meant.

'You'd better take up with Peppermint and have done with it,' said the widow. 'What's the good of your shilly-shallying till you're as thin as a whipping-post? If you don't mind what you're after he'll be off too.'

'And the d—— go along with him,' said Miss Geraghty, who had still about her a twang of the County Clare, from whence she came.

'With all my heart,' said Mrs. Davis; 'I shall save my hundred pounds: but if you'll be led by me you'll not throw Peppermint over till you're sure of the other; and, take my word for it, you're——'

'I hate Peppermint.'

'Nonsense; he's an honest good sort of man, and a deal more likely to keep you out of want than the other.'

Hereupon Norah began to cry, and to wipe her beautiful eyes with the glass-cloth. Hers, indeed, was a cruel position. Her face was her fortune, and her fortune she knew was deteriorating from day to day. She could not afford to lose the lover that she loved, and also the lover that she did not love. Matrimony with her was extremely desirable, and she was driven to confess that it might very probably be either now or never. Much as she hated Peppermint, she was quite aware that she would take him if she could not do better. But then, was it absolutely certain that she must lose the lover that so completely suited her taste ? Mrs. Davis said it was. Norah herself, confiding, as it is so natural that ladies should do, a little too much in her own beauty, thought that she couldn't but have a chance left. She also had her high aspirations ; she desired to rise in the world, to leave goes of gin and screws of tobacco behind her, and to reach some position more worthy of the tastes of a woman. ' Excelsior,' translated doubtless into excellent Irish, was her motto also. It would be so great a thing to be the wife of Charles Tudor, Esq., of the Civil Service, and more especially as she dearly and truly loved the same Charles Tudor in her heart of hearts.

She knew, however, that it was not for her to indulge in the luxury of a heart, if circumstances absolutely forbade it. To eat and drink and clothe herself, and, if possible, to provide eating and drinking and clothes for her future years, this was the business of life, this was the only real necessity. She had nothing to say in opposition to Mrs. Davis, and therefore she went on crying, and again wiped her eyes with the glass-cloth.

Mrs. Davis, however, was no stern monitor, unindulgent to the weakness of human nature. When she saw how Norah took to heart her sad fate, she resolved to make one more effort in her favour. She consequently dressed herself very nicely, put on her best bonnet, and took the unprecedented step of going off to the Internal Navigation, and calling on Charley in the middle of his office.

Charley was poking over the Kennett and Avon lock entries, with his usual official energy, when the office messenger came up and informed him that a lady was waiting to see him.

'A lady!' said Charley: 'what lady?' and he immediately began thinking of the Woodwards, whom he was to meet that afternoon at Chiswick.

'I'm sure I can't say, sir: all that she said was that she was a lady,' answered the messenger, falsely, for he well knew that the woman was Mrs. Davis, of the 'Cat and Whistle.'

Now the clerks at the Internal Navigation were badly off for a waiting-room; and in no respect can the different ranks of different public offices be more plainly seen than in the presence or absence of such little items of accommodation as this. At the Weights and Measures there was an elegant little chamber, carpeted, furnished with leathern-bottomed chairs, and a clock, supplied with cream-laid note-paper, new pens, and the *Times* newspaper, quite a little Elysium, in which to pass half an hour, while the Secretary, whom one had called to see, was completing his last calculation on the matter of the decimal coinage. But there were no such comforts at the Internal Navigation. There was, indeed, a little room at the top of the stairs, in which visitors were requested to sit down; but even here two men were always at work —at work, or else at play.

Into this room Mrs. Davis was shown, and there Charley found her. Long and intimately as the young navvy had been acquainted with the landlady of the 'Cat and Whistle,' he had never before seen her arrayed for the outer world. It may be doubted whether Sir John Falstaff would, at the first glance, have known even Dame Quickly in her bonnet, that is, if Dame Quickly in those days had had a bonnet. At any rate Charley was at fault for a moment, and was shaking hands with the landlady before he quite recognized who she was.

The men in the room, however, had recognized her, and Charley well knew that they had done so.

'Mr. Tudor,' she began, not a bit abashed, 'I want to know what it is you are a-going to do?'

Though she was not abashed, Charley was, and very much so. However, he contrived to get her out of the room, so that he might speak to her somewhat more privately in the passage. The gentlemen at the Internal Navigation were well accustomed to this mode of colloquy, as their tradesmen not unfrequently called, with the view of having a little conversation, which could not conveniently be held in the public room.

'And, Mr. Tudor, what are you a-going to do about that poor girl there?' said Mrs. Davis, as soon as she found herself in the passage, and saw that Charley was comfortably settled with his back against the wall.

'She may go to Hong-Kong for me.' That is what Charley should have said. But he did not say it. He had neither the sternness of heart nor the moral courage to enable him to do so. He was very anxious, it is true, to get altogether quit of Norah Geraghty; but his present immediate care was confined to a desire of getting Mrs. Davis out of the office.

'Do!' said Charley. 'Oh, I don't know; I'll come and settle something some of these days; let me see when—say next Tuesday.'

'Settle something,' said Mrs. Davis. 'If you are an honest man, as I take you, there is only one thing to settle; when do you mean to marry her?'

'Hush!' said Charley; for, as she was speaking, Mr. Snape came down the passage leading from Mr. Oldeschole's room. 'Hush!' Mr. Snape as he passed walked very slowly, and looked curiously round into the widow's face. 'I'll be even with you, old fellow, for that,' said Charley to himself; and it may be taken for granted that he kept his word before long.

'Oh! it is no good hushing any more,' said Mrs. Davis, hardly waiting till Mr. Snape's erect ears were out of hearing. 'Hushing won't do no good; there's that girl a-dying, and her grave'll be a-top of your head, Mr. Tudor; mind I tell you that fairly; so now I want to know what it is you're a-going to do.' And then Mrs. Davis lifted up the lid of a market basket which hung on her left arm, took out her pocket-handkerchief, and began to wipe her eyes.

Unfortunate Charley! An idea occurred to him that he might bolt and leave her. But then the chances were

that she would make her way into his very room, and tell
her story there, out before them all. He well knew that
this woman was capable of many things if her temper were
fairly roused. And yet what could he say to her to induce
her to go out from that building, and leave him alone to
his lesser misfortunes ?

'She's a-dying, I tell you, Mr. Tudor,' continued the
landlady, 'and if she do die, be sure of this, I won't be
slow to tell the truth about it. I'm the only friend she's
got, and I'm not going to see her put upon. So just tell
me this in two words—what is it you're a-going to do ?'
And then Mrs. Davis replaced her kerchief in the basket,
stood boldly erect in the middle of the passage, waiting for
Charley's answer.

Just at this moment Mr. Snape again appeared in the
passage, going towards Mr. Oldeschole's room. The pernicious old man ! He hated Charley Tudor ; and, to tell
the truth, there was no love lost between them. Charley,
afflicted and out of spirits as he was at the moment, could
not resist the opportunity of being impertinent to his old
foe : 'I'm afraid you'll make yourself very tired, Mr.
Snape, if you walk about so much,' said he. Mr. Snape
merely looked at him, and then hard at Mrs. Davis, and
passed on to Mr. Oldeschole's room.

'Well, Mr. Tudor, will you be so good as to tell me
what it is you're a-going to do about this poor girl ?'

'My goodness, Mrs. Davis, you know how I am situated
—how can you expect me to give an answer to such a
question in such a place as this ? I'll come to the "Cat
and Whistle" on Tuesday.'

'Gammon !' said the eloquent lady. 'You know you
means gammon.'

Charley, perhaps, did mean gammon ; but he protested
that he had never been more truthfully in earnest in his
life. Mr. Oldeschole's door opened, and Mrs. Davis
perceiving it, whipped out her handkerchief in haste, and
again began wiping her eyes, not without audible sobs.
'Confound the woman !' said Charley to himself ; 'what
on earth shall I do with her ?'

Mr. Oldeschole's door opened, and out of it came Mr.
Oldeschole, and Mr. Snape following him. What means

the clerk had used to bring forth the Secretary need not now be inquired. Forth they both came, and passed along the passage, brushing close by Charley and Mrs. Davis; Mr. Oldeschole, when he saw that one of the clerks was talking to a woman who apparently was crying, looked very intently on the ground, and passed by with a quick step; Mr. Snape looked as intently at the woman, and passed very slowly. Each acted according to his lights.

'I don't mean gammon at all, Mrs. Davis—indeed, I don't—I'll be there on Tuesday night certainly, if not sooner—I will indeed—I shall be in a desperate scrape if they see me here talking to you any longer; there is a rule against women being in the office at all.'

'And there's a rule against the clerks marrying, I suppose,' said Mrs. Davis.

The colloquy ended in Charley promising to spend the Saturday evening at the 'Cat and Whistle,' with the view of then and there settling what he meant to do about 'that there girl'; nothing short of such an undertaking on his part would induce Mrs. Davis to budge. Had she known her advantage she might have made even better terms. He would almost rather have given her a written promise to marry her barmaid, than have suffered her to remain there till Mr. Oldeschole should return and see her there again. So Mrs. Davis, with her basket and pocket-handkerchief, went her way about her marketing, and Charley, as he returned to his room, gave the strictest injunctions to the messenger that not, on any ground or excuse whatever, was any woman to be again allowed to see him at the office.

When, therefore, on the fine summer morning, with the early daylight all bright around him, Charley walked home from Mrs. Val's party, he naturally felt sad enough. He had one sixpence left in his pocket; he was engaged to spend the evening of the following day with the delight-ful Norah at the 'Cat and Whistle,' then and there to plight her his troth, in whatever formal and most irre-trievable manner Mrs. Davis might choose to devise; and as he thought of these things he had ringing in his ears the last sounds of that angel voice, 'You will be

steady, Charley, won't you ? I know you will, dear
Charley—won't you now ? '

Steady ! Would not the best thing for him be to step
down to Waterloo Bridge and throw himself over ? He
still had money enough left to pay the toll—though not
enough to hire a pistol. And so he went home and got
into bed.

On that same day, the day that was to witness Charley's
betrothal to Miss Geraghty, and that of M. Jaquêtanàpe
with Miss Golightly, Alaric Tudor had an appointment
with Sir Gregory Hardlines at the new office of the Civil
Service Examination Board. Alaric had been invited to
wait upon the great man, in terms which made him perfectly understand that the communication to be made was
one which would not be unpleasing or uncomplimentary
to himself. Indeed, he pretty well guessed what was to be
said to him. Since his promotion at the Weights and
Measures he had gone on rising in estimation as a man of
value to the Civil Service at large. Nearly two years had
now passed since that date, and in these pages nothing
has been said of his official career during the time. It
had, however, been everything that he or his friends
could have wished it to be. He had so put himself forward
as absolutely to have satisfied the actual chief clerk of
his office, and was even felt by some of the secretaries to
be treading very closely on their heels.

And yet a great portion of his time had been spent, not
at the Weights and Measures, but in giving some sort of
special assistance to Sir Gregory's Board. The authorities
at the Weights and Measures did not miss him ; they
would have been well content that he should have remained for ever with Sir Gregory.

He had also become somewhat known to the official
world, even beyond the confines of the Weights and
Measures, or the Examination Board. He had changed
his club, and now belonged to the Downing. He had
there been introduced by his friend Undy to many
men, whom to know should be the very breath in the
nostrils of a rising official aspirant. Mr. Whip Vigil, of
the Treasury, had more than once taken him by the hand,
and even the Chancellor of the Exchequer usually nodded

to him whenever that o'ertasked functionary found a
moment to look in at the official club.

Things had not been going quite smoothly at the
Examination Board. Tidings had got about that Mr.
Jobbles was interfering with Sir Gregory, and that Sir
Gregory didn't like it. To be sure, when this had been
indiscreetly alluded to in the House by one of those gentlemen who pass their leisure hours in looking out for raws
in the hide of the Government carcass, some other gentleman, some gentleman from the Treasury bench, had been
able to give a very satisfactory reply. For why, indeed,
should any gentleman sit on the Treasury bench if he be
not able, when so questioned, to give very satisfactory
replies? Giving satisfactory replies to ill-natured questions
is, one may say, the constitutional work of such gentlemen, who have generally well learned how to do so, and
earned their present places by asking the selfsame questions themselves, when seated as younger men in other
parts of the House.

But though the answer given in this instance was so
eminently satisfactory as to draw down quite a chorus
of triumphant acclamations from the official supporters of
Government, nevertheless things had not gone on at the
Board quite as smoothly as might have been desirable.
Mr. Jobbles was enthusiastically intent on examining the
whole adult male population of Great Britain, and had
gone so far as to hint that female competitors might, at
some future time, be made subject to his all-measuring rule
and compass. Sir Gregory, however, who, having passed
his early days in an office, may, perhaps, be supposed to
have had some slight prejudice remaining in favour of
ancient customs, was not inclined to travel so quickly.
Moreover, he preferred following his own lead, to taking
any other lead whatever that Mr. Jobbles might point out
as preferable.

Mr. Jobbles wanted to crush all patronage at a blow;
any system of patronage would lamentably limit the
number of candidates among whom his examination papers
would be distributed. He longed to behold, crowding
around him, an attendance as copious as Mr. Spurgeon's,
and to see every head bowed over the posing questions

which he should have dictated. No legion could be too many for him. He longed to be at this great work; but his energies were crushed by the opposition of his colleagues. Sir Gregory thought—and Sir Warwick, though he hardly gave a firm support to Sir Gregory, would not lend his countenance to Mr. Jobbles—Sir Gregory thought that enough would be done for the present, if they merely provided that every one admitted into the Service should be educated in such a manner as to be fit for any profession or calling under the sun; and that, with this slight proviso, the question of patronage might for the present remain untouched. ' Do you,' he would have said to the great officers of Government, ' appoint whom you like. In this respect remain quite unfettered. I, however, I am the St. Peter to whom are confided the keys of the Elysium. Do you send whatever candidates you please: it is for me merely to say whether or not they shall enter.' But Mr. Jobbles would have gone much farther. He would have had all mankind for candidates, and have selected from the whole mass those most worthy of the high reward. And so there was a split at the Examination Board, which was not to be healed even by the very satisfactory reply given by the Treasury gentleman in the House of Commons.

Neither Sir Gregory nor his rival were men likely to give way, and it soon appeared manifest to the powers that be, that something must be done. It therefore came to light that Mr. Jobbles had found that his clerical position was hardly compatible with a seat at a lay board, and he retired to the more congenial duties of a comfortable prebendal stall at Westminster. ' So that by his close vicinity,' as was observed by a newspaper that usually supported the Government, ' he might be able to be of material use, whenever his advice should be required by the Board of Commissioners.' Sir Gregory in the meantime was instructed to suggest the name of another colleague; and, therefore, he sent for Alaric Tudor.

Alaric, of course, knew well what had been going on at the Board. He had been Sir Gregory's confidential man all through; had worked out cases for him, furnished him with arguments, backed his views, and had assisted him, whenever such a course had been necessary, in holding Mr. Jobbles' head under the pump. Alaric knew well on which side his bread was buttered, and could see with a glance which star was in the ascendant; he perfectly understood the points and merits of the winning horse. He went in to win upon Sir Gregory, and he won. When Mr. Jobbles made his last little speech at the Board, and retired to his house in the Dean's yard, Alaric felt tolerably certain that he himself would be invited to fill the vacant place.

And he was so invited. 'That is £1,200 a year, at any rate,' said he to himself, as with many words of submissive gratitude he thanked his patron for the nomination. 'That is £1,200 a year. So far, so good. And now what must be the next step? Excelsior! It is very nice to be a Commissioner, and sit at a Board at Sir Gregory's right hand: much nicer than being a junior clerk at the Weights and Measures, like Harry Norman. But there are nicer things even than that; there are greater men even than Sir Gregory; richer figures than even £1,200 a year!'

So he went to his old office, wrote his resignation, and walked home meditating to what next step above he should now aspire to rise. 'Excelsior!' he still said to himself, 'Excelsior!'

At the same moment Charley was leaving the Internal Navigation, and as he moved with unusual slowness down the steps, he bethought himself how he might escape from the fangs of his Norah; how, if such might still be possible, he might fit himself for the love of Katie Woodward. Excelsior! such also was the thought of his mind; but he did not dare to bring the word to utterance. It was destined that his thoughts should be interrupted by no very friendly hand.

CHAPTER XXVIII

OUTERMAN v. TUDOR

CHARLEY sat at his office on the Saturday afternoon, very meditative and unlike himself. What was he to do when his office hours were over ? In the first place he had not a shilling in the world to get his dinner. His habit was to breakfast at home at his lodgings with Harry, and then to dine, as best he might, at some tavern, if he had not the good fortune to be dining out. He had a little dinner bill at a house which he frequented in the Strand ; but the bill he knew had reached its culminating point. It would, he was aware, be necessary that it should be decreased, not augmented, at the next commercial transaction which might take place between him and the tavern-keeper.

This was not the first time by many in which he had been in a similar plight—but his resource in such case had been to tell the truth gallantly to his friend Mrs. Davis ; and some sort of viands, not at all unprepossessing to him in his hunger, would always be forthcoming for him at the ' Cat and Whistle.' This supply was now closed to him. Were he, under his present circumstances, to seek for his dinner from the fair hands of Norah Geraghty, it would be tantamount to giving himself up as lost for ever.

This want of a dinner, however, was a small misfortune in comparison with others which afflicted him. Should or should he not keep his promise to Mrs. Davis, and go to the ' Cat and Whistle ' that evening ? That was the question which disturbed his equanimity, and hindered him from teasing Mr. Snape in his usual vivacious manner.

And here let it not be said that Charley must be altogether despicable in being so weak ; that he is not only a vulgar rake in his present habits, but a fool also, and altogether spiritless, and of a low disposition. Persons who may so argue of him, who so argue of those whom they meet in the real living world, are ignorant of the twists and turns, and rapid changes in character which are brought about by outward circumstances. Many a youth, abandoned by his friends to perdition on account of his folly, might have yet prospered, had his character not been set down as gone, before, in truth, it was well formed. It is not one calf only that should be killed for the returning prodigal. Oh, fathers, mothers, uncles, aunts, guardians, and elderly friends in general, kill seven fatted calves if seven should unfortunately be necessary !

And then there was a third calamity. Charley had, at this moment, in his pocket a certain document, which in civil but still somewhat peremptory language invited him to meet a very celebrated learned pundit, being no less than one of Her Majesty's puisne judges, at some court in Westminster, to explain why he declined to pay to one Nathaniel Outerman, a tailor, the sum of &c., &c., &c. ; and the document then went on to say, that any hesitation on Charley's part to accept this invitation would be regarded as great contempt shown to the said learned pundit, and would be treated accordingly. Now Charley had not paid the slightest attention to this requisition from the judge. It would, he conceived, have been merely putting his head into the lion's mouth to do so. But yet he knew that such documents meant something ; that the day of grace was gone by, and that Mr. Nathaniel Outerman would very speedily have him locked up.

So Charley sat meditative over his lock entries, and allowed even his proposed vengeance on Mr. Snape to be delayed.

'I say, Charley,' said Scatterall, coming over and whispering to him, 'you couldn't lend me half a crown, could you ? '

Charley said nothing, but looked on his brother navvy in a manner that made any other kind of reply quite unnecessary.

'I was afraid it was so,' said Scatterall, in a melancholy voice. And then, as if by the brilliance of his thought he had suddenly recovered his spirits, he made a little proposition.

'I'll tell you what you might do, Charley. I put my

watch up the spout last week. It's a silver turnip, so I
only got fifteen shillings; yours is a Cox and Savary, and
it's gold. I'm sure you'd get £3 for it easily—perhaps
£3 3s. Now, if you'll do that, and take my turnip down,
I'll let you have the turnip to wear, if you'll let me have
ten shillings of the money. You see, you'd get clear—let
me see how much.' And Scatterall went to work with
a sheet of foolscap paper, endeavouring to make some
estimate of what amount of ready cash Charley might
have in his pocket on completion of this delicate little
arrangement.

'You be d——,' said Charley.

'You'll not do it, then?' said Dick.

Charley merely repeated with a little more emphasis the
speech which he had just before made.

'Oh, very well,' said Scatterall; 'there couldn't have
been a fairer bargain; at least it was all on your side; for
you would have had the watch to wear, and nearly all the
money too.'

Charley still repeated the same little speech. This was
uncivil; for it had evidently been looked on by Scatterall
as unsatisfactory.

'Oh, very well,' said that gentleman, now in a state of
mild anger—'only I saw that you had a fine new purse,
and I thought you'd wish to have something to put in it.'

Charley again repeated his offensive mandate; but he
did it in a spirit of bravado, in order to maintain his
reputation. The allusion to the purse made him sadder
than ever. He put his hand into his breast-pocket, and
felt that it was near his heart: and then he fancied that
he again heard her words—'You will be steady; won't
you, dear Charley?'

At four o'clock, he was by no means in his usual hurry
to go away, and he sat there drawing patterns on his
blotting-paper, and chopping up a stick of sealing-wax
with his penknife, in a very disconsolate way. Scatterall
went. Corkscrew went. Mr. Snape, having carefully
brushed his hat and taken down from its accustomed peg
the old cotton umbrella, also took his departure; and the
fourth navvy, who inhabited the same room, went also.
The iron-fingered hand of time struck a quarter past four

on the Somerset House clock, and still Charley Tudor lingered at his office. The maid who came to sweep the room was thoroughly amazed, and knew that something must be wrong.

Just as he was about to move, Mr. Oldeschole came bustling into the room. 'Where is Corkscrew?' said he. 'Gone,' said Charley. 'And Scatterall?' asked Oldeschole. 'Gone, sir,' said Charley. 'And Mr. Snape?' said the Secretary. 'Oh, he is gone, of course,' said Charley, taking his revenge at last.

'Then, Mr. Tudor, I must trouble you to copy these papers for me at once. They are wanted immediately for Sir Gregory Hardlines.' It was quite clear that Mr. Oldeschole was very much in earnest about the job, and that he was rejoiced to find that he still had one clerk to aid him.

Charley sat down and did the required work. On any other day he would greatly have disliked such a summons, but now he did not care much about it. He made the copies, however, as quickly as he could, and then took them in to Mr. Oldeschole.

The worthy Secretary rewarded him by a lecture; a lecture, however, which, as Charley well understood, was intended all in kindness. He told him how Mr. Snape complained of him, how the office books told against him, how the clerks talked, and all Somerset House made stories of his grotesque iniquities. With penitential air Charley listened and promised. Mr. Oldeschole promised also that bygones should be bygones. 'I wonder whether the old cock would lend me a five-pound note! I dare say he would,' said Charley to himself, as he left the office. He abstained, however, from asking for it.

Returning to his room, he took his hat and went downstairs. As he was sauntering forth through the archway into the Strand, a man with a decent coat but a very bad hat came up to him.

'I'm afraid I must trouble you to go with me, Mr. Tudor,' said the man.

'All right,' said Charley; 'Outerman, I suppose; isn't it?'

'All right,' said the bailiff.

And away the two walked together to a sponging-house in Cursitor Street.

Charley had been arrested at the suit of Mr. Outerman, the tailor. He perfectly understood the fact, and made no special objection to following the bailiff. One case was at any rate off his mind; he could not now, be his will to do so ever so good, keep his appointment with Norah Geraghty. Perhaps it was quite as well for him to be arrested just at this moment, as be left at liberty. It must have come sooner or later. So he walked on with the bailiff not without some feeling of consolation.

The man had suggested to him a cab; but Charley had told him, without the slightest *mauvaise honte*, that he had not about him the means of paying for a cab. The man again suggested that perhaps he had better go home and get some money, as he would find it in Cursitor Street very desirable to have some. To this Charley replied that neither had he any money at home.

'That's blue,' said the man.

'It is rather blue,' said Charley; and on they went very amicably arm-in-arm.

We need not give any detailed description of Charley's prison-house. He was luckily not detained there so long as to make it necessary that we should become acquainted with his fellow-captives, or even have much intercourse with his jailers. He was taken to the sponging-house, and it was there imparted to him that he had better send for two things—first of all for money, which was by far the more desirable of the two; and secondly, for bail, which even if forthcoming was represented as being at best but a dubious advantage.

'There's Mrs. Davis, she'd bail you, of course, and willing,' said the bailiff.

'Mrs. Davis!' said Charley, surprised that the man should know aught of his personal acquaintances.

'Yes, Mrs. Davis of the "Cat and Whistle." She'd do it in course, along of Miss Geraghty.'

Charley perceived with a shudder that his matrimonial arrangements were known and talked of even in the distant world of Cursitor Street. He declined, however, the assistance of the landlady, which no doubt would have been willingly forthcoming, and was divided between his three friends, Alaric, Harry, and Mr. M'Ruen. Alaric was his cousin and his natural resource in such a position, but he had lately rejected Alaric's advice, and now felt a disinclination to call upon him in his difficulty. Harry he knew would assist him, would at once pay Mr. Outerman's bill, and relieve him from all immediate danger; but the sense of what he already owed to Norman made him unwilling to incur further obligations;—so he decided on sending for Mr. M'Ruen. In spite of his being so poorly supplied with immediate cash, it was surmised from his appearance, clothes, and known rank, that any little outlay made in his behalf would be probably repaid, and he was therefore furnished with a messenger on credit. This man was first to call at Mr. M'Ruen's with a note, and then to go to Charley's lodgings and get his brushes, razors, &c., these being the first necessaries of life for which a man naturally looks when once overtaken by such a misfortune as that with which Charley was now afflicted.

In the process of time the brushes and razors came, and so did Mr. M'Ruen.

'This is very kind of you,' said Charley, in rather a doleful voice, for he was already becoming tired of Cursitor Street.

Mr. M'Ruen twisted his head round inside his cravat, and put out three fingers by way of shaking hands with the prisoner.

'You seem pretty comfortable here,' said M'Ruen. Charley dissented to this, and said that he was extremely uncomfortable.

'And what is it that I can do for you, Mr. Tudor?' said M'Ruen.

'Do for me! Why, bail me, to be sure; they won't let me out unless somebody bails me. You know I shan't run away.'

'Bail you!' said M'Ruen.

'Yes, bail me,' said Charley. 'You don't mean to say that you have any objection?'

Mr. M'Ruen looked very sharply at his young client from head to foot. 'I don't know about bail,' he said:

'it's very dangerous, very; why didn't you send for
Mr. Norman or your cousin?'

'Because I didn't choose,' said Charley—'because
I preferred sending to some one I could pay for the
trouble.'

'Ha—ha—ha,' laughed M'Ruen; 'but that's just it—
can you pay? You owe me a great deal of money,
Mr. Tudor. You are so unpunctual, you know.'

'There are two ways of telling that story,' said Charley;
'but come, I don't want to quarrel with you about that
now—you go bail for me now, and you'll find your advantage in it. You know that well enough.'

'Ha—ha—ha,' laughed the good-humoured usurer;
'ha—ha—ha—well, upon my word I don't know. You
owe me a great deal of money, Mr. Tudor. Now, what
o'clock is it by you, I wonder?'

Charley took out his watch—the Cox and Savary, before
alluded to—and said that it was past seven.

'Aye; you've a very nice watch, I see. Come, Mr.
Tudor, you owe me a great deal of money, and you are
the most unpunctual young man I know; but yet I don't
like to see you distressed. I'll tell you what, now—do
you hand over your watch to me, just as a temporary
loan—you can't want it here, you know; and I'll come
down and bail you out to-morrow.'

Charley declined dealing on these terms; and then
Mr. M'Ruen at last went away, leaving Charley to his
fate, and lamenting quite pathetically that he was such
an unpunctual young man, so very unpunctual that it
was impossible to do anything to assist him. Charley,
however, manfully resisted the second attack upon his
devoted watch.

'That's very blue, very blue indeed,' said the master of
the house, as Mr. M'Ruen took his departure—'ha'n't you
got no huncles nor hants, nor nothin' of that sort?'

Charley declared that he had lots of uncles and aunts,
grandfathers and grandmothers, and a perfect wealth of
cousins, and that he would send for some of the leading
members of his family to-morrow. Satisfied with this,
the man supplied him with bread and cheese, gin and
water, and plenty of tobacco; and, fortified with these

comforts, Charley betook himself at last very lugubriously, to a filthy, uninviting bed.

He had, we have seen, sent for his brushes, and hence came escape; but in a manner that he had little recked of, and of which, had he been asked, he would as little have approved. Mrs. Richards, his landlady, was not slow in learning from the messenger how it came to pass that Charley wanted the articles of his toilet so suddenly demanded. 'Why, you see, he's just been quodded,' said the boy.

Mrs. Richards was quite enough up to the world, and had dealt with young men long enough, to know what this meant; nor indeed was she much surprised. She had practical knowledge that Charley had no strong propensity to pay his debts, and she herself was not unaccustomed to answer the emissaries of Mr. Outerman and other greedy tradesmen who were similarly situated. To Mrs. Richards herself Charley was not in debt, and she had therefore nothing to embitter her own feelings against him. Indeed, she had all that fondness for him which a lodging-house keeper generally has for a handsome, dissipated, easy-tempered young man; and when she heard that he had been 'quodded,' immediately made up her mind that steps must be taken for his release.

But what was she to do? Norman, who she was aware would 'unquod' him immediately, if he were in the way, was down at Hampton, and was not expected to be at his lodgings for two or three days. After some cogitation, Mrs. Richards resolved that there was nothing for it but to go down to Hampton herself, and break the news to his friends. Charley would not have been a bit obliged to her had he known it, but Mrs. Richards acted for the best. There was a train down to Hampton Court that night, and a return train to bring her home again—so off she started.

Mrs. Woodward had on that same afternoon taken down Katie, who was still an invalid;—Norman had gone down with them, and was to remain there for some few days—going up and down every morning and evening. Mrs. Woodward was sitting in the drawing-room; Linda and Katie were with her, the latter lying in state on her sofa as invalid young ladies should do; Captain Cuttwater was at Hampton Court, and Norman was on the water; when a fly from the railway made its way up to the door of the Cottage.

'Mrs. Richards, ma'am,' said the demure parlour-maid, ushering in the lodging-house keeper, who in her church-going best made a very decent appearance.

'Oh, Mrs. Richards, how are you?' said Mrs. Woodward, who knew the woman very well—'pray sit down—are there any news from London?'

'Oh, ma'am, such news—such bad news—Mister Charley——.' Up jumped Katie from her sofa and stood erect upon the floor. She stood there, with her mouth slightly open, with her eyes intently fixed on Mrs. Richards, with her little hands each firmly clenched, drawing her breath with hard, short, palpitating efforts. There she stood, but said nothing.

'Oh, Mrs. Richards—what is it?' said Mrs. Woodward; 'for Heaven's sake what is the matter?'

'Oh, ma'am; he's been took,' said Mrs. Richards.

'Took!' repeated Mrs. Woodward. 'Katie, dear Katie—sit down, my child—sit down.'

'Oh, mamma! oh, mamma!' said she, apparently unable to move, and certainly all but unable to stand.

'Tell us, Mrs. Richards, what is it—what has happened to Mr. Tudor?' and as she spoke Mrs. Woodward got up and passed her arm around her younger daughter's waist —Linda also got up and joined the group.

'Why, ma'am,' said Mrs. Richards, 'he's been took by the bailiffs, and now he's in prison.'

Katie did not faint. She never had fainted, and probably did not know the way; but she clenched her hands still tighter, breathed harder than before, and repeated her appeal to her mother in a voice of agony. 'Oh, mamma! oh, mamma!'

Katie had no very accurate conception of what an arrest for debt meant. She knew that next to death imprisonment was the severest punishment inflicted on erring mortals, and she now heard that Charley was in prison. She did not stop to think whether it was for his life, or for some more limited period. It was enough for her to know that this terrible misfortune had come upon him, to him who, to her young fancy, was so bright, so good, so clever, so excellent, upon him who had saved her life—upon him whom she so dearly loved.

'Oh, mamma! oh, mamma!' she said, and then in agony she shut her eyes and shuddered violently.

Mrs. Woodward was greatly afflicted. She was indeed sorry to hear such tidings of Charley Tudor; but her grief was now deeper even than that. She could not be longer blind to the sort of feeling which her child evinced for this young man; she could not think that these passionate bursts of overpowering sorrow were the result of mere childish friendship; she could not but see that her Katie's bosom now held a woman's heart, and that that heart was no longer her own.

And then Mrs. Woodward reflected of what nature, of what sort, was this man whom she had allowed to associate with her darling, almost as a brother does with his sister; whom she had warmed in her bosom till he had found an opportunity of inflicting this deadly wound. With terrible bitterness she upbraided herself as she sat down and bade Mrs. Richards go on with her tale. She knew that nothing which could now be said would add to Katie's anguish.

Mrs. Richards' story was soon told. It simply amounted to this—that 'Mister Charley,' as she always called him, had been arrested for debt at the suit of a tailor, and that she had learnt the circumstances from the fact of the prisoner having sent for his brushes.

'And so I thought the best thing was to come and tell Mr. Norman,' said Mrs. Richards, concluding her speech.

Nothing could be done till Norman came in. Linda went out with Mrs. Richards to get some refreshment in the dining-room, and Mrs. Woodward sat with her arm round Katie's neck on the sofa, comforting her with kisses and little caressing touches, but saying nothing. Katie, still unconscious of her passion, gave way to spasmodic utterance of her own grief.

'Oh, mamma!' she said—'what can be done? What can we do? You will do something, mamma, won't you? Poor Charley! Dear Charley! Harry will do something—

won't he ? Won't Harry go to London and do something ? '

Mrs. Woodward did what she could to quiet her. Something should be done, she said. They must wait till Harry came in, and then settle what was best. Nothing could be done till Harry came in. ' You must be patient, Katie, or else you will make yourself really ill.'

Katie became afraid that she would be sent off to bed on the score of her illness before Harry had come, and thus lose the advantage of hearing what was the step decided on. So she sat silent in the corner of her sofa feigning to be asleep, but pondering in her mind what sort of penalties were the penalties of imprisonment, how dreadful, how endurable, or how unendurable. Would they put chains on him ? would they starve him ? would they cut off his beautiful brown hair ?

Mrs. Woodward sat silent waiting for Harry's return. When first she had watched Katie's extreme misery, and guessed the secret of her child's heart, she had felt something like hard, bitter anger against Charley. But by degrees this feeling softened down. It was by no means natural to her, nor akin to her usual tenderness. After all, the fault hitherto was probably more her own than his.

Mrs. Richards was sent back to town. She was thanked for the trouble she had taken, and told that Mr. Norman would do in the matter all that was necessary to be done. So she took her departure, and Linda returned to the drawing-room.

Unfortunately Captain Cuttwater came in first. They none of them mentioned Charley's misfortune to him. Charley was no favourite with Uncle Bat, and his remarks would not have been of the most cheering tendency.

At last Norman came also. He came, as was his wont, through the drawing-room window, and, throwing himself into a chair, began to tell the girls how much they had lost by not joining him on the river.

' Harry,' said Mrs. Woodward, ' step into the dining-room with me for a moment.'

Harry got up to follow her. Katie and Linda also instantly jumped from their seats to do the same. Mrs. Woodward looked round, and motioned to them to stay with their uncle. Linda obediently, though reluctantly, remained ; but Katie's impulse was too strong for her. She gave one imploring look at her mother, a look which Mrs. Woodward well understood, and then taking silence for consent, crept into the dining-room.

'Harry,' said Mrs. Woodward, as soon as the dining-room door was closed, 'Charley has been arrested ; ' and then she told him how Mrs. Richards had been at the Cottage, and what was the nature of the tidings she had brought.

Norman was not much surprised, nor did he feign to be so. He took the news so coolly that Katie almost hated him. 'Did she say who had arrested him, or what was the amount ?' he asked.

Mrs. Woodward replied that she knew no more than what she had already told. Katie stood in the shade with her eyes fixed upon her cousin, but as yet she said nothing. How cruel, how stony-hearted must he be to hear such dreadful tidings and remain thus undisturbed ! Had Charley heard that Norman was arrested, he would have been half way to London by this time. So, at least, thought Katie.

'Something can be done for him, Harry, can there not ? We must contrive to do something—eh, Harry ?' said Mrs. Woodward.

'I fear it is too late to do anything to-night,' said Harry, looking at his watch. 'The last train is gone, and I could not possibly find him out before twelve.'

'And to-morrow is Sunday,' said Mrs. Woodward.

'Oh, Harry, pray do something !' said Katie, 'pray, pray, pray, do ! Oh, Harry, think of Charley being in prison ! Oh, Harry, he would do anything for you !' and then she burst into tears, and caught hold of Harry's arm and the front of his coat to add force to her entreaty.

'Katie,' said her mother, 'don't be so foolish. Harry will, of course, do whatever is best.'

'But, mamma, he says he will do nothing ; why does he not go at once ?'

'I will go at once, dear Katie,' said he ; 'I will go now directly. I don't know whether we can set him free to-night, or even to-morrow, as to-morrow is Sunday ; but it certainly shall be done on Monday, you may be sure of that at any rate. Whatever can be done shall be done; and, without further talk upon the subject, he took his hat and went his way.

'May God Almighty bless him!' said Mrs. Woodward. 'How infinitely greater are truth and honesty than any talent, however brilliant!' She spoke only to herself and no one even guessed what was the nature of the comparison which she thus made.

As soon as Norman was gone, Katie went to bed; and in the morning she was pronounced to be too unwell to get up. And, indeed, she was far from well. During the night she only slept by short starts, and in her sleep she was restless and uneasy; then, when she woke, she would burst out into fits of tears, and lie sobbing hysterically till she slept again. In the morning, Mrs. Woodward said something about Charley's misconduct, and this threw her into a wretched state of misery, from which nothing would rouse her till her mother promised that the prodigal should not be thrown over and abandoned.

Poor Mrs. Woodward was in a dreadful state of doubt as to what it now behoved her to do. She felt that, however anxious she might be to assist Charley for his own sake, it was her bounden duty to separate him from her child. Whatever merits he might have—and in her eyes he had many—at any rate he had not those which a mother would desire to see in the future husband of her daughter. He was profligate, extravagant, careless, and idle; his prospects in life were in every respect bad; he had no self-respect, no self-reliance, no moral strength. Was it not absolutely necessary that she should put a stop to any love that might have sprung up between such a man as this and her own young bright-eyed darling?

Put a stop to it! Yes, indeed, most expedient; nay, absolutely necessary—if it were only possible. Now, when it was too late, she began to perceive that she had not known of what material her own child was formed. At sixteen, Gertrude and Linda had in reality been little more than children. In manner, Katie had been more childish even than them, and yet—Mrs. Woodward, as she thought of these things, felt her heart faint within her.

She was resolved that, cost what it might, Charley must be banished from the Cottage. But at the first word of assumed displeasure that she uttered, Katie fell into such an agony of grief that her soft heart gave way, and she found herself obliged to promise that the sinner should be forgiven. Katie the while was entirely unconscious of the state of her own feelings. Had she thought that she loved him as women love, had any thought of such love and of him together even entered her mind, she could not have talked of him as she now talked. Had he been her brother, she could not have been less guarded in her protestations of affection, or more open in her appeals to her mother that he might be forgiven. Such was her present state ; but it was doomed that her eyes should soon be opened, and that she should know her own sorrow.

On the Sunday afternoon, Norman returned to Hampton with the tidings that Charley was once more a free man. The key of gold which he had taken with him had been found potent enough to open all barriers, even those with which the sanctity of Sunday had surrounded the prisoner. Mr. Outerman, and the bailiff, and the messenger, had all been paid their full claims, and Charley, with his combs and brushes, had returned to the more benign custody of Mrs. Richards.

' And why didn't he come down with you ? ' said Katie to Norman, who had gone up to her bedroom to give her the good tidings.

Norman looked at Mrs. Woodward, but made no reply.

' He would probably prefer remaining in town at present,' said Mrs. Woodward. ' It will be more comfortable for him to do so.'

And then Katie was left alone to meditate why Charley should be more comfortable after his arrest in London than at Hampton ; and after a while she thought that she had surmised the truth. ' Poor Charley ! perhaps he is ashamed. He need not be ashamed to come at any rate to me.'

CHAPTER XXIX

EASY IS THE SLOPE OF HELL

THE electors for the Tillietudlem district burghs, disgusted by the roguery of Mr. M'Buffer, and anxiously on the alert to replace him by a strictly honest man, returned our friend Undy by a glorious majority. He had no less than 312 votes, as opposed to 297, and though threatened with the pains and penalties of a petition, he was not a little elated by his success. A petition with regard to the Tillietudlem burghs was almost as much a matter of course as a contest; at any rate the threat of a petition was so. Undy, however, had lived through this before, and did not fear but that he might do so again. Threatened folks live long; parliamentary petitions are very costly, and Undy's adversaries were, if possible, even in more need of money than himself.

He communicated his good fortune to his friend Alaric in the following letter :—

'Bellenden Arms, Tillietudlem, July, 185—.

' MY DEAR DIRECTOR,

' Here I am once more a constituent part of the legislative wisdom of the United Kingdom, thanks to the patriotic discretion of the pot-wallopers, burgage-tenants, and ten-pound freeholders of these loyal towns. The situation is a proud one; I could only wish that it had been less expensive. I am plucked as clean as ever was pigeon; and over and above the loss of every feather I carried, old M'Cleury, my agent here, will have a bill against me that will hardly be settled before the next election. I do not complain, however; a man cannot have luxuries without paying for them; and this special luxury of serving one's country in Parliament is one for which a man has so often to pay, without the subsequent fruition of the thing paid for, that a successful candidate should never grumble, however much he may have been mulcted. They talk of a petition; but, thank God, there are still such things as recognizances ; and, moreover, to give M'Cleury his due, I do not think he has left a hole open for them to work at. He is a thorough rascal, but no man does better work.

'I find there is already a slight rise in the West Corks. Keep your eye open. If you find you can realize £4 4s. or even £4, sell, and let the West of Cork and Ballydehob go straight to the devil. We should then be able to do better with our money. But I doubt of such a sale with so large a stock as we hold. I got a letter yesterday from that Cork attorney, and I find that he is quite prepared to give way about the branch. He wants his price, of course ; and he must have it. When once we have carried that point, then it will be plain sailing ; our only regret then will be that we didn't go further into it. The calls, of course, must be met ; I shall be able to do something in October, but shall not have a shilling sooner— unless I sell, which I will not do under 80s.

'I was delighted to hear of your promotion ; not that you'll remain in the shop long, but it gives you a better name and a better claim. Old Golightly was buried yesterday, as of course you have heard. Mrs. Val quite agrees with me that your name had better be put in as that of Clem's trustee. She's going to marry that d—— Frenchman. What an unmitigated ass that cousin of yours must be ! I can't say I admire her taste ; but nevertheless she is welcome for me. It would, however, be most scandalous if we were to allow him to get possession of her money. He would, as a matter of course, make ducks and drakes of it in no time. Speculate probably in some Russian railway, or Polish mine, and lose every shilling. You will of course see it tied up tight in the hands of the trustees, and merely pay him, or if possible her, the interest of it. Now that I am once more in, I hope we shall be able to do something to protect the fortunes of married women.

'You will be quite safe in laying out Clem's money, or a portion of it, in the West Corks. Indeed, I don't know how you could well do better with it. You will find Figgs a mere shadow. I think we can pull through in this manner. If not we must get —— to take our joint bill. He would sooner do that than have the works stopped. But then we should have to pay a tremendous price for it.

'So we were well out of the Mary Janes at last. The take last month was next to nothing, and now she's full of water. Manylodes hung on till just the last, and yet got out on his feet after all. That fellow will make a mint of money yet. What a pity that he should be such a rogue! If he were honest, honest enough I mean to be trusted, he might do anything.

'I shall leave this on Wednesday night, take the oaths on Thursday, and will see you in the evening. M'Carthy Desmond will at once move that I be put on the West Cork Committee, in place of Nogo, who won't act. My shares are all at present registered in Val's name. It will be well, however, to have them all transferred to you.

'Yours ever,

'U. S.

'M'Cleury has pledged himself to put me in again without further expense, if I have to stand before the next general election, in consequence of taking place under Government. I earnestly hope his sincerity may be tried.'

During the month of July, Alaric was busy enough. He had to do the work of his new office, to attend to his somewhat critical duties as director of the West Cork Railway, to look after the interests of Miss Golightly, whose marriage was to take place in August, and to watch the Parliamentary career of his friend Undy, with whose pecuniary affairs he was now bound up in a manner which he could not avoid feeling to be very perilous.

July passed by, and was now over, and members were looking to be relieved from their sultry labours, and to be allowed to seek air and exercise on the mountains. The Ballydehob branch line had received the sanction of Parliament through the means which the crafty Undy had so well understood how to use; but from some cause hitherto not sufficiently fathomed, the shares had continued to be depressed in value in spite of that desirable event. It was necessary, however, that calls should be paid up to the amount of £5 a share, and as Undy and Alaric held nearly a thousand shares between them, a large amount of money was required. This, however, was made to be forthcoming from Miss Golightly's fortune.

On the first of August that interesting young lady was married to the man—shall we say of her heart or of her feet ? The marriage went off very nicely, but as we have already had one wedding, and as others may perhaps be before us, we cannot spare much time or many pages to describe how Miss Golightly became Madame Jaquêtanàpe. The lady seemed well pleased with everything that was done, and had even in secret but one care in the world. There was to be a dance after she and her Victoire were gone, and she could not join in it !

We, however, are in the position, as regards Clementina, in which needy gentlemen not unfrequently place themselves with reference to rich heiresses. We have more concern with her money than herself. She was married, and M. Jaquêtanàpe became the happy possessor of an income of £800 a year. Everybody conceived him to behave well on the occasion. He acknowledged that he had very little means of his own—about 4,000 francs a year, from rents in Paris. He expressed himself willing to agree to any settlement, thinking, perhaps with wisdom, that he might in this way best make sure of his wife's income, and was quite content when informed that he would receive his quarterly payments from so respectable a source as one of Her Majesty's Commissioners for the regulation of the Civil Service. The Bank of France could not have offered better security.

Thus Alaric obtained full control of Miss Golightly's fortune : for Figgs, his co-trustee, was, as has been said, a shadow. He obtained the full control of £20,000, and out of it he paid the calls due upon the West Cork shares, held both by himself and Undy Scott. But he put a salve upon his conscience, and among his private memoranda appertaining to that lady's money affairs he made an entry, intelligible to any who might read it, that he had so invested this money on her behalf. The entry was in itself a lie—a foolish, palpable lie—and yet he found

in it something to quiet remorse and stupefy his conscience.

Undy Scott had become tyrannical in his logic as soon
as he had persuaded Alaric to make use of a portion of
Madame Jaquêtanàpe's marriage portion. 'You have
taken part of the girl's money,' was Undy's argument ;
' you have already converted to your own purposes so
much of her fortune ; it is absurd for you now to talk of
conscience and honesty, of your high duties as a trustee,
of the inviolable distinction between meum and tuum.
You have already shown that the distinction is not inviolable ; let us have no more such nonsense ; there are
still left £15,000 on which we can trade ; open the till,
and let us go on swimmingly with the business.'

Alaric was not addressed absolutely in these words ;
he would not probably have allowed the veil with which
he still shrouded his dishonesty to be withdrawn with so
rough a hand ; but that which was said was in effect the
same. In September he left town for a few weeks and
went down to Scotland, still with Undy Scott. He had
at first much liked this man's society, for Scott was
gay, lively, clever, and a good companion at all points.
But latterly he had become weary of him. He now put
up with him as men in business have to put up with
partners whom they may not like ; or, perhaps, to speak
the truth openly, he bore with him as a rogue bears with
his confederate, though he absolutely hates his brother
rogue on account of his very roguery. Alaric Tudor was
now a rogue ; despite his high office, his grand ideas,
his exalted ambition ; despite his talent, zeal, and well-
directed official labours, he was a rogue ; a thief, a villain
who had stolen the money of the orphan, who had undertaken a trust merely that he might break it ; a robber,
doubly disgraced by being a robber with an education,
a Bill Sykes without any of those excuses which a philanthropist cannot but make for wretches brought up in
infamy.

Alas, alas ! how is it that in these days such men
become rogues ? How is it that we see in such frightful
instances the impotency of educated men to withstand
the allurements of wealth ? Men are not now more keen

after the pleasures which wealth can buy than were their forefathers. One would rather say that they are less so. The rich labour now, and work with an assiduity that often puts to shame the sweat in which the poor man earns his bread. The rich rogue, or the rogue that would be rich, is always a laborious man. He allows himself but little recreation, for dishonest labour admits of no cessation. His wheel is one which cannot rest without disclosing the nature of the works which move it.

It is not for pleasure that men

> Put rancours in the vessel of their peace;

nor yet primarily for ambition. Men do not wish to rise by treachery, or to become great through dishonesty. The object, the ultimate object, which a man sets before himself, is generally a good one. But he sets it up in so enviable a point of view, his imagination makes it so richly desirable, by being gazed at it becomes so necessary to existence, that its attainment is imperative. The object is good, but the means of attaining it—the path to the object—ah! there is the slip. Expediency is the dangerous wind by which so many of us have wrecked our little boats.

And we do so more now than ever, because great ships, swimming in deepest waters, have unluckily come safe to haven though wafted there by the same pernicious wind. Every great man, who gains a great end by dishonest means, does more to deteriorate his country and lower the standard of his countrymen than legions of vulgar thieves, or nameless unaspiring rogues. Who has injured us so much in this way as he whose name still stands highest among modern politicians? Who has given so great a blow to political honesty, has done so much to banish from men's minds the idea of a life-ruling principle, as Sir Robert Peel?

It would shock many were we to attribute to him the roguery of the Sadleirs and Camerons, of the Robsons and Redpaths of the present day; but could we analyse causes and effects, we might perhaps do so with no injustice. He has taught us as a great lesson, that a man who has before him a mighty object may dispense with those old-fashioned rules of truth to his neighbours and honesty to his own principles, which should guide us in ordinary life. At what point ordinary life ends, at what crisis objects may be considered great enough to justify the use of a dispensing power, that he has not taught us; that no Sir Robert Peel can teach us; that must unfortunately be left to the judgement of the individual. How prone we are, each of us, to look on our own object as great, how ready to make excuses for receiving such a lesson for our guide; how willing to think that we may be allowed to use this dispensing power ourselves—this experience teaches us in very plain language.

Thrice in his political life did Sir Robert Peel change his political creed, and carry, or assist to carry, with more or less of self-gratulation, the measures of his adversaries. Thrice by doing so he kept to himself that political power which he had fairly forfeited by previous opposition to the requirements of his country. Such an apposition of circumstances is at any rate suspicious. But let us give him credit for the expression of a true belief; of a belief at first that the corn-laws should be maintained, and then of a belief that they should not; let us, with a forced confidence in his personal honesty, declare so much of him; nevertheless, he should surely have felt, had he been politically as well as personally honest, that he was not the man to repeal them.

But it was necessary, his apologist will say, that the corn-laws should be repealed; he saw the necessity, and yielded to it. It certainly was necessary, very necessary, very unavoidable; absolutely necessary one may say; a fact, which the united efforts of all the Peels of the day could in nowise longer delay, having already delayed it to the utmost extent of their power. It was essential that the corn-laws should be repealed; but by no means essential that this should be done by Sir Robert Peel.

It was a matter of indifference to us Englishmen who did the deed. But to Sir Robert Peel it was a matter of great moment that he should do it. He did it, and posterity will point at him as a politician without policy, as a statesman without a principle, as a worshipper at the altar of expediency, to whom neither vows sworn to friends, nor declarations made to his country, were in any way binding. Had Sir Robert Peel lived, and did the people now resolutely desire that the Church of England should be abandoned, that Lords and Commons should bow the neck, that the Crown should fall, who can believe that Sir Robert Peel would not be ready to carry out their views? Readers, it may be that to you such deeds as those are horrible even to be thought of or expressed; to me I own that they are so. So also to Sir Robert Peel was Catholic Emancipation horrible, so was Reform of Parliament, so was the Corn Law Repeal. They were horrible to him, horrible to be thought of, horrible to be expressed. But the people required these measures, and therefore he carried them, arguing on their behalf with all the astuteness of a practised statesman.

That Sir Robert Peel should be a worshipper of expediency might be matter of small moment to any but his biographer, were it not that we are so prone to copy the example of those whose names are ever in our mouths. It has now become the doctrine of a large class of politicians that political honesty is unnecessary, slow, subversive of a man's interests, and incompatible with quick onward movement. Such a doctrine in politics is to be deplored; but alas! who can confine it to politics? It creeps with gradual, but still with sure and quick motion, into all the doings of our daily life. How shall the man who has taught himself that he may be false in the House of Commons, how shall he be true in the Treasury chambers? or if false there, how true on the Exchange? and if false there, how shall he longer have any truth within him?

And thus Alaric Tudor had become a rogue, and was obliged, as it were in his own defence, to consort with a rogue. He went down to Scotland with Undy, leaving his wife and child at home, not because he could thus best amuse his few leisure days, but because this new work of his, this laborious trade of roguery, allowed him no leisure days. When can villainy have either days or hours of leisure?

Among other things to be done in the north, Alaric was to make acquaintance with the constituents of the little borough of Strathbogy, which it was his ambition to represent in the next Parliament. Strathbogy was on the confines of the Gaberlunzie property; and indeed the lord's eldest son, who was the present member, lived almost within the municipal boundary. Ca'stocks Cottage, as his residence was called, was but a humble house for a peer's eldest son; but Mr. Scott was not ashamed to live there, and there for a while he entertained his brother Undy and Alaric Tudor. Mr. Scott intended, when the present session was over, to retire from the labours of parliamentary life. It may be that he thought that he had done enough for his country; it may be that the men of Strathbogy thought that he had not done enough for them; it may be that there was some family understanding between him and his brother. This, however, was clear, that he did not intend to stand again himself, and that he professed himself ready to put forward Alaric Tudor as a worthy successor, and to give him the full benefit and weight of the Gaberlunzie interest.

But not for nothing was Alaric to receive such important assistance.

'There are but 312 electors altogether,' said Undy one morning as they went out shooting, 'and out of these we can command a hundred and twenty. It must be odd if you cannot get enough outsiders to turn them into a majority. Indeed you may look on it as a certain seat. No man in England or Scotland could give you one more certain.'

This was not the first occasion on which Undy had spoken of all that he was doing for his friend, and Alaric therefore, somewhat disgusted with the subject, made no reply.

'I never had things made so easy for me when I went in,' continued Undy; 'nor have I ever found them so easy since. I don't suppose it will cost you above £500 or at most £600, altogether.'

'Well, that will be a comfort,' said Alaric.

'A comfort! why I should say it would. What with the election and petition together, Tillietudlem never cost me less than £2,000. It cost me just as much, too, when I was thrown out.'

'That was a bore for you,' said Alaric.

'Upon my word you take it rather coolly,' said Undy; 'another man would thank a fellow for putting such a nice thing in his way.'

'If the obligation be so deep,' said Alaric, becoming very red in the face, 'I would rather not accept it. It is not too late for you to take the cheaper seat to yourself, if you prefer it; and I will look elsewhere.'

'Oh, of course; perhaps at Tillietudlem; but for Heaven's sake, my dear fellow, don't let us quarrel about it. You are perfectly welcome to whatever assistance we can give you at Strathbogy. I only meant to say that I hope it will be efficacious. And on the score of expense I'll tell you what we'll do—that is, if you think that fair; we'll put the cost of the two elections together, and share and share alike.'

'Considering that the election will not take place for at least more than twelve months, there will be time enough to settle that,' said Alaric.

'Well, that's true, too,' said Undy; and then they went on, and for some time separated on the mountain, complaining, when they met again, of the game being scarce and the dogs wild, as men always do. But as they walked home, Undy, who regretted the loss of good time, again began about money matters.

'How many of those bridge shares will you take?' said he. This was a projected bridge from Poplar to Rotherhithe, which had been got up by some city gentle-·men, and as to which Undy Scott was, or pretended to be, very sanguine.

'None,' said Alaric. 'Unless I can get rid of those confounded West Cork and Ballydehobs, I can buy nothing more of anything.'

'Believe me, my dear fellow, the Ballydehobs are no such confounded things at all. If you are ever a rich man it will be through the Ballydehobs. But what you say about the bridge shares is nonsense. You have a large command of capital, and you cannot apply it better.'

Alaric winced, and wished in his heart that Clementina

Jaquêtanàpe, *née* Golightly, with all her money, was buried deep in the bogs of Ballydehob. Though he was a rogue, he could not yet bear his roguery with comfort to himself. It sat, however, as easy on Undy as though he had been to the manner born.

'I have no capital now at my disposal,' said he; 'and I doubt whether I should be doing right to lay out a ward's money in such a manner.'

A slight smile came over Undy's gay unconcerned features; it was very slight, but nevertheless it was very eloquent and very offensive also. Alaric understood it well; it made him hate the owner of it, but it made him hate himself still more.

'It is as well to be hung for a sheep as for a lamb,' said Undy's smile; 'and, moreover,' continued the smile, 'is it not ridiculous enough for you, Alaric Tudor, rogue as you are, to profess to me, Undy Scott, rogue as I am, any solicitude as to your ward's welfare, seeing that you have already taken to yourself, for your own dishonest purposes, a considerable slice of the fortune that has been trusted to your keeping? You have done this, and yet you talk to me of not having capital at your disposal! You have capital, and you will dispose of that capital for your own purposes, as long as a shilling remains uninvested of your ward's money. We are both rogues. God knows it, and you and I know it; but I am not such a hypocritical rogue as to make mock boasts of my honesty to my brother rogue.'

This was certainly a long speech to have been made by a smile which crossed Mr. Scott's face but for a moment, but every word of it was there expressed, and every word of it was there read. Alaric did not at all like being addressed so uncivilly. It seemed to tend but little to that 'Excelsior' for which his soul panted; but what could he do? how could he help himself? Was it not all true? could he contradict the smile? Alas! it was true; it was useless for him now to attempt even to combat such smiles. 'Excelsior,' indeed! his future course might now probably be called by some very different designation. Easy, very easy, is the slope of hell.

Before they had returned to Ca'stocks Cottage, Undy

had succeeded in persuading his friend that the game must be played on—on and on, and out. If a man intends to make a fortune in the share-market he will never do it by being bold one day and timid the next. No turf betting-book can be made up safely except on consistent principles. Half-measures are always ruinous. In matters of speculation one attempt is made safe by another. No man, it is true, can calculate accurately what may be the upshot of a single venture ; but a sharp fellow may calculate with a fair average of exactness what will be the aggregate upshot of many ventures. All mercantile fortunes have been made by the knowledge and understanding of this rule. If a man speculates but once and again, now and then, as it were, he must of course be a loser. He will be playing a game which he does not understand, and playing it against men who do understand it. Men who so play always lose. But he who speculates daily puts himself exactly in the reversed position. He plays a game which experience teaches him to play well, and he plays generally against men who have no such advantage. Of course he wins.

All these valuable lessons did Undy Scott teach to Alaric Tudor, and the result was that Alaric agreed to order—for self and partner—a considerable number of shares in the Limehouse Bridge Company. Easy, very easy, is the slope of hell.

And then in the evening, on this evening and other evenings, on all evenings, they talked over the prospects of the West Cork and Ballydehob branch, and of the Limehouse Bridge, which according to Undy's theory is destined to work quite a revolution in the East-end circles of the metropolis. Undy had noble ideas about this bridge. The shares at the present moment were greatly at a discount—so much the better, for they could be bought at a cheaper rate ; and they were sure to rise to some very respectable figure as soon as Undy should have played out with reference to them the parliamentary game which he had in view.

And so from morning to morning, and from night to night, they talked over their unholy trade till the price of shares and the sounds of sums of money entered into

Alaric's soul. And this, perhaps, is one of the greatest penalties to which men who embark in such trade are doomed, that they can never shake off the remembrance of their calculations; they can never drop the shop; they have no leisure, no ease; they can never throw themselves with loose limbs and vacant mind at large upon the world's green sward, and call children to come and play with them. At the Weights and Measures Alaric's hours of business had been from ten to five. In Undy's office they continued from one noon till the next, incessantly; even in his dreams he was working in the share market.

On his return to town Alaric found a letter from Captain Cuttwater, pressing very urgently for the repayment of his money. It had been lent on the express understanding that it was to be repaid when Parliament broke up. It was now the end of October, and Uncle Bat was becoming uneasy.

Alaric, when he received the letter, crushed it in his hand, and cursed the strictness of the man who had done so much for him. On the next day another slice was taken from the fortune of Madame Jaquêtanàpe; and his money, with the interest, was remitted to Captain Cuttwater.

CHAPTER XXX

MRS. WOODWARD'S REQUEST

WE will now go back for a while to Hampton. The author, for one, does so with pleasure. Though those who dwell there be not angels, yet it is better to live with the Woodwards and Harry Norman, with Uncle Bat, or even with the unfortunate Charley, than with such as Alaric and Undy Scott. The man who is ever looking after money is fitting company only for the devils, of whom, indeed, he is already one.

But Charley cannot any longer be called one of the Cottage circle. It was now the end of October, and since the day of his arrest, he had not yet been there. He had not been asked; nor would he go uninvited, as after what

had passed at Hampton Court Bridge he surely might
have done.

And consequently they were all unhappy. No one was
more so than Charley. When the prospect of the happy
evening with Norah had been so violently interrupted by
his arrest, he had, among his other messages, sent word to
the 'Cat and Whistle,' excusing his absence by a statement
of the true cause. From that day to this of which we are
now speaking he had seen neither Mrs. Davis nor her fair
protégée.

Nor were they better contented at the Cottage. Mrs.
Woodward was harassed by different feelings and different
fears, which together made her very unhappy. Her Katie
was still ill; not ill indeed so that she was forced to keep
her bed and receive daily visits from pernicious doctors,
but, nevertheless, so ill as to make a mother very anxious.

She had never been quite strong, quite herself, from
the night of Mrs. Val's dance. The doctor who had
attended her declared that her ducking in the river had
given her cold: and that this, not having been duly
checked, still hung about her. Then she had been taken
to a physician in London, who poked her on the back and
tapped her on the breast, listened to her lungs through
a wooden pipe—such was the account which Katie gave
herself when she returned home—and prescribed rum and
milk and cod-liver oil, declaring, with an authoritative
nod, that there was no organic disease—as yet.

'And what shall we do with her, doctor?' asked Mrs.
Woodward.

'Go on with the rum and milk and cod-liver oil, you
can't do better.'

'And the cough, doctor?'

'Why, if that doesn't go before the cold weather begins,
you may as well take her to Torquay for the winter.'

Oh! consumption, thou scourge of England's beauty!
how many mothers, gasping with ill-suppressed fears, have
listened to such words as these—have listened and then
hoped; listened again and hoped again with fainter hopes;
have listened again, and then hoped no more!

But there was much on Mrs. Woodward's mind which
she could not bring herself to tell to any doctor, but which

still left in her breast an impression that she was perhaps
keeping back the true cause of Katie's illness. Charley
had not been at Hampton since his arrest, and it was
manifest to all that Katie was therefore wretched.

'But why do you not ask him, mamma?' she had
urged when her mother suggested that he stayed away
because he did not like to show himself after what had
occurred. 'What will he think of us? he that saved my
life, mamma! Oh, mamma! you promised to forgive
him. Do ask him. You know he will come if you ask
him.'

Mrs. Woodward could not explain to her—could not
explain to any one—why she did not invite him. Norman
guessed it all, and Mrs. Woodward saw that he had done
so; but still she could not talk to him of Katie's feelings,
could not tell him that she feared her child was heart-
laden with so sad a love. So Mrs. Woodward had no
confidant in her sorrow, no counsel which she could seek
to aid her own wavering judgement. It was prudent, she
thought, that Katie and Charley should be kept apart.
Prudent! was it not even imperative on her to save her
child from such a fate? But then, when she saw the rosy
cheek grow pale by degrees, as she watched the plump
little arms grow gradually thin and wan, as those high
spirits fell, and that voice which had ever been so frequent
in the house and so clear, when the sound of it became
low and rare, then her heart would misgive her, and she
would all but resolve to take the only step which she
knew would bring a bright gleam on her child's face, and
give a happy tone to her darling's voice.

During the earlier portion of these days, Katie had with
eager constancy reiterated her request that Charley should
be asked to Hampton; but of a sudden her prayers ceased.
She spoke no more of Charley, asked no longer after his
coming, ceased even to inquire frequently of his welfare.
But yet, when his name was mentioned, she would open
wide her bright eyes, would listen with all her ears, and
show only too plainly to one who watched her as a mother
only can watch, what were the thoughts which filled her
heart.

'Linda,' she had said one night, as they sat in their

room, preparing themselves for bed, ' Linda, why does not mamma invite Charley to come down to Hampton ? '

' Oh ! I don't know,' said Linda ; who, however, if she did not know, was not far wrong in the guess she made. ' I suppose she thinks he'd be ashamed to show himself after having been in prison.'

' Ashamed ! Why should he be ashamed after so long ? Didn't you hear Harry say that the same thing often happens to young men ? Is he never to come here again ? Dear Linda, I know you know ; do tell me.'

' Well, I'm sure I do not know, if that's not the reason.'

' Oh ! Linda, dear Linda, yes, you do,' said Katie, throwing herself on her knees, resting her arms on her sister's lap, and looking up wistfully into her sister's face. Her long hair was streaming down her back ; her white, naked feet peeped out from beneath her bedroom dress, and large tears glistened in her eyes. Who could have resisted the prayers of such a suppliant ? Certainly not Linda, the soft-hearted Linda.

' Do tell me,' continued Katie, ' do tell me—I am sure you know ; and, Linda, if it is wrong to ask mamma about it, I'll never, never ask her again. I know mamma is unhappy about it. If my asking is wrong, I'll not make her unhappy any more in that way.'

Linda, for a while, did not know what to answer. Her hesitating manner immediately revealed to Katie that there was a secret, and that her sister could tell it if she would.

' Oh ! Linda, do tell me, do tell me, dear Linda ; you ought to tell me for mamma's sake.'

At last, with much hesitation, Linda told her the whole tale.

' Perhaps mamma thinks that you are too fond of Charley.'

An instant light flashed across Katie's heart—across her heart, and brain, and senses. Not another word was necessary to explain to her the whole mystery, to tell the whole tale, to reveal to her the secret of her own love, of her mother's fears, and of his assumed unwillingness. She got up slowly from her knees, kissed her sister's cheek and neck, smiled at her so sweetly, so sadly, and then sitting on her old seat, began playing with her long hair, and gazing at vacancy.

'It is only what I guess, you know, Katie—you would make me tell you, but I am sure there is nothing in it.'

'Dear Linda,' said she, 'you are so good; I am so much obliged to you.'

After that Katie spoke no further of Charley. But it was evident to them all, that though she said nothing, she had not ceased to think of him. Nor did her cheek again become rosy, nor her arms round, nor her voice happy. She got weaker than ever, and poor Mrs. Woodward was overcome with sorrow.

Nor was this the only cause of grief at Surbiton Cottage. During the last few weeks a bitter estrangement had taken place between the Woodwards and the Tudors, Alaric Tudor, that is, and Gertrude. Two years had now passed since Norman had chosen to quarrel with Alaric, and during all that period the two had never spoken amicably together, though they had met on business very frequently; on all such occasions Alaric had been imperturbed and indifferent, whereas Norman had been gloomy, and had carried a hostile brow and angry eye. At their period of life, two years generally does much to quiet feelings of ill-will and pacify animosity; but Norman's feelings had by no means been quieted, nor his animosity pacified. He had loved Alaric with a close and manly love; now he hated him with a close and, I fear I may say, a manly hatred. Alaric had, as he thought, answered his love by treachery; and there was that in Norman's heart which would not allow him to forgive one who had been a traitor to him. He had that kind of selfishness so common to us, but of which we are so unconscious, which will not allow us to pardon a sin against our own *amour propre*. Alaric might have been forgiven, though he had taken his friend's money, distanced him in his office, though he had committed against him all offences which one friend can commit against another, all but this. Norman had been proud of his love, and yet ashamed of it—proud of loving such a girl as Gertrude, and ashamed of being known to be in love at all. He had confided his love to Alaric, and

Alaric had robbed him of his love, and wounded both his pride and his shame.

Norman lacked the charity which should have been capable of forgiving even this. He now looked at all Alaric's doings through a different glass from that which he had used when Alaric had been dear to him. He saw, or thought that he saw, that his successful rival was false, ambitious, treacherous, and dishonest; he made no excuses for him, gave him no credit for his industry, accorded no admiration to his talent. He never spoke ill of Alaric Tudor to others; but he fed his own heart with speaking and thinking ill of him to himself.

Of Gertrude he thought very differently. He had taught himself to disconnect her from the treachery of her husband—or rather her memory; for, from the day on which he had learnt that she was engaged to Alaric, he had never seen her. He still loved the remembrance of her. In his solitary walks with Mrs. Woodward he would still speak of her as he might of one in some distant clime, for whose welfare he was deeply interested. He had seen and caressed her baby at Hampton. She was still dear to him. Had Alaric been called to his long account, it would have been his dearest wish to have become at some future time the husband of his widow.

To all these feelings on Norman's part Alaric was very indifferent; but their existence operated as a drawback on his wife's comfort, and, to a certain degree, on his own. Mrs. Woodward would not banish Norman from the Cottage, even for her daughter's sake, and it came by degrees to be understood that the Tudors, man and wife, should not go there unless they were aware that Norman was absent. Norman, on the other hand, did absent himself when it was understood that Alaric and Gertrude were coming; and thus the Woodwards kept up their intercourse with both.

But this was a bore. Alaric thought it most probable that Norman would marry one of the younger sisters, and he knew that family quarrels are uncomfortable and injudicious. When therefore he became a Civil Service Commissioner, and was thus removed from business intercourse with Norman, he conceived that it would be wise

to arrange a reconciliation. He discussed the matter
with Gertrude, and she, fully agreeing with him, undertook the task of making the proposal through her mother.
This she did with all the kindness and delicacy of a woman.
She desired her mother to tell Harry how much she had
valued his friendship, how greatly she regretted the loss
of it, how anxious her husband was to renew, if possible,
their former terms of affection. Mrs. Woodward, by no
means sanguine, undertook the commission. She undertook it, and utterly failed; and when Gertrude, in her
disappointment, spoke bitterly of Norman's bitterness,
both mother and sister, both Mrs. Woodward and Linda,
took Norman's part.

'I wish it could be otherwise,' said Mrs. Woodward,
'I wish it for all our sakes; but he is a man not easily to
be turned, and I cannot blame him. He has suffered very
much.'

Gertrude became very red. Her mother's words contained a reproach against herself, tacit and unintended
indeed, but not the less keenly felt.

'I am not aware that Mr. Norman has any cause of
just complaint,' she said, 'against any one, unless it be
himself. For the sake of charity and old associations
we have wished that all ideas of injury should be forgiven and forgotten. If he chooses still to indulge his
rancour, he must do so. I had taken him to be a better
Christian.'

More words had sprung from these. Mrs. Woodward,
who, in truth, loved Norman the better for the continuance
of his sorrow, would not give up his part; and so the
mother and child parted, and the two sisters parted, not
quarrelling indeed, not absolutely with angry words, but
in a tone of mind towards each other widely differing
from that of former years. Mrs. Woodward had lost none
of the love of the parent; but Gertrude had forgotten
somewhat of the reverence of the child.

All this had added much to the grief created by Katie's
illness.

And then of a sudden Katie became silent, as well as
sad and ill—silent and sad, but so soft, so loving in her
manner. Her gentle little caresses, the tender love ever

lying in her eye, the constant pressure of her thin small hand, would all but break her mother's heart. Katie would sit beside her on the sofa in the drawing-room for hours; a book, taken up as an excuse, would be in her lap, and she would sit there gazing listlessly into the vacant daylight till the evening would come; and then, when the room was shaded and sombre, when the light of the fire merely served to make the objects indistinct, she would lean gently and by degrees upon her mother's bosom, would coax her mother's arm round her neck, and would thus creep as it were into her mother's heart of hearts. And then slow tears would trickle down her cheeks, very slow, one by one, till they would fall as tell-tales on her mother's hand.

'Katie, my darling Katie,' the mother would say.

'I'm only tired, mamma,' would be her answer. 'Don't move, mamma; pray don't move. I am so comfortable.'

And then at night she would put herself to rest close circled in Linda's arms. She would twist up her little feet, and lie so quiet there, that Linda would remain motionless that she might not disturb her Katie's sleep; but soon warm tears would be running on her bosom, and she would know that Katie was still thinking of her love.

Linda, among all her virtues, had not that of reticence, and her mother had soon learnt from her what had been said that night in their bedroom about Charley. But this violation of confidence, if it was a violation, was hardly necessary to make Mrs. Woodward aware of what was passing in her daughter's bosom. When Katie ceased to ask that Charley might be sent for, when she ceased to plead for his pardon and to praise his virtues, Mrs. Woodward knew well the cause of her silence. It was not that others suspected her love, but that she had learned to suspect it herself. It was not that she was ashamed of loving Charley, but that she felt at once that such love would distress her mother's heart.

As she sat there that night fingering her silken hair, she had asked herself whether in truth this man was master of her heart; she had probed her young bosom, which now, by a sudden growth, became quick with a woman's impulse, and she had owned to herself that she did love him. He was dearer to her, she found, than all in the world beside. Fondly as she loved her sister, sweet to her as were her mother's caresses, their love was not as precious to her as his might be. And then she remembered what he was, what was the manner of his life, what his character; how different he was from Alaric or Harry Norman; she remembered this, and knew that her love was an unhappy passion. Herself she would have sacrificed: prisoner as he had been, debtor as he was, drunkard, penniless, and a spendthrift, she would not have hesitated to take him for her guide through life, and have done what a woman might to guide him in return. But she would not sacrifice her mother. She saw now why Charley was not asked, and silently acquiesced in his banishment.

She was not yet quite seventeen. Not yet seventeen! the reader will say. She was still such a child, and yet arguing to herself about spendthrift debtors and self-sacrifice! All this bombast at sixteen and a half. No, my ungentle reader, not all this bombast at sixteen and a half. The bombast is mine. It is my fault if I cannot put into fitting language the thoughts which God put into her young heart. In her mind's soliloquy, Charley's vices were probably all summed up in the one word, unsteady. 'Why is he so unsteady? Why does he like these wicked things?' And then as regarded Mrs. Woodward, she did but make a resolve that not even for her love would she add to the unhappiness of that loving, tenderest mother. There was no bombast in Katie, either expressed or unexpressed.

After much consideration on the matter, Mrs. Woodward determined that she should ask Charley down to the Cottage. In the first place, she felt bitterly her apparent ingratitude to him. When last they had been together, the day after Katie's escape at the bridge, when his tale had just been read, she had told him, with the warmth of somewhat more than friendly affection, that henceforth they must be more than common friends. She had promised him her love, she had almost promised him the affection and care of a mother; and now how was she keeping her promise? He had fallen into misfortune, and she had immediately deserted him. Over and over again she said to herself that her first duty was to her own child; but even with this reflection, she could hardly reconcile herself to her neglect of him.

And then, moreover, she felt that it was impossible that all their friendship, all their mutual regard, should die away suddenly without any explanation. An attempt to bring about this would not cure Katie's love. If this were done, would not Katie always think of Charley's wrong?

And, lastly, it was quite clear that Katie had put a check on her own heart. A meeting now might be the reverse of dangerous. It would be well that Katie should use herself to be with him now again; well, at any rate, that she should see him once before their proposed journey to Torquay; for, alas, the journey to Torquay was now insisted on by the London physician—insisted on, although he opined with a nod, somewhat less authoritative than his former nod, that the young lady was touched by no organic disease.

'And then,' said Mrs. Woodward to herself, 'his heart is good, and I will speak openly to him.' And so Charley was again invited to the cottage. After some demurring between him and Norman, he accepted the invitation.

Mrs. Val's dance had taken place in June, and it was now late in October. Four months had intervened, and during that period Charley had seen none of the Woodwards. He had over and over again tried to convince himself that this was his own fault, and that he had no right to accuse Mrs. Woodward of ingratitude. But he was hardly successful. He did feel, in spite of himself, that he had been dropped because of the disgrace attaching to his arrest; that Mrs. Woodward had put him aside as being too bad to associate with her and her daughters; and that it was intended that henceforth they should be strangers.

He still had Katie's purse, and he made a sort of resolve that as long as he kept that in his possession, as long as he had that near his heart, he would not go near Norah Geraghty. This resolution he had kept; but though he did not go to the 'Cat and Whistle,' he frequented other

places which were as discreditable, or more so. He paid
many very fruitless visits to Mr. M'Ruen; contrived to
run up a score with the proprietor of the dancing saloon
in Holborn; and was as negligent as ever in the matter
of the lock entries.

'It is no use now,' he would say to himself, when some
aspirations for higher things came across his heart; 'it is
too late now to go back. Those who once cared for me
have thrown me over.' And then he would again think of
Waterloo Bridge, and the Monument, and of what might
be done for threepence or fourpence in a pistol gallery.

And then at last came the invitation to Hampton. He
was once more to talk to Mrs. Woodward, and associate
with Linda—to see Katie once more. When he had last
left the house he had almost been as much at home as any
one of the family; and now he was to return to it as
a perfect stranger. As he travelled down with Norman by
the railway, he could not help feeling that the journey
was passing over too quickly. He was like a prisoner
going to his doom. As he crossed the bridge, and remembered how Katie had looked when she lay struggling in
the water, how he had been fêted and caressed after
pulling her out, he made a bitter contrast between his
present position and that which he then enjoyed. Were
it not for very shame, he would have found it in his heart
to return to London.

And then in a moment they were at the Cottage door.
The road had never been so short. Norman, who had
not fathomed Charley's feelings, was happy and light-
hearted—more so than was usual with him, for he was
unaffectedly glad to witness Charley's return to Hampton.
He rang sharply at the door, and when it was opened,
walked with happy confidence into the drawing-room.
Charley was bound to follow him, and there he found
himself again in presence of Mrs. Woodward and her
daughters. Katie would fain have absented herself, but
Mrs. Woodward knew that the first meeting could take
place in no more favourable manner.

Mrs. Woodward bade him welcome with a collected
voice, and assured, if not easy manner. She shook hands
with him cordially, and said a few words as to her pleasure

of seeing him again. Then he next took Linda's hand, and she too made a little speech, more awkwardly than her mother, saying something mal à propos about the very long time he had been away; and then she laughed with a little titter, trying to recover herself. And at last he came to Katie. There was no getting over it. She also stretched out her now thin hand, and Charley, as he touched it, perceived how altered she was. Katie looked up into his face, and tried to speak, but she could not articulate a word. She looked into his face, and then at Mrs. Woodward, as though imploring her mother's aid to tell her how to act or what to say; and then finding her power of utterance impeded by rising sobs, she dropped back again on her seat, and hid her face upon the arm of the sofa.

'Our Katie is not so well as when you last saw her— is she, Charley?' said Mrs. Woodward. 'She is very weak just now; but thank God she has, we believe, no dangerous symptoms about her. You have heard, perhaps, that we are going to Torquay for the winter?'

And so they went on talking. The ice was broken and the worst was over. They did not talk, it is true, as in former days; there was no confidence between them now, and each of them felt that there was none; but they nevertheless fell into a way of unembarrassed conversation, and were all tolerably at their ease.

And then they went to dinner, and Charley was called on to discuss Admiralty matters with Uncle Bat; and then he and Norman sat after dinner a little longer than usual; and then they had a short walk, during which Katie remained at home; but short as it was, it was quite long enough, for it was very dull; and then there was tea; and then more constrained conversation, in which Katie took no part whatever; and then Mrs. Woodward and the girls took their candles, and Charley went over to the inn on the other side of the road. Oh! how different was this from the former evenings at Surbiton Cottage.

Charley had made no plan for any special interview with Katie; had, indeed, not specially thought about it at all; but he could not but feel an intense desire to say one word to her in private, and learn whether all her solicitude for him was over. 'Dear Charley, you will be steady; won't you?' Those had been her last words to him. Nothing could have been sweeter; although they brought before his mind the remembrance of his own unworthy career, they had been inexpressibly sweet, as testifying the interest she felt in him. And was that all over now? Had it all been talked away by Mrs. Woodward's cautious wisdom, because he had lain for one night in a sponging-house?

But the next day came, and as it passed, it appeared to him that no opportunity of speaking one word to her was to be allowed to him.

She did not, however, shun him. She was not up at breakfast, but she sat next to him at lunch, and answered him when he spoke to her.

In the evening they again went out to walk, and then Charley found that Linda and Norman went one way, and that he was alone with Mrs. Woodward. It was manifest to him that this arrangement had been made on purpose, and he felt that he was to undergo some private conversation, the nature of which he dreaded. He dreaded it very much; when he heard it, it made him very wretched; but it was not the less full of womanly affection and regard for him.

'I cannot let you go from us, Charley,' began Mrs. Woodward, 'without telling you how deep a sorrow it has been to me to be so long without seeing you. I know you have thought me very ungrateful.'

'Ungrateful, Mrs. Woodward! O no! I have done nothing to make gratitude necessary.'

'Yes, Charley, you have—you have done much, too much. You have saved my child's life.'

'O no, I did not,' said he; 'besides, I hate gratitude. I don't want any one to be grateful to me. Gratitude is almost as offensive as pity. Of course I pulled Katie out of the water when she fell in; and I would have done as much for your favourite cat.' He said this with something of bitterness in his tone; it was not much, for though he felt bitterly he did not intend to show it; but Mrs. Woodward's ear did not fail to catch it.

'Don't be angry with us, Charley; don't make us more unhappy than we already are.'

'Unhappy!' said he, as though he thought that all the unhappiness in the world was at the present moment reserved for his own shoulders.

'Yes, we are not so happy now as we were when you were last with us. Poor Katie is very ill.'

'But you don't think there is any danger, Mrs. Woodward?'

There are many tones in which such a question may be asked—and is asked from day to day—all differing widely from each other, and giving evidence of various shades of feeling in the speaker. Charley involuntarily put his whole heart into it. Mrs. Woodward could not but love him for feeling for her child, though she would have given so much that the two might have been indifferent to each other.

'I do not know,' she said. 'We hope not. But I should not be sent with her to Torquay if she were not very ill. She is very ill, and it is absolutely essential that nothing should be allowed to excite her painfully. I tell you this, Charley, to excuse our apparent unkindness in not having you here sooner.'

Charley walked by her in silence. Why should his coming excite her more than Norman's? What could there be painful to her in seeing him? Did the fact of his having been arrested attach to his visit any peculiar probability of excitement?

'Do not suppose that we have not thought of you,' continued Mrs. Woodward. 'We have all done so daily. Nay, I have done so myself all but hourly. Ah, Charley, you will never know how truly I love you.'

Charley's heart was as soft as it was inflammable. He was utterly unable to resist such tenderness as Mrs. Woodward showed to him. He had made a little resolution to be stiff and stern, to ask for no favour and to receive none, not to palliate his own conduct, or to allow Mrs. Woodward to condemn it. He had felt that as the Woodwards had given him up, they had no longer any right to criticize him. To them at least, one and all, to Mrs. Woodward and her daughters, his conduct had been *sans reproche.* They had no cause to upbraid him on their own account; and they had now abandoned the right to do so on his own. With such assumed sternness he began his walk; but now it had all melted before the warmth of one tender word from a woman's mouth.

'I know I am not worth thinking about,' said he.

'Do not say so; pray do not say so. Do not think that we say so to ourselves. I grieve for your faults, Charley; I know they are grievous and wicked; but I know how much there is of good in you. I know how clever you are, how excellent your heart is, how sweet your disposition. I trust, I trust in God, you may reform, and be the pride of your friends. I trust that I yet may be proud of knowing you——'

'No one will ever be proud of me,' said Charley.

'We shall all be proud of you, if you will resolve to turn away from childish things now that you are no longer a child—your faults are faults which as yet may be so easily relinquished. But, oh, Charley——' and then Mrs. Woodward paused and looked wistfully into his face. She had now come to the point at which she had to make her prayer to him. She had resolved to tell him the cause of her fears, and to trust to his honour to free her from them. Now was the moment for her to speak out; but now that the moment was come, the words were wanting.

She looked wistfully into his face, but he did not even guess what was her meaning. He knew the secret of his own love; but he did not know that Katie also had her secret. He had never dreamt that his faults, among all their ill effects, had paled her cheek, made wan her arm, silenced her voice, and dimmed her eye. When he had heard Katie cough, he had in nowise connected the hated sound with his own arrest. He had thought only of his own love.

'Oh! Charley—I know I can trust you,' said Mrs. Woodward. 'I know you are gentle and good. You will be gentle and good to us, will you not? you will not make us all wretched?'

Charley declared that he would not willingly do anything to cause pain to any of them.

'No—I am sure you will not. And therefore, Charley, you must not see Katie any more.'

At this time they had turned off the road into a shady lane, in which the leaves of autumn were beginning to fall. A path led over a stile away from the lane into the fields, and Mrs. Woodward had turned towards it, as though intending to continue their walk in that direction. But when she had reached the stile, she had sat down upon the steps of it, and Charley had been listening to her, standing by, leaning on the top rail.

'And therefore, Charley, you must not see Katie any more.' So much she said, and then she looked into his face with imploring eyes.

It was impossible that he should answer her at once. He had to realize so much that had hitherto not been expressed between them, before he could fully understand what she meant; and then he was called on to give up so much that he now learnt for the first time was within his reach! Before he could answer her he had to assure himself that Katie loved him; he had to understand that her love for one so abandoned was regarded as fatal; and he had to reply to a mother's prayer that he would remove himself from the reach of a passion which to him was worth all the world beside.

He turned his face away from her, but still stood leaning on the stile, with his arms folded on it. She watched him for a while in silence, and at last she saw big tears drop from his face on to the dust of the path on the farther side. There came rolling down, large globules of sorrow. Nothing is so painful to a woman as a man in tears, and Mrs. Woodward's heart was wrung to its very core. Why was he not like Alaric or Norman, so that she might make him welcome to her daughter's heart?

She leant towards him and put her hand caressingly on his arm. 'It shall be so, shall it not, Charley?'

'Oh, of course, if you say so.'

'I have your word, then? If I have your word, that will be a perfect bond. I have your word, have I not, Charley?'

'What!—never see her in my life?' said he, turning almost fiercely on Mrs. Woodward.

'That, you know, is more than you can promise,' said she, very gently. 'It is not to the letter of the promise that I would bind you, but to its spirit. You understand well what I mean; you know what I wish, and why I wish it. Say that you will obey my wish, and I will leave the mode of doing it to your own honour. Have I your promise?'

He shook her hand off his arm almost roughly, though unintentionally, and turning sharply round leant with his back against the stile. The traces of tears were still on his cheeks, but he was no longer crying; there was, however, a look on his face of heart-rending sorrow which Mrs. Woodward could hardly endure.

'I do understand you,' said he, 'and since you demand it, I will promise;' and then they walked home side by side, without interchanging a single word.

When they reached the house, Mrs. Woodward went to her room, and Charley found himself alone with Katie.

'I hope you find yourself better this evening,' said he.

'Oh, I am quite well,' she answered, with her sweetest, kindest voice; 'I am quite well, only sometimes I am a little weak.'

He walked up to the window as though to pass on to the lawn; but the season was too far advanced for that, and the window was locked. He retraced his steps, therefore, and passing out of the drawing-room into the hall, stood at the open front door till he heard Mrs. Woodward come down. Then he followed her into the room.

'Good-bye,' he said to her suddenly; 'I shall start by the early train to-morrow, and shall not see you.' She pressed his hand, but he in nowise returned the pressure. 'Good-bye, Linda; good-bye, Katie; good night, Captain Cuttwater.' And so he went his way, as Adam did when he was driven out of Paradise.

Early on the following morning, the cook, while engaged in her most matutinal duties, was disturbed by a ring at the front door. She, and she only of the household, was up, and as she had not completed her toilet with much minuteness, she was rather embarrassed when, on opening the door, she saw Mr. Charles Tudor.

'I beg your pardon, cook, for troubling you so early;

but I have left something in the drawing-room. I can find it myself;' and, so saying, he hurried into the room, so as to prevent the servant from following him.

Katie had a well-worn, well-known little workbox, which, in years now long past, had been given to her either by Alaric or Harry. Doubtless she had now workboxes grander both in appearance and size; but, nevertheless, whether from habit or from choice, her custom was, in her daily needlework, to use this old friend. Often and often had Charley played with it many wicked pranks. Once, while Katie had as yet no pretension to be grown up, he had put a snail into it, and had incurred her severe displeasure. He had stuffed it full of acorns, and been rewarded by being pelted with them round the lawn; and had filled it with nuts, for which he had not found it so difficult to obtain pardon. He knew every hole and corner in it! he was intimate with all her little feminine nicknacks—her silver thimble, her scissors, her bit of wax, and the yard-measure, which twisted itself in and out of an ivory cottage—he knew them all, as well as though they were his own; and he knew also where the workbox stood.

He closed the door behind him, and then, with his quickest motion, raised the lid and put within the box, just under the bit of work on which she was employed, a light small paper parcel. It contained the purse which she had worked for him, and had given to him with such sweet affection at the Chiswick flower-show.

CHAPTER XXXI

HOW APOLLO SAVED THE NAVVY

About the middle of November, the Woodwards went to Torquay, and remained there till the following May. Norman went with them to see them properly settled in their new lodgings, and visited them at Christmas, and once again during their stay there. He then went down to fetch them home, and when they all returned, informed Charley, with whom he was still living, that he was engaged to Linda. It was arranged, he said, that they were to be married in August.

On the whole, the journey to Torquay was considered to have been successful. Katie's health had been the only object in going there, and the main consideration while they remained. She returned, if not well, at any rate not worse. She had got through the winter, and her lungs were still pronounced to be free from those dreadful signs of decay, the name of which has broken so many mothers' hearts, and sent dismay into the breasts of so many fathers. During her sojourn at Torquay she had grown much, and, as is often the case with those who grow quickly, she had become weak and thin. People at Torquay are always weak and thin, and Mrs. Woodward had not, therefore, been greatly frightened at this. Her spirits, though by no means such as they had been in former days, had improved, she had occupied herself more than she had done during the last two months at Hampton, and had, at least so Mrs. Woodward fondly flattered herself, ceased to be always thinking of Charley Tudor. It was quite clear that she had firmly made up her mind to some certain line of conduct with reference to him; she never mentioned his name, nor was it mentioned in her hearing by either her mother or sister during their stay at Torquay. When Norman came down, she always found some opportunity of inquiring from him as to Charley's health and welfare; but she did this in a

manner which showed that she had succeeded in placing
her feelings wonderfully under control.

On that Monday morning, on which Charley had returned to town after his early visit to her workbox, she
had not failed to find the purse. Linda was with her
when she did so, but she had contrived so to conceal her
emotion, that nothing was seen and nothing suspected.
She felt at once that it was intended that all intercourse
should be broken off between them. She knew instinctively that this was the effect of some precaution on
her mother's part, and with a sad bosom and a broken
heart, she acquiesced in it. She said nothing, even to
herself, of the truth and constancy of her love; she made
no mental resolution against any other passion; she did
not even think whether or not she might ever be tempted
to love another; but she felt a dumb aching numbness
about her heart; and, looking round about her, she
seemed to feel that all was dark and dismal.

And so they sojourned through the winter at Torquay.
The effort which Katie made was undoubtedly salutary
to her. She took again to her work and her lessons—
studies we should probably now call them—and before
she left Torquay, she had again learned how to smile;
but not to laugh with that gay ringing silver laughter,
ringing, but yet not loud, which to Charley's ear had been
as sweet as heavenly music. During this time Uncle
Bat remained at Hampton, keeping bachelor's house by
himself.

And then while they were at Torquay, Linda and
Norman became engaged to each other. Their loves were
honest, true, and happy; but not of a nature to give much
scope to a novelist of a romantic turn. Linda knew she
was not Norman's first love, and requited Norman, of
course, by telling him something, not much, of Alaric's
falseness to her. Norman made but one ungenerous
stipulation. It was this: that in marrying him Linda
must give up all acquaintance with her brother-in-law.
He would never, he said, be the means of separating two
sisters; she and Gertrude might have such intercourse
together as their circumstances might render possible;
but it was quite out of the question that either he, Harry

Norman, or his wife, should ever again associate with Alaric Tudor.

In such matters Linda had always been guided by others; so she sighed and promised, and the engagement was duly ratified by all the parties concerned.

We must now return to Charley. When he got back to town, he felt that he had lost his amulet; his charm had gone from him, and he had nothing now left whereby to save himself from ruin and destruction. He was utterly flung over by the Woodwards; that now was to him an undoubted fact. When Mrs. Woodward told him that he was never again to see Katie, that was, of course, tantamount to turning him out of the Cottage. It might be all very well to talk to him of affection and friendship; but it was manifest that no further signs of either were to be shown to him. He had proved himself to be unworthy, and was no more to be considered as one of the circle which made the drawing-room at Surbiton Cottage its centre. He could not quite explain all this to Norman, as he could not tell him what had passed between him and Mrs. Woodward; but he said enough to make his friend know that he intended to go to Hampton no more.

It would be wrong, perhaps, to describe Charley as being angry with Mrs. Woodward. He knew that she was only doing her duty by her child; he knew that she was actuated by the purest and best of motives; he was not able to say a word against her even to himself; but, nevertheless, he desired to be revenged on her—not by injuring her, not by injuring Katie—but by injuring himself. He would make Mrs. Woodward feel what she had done, by rushing, himself, on his own ruin. He would return to the 'Cat and Whistle'—he would keep his promise and marry Norah Geraghty—he would go utterly to destruction, and then Mrs. Woodward would know and feel what she had done in banishing him from her daughter's presence!

Having arrived at this magnanimous resolution after a fortnight's doubt and misery, he proceeded to put his purpose into execution. It was now some considerable time since he had been at the 'Cat and Whistle;' he had had no further visit from Mrs. Davis, but he had

received one or two notes both from her and Norah, to
which, as long as he had Katie's purse, he was resolute
in not replying; messages also had reached him from
the landlady through Dick Scatterall, in the last of which
he was reminded that there was a trifle due at the bar,
and another trifle for money lent.

One night, having lashed himself up to a fit state of
wretched desperation, he found himself at the well-known
corner of the street leading out of the Strand. On his
journey thither he had been trying to realize to himself
what it would be to be the husband of Norah Geraghty;
what would be the joy of returning to a small house in
some dingy suburb and finding her to receive him. Could
he really love her when she would be bone of his bone
and flesh of his flesh, the wife of his bosom and the mother
of his children? In such a case would he ever be able to
forget that he had known Katie Woodward? Would
those words of hers ever ring in his ears, then as now—
'You will be steady, dear Charley; won't you?'

There are those who boast that a gentleman must
always be a gentleman; that a man, let him marry whom
he will, raises or degrades his wife to the level of his own
condition, and that King Cophetua could share his throne
with a beggar-woman without sullying its splendour or
diminishing its glory. How a king may fare in such a
condition, the author, knowing little of kings, will not
pretend to say; nor yet will he offer an opinion whether
a lowly match be fatally injurious to a marquess, duke, or
earl; but this he will be bold to affirm, that a man from
the ordinary ranks of the upper classes, who has had the
nurture of a gentleman, prepares for himself a hell on
earth in taking a wife from any rank much below his
own—a hell on earth, and, alas! too often another hell
elsewhere also. He must either leave her or loathe her.
She may be endowed with all those moral virtues which
should adorn all women, and which, thank God, are
common to women in this country; but he will have to
endure habits, manners, and ideas, which the close
contiguity of married life will force upon his disgusted
palate, and which must banish all love. Man by instinct
desires in his wife something softer, sweeter, more refined

than himself; and though in failing to obtain this, the fault may be all his own, he will not on that account the more easily reconcile himself to the want.

Charley knew that he was preparing such misery for himself. As he went along, determined to commit a moral suicide by allying himself to the barmaid, he constrained himself to look with his mind's eye 'upon this picture and on that.'

He had felt of what nature was the sort of love with which Katie Woodward had inspired his heart; and he felt also what was that other sort of love to which the charms of Norah Geraghty had given birth.

Norah was a fine girl, smart enough in her outward apparel, but apt occasionally to disclose uncomfortable secrets, if from any accident more than her outward apparel might momentarily become visible. When dressed up for a Sunday excursion she had her attractions, and even on ordinary evenings, a young man such as Charley, after imbibing two or three glasses of spirits and water, and smoking two or three cigars, might find her to be what some of her friends would have called 'very good company.' As to her mind, had Charley been asked about it, he would probably have said that he was ignorant whether she had any; but this he did know, that she was sharp and quick, alert in counting change, and gifted with a peculiar power of detecting bad coin by the touch. Such was Norah Geraghty, whom Charley was to marry.

And then that other portrait was limned with equal accuracy before his eyes. Katie, with all her juvenile spirit, was delightfully feminine; every motion of hers was easy, and every form into which she could twist her young limbs was graceful. She had all the nice ideas and ways which a girl acquires when she grows from childhood to woman's stature, under the eye of a mother who is a lady. Katie could be untidy on occasions; but her very untidiness was inviting. All her belongings were nice; she had no hidden secrets, the chance revealing of which would disgrace her. She might come in from her island palaces in a guise which would call down some would-be-censorious exclamation from her mother ; but all others but her mother would declare that Katie in such moments was more lovely than ever. And Katie's beauty pleased more than the eye— it came home to the mind and heart of those who saw her. It spoke at once to the intelligence, and required, for its full appreciation, an exercise of the mental faculties, as well as animal senses. If the owner of that outward form were bad or vile, one would be inclined to say that Nature must have lied when she endowed her with so fair an index. Such was Katie Woodward, whom Charley was not to marry.

As he turned down Norfolk Street, he thought of all this, as the gambler, sitting with his razor before him with which he intends to cut his throat, may be supposed to think of the stakes which he has failed to win, and the fortune he has failed to make. Norah Geraghty was Charley's razor, and he plunged boldly into the 'Cat and Whistle,' determined to draw it at once across his weasand, and sever himself for ever from all that is valuable in the world.

It was now about eleven o'clock, at which hour the 'Cat and Whistle' generally does its most stirring trade. This Charley knew ; but he also knew that the little back parlour, even if there should be an inmate in it at the time of his going in, would soon be made private for his purposes.

When he went in, Mrs. Davis was standing behind the counter, dressed in a cap of wonderful grandeur, and a red tabinet gown, which rustled among the pots and jars, sticking out from her to a tremendous width, inflated by its own magnificence and a substratum of crinoline. Charley had never before seen her arrayed in such royal robes. Her accustomed maid was waiting as usual on the guests, and another girl also was assisting ; but Norah did not appear to Charley's first impatient glance.

He at once saw that something wonderful was going on. The front parlour was quite full, and the ministering angel was going in and out quickly, with more generous supplies of the gifts of Bacchus than were usual at the 'Cat and Whistle.' Gin and water was the ordinary tipple in the front parlour ; and any one of its denizens inclined to cut a dash above his neighbours generally did so with a bottom of brandy. But now Mrs. Davis was mixing port-wine negus as fast as her hands could make it.

And then there were standing round the counter four or five customers, faces well known to Charley, all of whom seemed to be dressed with a splendour second only to that of the landlady. One man had on an almost new brown frock coat with a black velvet collar, and white trousers. Two had blue swallow-tailed coats with brass buttons ; and a fourth, a dashing young lawyer's clerk from Clement's Inn, was absolutely stirring a mixture, which he called a mint julep, with a yellow kid glove dangling out of his hand.

They all stood back when Charley entered ; they had been accustomed to make way for him in former days, and though he had latterly ceased to rule at the ' Cat and Whistle ' as he once did, they were too generous to trample on fallen greatness. He gave his hand to Mrs. Davis across the counter, and asked her in the most unconcerned voice which he could assume what was in the wind. She tittered and laughed, told him he had come too late for the fun, and then retreated into the little back parlour, whither he followed her. She was at any rate in a good humour, and seemed quite inclined to forgive his rather uncivil treatment of her notes and messages.

In the back parlour Charley found more people drinking, and among them three ladies of Mrs. Davis's acquaintance. They were all very fine in their apparel, and very comfortable as to their immediate employment, for each had before her a glass of hot tipple. One of them, a florid-faced dame about fifty, Charley had seen before, and knew to be the wife of a pork butcher and sausage maker in the neighbourhood. Directly he entered the room, Mrs. Davis formally introduced him to them all. ' A very particular friend of mine, Mrs. Allchops ; and of Norah's too, I can assure you,' said Mrs. Davis.

' Ah, Mr. Tudor, and how be you ? A sight of you is good for sore eyes,' said she of the sausages, rising with some difficulty from her chair, and grasping Charley's

hand with all the pleasant cordiality of old friendship.

'The gen'leman seems to be a little too late for the fair,'
said a severe lodging-house keeper from Cecil Street.

> 'Them as wills not, when they may,
> When they wills they shall have nay,'

said a sarcastic rival barmaid from a neighbouring public,
to whom all Norah's wrongs and all Mr. Tudor's false
promises were fully known.

Charley was not the fellow to allow himself to be put
down, even by feminine raillery; so he plucked up his
spirit, sad as he was at heart, and replied to them all
en masse.

'Well, ladies, what's in the wind now? You seem to
be very cosy here, all of you; suppose you allow me to
join you.'

'With a 'eart and a 'alf,' said Mrs. Allchops, squeezing
her corpulence up to the end of the horsehair sofa, so as
to make room for him between herself and the poetic
barmaid. 'I'd sooner have a gentleman next to me nor
a lady hany day of the week; so come and sit down, my
birdie.'

But Charley, as he was about to accept the invitation
of his friend Mrs. Allchops, caught Mrs. Davis's eye, and
followed her out of the room into the passage. 'Step up
to the landing, Mr. Tudor,' said she; and Charley stepped
up. 'Come in here, Mr. Tudor—you won't mind my
bedroom for once.' And Charley followed her in, not
minding her bedroom.

'Of course you know what has happened, Mr. Tudor?'
said she.

'Devil a bit,' said Charley.

'Laws, now—don't you indeed? Well, that is odd.'

'How the deuce should I know? Where's Norah?'

'Why—she's at Gravesend.'

'At Gravesend—you don't mean to say she's——'

'I just do then; she's just gone and got herself spliced
to Peppermint this morning. They had the banns said
these last three Sundays; and this morning they was at

St. Martin's at eight o'clock, and has been here junketing ever since, and now they're away to Gravesend.'

'Gravesend!' said Charley, struck by the suddenness of his rescue, as the gambler would have been had some stranger seized the razor at the moment when it was lifted to his throat.

'Yes, Gravesend,' said Mrs. Davis; 'and they'll come up home to his own house by the first boat to-morrow.'

'So Norah's married!' said Charley, with a slight access of sentimental softness in his voice.

'She's been and done it now, Mr. Tudor, and no mistake; and it's better so, ain't it? Why, Lord love you, she'd never have done for you, you know; and she's the very article for such a man as Peppermint.'

There was something good-natured in this, and so Charley felt it. As long as Mrs. Davis could do anything to assist her cousin's views, by endeavouring to seduce or persuade her favourite lover into a marriage, she left no stone unturned, working on her cousin's behalf. But now, now that all those hopes were over, now that Norah had consented to sacrifice love to prudence, why should Mrs. Davis quarrel with an old friend any longer?— why should not things be made pleasant to him as to the others?

'And now, Mr. Tudor, come down, and drink a glass to their healths, and wish 'em both well, and don't mind what them women says to you. You're well out of a mess; and now it's all over, I'm glad it is as it is.'

Charley went down and took his glass and drank 'prosperity to the bride and bridegroom.' The sarcastic rival barmaid said little snappish things to him, offered him a bit of green ribbon, and told him that if he 'minded hisself,' somebody might, perhaps, take him yet. But Charley was proof against this.

He sat there about half an hour, and then went his way, shaking hands with all the ladies and bowing to the gentlemen. On the following day, as soon as he left his office, he called at the 'Cat and Whistle,' and paid his little bill there, and said his last farewell to Mrs. Davis. He never visited the house again. Now that Norah was gone the attractions were not powerful. Reader, you and I will at the same time say our farewells to Mrs. Davis, to Mr. Peppermint also, and to his bride. If thou art an elegant reader, unaccustomed to the contamination of pipes and glasses, I owe thee an apology in that thou hast been caused to linger a while among things so unsavoury. But if thou art one who of thine own will hast taken thine ease in thine inn, hast enjoyed the freedom of a sanded parlour, hast known ' that ginger is hot in the mouth,' and made thyself light-hearted with a yard of clay, then thou wilt confess there are worse establishments than the ' Cat and Whistle,' less generous landladies than Mrs. Davis.

When all this happened the Woodwards had not been long at Torquay. Mr. Peppermint was made a happy man before Christmas; and therefore Charley was left to drift before the wind without the ballast of any lady's love to keep him in sailing trim. Poor fellow ! he had had wealth on one side, beauty and love on another, and on the third all those useful qualities which Miss Geraghty has been described as possessing. He had been thus surrounded by feminine attractions, and had lost them all. Two of those, from whom he had to choose, had married others, and he was banished from the presence of the third. Under such circumstances what could he do but drift about the gulfs and straits of the London ocean without compass or rudder, and bruise his timbers against all the sunken rocks that might come in his way ?

And then Norman told him of his coming marriage, and Charley was more sad than ever. And thus matters went on with him till the period at which our story will be resumed at the return of the Woodwards to Hampton.

In the meantime another winter and another spring had passed over Alaric's head, and now the full tide of the London season found him still rising, and receiving every day more of the world's homage. Sir Gregory Hardlines had had every reason to praise his own judgement in selecting Mr. Tudor for the vacant seat among the Magi.

From that moment all had gone smooth with Sir Gregory ; there was no one to interfere with his hobby, or run counter to his opinion. Alaric was all that was conciliatory and amiable in a colleague. He was not submissive and cringing ; and had he been so, Sir Gregory, to do him justice, would have been disgusted ; but neither was he self-opinionated nor obstinate like Mr. Jobbles. He insisted on introducing no crotchets of his own, and allowed Sir Gregory all the credit of the Commission.

This all went on delightfully for a while ; but on one morning, early in May, Alaric somewhat disturbed the equanimity of his chief by communicating to him his intention of becoming a candidate for the representation of the borough of Strathbogy, at the next general election, which was to take place very shortly after the close of the session. Sir Gregory was dumbfounded, and expressed himself as incapable of believing that Tudor really meant to throw up £1,200 a year on the mere speculation of its being possible that he should get into Parliament. Men in general, as Sir Gregory endeavoured to explain with much eloquence, go into Parliament for the sake of getting places of £1,200 a year. For what earthly reason should Alaric again be going to the bottom of the ladder, seeing that he had already attained a rung of such very respectable altitude ? Alaric said to himself, ' Excelsior !' To Sir Gregory he suggested that it might be possible that he should get into Parliament without giving up his seat at the Board. Earth and heaven, it might be hoped, would not come together, even though so great a violence as this should be done to the time-honoured practices of the Government. Sir Gregory suggested that it was contrary to the constitution. Alaric replied that the constitution had been put upon to as great an extent before this, and had survived. Sir Gregory regarded it as all but impossible, and declared it to be quite unusual. Alaric rejoined that something of the same kind had been done at the Poor Law Board. To this Sir Gregory replied, gently pluming his feathers with conscious greatness, that at the Poor Law Board the chief of the Commission was the Parliamentary officer. Alaric declared that he was perfectly willing to give way if Sir Gregory would go into the House himself. To this Sir Gregory demurred ; not feeling himself called on to change the sphere of his utility. And so the matter was debated between them, till at last Sir Gregory promised to consult his friend the Chancellor of the Exchequer. The ice was thus broken, and Alaric was quite contented with the part which he had taken in the conversation.

With his own official prospects, in spite of the hazardous step which he now meditated, he was quite contented. He had an idea that in the public service of the Government, as well as in all other services, men who were known to be worth their wages would find employment. He was worth his wages. Men who could serve their country well, who could adapt themselves to work, who were practical, easy in harness, able to drive and patient to be driven, were not, unfortunately, as plentiful as blackberries. He began to perceive that a really useful man could not be found miscellaneously under every hat in Pall Mall. He knew his own value, and did not fear but that he should find a price for it in some of the world's markets. He would not, therefore, allow himself to be deterred from further progress by any fear that in doing so he risked the security of his daily bread; no, not though the risk extended to his wife; she had taken him for better or worse; if the better came she should share it; if the worse, why let her share that also, with such consolation as his affection might be able to offer.

There was something noble in this courage, in this lack of prudence. It may be a question whether men, in marrying, do not become too prudent. A single man may risk anything, says the world; but a man with a wife should be sure of his means. Why so? A man and a woman are but two units. A man and a woman with ten children are but twelve units. It is sad to see a man starving—sad to see a woman starving—very sad to see children starving. But how often does it come to pass that the man who will work is seen begging his bread? we may almost say never—unless, indeed, he be a clergyman. Let the idle man be sure of his wife's bread before he marries her; but the working man, one would say, may generally trust to God's goodness without fear.

With his official career Alaric was, as we have said, well contented; in his stock-jobbing line of business

he also had had moments of great exaltation, and some
moments of considerable depression. The West Corks
had vacillated. Both he and Undy had sold and bought
and sold again; and on the whole their stake in that
stupendous national line of accommodation was not so
all-absorbing as it had once been. But if money had been
withdrawn from this, it had been invested elsewhere,
and the great sum borrowed from Madame Jaquêtanàpe's
fortune had been in no part replaced—one full moiety
of it had been taken—may one not say stolen?—
to enable Alaric and Undy to continue their speculations.

The undertaking to which they were now both wedded
was the Limehouse and Rotherhithe Bridge. Of this
Undy was chairman, and Alaric was a director, and at
the present moment they looked for ample fortune, or
what would nearly be ample ruin, to the decision of a
committee of the House of Commons which was about to
sit with the view of making inquiry as to the necessity
of the bridge in question.

Mr. Nogo, the member for Mile End, was the parent of
this committee. He asserted that the matter was one
of such vital importance not only to the whole metropolis,
but to the country at large, that the Government were
bound in the first place to give a large subsidy towards
building the bridge, and afterwards to pay a heavy annual
sum towards the amount which it would be necessary to
raise by tolls. Mr. Whip Vigil, on the other hand, declared on the part of Government that the bridge was
wholly unnecessary; that if it were built it ought to be
pulled down again; and that not a stiver could be given
out of the public purse with such an object.

On this they joined issue. Mr. Nogo prayed for a
committee, and Mr. Vigil, having duly consulted his
higher brethren in the Government, conceded this point.
It may easily be conceived how high were now the hopes
both of Undy Scott and Alaric Tudor. It was not at all
necessary for them that the bridge should ever be built;
that, probably, was out of the question; that, very
likely, neither of them regarded as a possibility. But if
a committee of the House of Commons could be got to

say that it ought to be built, they might safely calculate on selling out at a large profit.

But who were to·sit on the committee ? That was now the all-momentous question.

CHAPTER XXXII

THE PARLIAMENTARY COMMITTEE

THERE is a sport prevalent among the downs in Hampshire to which, though not of a high degree, much interest is attached. Men and boys, with social glee and happy boyish shouts, congregate together on a hill-side, at the mouth of a narrow hole, and proceed, with the aid of a well-trained bull-dog, to draw a badger. If the badger be at all commendable in his class this is by no means an easy thing to do. He is a sturdy animal, and well fortified with sharp and practised teeth ; his hide is of the toughest; his paws of the strongest, and his dead power of resistance so great as to give him more than an equal chance with the bull-dog. The delighted sportsmen stand round listening to the growls and snarls, the tearings, gnawings, and bloody struggles of the combatants within.—'Well done, badger !—Well done, bull-dog !—Draw him, bull-dog !—Bite him, badger ! ' Each has his friends, and the interest of the moment is intense. The badger, it is true, has done no harm. He has been doing as it was appointed for him to do, poor badger, in that hole of his. But then, why were badgers created but to be drawn ? Why, indeed, but to be drawn, or not to be drawn, as the case may be ? See ! the bull-dog returns minus an ear, with an eye hanging loose, his nether lip torn off, and one paw bitten through and through. Limping, dejected, beaten, glaring fearfully from his one remaining eye. the dog comes out ; and the badger within rolls himself up with affected ease, hiding his bloody wounds from the public eye.

So it is that the sport is played in Hampshire ; and so also at Westminster—with a difference, however. In

Hampshire the two brutes retain ever their appointed natures. The badger is always a badger, and the bull-dog never other than a bull-dog. At Westminster there is a juster reciprocity of position. The badger when drawn has to take his place outside the hole, and fight again for the home of his love ; while the victorious bull-dog assumes a state of badgerdom, dons the skin of his enemy, and, in his turn, submits to be baited.

The pursuit is certainly full of interest, but it is some-what deficient in dignity.

The parliamentary committee, which was to sit with reference to the Limehouse and Rotherhithe Bridge, had been one of the effects of a baiting-match such as that above described. In this contest the enemies of the proud occupier of the den on the mountain-side had not been contented to attempt to expel him with a single bull-dog. A whole pack had been let loose at his devoted throat. Bull-dogs had been at him, and terriers, mastiffs, blood-hounds, lurchers, and curs ; but so accustomed was he to the contest, so knowing in his fence, so ready with all the weapons given to him by nature, that, in spite of the numbers and venom of his enemies, he had con-trived to hold his own. Some leading hounds had fallen to rise no more ; others had retreated, yelping to their kennels, to lie quiet for a while, till time might give them courage for a new attack. The country round was filled with the noise of their plaints, and the yowling and howling of canine defeat. The grey old badger meanwhile sat proud in his hole, with all his badger kin around him, and laughed his well-known badger laugh at his disconsolate foes. Such a brock had not for years been seen in the country-side ; so cool, .so resolute, so knowing in his badger ways, so impregnable in his badger hole, and so good-humoured withal. He could bite full sore with those old teeth of his, and yet he never condescended to show them. A badger indeed of whom the country might well be proud !

But in the scramble of the fight some little curs had been permitted to run away with some little bones ; and, in this way, Mr. Nogo, the member for Mile End, had been allowed to carry his motion for a committee to inquire as to the expediency of the Government's advancing a quarter of a million towards the completion of that momentous national undertaking, the building of a bridge from Limehouse to Rotherhithe.

Very much had been said about this bridge, till men living out of the light of parliamentary life, nine hundred and ninety-nine men, that is, out of every thousand in the Queen's dominions, had begun to think that it was the great want of the age. Men living in the light, the supporters of the bridge as well as its enemies, knew very well that such an erection was quite unneeded, and would in all probability never be made. But then the firm of Blocks, Piles, and Cofferdam, who held a vast quantity of the bridge shares, and who were to be the contractors for building it, had an all-powerful influence in the borough of Limehouse. Where would Mr. Nogo be if he did not cultivate the friendship of such men as Blocks, Piles, and Cofferdam ?

And so Mr. Nogo, and those who acted with Mr. Nogo —men, that is, who had little jobs of their own to do, and in the doing of which Mr. Nogo occasionally assisted, Undy Scott, for instance, and such-like—these men, I say, had talked much about the bridge ; and gentlemen on the Treasury bench, who could have afforded to show up the folly of the scheme, and to put Mr. Nogo down at once, had he been alone, felt themselves under the necessity of temporizing. As to giving a penny of the public money for such a purpose, that they knew was out of the question ; that Mr. Nogo never expected ; that they all knew Mr. Nogo never expected. But as Mr. Nogo's numbers were so respectable, it was necessary to oppose him in a respectable parliamentary steady manner. He had fifteen with him ! Had he been quite alone, Mr. Vigil would have sneered him off ; had he had but four to back him, the old badger would have laughed them out of face with a brace of grins. But fifteen——! Mr. Whip Vigil thought that the committee would be the most safe. So would the outer world be brought to confess that the interests of Limehouse and Poplar, Rotherhithe and Deptford, had not been overlooked by a careful Government.

But of whom was the committee to be made up ?
That was now the question which to Mr. Nogo, in his
hour of temporary greatness, was truly momentous. He
of course was to be the chairman, and to him appertained
the duty of naming the other members ; of naming them
indeed—so much he could undoubtedly do by the strength
of his own privilege. But of what use to name a string
of men to whom Mr. Vigil would not consent ? Mr.
Nogo, did he do so, would have to divide on every name,
and be beaten at every division. There would be no
triumph in that. No ; Mr. Nogo fully understood that
his triumph must be achieved—if he were destined to
a triumph—by an astute skill in his selection, not by an
open choice of friends. He must obtain a balance on
his side, but one in which the scale would lean so slightly
to his side that Mr. Vigil's eyes might be deceived. Those
who knew Mr. Vigil best were inclined to surmise that
such an arrangement was somewhat beyond Mr. Nogo's
political capacity. There is a proverb which goes to
show that a certain little lively animal may be shaved
if he be caught napping ; but then the difficulty of so
catching him is extreme.

Mr. Nogo, at the head of the list, put Mr. Vigil himself.
This, of course, was a necessity to him—would that he
could have dispensed with it ! Then he named sundry
supporters of the Government, sundry members also of
the opposition ; and he filled up the list with certain
others who could not be regarded as sure supporters of
one side or the other, but with whom, for certain reasons,
he thought he might in this particular case be safe. Undy
Scott was of course not among the number, as Mr. Nogo
would only have damaged his cause by naming a man
known to have a pecuniary interest in the concern.

The member for Mile End was doubtless sharp, but
Mr. Vigil was sharper. His object was, in fact, merely
to do his duty to the country by preventing a profuse and
useless expenditure of money. His anxiety was a perfectly honest one—to save the Exchequer namely. But
the circumstances of the case required that he should
fight the battle according to the tactics of the House, and
he well understood how to do so.

When the list was read he objected to two or three names—only to two or three. They were not those of staunch enemies of the Government; nor did he propose in their places the names of staunch supporters. He suggested certain gentlemen who, from their acquaintance with bridges, tolls, rivers, &c., would, as he said, be probably of use. He, also, was sure of his men, and as he succeeded with two of them, he was also pretty sure of his committee.

And then the committee met, and a lot of witnesses were in attendance. The chairman opened his case, and proceeded to prove, by the evidence of sundry most respectable men connected with Limehouse, and with the portions of Surrey and Kent lying immediately opposite to it, that the most intense desire for friendly and commercial intercourse was felt; but that, though absolutely close to each other, the districts were so divided by adverse circumstances, circumstances which were monstrous considering the advance of science in the nineteenth century, that the dearest friends were constrained to perpetual banishment from each other; and that the men of Kent were utterly unable to do any trade at Limehouse, and the Limehousians equally unable to carry on traffic in Surrey.

It was wonderful that the narrow river should be so effective for injury. One gentleman from Poplar proved that, having given his daughter in marriage to a man of Deptford two years since, he had not yet been able to see her since that day. Her house, by the crow's flight, was but seven furlongs from his own; but, as he kept no horse, he could not get to her residence without a four hours' walk, for which he felt himself to be too old. He was, however, able to visit his married daughter at Reading, and be back to tea. The witness declared that his life was made miserable by his being thus debarred from his child, and he wiped his eyes with his pocket-handkerchief piteously, sitting there in front of the committee. In answer to Mr. Vigil he admitted that there might be a ferry, but stated that he did not know. Having had, from childhood, an aversion to the water, he had not inquired. He was aware that some rash people had gone through the Tunnel, but for himself he did not think the Tunnel a safe mode of transit.

Another gentleman belonging to Rotherhithe, who was obliged to be almost daily at Blackwall, maintained two horses for the express purpose of going backwards and forwards, round by London Bridge. They cost him £70 per annum each. Such a bridge as that now proposed, and which the gentleman declared that he regarded as an embryo monument of national glory, would save him £140 per annum. He then proceeded to make a little speech about the spirit of the age, and the influence of routine, which he described as a gloomy gnome. But his oratory was cruelly cut short by Mr. Vigil, who demanded of him whether he ever used the river steamers. The witness shuddered fearfully as he assured the committee that he never did, and referred to the *Cricket*, whose boilers burst in the year 1842; besides, he had, he said, his things to carry with him.

Another witness told how unsafe was the transit of heavy goods by barge from one side of the river to another. He had had a cargo of marine stores which would go to sea before their time. The strong ebb of the tide, joined to the river current, had positively carried the barge away, and its course had not been stopped till it had drifted on shore at Purfleet. He acknowledged that something had transpired of the bargemen being drunk, but he had no knowledge himself that such had been the case. No other cargoes of his own had been carried away, but he had heard that such was often the case. He thought that the bridge was imperatively demanded. Would the tolls pay? He felt sure that they would. Why, then, should not the bridge be built as a commercial speculation, without Government aid? He thought that in such cases a fostering Government was bound to come forward and show the way. He had a few shares in the bridge himself. He had paid up £1 a share. They were now worth 2s. 6d. each. They had been worth nothing before the committee had been ordered to sit. He declined to give any opinion as to what the shares would be worth if the money were granted.

Ladies at Limehouse proved that if there were a bridge

they could save 30s. a year each, by buying their tea and sugar at Rotherhithe ; and so singular are the usages of trade, that the ladies of Rotherhithe would benefit their husbands equally, and return the compliment, by consuming the bread of Limehouse. The shores of Kent were pining for the beef of the opposite bank, and only too anxious to give in return the surplus stock of their own poultry.

'Let but a bridge be opened,' as was asserted by one animated vendor of rope, 'and Poplar would soon rival Pimlico. Perhaps that might not be desirable in the eyes of men who lived in the purlieus of the Court, and who were desirous to build no new bridge, except that over the ornamental water in St. James's Park.' Upon uttering which the rope-vendor looked at Mr. Vigil as though he expected him to sink at once under the table.

Mr. Blocks, of the great firm of Blocks, Piles, and Cofferdam, then came forward. He declared that a large sum of money was necessary before this great national undertaking could be begun in a spirit worthy of the nineteenth century. It was intended to commence the approaches on each side of the river a quarter of a mile from the first abutment of the bridge, in order to acquire the necessary altitude without a steep ascent. He then described what a glorious bridge this bridge would be ; how it would eclipse all bridges that had ever been built ; how the fleets of all nations would ride under it ; how many hundred thousand square feet of wrought iron would be consumed in its construction ; how many tons of Portland stone in the abutments, parapets, and supporting walls ; how much timber would be buried twenty fathoms deep in the mud of the river ; how many miles of paving-stone would be laid down. Mr. Blocks went on with his astonishing figures till the committee were bewildered, and even Mr. Vigil, though well used to calculations, could hardly raise his mind to the dimensions of the proposed undertaking.

The engineer followed, and showed how easily this great work could be accomplished. There was no difficulty, literally none. The patronage of the Crown was all that was required. The engineer was asked whether by the

word patronage he meant money, and after a little laughing and a few counter questions, he admitted that, in
his estimation, patronage and money did mean the same
thing.

Such was the case made out by the promoters of the
bridge, and the chairman and his party were very sanguine of success. They conceived that Mr. Blocks' figures
had completely cowed their antagonists.

Mr. Vigil then took his case in hand, and brought forward his witnesses. It now appeared that the intercourse
between the people living on each side of the river was
immense, and ever on the increase. Limehouse, it would
seem, had nothing to do but to go to Deptford, and that
Deptford consumed all its time in returning the visit.
Little children were sent across continually on the most
trifling errands, going and coming for one halfpenny. An
immense income was made by the owners of the ferry.
No two adjacent streets in London had more to do with
each other than had the lanes of Rotherhithe and the lanes
of Limehouse. Westminster and Lambeth were further
apart, and less connected by friendly intercourse. The
frequenters of the ferry were found to outnumber the
passengers over Waterloo Bridge by ten to one.

Indeed, so lamentable a proposition as this of building
a bridge across the river had never before been mooted
by the public. Men conversant with such matters gave
it as their opinion that no amount of tolls that could
reasonably be expected would pay one per cent on the
money which it was proposed to expend; that sum,
however, they stated, would not more than half cover
the full cost of the bridge. Traffic would be prohibited
by the heavy charges which would be necessary, and the
probability would be that the ferry would still continue
to be the ordinary mode of crossing the river.

A gentleman, accustomed to use strong figures of
speech, declared that if such a bridge were built, the
wisest course would be to sow the surface with grass, and
let it out for grazing. This witness was taken specially
in hand by Mr. Nogo, and targed very tightly. Mr. Vigil
had contrived to prove, out of the mouths of inimical
witnesses, the very reverse of that which they had been

summoned thither to assert. The secret of the ferry had
been first brought to the light by the gentleman who
could not visit his daughter at Deptford, and so on.
These triumphs had evidently been very pleasant to Mr.
Vigil, and Mr. Nogo thought that he might judiciously
take a leaf out of the Treasury book. Actuated by this
ambition, he, with the assistance of his friend, the M'Carthy
Desmond, put no less than 2,250 questions to the gentleman who suggested the grazing, in order to induce him to
say, that if there were a bridge, men would probably walk
over it. But they could not bring him to own to a single
passenger, unless they would abandon the tolls. The
most that they could get from him was, that perhaps an
old woman, with more money than wit, might go over it
on a Sunday afternoon, if—which he did not believe—
any old woman existed, *in that part of the world,* who had
more money than wit.

This witness was kept in the chair for three days,
during which Mr. Vigil was nearly driven wild by the
loss of his valuable time. But he did not complain.
Nor would he have complained, though he might have
absented himself, had the witness been kept in the chair
three weeks instead of three days. The expense of the
committee, including witnesses, shorthand-writers, and
printing, was about £60 a day, but it never occurred to
any one of the number to get up and declare with indignation, that such a waste of money and time on so palpably
absurd a scheme was degrading, and to demand an immediate close of their labours. It all went smoothly to
the end, and Mr. Nogo walked off from his task with the
approving conscience of a patriotic legislator.

At the close the members met to prepare their report.
It was then the first week in August, and they were
naturally in a hurry to finish their work. It was now
their duty to decide on the merits of what they had
heard, to form a judgement as to the veracity of the witnesses, and declare, on behalf of the country which they
represented, whether or no this bridge should be built at
the expense of the nation.

With his decision each was ready enough ; but not one
of them dreamed of being influenced by anything which

had been said before them. All the world—that is, all that were in any way concerned in the matter—knew that the witnesses for the bridge were anxious to have it built, and that the witnesses against the bridge were anxious to prevent the building. It would be the worst of ignorance, ignorance of the usage of the world we live in, to suppose that any member of Parliament could be influenced by such manœuvres. Besides, was not the mind of each man fully known before the committee met ?

Various propositions were made by the members among themselves, and various amendments moved. The balance of the different parties had been nearly preserved. A decided victory was not to be expected on either side. At last the resolution to which the committee came was this : ' That this committee is not prepared, under existing circumstances, to recommend a grant of public money for the purpose of erecting a bridge at Limehouse ; but that the committee consider that the matter is still open to consideration should further evidence be adduced.'

Mr. Vigil was perfectly satisfied. He did not wish to acerbate the member for Mile End, and was quite willing to give him a lift towards keeping his seat for the borough, if able to do so without cost to the public exchequer. At Limehouse the report of the committee was declared by certain persons to be as good as a decision in their favour ; it was only postponing the matter for another session. But Mr. Vigil knew that he had carried his point, and the world soon agreed with him. He at least did his work successfully, and, considering the circumstances of his position, he did it with credit to himself.

A huge blue volume was then published, containing, among other things, all Mr. Nogo's 2,250 questions and their answers ; and so the Limehouse and Rotherhithe bridge dropped into oblivion and was forgotten.

CHAPTER XXXIII

TO STAND, OR NOT TO STAND

Sir Gregory Hardlines had been somewhat startled by Alaric's announcement of his parliamentary intentions. It not unnaturally occurred to that great man that should Mr. Tudor succeed at Strathbogy, and should he also succeed in being allowed to hold his office and seat together, he, Tudor, would very soon become first fiddle at the Civil Service Examination Board. This was a view of the matter which was by no means agreeable to Sir Gregory. Not for this had he devoted his time, his energy, and the best powers of his mind to the office of which he was at present the chief; not for this had he taken by the hand a young clerk, and brought him forward, and pushed him up, and seated him in high places. To have kept Mr. Jobbles would have been better than this; he, at any rate, would not have aspired to parliamentary honours.

And when Sir Gregory came to look into it, he hardly knew whether those bugbears with which he had tried to frighten Tudor were good serviceable bugbears, such as would stand the strain of such a man's logic and reason. Was there really any reason why one of the commissioners should not sit in Parliament? Would his doing so be subversive of the constitution? Or would the ministers of the day object to an additional certain vote? This last point of view was one in which it did not at all delight Sir Gregory to look at the subject in question. He determined that he would not speak on the matter to the Chancellor of the Exchequer, or to any of the Government wigs who might be considered to be bigger wigs than himself.

And Alaric thought over the matter coolly also. He looked at it till the bugbears shrank into utter insignificance; till they became no more than forms of shreds and patches put up to frighten birds out of cherry-orchards.

Why should the constitution be wounded by the presence
of one more commissioner in Parliament ? Why should
not he do his public duty and hold his seat at the same
time, as was done by so many others ? But he would
have to go out if the ministry went out. That was
another difficulty, another bugbear, more substantial
perhaps than the others ; but he was prepared to meet
even that. He was a poor man ; his profession was
that of the Civil Service ; his ambition was to sit in
Parliament. He would see whether he could not combine
his poverty with his profession, and with his ambition
also. Sir Gregory resolved in his fear that he would not
speak to the Chancellor of the Exchequer on the matter ;
Alaric, on the other hand, in his audacity, resolved that
he would do so.

It was thus that Sir Gregory regarded the matter.
' See all that I have done for this man,' said he to himself ;
' see how I have warmed him in my bosom, how I have
lifted him to fortune and renown, how I have heaped
benefits on his head ! If gratitude in this world be
possible, that man should be grateful to me ; if one man
can ever have another's interest at heart, that man should
have a heartfelt anxiety as to my interest. And yet how
is it ? I have placed him in the chair next to my own,
and now he is desirous of sitting above me ! '

'Twas thus Sir Gregory communed with himself. But
Alaric's soliloquy was very different. A listener who
could have overheard both would hardly have thought
that the same question was being discussed by the two.
' I have got so high,' said Alaric, ' by my own labour,
by my own skill and tact ; and why should I stop here ?
I have left my earliest colleagues far behind me ; have
distanced those who were my competitors in the walk of
life ; why should I not still go on and distance others
also ? why stop when I am only second or third ? It is
very natural that Sir Gregory should wish to keep me
out of Parliament ; I cannot in the least blame him ;
let us all fight as best each may for himself. He does
not wish a higher career ; I do. Sir Gregory will now
do all that he can to impede my views, because they
are antagonistic to his own ; very well ; I must only

work the harder to overcome his objections.' There was
no word in all this of gratitude ; there was no thought in
Alaric's mind that it behoved him to be grateful to Sir
Gregory. It was for his own sake, not for his pupil's,
that Sir Gregory had brought this pupil forward. Grateful, indeed ! In public life when is there time for gratitude ? Who ever thinks of other interest than his own ?

Such was Alaric's theory of life. But not the less
would he have expected gratitude from those whom he
might serve. Such also very probably was Sir Gregory's
theory when he thought of those who had helped him,
instead of those whom he himself had helped.

And so they met, and discussed Alaric's little proposition.

'Since I saw you yesterday,' said Sir Gregory, 'I have
been thinking much of what you were saying to me of
your wish to go into Parliament.'

'I am very much obliged to you,' said Alaric.

'I need hardly tell you, Tudor, how anxious I am to
further your advancement. I greatly value your ability
and diligence, and have shown that I am anxious to make
them serviceable to the public.'

'I am fully aware that I owe you a great deal, Sir
Gregory.'

'Oh, I don't mean that ; that's nothing ; I am not
thinking of myself. I only want you to understand that
I am truly anxious to see you take that line in public
matters which may make your services most valuable to
the public, and which may redound the most to your own
advantage. I have thought of what you said to me with
the most mature deliberation, and I am persuaded that
I shall best do my duty to you, and to the service, by
recommending you to abandon altogether your idea of
going into Parliament.'

Sir Gregory said this in his weightiest manner. He
endeavoured to assume some of that authority with
which he had erst cowed the young Tudor at the Weights
and Measures, and as he finished his speech he assumed
a profound look which ought to have been very convincing.

But the time was gone by with Alaric when such tricks
of legerdemain were convincing to him. A grave brow,

compressed lips, and fixed eyes, had no longer much
effect upon him. He had a point to gain, and he was
thinking of that, and not of Sir Gregory's grimaces.

'Then you will not see the Chancellor of the Exchequer
on the subject ? '

'No,' said Sir Gregory ; 'it would be useless for me to
do so. I could not advocate such a scheme, feeling
certain that it would be injurious both to yourself and to
the service ; and I would not desire to see the Chancellor
with the view of opposing your wishes.'

'I am much obliged to you for that, at any rate,' said
Alaric.

'But I do hope that you will not carry your plan any
farther. When I tell you, as I do with the utmost sincerity, that I feel certain that an attempt to seat yourself
in Parliament can only lead to the ruin of your prospects
as a Civil servant—prospects which are brighter now than
those of any other young man in the service—I cannot
but think that you must hesitate before you take any
step which will, in my opinion, render your resignation
necessary.'

'I shall be sorry to resign, Sir Gregory, as I have such
true pleasure in serving with you.'

'And, I presume, a salary of £1,200 a year is not un-
acceptable ? ' said Sir Gregory, with the very faintest of
smiles.

'By no means,' said Alaric ; 'I am a poor man, de-
pending altogether on my own exertions for an income.
I cannot afford to throw away a chance.'

'Then take my word for it, you should give up all
idea of Parliament,' said Sir Gregory, who thought that
he had carried his point.

'But I call a seat in Parliament a chance,' said Alaric ;
'the best chance that a man, circumstanced as I am, can
possibly have. I have the offer of a seat, Sir Gregory,
and I can't afford to throw it away.'

'Then it is my duty to tell you, as the head of your
office, that it will be your duty to resign before you offer
yourself as a candidate.'

'That you mean is your present opinion, Sir Gregory ? '

'Yes, Mr. Tudor, that is my opinion—an opinion which

I shall be forced to express to the Chancellor of the Exchequer, if you persist in this infatuation.'

Alaric looked very grave, but not a whit angry. 'I am sorry for it, Sir Gregory, very sorry; I had hoped to have had your countenance.'

'I would give it you, Mr. Tudor, if I could consistently with my duty as a public servant; but as I cannot, I am sure you will not ask for it.' How Fidus Neverbend would have admired the chief commissioner could he have seen and heard him at this moment! 'But,' he continued, relaxing for a while the muscles of his face, 'I hope, I do hope, you will think better of this. What are you to gain? Come, Tudor, think of it that way. What are you to gain? You, with a wife and young family coming up about your heels, what are you to gain by going into Parliament? That is what I ask you. What are you to gain?' It was delightful to see how pleasantly practical Sir Gregory could become when he chose to dismount from his high horse.

'It is considered a high position in this country, that of a member of Parliament,' said Alaric. 'A man in gaining that is generally supposed to have gained something.'

'True, quite true. It is a desirable position for a rich man, or a rich man's eldest son, or even for a poor man, if by getting into Parliament he can put himself in the way of improving his income. But, my dear Tudor, you are in none of these positions. Abandon the idea, my dear Tudor—pray abandon it. If not for your own sake, at any rate do so for that of your wife and child.'

Sir Gregory might as well have whistled. Not a word that he said had the slightest effect on Alaric. How was it possible that his words should have any effect, seeing that Alaric was convinced that Sir Gregory was pleading for his own advantage, and not for that of his listener? Alaric did listen. He received all that Sir Gregory said with the most profound attention; schooled his face into a look of the most polite deference; and then, with his most cruel tone, informed Sir Gregory that his mind was quite made up, and that he did intend to submit himself to the electors of Strathbogy.

'And as to what you say about my seat at the board, Sir Gregory, you may probably be right. Perhaps it will be as well that I should see the Chancellor of the Exchequer myself.'

'"Who will to Cupar maun to Cupar,"' said Sir Gregory; 'I can only say, Mr. Tudor, that I am very sorry for you, and very sorry for your wife—very sorry, very sorry indeed.'

'And who will to Strathbogy maun to Strathbogy,' said Alaric, laughing; 'there is certainly an air of truth about the proverb as applied to myself just at present. But the fact is, whether for good or for bad, I maun to Strathbogy. That is my present destiny. The fact that I have a wife and a child does make the step a most momentous one. But, Sir Gregory, I should never forgive myself were I to throw away such an opportunity.'

'Then I have nothing more to say, Mr. Tudor.'

'Of course I shall try to save my place,' continued Alaric.

'I look upon that as quite impossible,' said Sir Gregory.

'It can do me no harm at any rate to see the Chancellor of the Exchequer. If he tells me that a seat in Parliament and a seat at the board are incompatible, and that as one of the Civil Service Commissioners I am not free to stand for the borough, I will in that case, Sir Gregory, put my resignation in your hands before I publish my address.'

And so they parted, each determined to do all that in him lay to thwart the wishes of the other. Alaric was not in the least influenced by anything that Sir Gregory had said to him; he had made up his mind, and was determined to be turned from it by no arguments that his colleague could use; but nevertheless he could not but be meditative, as, walking home across the Parks, he thought of his wife and child. It is true that he had a second trade; he was a stock-jobber as well as a Civil Service Commissioner; but he already perceived how very difficult it was to realize an income to which he could trust from that second precarious pursuit. He had also lived in a style considerably beyond that which his official income would have enabled him to assume. He had on the whole, he thought, done very well; but yet it would be a dreadful thing to have to trust to so precarious a livelihood. He had realized nothing; he had not yet been able to pay back the money which he had so fraudulently taken, and to acquit himself of a debt which now lay daily heavier and heavier on his soul. He felt that he must repay not only that but Undy's share also, before he could again pass a happy day or a quiet night. This plan of throwing up £1,200 a year would badly assist him in getting rid of this incubus.

But still that watchword of his goaded him on— 'Excelsior!' he still said to himself; 'Excelsior!' If he halted now, now when the ball was at his foot, he might never have another chance. Very early in life, before a beard was on his chin, before he could style himself a man according to the laws of his country, he had determined within himself that a seat in Parliament was the only fitting ambition for an Englishman. That was now within his reach. Would he be such a dastard as to draw back his hand, and be deterred from taking it, by old women's tales of prudence, and the self-interested lectures of Sir Gregory Hardlines?

'Excelsior!' There was not much that could be so styled in that debt of his to M. and Madame Jaquêtanàpe. If he could only pay that off he felt that he could brave the world without a fear. Come what come might he would sell out and do so. The bridge committee was sitting, and his shares were already worth more than he had paid for them. Mr. Blocks had just given his evidence, and the commercial world was willing enough to invest in the Limehouse bridge. He would sell out and put his conscience at rest.

But then to do so successfully, he must induce Undy to do so too; and that he knew would not at present be an easy task. Who had ever been successful in getting back money from Undy Scott? He had paid the last half-year's interest with most commendable punctuality, and was not that a great deal from Undy Scott?

But what if this appropriation of another's money, what if this fraud should be detected and exposed before he had succeeded in paying back the £10,000. What if he should wake some morning and find himself in the grip of some Newgate myrmidon? A terrible new law had just been passed for the protection of trust property; a law in which he had not felt the slightest interest when he had first seen in the daily newspapers some tedious account of the passing of the various clauses, but which was now terrible to his innermost thoughts.

His walk across the Parks was not made happy by much self-triumph. In spite of his commissionership and coming parliamentary honours, his solitary moments were seldom very happy. It was at his club, when living with Undy and Undy's peers, that he was best able to throw off his cares and enjoy himself. But even then, high as he was mounted on his fast-trotting horse, black Care would sit behind him, ever mounted on the same steed.

And bitterly did poor Gertrude feel the misery of these evenings which her husband passed at his club; but she never reviled him or complained; she never spoke of her sorrow even to her mother or sister. She did not even blame him in her own heart. She knew that he had other business than that of his office, higher hopes than those attached to his board; and she taught herself to believe that his career required him to be among public men.

He had endeavoured to induce her to associate constantly with Mrs. Val, so that her evenings might not be passed alone; but Gertrude, after trying Mrs. Val for a time, had quietly repudiated the closeness of this alliance. Mrs. Val had her ideas of 'Excelsior,' her ambition to rule, and these ideas and this ambition did not at all suit Gertrude's temper. Not even for her husband's sake could she bring herself to be patronized by Mrs. Val. They were still very dear friends, of course; but they did not live in each other's arms as Alaric had intended they should do.

He returned home after his interview with Sir Gregory, and found his wife in the drawing-room with her child. He usually went down from his office to his club, and she was therefore the more ready to welcome him for having broken through his habit on the present occasion.

She left her infant sprawling on the floor, and came up to greet him with a kiss.

'Ger,'—said he, putting his arm round her and embracing her—'I have come home to consult you on business;' and then he seated himself on the sofa, taking her with him, and still in his arms. There was but little doubt that she would consent to anything which he could propose to her after such a fashion, in such a guise as this; that he knew full well.

'Well, love,' said she, 'and what is the business about? You know that I always think that to be best which you think to be best.'

'Yes, Ger; but this is a very important matter;' and then he looked grave, but managed at the same time to look happy and contented. 'This is a matter of vital importance to you, and I will do nothing in it without your consent.'

'What is best for you must be best for me,' said Gertrude, kissing his forehead.

Then he explained to her what had passed between himself and Sir Gregory, and what his own ideas were as regarded the borough of Strathbogy. 'Sir Gregory,' said he, 'is determined that I shall not remain at the board and sit in Parliament at the same time; but I do not see why Sir Gregory is to have his own way in everything. If you are not afraid of the risk, I will make up my mind to stand it at all events, and to resign if the Minister makes it imperative. If, however, you fear the result, I will let the matter drop, and tell the Scotts to find another candidate. I am anxious to go into Parliament, I confess; but I will never do so at the expense of your peace of mind.'

The way in which he put upon her the whole weight of the decision was not generous. Nor was the mode he adopted of inducing her to back his own wishes. If there were risk to her—and in truth there was fearful risk—it was his duty to guard her from the chance, not hers to say whether such danger should be encountered or no. The nature of her answer may be easily surmised. She was generous, though he was not. She would never retard his advance, or be felt as a millstone round his neck. She encouraged him with all her enthusiasm, and bade him throw prudence to the winds. If he rose, must she not rise also ? Whatever step in life was good for him, must it not be good for her as well ? And so that matter was settled between them—pleasantly enough.

He endured a fortnight of considerable excitement, during which he and Sir Gregory did not smile at each other, and then he saw the Chancellor of the Exchequer. That gentleman promised to speak to the Prime Minister, feeling himself unable to answer the question put to him, definitely out of his own head ; and then another fortnight passed on. At the end of that time the Chancellor of the Exchequer sent for Alaric, and they had a second interview.

'Well, Mr. Tudor,' said the great man, 'this is a matter of very considerable importance, and one on which I am not even yet prepared to give you a positive answer.'

This was very good news for Alaric. Sir Gregory had spoken of the matter as one on which there could be no possible doubt. He had asserted that the British lion would no longer sleep peaceably in his lair, if such a violence were put on the constitution as that meditated by the young commissioner. It was quite clear that the Chancellor of the Exchequer, and the Prime Minister also, looked at it in a very different light. They doubted, and Alaric was well aware that their doubt was as good as certainty to him.

The truth was that the Prime Minister had said to the Chancellor of the Exchequer, in a half-serious, half-jocular way, that he didn't see why he should reject a vote when offered to him by a member of the Civil Service. The man must of course do his work—and should it be found that his office work and his seat in Parliament interfered with each other, why, he must take the consequences. And if ——— or ——— or ——— made a row about it in the House and complained, why in that case also Mr. Tudor must take the consequences. And then, enough having been said on that matter, the conversation dropped.

'I am not prepared to give a positive answer,' said

the Chancellor of the Exchequer, who of course did not choose to commit himself.

Alaric assured the great man that he was not so unreasonable as to expect a positive answer. Positive answers, as he well knew, were not often forthcoming among official men; official men, as he had already learnt, prefer to do their business by answers which are not positive. He himself had become adverse to positive answers since he had become a commissioner, and was quite prepared to dispense with them in the parliamentary career which he hoped that he was now about to commence. This much, however, was quite clear, that he might offer himself as a candidate to the electors of Strathbogy without resigning; and that Sir Gregory's hostile remonstrance on the subject, should he choose to make one, would not be received as absolute law by the greater powers.

Accordingly as Alaric was elated, Sir Gregory was depressed. He had risen high, but now this young tyro whom he had fostered was about to climb above his head. O the ingratitude of men!

Alaric, however, showed no triumph. He was more submissive, more gracious than ever to his chief. It was only to himself that he muttered ' Excelsior !

CHAPTER XXXIV

WESTMINSTER HALL

THE parliamentary committee pursued their animated inquiries respecting the Limehouse bridge all through the sultry month of July. How Mr. Vigil must have hated Mr. Nogo, and the M'Carthy Desmond! how sick he must have been of that eternal witness who, with imperturbable effrontery, answered the 2,250 questions put to him without admitting anything! To Mr. Vigil it was all mere nonsense, sheer waste of time. Had he been condemned to sit for eight days in close contiguity to the clappers of a small mill, he would have learnt as much as he did from the witnesses before the committee. Nevertheless he went through it and did not lose his temper. He smiled sweetly on Mr. Nogo every morning, and greeted the titled Irishman with his easy familiar nod, as though the continued sitting of this very committee was of all things to him the most desirable. Such is Mr. Vigil's peculiar tact, such his special talent ; these are the gifts—gifts by no means ordinary—which have made him Right Honourable, and recommended him to the confidence of successive badgers.

But though the committee was uninteresting to Mr. Vigil, it was not so to the speculative inhabitants of Limehouse, or to the credulous shopkeepers of Rother-hithe. On the evening of the day on which Mr. Blocks was examined, the shares went up 20 per cent ; and when his evidence was published *in extenso* the next Saturday morning by the *Capel Court Share-buyer*, a periodical which served for Bible and Prayer-book, as well as a Compendium of the Whole Duty of Man, to Undy Scott and his friends, a further rise in the price of this now valuable property was the immediate consequence.

Now, then, was the time for Alaric to sell and get out of his difficulties if ever he could do so. Shares which he bought for 30s. were now worth nearly £2 10s. He was strongly of opinion that they would fall again, and that the final result of the committee would leave them of a less value than their original purchase-money, and probably altogether valueless. He could not, however, act in the matter without consulting Undy, so closely linked were they in the speculation ; and even at the present price his own shares would not enable him to pay back the full amount of what he had taken.

The joint property of the two was, however, at its present market price, worth £12,000—£10,000 would make him a free man. He was perfectly willing to let Undy have the full use of the difference in amount ; nay, he was ready enough to give it to him altogether, if by so doing he could place the whole of his ward's money once more in safety. With the power of offering such a douceur to his friend's rapacity, he flattered himself that he might have a chance of being successful. He was thus prepared to discuss the matter with his partner.

It so happened that at the same moment Undy was desirous of discussing the same subject, their joint interest, namely, in the Limehouse bridge; there was no difficulty therefore in their coming together. They met at the door of the committee-room when Mr. Nogo had just put his 999th question to the adverse witness; and as the summons to prayers prevented the 1,000th being proceeded with at that moment, Undy and Alaric sauntered back along the passages, and then walking up and down the immense space of Westminster Hall, said each to the other what he had to say on the matter mooted between them.

Undy was in great glee, and seemed to look on his fortune as already made. They had at first confined their remarks to the special evidence of the witness who had last been in the chair; and Undy, with the volubility which was common to him when he was in high spirits, had been denouncing him as an ass who was injuring his own cause by his over obstinacy.

'Nothing that he can say,' said Undy, 'will tell upon the share-market. The stock is rising from hour to hour; and Piles himself told me that he knew from sure intelligence that the Chancellor of the Exchequer is prepared to give way, whatever Vigil may say to the contrary. Their firm, Piles says, is buying every share they can lay their hands on.'

'Then in God's name let them buy ours,' said Alaric.

'Buy ours!' said Undy. 'You don't mean to tell me that you wish to sell now? You don't mean to say that you want to back out, now that the game is all going our own way?'

'Indeed I do, and I intend to do so; just listen to me, Undy——'

'I tell you fairly, Tudor, I will not sell a share; what you may choose to do with your own I cannot say. But if you will be guided by me you will keep every share you have got. Instead of selling we should both add to our stock. I at any rate am resolved to do so.'

'Listen to me, Undy,' said Alaric.

'The truth is,' said Undy—who at the present moment preferred talking to listening—'the truth is, you do not understand buying and selling shares. We should both be ruined very quickly were I to allow myself to be led by you; you are too timid, too much afraid of risking your money; your speculative pluck hardly rises higher than the Three per cents, and never soars above a first-class mortgage on land.'

'I could be as sanguine as you are, and as bold,' said Alaric, 'were I venturing with my own money.'

'In the name of goodness get that bugbear out of your head,' said Undy. 'Whatever good it might have done you to think of that some time ago, it can do you no good now.' There was a bitter truth in this which made Alaric's heart sink low within his breast. 'Wherever the money came from, whose property it may have been or be, it has been used; and now your only safety is in making the best use of it. A little daring, a little audacity—it is that which ruins men. When you sit down to play brag, you must brag it out, or lose your money.'

'But, my dear fellow, there is no question here of losing money. If we sell now we shall realize about £2,000.'

'And will that, or the half of that, satisfy you? Is that your idea of a good thing? Will that be sufficient to pay for the dozen of bad things which a fellow is always putting his foot into? It won't satisfy me. I can tell you that, at any rate.'

Alaric felt very desirous of keeping Undy in a good humour. He wished, if possible, to persuade him rather than to drive him; to coax him into repaying this money, and not absolutely to demand the repayment. 'Come,' said he, 'what do you call a good thing yourself?'

'I call cent per cent a good thing, and I'll not sell a share till they come up to that.'

'They'll never do that, Undy.'

'That's your opinion. I think differently. And I'm sure you will own I have had more experience of the share-market than you have. When I see such men as Blocks and Piles buying fast, I know very well which way the wind blows. A man may be fishing a long time,

Tudor, in these waters, before he gets such a haul as this ; but he must be a great fool to let go his net when he does get it.'

They both then remained silent for a time, for each was doubtful how best to put forward the view which he himself wished to urge. Their projects were diametrically different, and yet neither could carry his own without the assistance of the other.

' I tell you what I propose,' said Undy.

' Wait a moment, Undy,' said Alaric ; ' listen to me for one moment. I can hear nothing till you do so, and then I will hear anything.'

' Well, what is it ? '

' We have each of us put something near to £5,000 into this venture.'

' I have put more,' said Scott.

' Very well. But we have each of us withdrawn a sum equal to that I have named from my ward's fortune for this purpose.'

' I deny that,' said Undy. ' I have taken nothing from your ward's fortune. I have had no power to do so. You have done as you pleased with that fortune. But I am ready to admit that I have borrowed £5,000— not from your ward, but from you.'

Alaric was nearly beside himself ; but he still felt that he should have no chance of carrying his point if he lost his temper.

' That is ungenerous of you, Scott, to say the least of it ; but we 'll let that pass. To enable me to lend you the £5,000, and to enable me to join you in this speculation, £10,000 has been withdrawn from Clementina's fortune.'

' I know nothing about that,' said Scott.

' Know nothing about it ! ' said Alaric, looking at him with withering scorn. But Undy was not made of withering material, and did not care a straw for his friend's scorn.

' Nothing whatever,' said he.

' Well, so be it,' said Alaric ; ' but the fact is, the money has been withdrawn.'

' I don't doubt that in the least,' said Undy.

'I am not now going to argue whether the fault has been most mine or yours,' continued Alaric.

'Well, that is kind of you,' said Undy, 'considering that you are the girl's trustee, and that I have no more to do with it than that fellow in the wig there.'

'I wish at any rate you would let me explain myself,' said Alaric, who felt that his patience was fast going, and who could hardly resist the temptation of seizing his companion by the throat, and punishing him on the spot for his iniquity.

'I don't prevent you, my dear fellow—only remember this: I will not permit you to assert, without contradicting you, that I am responsible for Clem's fortune. Now, go on, and explain away as hard as you like.'

Alaric, under these circumstances, found it not very easy to put what he had to say into any words that his companion would admit. He fully intended at some future day to thrust Scott's innocence down his throat, and tell him that he was not only a thief, but a mean, lying, beggarly thief. But the present was not the time. Too much depended on his inducing Undy to act with him.

'Ten thousand pounds has at any rate been taken.'

'That I won't deny.'

'And half that sum has been lent to you.'

'I acknowledge a debt of £5,000.'

'It is imperative that £10,000 should at once be repaid.'

'I have no objection in life.'

'I can sell my shares in the Limehouse bridge,' continued Alaric, 'for £6,000, and I am prepared to do so.'

'The more fool you,' said Undy, 'if you do it; especially as £6,000 won't pay £10,000, and as the same property, if overheld another month or two, in all probability will do so.'

'I am ready to sacrifice that and more than that,' said Alaric. 'If you will sell out £4,000, and let me at once have that amount, so as to make up the full sum I owe, I will make you a free present of the remainder of the debt. Come, Undy, you cannot but call that a good thing. You will have pocketed two thousand pounds, according to the present market value of the shares, and that without the slightest risk.'

Undy for a while seemed staggered by the offer. Whether it was Alaric's extreme simplicity in making it, or his own good luck in receiving it, or whether by any possible chance some all but dormant remnant of feeling within his heart was touched, we will not pretend to say. But for a while he walked on silent, as though wavering in his resolution, and looking as if he wished to be somewhat more civil, somewhat less of the bully, than he had been.

There was no one else to whom Alaric could dare to open his heart on this subject of his ward's fortune; there was none other but this ally of his to whom he could confide, whom he could consult. Unpromising, therefore, though Undy was as a confederate, Alaric, when he thought he saw this change in his manner, poured forth at once the full tide of his feelings.

'Undy,' said he, 'pray bear with me a while. The truth is, I cannot endure this misery any longer. I do not now want to blame anyone but myself. The thing has been done, and it is useless now to talk of blame. The thing has been done, and all that now remains for me is to undo it; to put this girl's money back again, and get this horrid weight from off my breast.'

'Upon my word, my dear fellow, I did not think that you took it in such a light as that,' said Undy.

'I am miserable about it,' said Alaric. 'It keeps me awake all night, and destroys all my energy during the day.'

'Oh, that's all bile,' said Undy. 'You should give up fish for a few days, and take a blue pill at night.'

'Scott, this money must be paid back at once, or I shall lose my senses. Fortune has so far favoured me as to enable me to put my hand at once on the larger portion of it. You must let me have the remainder. In God's name say that you will do so.'

Undy Scott unfortunately had not the power to do as he was asked. Whether he would have done so, had he had the power, may be doubtful. He was somewhat gravelled for an answer to Alaric's earnest supplication, and therefore made none till the request was repeated.

' In God's name let me have this money,' repeated Alaric.
' You will then have made two thousand pounds by the
transaction.'

' My dear Tudor,' said he, ' your stomach is out of order,
I can see it as well as possible from the way you talk.'

Here was an answer for a man to get to the most earnest
appeal which he could make ! Here was comfort for
a wretch suffering from fear, remorse, and shame, as
Alaric was suffering. He had spoken of his feelings and
his heart, but these were regions quite out of Undy Scott's
cognizance. ' Take a blue pill,' said he, ' and you'll be as
right as a trivet in a couple of days.'

What was Alaric to say ? What could he say to a man
who at such a crisis could talk to him of blue pills ? For
a while he said nothing ; but the form of his face changed,
a darkness came over his brow which Scott had never
before seen there, the colour flew from his face, his eyes
sparkled, and a strange appearance of resolute defiance
showed itself round his mouth. Scott began to perceive
that his medical advice would not be taken in good part.

' Scott,' said he, stopping short in his walk and taking
hold of the collar of his companion's coat, not loosely by
the button, but with a firm grip which Undy felt that it
would be difficult to shake off—' Scott, you will find that
I am not to be trifled with. You have made a villain of
me. I can see no way to escape from my ruin without
your aid ; but by the living God, if I fall, you shall fall
with me. Tell me now ; will you let me have the sum
I demand ? If you do not, I will go to your brother's
wife and tell her what has become of her daughter's
money.'

' You may go to the devil's wife if you like it,' said
Undy, ' and tell her whatever you please.'

' You refuse, then ? ' said Alaric, still keeping hold of
Undy's coat.

' Come, take your hand off,' said Undy. ' You will
make me think your head is wrong as well as your stomach,
if you go on like this. Take your hand off and listen to
me. I will then explain to you why I cannot do what you
would have me. Take your hand away, I say ; do you
not see that people are looking at us.'

They were now standing at the upper end of the hall—close under the steps which lead to the Houses of Parliament ; and, as Undy said, the place was too public for a display of physical resentment. Alaric took his hand away. 'Well,' said he, 'now tell me what is to hinder you from letting me have the money you owe me ?'

'Only this,' said Undy, 'that every share I have in the concern is made over by way of security to old M'Cleury, and he now holds them. Till I have redeemed them, I have no power of selling.'

Alaric, when he heard these words, could hardly prevent himself from falling in the middle of the hall. All his hopes were then over ; he had no chance of shaking this intolerable burden from his shoulders ; he had taken the woman's money, this money which had been entrusted to his honour and safe-keeping, and thrown it into a bottom-less gulf.

'And now listen to me,' said Undy, looking at his watch. 'I must be in the House in ten or fifteen minutes, for this bill about married women is on, and I am in-terested in it : listen to me now for five minutes. All this that you have been saying is sheer nonsense.'

'I think you'll find that it is not all nonsense,' said Alaric.

'Oh, I am not in the least afraid of your doing any-thing rash. You'll be cautious enough I know when you come to be cool ; especially if you take a little physic. What I want to say is this—Clem's money is safe enough. I tell you these bridge shares will go on rising till the beginning of next session. Instead of selling, what we should do is to buy up six or seven thousand pounds more.'

'What, with Clementina's money ?'

'It's as well to be hung for a sheep as a lamb. Besides, your doing so is your only safety. My brother Val insists upon having 250 shares.'

'Your brother Val !' said Alaric.

'Yes, Val ; and why shouldn't he ? I would give them to him if I could, but I can't. M'Cleury, as I tell you, has every share of mine in his possession.'

' Your brother Val wants 250 shares ! And does he expect me to give them to him ? '

' Well—I rather think he does. That is, not to give them, of course ; you don't suppose he wants you to make him a present of money. But he wants you to accommodate him with the price of them. You can either do that, or let him have so many of your own ; it will be as broad as it is long ; and he'll give you his note of hand for the amount.'

Now it was well known among the acquaintance of the Scott family, that the note of hand of the Honourable Captain Val was not worth the paper on which it was written.

Alaric was so astonished at this monstrous request, coming as it did after such a conversation, that he did not well know how to take it.

Was Undy mad, or was he in joke ? What man in his senses would think of lending six or seven hundred pounds to Val Scott ! ' I suppose you are in jest,' said he, somewhat bitterly.

' I never was more in earnest in my life,' said Undy. ' I'll just explain how the matter is ; and as you are sharp enough, you'll see at once that you had better oblige him. Val, you know, is always hard up ; he can't touch a shilling of that woman's money, and just at present he has none of his own. So he came to me this morning to raise the wind.'

' And you are kind enough to pass him on to me.'

' Listen a moment. I did not do anything of the kind. I never lend money to Val. It 's a principle with me not to do so, and he knows it.'

' Then just tell him that my principles in this respect are identical with your own.'

' That 's all very well ; and you may tell him so yourself, if you like it ; but hear first of all what his arguments are. Of course I told him I could do nothing for him. "But," said he, "you can get Tudor to do it." I told him, of course, that I could do nothing of the kind. "Oh !" said Val, "I know the game you are both playing. I know all about Clem's money." Val, you know, never says much. He was playing pool at the time, at the club ;

but he came back after his stroke, and whispered to me—
" You and Tudor must let me have 250 of those shares,
and then it'll be all right." Now Val, you know, is a most
determined fellow.'

Alaric, when he heard this, looked up into his companion's face to see whether he was talking to the Evil
One himself. Oh, what a net of ruin was closing round
him !—how inextricable were the toils into which he had
fallen !

' After all,' continued Undy, ' what he asks is not
much, and I really think you should do it for him. He is
quite willing to give you his assistance at Strathbogy, and
he is entitled to some accommodation.'

' Some accommodation!' repeated Alaric, almost lost
in the consideration of his own misery.

' Yes ; I really think he is. And, Tudor, you may be
sure of this, you know ; you will be quite safe with him.
Val is the very soul of honour. Do this for him, and
you'll hear no more about it. You may be quite sure
he'll ask for nothing further, and that he'll never say
a word to annoy you. He 's devilish honourable is Val ;
no man can be more so ; though, perhaps, you wouldn't
think it.'

' Devilish honourable !' said Alaric. ' Only he would
like to have a bribe.'

' A bribe !' said Scott. ' Come, my dear fellow, don't
you make an ass of yourself. Val is like the rest of us ;
when money is going, he likes to have a share of it. If
you come to that, every man who is paid either for talking
or for not talking is bribed.'

' I don't know that I ever heard of a much clearer case
of a bribe than this which you now demand for your
brother.'

' Bribe or no bribe,' said Undy, looking at his watch,
' I strongly advise you to do for him what he asks ; it
will be better for all of us. And let me give you another
piece of advice : never use hard words among friends.
Do you remember the Mary Janes which Manylodes
brought for you in his pocket to the hotel at Tavistock ?'
Here Alaric turned as pale as a spectre. ' Don't talk of
bribes, my dear fellow. We are all of us giving and taking

bribes from our cradles to our graves; but men of the world generally call them by some prettier names. Now, if you are not desirous to throw your cards up altogether, get these shares for Val, and let him or me have them to-morrow morning.' And so saying Undy disappeared into the House, through the side door out of the hall, which is appropriated to the use of honourable members.

And then Alaric was left alone. He had never hitherto realized the true facts of the position in which he had placed himself; but now he did so. He was in the hands of these men, these miscreants, these devils; he was completely at their mercy, and he already felt that they were as devoid of mercy as they were of justice. A cold sweat broke out all over him, and he continued walking up and down the hall, ignorant as to where he was and what he was doing, almost thoughtless, stunned, as it were, by his misery and the conviction that he was a ruined man. He had remained there an hour after Undy had left him, before he roused himself sufficiently to leave the hall and think of returning home. It was then seven o'clock, and he remembered that he had asked his cousin to dine with him. He got into a cab, therefore, and desired to be driven home.

What was he to do? On one point he instantly made up his mind. He would not give one shilling to Captain Val; he would not advance another shilling to Undy; and he would at once sell out his own shares, and make such immediate restitution as might now be in his power. The mention of Manylodes and the mining shares had come home to him with frightful reality, and nearly stunned him. What right, indeed, had he to talk of bribes with scorn—he who so early in his own life had allowed himself to be bought? How could he condemn the itching palm of such a one as Val Scott—he who had been so ready to open his own when he had been tempted by no want, by no poverty?

He would give nothing to Captain Val to bribe him to silence. He knew that if he did so, he would be a slave for ever. The appetite of such a shark as that, when once he has tasted blood, is unappeasable. There is nothing so ruinous as buying the silence of a rogue who has a secret.

What you buy you never possess ; and the price that is
once paid must be repaid again and again, as often as the
rogue may demand it. Any alternative must be better
than this.

And yet what other alternative was there ? He did
not doubt that Val, when disappointed of his prey, would
reveal whatever he might know to his wife, or to his
stepson. Then there would be nothing for Alaric but
confession and ruin. And how could he believe what
Undy Scott had told him ? who else could have given
information against him but Undy himself ? who else
could have put up so heavily stupid a man as Captain
Scott to make such a demand ? Was it not clear that his
own colleague, his own partner, his own intimate associate,
Undy Scott himself, was positively working out his ruin ?
Where were now his high hopes, where now his seat in
Parliament, his authority at the board, his proud name,
his soaring ambition, his constant watchword ? 'Excelsior'
—ah me—no! no longer 'Excelsior'; but he thought of
the cells of Newgate, of convict prisons, and then of his
young wife and of his baby.

He made an effort to assume his ordinary demeanour,
and partially succeeded. He went at once up to his
drawing-room, and there he found Charley and Gertrude
waiting dinner for him ; luckily he had no other
guests.

'Are you ill, Alaric ? ' said Gertrude, directly she saw
him.

'Ill ! No,' said he ; 'only fagged, dearest ; fagged and
worried, and badgered and bored ; but, thank God, not
ill ; ' and he endeavoured to put on his usual face, and
speak in his usual tone. 'I have kept you waiting most
unmercifully for your dinner, Charley ; but then I know
you navvies always lunch on mutton chops.'

'Oh, I am not particularly in a hurry,' said Charley ;
'but I deny the lunch. This has been a bad season for
mutton chops in the neighbourhood of Somerset House ;
somehow they have not grown this year.'

Alaric ran up to prepare for dinner, and his wife followed
him.

'Oh ! Alaric,' said she, 'you are so pale : what is the

matter ? Do tell me,' and she put her arm through his, took hold of his hand, and looked up into his face.

'The matter! nothing is the matter—a man can't always be grinning;' and he gently shook her off, and walked through their bedroom to his own dressing-room. Having entered it he shut the door, and then, sitting down, bowed his head upon a small table and buried it in his hands. All the world seemed to go round and round with him; he was giddy, and he felt that he could not stand.

Gertrude paused a moment in the bedroom to consider, and then followed him. 'What is it you want?' said he, as soon as he heard the handle turn, 'do leave me alone for one moment. I am fagged with the heat, and I want one minute's rest.'

'Oh, Alaric, I see you are ill,' said she. 'For God's sake do not send me from you,' and coming into the room she knelt down beside his chair. 'I know you are suffering, Alaric; do let me do something for you.'

He longed to tell her everything. He panted to share his sorrows with one other bosom; to have one near him to whom he could speak openly of everything, to have one counsellor in his trouble. In that moment he all but resolved to disclose everything to her, but at last he found that he could not do it. Charley was there waiting for his dinner; and were he now to tell his secret to his wife, neither of them, neither he nor she, would be able to act the host or hostess. If done at all, it could not at any rate be done at the present moment.

'I am better now,' said he, giving a long and deep sigh; and then he threw his arms round his wife and passionately embraced her. 'My own angel, my best, best love, how much too good or much too noble you are for such a husband as I am!'

'I wish I could be good enough for you,' she replied, as she began to arrange his things for dressing. 'You are so tired, dearest; wash your hands and come down—don't trouble yourself to dress this evening; unless, indeed, you are going out again.'

'Gertrude,' said he, 'if there be a soul on earth that has not in it a spark of what is good or generous, it is the soul of Undy Scott ; ' and so saying he began the operations of his toilet.

Now Gertrude had never liked Undy Scott ; she had attributed to him whatever faults her husband might have as a husband ; and at the present moment she was not inclined to fight for any of the Scott family.

' He is a very worldly man, I think,' said she.

' Worldly !—no—but hellish,' said Alaric ; ' hellish, and damnable, and fiendish.'

' Oh, Alaric, what has he done ? '

' Never mind ; I cannot tell you ; he has done nothing. It is not that he has done anything, or can do anything to me—but his heart—but never mind—I wish—I wish I had never seen him.'

' Alaric, if it be about money tell me the worst, and I'll bear it without a murmur. As long as you are well I care for nothing else—have you given up your place ? '

' No, dearest, no ; I can keep my place. It is nothing about that. I have lost no money ; I have rather made money. It is the ingratitude of that man which almost kills me. But come, dearest, we will go down to Charley. And Gertrude, mind this, be quite civil to Mrs. Val at present. We will break from the whole set before long ; but in the meantime I would have you be very civil to Mrs. Val.'

And so they went down to dinner, and Alaric, after taking a glass of wine, played his part almost as though he had no weight upon his soul. After dinner he drank freely, and as he drank his courage rose. ' Why should I tell her ? ' he said to himself as he went to bed. ' The chances are that all will yet go well.'

CHAPTER XXXV

MRS. VAL'S NEW CARRIAGE

On the next morning Alaric went to his office without speaking further as to the trouble on his mind, and endeavoured to comfort himself as best he might as he walked down to his office. Then he had also to decide whether it would better suit his purpose to sell out at once and pay up every shilling that he could, or whether he would hold on, and hope that Undy's predictions would be fulfilled, and that the bridge shares would go on rising till they would sell for all that was required of him.

Unfortunate man! what would he have given now to change his position for Norman's single clerkship, or even for Charley's comparative poverty!

Gertrude stayed within all day; but not all day in solitude. About four in the afternoon the Hon. Mrs. Val called, and with her came her daughter Clem, now Madame Jaquêtanàpe, and the two Misses Neverbend. M. Jaquêtanàpe had since his marriage made himself very agreeable to his honourable mother-in-law, so much so that he now occupied the place in her good graces which Undy had formerly filled, and which after Undy's reign had fallen to Alaric's lot. Mrs. Val liked to have about her some confidential gentleman; and as she never thought of placing her confidence in her husband, she was prone to select first one man and then another as her taste and interest dictated. Immediately after their marriage, Victoire and Clem had consented to join housekeeping with their parent. Nothing could be more pleasant than this; their income was unembarrassed, and Mrs. Val, for the first time in her life, was able to set up her carriage. Among the effects arising from this cause, the female Neverbends, who had lately been worshippers of Gertrude, veered round in their idolatry, and paid their vows before Mrs. Val's new yellow panels. In this new carriage now came the four ladies to pay a morning visit to Mrs. Tudor. It was wonderful to see into how small dimensions the Misses Neverbend had contrived to pack, not themselves, but their crinoline.

As has before been hinted, Gertrude did not love Mrs. Val; nor did she love Clem the danseuse; nor did she specially love the Misses Neverbend. They were all of a class essentially different from that in which she had been brought up; and, moreover, Mrs. Val was not content to allow Gertrude into her set without ruling over her, or at any rate patronizing her. Gertrude had borne with them all for her husband's sake; and was contented to do so yet for a while longer, but she thought in her heart that she would be able to draw some consolation from her husband's misfortune if it should be the means of freeing her from Mrs. Val.

'Oh, my dear,' said Mrs. Val, throwing herself down into a sofa as though she were exhausted—' what a dreadful journey it is to you up here! How those poor horses will stand it this weather I don't know, but it nearly kills me; it does indeed.' The Tudors, as has been said, lived in one of the quiet streets of Westbournia, not exactly looking into Hyde Park, but very near to it; Mrs. Val, on the other hand, lived in Ebury Street, Pimlico; her house was much inferior to that of the Tudors; it was small, ill built, and afflicted with all the evils which bad drainage and bad ventilation can produce; but then it was reckoned to be within the precincts of Belgravia, and was only five minutes' walk from Buckingham Palace. Mrs. Val, therefore, had fair ground for twitting her dear friend with living so far away from the limits of fashion. 'You really must come down somewhat nearer to the world; indeed you must, my dear,' said the Hon. Mrs. Val.

'We are thinking of moving; but then we are talking of going to St. John's Wood, or Islington,' said Gertrude, wickedly.

'Islington!' said the Honourable Mrs. Val, nearly fainting.

'Is not Islington and St. Giles' the same place?' asked the innocent Clem, with some malice, however, to counterbalance her innocence.

'O no!' said Lactimel. 'St. Giles' is where the poor wretched starving Irish dwell. Their utter misery in the middle of this rich metropolis is a crying disgrace to the Prime Minister.' Poor Badger, how much he has to bear! 'Only think,' continued Lactimel, with a soft pathetic drawl, 'they have none to feed them, none to clothe them, none to do for them!'

'It is a great question,' said Ugolina, 'whether promiscuous charity is a blessing or a curse. It is probably the greatest question of the age. I myself am inclined to think——'

'But, ma,' said Madame Jaquêtanàpe, 'Mrs. Tudor doesn't really mean that she is going to live at St. Giles', does she?'

'I said Islington,' said Gertrude. 'We may go to St. Giles' next, perhaps.' Had she known all, how dreadful would such jokes have been to her!

Mrs. Val saw that she was being quizzed, and, not liking it, changed the conversation. 'Ugolina,' said she, 'might I trouble you to look out of the front window? I hope those stupid men of mine are not letting the horses stand still. They were so warm coming here, that they will be sure to catch cold.' The stupid men, however, were round the corner at the public-house, and Ugolina could only report that as she did not see them she supposed the horses were walking about.

'And so,' said Mrs. Val, 'Mr. Tudor is thinking of resigning his place at the Civil Service Board, and standing for that borough of Lord Gaberlunzie's, in Aberdeenshire?'

'I really cannot say,' said Gertrude; 'but I believe he has some idea of going into Parliament. I rather believe he will continue to hold his place.'

'Oh, that I know to be impossible! I was told that by a gentleman who has been much longer in the service than Mr. Tudor, and who understands all its bearings.' She here alluded to Fidus Neverbend.

'I cannot say,' said Gertrude. 'I do not think Mr. Tudor has quite made up his mind yet.'

'Well, my dear, I'll tell you fairly what I think about it. You know the regard I have for you and Mr. Tudor. He, too, is Clementina's trustee; that is to say, her fortune is partly consigned to his care; so I cannot but have a very great interest about him, and be very anxious that he should do well. Now, my dear, I'll tell you fairly what I think, and what all the world is saying. He ought not to think of Parliament. He ought not, indeed, my dear. I speak for your sake, and your child's. He is not a man of fortune, and he ought not to think of Parliament. He has a very fine situation, and he really should be contented.'

This was intolerable to Gertrude. She felt that she must put Mrs. Val down, and yet she hardly knew how to do it without being absolutely rude; whereas her husband had specially begged her to be civil to this woman at present. 'Oh,' said she, with a slight smile, 'Mr. Tudor will be able to take care of himself; you will find, I hope, that there is no cause for uneasiness.'

'Well, I hope not, I am sure I hope not,' said Mrs. Val, looking very grave. 'But I tell you fairly that the confidence which we all have in your husband will be much shaken if he does anything rash. He should think of this, you know. He has no private fortune to back him; we must remember that.'

Gertrude became very red in the face; but she would not trust herself to answer Mrs. Val at the spur of the moment.

'It makes such a difference, when one has got no private fortune,' said Madame Jaquêtanàpe, the heiress. 'Does it not, Lactimel?'

'Oh, indeed it does,' said Lactimel. 'I wish every one had a private fortune; it would be so nice, wouldn't it?'

'There would be very little poetry in the world if you were to banish poverty,' said Ugolina. 'Poverty may be called the parent of poetry. Look at Milton, how poor he was; and Homer, he begged his bread.'

'But Lord Byron was not a beggar,' said Clem, contemptuously.

'I do hope Mr. Tudor will think of what he is doing,' continued Mrs. Val. 'It is certainly most good-natured and most disinterested of my dear father-in-law, Lord Gaberlunzie, to place his borough at Mr. Tudor's disposal. It is just like him, dear good old nobleman. But, my

dear, it will be a thousand pities if Mr. Tudor should be
led on by his lordship's kindness to bring about his own
ruin.'

Mrs. Val had once in her life seen his good-natured
lordship. Soon after her marriage she had insisted on
Captain Val taking her down to the family mansion. She
stayed there one night, and then left it, and since that had
shown no further desire to visit Cauldkail Castle. She
did not the less delight to talk about her dear good father-
in-law, the lord. Why should she give his son Val board
and lodging, but that she might be enabled to do so ?
She was not the woman to buy an article, and not make
of it all the use of which it might be capable.

'Pray do not concern yourself,' said Gertrude. 'I can
assure you Mr. Tudor will manage very well for himself—
but should any misfortune happen to him he will not, you
may be certain, attribute it to Lord Gaberlunzie.'

'I am told that Sir Gregory is most opposed to it,'
continued Mrs. Val. 'I heard that from Mr. Neverbend,
who is altogether in Sir Gregory's confidence—did not
you, my dears ? ' and she turned round to the sisters of
Fidus for confirmation.

'I heard my brother say that as Mr. Tudor's office is
not parliamentary but permanent, and as he has to attend
from ten till four—— '

'Alaric has not to attend from ten till four,' said
Gertrude, who could not endure the idea that her husband
should be ranked with common clerks, like Fidus Neverbend.

'Oh, I didn't know,' said Lactimel, meekly. 'Perhaps
Fidus only meant that as it is one of those offices where
the people have something to do, the commissioners
couldn't be in their offices and in Parliament at the same
time.'

'I did understand,' said Ugolina, 'that Sir Gregory
Hardlines had put his veto upon it ; but I must confess
that it is a subject which I have not sufficiently studied to
enable me—— '

'It's £1,200 a year, isn't it ? ' asked the bride.

'Twelve hundred pounds a year,' said her mother—
'a very serious consideration when there is no private

fortune to back it, on either side. Now if it were
Victoire——'

'He couldn't sit in Parliament, ma, because he's an
alien—only for that I shouldn't think of his doing anything else.'

'Perhaps that may be altered before long,' said Lactimel, graciously.

'If Jews are to be admitted,' said Ugolina, 'who
certainly belong to an alien nation; a nation expressly
set apart and separated from all people—a peculiar nation
distinct from all others, I for one cannot discern——'

What Ugolina could or could not discern about the
Jews was communicated perhaps to Madame Jaquêtanàpe
or to Lactimel, but not to Gertrude or to Mrs. Val; for
the latter, taking Gertrude apart into a corner as it were
of the sofa, began confidentially to repeat to her her fears
about her husband.

'I see, my dear,' said she, 'that you don't like my
speaking about it.'

'Upon my word,' said Gertrude, 'I am very indifferent
about it. But would it not be better if you said what you
have to say to my husband?'

'I intend to do so. I intend to do that also. But
I know that a wife ought to have influence over her
husband, and I believe that you have influence over
yours.'

'Not the least,' said Gertrude, who was determined to
contradict Mrs. Val in everything.

'I am sorry to hear it,' said Mrs. Val, who among all
her excellent acquirements, did not possess that specially
excellent one of understanding repartee. 'I am very
sorry to hear it, and I shall certainly speak to him the
more seriously on that account. I think I have some
influence over him: at any rate I ought to have.'

'I dare say you have,' said Gertrude; 'Alaric always
says that no experience is worth anything that is not
obtained by years.'

Mrs. Val at least understood this, and continued her
lecture with some additional severity. 'Well, my dear,
I am glad he has so much wisdom. But what I was
going to say is this: you know how much we have at stake

with Mr. Tudor—what a very large sum of Clementina's
money lies in his hands.   Now I really should not have
consented to the arrangement had I thought it possible
that Mr. Tudor would have given up his income with the
idea of going into Parliament.   It wouldn't have been
right or prudent of me to do so.   I have the greatest
opinion of your husband's talents and judgement, or
I should not of course have entrusted him with the management of Clementina's fortune ; but I really shall think
it right to make some change if this project of his goes on.'
    'Why, what is it you suspect ?' said Gertrude.   'Do
you think that Mr. Tudor intends to use your daughter's
income if he loses a portion of his own ?   I never heard
such a thing in my life.'
    'Hush ! my dear—gently—I would not for worlds let
Clementina hear a word of this ; it might disturb her
young happiness.   She is so charmed with her husband ;
her married life is so fortunate ; Victoire is so—so—so
everything that we all wish, that I would not for the world
breathe in her hearing a shadow of a suspicion.'
    'Good gracious !   Mrs. Scott, what do you mean ?
Suspicion !—what suspicion ?   Do you suspect my husband
of robbing you ?'   Oh, Gertrude ; poor Gertrude ! she
was doomed to know it all before long.
    'Oh dear, no,' said Mrs. Val ; 'nothing of the kind,
I assure you.   Of course we suspect nothing of the sort.
But one does like to have one's money in safe hands.   Of
course Mr. Tudor wouldn't have been chosen as trustee
if he hadn't had a good income of his own ; and look here,
my dear,'—and Mrs. Val whispered very confidentially,—
'Mr. Tudor we all know is greatly concerned in this bridge
that the committee is sitting about ; and he and my
brother-in-law, Undecimus, are always dealing in shares.
Gentlemen do, I know ; and therefore I don't say that
there is anything against it.   But considering all, I hope
Mr. Tudor won't take it ill if we propose to change our
trustee.'
    'I am very certain he will not,' said Gertrude.   'It is
a laborious business, and he will be glad enough to be rid
of it.   When he was asked to accept it, he thought it
would be ill-natured to refuse ; I am certain, however, he

will be very glad to give up the work to any other person
who may be appointed. I will be sure to tell him this
evening what you have said.'

'You need not trouble yourself to do that,' said Mrs.
Val. 'I shall see him myself before long.'

'It will be no trouble,' said Gertrude, very indignantly,
for she was very angry, and had, as she thought, great
cause for anger. 'I shall certainly think it my duty to do
so after what has passed. Of course you will now take
steps to relieve him as soon as possible.'

'You have taken me up a great deal too quick, my
dear,' said Mrs. Val. 'I did not intend—— '

'Oh—one can't be too quick on such a matter as this,'
said Gertrude. 'When confidence is once lost between
two persons it is better that the connexion which has
grown out of confidence should be put an end to as soon
as possible.'

'Lost confidence! I said nothing about lost confidence!'

'Alaric will so understand it, I am quite sure; at any
rate I will tell him what you have said. Suspicion indeed!
who has dared to suspect him of anything not honest or
upright?'

Gertrude's eyes flashed with anger as she vindicated
her absent lord. Mrs. Val had been speaking with bated
breath, so that no one had heard her but she to whom she
was speaking; but Gertrude had been unable so to confine
her answers, and as she made her last reply Madame
Jaquêtanàpe and the Misses Neverbend were all ears.

'Ha, ha, ha!' laughed Mrs. Val. 'Upon my word, my
dear, it is amusing to hear you take it up. However,
I assure you I meant nothing but what was kind and
friendly. Come, Clementina, we have been sitting here
a most unconscionable time. Will you allow me, my dear,
to ring for my carriage?'

'Mamma,' said Clem, 'have you asked Mrs. Tudor to
our little dance?'

'No, my dear; I have left that for you to do. It's
your party, you know—but I sincerely hope Mrs. Tudor
will come.'

'Oh yes,' said Clementina, the tongue of whose eloquence

was now loosened. 'You must come, Mrs. Tudor; indeed you must. It will be so charming; just a few nice people, you know, and nothing more.'

'Thank you,' said Gertrude; 'but I never dance now.' She had inwardly resolved that nothing should ever induce her again to enter Mrs. Val's house.

'Oh, but you must come,' said Clementina. 'It will be so charming. We only mean to dance one kind of dance—that new thing they have just brought over from Spain—the Contrabandista. It is a polka step, only very quick, and you take every other turn by yourself; so you have to take your partner up and let him go as quick as possible. You don't know how charming it is, and it will be all the rage. We are to have the music out in the street, just as they have in Spain.'

'It would be much too difficult for me,' said Gertrude.

'It is difficult,' said the enthusiastic Clem; 'but Victoire gives us lessons in it everyday from twelve to two—doesn't he, Ugolina?'

'I'm afraid I shouldn't have time to go to school,' said Gertrude.

'Oh, it doesn't take much time—six or seven or eight lessons will do it pretty well. I have almost learnt it already, and Ugolina is coming on very fast. Lactimel is not quite so perfect. She has learnt the step, but she cannot bring herself to let Victoire go quick enough. Do come, and bring Mr. Tudor with you.'

'As he has not to attend from ten till four, he could come and take lessons too,' said Lactimel, who, now that she was no longer a hanger-on of Gertrude's, could afford to have her little revenge.

'That would be delightful,' said Clem. 'Mr. Charles Tudor does come in sometimes at twelve o'clock, and I think he does it almost as well as Victoire.'

Gertrude, however, would go neither to the rehearsals nor to the finished performance; and as Mrs. Val's men had by this time been induced to leave the beershop, the whole party went away, leaving Gertrude to her meditations.

CHAPTER XXXVI

TICKLISH STOCK

ALARIC returned from his office worn and almost as wretched as he had been on the day before. He had spent a miserable day. In the morning Sir Gregory had asked him whether he had finally made up his mind to address the electors of Strathbogy. 'No, not finally,' said Alaric, ' but I think I shall do so.'

'Then I must tell you, Tudor,' said Sir Gregory, speaking more in sorrow than in anger, 'that you will not have my countenance. I cannot but think also that you are behaving with ingratitude.' Alaric prepared to make some petulant answer, but Sir Gregory, in the meantime, left the room.

Every one was falling away from him. He felt inclined to rush after Sir Gregory, and promise to be guided in this matter solely by him, but his pride prevented him : though he was no longer sanguine and confident as he had been a week ago, still his ambition was high. 'Those who play brag must brag it out, or they will lose their money.' This had been said by Undy ; but it was not the less true on that account. Alaric felt that he was playing brag, and that his only game was to brag it out.

He walked home slowly through the Parks. His office and house were so circumstanced that, though they were some two miles distant, he could walk from one to the other almost without taking his feet off the grass. This had been the cause of great enjoyment to him ; but now he sauntered on with his hands behind his back, staring straight before him, with fixed eyes, going by his accustomed route, but never thinking for a moment where he was. The time was gone when he could watch the gambols of children, smile at the courtships of nursery-maids, watch the changes in the dark foliage of the trees, and bend from his direct path hither and thither to catch the effects of distant buildings, and make for his eye half-

rural landscapes in the middle of the metropolis. No
landscapes had beauty for him now ; the gambols even of
his own baby were unattractive to him ; leaves might bud
forth and flourish and fall without his notice. How went
the share-market ? that was the only question that had
an interest for him. The dallyings of Capel Court were
the only courtships that he now cared to watch.

And with what a terribly eager eye had he now to watch
them ! If his shares went up quickly, at once, with an
unprecedented success, he might possibly be saved. That
was all. But if they did not—— ! Such was the phase
of life under which at the present moment it behoved him
to exist.

And then, when he reached his home, how was he
welcomed ? With all the fond love which a loving wife
can show ; so much at least was his ; but before he had
felt the sweetness of her caresses, before he had acknowledged how great was the treasure that he possessed, forth
from her eager lips had come the whole tale of Mrs. Val's
impertinence.

'I will never see her again, Alaric ! never ; she talked
of her daughter's money, and said something of suspicion !'
Suspicion ! Gertrude's eye again flashed fire with anger ;
and she all but stamped with her little foot upon the
ground. Suspicion ! suspect him, her husband, the choice
of her heart, her Alaric, the human god whom she worshipped ! suspect him of robbery ! her lord, her heart,
her soul, the strong staff on which she leaned so securely,
with such true feminine confidence ! Suspect him of
common vile dishonesty !—'You will never ask me to
see her again—will you, Alaric ?'

What was he to say to her ? how was he to bear this ?
His heart yearned to tell her all ; he longed for the luxury
of having one bosom to whom he could entrust his misery,
his slight remaining hope. But how could he himself, at
one blow, by one word, destroy the high and polished
shaft on which she whom he loved had placed him ? He
could not do it. He would suffer by himself ; hope by
himself, cease to hope by himself, and endure all, till either
his sufferings or his hopes should be over.

He had to pretend that he was indignant at Mrs. Val's

interference ; he had to counterfeit the feelings of outraged
honour, which was so natural to Gertrude. This he failed
to do well. Had he been truly honest—had that woman's
suspicion really done him injustice—he would have received his wife's tidings with grave displeasure, and have
simply resolved to acquit himself as soon as possible of
the disagreeable trust which had been reposed in him.
But such was not now his conduct. He contented himself by calling Mrs. Val names, and pretended to laugh at
her displeasure.

'But you will give up this trust, won't you ?' said
Gertrude.

'I will think about it,' said he. 'Before I do anything
I must consult old Figgs. Things of that kind can't be
put out of their course by the spleen of an old woman like
Mrs. Val.'

'Oh, Alaric, I do so wish you had had nothing to do
with these Scotts !'

'So do I,' said he, bitterly ; 'I hate them—but, Gertrude, don't talk about them now ; my head aches, and
I am tired.'

He sat at home the whole evening ; and though he was
by no means gay, and hardly affectionate in his demeanour
to her, yet she could not but feel that some good effect
had sprung from his recent dislike to the Scotts, since it
kept him at home with her. Lately he had generally
spent his evenings at his club. She longed to speak to
him of his future career, of his proposed seat in Parliament,
of his office-work ; but he gave her no encouragement to
speak of such things, and, as he pleaded that he was ill,
she left him in quiet on the sofa.

On the next morning he again went to his office, and in
the course of the morning a note was brought to him
from Undy. It ran as follows :—

'My dear Tudor,

'Is Val to have the shares ? Let me have a line by
the bearer.

'Yours ever,

'U. S.'

To this he replied by making an appointment to meet
Undy before dinner at his own office.

At the time fixed Undy came, and was shown by the
sole remaining messenger into Alaric's private room. The
two shook hands together in their accustomed way. Undy
smiled good-humouredly, as he always did ; and Alaric
maintained his usual composed and uncommunicative
look.

'Well,' said Undy, sitting down, 'how about those
shares ? '

'I am glad you have come,' said Alaric, 'because I want
to speak to you with some earnestness.'

'I am quite in earnest myself,' said Undy ; 'and so, by
G—, is Val. I never saw a fellow more in earnest—nor
yet apparently more hard up. I hope you have the shares
ready, or else a cheque for the amount.'

'Look here, Undy ; if my doing this were the only
means of saving both you and me from rotting in gaol, by
the Creator that made me I would not do it ! '

'I don't know that it will have much effect upon me,
one way or the other,' said Undy, coolly ; 'but it seems to
me to be the only way that can save yourself from some
such fate. Shall I tell you what the clauses are of this
new bill about trust property ? '

'I know the clauses well enough ; I know my own
position ; and I know yours also.'

'D— your impudence ! ' said Undy ; 'how do you
dare to league me with your villainy ? Have I been the
girl's trustee ? have I drawn, or could I have drawn,
a shilling of her money ? I tell you, Tudor, you are in the
wrong box. You have one way of escape, and one only.
I don't want to ruin you ; I'll save you if I can ; I think
you have treated the girl in a most shameful way, nevertheless I'll save you if I can ; but mark this, if this money
be not at once produced I cannot save you.'

Alaric felt that he was covered with cold perspiration.
His courage did not fail him ; he would willingly have
taken Undy by the throat, could his doing so have done
himself or his cause any good ; but he felt that he was
nearly overset by the cool deep villainy of his companion.

'I have treated the girl badly—very badly,' he said,

after a pause; 'whether or no you have done so too
I leave to your own conscience, if you have a conscience.
I do not now mean to accuse you; but you may know
this for certain—my present anxiety is to restore to her
that which I have taken from her; and for no earthly
consideration—not to save my own wife—will I increase
the deficiency.'

'Why, man, what nonsense you talk—as if I did not
know all the time that you have your pocket full of these
shares.'

'Whatever I have, I hold for her. If I could succeed
in getting out of your hands enough to make up the full
sum that I owe her——'

'You will succeed in getting nothing from me. When
I borrowed £5,000 from you, it was not understood that
I was to be called upon for the money in three or four
months' time.'

'Now look here, Scott; you have threatened me with
ruin and a prison, and I will not say but your threats may
possibly prove true. It may be that I am ruined; but, if
I fall, you shall share my fall.'

'That's false,' said Undy. 'I am free to hold my head
before the world, which you are not. I have done nothing
to bring me to shame.'

'Nothing to bring you to shame, and yet you would now
have me give you a further portion of this girl's money!'

'Nothing! I care nothing about the girl's money.
I have not touched it, nor do I want to touch it. I bring
you a message from my brother; you have ample means
of your own to comply with his request.'

'Then tell your brother,' said Alaric, now losing all
control over his temper—'tell your brother, if indeed he
have any part in this villany—tell your brother that if
it were to save me from the gallows, he should not have
a shilling. I have done very badly in this matter; I have
acted shamefully, and I am ashamed, but——'

'Oh, I want to hear none of your rhapsodies,' said
Undy. 'If you will not now do what I ask you, I may as
well go, and you may take the consequences;' and he
lifted his hat as though preparing to take his leave.

'But you shall hear me,' said Alaric, rising quickly

from his seat, and standing between Undy and the door. Undy very coolly walked to the bell and rang it. 'I have much to answer for,' continued Alaric, 'but I would not have your sin on my soul, I would not be as black as you are, though, by being so, I could save myself with certainty from all earthly punishment.'

As he finished, the messenger opened the door. 'Show Mr. Scott out,' said Alaric.

'By, by,' said Undy. 'You will probably hear from Mrs. Val and her daughter to-morrow,' and so saying he walked jauntily along the passage, and went jauntily to his dinner at his club. It was part of his philosophy that nothing should disturb the even tenor of his way, or interfere with his animal comforts. He was at the present moment over head and ears in debt; he was playing a game which, in all human probability, would end in his ruin; the ground was sinking beneath his feet on every side; and yet he thoroughly enjoyed his dinner. Alaric Scott could not make such use of his philosophy. Undy Scott might be the worse man of the two, but he was the better philosopher.

Not on the next day, or on the next, did Alaric hear from Mrs. Val, but on the following Monday he got a note from her begging him to call in Ebury Street. She underscored every line of it once or twice, and added, in a postscript, that he would, she *was sure, at once acknowledge* the NECESSITY of her *request*, as she *wished to communicate* with *him* on the *subject* of her DAUGHTER'S FORTUNE.

Alaric immediately sent an answer to her by a messenger. 'My dear Mrs. Scott,' said he, 'I am very sorry that an engagement prevents my going to you this evening; but, as I judge by your letter, and by what I have heard from Gertrude, that you are anxious about this trust arrangement, I will call at ten to-morrow morning on my way to the office.'

Having written and dispatched this, he sat for an hour leaning with his elbows on the table and his hands clasped, looking with apparent earnestness at the rows of books which stood inverted before him, trying to make up his mind as to what step he should now take.

Not that he sat an hour undisturbed. Every five

minutes some one would come knocking at the door ; the
name of some aspirant to the Civil Service would be
brought to him, or the card of some influential gentleman
desirous of having a little job perpetrated in favour of
his own peculiarly interesting, but perhaps not very
highly-educated, young candidate. But on this morning
Alaric would see no one ; to every such intruder he sent
a reply that he was too deeply engaged at the present
moment to see any one. After one he would be at
liberty, &c., &c.

And so he sat and looked at the books ; but he could
in nowise make up his mind. He could in nowise bring
himself even to try to make up his mind—that is, to
make any true effort towards doing so. His thoughts would
would run off from him, not into the happy outer world,
but into a multitude of noisy, unpleasant paths, all
intimately connected with his present misery, but none
of which led him at all towards the conclusions at which
he would fain arrive. He kept on reflecting what Sir
Gregory would think when he heard of it ; what all those
clerks would say at the Weights and Measures, among
whom he had held his head so high ; what shouts there
would be among the navvies and other low pariahs of the
service ; how Harry Norman would exult—(but he did
not yet know Harry Norman) ;—how the Woodwards
would weep ; how Gertrude—and then as he thought of
that he bowed his head, for he could no longer endure the
open light of day. At one o'clock he was no nearer to any
decision than he had been when he reached his office.

At three he put himself into a cab, and was taken to
the city. Oh, the city, the weary city, where men go
daily to look for money, but find none ; where every
heart is eaten up by an accursed famishing after gold ;
where dark, gloomy banks come thick on each other, like
the black, ugly apertures to the realms below in a mining
district, each of them a separate little pit-mouth into hell.
Alaric went into the city, and found that the shares were
still rising. That imperturbable witness was still in the
chair at the committee, and men said that he was dis-
gusting the members by the impregnable endurance of
his hostility. A man who could answer 2,250 questions

without admitting anything must be a liar ! Such a one could convince no one ! And so the shares went on rising, rising, and rising, and Messrs. Blocks, Piles, and Cofferdam were buying up every share ; either doing that openly— or else selling on the sly.

Alaric found that he could at once realize £7,500. Were he to do this, there would be at any rate seven-eighths of his ward's fortune secure.

Might he not, in such a case, calculate that even Mrs. Val's heart would be softened, and that time would be allowed him to make up the small remainder ? Oh, but in such case he must tell Mrs. Val ; and could he calculate on her forbearance ? Might he not calculate with much more certainty on her love of triumphing ? Would he not be her slave if she had the keeping of his secret ? And why should he run so terrible a risk of destroying himself ? Why should he confide in Mrs. Val, and deprive himself of the power of ever holding up his head again, when, possibly, he might still run out his course with full sails, and bring his vessel into port, giving no knowledge to the world of the perilous state in which she had been thus ploughing the deep ? He need not, at any rate, tell everything to Mrs. Val at his coming visit on the morrow.

He consulted his broker with his easiest air of common concern as to his money ; and the broker gave him a dubious opinion. 'They may go a little higher, sir ; indeed I think they will. But they are ticklish stock, sir—uncommon ticklish. I should not like to hold many myself, sir.' Alaric knew that the man was right ; they were ticklish stock : but nevertheless he made up his mind to hold on a little longer.

He then got into another cab and went back to his office ; and as he went he began to bethink himself to whom of all his friends he might apply for such a loan as would enable him to make up this sum of money, if he sold his shares on the morrow. Captain Cuttwater was good for £1,000, but he knew that he could not get more from him. It would be bad borrowing, he thought, from Sir Gregory. Intimate as he had been with that great man, he knew nothing of his money concerns ; but he had always heard that Sir Gregory was a close man. Sir Warwick, his other colleague, was in easy circumstances; but then he had never been intimate with Sir Warwick. Norman—ah, if he had known Norman now, Norman would have pulled him through; but hope in that quarter there was, of course, none. Norman was gone, and Norman's place had been filled by Undy Scott! What could be done with Undy Scott he had already tried. Fidus Neverbend! he had a little money saved; but Fidus was not the man to do anything without security. He, he, Alaric Tudor, he, whose credit had stood, did stand, so high, did not know where to borrow, how to raise a thousand pounds; and yet he felt that had he not wanted it so sorely, he could have gotten it easily.

He was in a bad state for work when he got back to the office on that day. He was flurried, ill at ease, wretched, all but distracted; nevertheless he went rigidly to it, and remained there till late in the evening. He was a man generally blessed with excellent health; but now he suddenly found himself ill, and all but unable to accomplish the task which he had prescribed to himself. His head was heavy and his eyes weak, and he could not bring himself to think of the papers which lay before him.

Then at last he went home, and had another sad and solitary walk across the Parks, during which he vainly tried to rally himself again, and collect his energies for the work which he had to do. It was in such emergencies as this that he knew that it most behoved a man to fall back upon what manliness there might be within him; now was the time for him to be true to himself; he had often felt proud of his own energy of purpose; and now was the opportunity for him to use such energy, if his pride in this respect had not been all in vain.

Such were the lessons with which he endeavoured to strengthen himself, but it was in vain; he could not feel courageous—he could not feel hopeful—he could not do other than despair. When he got home, he again prostrated himself, again declared himself ill, again buried his face in his hands, and answered the affection of his wife by saying that a man could not always be cheerful, could not always laugh. Gertrude, though she was very far indeed from guessing the truth, felt that something extraordinary was the matter, and knew that her husband's uneasiness was connected with the Scotts.

He came down to dinner, and though he ate but little, he drank glass after glass of sherry. He thus gave himself courage to go out in the evening and face the world at his club. He found Undy there as he expected, but he had no conversation with him, though they did not absolutely cut each other. Alaric fancied that men stared at him, and sat apart by himself, afraid to stand up among talking circles, or to put himself forward as it was his wont to do. He himself avoided other men, and then felt that others were avoiding him. He took up one evening paper after another, pretending to read them, but hardly noticing a word that came beneath his eye: at last, however, a name struck him which riveted his attention, and he read the following paragraph, which was among many others, containing information as to the coming elections.

'STRATHBOGY.—We hear that Lord Gaberlunzie's eldest son will retire from this borough, and that his place will be filled by his brother, the Honourable Captain Valentine Scott. The family have been so long connected with Strathbogy by ties of friendship and near neighbourhood, and the mutual alliance has been so much to the taste of both parties, that no severance need be anticipated.'

Alaric's first emotion was one of anger at the whole Scott tribe, and his first resolve was to go down to Strathbogy and beat that inanimate fool, Captain Val, on his own ground; but he was not long in reflecting that, under his present circumstances, it would be madness in him to bring his name prominently forward in any quarrel with the Scott family. This disappointment he might at any rate bear; it would be well for him if this were all. He put the paper down with an affected air of easy composure, and walked home through the glaring gas-lights, still trying to think—still trying, but in vain, to come to some definite resolve.

And then on the following morning he went off to call on Mrs. Val. He had as yet told Gertrude nothing. When she asked him what made him start so early, he merely replied that he had business to do on his road. As he went, he had considerable doubt whether or no it would be better for him to break his word to Mrs. Val, and not go near her at all. In such event he might be sure that she would at once go to work and do her worst; but, nevertheless, he would gain a day, or probably two, and one or two days might do all that he required; whereas he could not see Mrs. Val without giving her some explanation, which if false would be discovered to be false, and if true would be self-condemnatory. He again, however, failed to decide, and at last knocked at Mrs. Val's door merely because he found himself there.

He was shown up into the drawing-room, and found, of course, Mrs. Val seated on a sofa; and he also found, which was not at all of course, Captain Val, on a chair on one side of the table, and M. Victoire Jacquêtanàpe on the other. Mrs. Val shook hands with him much in her usual way, but still with an air of importance in her face; the Frenchman was delighted to see M. Tudere, and the Honourable Val got up from his chair, said 'How do?' and then sat down again.

'I requested you to call, Mr. Tudor,' said Mrs. Val, opening her tale in a most ceremonious manner, 'because we all think it necessary to know somewhat more than has yet been told to us of the manner in which my daughter's money has been invested.'

Captain Val wiped his moustache with the middle finger of his right hand, by way of saying that he quite assented to his wife's proposition; and Victoire remarked that 'Madame was a leetle anxious, just a leetle anxious; not that anything could be wrong with M. Tudere, but because she was one excellent mamma.'

'I thought you knew, Mrs. Scott,' said Alaric, 'that your daughter's money is in the funds.'

'Then I may understand clearly that none of the amount so invested has been sold out or otherwise appropriated by you,' said Mrs. Val.

'Will you allow me to inquire what has given rise to these questions just at the present moment?' asked Alaric.

'Yes, certainly,' said Mrs. Val; 'rumours have reached

my husband—rumours which, I am happy to say, I do not believe—that my daughter's money has been used for purposes of speculation.' Whereupon Captain Val again wiped his upper lip, but did not find it necessary to speak.

'May I venture to ask Captain Scott from what source such rumours have reached him?'

'Ah—ha—what source? d—— lies, very likely; d—— lies, I dare say; but people do talk—eh—you know,' so much the eloquent embryo member for Strathbogy vouchsafed.

'And therefore, Mr. Tudor, you mustn't be surprised that we should ask you this question.'

'It is one simple, simple question,' said Victoire, 'and if M. Tudere will say that it is all right, I, for myself, will be satisfied.' The amiable Victoire, to tell the truth, was still quite satisfied to leave his wife's income in Alaric's hands, and would not have been at all satisfied to remove it to the hands of his respected step-papa-in-law, or even his admired mamma-in-law.

'When I undertook this trust,' said Alaric, 'which I did with considerable hesitation, I certainly did not expect to be subjected to any such cross-examination as this. I consider such questions as insults, and therefore I shall refuse to answer them. You, Mrs. Scott, have of course a right to look after your daughter's interests, as has M. Jaquêtanàpe to look after those of his wife; but I will not acknowledge that Captain Scott has any such right whatsoever, nor can I think that his conduct in this matter is disinterested;' and as he spoke he looked at Captain Val, but he might just as well have looked at the door; Captain Val only wiped his moustache with his finger once more. 'My answer to your inquiries, Mrs. Scott, is this—I shall not condescend to go into any details as to Madame Jaquêtanàpe's fortune with anyone but my co-trustee. I shall, however, on Saturday next, be ready to give up my trust to any other person who may be legally appointed to receive it, and will then produce all the property that has been entrusted to my keeping:' and so saying, Alaric got up and took his hat as though to depart.

'And do you mean to say, Mr. Tudor, that you will not answer my question?' said Mrs. Scott.

'I mean to say, most positively, that I will answer no questions,' said Alaric.

'Oh, confound, not do at all; d——,' said the captain. 'The girl's money all gone, and you won't answer questions!'

'No!' shouted Alaric, walking across the room till he closely confronted the captain. 'No—no—I will answer no questions that may be asked in your hearing. But that your wife's presence protects you, I would kick you down your own stairs before me.'

Captain Val retreated a step—he could retreat no more—and wiped his moustache with both hands at once. Mrs. Val screamed. Victoire took hold of the back of a chair, as though he thought it well that he should be armed in the general battle that was to ensue; and Alaric, without further speech, walked out of the room, and went away to his office.

'So you have given up Strathbogy?' said Sir Gregory to him, in the course of the day.

'I think I have,' said Alaric; 'considering all things, I believe it will be the best for me to do so.'

'Not a doubt of it,' said Sir Gregory—'not a doubt of it, my dear fellow;' and then Sir Gregory began to evince, by the cordiality of his official confidence, that he had fully taken Alaric back into his good graces. It was nothing to him that Strathbogy had given up Alaric instead of Alaric giving up Strathbogy. He was sufficiently pleased at knowing that the danger of his being supplanted by his own junior was over.

And then Alaric again went into the weary city, again made inquiries about his shares, and again returned to his office, and thence to his home.

But on his return to his office, he found lying on his table a note in Undy's handwriting, but not signed, in which he was informed that things would yet be well, if the required shares should be forthcoming on the following day.

He crumpled the note tight in his hand, and was about to fling it among the waste paper, but in a moment he thought better of it, and smoothing the paper straight, he folded it, and laid it carefully on his desk.

That day, on his visit into the city, he had found that the bridge shares had fallen to less than the value of their original purchase-money ; and that evening he told Gertrude everything. The author does not dare to describe the telling.

CHAPTER XXXVII

TRIBULATION

WE must now return for a short while to Surbiton Cottage. It was not so gay a place as it once had been ; merry laughter was not so often heard among the shrubbery walks, nor was a boat to be seen so often glancing in and out between the lawn and the adjacent island. The Cottage had become a demure, staid abode, of which Captain Cuttwater was in general the most vivacious inmate ; and yet there was soon to be marrying, and giving in marriage.

Linda's wedding-day had twice been fixed. That first-named had been postponed in consequence of the serious illness of Norman's elder brother. The life of that brother had been very different in its course from Harry's ; it had been dissipated at college in riotous living, and had since been stained with debauchery during the career of his early manhood in London. The consequence had been that his health had been broken down, and he was now tottering to an early grave.

Cuthbert Norman was found to be so ill when the day first named for Linda's marriage approached, that it had been thought absolutely necessary to postpone the ceremony. What amount of consolation Mrs. Woodward might have received from the knowledge that her daughter, by this young man's decease, would become Mrs. Norman of Normansgrove, we need not inquire ; but such consolation, if it existed at all, did not tend to dispel the feeling of sombre disappointment which such delay was sure to produce. The heir, however, rallied, and another day, early in August, was fixed.

Katie, the while, was still an invalid ; and, as such, puzzled all the experience of that very experienced medical gentleman, who has the best aristocratic practice in the neighbourhood of Hampton Court. He, and the London physician, agreed that her lungs were not affected ; but yet she would not get well. The colour would not come to her cheeks, the flesh would not return to her arms, nor the spirit of olden days shine forth in her eyes. She did not keep her bed, or confine herself to her room, but she went about the house with a slow, noiseless, gentle tread, so unlike the step of that Katie whom we once knew.

But that which was a mystery to the experienced medical gentleman, was no mystery to her mother. Mrs. Woodward well knew why her child was no longer rosy, plump, and *débonnaire*. As she watched her Katie move about so softly, as she saw her constant attempt to smile whenever her mother's eye was on her, that mother's heart almost gave way ; she almost brought herself to own that she would rather see her darling the wife of an idle, ruined spendthrift, than watch her thus drifting away to an early grave. These days were by no means happy days for Mrs. Woodward.

When that July day was fixed for Linda's marriage, certain invitations were sent out to bid the family friends to the wedding. These calls were not so numerous as they had been when Gertrude became a bride. No Sir Gregory was to come down from town, no gallant speech-makers from London clubs were to be gathered there, to wake the echoes of the opposite shore with matrimonial wit. Mrs. Woodward could not bear that her daughter should be married altogether, as it were, in the dark ; but for many considerations the guests were to be restricted in numbers, and the mirth was to be restrained and quiet.

When the list was made out, Katie saw it, and saw that Charley's name was not there.

'Mamma,' she said, touching her mother's arm in her sweet winning way, 'may not Charley come to Linda's wedding ? You know how fond Harry is of him : would not Harry wish that he should be here ? '

Mrs. Woodward's eyes immediately filled with tears, and she looked at her daughter, not knowing how to answer her. She had never spoken to Katie of her love; no word had ever passed between them on the subject which was now always nearest to the hearts of them both. Mrs. Woodward had much in her character, as a mother, that was excellent, nay, all but perfect; but she could not bring herself to question her own children as to the inward secrets of their bosoms. She knew not at once how to answer Katie's question; and so she looked up at her with wistful eyes, laden with tears.

'You may do so, mamma,' said Katie. Katie was already a braver woman than her mother. 'I think Harry would like it, and poor Charley will feel hurt at being left out; you may do it, mamma, if you like; it will not do any harm.'

Mrs. Woodward quite understood the nature of the promise conveyed in her daughter's assurance, and replied that Charley should be asked. He was asked, and promised, of course, to come. But when the wedding was postponed, when the other guests were put off, he also was informed that his attendance at Hampton was not immediately required; and so he still remained a stranger to the Cottage.

And then after a while another day was named, the guests, and Charley with them, were again invited, and Norman was again assured that he should be made happy. But, alas! his hopes were again delusive. News arrived at Surbiton Cottage which made it indispensable that the marriage should be again postponed, news worse than any which had ever yet been received there, news which stunned them all, and made it clear to them that this year was no time for marrying. Alaric had been arrested. Alaric, their own Gertrude's own husband, their son-in-law and brother-in-law, the proud, the high, the successful, the towering man of the world, Alaric had been arrested, and was to be tried for embezzling the money of his ward.

These fatal tidings were brought to Hampton by Harry Norman himself; how they were received we must now endeavour to tell.

But that it would be tedious we might describe the

amazement with which that news was received at the
Weights and Measures. Though the great men at the
Weights were jealous of Alaric, they were not the less
proud of him. They had watched him rise with a certain
amount of displeasure, and yet they had no inconsiderable
gratification in boasting that two of the Magi, the two
working Magi of the Civil Service, had been produced by
their own establishment. When therefore tidings reached
them that Tudor had been summoned in a friendly way
to Bow Street, that he had there passed a whole morning,
and that the inquiry had ended in his temporary suspen-
sion from his official duties, and in his having to provide
two bailsmen, each for £1,000, as security that he would
on a certain day be forthcoming to stand his trial at the
Old Bailey for defrauding his ward—when, I say, these
tidings were carried from room to room at the Weights
and Measures, the feelings of surprise were equalled by
those of shame and disappointment.

No one knew who brought this news to the Weights
and Measures. No one ever does know how such tidings
fly; one of the junior clerks had heard it from a messenger, to whom it had been told downstairs; then another
messenger, who had been across to the Treasury Chambers
with an immediate report as to a projected change in the
size of the authorized butter-firkin, heard the same thing,
and so the news by degrees was confirmed.

But all this was not sufficient for Norman. As soon as
the rumour reached him, he went off to Bow Street, and
there learnt the actual truth as it has been above stated.
Alaric was then there, and the magistrates had decided
on requiring bail; he had, in fact, been committed.

It would be dreadful that the Woodwards should first
hear all this from the lips of a stranger, and this reflection
induced Norman at once to go to Hampton; but it was
dreadful, also, to find himself burdened with the task of
first telling such tidings. When he found himself knocking
at the Cottage door he was still doubtful how he might
best go through the work he had before him.

He found that he had a partial reprieve; but then it
was so partial that it would have been much better for
him to have had no such reprieve at all. Mrs. Woodward

was at Sunbury with Linda, and no one was at home but
Katie. What was he to do ? was he to tell Katie ? or
was he to pretend that all was right, that no special
business had brought him unexpectedly to Hampton ?

'Oh, Harry, Linda will be so unhappy,' said Katie as
soon as she saw him. 'They have gone to dine at Sunbury,
and they won't be home till ten or eleven. Uncle Bat
dined early with me, and he has gone to Hampton Court.
Linda will be so unhappy. But, good gracious, Harry,
is there anything the matter ? '

'Mrs. Woodward has not heard from Gertrude to-day,
has she ? '

'No—not a word—Gertrude is not ill, is she ? Oh, do
tell me,' said Katie, who now knew that there was some
misfortune to be told.

'No ; Gertrude is not ill.'

'Is Alaric ill, then ? Is there anything the matter with
Alaric ? '

'He is not ill,' said Norman, ' but he is in some trouble.
I came down as I thought your mother should be told.'

So much he said, but would say no more. In this he
probably took the most unwise course that was open to
him. He might have held his tongue altogether, and let
Katie believe that love alone had brought him down, as it
had done so often before ; or he might have told her all,
feeling sure that all must be told her before long. But he
did neither ; he left her in suspense, and the consequence
was that before her mother's return she was very ill.

It was past eleven before the fly was heard in which
Linda and her mother returned home. Katie had then
gone upstairs, but not to bed. She had seated herself in
the armchair in her mother's dressing-room, and sitting
there waited till she should be told by her mother what
had occurred. When the sound of the wheels caught her
ears, she came to the door of the room and held it in her
hand that she might learn what passed. She heard
Linda's sudden and affectionate greeting ; she heard
Mrs. Woodward's expression of gratified surprise ; and
then she heard also Norman's solemn tone, by which, as
was too clear, all joy, all gratification, was at once suppressed. Then she heard the dining-room door close, and

she knew that he was telling his tale to Linda and her mother.

O the misery of that next hour ! For an hour they remained there talking, and Katie knew nothing of what they were talking ; she knew only that Norman had brought unhappiness to them all. A dozen different ideas passed across her mind. First she thought that Alaric was dismissed, then that he was dead ; was it not possible that Harry had named Alaric's name to deceive her ? might not this misfortune, whatever it was, be with Charley ? might not he be dead ? Oh ! better so than the other. She knew, and said as much to herself over and over again ; but she did not the less feel that his death must involve her own also.

At last the dining-room door opened, and she heard her mother's step on the stairs. Her heart beat so that she could hardly support herself. She did not get up, but sat quite quiet, waiting for the tidings which she knew that she should now hear. Her mother's face, when she entered the room, nearly drove her to despair ; Mrs. Woodward had been crying, bitterly, violently, convulsively crying ; and when one has reached the age of forty, the traces of such tears are not easily effaced even from a woman's cheek.

'Mamma, mamma, what is it ? pray, pray tell me ; oh ! mamma, what is it ? ' said Katie, jumping up and rushing into her mother's arms.

'Oh ! Katie,' said Mrs. Woodward, ' why are you not in bed ? Oh ! my darling, I wish you were in bed ; I do so wish you were in bed—my child, my child ! ' and, seating herself in the nearest chair, Mrs. Woodward again gave herself up to uncontrolled weeping.

Then Linda came up with the copious tears still streaming down her face. She made no effort to control them ; at her age tears are the easiest resource in time of grief. Norman had kept her back a moment to whisper one word of love, and she then followed her mother into the room.

Katie was now kneeling at her mother's feet. ' Linda,' she said, with more quietness than either of the others was able to assume, ' what has happened ? what makes

mamma so unhappy ? Has anything happened to Alaric ?'
But Linda was in no state to tell anything.

'Do tell me, mamma,' said Katie; 'do tell me all
at once. Has anything—anything happened to—to
Charley ?'

'Oh, it is worse than that, a thousand times worse than
that !' said Mrs. Woodward, who, in the agony of her own
grief, became for the instant ungenerous.

Katie's blood rushed back to her heart, and for a
moment her own hand relaxed the hold which she had on
that of her mother. She had never spoken of her love ;
for her mother's sake she had been silent ; for her mother's
sake she had determined to suffer and be silent—now, and
ever ! Well ; she would bear this also. It was but for
a moment she relaxed her hold ; and then again she
tightened her fingers round her mother's hand, and held
it in a firmer grasp. 'It is Alaric, then ?' she said.

'God forgive me,' said Mrs. Woodward, speaking
through her sobs—'God forgive me ! I am a broken-
hearted woman, and say I know not what. My Katie,
my darling, my best of darlings—will you forgive
me ?'

'Oh, mamma,' said Katie, kissing her mother's hands,
and her arms, and the very hem of her garment, 'oh,
mamma, do not speak so. But I wish I knew what this
sorrow is, so that I might share it with you ; may I not
be told, mamma ? is it about Alaric ?'

'Yes, Katie. Alaric is in trouble.'

'What trouble—is he ill ?'

'No—he is not ill. It is about money.'

'Has he been arrested ?' asked Katie, thinking of
Charley's misfortune. 'Could not Harry get him out ?
Harry is so good ; he would do anything, even for Alaric,
when he is in trouble.'

'He will do everything for him that he can,' said Linda,
through her tears.

'He has not been arrested,' said Mrs. Woodward ; 'he
is still at home ; but he is in trouble about Miss Golightly's
money—and—and he is to be tried.'

'Tried,' said Katie ; 'tried like a criminal !'

Katie might well express herself as horrified. Yes, he

had to be tried like a criminal; tried as pickpockets, housebreakers, and shoplifters are tried, and for a somewhat similar offence; with this difference, however, that pickpockets, housebreakers, and shoplifters, are seldom educated men, and are in general led on to crime by want. He was to be tried for the offence of making away with some of Miss Golightly's money for his own purposes. This was explained to Katie, with more or less perspicuity; and then Gertrude's mother and sisters lifted up their voices together and wept.

He might, it is true, be acquitted; they would none of them believe him to be guilty, though they all agreed that he had probably been imprudent; but then the public shame of the trial! the disgrace which must follow such an accusation! What a downfall was here! 'Oh, Gertrude! oh, Gertrude!' sobbed Mrs. Woodward; and indeed, at that time, it did not fare well with Gertrude.

It was very late before Mrs. Woodward and her daughters went to bed that night; and then Katie, though she did not specially complain, was very ill. She had lately received more than one wound, which was still unhealed; and now this additional blow, though she apparently bore it better than the others, altogether upset her. When the morning came, she complained of headache, and it was many days after that before she left her bed.

But Mrs. Woodward was up early. Indeed, she could hardly be said to have been in bed at all; for though she had lain down for an hour or two, she had not slept. Early in the morning she knocked at Harry's door, and begged him to come out to her. He was not long in obeying her summons, and soon joined her in the little breakfast parlour.

'Harry,' said she, 'you must go and see Alaric.'

Harry's brow grew black. On the previous evening he had spoken of Alaric without bitterness, nay, almost with affection; of Gertrude he had spoken with the truest brotherly love; he had assured Mrs. Woodward that he would do all that was in his power for them; that he would spare neither his exertions nor his purse.

He had a truer idea than she had of what might probably be the facts of the case, and was prepared, by all the means at his disposal, to help his sister-in-law, if such aid would help her. But he had not thought of seeing Alaric.

'I do not think it would do any good,' said he.

'Yes, Harry, it will; it will do the greatest good; whom else can I get to see him? who else can find out and let us know what really is required of us, what we ought to do? I would do it myself, but I could not understand it; and he would never trust us sufficiently to tell me all the truth.'

'We will make Charley go to him. He will tell everything to Charley, if he will to anyone.'

'We cannot trust Charley; he is so thoughtless, so imprudent. Besides, Harry, I cannot tell everything to Charley as I can to you. If there be any deficiency in this woman's fortune, of course it must be made good; and in that case I must raise the money. I could not arrange all this with Charley.'

'There cannot, I think, be very much wanting,' said Norman, who had hardly yet realized the idea that Alaric had actually used his ward's money for his own purposes. 'He has probably made some bad investment, or trusted persons that he should not have trusted. My small property is in the funds, and I can get the amount at a moment's notice. I do not think there will be any necessity to raise more money than that. At any rate, whatever happens, you must not touch your own income; think of Katie.'

'But, Harry—dear, good, generous Harry—you are so good, so generous! But, Harry, we need not talk of that now. You will see him, though, won't you?'

'It will do no good,' said Harry; 'we have no mutual trust in each other.'

'Do not be unforgiving, Harry, now that he requires forgiveness.'

'If he does require forgiveness, Mrs. Woodward, if it shall turn out that he has been guilty, God knows that I will forgive him. I trust this may not be the case; and it would be useless for me to thrust myself upon him now, when a few days may replace us again in our present relations to each other.'

'I don't understand you, Harry; why should there always be a quarrel between two brothers, between the husbands of two sisters? I know you mean to be kind, I know you are most kind, most generous; but why should you be so stern?'

'What I mean is this—if I find him in adversity, I shall be ready to offer him my hand; it will then be for him to say whether he will take it. But if the storm blow over, in such case I would rather that we should remain as we are.'

Norman talked of forgiveness, and accused himself of no want of charity in this respect. He had no idea that his own heart was still hard as the nether millstone against Alaric Tudor. But yet such was the truth. His money he could give; he could give also his time and mind, he could lend his best abilities to rescue his former friend and his own former love from misfortune. He could do this, and he thought therefore that he was forgiving; but there was no forgiveness in such assistance. There was generosity in it, for he was ready to part with his money; there was kindness of heart, for he was anxious to do good to his fellow-creature; but there were with these both pride and revenge. Alaric had out-topped him in everything, and it was sweet to Norman's pride that his hand should be the one to raise from his sudden fall the man who had soared so high above him. Alaric had injured him, and what revenge is so perfect as to repay gross injuries by great benefits? Is it not thus that we heap coals of fire on our enemies' heads? Not that Norman indulged in thoughts such as these; not that he resolved thus to gratify his pride, thus to indulge his revenge. He was unconscious of his own sin, but he was not the less a sinner.

'No,' said he, 'I will not see him myself; it will do no good.'

Mrs. Woodward found that it was useless to try to bend him. That, indeed, she knew from a long experience. It was then settled that she should go up to Gertrude that morning, travelling up to town together with Norman, and that when she had learned from her daughter, or from Alaric—if Alaric would talk to her about his concerns—what was really the truth of the matter, she should come to Norman's office, and tell him what it would be necessary for him to do.

And then the marriage was again put off. This, in itself, was a great misery, as young ladies who have just been married, or who may now be about to be married, will surely own. The words 'put off' are easily written, the necessity of such a 'put off' is easily arranged in the pages of a novel; an enforced delay of a month or two in an affair which so many folk willingly delay for so many years, sounds like a slight thing; but, nevertheless, a matrimonial 'put off' is, under any circumstances, a great grief. To have to counter-write those halcyon notes which have given glad promise of the coming event; to pack up and put out of sight, and, if possible, out of mind, the now odious finery with which the house has for the last weeks been strewed; to give the necessary information to the pastry-cook, from whose counter the sad tidings will be disseminated through all the neighbourhood; to annul the orders which have probably been given for rooms and horses for the happy pair; to live, during the coming interval, a mark for Pity's unpitying finger; to feel, and know, and hourly calculate, how many slips there may be between the disappointed lip and the still distant cup; all these things in themselves make up a great grief, which is hardly lightened by the knowledge that they have been caused by a still greater grief.

These things had Linda now to do, and the poor girl had none to help her in the doing of them. A few hurried words were spoken on that morning between her and Norman, and for the second time she set to work to put off her wedding. Katie, the meantime, lay sick in bed, and Mrs. Woodward had gone to London to learn the worst and to do the best in this dire affliction that had come upon them.

CHAPTER XXXVIII

ALARIC TUDOR TAKES A WALK

THERE is, undoubtedly, a propensity in human love to attach itself to excellence; but it has also, as undoubtedly, a propensity directly antagonistic to this, and which teaches it to put forth its strongest efforts in favour of inferiority. Watch any fair flock of children in which there may be one blighted bud, and you will see that that blighted one is the mother's darling. What 'filial affection is ever so strong as that evinced by a child for a parent in misfortune? Even among the rough sympathies of schoolboys, the cripple, the sickly one, or the orphan without a home, will find the warmest friendship and a stretch of kindness. Love, that must bow and do reverence to superiority, can protect and foster inferiority; and what is so sweet as to be able to protect?

Gertrude's love for her husband had never been so strong as when she learnt that that love must now stand in the place of all other sympathies, of all other tenderness. Alaric told her of his crime, and in his bitterness he owned that he was no longer worthy of her love. She answered by opening her arms to him with more warmth than ever, and bidding him rest his weary head upon her breast. Had they not taken each other for better or for worse? had not their bargain been that they would be happy together if such should be their lot, or sad together if God should so will it?—and would she be the first to cry off from such a bargain?

It seldom happens that a woman's love is quenched by a man's crime. Women in this respect are more enduring than men; they have softer sympathies, and less acute, less selfish, appreciation of the misery of being joined to that which has been shamed. It was not many hours since Gertrude had boasted to herself of the honour and honesty of her lord, and tossed her head with defiant scorn when a breath of suspicion had been muttered against

his name. Then she heard from his own lips the whole
truth, learnt that that odious woman had only muttered
what she soon would have a right to speak out openly,
knew that fame and honour, high position and pride of
life, were all gone ; and then in that bitter hour she felt
that she had never loved him as she did then.

He had done wrong, he had sinned grievously ; but no
sooner did she acknowledge so much than she acknowledged also that a man may sin and yet not be all sinful ;
that glory may be tarnished, and yet not utterly destroyed;
that pride may get a fall, and yet live to rise again. He
had sinned, and had repented ; and now to her eyes he
was again as pure as snow. Others would now doubt him,
that 'must needs be the case ; but she would never doubt
him ; no, not a whit the more in that he had once fallen.
He should still be the cynosure of her eyes, the pride of
her heart, the centre of her hopes. Marina said of her
lord, when he came to her shattered in limb, from the
hands of the torturer—

> ' I would not change
> My exiled, mangled, persecuted husband,
> Alive or dead, for prince or paladin,
> In story or in fable, with a world
> To back his suit.'

Gertrude spoke to herself in the same language. She
would not have changed her Alaric, branded with infamy
as he now was, or soon would be, for the proudest he that
carried his head high among the proud ones of the earth.
Such is woman's love ; such is the love of which a man's
heart is never capable !

Alaric's committal had taken place very much in the
manner in which it was told at the Weights and Measures.
He had received a note from one of the Bow Street
magistrates, begging his attendance in the private room
at the police-office. There he had passed nearly the
whole of one day ; and he was also obliged to pass nearly
the whole of another in the same office. On this second
day the proceedings were not private, and he was accompanied by his own solicitor.

It would be needless to describe how a plain case was,

as usual, made obscure by the lawyers, how Acts of Parliament were consulted, how the magistrate doubted, how indignant Alaric's attorney became when it was suggested that some insignificant piece of evidence should be admitted, which, whether admitted or rejected, could have no real bearing on the case. In these respects this important examination was like other important examinations of the same kind, such as one sees in the newspapers whenever a man above the ordinary felon's rank becomes amenable to the outraged laws. It ended, however, in Alaric being committed, and giving bail to stand his trial in about a fortnight's time ; and in his being assured by his attorney that he would most certainly be acquitted. That bit of paper on which he had made an entry that certain shares bought by him had been bought on behalf of his ward, would save him ; so said the attorney : to which, however, Alaric answered not much. Could any acutest lawyer, let him be made of never so fine an assortment of forensic indignation, now whitewash his name and set him again right before the world ? He, of course, communicated with Sir Gregory, and agreed to be suspended from his commissionership till the trial should be over. His two colleagues then became bail for him.

So much having been settled, he got into a cab with his attorney, and having dropped that gentleman on the road, he returned home. The excitement of the examination and the necessity for action had sustained him ? but now—what was to sustain him now ? How was he to get through the intervening fortnight, banished as he was from his office, from his club, and from all haunts of men ? His attorney, who had other rogues to attend to besides him, made certain set appointments with him—and for the rest, he might sit at home and console himself as best he might with his own thoughts. 'Excelsior !' This was the pass to which ' Excelsior ' had brought *Sic itur ad astra !*—Alas, his road had taken him hitherto in quite a different direction.

He sent for Charley, and when Charley came he made Gertrude explain to him what had happened. He had confessed his own fault once, to his own wife, and he could not bring himself to do it again. Charley was thunderstruck at the greatness of the ruin, but he offered what assistance he could give. Anything that he could do, he would. Alaric had sent for him for a purpose, and that purpose at any rate Charley could fulfil. He went into the city to ascertain what was now the price of the Limehouse bridge shares, and returned with the news that they were falling, falling, falling.

No one else called at Alaric's door that day. Mrs. Val, though she did not come there, by no means allowed her horses to be idle; she went about sedulously among her acquaintance, dropping tidings of her daughter's losses. 'They will have enough left to live upon, thank God,' said she; 'but did you ever hear of so barefaced, so iniquitous a robbery? Well, I am not cruel; but my own opinion is that he should certainly be hanged.'

To this Ugolina assented fully, adding, that she had been so shocked by the suddenness and horror of the news, as to have become perfectly incapacitated ever since for any high order of thought.

Lactimel, whose soft bosom could not endure the idea of putting an end to the life of a fellow-creature, suggested perpetual banishment to the penal colonies; perhaps Norfolk Island. 'And what will she do?' said Lactimel.

'Indeed I cannot guess,' said Ugolina; 'her education has been sadly deficient.'

None but Charley called on Alaric that day, and he found himself shut up alone with his wife and child. His own house seemed to him a prison. He did not dare to leave it; he did not dare to walk out and face the public as long as daylight continued; he was ashamed to show himself, and so he sat alone in his dining-room thinking, thinking, thinking. Do what he would, he could not get those shares out of his mind; they had entered like iron into his soul, as poison into his blood; they might still rise, they might yet become of vast value, might pay all his debts, and enable him to begin again. And then this had been a committee day; he had had no means of knowing how things had gone there, of learning the opinions of the members, of whispering to Mr. Piles, or hearing the law on the matter laid down by the heavy deep voice of the great Mr. Blocks. And so he went on

thinking, thinking, thinking, but ever as though he had
a clock-weight fixed to his heart and pulling at its strings.
For, after all, what were the shares or the committee to
him ? Let the shares rise to ever so fabulous a value, let
the Chancellor of the Exchequer be ever so complaisant
in giving away his money, what avail would it be to him ?
what avail now ? He must stand his trial for the crime
of which he had been guilty.

With the utmost patience Gertrude endeavoured to
soothe him, and to bring his mind into some temper in
which it could employ itself. She brought him his baby,
thinking that he would play with his child, but all that
he said was—' My poor boy ! I have ruined him already ;'
and then turning away from the infant, he thrust his hands
deep into his trousers-pockets, and went on calculating
about the shares.

When the sun had well set, and the daylight had, at last,
dwindled out, he took up his hat and wandered out among
the new streets and rows of houses which lay between
his own house and the Western Railway. He got into a
district in which he had never been before, and as he
walked about here, he thought of the fate of other such
swindlers as himself ;—yes, though he did not speak the
word, he pronounced it as plainly, and as often, in the
utterance of his mind, as though it was being rung out
to him from every steeple in London ; he thought of the
fate of such swindlers as himself ; how one had been
found dead in the streets, poisoned by himself ; how
another, after facing the cleverest lawyers in the land,
was now dying in a felon's prison ; how a third had
vainly endeavoured to fly from justice by aid of wigs, false
whiskers, painted furrows, and other disguises. Should
he try to escape also, and avoid the ignominy of a trial ?
He knew it would be in vain ; he knew that, at this
moment, he was dogged at the distance of some thirty
yards by an amiable policeman in mufti, placed to watch
his motions by his two kind bailsmen, who preferred this
small expense to the risk of losing a thousand pounds
a-piece.

As he turned short round a corner, into the main road
leading from the railway station to Bayswater, he came

close upon a man who was walking quickly in the opposite direction, and found himself face to face with Undy Scott. How on earth should Undy Scott have come out there to Bayswater, at that hour of the night, he, the constant denizen of clubs, the well-known frequenter of Pall Mall, the member for the Tillietudlem burghs, whose every hour was occupied in the looking after things political, or things commercial ? Who could have expected him in a back road at Bayswater ? There, however, he was, and Alaric, before he knew of his presence, had almost stumbled against him.

'Scott !' said Alaric, starting back.

'Hallo, Tudor, what the deuce brings you here ? but I suppose you'll ask me the same question ?' said Undy.

Alaric Tudor could not restrain himself. 'You scoundrel,' said he, seizing Undy by the collar ; 'you utterly unmitigated scoundrel ! You premeditated, wilful villain !' and he held Undy as though he intended to choke him.

But Undy Scott was not a man to be thus roughly handled with impunity ; and in completing the education which he had received, the use of his fists had not been overlooked. He let out with his right hand, and struck Alaric twice with considerable force on the side of his jaw, so that the teeth rattled in his mouth.

But Alaric, at the moment, hardly felt it. 'You have brought me and mine to ruin,' said he ; 'you have done it purposely, like a fiend. But, low as I have fallen, I would not change places with you for all that the earth holds. I have been a villain ; but such villany as yours—ugh——' and so saying, he flung his enemy from him, and Undy, tottering back, saved himself against the wall.

In a continued personal contest between the two men, Undy would probably have had the best of it, for he would certainly have been the cooler of the two, and was also the more skilful in such warfare ; but he felt in a moment that he could gain nothing by thrashing Tudor, whereas he might damage himself materially by having his name brought forward at the present moment in connexion with that of his old friend.

'You reprobate !' said he, preparing to pass on ; 'it has been my misfortune to know you, and one cannot touch pitch and not be defiled. But, thank God, you'll come by your deserts now. If you will take my advice you'll hang yourself ; ' and so they parted.

The amiable policeman in mufti remained at a convenient distance during this little interview, having no special mission to keep the peace, pending his present employment ; but, as he passed by, he peered into Undy's face, and recognized the honourable member for the Tillietudlem burghs. A really sharp policeman knows every one of any note in London. It might, perhaps, be useful that evidence should be given at the forthcoming trial of the little contest which we have described. If so, our friend in mufti was prepared to give it.

On the following morning, at about eleven, a cab drove up to the door, and Alaric, standing at the dining-room window, saw Mrs. Woodward get out of it.

'There's your mother,' said Alaric to his wife. 'I will not see her—let her go up to the drawing-room.'

'Oh ! Alaric, will you not see mamma ? '

'How can I, with my face swollen as it is now ? Besides, what would be the good ? What can I say to her ? I know well enough what she has to say to me, without listening to it.'

'Dear Alaric, mamma will say nothing to you that is not kind ; do see her, for my sake, Alaric.'

But misery had not made him docile. He merely turned from her, and shook his head impatiently. Gertrude then ran out to welcome her mother, who was in the hall.

And what a welcoming it was ! 'Come upstairs, mamma, come into the drawing-room,' said Gertrude, who would not stop even to kiss her mother till they found themselves secured from the servants' eyes. She knew that one word of tenderness would bring her to the ground.

'Mamma, mamma ! ' she almost shrieked, and throwing herself into her mother's arms wept convulsively. Mrs. Woodward wanted no more words to tell her that Alaric had been guilty.

'But, Gertrude, how much is it ? ' whispered the mother, as, after a few moments of passionate grief, they sat holding each other's hands on the sofa. 'How much money is wanting? Can we not make it up? If it be all paid before the day of trial, will not that do? will not that prevent it?'

Gertrude could not say. She knew that £10,000 had been abstracted. Mrs. Woodward groaned as she heard the sum named. But then there were those shares, which had not long since been worth much more than half that sum, which must still be worth a large part of it.

'But we must know, dearest, before Harry can do anything,' said Mrs. Woodward.

Gertrude blushed crimson when Harry Norman's name was mentioned. And had it come to that—that they must look to him for aid?

'Can you not ask him, love?' said Mrs. Woodward. 'I saw him in the dining-room; go and ask him; when he knows that we are doing our best for him, surely he will help us.'

Gertrude, with a heavy heart, went down on her message, and did not return for fifteen or twenty minutes. It may easily be conceived that Norman's name was not mentioned between her and her husband, but she made him understand that an effort would be made for him if only the truth could be ascertained.

'It will be of no use,' said he.

'Don't say so, Alaric; we cannot tell what may be of use. But at any rate it will be weight off your heart to know that this money has been paid. It is that which overpowers you now, and not your own misfortune.'

At last he suffered her to lead him, and she put down on paper such figures as he dictated to her. It was, however, impossible to say what was the actual deficiency; that must depend upon the present value of the shares; these he said he was prepared to give over to his own attorney, if it was thought that by so doing he should be taking the best steps towards repairing the evil he had done; and then he began calculating how much the shares might possibly be worth, and pointing out under what circumstances they should be sold, and under what again they should be overheld till the market had improved. All this was worse than Greek to Gertrude;

but she collected what facts she could, and then returned
to her mother.

And they discussed the matter with all the wit and all
the volubility which women have on such occasions.
Paper was brought forth, and accounts were made out
between them, not such as would please the eyes of a
Civil Service Examiner, but yet accurate in their way.
How they worked and racked their brains, and strained
their women's nerves in planning how justice might be
defeated, and the dishonesty of the loved one covered
from shame ! Uncle Bat was ready with his share. He
had received such explanation as Mrs. Woodward had
been able to give, and though when he first heard the
news he had spoken severely of Alaric, still his money
should be forthcoming for the service of the family. He
could produce some fifteen hundred pounds ; and would
if needs be that he should do so. Then Harry—but the
pen fell from Gertrude's fingers as she essayed to write
down Harry Norman's contribution to the relief of her
husband's misery.

'Remember, Gertrude, love, in how short a time he
will be your brother.'

'But when will it be, mamma ? Is it to be on Thursday, as we had planned ? Of course, mamma, I cannot
be there.'

And then there was a break in their accounts, and Mrs.
Woodward explained to Gertrude that they had all
thought it better to postpone Linda's marriage till after
the trial ; and this, of course was the source of fresh
grief. When men such as Alaric Tudor stoop to dishonesty, the penalties of detection are not confined to
their own hearthstone. The higher are the branches of
the tree and the wider, the greater will be the extent of
earth which its fall will disturb.

Gertrude's pen, however, again went to work. The
shares were put down at £5,000. 'If they can only be
sold for so much, I think we may manage it,' said
Mrs. Woodward ; 'I am sure that Harry can get the
remainder—indeed he said he could have more than
that.'

'And what will Linda do ?'

'Linda will never want it, love; and if she did, what of that? would she not give all she has for you?'

And then Mrs. Woodward went her way to Norman's office, without having spoken to Alaric. 'You will come again soon, mamma,' said Gertrude. Mrs. Woodward promised that she would.

'And, mamma,' and she whispered close into her mother's ear, as she made her next request; 'and, mamma, you will be with me on that day?'

We need not follow Norman in his efforts to have her full fortune restored to Madame Jaquêtanàpe. He was daily in connexion with Alaric's lawyer, and returned sometimes with hope and sometimes without it. Mrs. Val's lawyer would receive no overtures towards a withdrawal of the charge, or even towards any mitigation in their proceedings, unless the agent coming forward on behalf of the lady's late trustee, did so with the full sum of £20,000 in his hands.

We need not follow Charley, who was everyday with Alaric, and who was, unknown to Alaric, an agent between him and Norman. 'Well, Charley, what are they doing to-day?' was Alaric's constant question to him, even up to the very eve of his trial.

If any spirit ever walks it must be that of the stock-jobber, for how can such a one rest in its grave without knowing what shares are doing?

CHAPTER XXXIX

THE LAST BREAKFAST

AND that day was not long in coming; indeed, it came with terrible alacrity; much too quickly for Gertrude, much too quickly for Norman; and much too quickly for Alaric's lawyer. To Alaric only did the time pass slowly, for he found himself utterly without employment.

Norman and Uncle Bat between them had raised something about £6,000; but when the day came on which they were prepared to dispose of the shares, the

Limehouse bridge was found to be worth nothing. They were, as the broker had said, ticklish stock; so ticklish that no one would have them at any price. When Undy, together with his agent from Tillietudlem, went into the market about the same time to dispose of theirs, they were equally unsuccessful. How the agent looked and spoke and felt may be imagined; for the agent had made large advances, and had no other security; but Undy had borne such looks and speeches before, and merely said that it was very odd—extremely odd; he had been greatly deceived by Mr. Piles. Mr. Piles also said it was very odd; but he did not appear to be nearly so much annoyed as the agent from Tillietudlem; and it was whispered that, queer as things now looked, Messrs. Blocks, Piles, and Cofferdam, had not made a bad thing of the bridge.

Overture after overture was made to the lawyer employed by Mrs. Val's party. Norman first offered the £6,000 and the shares; then when the shares were utterly rejected by the share-buying world, he offered to make himself personally responsible for the remainder of the debt, and to bind himself by bond to pay it within six months. At first these propositions were listened to, and Alaric's friends were led to believe that the matter would be handled in such a way that the prosecution would fall to the ground. But at last all composition was refused. The adverse attorney declared, first, that he was not able to accept any money payment short of the full amount with interest, and then he averred, that as criminal proceedings had been taken they could not now be stayed. Whether or no Alaric's night attack had anything to do with this, whether Undy had been the means of instigating this rigid adherence to justice, we are not prepared to say.

That day for which Gertrude had prayed her mother's assistance came all too soon. They had become at last aware that the trial must go on. Charley was with them on the last evening, and completed their despair by telling them that their attorney had resolved to make no further efforts at a compromise.

Perhaps the most painful feeling to Gertrude through the whole of the last fortnight had been the total prostra-

tion of her husband's energy, and almost of his intellect ;
he seemed to have lost the power of judging for himself,
and of thinking and deciding what conduct would be best
for him in his present condition. He who had been so
energetic, so full of life, so ready for all emergencies, so
clever at devices, so able to manage not only for himself
but for his friends, he was, as it were, paralysed and
unmanned. He sat from morning to night looking at
the empty fire-grate, and hardly ventured to speak of the
ordeal that he had to undergo.

His lawyer was to call for him on the morning of the
trial, and Mrs. Woodward was to be at the house soon
after he had left it. He had not yet seen her since the
inquiry had commenced, and it was very plain that he
did not wish to do so. Mrs. Woodward was to be there
and to remain till his fate had been decided, and then——
Not a word had yet been said as to the chance of his not
returning ; but Mrs. Woodward was aware that he would
probably be unable to do so, and felt, that if such
should be the case, she could not leave her daughter
alone.

And so Alaric and his wife sat down to breakfast on
that last morning. She had brought their boy down ;
but as she perceived that the child's presence did not
please his father, he had been sent back to the nursery,
and they were alone. She poured out his tea for him,
put bread upon his plate, and then sat down close beside
him, endeavouring to persuade him to eat. She had
never yet found fault with him, she had never even
ventured to give him counsel, but now she longed to
entreat him to collect himself and take a man's part in
the coming trial. He sat in the seat prepared for him,
but, instead of eating, he thrust his hands after his accustomed manner into his pockets and sat glowering at the
teacups.

'Come, Alaric, won't you eat your breakfast ?' said
she.

'No; breakfast! no—how can I eat now ? how can you
think that I could eat at such a time as this ? Do you
take yours ; never mind me.'

'But, dearest, you will be faint if you do not eat ;

think what you have to go through ; remember how
many eyes will be on you to-day.'

He shuddered violently as she spoke, and motioned
to her with his hand not to go on with what she was
saying.

'I know, I know,' said she passionately, 'dearest,
dearest love—I know how dreadful it is ; would that I
could bear it for you ! would that I could ! '

He turned away his head, for a tear was in his eye. It
was the first that had come to his assistance since this
sorrow had come upon him.

'Don't turn from me, dearest Alaric ; do not turn
from me now at our last moments. To me at least you
are the same noble Alaric that you ever were.'

'Noble ! ' said he, with all the self-scorn which he so
truly felt.

'To me you are, now as ever ; but, Alaric, I do so fear
that you will want strength, physical strength, you know,
to go through all this. I would have you bear yourself
like a man before them all.'

'It will be but little matter,' said he.

'It will be matter. It will be matter to me. My
darling, darling husband, rouse yourself,' and she knelt
before his knees and prayed to him ; 'for my sake do it ;
eat and drink that you may have the power of a man
when all the world is looking at you. If God forgives us
our sins, surely we should so carry ourselves that men
may not be ashamed to do so.'

He did not answer her, but he turned to the table and
broke the bread, and put his lips to the cup. And then
she gave him food as she would give it to a child, and he
with a child's obedience ate and drank what was put
before him. As he did so, every now and again a single
tear forced itself beneath his eyelid and trickled down his
face, and in some degree Gertrude was comforted.

He had hardly finished his enforced breakfast when the
cab and the lawyer came to the door. The learned
gentleman had the good taste not to come in, and so the
servant told them that Mr. Gitemthruet was there.

'Say that your master will be with him in a minute,'
said Gertrude, quite coolly ; and then the room door was

474 THE THREE CLERKS

again closed, and the husband and wife had now to say adieu.

Alaric rose from his chair and made a faint attempt to smile. 'Well, Gertrude,' said he, 'it has come at last.'

She rushed into his embrace, and throwing her arms around him, buried her face upon his breast. 'Alaric, Alaric, my husband ! my love, my best, my own, my only love ! '

'I cannot say much now, Gertrude, but I know how good you are ; you will come and see me, if they will let you, won't you ? '

'See you ! ' said she, starting back, but still holding him and looking up earnestly into his face. 'See you ! ' and then she poured out her love with all the passion of a Ruth : ' '' Whither thou goest, I will go ; and where thou lodgest, I will lodge. . . . Where thou diest, will I die, and there will I be buried ; the Lord do so to me, and more also, if aught but death part thee and me.'' See you, Alaric ; oh, it cannot be that they will hinder the wife from being with her husband. But, Alaric,' she went on, 'do not droop now, love—will you ? '

'I cannot brazen it out,' said he. 'I know too well what it is that I have done.'

'No, not that, Alaric ; I would not have that. But remember, all is not over, whatever they may do. Ah, how little will really be over, whatever they can do ! You have repented, have you not, Alaric ? '

'I think so, I hope so,' said Alaric, with his eyes upon the ground.

'You have repented, and are right before God ; do not fear then what man can do to you. I would not have you brazen, Alaric ; but be manly, be collected, be your own self, the man that I have loved, the man that I do now love so well, better, better than ever ; ' and she threw herself on him and kissed him and clung to him, and stroked his hair and put her hand upon his face, and then holding him from her, looked up to him as though he were a hero whom she all but worshipped.

'Gertrude, Gertrude—that I should have brought you to this ! '

'Never mind,' said she ; 'we will win through it yet—we will yet be happy together, far, far away from here—remember that—let that support you through all.   And now, Alaric, you will come up for one moment and kiss him before you go.'

'The man will be impatient.'

'Never mind; let him be impatient—you shall not go away without blessing your boy ; come up, Alaric.'   And she took him by the hand and led him like a child into the nursery.

'Where is the nurse ?   bring him here—papa is going away—Alley, boy, give papa a big kiss.'

Alaric, for the first time for the fortnight, took the little fellow into his arms and kissed him.   'God bless you, my bairn,' said he, 'and grant that all this may never be visited against you, here or hereafter ! '

'And now go,' said Gertrude, as they descended the stairs together, 'and may God in His mercy watch over and protect you and give you back to me !   And, Alaric, wherever you are I will be close to you, remember that. I will be quite, quite close to you.   Now, one kiss—oh, dearest, dearest Alaric—there—there—now go.'   And so he went, and Gertrude shutting herself into her room threw herself on to the bed, and wept aloud.

CHAPTER XL

MR. CHAFFANBRASS

WE must now follow Alaric to his trial.   He was, of course, much too soon at court.   All people always are, who are brought to the court perforce, criminals for instance, and witnesses, and other such-like unfortunate wretches ; whereas many of those who only go there to earn their bread are very often as much too late.   He was to be tried at the Old Bailey.   As I have never seen the place, and as so many others have seen it, I will not attempt to describe it.   Here Mr. Gitemthruet was quite at home ; he hustled and jostled, elbowed and ordered,

as though he were the second great man of the place, and
the client whom he was to defend was the first.   In this
latter opinion he was certainly right.   Alaric was the
hero of the day, and people made way for him as though
he had won a victory in India, and was going to receive
the freedom of the city in a box.   As he passed by, a
gleam of light fell on him from a window, and at the
instant three different artists had him photographed,
daguerreotyped, and bedevilled; four graphic members
of the public press took down the details of his hat,
whiskers, coat, trousers, and boots ; and the sub-editor
of the *Daily Delight* observed that ' there was a slight
tremor in the first footstep which he took within the
precincts of the prison, but in every other respect his
demeanour was dignified and his presence manly ; he
had light-brown gloves, one of which was on his left hand,
but the other was allowed to swing from his fingers.
The court was extremely crowded, and some fair ladies
appeared there to grace its customarily ungracious walls.
On the bench we observed Lord Killtime, Sir Gregory
Hardlines, and Mr. Whip Vigil.   Mr. Undecimus Scott,
who had been summoned as a witness by the prisoner,
was also accommodated by the sheriffs with a seat.'
Such was the opening paragraph of the seven columns
which were devoted by the *Daily Delight* to the all-
absorbing subject.

But Mr. Gitemthruet made his way through artists,
reporters, and the agitated crowd with that happy air of
command which can so easily be assumed by men at a
moment's notice, when they feel themselves to be for that
moment of importance.   ' Come this way, Mr. Tudor ;
follow me and we will get on without any trouble ; just
follow me close,' said Mr. Gitemthruet to his client, in
a whisper which was audible to not a few.   Tudor, who
was essaying, and not altogether unsuccessfully, to bear
the public gaze undismayed, did as he was bid, and
followed Mr. Gitemthruet.

' Now,' said the attorney, ' we'll sit here—Mr. Chaffanbrass will be close to us, there ; so that I can touch him
up as we go along ; of course, you know, you can make
any suggestion, only you must do it through me.   Here 's

his lordship; uncommon well he looks, don't he? You'd hardly believe him to be seventy-seven, but he's not a day less, if he isn't any more; and he has as much work in him yet as you or I, pretty nearly. If you want to insure a man's life, Mr. Tudor, put him on the bench; then he'll never die. We lawyers are not like bishops, who are always for giving up, and going out on a pension.'

But Alaric was not at the moment inclined to meditate much on the long years of judges. He was thinking, or perhaps trying to think, whether it would not be better for him to save this crowd that was now gathered together all further trouble, and plead guilty at once. He knew he was guilty, he could not understand that it was possible that any juryman should have a doubt about it; he had taken the money that did not belong to him; that would be made quite clear; he had taken it, and had not repaid it; there was the absolute *corpus delicti* in court, in the shape of a deficiency of some thousands of pounds. What possible doubt would there be in the breast of any-one as to his guilt? Why should he vex his own soul by making himself for a livelong day the gazing-stock for the multitude? Why should he trouble all those wigged counsellors, when one word from him would set all at rest?

'Mr. Gitemthruet, I think I'll plead guilty,' said he.

'Plead what!' said Mr. Gitemthruet, turning round upon his client with a sharp, angry look. It was the first time that his attorney had shown any sign of disgust, displeasure, or even disapprobation since he had taken Alaric's matter in hand. 'Plead what! Ah, you're joking, I know; upon my soul you gave me a start.'

Alaric endeavoured to explain to him that he was not joking, nor in a mood to joke; but that he really thought the least vexatious course would be for him to plead guilty.

'Then I tell you it would be the most vexatious proceeding ever I heard of in all my practice. But you are in my hands, Mr. Tudor, and you can't do it. You have done me the honour to come to me, and now you must be ruled by me. Plead guilty! Why, with such a case as you have got, you would disgrace yourself for ever if you did so. Think of your friends, Mr. Tudor, if you won't think of me or of yourself.'

His lawyer's eloquence converted him, and he resolved that he would run his chance. During this time all manner of little legal preliminaries had been going on; and now the court was ready for business; the jury were in their box, the court-keeper cried silence, and Mr. Gitemthruet was busy among his papers with frantic energy. But nothing was yet seen of the great Mr. Chaffanbrass.

'I believe we may go on with the trial for breach of trust,' said the judge. 'I do not know why we are waiting.'

Then up and spoke Mr. Younglad, who was Alaric's junior counsel. Mr. Younglad was a promising common-law barrister, now commencing his career, of whom his friends were beginning to hope that he might, if he kept his shoulders well to the collar, at some distant period make a living out of his profession. He was between forty and forty-five years of age, and had already over-come the natural diffidence of youth in addressing a learned bench and a crowded court.

'My lud,' said Younglad, 'my learned friend, Mr. Chaffanbrass, who leads for the prisoner, is not yet in court. Perhaps, my lud, on behalf of my client, I may ask for a few moments' delay.'

'And if Mr. Chaffanbrass has undertaken to lead for the prisoner, why is he not in court?' said the judge, looking as though he had uttered a poser which must altogether settle Mr. Younglad's business.

But Mr. Younglad had not been sitting, and walking and listening, let alone talking occasionally, in criminal courts, for the last twenty years, to be settled so easily.

'My lud, if your ludship will indulge me with five minutes' delay—we will not ask more than five minutes—your ludship knows, no one better, the very onerous duties——'

'When I was at the bar I took no briefs to which I could not attend,' said the judge.

'I am sure you did not, my lud; and my learned friend, should he ever sit in your ludship's seat, will be able to say as much for himself, when at some future time he may be———; but, my lud, Mr. Chaffanbrass is now in court.' And as he spoke, Mr. Chaffanbrass, carrying in his hand a huge old blue bag, which, as he entered, he took from his clerk's hands, and bearing on the top of his head a wig that apparently had not been dressed for the last ten years, made his way in among the barristers, caring little on whose toes he trod, whose papers he upset, or whom he elbowed on his road. Mr. Chaffanbrass was the cock of this dunghill, and well he knew how to make his crowing heard there.

'And now, pray, let us lose no more time,' said the judge.

'My lord, if time has been lost through me, I am very sorry; but if your lordship's horse had fallen down in the street as mine did just now———'

'My horse never falls down in the street, Mr. Chaffanbrass.'

'Some beasts, my lord, can always keep their legs under them, and others can't; and men are pretty much in the same condition. I hope the former may be the case with your lordship and your lordship's cob for many years.' The judge, knowing of old that nothing could prevent Mr. Chaffanbrass from having the last word, now held his peace, and the trial began.

There are not now too many pages left to us for the completion of our tale; but, nevertheless, we must say a few words about Mr. Chaffanbrass. He was one of an order of barristers by no means yet extinct, but of whom it may be said that their peculiarities are somewhat less often seen than they were when Mr. Chaffanbrass was in his prime. He confined his practice almost entirely to one class of work, the defence, namely, of culprits arraigned for heavy crimes, and in this he was, if not unrivalled, at least unequalled. Rivals he had, who, thick as the skins of such men may be presumed to be, not unfrequently writhed beneath the lashes which his tongue could inflict. To such a perfection had he carried his skill and power of fence, so certain was he in attack, so invulnerable when attacked, that few men cared to come within the reach of his forensic flail. To the old stagers

who were generally opposed to him, the gentlemen who
conducted prosecutions on the part of the Crown, and
customarily spent their time and skill in trying to hang
those marauders on the public safety whom it was the
special business of Mr. Chaffanbrass to preserve unhung,
to these he was, if not civil, at least forbearing ; but
when any barrister, who was comparatively a stranger to
him, ventured to oppose him, there was no measure to
his impudent sarcasm and offensive sneers.

Those, however, who most dreaded Mr. Chaffanbrass,
and who had most occasion to do so, were the witnesses.
A rival lawyer could find a protection on the bench when
his powers of endurance were tried too far ; but a witness
in a court of law has no protection. He comes there
unfeed, without hope of guerdon, to give such assistance
to the State in repressing crime and assisting justice as
his knowledge in this particular case may enable him to
afford ; and justice, in order to ascertain whether his
testimony be true, finds it necessary to subject him to
torture. One would naturally imagine that an undisturbed thread of clear evidence would be best obtained
from a man whose position was made easy and whose
mind was not harassed ; but this is not the fact : to turn
a witness to good account, he must be badgered this way
and that till he is nearly mad ; he must be made a laughing-
stock for the court ; his very truths must be turned into
falsehoods, so that he may be falsely shamed ; he must
be accused of all manner of villany, threatened with all
manner of punishment ; he must be made to feel that
he has no friend near him, that the world is all against him ;
he must be confounded till he forget his right hand from
his left, till his mind be turned into chaos, and his heart
into water ; and then let him give his evidence. What
will fall from his lips when in this wretched collapse must
be of special value, for the best talents of practised
forensic heroes are daily used to bring it about ; and no
member of the Humane Society interferes to protect the
wretch. Some sorts of torture are, as it were, tacitly
allowed even among humane people. Eels are skinned
alive, and witnesses are sacrificed, and no one's blood
curdles at the sight, no soft heart is sickened at the cruelty.

To apply the thumbscrew, the boot, and the rack to the victim before him was the work of Mr. Chaffanbrass's life. And it may be said of him that the labour he delighted in physicked pain. He was as little averse to this toil as the cat is to that of catching mice. And, indeed, he was not unlike a cat in his method of proceeding; for he would, as it were, hold his prey for a while between his paws, and pat him with gentle taps before he tore him. He would ask a few civil little questions in his softest voice, glaring out of his wicked old eye as he did so at those around him, and then, when he had his mouse well in hand, out would come his envenomed claw, and the wretched animal would feel the fatal wound in his tenderest part.

Mankind in general take pleasure in cruelty, though those who are civilized abstain from it on principle. On the whole Mr. Chaffanbrass is popular at the Old Bailey. Men congregate to hear him turn a witness inside out, and chuckle with an inward pleasure at the success of his cruelty. This Mr. Chaffanbrass knows, and, like an actor who is kept up to his high mark by the necessity of maintaining his character, he never allows himself to grow dull over his work. Therefore Mr. Chaffanbrass bullies when it is quite unnecessary that he should bully; it is a labour of love; and though he is now old, and stiff in his joints, though ease would be dear to him, though like a gladiator satiated with blood, he would as regards himself be so pleased to sheathe his sword, yet he never spares himself. He never spares himself, and he never spares his victim.

As a lawyer, in the broad and high sense of the word, it may be presumed that Mr. Chaffanbrass knows little or nothing. He has, indeed, no occasion for such knowledge. His business is to perplex a witness and bamboozle a jury, and in doing that he is generally successful. He seldom cares for carrying the judge with him: such tactics, indeed, as his are not likely to tell upon a judge. That which he loves is, that a judge should charge against him, and a jury give a verdict in his favour. When he achieves that he feels that he has earned his money. Let others, the young lads and spooneys of his profession, undertake the milk-and-water work of defending injured innocence;

it is all but an insult to his practised ingenuity to invite his assistance to such tasteless business. Give him a case in which he has all the world against him; Justice with her sword raised high to strike; Truth with open mouth and speaking eyes to tell the bloody tale; outraged humanity shrieking for punishment; a case from which Mercy herself, with averted eyes, has loathing turned and bade her sterner sister do her work; give him such a case as this, and then you will see Mr. Chaffanbrass in his glory. Let him, by the use of his high art, rescue from the gallows and turn loose upon the world the wretch whose hands are reeking with the blood of father, mother, wife, and brother, and you may see Mr. Chaffanbrass, elated with conscious worth, rub his happy hands with infinite complacency. Then will his ambition be satisfied, and he will feel that in the verdict of the jury he has received the honour due to his genius. He will have succeeded in turning black into white, in washing the blackamoor, in dressing in the fair robe of innocence the foulest, filthiest wretch of his day; and as he returns to his home, he will be proudly conscious that he is no little man.

In person, however, Mr. Chaffanbrass is a little man, and a very dirty little man. He has all manner of nasty tricks about him, which make him a disagreeable neighbour to barristers sitting near to him. He is profuse with snuff, and very generous with his handkerchief. He is always at work upon his teeth, which do not do much credit to his industry. His wig is never at ease upon his head, but is poked about by him, sometimes over one ear, sometimes over the other, now on the back of his head, and then on his nose; and it is impossible to say in which guise he looks most cruel, most sharp, and most intolerable. His linen is never clean, his hands never washed, and his clothes apparently never new. He is about five feet six in height, and even with that stoops greatly. His custom is to lean forward, resting with both hands on the sort of desk before him, and then to fix his small brown basilisk eye on the victim in the box before him. In this position he will remain unmoved by the hour together, unless the elevation and fall of his thick eye-

brows and the partial closing of his wicked eyes can be
called motion. But his tongue! that moves; there is
the weapon which he knows how to use!

Such is Mr. Chaffanbrass in public life; and those who
only know him in public life can hardly believe that at
home he is one of the most easy, good-tempered, amiable
old gentlemen that ever was pooh-poohed by his grown-up
daughters, and occasionally told to keep himself quiet in
a corner. Such, however, is his private character. Not
that he is a fool in his own house; Mr. Chaffanbrass can
never be a fool; but he is so essentially good-natured, so
devoid of any feeling of domestic tyranny, so placid in
his domesticities, that he chooses to be ruled by his own
children. But in his own way he is fond of hospitality;
he delights in a cosy glass of old port with an old friend
in whose company he may be allowed to sit in his old
coat and old slippers. He delights also in his books, in
his daughters' music, and in three or four live pet dogs,
and birds, and squirrels, whom morning and night he
feeds with his own hands. He is charitable, too, and
subscribes largely to hospitals founded for the relief of
the suffering poor.

Such was Mr. Chaffanbrass, who had been selected by
the astute Mr. Gitemthruet to act as leading counsel on
behalf of Alaric. If any human wisdom could effect the
escape of a client in such jeopardy, the wisdom of Mr.
Chaffanbrass would be likely to do it; but, in truth, the
evidence was so strong against him, that even this Newgate hero almost feared the result.

I will not try the patience of anyone by stating in
detail all the circumstances of the trial. In doing so
I should only copy, or, at any rate, might copy, the
proceedings at some of those modern *causes célèbres* with
which all those who love such subjects are familiar. And
why should I force such matters on those who do not love
them? The usual opening speech was made by the chief
man on the prosecuting side, who, in the usual manner,
declared 'that his only object was justice; that his
heart bled within him to see a man of such acknowledged
public utility as Mr. Tudor in such a position; that he
sincerely hoped that the jury might find it possible to

acquit him, but that——' And then went into his ' but '
with so much venom that it was clearly discernible to all,
that in spite of his protestations, his heart was set upon
a conviction.

When he had finished, the witnesses for the prosecution
were called—the poor wretches whose fate it was to be
impaled alive that day by Mr. Chaffanbrass. They gave
their evidence, and in due course were impaled. Mr.
Chaffanbrass had never been greater. The day was hot,
and he thrust his wig back till it stuck rather on the top
of his coat-collar than on his head ; his forehead seemed
to come out like the head of a dog from his kennel, and
he grinned with his black teeth, and his savage eyes
twinkled, till the witnesses sank almost out of sight as
they gazed at him.

And yet they had very little to prove, and nothing that
he could disprove. They had to speak merely to certain
banking transactions, to say that certain moneys had been
so paid in and so drawn out, in stating which they had
their office books to depend on. But not the less on this
account were they made victims. To one clerk it was
suggested that he might now and then, once in three
months or so, make an error in a figure ; and, having
acknowledged this, he was driven about until he admitted
that it was very possible that every entry he made in the
bank books in the course of the year was false. ' And
you, such as you,' said Mr. Chaffanbrass, ' do you dare
to come forward to give evidence on commercial affairs ?
Go down, sir, and hide your ignominy.' The wretch,
convinced that he was ruined for ever, slunk out of court,
and was ashamed to show himself at his place of business
for the next three days.

There were ten or twelve witnesses, all much of the
same sort, who proved among them that this sum of
twenty thousand pounds had been placed at Alaric's disposal, and that now, alas ! the twenty thousand pounds
were not forthcoming. It seemed to be a very simple
case ; and, to Alaric's own understanding, it seemed
impossible that his counsel should do anything for him.
But as each impaled victim shrank with agonized terror
from the torture, Mr. Gitemthruet would turn round to

Alaric and assure him that they were going on well, quite
as well as he had expected. Mr. Chaffanbrass was really
exerting himself; and when Mr. Chaffanbrass did really
exert himself he rarely failed.

And so the long day faded itself away in the hot sweltering court, and his lordship, at about seven o'clock, declared
his intention of adjourning. Of course a *cause célèbre* such
as this was not going to decide itself in one day. Alaric's
guilt was clear as daylight to all concerned; but a man
who had risen to be a Civil Service Commissioner, and
to be entrusted with the guardianship of twenty thousand
pounds, was not to be treated like a butcher who had
merely smothered his wife in an ordinary way, or a house-
breaker who had followed his professional career to its
natural end; more than that was due to the rank and
station of the man, and to the very respectable retaining
fee with which Mr. Gitemthruet had found himself enabled
to secure the venom of Mr. Chaffanbrass. So the jury
retired to regale themselves *en masse* at a neighbouring
coffee-house; Alaric was again permitted to be at large
on bail (the amiable policeman in mufti still attending
him at a distance); and Mr. Chaffanbrass and his lordship
retired to prepare themselves by rest for the morrow's
labours.

But what was Alaric to do? He soon found himself
under the guardianship of the constant Gitemthruet in
a neighbouring tavern, and his cousin Charley was with
him. Charley had been in court the whole day, except
that he had twice posted down to the West End in a cab
to let Gertrude and Mrs. Woodward know how things were
going on. He had posted down and posted back again,
and, crowded as the court had been, he had contrived to
make his way in, using that air of authority to which the
strongest-minded policeman will always bow; till at last
the very policemen assisted him, as though he were in
some way connected with the trial.

On his last visit at Gertrude's house he had told her
that it was very improbable that the trial should be
finished that day. She had then said nothing as to Alaric's
return to his own house; it had indeed not occurred to
her that he would be at liberty to do so: Charley at once

caught at this, and strongly recommended his cousin to remain where he was. ' You will gain nothing by going home,' said he ; ' Gertrude does not expect you ; Mrs. Woodward is there ; and it will be better for all parties that you should remain.' Mr. Gitemthruet strongly backed his advice, and Alaric, so counselled, resolved to remain where he was. Charley promised to stay with him, and the policeman in mufti, without making any promise at all, silently acquiesced in the arrangement. Charley made one more visit to the West, saw Norman at his lodgings, and Mrs. Woodward and Gertrude in Albany Place, and then returned to make a night of it with Alaric. We need hardly say that Charley made a night of it in a very different manner from that to which he and his brother navvies were so well accustomed.

CHAPTER XLI

THE OLD BAILEY

THE next morning, at ten o'clock, the court was again crowded. The judge was again on his bench, prepared for patient endurance ; and Lord Killtime and Sir Gregory Hardlines were alongside of him. The jury were again in their box, ready with pen and paper to give their brightest attention—a brightness which will be dim enough before the long day be over ; the counsel for the prosecution were rummaging among their papers ; the witnesses for the defence were sitting there among the attorneys, with the exception of the Honourable Undecimus Scott, who was accommodated with a seat near the sheriff, and whose heart, to tell the truth, was sinking somewhat low within his breast, in spite of the glass of brandy with which he had fortified himself. Alaric was again present under the wings of Mr. Gitemthruet ; and the great Mr. Chaffanbrass was in his place. He was leaning over a slip of paper which he held in his hand, and with compressed lips was meditating his attack upon his enemies ; on this occasion his wig was well over his eyes, and as he peered up from under it to the judge's face, he cocked his nose with an air of supercilious contempt for all those who were immediately around him.

It was for him to begin the day's sport by making a speech, not so much in defence of his client as in accusation of the prosecutors. ' It had never,' he said, ' been his fate, he might say his misfortune, to hear a case against a man in a respectable position, opened by the Crown with such an amount of envenomed virulence.' He was then reminded that the prosecution was not carried on by the Crown. ' Then,' said he, ' we may attribute this virulence to private malice ; that it is not to be attributed to any fear that this English bride should lose her fortune, or that her French husband should be deprived of any portion of his spoil, I shall be able to prove to a certainty. Did I allow myself that audacity of denunciation which my learned friend has not considered incompatible with the dignity of his new silk gown ? Could I permit myself such latitude of invective as he has adopted ? '—a slight laugh was here heard in the court, and an involuntary smile played across the judge's face—' yes,' continued Mr. Chaffanbrass, ' I boldly aver that I have never forgotten myself, and what is due to humanity, as my learned friend did in his address to the jury. Gentlemen of the jury, you will not confound the natural indignation which counsel must feel when defending innocence from the false attacks, with the uncalled-for, the unprofessional acerbity which has now been used in promoting such an accusation as this. I may at times be angry, when I see mean false-hood before me in vain assuming the garb of truth—for with such juries as I meet here it generally is in vain—I may at times forget myself in anger ; but, if we talk of venom, virulence, and eager hostility, I yield the palm, without a contest, to my learned friend in the new silk gown.'

He then went on to dispose of the witnesses whom they had heard on the previous day, and expressed a regret that an *exposé* should have been made so disgraceful to the commercial establishments of this great commercial city. It only showed what was the effect on such establishments

of that undue parsimony which was now one of the crying
evils of the times. Having thus shortly disposed of them,
he came to what all men knew was the real interest of
the day's doings. 'But,' said he, 'the evidence in this
case, to which your attention will be chiefly directed,
will be, not that for the accusation, but that for the
defence. It will be my business to show to you, not only
that my client is guiltless, but to what temptations to
be guilty he has been purposely and wickedly subjected.
I shall put into that bar an honourable member of the
House of Commons, who will make some revelations as to
his own life, who will give us an insight into the ways and
means of a legislator, which will probably surprise us all,
not excluding his lordship on the bench. He will be able
to explain to us—and I trust I may be able to induce him
to do so, for it is possible that he may be a little coy—he
will be able to explain to us why my client, who is in no
way connected either with the Scotts, or the Golightlys,
or the Figgs, or the Jaquêtanàpes, why he was made the
lady's trustee ; and he will also, perhaps, tell us, after some
slight, gentle persuasion, whether he has himself handled,
or attempted to handle, any of this lady's money.'

Mr. Chaffanbrass then went on to state that, as the
forms of the court would not give him the power of addressing the jury again, he must now explain to them what
he conceived to be the facts of the case. He then admitted
that his client, in his anxiety to do the best he could with
the fortune entrusted to him, had invested it badly. The
present fate of these unfortunate bridge shares, as to
which the commercial world had lately held so many
different opinions, proved that : but it had nevertheless
been a *bona fide* investment, made in conjunction with,
and by the advice of, Mr. Scott, the lady's uncle, who
thus, for his own purposes, got possession of money which
was in truth confided to him for other purposes. His
client, Mr. Chaffanbrass acknowledged, had behaved with
great indiscretion ; but the moment he found that the
investment would be an injurious one to the lady whose
welfare was in his hands, he at once resolved to make
good the whole amount from his own pocket. That he
had done so, or, at any rate, would have done so, but for

this trial, would be proved to them. Nobler conduct than this it was impossible to imagine. Whereas, the lady's uncle, the honourable member of Parliament, the gentleman who had made a stalking-horse of his, Mr. Chaffanbrass's, client, refused to refund a penny of the spoil, and was now the instigator of this most unjust proceeding.

As Mr. Chaffanbrass thus finished his oration, Undy Scott tried to smile complacently on those around him. But why did the big drops of sweat stand on his brow as his eye involuntarily caught those of Mr. Chaffanbrass? Why did he shuffle his feet, and uneasily move his hands and feet hither and thither, as a man does when he tries in vain to be unconcerned? Why did he pull his gloves on and off, and throw himself back with that affected air which is so unusual to him? All the court was looking at him, and every one knew that he was wretched. Wretched! aye, indeed he was; for the assurance even of an Undy Scott, the hardened man of the clubs, the thrice elected and twice rejected of Tillietudlem, fell prostrate before the well-known hot pincers of Chaffanbrass, the torturer!

The first witness called was Henry Norman. Alaric looked up for a moment with surprise, and then averted his eyes. Mr. Gitemthruet had concealed from him the fact that Norman was to be called. He merely proved this, that having heard from Mrs. Woodward, who was the prisoner's mother-in-law, and would soon be his own mother-in-law, that a deficiency had been alleged to exist in the fortune of Madame Jaquêtanàpe, he had, on the part of Mrs. Woodward, produced what he believed would cover this deficiency, and that when he had been informed that more money was wanting, he had offered to give security that the whole should be paid in six months. Of course, on him Mr. Chaffanbrass exercised none of his terrible skill, and as the lawyers on the other side declined to cross-examine him, he was soon able to leave the court. This he did speedily, for he had no desire to witness Alaric's misery.

And then the Honourable Undecimus Scott was put into the witness-box. It was suggested, on his behalf, that he might give his evidence from the seat which he then occupied, but this Mr. Chaffanbrass would by no means allow. His intercourse with Mr. Scott, he said, must be of a nearer, closer, and more confidential nature than such an arrangement as that would admit. A witness, to his way of thinking, was never an efficient witness till he had his arm on the rail of a witness-box. He must trouble Mr. Scott to descend from the grandeur of his present position; he might return to his seat after he had been examined—if he then should have a mind to do so. Our friend Undy found that he had to obey, and he was soon confronted with Mr. Chaffanbrass in the humbler manner which that gentleman thought so desirable.

'You are a member of the House of Commons, I believe, Mr. Scott?' began Mr. Chaffanbrass.

Undy acknowledged that he was so.

'And you are the son of a peer, I believe?'

'A Scotch peer,' said Undy.

'Oh, a Scotch peer,' said Mr. Chaffanbrass, bringing his wig forward over his left eye in a manner that was almost irresistible—'a Scotch peer—a member of Parliament, and son of a Scotch peer; and you have been a member of the Government, I believe, Mr. Scott?'

Undy confessed that he had been in office for a short time.

'A member of Parliament, a son of a peer, and one of the Government of this great and free country. You ought to be a proud and a happy man. You are a man of fortune, too, I believe, Mr. Scott?'

'That is a matter of opinion,' said Undy; 'different people have different ideas. I don't know what you call fortune.'

'Why I call £20,000 a fortune—this sum that the lady had who married the Frenchman. Have you £20,000?'

'I shall not answer that question.'

'Have you £10,000? You surely must have as much as that, as I know you married a fortune yourself,—unless, indeed, a false-hearted trustee has got hold of your money also. Come, have you got £10,000?'

'I shall not answer you.'

'Have you got any income at all ? Now, I demand an answer to that on your oath, sir.'

'My lord, must I answer such questions ?' said Undy.

'Yes, sir ; you must answer them, and many more like them,' said Mr. Chaffanbrass. 'My lord, it is essential to my client that I should prove to the jury whether this witness is or is not a penniless adventurer ; if he be a respectable member of society, he can have no objection to let me know whether he has the means of living.'

'Perhaps, Mr. Scott,' said the judge, 'you will not object to state whether or no you possess any fixed income.'

'Have you, or have you not, got an income on which you live ?' demanded Mr. Chaffanbrass.

'I have an income,' said Undy, not, however, in a voice that betokened much self-confidence in the strength of his own answer.

'You have an income, have you ? And now, Mr. Scott, will you tell us what profession you follow at this moment with the object of increasing your income ? I think we may surmise, by the tone of your voice, that your income is not very abundant.'

'I have no profession,' said Undy.

'On your oath, you are in no profession ?'

'Not at present.'

'On your oath, you are not a stock-jobber ?'

Undy hesitated for a moment.

'By the virtue of your oath, sir, are you a stock-jobber, or are you not ?'

'No, I am not. At least, I believe not.'

'You believe not !' said Mr. Chaffanbrass—and it would be necessary to hear the tone in which this was said to understand the derision which was implied. 'You believe you are not a stock-jobber ! Are you, or are you not, constantly buying shares and selling shares—railway shares—bridge shares—mining shares—and such-like ?'

'I sometimes buy shares.'

'And sometimes sell them ?'

'Yes—and sometimes sell them.'

Where Mr. Chaffanbrass had got his exact information, we cannot say ; but very exact information he had acquired respecting Undy's little transactions. He questioned him about the Mary Janes and Old Friendships, about the West Corks and the Ballydehob Branch, about sundry other railways and canals, and finally about the Limehouse bridge; and then again he asked his former question. 'And now,' said he, 'will you tell the jury whether you are a stock-jobber or no?'

'It is all a matter of opinion,' said Undy. 'Perhaps I may be, in your sense of the word.'

'My sense of the word!' said Mr. Chaffanbrass. 'You are as much a stock-jobber, sir, as that man is a policeman, or his lordship is a judge. And now, Mr. Scott, I am sorry that I must go back to your private affairs, respecting which you are so unwilling to speak. I fear I must trouble you to tell me this—How did you raise the money with which you bought that latter batch— the large lump of the bridge shares—of which we were speaking?'

'I borrowed it from Mr. Tudor,' said Undy, who had prepared himself to answer this question glibly.

'You borrowed it from Mr. Alaric Tudor—that is, from the gentleman now upon his trial. You borrowed it, I believe, just at the time that he became the lady's trustee?'

'Yes,' said Undy; 'I did so.'

'You have not repaid him as yet?'

'No—not yet,' said Undy.

'I thought not. Can you at all say when Mr. Tudor may probably get his money?'

'I am not at present prepared to name a day. When the money was lent it was not intended that it should be repaid at an early day.'

'Oh! Mr. Tudor did not want his money at an early day—didn't he? But, nevertheless, he has, I believe, asked for it since, and that very pressingly?'

'He has never asked for it,' said Undy.

'Allow me to remind you, Mr. Scott, that I have the power of putting my client into that witness-box, although he is on his trial; and, having so reminded you, let me again beg you to say whether he has not asked you for repayment of this large sum of money very pressingly.'

' No ; he has never done so.'

' By the value of your oath, sir—if it has any value—
did not my client beseech you to allow these shares to
be sold while they were yet saleable, in order that your
niece's trust money might be replaced in the English
funds ? '

' He said something as to the expediency of selling
them, and I differed from him.'

' You thought it would be better for the lady's interest
that they should remain unsold ? '

' I made no question of the lady's interest. I was not
her trustee.'

' But the shares were bought with the lady's money.'

' What shares ? ' asked Undy.

' What shares, sir ? Those shares which you had professed to hold on the lady's behalf, and which afterwards
you did not scruple to call your own. Those shares of
yours—since you have the deliberate dishonesty so to call
them—those shares of yours, were they not bought with
the lady's money ? '

' They were bought with the money which I borrowed
from Mr. Tudor.'

' And where did Mr. Tudor get that money ? '

' That is a question you must ask himself,' said Undy.

' It is a question, sir, that just at present I prefer to
ask you. Now, sir, be good enough to tell the jury,
whence Mr. Tudor got that money ; or tell them, if you
dare do so, that you do not know.'

Undy for a minute remained silent, and Mr. Chaffanbrass remained silent also. But if the fury of his tongue
for a moment was at rest, that of his eyes was as active
as ever. He kept his gaze steadily fixed upon the witness,
and stood there with compressed lips, still resting on his
two hands, as though he were quite satisfied thus to watch
the prey that was in his power. For an instant he glanced
up to the jury, and then allowed his eyes to resettle on
the face of the witness, as though he might have said,
' There, gentlemen, there he is—the son of a peer, a
member of Parliament ; what do you think of him ? '

The silence of that minute was horrible to Undy, and
yet he could hardly bring himself to break it. The judge

looked at him with eyes which seemed to read his inmost soul; the jury looked at him, condemning him one and all; Alaric looked at him with fierce, glaring eyes of hatred, the same eyes that had glared at him that night when he had been collared in the street; the whole crowd looked at him derisively; but the eyes of them all were as nothing to the eyes of Mr. Chaffanbrass.

'I never saw him so great; I never did,' said Mr. Gitemthruet, whispering to his client; and Alaric, even he, felt some consolation in the terrible discomfiture of his enemy.

'I don't know where he got it,' said Undy, at last breaking the terrible silence, and wiping the perspiration from his brow.

'Oh, you don't!' said Mr. Chaffanbrass, knocking his wig back, and coming well out of his kennel. 'After waiting for a quarter of an hour or so, you are able to tell the jury at last that you don't know anything about it. He took the small trifle of change out of his pocket, I suppose?'

'I don't know where he took it from.'

'And you didn't ask?'

'No.'

'You got the money; that was all you know. But this was just at the time that Mr. Tudor became the lady's trustee; I think you have admitted that.'

'It may have been about the time.'

'Yes; it may have been about the time, as you justly observe, Mr. Scott. Luckily, you know, we have the dates of the two transactions. But it never occurred to your innocent mind that the money which you got into your hands was a part of the lady's fortune; that never occurred to your innocent mind—eh, Mr. Scott?'

'I don't know that my mind is a more innocent mind than your own,' said Undy.

'I dare say not. Well, did the idea ever occur to your guilty mind?'

'Perhaps my mind is not more guilty than your own, either.'

'Then may God help me,' said Mr. Chaffanbrass, 'for I must be at a bad pass. You told us just now, Mr. Scott, that some time since Mr. Tudor advised you to sell these shares—what made him give you this advice ? '

' He meant, he said, to sell his own.'

' And he pressed you to sell yours ? '

' Yes.'

' He urged you to do so more than once ? '

' Yes ; I believe he did.'

' And now, Mr. Scott, can you explain to the jury why he was so solicitous that you should dispose of your property ? '

' I do not know why he should have done so, unless he wanted back his money.'

' Then he did ask for his own money ? '

' No ; he never asked for it. But if I had sold the shares perhaps he might have asked for it.'

' Oh ! ' said Mr. Chaffanbrass ; and as he uttered the monosyllable he looked up at the jury, and gently shook his head, and gently shook his hands. Mr. Chaffanbrass was famous for these little silent addresses to the jury-box.

But not even yet had he done with this suspicious loan. We cannot follow him through the whole of his examination ; for he kept our old friend under the harrow for no less than seven hours. Though he himself made no further statement to the jury, he made it perfectly plain, by Undy's own extracted admissions, or by the hesitation of his denials, that he had knowingly received this money out of his niece's fortune, and that he had refused to sell the shares bought with this money, when pressed to do so by Tudor, in order that the trust-money might be again made up.

There were those who blamed Mr. Chaffanbrass for thus admitting that his client had made away with his ward's money by lending it to Undy ; but that acute gentleman saw clearly that he could not contend against the fact of the property having been fraudulently used ; but he saw that he might induce the jury to attach so much guilt to Undy, that Tudor would, as it were, be whitened by the blackness of the other's villainy. The judge, he well knew, would blow aside all this froth ; but then the judge could not find the verdict.

Towards the end of the day, when Undy was thoroughly worn out—at which time, however, Mr. Chaffanbrass was as brisk as ever, for nothing ever wore him out when he was pursuing his game—when the interest of those who had been sweltering in the hot court all the day was observed to flag, Mr. Chaffanbrass began twisting round his finger a bit of paper, of which those who were best acquainted with his manner knew that he would soon make use.

'Mr. Scott,' said he, suddenly dropping the derisive sarcasm of his former tone, and addressing him with all imaginable courtesy, 'could you oblige me by telling me whose handwriting that is?' and he handed to him the scrap of paper. Undy took it, and saw that the writing was his own; his eyes were somewhat dim, and he can hardly be said to have read it. It was a very short memorandum, and it ran as follows: 'All will yet be well, if those shares be ready to-morrow morning.'

'Well, Mr. Scott,' said the lawyer, 'do you recognize the handwriting?'

Undy looked at it, and endeavoured to examine it closely, but he could not; his eyes swam, and his head was giddy, and he felt sick. Could he have satisfied himself that the writing was not clearly and manifestly his own, he would have denied the document altogether; but he feared to do this; the handwriting might be proved to be his own.

'It is something like my own,' said he.

'Something like your own, is it?' said Mr. Chaffanbrass, as though he were much surprised. 'Like your own! Well, will you have the goodness to read it?'

Undy turned it in his hand as though the proposed task were singularly disagreeable to him. Why, thought he to himself, should he be thus browbeaten by a dirty old Newgate lawyer? Why not pluck up his courage, and, at any rate, show that he was a man? 'No,' said he, 'I will not read it.'

'Then I will. Gentlemen of the jury, have the goodness to listen to me.' Of course there was a contest then between him and the lawyers on the other side whether the document might or might not be read; but equally of course the contest ended in the judge's decision that it should be read. And Mr. Chaffanbrass did read it in a voice audible to all men. '"All will yet be well, if those shares be ready to-morrow morning." We may take it as admitted, I suppose, that this is in your hand-writing, Mr. Scott?'

'It probably may be, though I will not say that it is.'

'Do you not know, sir, with positive certainty that it is your writing?'

To this Undy made no direct answer. 'What is your opinion, Mr. Scott?' said the judge; 'you can probably give an opinion by which the jury would be much guided.'

'I think it is, my lord,' said Undy.

'He thinks it is,' said Mr. Chaffanbrass, addressing the jury. 'Well, for once I agree with you. I think it is also—and now will you have the goodness to explain it. To whom was it addressed?'

'I cannot say.'

'When was it written?'

'I do not know.'

'What does it mean?'

'I cannot remember.'

'Was it addressed to Mr. Tudor?'

'I should think not.'

'Now, Mr. Scott, have the goodness to look at the jury, and to speak a little louder. You are in the habit of addressing a larger audience than this, and cannot, therefore, be shamefaced. You mean to tell the jury that you think that that note was not intended by you for Mr. Tudor?'

'I think not,' said Undy.

'But you can't say who it was intended for?'

'No.'

'And by the virtue of your oath, you have told us all that you know about it?' Undy remained silent, but Mr. Chaffanbrass did not press him for an answer. 'You have a brother, named Valentine, I think.' Now Captain Val had been summoned also, and was at this moment in court. Mr. Chaffanbrass requested that he might be desired to leave it, and, consequently, he was ordered out in charge of a policeman.

'And now, Mr. Scott—was that note written by you to Mr. Tudor, with reference to certain shares, which you proposed that Mr. Tudor should place in your brother's hands? Now, sir, I ask you, as a member of Parliament, as a member of the Government, as the son of a peer, to give a true answer to that question.' And then again Undy was silent; and again Mr. Chaffanbrass leant on the desk and glared at him. 'And remember, sir, member of Parliament and nobleman as you are, you shall be indicted for perjury, if you are guilty of perjury.'

'My lord,' said Undy, writhing in torment, 'am I to submit to this?'

'Mr. Chaffanbrass,' said the judge, 'you should not threaten your witness. Mr. Scott—surely you can answer the question.'

Mr. Chaffanbrass seemed not to have even heard what the judge said, so intently were his eyes fixed on poor Undy. 'Well, Mr. Scott,' he said at last, very softly, 'is it convenient for you to answer me? Did that note refer to a certain number of bridge shares, which you required Mr. Tudor to hand over to the stepfather of this lady?'

Undy had no trust in his brother. He felt all but sure that, under the fire of Mr. Chaffanbrass, he would confess everything. It would be terrible to own the truth, but it would be more terrible to be indicted for perjury. So he sat silent.

'My lord, perhaps you will ask him,' said Mr. Chaffanbrass.

'Mr. Scott, you understand the question—why do you not answer it?' asked the judge. But Undy still remained silent.

'You may go now,' said Mr. Chaffanbrass. 'Your eloquence is of the silent sort; but, nevertheless, it is very impressive. You may go now, and sit on that bench again, if, after what has passed, the sheriff thinks proper to permit it.'

Undy, however, did not try that officer's complaisance. He retired from the witness-box, and was not again seen during the trial in any conspicuous place in the court.

It was then past seven o'clock; but Mr. Chaffanbrass

insisted on going on with the examination of Captain Val.
It did not last long. Captain Val, also, was in that disagreeable position, that he did not know what Undy had
confessed, and what denied. So he, also, refused to
answer the questions of Mr. Chaffanbrass, saying that he
might possibly damage himself should he do so. This
was enough for Mr. Chaffanbrass, and then his work was
done.

At eight o'clock the court again adjourned; again
Charley posted off—for the third time that day—to let
Gertrude know that, even as yet, all was not over; and
again he and Alaric spent a melancholy evening at the
neighbouring tavern; and then, again, on the third
morning, all were re-assembled at the Old Bailey.

Or rather they were not all re-assembled. But few
came now, and they were those who were obliged to
come. The crack piece of the trial, that portion to which,
among the connoisseurs, the interest was attached, that
was all over. Mr. Chaffanbrass had done his work. Undy
Scott, the member of Parliament, had been gibbeted, and
the rest was, in comparison, stale, flat, and unprofitable.
The judge and jury, however, were there, so were the
prosecuting counsel, so were Mr. Chaffanbrass and Mr.
Younglad, and so was poor Alaric. The work of the day
was commenced by the judge's charge, and then Alaric,
to his infinite dismay, found how all the sophistry and
laboured arguments of his very talented advocate were
blown to the winds, and shown to be worthless. 'Gentlemen,' said the judge to the jurors, after he had gone
through all the evidence, and told them what was ad-
missible, and what was not—' gentlemen, I must especially
remind you, that in coming to a verdict in the matter,
no amount of guilt on the part of any other person can
render guiltless him whom you are now trying, or palliate
his guilt if he be guilty. An endeavour has been made
to affix a deep stigma on one of the witnesses who has
been examined before you; and to induce you to feel,
rather than to think, that Mr. Tudor is, at any rate,
comparatively innocent—innocent as compared with that
gentleman. That is not the issue which you are called
on to decide; not whether Mr. Scott, for purposes of

his own, led Mr. Tudor on to guilt, and then turned against him ; but whether Mr. Tudor himself has, or has not, been guilty under this Act of Parliament that has been explained to you.

'As regards the evidence of Mr. Scott, I am justified in telling you, that if the prisoner's guilt depended in any way on that evidence, it would be your duty to receive it with the most extreme caution, and to reject it altogether if not corroborated. That evidence was not trustworthy, and in a great measure justified the treatment which the witness encountered from the learned barrister who examined him. But Mr. Scott was a witness for the defence, not for the prosecution. The case for the prosecution in no way hangs on his evidence.

'If it be your opinion that Mr. Tudor is guilty, and that he was unwarily enticed into guilt by Mr. Scott ; that the whole arrangement of this trust was brought about by Mr. Scott or others, to enable him or them to make a cat's-paw of this new trustee, and thus use the lady's money for their own purposes, such an opinion on your part may justify you in recommending the prisoner to the merciful consideration of the bench ; but it cannot justify you in finding a verdict of not guilty.'

As Alaric heard this, and much more to the same effect, his hopes, which certainly had been high during the examination of Undy Scott, again sank to zero, and left him in despair. He had almost begun to doubt the fact of his own guilt, so wondrously had his conduct been glossed over by Mr. Chaffanbrass, so strikingly had any good attempt on his part been brought to the light, so black had Scott been made to appear. Ideas floated across his brain that he might go forth, not only free of the law, but whitewashed also in men's opinions, that he might again sit on his throne at the Civil Service Board, again cry to himself 'Excelsior,' and indulge the old dreams of his ambition.

But, alas ! the deliberate and well-poised wisdom of the judge seemed to shower down cold truth upon the jury from his very eyes. His words were low in their tone, though very clear, impassive, delivered without gesticulation or artifice, such as that so powerfully used by Mr. Chaffanbrass; but Alaric himself felt that it was impossible to doubt the truth of such a man; impossible to suppose that any juryman should do so. Ah me! why had he brought himself thus to quail beneath the gaze of an old man seated on a bench? with what object had he forced himself to bend his once proud neck? He had been before in courts such as this, and had mocked within his own spirit the paraphernalia of the horsehair wigs, the judges' faded finery, and the red cloth; he had laughed at the musty, stale solemnity by which miscreants were awed, and policemen enchanted; now, these things told on himself heavily enough; he felt now their weight and import.

And then the jury retired from the court to consider their verdict, and Mr. Gitemthruet predicted that they would be hungry enough before they sat down to their next meal. 'His lordship was dead against us,' said Mr. Gitemthruet; 'but that was a matter of course; we must look to the jury, and the city juries are very fond of Mr. Chaffanbrass; I am not quite sure, however, that Mr. Chaffanbrass was right: I would not have admitted so much myself; but then no one knows a city jury so well as Mr. Chaffanbrass.'

Other causes came on, and still the jury did not return to court. Mr. Chaffanbrass seemed to have forgotten the very existence of Alaric Tudor, and was deeply engaged in vindicating a city butcher from an imputation of having vended a dead ass by way of veal. All his indignation was now forgotten, and he was full of boisterous fun, filling the court with peals of laughter. One o'clock came, two, three, four, five, six, seven, and still no verdict. At the latter hour, when the court was about to be adjourned, the foreman came in, and assured the judge that there was no probability that they could agree; eleven of them thought one way, while the twelfth was opposed to them. 'You must reason with the gentleman,' said the judge. 'I have, my lord,' said the foreman, 'but it's all thrown away upon him.' 'Reason with him again,' said the judge, rising from his bench and preparing to go to his dinner.

And then one of the great fundamental supports of the

British constitution was brought into play. Reason was thrown away upon this tough juryman, and, therefore, it was necessary to ascertain what effect starvation might have upon him. A verdict, that is, a unanimous decision from these twelve men as to Alaric's guilt, was necessary; it might be that three would think him innocent, and nine guilty, or that any other division of opinion might take place; but such divisions among a jury are opposed to the spirit of the British constitution. Twelve men must think alike; or, if they will not, they must be made to do so. 'Reason with him again,' said the judge, as he went to his own dinner. Had the judge bade them remind him how hungry he would soon be if he remained obstinate, his lordship would probably have expressed the thought which was passing through his mind. 'There is one of us, my lord,' said the foreman, 'who will I know be very ill before long; he is already so bad that he can't sit upright.'

There are many ludicrous points in our blessed constitution, but perhaps nothing so ludicrous as a juryman praying to a judge for mercy. He has been caught, shut up in a box, perhaps, for five or six days together, badgered with half a dozen lawyers till he is nearly deaf with their continual talking, and then he is locked up until he shall die or find a verdict. Such at least is the intention of the constitution. The death, however, of three or four jurymen from starvation would not suit the humanity of the present age, and therefore, when extremities are nigh at hand, the dying jurymen, with medical certificates, are allowed to be carried off. It is devoutly to be wished that one juryman might be starved to death while thus serving the constitution; the absurdity then would cure itself, and a verdict of a majority would be taken.

But in Alaric's case, reason or hunger did prevail at the last moment, and as the judge was leaving the court, he was called back to receive the verdict. Alaric, also, was brought back, still under Mr. Gitemthruet's wing, and with him came Charley. A few officers of the court were there, a jailer and a policeman or two, those whose attendance was absolutely necessary, but with these exceptions the place was empty. Not long since men were crowding for seats, and the policemen were hardly able to restrain the pressure of those who pushed forward; but now there was no pushing; the dingy, dirty benches, a few inches of which had lately been so desirable, were not at all in request, and were anything but inviting in appearance; Alaric sat himself down on the very spot which had lately been sacred to Mr. Chaffanbrass, and Mr. Gitemthruet, seated above him, might also fancy himself a barrister. There they sat for five minutes in perfect silence; the suspense of the moment cowed even the attorney, and Charley, who sat on the other side of Alaric, was so affected that he could hardly have spoken had he wished to do so.

And then the judge, who had been obliged to re-array himself before he returned to the bench, again took his seat, and an officer of the court inquired of the foreman of the jury, in his usual official language, what their finding was.

' Guilty on the third count,' said the foreman. ' Not guilty on the four others. We beg, however, most strongly to recommend the prisoner to your lordship's merciful consideration, believing that he has been led into this crime by one who has been much more guilty than himself.'

' I knew Mr. Chaffanbrass was wrong,' said Mr. Gitemthruet. ' I knew he was wrong when he acknowledged so much. God bless my soul! in a court of law one should never acknowledge anything! what's the use?'

And then came the sentence. He was to be confined at the Penitentiary at Millbank for six months. ' The offence,' said the judge, ' of which you have been found guilty, and of which you most certainly have been guilty, is one most prejudicial to the interests of the community. That trust which the weaker of mankind should place in the stronger, that reliance which widows and orphans should feel in their nearest and dearest friends, would be destroyed, if such crimes as these were allowed to pass unpunished. But in your case there are circumstances which do doubtless palliate the crime of which you have been guilty; the money which you took will,

I believe, be restored ; the trust which you were courted to undertake should not have been imposed on you ; and in the tale of villainy which has been laid before us, you have by no means been the worst offender. I have, therefore, inflicted on you the slightest penalty which the law allows me. Mr. Tudor, I know what has been your career, how great your services to your country, how unexceptionable your conduct as a public servant ; I trust, I do trust, I most earnestly, most hopefully trust, that your career of utility is not over. Your abilities are great, and you are blessed with the power of thinking ; I do beseech you to consider, while you undergo that confinement which you needs must suffer, how little any wealth is worth an uneasy conscience.'

And so the trial was over. Alaric was taken off in custody ; the policeman in mufti was released from his attendance ; and Charley, with a heavy heart, carried the news to Gertrude and Mrs. Woodward.

'And as for me,' said Gertrude, when she had so far recovered from the first shock as to be able to talk to her mother—'as for me, I will have lodgings at Mill-bank.'

CHAPTER XLII

A PARTING INTERVIEW

Mrs. Woodward remained with her eldest daughter for two days after the trial, and then she was forced to return to Hampton. She had earnestly entreated Gertrude to accompany her, with her child ; but Mrs. Tudor was inflexible. She had, she said, very much to do ; so much, that she could not possibly leave London ; the house and furniture were on her hands, and must be disposed of ; their future plans must be arranged ; and then nothing, she said, should induce her to sleep out of sight of her husband's prison, or to omit any opportunity of seeing him which the prison rules would allow her.

Mrs. Woodward would not have left one child in such

extremity, had not the state of another child made her presence at the Cottage indispensable. Katie's anxiety about the trial had of course been intense, so intense as to give her a false strength, and somewhat to deceive Linda as to her real state. Tidings of course passed daily between London and the Cottage, but for three days they told nothing. On the morning of the fourth day, however, Norman brought the heavy news, and Katie sank completely under it. When she first heard the result of the trial she swooned away, and remained for some time nearly unconscious. But returning consciousness brought with it no relief, and she lay sobbing on her pillow, till she became so weak, that Linda in her fright wrote up to her mother begging her to return at once. Then, wretched as it made her to leave Gertrude in her trouble, Mrs. Woodward did return.

For a fortnight after this there was an unhappy household at Surbiton Cottage. Linda's marriage was put off till the period of Alaric's sentence should be over, and till something should be settled as to his and Gertrude's future career. It was now August, and they spoke of the event as one which perhaps might occur in the course of the following spring. At this time, also, they were deprived for a while of the comfort of Norman's visits by his enforced absence at Normansgrove. Harry's eldest brother was again ill, and at last the news of his death was received at Hampton. Under other circumstances such tidings as those might, to a certain extent, have brought their own consolation with them. Harry would now be Mr. Norman of Normansgrove, and Linda would become Mrs. Norman of Normansgrove; Harry's mother had long been dead, and his father was an infirm old man, who would be too glad to give up to his son the full management of the estate, now that the eldest son was a man to whom that estate could be trusted. All those circumstances had, of course, been talked over between Harry and Linda, and it was understood that Harry was now to resign his situation at the Weights and Measures. But Alaric's condition, Gertrude's misery, and Katie's illness, threw all such matters into the background.

Katie became no better; but then the doctors said that she did not become any worse, and gave it as their opinion that she ought to recover. She had youth, they said, on her side; and then her lungs were not affected. This was the great question which they were all asking of each other continually. The poor girl lived beneath a stethoscope, and bore all their pokings and tappings with exquisite patience. She herself believed that she was dying, and so she repeatedly told her mother. Mrs. Woodward could only say that all was in God's hands, but that the physicians still encouraged them to hope the best.

One day Mrs. Woodward was sitting with a book in her usual place at the side of Katie's bed; she looked every now and again at her patient, and thought that she was slumbering; and at last she rose from her chair to creep away, so sure was she that she might be spared for a moment. But just as she was silently rising, a thin, slight, pale hand crept out from beneath the clothes, and laid itself on her arm.

' I thought you were asleep, love,' said she.

' No, mamma, I was not asleep. I was thinking of something. Don't go away, mamma, just now. I want to ask you something.'

Mrs. Woodward again sat down, and taking her daughter's hand in her own, caressed it.

' I want to ask a favour of you, mamma,' said Katie.

' A favour, my darling! what is it? you know I will do anything in my power that you ask me.'

' Ah, mamma, I do not know whether you will do this.'

' What is it, Katie? I will do anything that is for your good. I am sure you know that, Katie.'

' Mamma, I know I am going to die. Oh, mamma, don't say anything now, don't cry now—dear, dear mamma; I don't say it to make you unhappy; but you know when I am so ill I ought to think about it, ought I not, mamma?'

' But, Katie, the doctor says that he thinks you are not so dangerously ill; you should not, therefore, despond; it will increase your illness, and hinder your chance of getting well. That would be wrong, wouldn't it, love?'

'Mamma, I feel that I shall never again be well, and therefore——' It was useless telling Mrs. Woodward not to cry; what else could she do? 'Dear mamma, I am so sorry to make you unhappy, but you are my own mamma, and therefore I must tell you. I can be happy still, mamma, if you will let me talk to you about it.'

'You shall talk, dearest; I will hear what you say; but oh, Katie, I cannot bear to hear you talk of dying. I do not think you are dying. If I did think so, my child, my trust in your goodness is so strong that I should tell you.'

'You know, mamma, it might have been much worse; suppose I had been drowned, when he, when Charley, you know, saved me;' and as she mentioned his name a tear for the first time ran down each cheek; 'how much worse that would have been! think, mamma, what it would be to be drowned without a moment for one's prayers.'

'It is quite right we should prepare ourselves for death. Whether we live, or whether we die, we shall be better for doing that.'

Katie still held her mother's hand in hers, and lay back against the pillows which had been placed behind her back. 'And now, mamma,' she said at last, 'I am going to ask you this favour—I want to see Charley once more.'

Mrs. Woodward was so much astonished at the request that at first she knew not what answer to make. 'To see Charley!' she said at last.

'Yes, mamma; I want to see Charley once more; there need be no secrets between us now, mamma.'

'There have never been any secrets between us,' said Mrs. Woodward, embracing her. 'You have never had any secrets from me?'

'Not intentionally, mamma; I have never meant to keep anything secret from you. And I know you have known what I felt about Charley.'

'I know that you have behaved like an angel, my child; I know your want of selfishness, your devotion to others, has been such as to shame me; I know your

conduct has been perfect : oh, my Katie, I have understood it, and I have so loved you, so admired you.'

Katie smiled through her tears as she returned her
mother's embrace. 'Well, mamma,' she said, 'at any
rate you know that I love him. Oh, mamma, I do love
him so dearly. It is not now like Gertrude's love, or
Linda's. I know that I can never be his wife. I did
know before, that for many reasons I ought not to wish
to be so ; but now I know I never, never can be.'

Mrs. Woodward was past the power of speaking, and
so Katie went on.

'But I do not love him the less for that reason ;
I think I love him the more. I never, never, could have
loved anyone else, mamma ; never, never ; and that is
one reason why I do not so much mind being ill now.'

Mrs. Woodward bowed forward, and hid her face in
the counterpane, but she still kept hold of her daughter's
hand.

'And, mamma,' she continued, 'as I do love him so
dearly, I feel that I should try to do something for him.
I ought to do so ; and, mamma, I could not be happy
without seeing him. He is not just like a brother or
a brother-in-law, such as Harry and Alaric ; we are not
bound to each other as relations are ; but yet I feel that
something does bind me to him. I know he doesn't love
me as I love him ; but yet I think he loves me dearly ;
and if I speak to him now, mamma, now that I am—that
I am so ill, perhaps he will mind me. Mamma, it will be
as though one came unto him from the dead.'

Mrs. Woodward did not know how to refuse any request
that Katie might now make to her, and felt herself
altogether unequal to the task of refusing this request.
For many reasons she would have done so, had she been
able ; in the first place she did not think that all chance
of Katie's recovery was gone ; and then at the present
moment she felt no inclination to draw closer to her any
of the Tudor family. She could not but feel that Alaric
had been the means of disgracing and degrading one
child ; and truly, deeply, warmly, as she sympathized
with the other, she could not bring herself to feel the same
sympathy for the object of her love. It was a sore day

for her and hers, that on which the Tudors had first entered her house.

Nevertheless she assented to Katie's proposal, and undertook the task of asking Charley down to Hampton.

Since Alaric's conviction Charley led a busy life ; and as men who have really something to do have seldom time to get into much mischief, he had been peculiarly moral and respectable. It is not surprising that at such a moment Gertrude found that Alaric's newer friends fell off from him. Of course they did ; nor is it a sign of ingratitude or heartlessness in the world that at such a period of great distress new friends should fall off. New friends, like one's best coat and polished patent-leather dress boots, are only intended for holiday wear. At other times they are neither serviceable nor comfortable ; they do not answer the required purposes, and are ill adapted to give us the ease we seek. A new coat, however, has this advantage, that it will in time become old and comfortable ; so much can by no means be predicted with certainty of a new friend. Woe to those men who go through the world with none but new coats on their backs, with no boots but those of polished leather, with none but new friends to comfort them in adversity.

But not the less, when misfortune does come, are we inclined to grumble· at finding ourselves deserted. Gertrude, though she certainly wished to see no Mrs. Val and no Miss Neverbends, did feel lonely enough when her mother left her, and wretched enough. But she was not altogether deserted. At this time Charley was true to her, and did for her all those thousand nameless things which a woman cannot do for herself. He came to her everyday after leaving his office, and on one excuse or another remained with her till late every evening.

He was not a little surprised one morning on receiving Mrs. Woodward's invitation to Hampton. Mrs. Woodward in writing had had some difficulty in wording her request. She hardly liked asking Charley to come because Katie was ill ; nor did she like to ask him without mentioning Katie's illness. ' I need not explain to you,' she said in her note, ' that we are all in great distress ; poor Katie is very ill, and you will understand what we must feel about

Alaric and Gertrude. Harry is still at Normansgrove.
We shall all be glad to see you, and Katie, who never
forgets what you did for her, insists on my asking you
at once. I am sure you will not refuse her, so I shall
expect you to-morrow.' Charley would not have refused
her anything, and it need hardly be said that he accepted
the invitation.

Mrs. Woodward was at a loss how to receive him, or
what to say to him. Though Katie was so positive that
her own illness would be fatal—a symptom which might
have confirmed those who watched her in their opinion
that her disease was not consumption—her mother was
by no means so desponding. She still thought it not
impossible that her child might recover, and so thinking
could not but be adverse to any declaration on Katie's
part of her own feelings. She had endeavoured to explain
this to her daughter ; but Katie was so carried away by
her enthusiasm, was at the present moment so devoted,
and, as it were, exalted above her present life, that all
that her mother said was thrown away upon her. Mrs.
Woodward might have refused her daughter's request,
and have run the risk of breaking her heart by the refusal ;
but now that the petition had been granted, it was useless
to endeavour to teach her to repress her feelings.

' Charley,' said Mrs. Woodward, when he had been some
little time in the house, ' our dear Katie wants to see you ;
she is very ill, you know.'

Charley said he knew she was ill.

' You remember our walk together, Charley.'

' Yes,' said Charley, ' I remember it well. I made you
a promise then, and I have kept it. I have now come here
only because you have sent for me.' This he said in the
tone which a man uses when he feels himself to have been
injured.

' I know it, Charley ; you have kept your promise ; I
knew you would, and I know you will. I have the fullest
trust in you ; and now you shall come and see her.'

Charley was to return to town that night, and they had
not therefore much time to lose ; they went upstairs at
once, and found Linda and Uncle Bat in the patient's
room. It was a lovely August evening, and the bedroom

window opening upon the river was unclosed. Katie, as
she sat propped up against the pillows, could look out upon
the water and see the reedy island, on which in happy
former days she had so delighted to let her imagination
revel.

'It is very good of you to come and see me, Charley,'
said she, as he made his way up to her bedside.

He took her wasted hand in his own and pressed it,
and, as he did so, a tear forced itself into each corner of
his eyes. She smiled as though to cheer him, and said
that now she saw him she could be quite happy, only for
poor Alaric and Gertrude. She hoped she might live to
see Alaric again ; but if not, Charley was to give him her
best—best love.

'Live to see him ! of course you will,' said Uncle Bat.

'What's to hinder you ?' Uncle Bat, like the rest of
them, tried to cheer her, and make her think that she
might yet live.

After a while Uncle Bat went out of the room, and
Linda followed him. Mrs. Woodward would fain have
remained, but she perfectly understood that it was part
of the intended arrangement with Katie, that Charley
should be alone with her. 'I will come back in a quarter
of an hour,' she said, rising to follow the others. 'You
must not let her talk too much, Charley : you see how
weak she is.'

'Mamma, when you come, knock at the door, will you ?'
said Katie. Mrs. Woodward, who found herself obliged
to act in complete obedience to her daughter, promised
that she would ; and then they were left alone.

'Sit down, Charley,' said she ; he was still standing by
her bedside, and now at her bidding he sat in the chair
which Captain Cuttwater had occupied. 'Come here
nearer to me,' said she ; 'this is where mamma always
sits, and Linda when mamma is not here.' Charley did
as he was bid, and, changing his seat, came and sat down
close to her bed-head.

'Charley, do you remember how you went into the
water for me ?' said she, again smiling, and pulling her
hand out and resting it on his arm which lay on the bed
beside her.

' Indeed I do, Katie—I remember the day very well.'

' That was a very happy day in spite of the tumble, was it not, Charley ? And do you remember the flower-show, and the dance at Mrs. Val's ? '

Charley did remember them all well. Ah me ! how often had he thought of them !

' I think of those days so often—too often,' continued Katie. ' But, dear Charley, I cannot remember too often that you saved my life.'

Charley once more tried to explain to her that there was nothing worthy of notice in his exploit of that day.

' Well, Charley, I may think as I like, you know,' she said, with something of the obstinacy of old days. ' I think you did save my life, and all the people in the world won't make me think anything else ; but, Charley, I have something now to tell you.'

He sat and listened. It seemed to him as though he were only there to listen ; as though, were he to make his own voice audible, he would violate the sanctity of the place. His thoughts were serious enough, but he could not pitch his voice so as to suit the tone in which she addressed him.

' We were always friends, were we not ? ' said she ; ' we were always good friends, Charley. Do you remember how you were to build a palace for me in the dear old island out there ? You were always so kind, so good to me.'

Charley said he remembered it all—they were happy days ; the happiest days, he said, that he had ever known.

' And you used to love me, Charley ? '

' Used ! ' said he, ' do you think I do not love you now ? '

' I am sure you do. And, Charley, I love you also. That it is that I want to tell you. I love you so well that I cannot go away from this world in peace without wishing you farewell. Charley, if you love me, you will think of me when I am gone ; and then for my sake you will be steady.'

Here were all her old words over again—' You will be steady, won't you, Charley ? I know you will be steady, now.' How much must she have thought of him ! How

often must his career have caused her misery and pain!
How laden must that innocent bosom have been with
anxiety on his account! He had promised her then that
he would reform; but he had broken his promise. He
now promised her again, but how could he hope that she
would believe him?

'You know how ill I am, don't you? You know that
I am dying, Charley?'

Charley of course declared that he still hoped that she
would recover.

'If I thought so,' said she, 'I should not say what
I am now saying; but I feel that I may tell the truth.
Dear Charley, dearest Charley, I love you with all my
heart—I do not know how it came so; I believe I have
always loved you since I first knew you; I used to think
it was because you saved my life; but I know it was not
that. I was so glad it was you that came to me in the
water, and not Harry; so that I know I loved you before
that.'

'Dear Katie, you have not loved me, or thought of
me, more than I have loved and thought of you.'

'Ah, Charley,' she said, smiling in her sad sweet way—
' I don't think you know how a girl can love; you have so
many things to think of, so much to amuse you up in
London; you don't know what it is to think of one
person for days and days, and nights and nights together.
That is the way I have thought of you. I don't think
there can be any harm,' she continued, ' in loving a person
as I have loved you. Indeed, how could I help it? I did
not love you on purpose. But I think I should be wrong
to die without telling you. When I am dead, Charley,
will you think of this, and try—try to give up your bad
ways? When I tell you that I love you so dearly, and
ask you on my deathbed, I think you will do this.'

Charley went down on his knees, and bowing his head
before her and before his God, he made the promise. He
made it, and we may so far anticipate the approaching
end of our story as to declare that the promise he then
made was faithfully kept.

'Katie, Katie, my own Katie, my own, own, own Katie—
—oh, Katie, you must not die, you must not leave me!

Oh, Katie, I have so dearly loved you ! Oh, Katie, I do so dearly love you ! If you knew all, if you could know all, you would believe me.'

At this moment Mrs. Woodward knocked at the door, and Charley rose from his knees. 'Not quite yet, mamma,' said Katie, as Mrs. Woodward opened the door. 'Not quite yet ; in five minutes, mamma, you may come.' Mrs. Woodward, not knowing how to refuse, again went away.

'Charley, I never gave you anything but once, and you returned it to me, did you not ? '

'Yes,' said he, 'the purse—I put it in your box, because—— '

And then he remembered that he could not say why he had returned it without breaking in a manner that confidence which Mrs. Woodward had put in him.

'I understand it all. You must not think I am angry with you. I know how good you were about it. But Charley, you may have it back now ; here it is ; ' and putting her hand under the pillow, she took it out, carefully folded up in new tissue paper. 'There, Charley, you must never part with it again as long as there are two threads of it together ; but I know you never will ; and Charley, you must never talk of it to anybody but to your wife ; and you must tell her all about it.'

He took the purse, and put it to his lips, and then pressed it to his heart. 'No,' said he, 'I will never part with it again. I think I can promise that.'

'And now, dearest, good-bye,' said she ; 'dearest, dearest Charley, good-bye ; perhaps we shall know each other in heaven. Kiss me, Charley, before you go,' So he stooped down over her, and pressed his lips to hers.

Charley, leaving the room, found Mrs. Woodward at the other end of the passage, standing at the door of her own dressing-room. 'You are to go to her now,' he said. 'Good-bye,' and without further speech to any of them he hurried out of the house.

None but Mrs. Woodward had seen him ; but she saw that the tears were streaming down his cheeks as he passed her, and she expressed no surprise that he had left the Cottage without going through the formality of making his adieux.

And then he walked up to town, as Norman once had done after a parting interview with her whom he had loved. It might be difficult to say which at the moment suffered the bitterest grief.

CHAPTER XLIII

MILLBANK

THE immediate neighbourhood of Millbank Penitentiary is not one which we should, for its own sake, choose for our residence, either on account of its natural beauty, or the excellence of its habitations. That it is a salubrious locality must be presumed from the fact that it has been selected for the site of the institution in question ; but salubrity, though doubtless a great recommendation, would hardly reconcile us to the extremely dull, and one might almost say, ugly aspect which this district bears.

To this district, however, ugly as it is, we must ask our readers to accompany us, while we pay a short visit to poor Gertrude. It was certainly a sad change from her comfortable nursery and elegant drawing-room near Hyde Park. Gertrude had hitherto never lived in an ugly house. Surbiton Cottage and Albany Place were the only two homes that she remembered, and neither of them was such as to give her much fitting preparation for the melancholy shelter which she found at No. 5, Paradise Row, Millbank.

But Gertrude did not think much of this when she changed her residence. Early one morning, leaning on Charley's arm, she had trudged down across the Park, through Westminster, and on to the close vicinity of the prison ; and here they sought for and obtained such accommodation as she thought fitting to her present situation. Charley had begged her to get into a cab, and when she refused that, had implored her to indulge in the luxury of an omnibus ; but Gertrude's mind was now set upon economy ; she would come back, she said, in an omnibus when the day would be hotter, and she would be alone, but she was very well able to walk the distance once.

She procured for seven shillings a week a sitting-room and bedroom, from whence she could see the gloomy prison walls, and also a truckle-bed for the young girl whom she was to bring with her as her maid. This was a little Hampton maiden, whom she had brought from the country to act as fag and deputy to her grand nurse ; but the grand nurse was now gone, and the fag was promoted to the various offices of nurse, lady's-maid, and parlour servant. The rest of the household in Albany Place had already dispersed with the discreet view of bettering their situations.

Everything in the house was given up to pay what Alaric owed. Independently of his dreadful liability to Madame Jaquêtanàpe, he could not have been said to be in debt ; but still, like most other men who live as he had done, when his career was thus brought to a sudden close, it was found that there were many people looking for money. There were little bills, as the owners said of them, which had been forgotten, of course, on account of their insignificance, but which being so very little might now be paid, equally of course, without any trouble. It is astonishing how easy it is to accumulate three or four hundred pounds' worth of little bills, when one lives before the world in a good house and in visible possession of a good income.

At the moment of Alaric's conviction, there was but a slender stock of money forthcoming for these little bills. The necessary expense of his trial,—and it had been by no means trifling,—he had, of course, been obliged to pay. His salary had been suspended, and all the money that he could lay his hands on had been given up towards making restitution towards the dreadful sum of £20,000 that had been his ruin. The bills, however, did not come in till after his trial, and then there was but little left but the furniture.

As the new trustees employed on behalf of Madame

Jaquêtanàpe and Mr. Figgs were well aware that they had much more to expect from the generosity of Tudor's friends than from any legal seizure of his property, they did not interfere in the disposal of the chairs and tables. But not on that account did Gertrude conceive herself entitled to make any use on her own behalf of such money as might come into her hands. The bills should be paid, and then every farthing that could be collected should be given towards lessening the deficiency. Six thousand pounds had already been made up by the joint efforts of Norman and Captain Cuttwater. Undy Scott's acknowledgement for the other four thousand had been offered, but the new trustees declined to accept it as of any value whatsoever. They were equally incredulous as to the bridge shares, which from that day to this have never held up their heads, even to the modest height of half a crown a share.

Gertrude's efforts to make the most of everything had been unceasing. When her husband was sentenced, she had in her possession a new dress and some finery for her baby, which were not yet paid for; these she took back with her own hand, offering to the milliners her own trinkets by way of compensation for their loss. When the day for removal came, she took with her nothing that she imagined could be sold. She would have left the grander part of her own wardrobe, if the auctioneers would have undertaken to sell it. Some few things, books and trifling household articles, which she thought were dear to Alaric, she packed up; and such were sent to Hampton. On the day of her departure she dressed herself in a plain dark gown, one that was almost mourning, and then, with her baby in her lap, and her young maid beside her, and Charley fronting her in the cab, she started for her new home.

I had almost said that her pride had left her. Such an assertion would be a gross libel on her. No; she was perhaps prouder than ever, as she left her old home. There was a humility in her cheap dress, in her large straw bonnet coming far over her face, in her dark gloves and little simple collar; nay, there was a humility in her altered voice, and somewhat chastened mien; but the spirit of the woman was wholly unbroken. She had even a pride in her very position, in her close and dear tie with the convicted prisoner. She was his for better and for worse; she would now show him what was her idea of the vow she had made. To the men who came to ticket and number the furniture, to the tradesmen's messengers who called for money, to the various workmen with whom the house was then invaded, she was humble enough; but had Mrs. Val come across her with pity, or the Miss Neverbends with their sententious twaddlings, she would have been prouder than ever. Fallen indeed! She had had no fall; nor had he; he was still a man, with a greater aggregate of good in him than falls to the average lot of mortals. Who would dare to tell her that he had fallen? 'Twas thus that her pride was still strong within her; and as it supported her through this misery, who can blame her for it?

She was allowed into the prison twice a week; on Tuesdays and Fridays she was permitted to spend one hour with her husband, and to take her child with her. It is hardly necessary to say that she was punctual to the appointed times. This, however, occupied but a short period, even of those looked-for days; and in spite of her pride, and her constant needle, the weary six months went from her all too slowly.

Nor did they pass with swifter foot within the prison. Alaric was allowed the use of books and pens and paper, but even with these he found a day in prison to be almost an unendurable eternity. This was the real punishment of his guilt; it was not that he could not eat well, and lie soft, or enjoy the comforts which had always surrounded him; but that the day would not pass away. The slowness of the lagging hours nearly drove him mad. He made a thousand resolutions as to reading, writing, and employment for his mind. He attempted to learn whole pages by rote, and to fatigue himself to rest by exercise of his memory. But his memory would not work; his mind would continue idle; he was impotent over his own faculties. Oh, if he could only sleep while these horrid weeks were passing over him!

All hope of regaining his situation had of course passed

from him, all hope of employment in England. Emigration must now be his lot; and hers also, and the lot of that young one that was already born to them, and of that other one who was, alas! now coming to the world, whose fate it would be first to see the light under the walls of its father's prison.—Yes, they must emigrate.—But there was nothing so very terrible in that. Alaric felt that even his utter poverty would be no misfortune if only his captivity were over. Poverty!—how could any man be poor who had liberty to roam the world?

We all of us acknowledge that the educated man who breaks the laws is justly liable to a heavier punishment than he who has been born in ignorance, and bred, as it were, in the lap of sin; but we hardly realize how much greater is the punishment which, when he be punished, the educated man is forced to undergo. Confinement to the man whose mind has never been lifted above vacancy is simply remission from labour. Confinement, with labour, is simply the enforcement of that which has hitherto been his daily lot. But what must a prison be to him whose intellect has received the polish of the world's poetry, who has known what it is to feed more than the belly, to require other aliment than bread and meat?

And then, what does the poor criminal lose? His all, it will be said; and the rich can lose no more. But this is not so. No man loses his all by any sentence which a human judge can inflict. No man so loses anything approaching to his all, however much he may have lost before. But the one man has too often had no self-respect to risk; the other has stood high in his own esteem, has held his head proudly before the world, has aspired to walk in some way after the fashion of a god. Alaric had so aspired, and how must he have felt during those prison days! Of what nature must his thoughts have been when they turned to Gertrude and his child! His sin had indeed been heavy, and heavy was the penalty which he suffered.

When they had been thus living for about three months, Gertrude's second child was born. Mrs. Woodward was with her at the time, and she had suffered but little except that for three weeks she was unable to see her husband; then, in the teeth of all counsel, and in opposition to all

medical warning, she could resist no longer, and carried
the newborn stranger to his father.

'Poor little wretch!' said Alaric, as he stooped to kiss
him.

'Wretch!' said Gertrude, looking up to him with
a smile upon her face—'he is no wretch. He is a sturdy
little man, that shall yet live to make your heart dance
with joy.'

Mrs. Woodward came often to see her. She did not
stay, for there was no bed in which she could have slept;
but the train put her down at Vauxhall, and she had but
to pass the bridge, and she was close to Gertrude's lodgings.
And now the six months had nearly gone by, when, by
appointment, she brought Norman with her. At this time
he had given up his clerkship at the Weights and Measures,
and was about to go to Normansgrove for the remainder
of the winter. Both Alaric and Norman had shown a great
distaste to meet each other. But Harry's heart softened
towards Gertrude. Her conduct during her husband's
troubles had been so excellent, that he could not but
forgive her the injuries which he fancied he owed to her.

Everything was now prepared for their departure. They
were to sail on the very day after Alaric's liberation, so as
to save him from the misery of meeting those who might
know him. And now Harry came with Mrs. Woodward to
bid farewell, probably for ever on this side the grave, to
her whom he had once looked on as his own. How different were their lots now! Harry was Mr. Norman of
Normansgrove, immediately about to take his place as
the squire of his parish, to sit among brother magistrates,
to decide about roads and poachers, parish rates and other
all-absorbing topics, to be a rural magistrate, and fill
a place among perhaps the most fortunate of the world's
inhabitants. Gertrude was the wife of a convicted felon,
who was about to come forth from his prison in utter
poverty, a man who, in such a catalogue as the world
makes of its inhabitants, would be ranked among the very
lowest.

And did Gertrude even now regret her choice? No, not
for a moment! She still felt certain in her heart of hearts
that she had loved the one who was the most worthy of

a woman's love. We cannot, probably, all agree in her
opinion ; but we will agree in this, at least, that she was
now right to hold such opinion. Had Normansgrove
stretched from one boundary of the county to the other,
it would have weighed as nothing. Had Harry's virtues
been as bright as burnished gold—and indeed they had
been bright—they would have weighed as nothing.
A nobler stamp of manhood was on her husband—so at
least Gertrude felt ;—and manhood is the one virtue
which in a woman's breast outweighs all others.

They had not met since the evening on which Gertrude
had declared to him that she never could love him ; and
Norman, as he got out of the cab with Mrs. Woodward,
at No. 5, Paradise Row, Millbank, felt his heart beat
within him almost as strongly as he had done when he
was about to propose to her. He followed Mrs. Woodward
into the dingy little house, and immediately found himself
in Gertrude's presence.

I should exaggerate the fact were I to say that he
would not have known her ; but had he met her elsewhere,
met her where he did not expect to meet her, he would
have looked at her more than once before he felt assured
that he was looking at Gertrude Woodward. It was not
that she had grown pale, or worn, or haggard ; though,
indeed, her face had on it that weighty look of endurance
which care will always give ; it was not that she had lost
her beauty, and become unattractive in his eyes ; but that
the whole nature of her mien and form, the very trick of
her gait was changed. Her eye was as bright as ever,
but it was steady, composed, and resolved ; her lips were
set and compressed, and there was no playfulness round
her mouth. Her hair was still smooth and bright, but
it was more brushed off from her temples than it had been
of yore, and was partly covered by a bit of black lace,
which we presume we must call a cap ; here and there,
too, through it, Norman's quick eye detected a few grey
hairs. She was stouter too than she had been, or else she
seemed to be so from the changes in her dress. Her step
fell heavier on the floor than it used to do, and her voice
was quicker and more decisive in its tones. When she
spoke to her mother, she did so as one sister might do to

another; and, indeed, Mrs. Woodward seemed to exercise over her very little of the authority of a parent. The truth was that Gertrude had altogether ceased to be a girl, had altogether become a woman. Linda, with whom Norman at once compared her, though but one year younger, was still a child in comparison with her elder sister. Happy, happy Linda!

Gertrude had certainly proved herself to be an excellent wife; but perhaps she might have made herself more pleasing to others if she had not so entirely thrown off from herself all traces of juvenility. Could she, in this respect, have taken a lesson from her mother, she would have been a wiser woman. We have said that she consorted with Mrs. Woodward as though they had been sisters; but one might have said that Gertrude took on herself the manners of the elder sister. It is true that she had hard duties to perform, a stern world to overcome, an uphill fight before her with poverty, distress, and almost, nay, absolutely, with degradation. It was well for her and Alaric that she could face it all with the true courage of an honest woman. But yet those who had known her in her radiant early beauty could not but regret that the young freshness of early years should all have been laid aside so soon.

'Linda, at any rate, far exceeds her in beauty,' was Norman's first thought, as he stood for a moment to look at her—'and then Linda too is so much more feminine.' 'Twas thus that Harry Norman consoled himself in the first moment of his first interview with Alaric's wife. And he was right in his thoughts. The world would now have called Linda the more lovely of the two, and certainly the more feminine in the ladylike sense of the word. If, however, devotion be feminine, and truth to one selected life's companion, if motherly care be so, and an indomitable sense of the duties due to one's own household, then Gertrude was not deficient in feminine character.

'You find me greatly altered, Harry, do you not?' said she, taking his hand frankly, and perceiving immediately the effect which she had made upon him. 'I am a steady old matron, am I not?—with a bairn on each side of me,' and she pointed to her baby in the cradle, and to her other boy sitting on his grandmother's knee.

Harry said he did find her altered. It was her dress, he said, and the cap on her head.

'Yes, Harry; and some care and trouble too. To you, you know, to a friend such as you are, I must own that care and trouble do tell upon one. Not, thank God, that I have more than I can bear; not that I have not blessings for which I cannot but be too thankful.'

'And so these are your boys, Gertrude?'

'Yes,' said she, cheerfully; 'these are the little men, that in the good times coming will be managing vast kingdoms, and giving orders to this worn-out old island of yours. Alley, my boy, sing your new song about the "good and happy land."' But Alley, who had got hold of his grandmother's watch, and was staring with all his eyes at the stranger, did not seem much inclined to be musical at the present moment.

'And this is Charley's godson,' continued Gertrude, taking up the baby. 'Dear Charley! he has been such a comfort to me.'

'I have heard all about you daily from him,' said Harry.

'I know you have—and he is daily talking of you, Harry. And so he should do; so we all should do. What a glorious change this is for him! is it not, Harry?'

Charley by this time had torn himself away from Mr. Snape and the navvies, and transferred the whole of his official zeal and energies to the Weights and Measures. The manner and reason of this must, however, be explained in a subsequent chapter.

'Yes,' said Harry, 'he has certainly got into a better office.'

'And he will do well there?'

'I am sure he will. It was impossible he should do well at that other place. No man could do so. He is quite an altered man now. The only fault I find with him is that he is so full of his heroes and heroines.'

'So he is, Harry; he is always asking me what he is to do with some forlorn lady or gentleman. "Oh, smother her!" I said the other day. "Well," said he, with a melancholy gravity, "I'll try it; but I fear it won't answer." Poor Charley! what a friend you have been to him, Harry!'

'A friend!' said Mrs. Woodward, who was still true to her adoration of Norman. 'Indeed he has been a friend—a friend to us all. Who is there like him?'

Gertrude could have found it in her heart to go back to the subject of old days, and tell her mother that there was somebody much better even than Harry Norman. But the present was hardly a time for such an assertion of her own peculiar opinion.

'Yes, Harry,' she said, 'we have all much, too much, to thank you for. I have to thank you on his account.'

'Oh no,' said he, ungraciously; 'there is nothing to thank me for,—not on his account. Your mother and Captain Cuttwater——' and then he stopped himself. What he meant was that he had sacrificed his little fortune—for at the time his elder brother had still been living—not to rescue, or in attempting to rescue, his old friend from misfortune—not, at least, because that man had been his friend; but because he was the husband of Gertrude Woodward, and of Mrs. Woodward's daughter. Could he have laid bare his heart, he would have declared that Alaric Tudor owed him nothing; that he had never forgiven, never could forgive, the wrongs he had received from him; but that he had forgiven Alaric's wife; and that having done so in the tenderness of his heart, he had been ready to give up all that he possessed for her protection. He would have spared Gertrude what pain he could; but he would not lie, and speak of Alaric Tudor with affection.

'But there is, Harry; there is,' said Gertrude; 'much—too much—greatly too much. It is that now weighs me down more than anything. Oh! Harry, how are we to pay to you all this money?'

'It is with Mrs. Woodward,' said he coldly, 'and Captain Cuttwater, net with me, that you should speak of that. Mr. Tudor owes me nothing.'

'Oh, Harry, Harry,' said she, 'do not call him Mr. Tudor—pray, pray; now that we are going—now that we shall never wound your sight again! do not call him Mr. Tudor.

He has done wrong ; I do not deny it ; but which of us
is there that has not ? '

' It was not on that account,' said he ; ' I could forgive
all that.'

Gertrude understood him, and her cheeks and brow
became tinged with red. It was not from shame, nor yet
wholly from a sense of anger, but mingled feelings filled
her heart; feelings which she could in nowise explain.
' If you have forgiven him that '—she would have said,
had she thought it right to speak out her mind—' if you
have forgiven him that, then there is nothing left for
further forgiveness.'

Gertrude had twice a better knowledge of the world than
he had, twice a quicker perception of how things were
going, and should be made to go. She saw that it was
useless to refer further to her husband. Norman had
come there at her request to say adieu to her ; that she
and he, who had been friends since she was a child, might
see each other before they were separated for ever by half
a world, and that they might part in love and charity.
She would be his sister-in-law, he would be son to her
mother, husband to her Linda ; he had been, though he
now denied it, her husband's staunchest friend in his
extremity ; and it would have added greatly to the
bitterness of her departure had she been forced to go
without speaking to him one kindly word. The opportunity was given to her, and she would not utterly mar its
sweetness by insisting on his injustice to her husband.

They all remained silent for a while, during which
Gertrude fondled her baby, and Norman produced before
the elder boy some present that he had brought for him.

' Now, Alley,' said Mrs. Woodward, ' you're a made
man ; won't that do beautifully to play with on board
the big ship ? '

' And so, Harry, you have given up official life altogether,' said Gertrude.

' Yes,' said he—' the last day of the last year saw my
finale at the Weights and Measures. I did not live long—
officially—to enjoy my promotion. I almost wish myself
back again.'

' You'll go in on melting days, like the retired tallow-

chandler,' said Gertrude ; ' but, joking apart, I wish you
joy on your freedom from thraldom ; a government office
in England is thraldom. If a man were to give his work
only, it would be well. All men who have to live by
labour must do that ; but a man has to give himself as
well as his work ; to sacrifice his individuality ; to become
body and soul a part of a lumbering old machine.'

This hardly came well from Gertrude, seeing that
Alaric at any rate had never been required to sacrifice
any of his individuality. But she was determined to hate
all the antecedents of his life, as though those antecedents,
and not the laxity of his own principles, had brought
about his ruin. She was prepared to live entirely for the
future, and to look back on her London life as bad, tasteless, and demoralizing. England to her was no longer
a glorious country ; for England's laws had made a felon
of her husband. She would go to a new land, new hopes,
new ideas, new freedom, new work, new life, and new
ambition. ' Excelsior !' there was no longer an excelsior
left for talent and perseverance in this effete country.
She and hers would soon find room for their energies in
a younger land ; and as she went she could not but pity
those whom she left behind. Her reasoning was hardly
logical, but, perhaps, it was not unfortunate.

' For myself,' said Norman, not quite following all
this—' I always liked the Civil Service, and now I leave
it with a sort of regret. I am quite glad that Charley has
my old desk ; it will keep up a sort of tie between me and
the place.'

' What does Linda say about it, mamma ? '

' Linda and I are both of Harry's way of thinking,'
said Mrs. Woodward, ' because Normansgrove is such
a distance.'

' Distance !' repeated Gertrude, with something of
sorrow, but more of scorn in her tone. ' Distance, mamma !
why you can get to her between breakfast and dinner.
Think where Melbourne is, mamma !'

' It has nearly broken my heart to think of it,' said
Mrs. Woodward.

' And you will still have Linda, mamma, and our darling
Katie, and Harry, and dear Charley. If the idea of

distance should frighten anyone it is me. But nothing
shall frighten me while I have my husband and children.
Harry, you must not let mamma be too often alone
when some other knight shall have come and taken away
Katie.'

'We will take her to Normansgrove for good and all,
if she will let us,' said Harry.

And now the time came for them to part. Harry was
to say good-bye to her, and then to see her no more.
Early on the following morning Gertrude was to go to
Hampton and see Katie for the last time; to see Katie
for the last time, and the Cottage, and the shining river,
and all the well-known objects among which she had
passed her life. To Mrs. Woodward, to Linda, and Katie,
all this was subject of inexpressible melancholy; but
with Gertrude every feeling of romance seemed to have been
absorbed by the realities of life. She would, of course, go
to Katie and give her a farewell embrace, since Katie
was still too weak to come to her; she would say farewell
to Uncle Bat, to whom she and Alaric owed so much;
she would doubtless shed a tear or two, and feel some
emotion at parting, even from the inanimate associations
of her youth; but all this would now impress no lasting
sorrow on her.

She was eager to be off, eager for her new career, eager
that he should stand on a soil where he could once more
face his fellow-creatures without shame. She panted to
put thousands of leagues of ocean between him and his
disgrace.

On the following morning Gertrude was to go to Hampton for two hours, and then to return to Millbank, with
her mother and sister, for whose accommodation a bed
had been hired in the neighbourhood. On that evening
Alaric would be released from his prison; and then before
daybreak on the following day they were to take their
way to the far-off docks, and place themselves on board
the vessel which was to carry them to their distant home.

'God bless you, Gertrude,' said Norman, whose eyes
were not dry.

'God Almighty bless you, Harry, you and Linda—and
make you happy. If Linda does not write constantly

very constantly, you must do it for her. We have delayed the happiness of your marriage, Harry—you must forgive us that, as well as all our other trespasses. I fear Linda will never forgive that.'

'You won't find her unmerciful on that score,' said he. 'Dear Gertrude, good-bye.'

She put up her face to him, and he kissed her, for the first time in his life. 'He bade me give you his love,' said she, in her last whisper; 'I must, you know, do his bidding.'

Norman's heart palpitated so that he could hardly compose his voice for his last answer; but even then he would not be untrue to his inexorable obstinacy; he could not send his love to a man he did not love. 'Tell him,' said he, 'that he has my sincerest wishes for success wherever he may be; and Gertrude, I need hardly say——' but he could get no further.

And so they parted.

CHAPTER XLIV

THE CRIMINAL POPULATION IS DISPOSED OF

BEFORE we put Alaric on board the ship which is to take him away from the land in which he might have run so exalted a career, we must say one word as to the fate and fortunes of his old friend Undy Scott. This gentleman has not been represented in our pages as an amiable or high-minded person. He has indeed been the bad spirit of the tale, the Siva of our mythology, the devil that has led our hero into temptation, the incarnation of evil, which it is always necessary that the novelist should have personified in one of his characters to enable him to bring about his misfortunes, his tragedies, and various requisite catastrophes. Scott had his Varney and such-like; Dickens his Bill Sykes and such-like; all of whom are properly disposed of before the end of those volumes in which are described their respective careers.

I have ventured to introduce to my readers, as my devil, Mr. Undy Scott, M.P. for the Tillietudlem district burghs ; and I also feel myself bound to dispose of him, though of him I regret I cannot make so decent an end as was done with Sir Richard Varney and Bill Sykes.

He deserves, however, as severe a fate as either of those heroes. With the former we will not attempt to compare him, as the vices and devilry of the days of Queen Elizabeth are in no way similar to those in which we indulge ; but with Bill Sykes we may contrast him, as they flourished in the same era, and had their points of similitude, as well as their points of difference.

They were both apparently born to prey on their own species ; they both resolutely adhered to a fixed rule that they would in nowise earn their bread, and to a rule equally fixed that, though they would earn no bread, they would consume much. They were both of them blessed with a total absence of sensibility and an utter disregard to the pain of others, and had no other use for a heart than that of a machine for maintaining the circulation of the blood. It is but little to say that neither of them ever acted on principle, on a knowledge, that is, of right and wrong, and a selection of the right ; in their studies of the science of evil they had progressed much further than this, and had taught themselves to believe that that which other men called virtue was, on its own account, to be regarded as mawkish, insipid, and useless for such purposes as the acquisition of money or pleasure ; whereas vice was, on its own account, to be preferred, as offering the only road to those things which they were desirous of possessing.

So far there was a great resemblance between Bill Sykes and Mr. Scott ; but then came the points of difference, which must give to the latter a great pre-eminence in the eyes of that master whom they had both so worthily served. Bill could not boast the merit of selecting the course which he had run ; he had served the Devil, having had, as it were, no choice in the matter ; he was born and bred and educated an evil-doer, and could hardly have deserted from the colours of his great Captain, without some spiritual interposition to enable him to do

so. To Undy a warmer reward must surely be due : he
had been placed fairly on the world's surface, with power
to choose between good and bad, and had deliberately
taken the latter ; to him had, at any rate, been explained
the theory of *meum* and *tuum,* and he had resolved that he
liked *tuum* better than *meum ;* he had learnt that there is
a God ruling over us, and a Devil hankering after us,
and had made up his mind that he would belong to the
latter. Bread and water would have come to him naturally
without any villainy on his part, aye, and meat and milk,
and wine and oil, the fat things of the world ; but he
elected to be a villain ; he liked to do the Devil's bidding.—
Surely he was the better servant ; surely he shall have the
richer reward.

And yet poor Bill Sykes, for whom here I would
willingly say a word or two, could I, by so saying, mitigate
the wrath against him, is always held as the more detestable scoundrel. Lady, you now know them both. Is it
not the fact, that, knowing him as you do, you could
spend a pleasant hour enough with Mr. Scott, sitting next
to him at dinner ; whereas your blood would creep within
you, your hair would stand on end, your voice would stick
in your throat, if you were suddenly told that Bill Sykes
was in your presence ?

Poor Bill ! I have a sort of love for him, as he walks
about wretched with that dog of his, though I know that
it is necessary to hang him. Yes, Bill ; I, your friend,
cannot gainsay that, must acknowledge that. Hard as
the case may be, you must be hung ; hung out of the way
of further mischief ; my spoons, my wife's throat, my
children's brains, demand that. You, Bill, and polecats,
and such-like, must be squelched when we can come
across you, seeing that you make yourself so universally
disagreeable. It is your ordained nature to be disagreeable ;
you plead silently. I know it ; I admit the hardship of
your case ; but still, my Bill, self-preservation is the first
law of nature. You must be hung. But, while hanging
you, I admit that you are more sinned against than
sinning. There is another, Bill, another, who will surely
take account of this in some way, though it is not for me
to tell you how.

Yes, I hang Bill Sykes with soft regret ; but with what a savage joy, with what exultation of heart, with what alacrity of eager soul, with what aptitude of mind to the deed, would I hang my friend, Undy Scott, the member of Parliament for the Tillietudlem burghs, if I could but get at his throat for such a purpose ! Hang him ! aye, as high as Haman ! In this there would be no regret, no vacillation of purpose, no doubt as to the propriety of the sacrifice, no feeling that I was so treating him, not for his own desert, but for my advantage.

We hang men, I believe, with this object only, that we should deter others from crime ; but in hanging Bill we shall hardly deter his brother. Bill Sykes must look to crime for his bread, seeing that he has been so educated, seeing that we have not yet taught him another trade.

But if I could hang Undy Scott, I think I should deter some others. The figure of Undy swinging from a gibbet at the broad end of Lombard Street would have an effect. Ah ! my fingers itch to be at the rope.

Fate, however, and the laws are averse. To gibbet him, in one sense, would have been my privilege, had I drunk deeper from that Castalian rill whose dark waters are tinged with the gall of poetic indignation ; but as in other sense I may not hang him, I will tell how he was driven from his club, and how he ceased to number himself among the legislators of his country.

Undy Scott, among his other good qualities, possessed an enormous quantity of that which schoolboys in these days call 'cheek.' He was not easily browbeaten, and was generally prepared to browbeat others. Mr. Chaffanbrass certainly did get the better of him ; but then Mr. Chaffanbrass was on his own dunghill. Could Undy Scott have had Mr. Chaffanbrass down at the clubs, there would have been, perhaps, another tale to tell.

Give me the cock that can crow in any yard ; such cocks, however, we know are scarce. Undy Scott, as he left the Old Bailey, was aware that he had cut a sorry figure, and felt that he must immediately do something to put himself right again, at any rate before his portion of the world. He must perform some exploit uncommonly cheeky in order to cover his late discomfiture. To get the better of

Mr. Chaffanbrass at the Old Bailey had been beyond him; but he might yet do something at the clubs to set aside the unanimous verdict which had been given against him in the city. Nay, he must do something, unless he was prepared to go to the wall utterly, and at once.

Going to the wall with Undy would mean absolute ruin; he lived but on the cheekiness of his gait and habits; he had become member of Parliament, Government official, railway director, and club aristocrat, merely by dint of cheek. He had now received a great blow; he had stood before a crowd, and been annihilated by the better cheek of Mr. Chaffanbrass, and, therefore, it behoved him at once to do something. When the perfume of the rose grows stale, the flower is at once thrown aside, and carried off as foul refuse. It behoved Undy to see that his perfume was maintained in its purity, or he, too, would be carried off.

The club to which Undy more especially belonged was called the Downing; and of this Alaric was also a member, having been introduced into it by his friend. Here had Alaric spent by far too many of the hours of his married life, and had become well known and popular. At the time of his conviction, the summer was far advanced; it was then August; but Parliament was still sitting, and there were sufficient club men remaining in London to create a daily gathering at the Downing.

On the day following that on which the verdict was found, Undy convened a special committee of the club, in order that he might submit to it a proposition which he thought it indispensable should come from him; so, at least, he declared. The committee did assemble, and when Undy met it, he saw among the faces before him not a few with whom he would willingly have dispensed. However, he had come there to exercise his cheek; no one there should cow him; the wig of Mr. Chaffanbrass was, at any rate, absent.

And so he submitted his proposition. I need not trouble my readers with the neat little speech in which it was made. Undy was true to himself, and the speech was neat. The proposition was this: that as he had

unfortunately been the means of introducing Mr. Alaric
Tudor to the club, he considered it to be his duty to
suggest that the name of that gentleman should be struck
off the books. He then expressed his unmitigated disgust
at the crime of which Tudor had been found guilty, uttered
some nice little platitudes in the cause of virtue, and
expressed a hope ' that he might so far refer to a personal
matter as to say that his father's family would take care
that the lady, whose fortune had been the subject of the
trial, should not lose one penny through the dishonesty
of her trustee.'

Oh, Undy, as high as Haman, if I could ! as high as
Haman ! and if not in Lombard Street, then on that open
ground where Waterloo Place bisects Pall Mall, so that all
the clubs might see thee !

' He would advert,' he said, ' to one other matter,
though, perhaps, his doing so was unnecessary. It was
probably known to them all that he had been a witness
at the late trial ; an iniquitous attempt had been made
by the prisoner's counsel to connect his name with the
prisoner's guilt. They all too well knew the latitude
allowed to lawyers in the criminal courts, to pay much
attention to this. Had he ' (Undy Scott) ' in any way
infringed the laws of his country, he was there to answer
for it. But he would go further than this, and declare
that if any member of that club doubted his probity in
the matter, he was perfectly willing to submit to such
member documents which would,' &c., &c.

He finished his speech, and an awful silence reigned
around him. No enthusiastic ardour welcomed the well-
loved Undy back to his club, and comforted him after
the rough usage of the unpolished Chaffanbrass. No ten
or twenty combined voices expressed, by their clamorous
negation of the last-proposed process, that their Undy
was above reproach. The eyes around looked into him
with no friendly alacrity. Undy, Undy, more cheek still,
still more cheek, or you are surely lost.

' If,' said he, in a well-assumed indignant tone of
injured innocence, ' there be any in the club who do
suspect me of anything unbecoming a gentleman in this
affair, I am willing to retire from it till the matter shall

have been investigated ; but in such case I demand that the investigation be immediate.'

Oh, Undy, Undy, the supply of cheek is not bad ; it is all but unlimited ; but yet it suffices thee not. ' Can there be positions in this modern West End world of mine,' thought Undy to himself, ' in which cheek, unbounded cheek, will not suffice ? ' Oh, Undy, they are rare ; but still there are such, and this, unfortunately for thee, seemeth to be one of them.

And then got up a discreet old baronet, one who moveth not often in the affairs around him, but who, when he moveth, stirreth many waters ; a man of broad acres, and a quiet, well-assured fame which has grown to him without his seeking it, as barnacles grow to the stout keel when it has been long a-swimming ; him, of all men, would Undy have wished to see unconcerned with these matters.

Not in many words, nor eloquent did Sir Thomas speak. ' He felt it his duty,' he said, ' to second the proposal made by Mr. Scott for removing Mr. Tudor from amongst them. He had watched this trial with some care, and he pitied Mr. Tudor from the bottom of his heart. He would not have thought that he could have felt so strong a sympathy for a man convicted of dishonesty. But Mr. Tudor had been convicted, and he must incur the penalties of his fault. One of these penalties must, undoubtedly, be his banishment from this club. He therefore seconded Mr. Scott's proposal.'

He then stood silent for a moment, having finished that task ; but yet he did not sit down. Why, oh, why does he not sit down ? why, O Undy, does he thus stand, looking at the surface of the table on which he is leaning ?

' And now,' he said, ' he had another proposition to make ; and that was that Mr. Undecimus Scott should also be expelled from the club,' and having so spoken, in a voice of unusual energy, he then sat down.

And now, Undy, you may as well pack up, and be off, without further fuss, to Boulogne, Ostend, or some such idle Elysium, with such money-scrapings as you may be able to collect together. No importunity will avail thee anything against the judges and jurymen who are now trying thee. One word from that silent old baronet was worse to thee than all that Mr. Chaffanbrass could say. Come! pack up; and begone.

But he was still a Member of Parliament. The Parliament, however, was about to be dissolved, and, of course, it would be useless for him to stand again; he, like Mr. M'Buffer had had his spell of it, and he recognized the necessity of vanishing. He at first thought that his life as a legislator might be allowed to come to a natural end, that he might die as it were in his bed, without suffering the acute pain of applying for the Chiltern Hundreds. In this, however, he found himself wrong. The injured honour of all the Tillietudlemites rose against him with one indignant shout; and a rumour, a horrid rumour, of a severer fate met his ears. He applied at once for the now coveted sinecure,—and was refused. Her Majesty could not consent to entrust to him the duties of the situation in question——; and in lieu thereof the House expelled him by its unanimous voice.

And now, indeed, it was time for him to pack up and begone. He was now liable to the vulgarest persecution from the vulgar herd; his very tailor and bootmaker would beleaguer him, and coarse unwashed bailiffs take him by the collar. Yes, now indeed, it was time to be off.

And off he was. He paid one fleeting visit to my Lord at Cauldkail Castle, collecting what little he might; another to his honourable wife, adding some slender increase to his little budget, and then he was off. Whither, it is needless to say—to Hamburg perhaps, or to Ems, or the richer tables of Homburg. How he flourished for a while with ambiguous success; how he talked to the young English tourists of what he had done when in Parliament, especially for the rights of married women; how he poked his 'Honourable' card in every one's way, and lugged Lord Gaberlunzie into all conversations; how his face became pimply and his wardrobe seedy; and how at last his wretched life will ooze out from him in some dark corner, like the filthy juice of a decayed fungus which makes hideous the hidden wall on which it bursts, all this is unnecessary more particularly to describe. He is probably still living, and those who desire his acquaintance will find him creeping round some gambling table, and trying to look as though he had in his pocket ample means to secure those hoards of money which men are so listlessly raking about. From our view he has now vanished.

It was a bitter February morning, when two cabs stood packing themselves at No. 5, Paradise Row, Millbank. It was hardly yet six o'clock, and Paradise Row was dark as Erebus ; that solitary gas-light sticking out from the wall of the prison only made darkness visible ; the tallow candles which were brought in and out with every article that was stuffed under a seat, or into a corner, would get themselves blown out ; and the sleet which was falling fast made the wicks wet, so that they could with difficulty be relighted.

But at last the cabs were packed with luggage, and into one got Gertrude with her husband, her baby, and her mother ; and into the other Charley handed Linda, then Alley, and lastly, the youthful maiden, who humbly begged his pardon as she stepped up to the vehicle ; and then, having given due directions to the driver, he not without difficulty squeezed himself into the remaining space.

Such journeys as these are always made at a slow pace. Cabmen know very well who must go fast, and who may go slow. Women with children going on board an emigrant vessel at six o'clock on a February morning may be taken very slowly. And very slowly Gertrude and her party were taken. Time had been—nay, it was but the other day—when Alaric's impatient soul would have spurned at such a pace as this. But now he sat tranquil enough. His wife held one of his hands, and the other he pressed against his eyes, as though shading them from the light. Light there was none, but he had not yet learnt to face Mrs. Woodward even in the darkness.

He had come out of the prison on the day before, and had spent an evening with her. It is needless to say that no one had upbraided him, that no one had hinted that his backslidings had caused all this present misery, had brought them all to that wretched cabin, and would on the morrow separate, perhaps for ever, a mother and a child who loved each other so dearly. No one spoke to him of this ; perhaps no one thought of it ; he, however, did so think of it that he could not hold his head up before them.

'He was ill,' Gertrude said ; 'his long confinement had prostrated him ; but the sea air would revive him in a day or two.' And then she made herself busy, and got the tea for them, and strove, not wholly in vain, ' to drive dull care away ! '

But slowly as the cabs went in spite of Charley's vocal execrations, they did get to the docks in time. Who, indeed, was ever too late at the docks ? Who, that ever went there, had not to linger, linger, linger, till every shred of patience was clean worn out ? They got to the docks in time, and got on board that fast-sailing, clipper-built, never-beaten, always-healthy ship, the *Flash of Lightning*, 5,500 tons, A 1. Why, we have often wondered, are ships designated as A 1, seeing that all ships are of that class ? Where is the excellence, seeing that all share it ? Of course the *Flash of Lightning* was A 1. The author has for years been looking out, and has not yet found a ship advertised as A 2, or even as B 1. What is this catalogue of comparative excellence, of which there is but one visible number ?

The world, we think, makes a great mistake on the subject of saying, or acting, farewell. The word or deed should partake of the suddenness of electricity ; but we all drawl through it at a snail's pace. We are supposed to tear ourselves from our friends ; but tearing is a process which should be done quickly. What is so wretched as lingering over a last kiss, giving the hand for the third time, saying over and over again, ' Good-bye, John, God bless you ; and mind you write ! ' Who has not seen his dearest friends standing round the window of a railway carriage, while the train would not start, and has not longed to say to them, ' Stand not upon the order of your going, but go at once ! ' And of all such farewells, the ship's farewell is the longest and the most dreary. One sits on a damp bench, snuffing up the odour of oil and ropes, cudgelling one's brains to think what further word of increased tenderness can be spoken. No tenderer word

can be spoken.   One returns again and again to the
weather, to coats and cloaks, perhaps even to sandwiches
and the sherry flask.   All effect is thus destroyed, and
a trespass is made even on the domain of feeling.

I remember a line of poetry, learnt in my earliest youth,
and which I believe to have emanated from a sentimental
Frenchman, a man of genius, with whom my parents were
acquainted.   It is as follows :—

Are you go ?—Is you gone ?—And I left ?—Vera vell !

Now the whole business of a farewell is contained in that
line.   When the moment comes, let that be said ; let that
be said and felt, and then let the dear ones depart.

Mrs. Woodward and Gertrude—God bless them !—had
never studied the subject.   They knew no better than to
sit in the nasty cabin, surrounded by boxes, stewards,
porters, children, and abominations of every kind, holding
each other's hands, and pressing damp handkerchiefs to
their eyes.   The delay, the lingering, upset even Gertrude,
and brought her for a moment down to the usual level of
leave-taking womanhood.   Alaric, the meanwhile, stood
leaning over the taffrail with Charley, as mute as the fishes
beneath him.

' Write to us the moment you get there,' said Charley.
How often had the injunction been given !   ' And now we
had better get off—you'll be better when we are gone,
Alaric,'—Charley had some sense of the truth about him—
' and, Alaric, take my word for it, I'll come and set the
Melbourne Weights and Measures to rights before long—
I'll come and weigh your gold for you.'

' We had better be going now,' said Charley, looking
down into the cabin ;   ' they may let loose and be off any
moment now.'

' Oh, Charley, not yet, not yet,' said Linda, clinging to
her sister.

' You'll have to go down to the Nore, if you stay ;
that's all,' said Charley.

And then again began the kissing and the crying.   Yes,
ye dear ones—it is hard to part—it is hard for the mother
to see the child of her bosom torn from her for ever ; it is
cruel that sisters should be severed ; it is a harsh sentence

for the world to give, that of such a separation as this. These, O ye loving hearts, are the penalties of love! Those that are content to love must always be content to pay them.

'Go, mamma, go,' said Gertrude; 'dearest, best, sweetest mother—my own, own mother; go, Linda, darling Linda. Give my kindest love to Harry—Charley, you and Harry will be good to mamma, I know you will. And mamma'—and then she whispered to her mother one last prayer in Charley's favour—'she may love him now, indeed she may.'

Alaric came to them at the last moment—'Mrs. Woodward,' said he, 'say that you forgive me.'

'I do,' said she, embracing him—'God knows that I do;—but, Alaric, remember what a treasure you possess.'

And so they parted. May God speed the wanderers!

CHAPTER XLV

THE FATE OF THE NAVVIES

AND now, having dispatched Alaric and his wife and bairns on their long journey, we must go back for a while and tell how Charley had been transformed from an impudent, idle young Navvy into a well-conducted, zealous young Weights.

When Alaric was convicted, Charley had, as we all know, belonged to the Internal Navigation; when the six months' sentence had expired, Charley was in full blow at the decorous office in Whitehall; and during the same period Norman had resigned and taken on himself the new duties of a country squire. The change which had been made had affected others than Charley. It had been produced by one of those far-stretching, world-moving commotions which now and then occur, sometimes twice or thrice in a generation, and, perhaps, not again for half a century, causing timid men to whisper in corners, and the brave and high-spirited to struggle with the struggling waves, so that when the storm subsides they may be found floating on the surface. A moral earth-quake had been endured by a portion of the Civil Service of the country.

The Internal Navigation had—— No, my prognostic reader, it had not been reformed; no new blood had been infused into it; no attempt had been made to produce a better discipline by the appointment of a younger secretary; there had been no carting away of decayed wood in the shape of Mr. Snape, or gathering of rank weeds in the form of Mr. Corkscrew; nothing of the kind had been attempted. No—the disease had gone too far either for phlebotomy, purging, or cautery. The Internal Navigation had ceased to exist! Its demise had been in this wise.—It may be remembered that some time since Mr. Oldeschole had mentioned in the hearing of Mr. Snape that things were going wrong. Sir Gregory Hard-lines had expressed an adverse opinion as to the Internal Navigation, and worse, ten times worse than that, there had been an article in the *Times*. Now, we all know that if anything is ever done in any way towards improve-ment in these days, the public press does it. And we all know, also, of what the public press consists. Mr. Olde-schole knew this well, and even Mr. Snape had a glimmering idea of the truth. When he read that article, Mr. Oldeschole felt that his days were numbered, and Mr. Snape, when he heard of it, began to calculate for the hundredth time to what highest amount of pension he might be adjudged to be entitled by a liberal-minded Treasury minute.

Mr. Oldeschole began to set his house in order, hope-lessly; for any such effort the time was gone by. It was too late for the office to be so done by, and too late for Mr. Oldeschole to do it. He had no aptitude for new styles and modern improvements; he could not under-stand Sir Gregory's code of rules, and was dumbfounded by the Civil Service requisitions that were made upon him from time to time. Then came frequent calls for him to attend at Sir Gregory's office. There a new broom had been brought in, in the place of our poor friend Alaric, a broom which seemed determined to sweep all before it with an unmitigable energy. Mr. Oldeschole found that he could not stand at all before this young Hercules, seeing that his special stall was considered to be the foulest in the whole range of the Augean stables. He soon saw that the river was to be turned in on him, and that he was to be officially obliterated in the flood.

The civility of those wonder-doing demigods—those Magi of the Civil Service office—was most oppressive to him. When he got to the board, he was always treated with a deference which he knew was but a prelude to barbaric tortures. They would ask him to sit down in a beautiful new leathern arm-chair, as though he were really some great man, and then examine him as they would a candidate for the Custom House, smiling always, but looking at him as though they were determined to see through him.

They asked him all manner of questions ; but there was one question which they put to him, day after day, for four days, that nearly drove him mad. It was always put by that horrid young lynx-eyed new commissioner, who sat there with his hair brushed high from off his forehead, peering out of his capacious, excellently-washed shirt-collars, a personification of conscious official zeal.

' And now, Mr. Oldeschole, if you have had leisure to consider the question more fully, perhaps you can define to us what is the—hum—hm—the use—hm—hm—the exact use of the Internal Navigation Office ? '

And then Sir Warwick would go on looking through his millstone as though now he really had a hope of seeing something, and Sir Gregory would lean back in his chair, and rubbing his hands slowly over each other, like a great Akinetos as he was, wait leisurely for Mr. Oldeschole's answer, or rather for his no answer.

What a question was this to ask of a man who had spent all his life in the Internal Navigation Office ! O reader ! should it chance that thou art a clergyman, imagine what it would be to thee, wert thou asked what is the exact use of the Church of England ; and that, too, by some stubborn catechist whom thou wert bound to answer ; or, if a lady, happy in a husband and family, say, what would be thy feelings if demanded to define the exact use of matrimony ? Use ! Is it not all in all to thee ?

Mr. Oldeschole felt a hearty inward conviction that his office had been of very great use. In the first place, had he not drawn from it a thousand a year for the last five-and-twenty years? had it not given maintenance and employment to many worthy men who might perhaps have found it difficult to obtain maintenance elsewhere? had it not always been an office, a public office of note and reputation, with proper work assigned to it? The use of it—the exact use of it? Mr. Oldeschole at last declared, with some indignation in his tone, that he had been there for forty years and knew well that the office was very useful; but that he would not undertake to define its exact use. 'Thank you, thank you, Mr. Oldeschole—that will do, I think,' said the very spruce-looking new gentleman out of his shirt-collars.

In these days there was a kind of prescience at the Internal Navigation that something special was going to be done with them. Mr. Oldeschole said nothing openly; but it may be presumed that he did whisper somewhat to those of the seniors around him in whom he most confided. And then, his frequent visits to Whitehall were spoken of even by the most thoughtless of the navvies, and the threatenings of the coming storm revealed themselves with more or less distinctness to every mind.

At last the thundercloud broke and the bolt fell. Mr. Oldeschole was informed that the Lords of the Treasury had resolved on breaking up the establishment and providing for the duties in another way. As the word duties passed Sir Gregory's lips a slight smile was seen to hover round the mouth of the new commissioner. Mr. Oldeschole would, he was informed, receive an official notification to this effect on the following morning; and on the following morning accordingly a dispatch arrived, of great length, containing the resolution of my Lords, and putting an absolute extinguisher on the life of every navvy.

How Mr. Oldeschole, with tears streaming down his cheeks, communicated the tidings to the elder brethren; and how the elder brethren, with palpitating hearts and quivering voices, repeated the tale to the listening juniors,

I cannot now describe. The boldest spirits were then cowed, the loudest miscreants were then silenced, there were but few gibes, but little jeering at the Internal Navigation on that day; though Charley, who had already other hopes, contrived to keep up his spirits. The men stood about talking in clusters, and old animosities were at an end. The lamb sat down with the wolf, and Mr. Snape and Dick Scatterall became quite confidential.

'I knew it was going to happen,' said Mr. Snape to him. 'Indeed, Mr. Oldeschole has been consulting us about it for some time; but I must own I did not think it would be so sudden; I must own that.'

'If you knew it was coming,' said Corkscrew, 'why didn't you tell a chap?'

'I was not at liberty,' said Mr. Snape, looking very wise.

'We shall all have liberty enough now,' said Scatterall; 'I wonder what they'll do with us; eh, Charley?'

'I believe they will send the worst of us to Spike Island or Dartmoor prison,' said Charley; 'but Mr. Snape, no doubt, has heard and can tell us.'

'Oh, come, Charley! It don't do to chaff now,' said a young navvy, who was especially down in the mouth. 'I wonder will they do anything for a fellow?'

'I heard my uncle, in Parliament Street, say, that when a chap has got any *infested* interest in a thing, they can't turn him out,' said Corkscrew; 'and my uncle is a parliamentary agent.'

'Can't they though!' said Scatterall. 'It seems to me that they mean to, at any rate; there wasn't a word about pensions or anything of that sort, was there, Mr. Snape?'

'Not a word,' said Snape. 'But those who are entitled to pensions can't be affected injuriously. As far as I can see they must give me my whole salary. I don't think they can do less.'

'You're all serene then, Mr. Snape,' said Charley; 'you're in the right box. Looking at matters in that light, Mr. Snape, I think you ought to stand something handsome in the shape of lunch. Come, what do you say to chops and stout all round ? Dick will go over and order it in a minute.'

'I wish you wouldn't, Charley,' said the navvy who seemed to be most affected, and who, in his present humour, could not endure a joke. As Mr. Snape did not seem to accede to Charley's views, the liberal proposition fell to the ground.

'Care killed a cat,' said Scatterall. 'I shan't break my heart about it. I never liked the shop—did you, Charley ?'

'Well, I must say I think we have been very comfortable here, under Mr. Snape,' said Charley. 'But if Mr. Snape is to go, why the office certainly would be deuced dull without him.'

'Charley !' said the broken-hearted young navvy, in a tone of reproach.

Sorrow, however, did not take away their appetite, and as Mr. Snape did not see fitting occasion for providing a banquet, they clubbed together, and among them managed to get a spread of beefsteaks and porter. Scatterall, as requested, went across the Strand to order it at the cookshop, while Corkscrew and Charley prepared the tables. 'And now mind it's the thing,' said Dick, who, with intimate familiarity, had penetrated into the eating-house kitchen ; 'not dry, you know, or too much done ; and lots of fat.'

And then, as the generous viands renewed their strength, and as the potent stout warmed their blood, happier ideas came to them, and they began to hope that the world was not all over. 'Well, I shall try for the Customs,' said the unhappy one, after a deep pull at the pewter. 'I shall try for the Customs ; one does get such stunning feeds for tenpence at that place in Thames Street.' Poor youth ! his ideas of earning his bread did not in their wildest flight spread beyond the public offices of the Civil Service.

For a few days longer they hung about the old office, doing nothing—how could men so circumstanced do anything ?—and waiting for their fate. At last their fate was announced. Mr. Oldeschole retired with his full salary. Secretaries and such-like always retire with full pay, as it is necessary that dignity should be supported. Mr. Snape and the other seniors were pensioned, with a careful respect to their years of service ; with which arrangement they all of them expressed themselves highly indignant, and loudly threatened to bring the cruelty of their treatment before Parliament, by the aid of sundry members, who were supposed to be on the look out for such work ; but as nothing further was ever heard of them, it may be presumed that the members in question did not regard the case as one on which the Government of the day was sufficiently vulnerable to make it worth their while to trouble themselves. Of the younger clerks, two or three, including the unhappy one, were drafted into other offices ; some others received one or more years' pay, and then tore themselves away from the fascinations of London life ; among those was Mr. R. Scatterall, who, in after years, will doubtless become a lawgiver in Hong-Kong ; for to that colony has he betaken himself. Some few others, more unfortunate than the rest, among whom poor Screwy was the most conspicuous, were treated with a more absolute rigour, and were sent upon the world portionless. Screwy had been constant in his devotion to pork chops, and had persisted in spelling blue without the final 'e.' He was therefore, declared unworthy of any further public confidence whatever. He is now in his uncle's office in Parliament Street ; and it is to be hoped that his peculiar talents may there be found useful.

And so the Internal Navigation Office came to an end, and the dull, dingy rooms were vacant. Ruthless men shovelled off as waste paper all the lock entries of which Charley had once been so proud ; and the ponderous ledgers, which Mr. Snape had delighted to haul about, were sent away into Cimmerian darkness, and probably to utter destruction. And then the Internal Navigation was no more.

Among those who were drafted into other offices was Charley, whom propitious fate took to the Weights and Measures. But it must not be imagined that chance took him there. The Weights and Measures was an Elysium, the door of which was never casually open.

Charley at this time was a much-altered man; not that he had become a good clerk at his old office—such a change one may say was impossible; there were no good clerks at the Internal Navigation, and Charley had so long been among navvies the most knavish or navviest, that any such transformation would have met with no credence—but out of his office he had become a much-altered man. As Katie had said, it was as though some one had come to him from the dead. He could not go back to his old haunts, he could not return like a dog to his vomit, as long as he had that purse so near his heart, as long as that voice sounded in his ear, while the memory of that kiss lingered in his heart.

He now told everything to Gertrude, all his debts, all his love, and all his despair. There is no relief for sorrow like the sympathy of a friend, if one can only find it. But then the sympathy must be real; mock sympathy always tells the truth against itself, always fails to deceive. He told everything to Gertrude, and by her counsel he told much to Norman. He could not speak to him, true friend as he was, of Katie and her love. There was that about the subject which made it too sacred for man's ears, too full of tenderness to be spoken of without feminine tears. It was only in the little parlour at Paradise Row, when the evening had grown dark, and Gertrude was sitting with her baby in her arms, that the boisterous young navvy could bring himself to speak of his love.

During these months Katie's health had greatly improved, and as she herself had gained in strength, she had gradually begun to think that it was yet possible for her to live. Little was now said by her about Charley, and not much was said of him in her hearing; but still she did learn how he had changed his office, and with his office his mode of life; she did hear of his literary efforts, and of his kindness to Gertrude, and it would seem as though it were ordained that his moral life and her physical life were to gain strength together.

CHAPTER XLVI

MR. NOGO'S LAST QUESTION

BUT at this time Charley was not idle. The fate of 'Crinoline and Macassar' has not yet been told; nor has that of the two rival chieftains, the 'Baron of Bally-poreen and Sir Anthony Allan-a-dale.' These heartrending tales appeared in due course, bit by bit, in the pages of the *Daily Delight*. On every morning of the week, Sundays excepted, a page and a half of Charley's narrative was given to the expectant public; and though I am not prepared to say that the public received the offering with any violent acclamations of applause, that his name became suddenly that of a great unknown, that literary cliques talked about him to the exclusion of other topics, or that he rose famous one morning as Byron did after the publication of the 'Corsair,' nevertheless something was said in his praise. The *Daily Delight*, on the whole, was rather belittled by its grander brethren of the press; but a word or two was said here and there to exempt Charley's fictions from the general pooh-poohing with which the remainder of the publication was treated.

Success, such as this even, is dear to the mind of a young author, and Charley began to feel that he had done something. The editor was proportionably civil to him, and he was encouraged to commence a third historiette.

'We have polished off poison and petticoats pretty well,' said the editor; 'what do you say to something political?'

Charley had no objection in life.

'This Divorce Bill, now—we could have half a dozen married couples all separating, getting rid of their ribs and buckling again, helter-skelter, every man to somebody else's wife; and the parish parson refusing to do the work; just to show the immorality of the thing.'

Charley said he'd think about it.

'Or the Danubian Principalities and the French Alliance—could you manage now to lay your scene in Constantinople?'

Charley doubted whether he could.

'Or perhaps India is the thing? The Cawnpore massacre would work up into any lengths you pleased. You could get a file of the *Times*, you know, for your facts.'

But while the editor was giving these various valuable hints as to the author's future subjects, the author himself, with base mind, was thinking how much he should be paid for his past labours. At last he ventured, in the mildest manner, to allude to the subject.

'Payment!' said the editor.

Charley said that he had understood that there was to be some fixed scale of pay; so much per sheet, or something of that sort.

'Undoubtedly there will,' said the editor; 'and those who will have the courage and perseverance to work through with us, till the publication has obtained that wide popularity which it is sure to achieve, will doubtless be paid,—be paid as no writers for any periodical in this metropolis have ever yet been paid. But at present, Mr. Tudor, you really must be aware that it is quite out of the question.'

Charley had not the courage and perseverance to work through with the *Daily Delight* till it had achieved its promised popularity, and consequently left its ranks like a dastard. He consulted both Gertrude and Norman on the subject, and on their advice set himself to work on his own bottom. 'You may perhaps manage to fly alone,' said Gertrude; 'but you will find it very difficult to fly if you tie the whole weight of the *Daily Delight* under your wings.' So Charley prepared himself for solitary soaring.

While he was thus working, the time arrived at which Norman was to leave his office, and it occurred to him that it might be possible that he should bequeath his vacancy to Charley. He went himself to Sir Gregory, and explained, not only his own circumstances, and his former friendship with Alaric Tudor, but also the relationship between Alaric and Charley. He then learnt, in the strictest confidence of course, that the doom of the Internal Navigation had just been settled, and that it would be necessary to place in other offices those young men who could in any way be regarded as worth their salt, and, after considerable manœuvring, had it so arranged that the ne'er-do-well young navvy should recommence his official life under better auspices.

Nor did Charley come in at the bottom of his office, but was allowed, by some inscrutable order of the great men who arranged those things, to take a position in the Weights and Measures equal in seniority and standing to that which he had held at the Navigation, and much higher, of course, in pay. There is an old saying, which the unenlightened credit, and which declares that that which is sauce for the goose is sauce also for the gander. Nothing put into a proverb since the days of Solomon was ever more untrue. That which is sauce for the goose is not sauce for the gander, and especially is not so in official life. Poor Screwy was the goose, and certainly got the sauce best suited to him when he was turned adrift out of the Civil Service. Charley was the gander, and fond as I am of him for his many excellent qualities, I am fain to own that justice might fairly have demanded that he should be cooked after the same receipt. But it suited certain potent personages to make a swan of him ; and therefore, though it had long been an assured fact through the whole service that no man was ever known to enter the Weights and Measures without the strictest examination, though the character of aspirants for that high office was always subjected to a rigid scrutiny, though knowledge, accomplishments, industry, morality, outward decency, inward zeal, and all the cardinal virtues were absolutely requisite, still Charley was admitted, without any examination or scrutiny whatever, during the commotion consequent upon the earthquake above described.

Charley went to the Weights some time during the recess. In the process of the next session Mr. Nogo gave notice that he meant to ask the Government a question as to a gross act of injustice which had been perpetrated —so at least the matter had been represented to him— on the suppression of the Internal Navigation Office.

Mr. Nogo did not at first find it very easy to get a fitting opportunity for asking his question. He had to give notice, and inquiries had to be made, and the responsible people were away, and various customary accidents happened, so that it was late in June before the question was put. Mr. Nogo, however, persevered ruthlessly, and after six months' labour, did deliver himself of an indignant, and, as his friends declared to him, a very telling speech.

It was reported at the time by the opposition newspapers, and need not therefore be given here. But the upshot was this: two men bearing equal character—Mr. Nogo would not say whether the characters of the gentlemen were good or bad; he would only say equal characters—sat in the same room at this now defunct office; one was Mr. Corkscrew and the other Mr. Tudor. One had no friends in the Civil Service, but the other was more fortunate. Mr. Corkscrew had been sent upon the world a ruined, blighted man, without any compensation, without any regard for his interests, without any consideration for his past services or future prospects. They would be told that the Government had no further need of his labours, and that they could not dare to saddle the country with a pension for so young a man. But what had been done in the case of the other gentleman? Why, he had been put into a valuable situation, in the best Government office in London, had been placed over the heads of a dozen others, who had been there before him, &c., &c., &c. And then Mr. Nogo ended with so vehement an attack on Sir Gregory, and the Government as connected with him, that the dogs began to whet their teeth and prepare for a tug at the great badger.

But circumstances were mischancy with Mr. Nogo, and all he said redounded only to the credit of our friend Charley. His black undoubtedly was black; the merits of Charley and Mr. Corkscrew, as public servants, had been about equal; but Mr. Whip Vigil turned the black into white in three minutes.

As he got upon his legs, smiling after the manner of his great exemplar, he held in his hand a small note and a newspaper. 'A comparison,' he said, 'had been instituted between the merits of two gentlemen formerly in the employment of the Crown, one of them had been selected for further employment, and the other rejected. The honourable member for Mile End had, he regretted to say, instituted this comparison. They all knew what was the proverbial character of a comparison. It was, however, ready made to his hands, and there was nothing left for him, Mr. Whip Vigil, but to go on with it. This, however, he would do in as light a manner as possible. It had been thought that the one gentleman would not suit the public service, and that the other would do so. It was for him merely to defend this opinion. He now held in his hand a letter written by the protégé of the honourable member for Limehouse ; he would not read it—' (cries of ' Read, read ! ') ' no, he would not read it, but the honourable member might if he would—and could. He himself was prepared to say that a gentleman who chose to express himself in such a style in his private notes—this note, however, was not private in the usual sense—could hardly be expected to command a proper supply of wholesome English, such as the service of the Crown demanded ! ' Then Mr. Vigil handed across to Mr. Nogo poor Screwy's unfortunate letter about the pork chops. ' As to the other gentleman, whose name was now respectably known in the lighter walks of literature, he would, if permitted, read the opinion expressed as to his style of language by a literary publication of the day ; and then the House would see whether or no the produce of the Civil Service field had not been properly winnowed ; whether the wheat had not been garnered, and the chaff neglected.' And then the right honourable gentleman read some half-dozen lines, highly eulogistic of Charley's first solitary flight.

Poor Mr. Nogo remained in silence, feeling that his black had become white to all intents and purposes ; and the big badger sat by and grinned, not deigning to notice the dogs around him. Thus it may be seen that that which is sauce for the goose is not sauce for the gander.

Early in the spring Norman was married ; and then, as had been before arranged, Charley once more went to Surbiton Cottage. The marriage was a very quiet affair. The feeling of disgrace which had fallen upon them all since the days of Alaric's trial had by no means worn

itself away. There were none of them yet—no, not one
of the Cottage circle, from Uncle Bat down to the parlour-
maid—who felt that they had a right to hold up their
faces before the light of day as they had formerly done.
There was a cloud over their house, visible perhaps with
more or less distinctness to all eyes, but which to themselves appeared black as night. That evil which Alaric
had done to them was not to be undone in a few moons.
We are all of us responsible for our friends, fathers-in-
law for their sons-in-law, brothers for their sisters, husbands for their wives, parents for their children, and
children even for their parents. We cannot wipe off
from us, as with a wet cloth, the stains left by the fault
of those who are near to us. The ink-spot will cling.
Oh! Alaric, Alaric, that thou, thou who knewest all this,
that thou shouldest have done this thing! They had
forgiven his offence against them, but they could not
forget their own involuntary participation in his disgrace.
It was not for them now to shine forth to the world with
fine gala doings, and gay gaudy colours, as they had
done when Gertrude had been married.

But still there was happiness—quiet, staid happiness—
at the Cottage. Mrs. Woodward could not but be happy
to see Linda married to Harry Norman, her own favourite,
him whom she had selected in her heart for her son-in-
law from out of all the world. And now, too, she was
beginning to be conscious that Harry and Linda were
better suited for each other than he and Gertrude would
have been. What would have been Linda's fate, how
unendurable, had she been Alaric's wife, when Alaric
fell? How would she have borne such a fall? What
could she have done, poor lamb, towards mending the
broken thread or binding the bruised limbs? What balm
could she have poured into such wounds as those which
fate had inflicted on Gertrude and her household? But
at Normansgrove, with a steady old housekeeper at her
back, and her husband always by to give her courage,
Linda would find the very place for which she was suited.

And then Mrs. Woodward had another source of joy,
of liveliest joy, in Katie's mending looks. She was at
the wedding, though hardly with her mother's approval.

As she got better her old spirit returned to her, and it became difficult to refuse her anything. It was in vain that her mother talked of the cold church, and easterly winds, and the necessary lightness of a bridesmaid's attire. Katie argued that the church was only two hundred yards off, that she never suffered from the cold, and that though dressed in light colours, as became a bridesmaid, she would, if allowed to go, wear over her white frock any amount of cloaks which her mother chose to impose on her. Of course she went, and we will not say how beautiful she looked, when she clung to Linda in the vestry-room, and all her mother's wrappings fell in disorder from her shoulders.

So Linda was married and carried off to Normans-grove, and Katie remained with her mother and Uncle Bat.

'Mamma, we will never part—will we, mamma?' said she, as they comforted each other that evening after the Normans were gone, and when Charley also had returned to London.

'When you go, Katie, I think you must take me with you,' said her mother, smiling through her tears. 'But what will poor Uncle Bat do? I fear you can't take him also.'

'I will never go from you, mamma.'

Her mother knew what she meant. Charley had been there, Charley to whom she had declared her love when lying, as she thought, on her bed of death—Charley had been there again, and had stood close to her, and touched her hand, and looked—oh, how much handsomer he was than Harry, how much brighter than Alaric!—he had touched her hand, and spoken to her one word of joy at her recovered health. But that had been all. There was a sort of compact, Katie knew, that there should be no other Tudor marriage. Charley was not now the scamp he had been, but still—it was understood that her love was not to win its object.

'I will never go from you, mamma.'

But Mrs. Woodward's heart was not hard as the nether millstone. She drew her daughter to her, and as she pressed her to her bosom, she whispered into her ears that she now hoped they might all be happy.

CHAPTER XLVII

CONCLUSION

OUR tale and toils have now drawn nigh to an end ; our loves and our sorrows are over ; and we are soon to part company with the three clerks and their three wives. Their three wives ? Why, yes. It need hardly be told in so many words to an habitual novel-reader that Charley did get his bride at last.

Nevertheless, Katie kept her promise to Mrs. Woodward. What promise did she ever make and not keep ? She kept her promise, and did not go from her mother. She married Mr. Charles Tudor, of the Weights and Measures, that distinguished master of modern fiction, as the *Literary Censor* very civilly called him the other day ; and Mr. Charles Tudor became master of Surbiton Cottage.

Reader ! take one last leap with me, and presume that two years have flown from us since the end of the last chapter ; or rather somewhat more than two years, for we would have it high midsummer when we take our last farewell of Surbiton Cottage.

But sundry changes had taken place at the Cottage, and of such a nature, that were it not for the old name's sake, we should now find ourselves bound to call the place Surbiton Villa, or Surbiton Hall, or Surbiton House. It certainly had no longer any right to the title of a cottage ; for Charley, in anticipation of what Lucina might do for him, had added on sundry rooms, a children's room on the ground floor, and a nursery above, and a couple of additional bedrooms on the other side, so that the house was now a comfortable abode for an increasing family.

At the time of which we are now speaking Lucina had not as yet done much ; for, in truth, Charley had been married but little over twelve months ; but there appeared every reason to believe that the goddess would be propitious. There was already one little rocking shrine, up

in that cosy temple opening out of Katie's bedroom—
we beg her pardon, we should have said Mrs. Charles
Tudor's bedroom—one precious tabernacle in which was
laid a little man-deity, a young Charley, to whom was
daily paid a multitude of very sincere devotions.

How precious are all the belongings of a first baby ;
how dear are the cradle, the lace-caps, the first coral, all
the little duds which are made with such punctilious care
and anxious efforts of nicest needlework to encircle that
small lump of pink humanity ! What care is taken that
all shall be in order ! See that basket lined with crimson
silk, prepared to hold his various garments, while the
mother, jealous of her nurse, insists on tying every string
with her own fingers. And then how soon the change
comes ; how different it is when there are ten of them,
and the tenth is allowed to inherit the well-worn wealth
which the ninth, a year ago, had received from the eighth.
There is no crimson silk basket then, I trow.

'Jane, Jane, where are my boots ?' 'Mary, I've lost
my trousers !' Such sounds are heard, shouted through
the house from powerful lungs.

'Why, Charley,' says the mother, as her eldest hope
rushes in to breakfast with dishevelled hair and dirty
hands, 'you've got no handkerchief on your neck—what
have you done with your handkerchief ?'

'No, mamma ; it came off in the hay-loft, and I can't
find it.'

'Papa,' says the lady wife, turning to her lord, who
is reading his newspaper over his coffee—'papa, you
really must speak to Charley ; he will not mind me.
He was dressed quite nicely an hour ago, and do see
what a figure he has made himself.'

'Charley,' says papa, not quite relishing this disturb-
ance in the midst of a very interesting badger-baiting—
'Charley, my boy, if you don't mind your P's and Q's,
you and I shall fall out ; mind that ;' and he again
goes on with his sport ; and mamma goes on with her
teapot, looking not exactly like Patience on a monument.

Such are the joys which await you, Mr. Charles Tudor ;
but not to such have you as yet arrived. As yet there
is but the one little pink deity in the rocking shrine

above; but one, at least, of your own. At the moment of which we are now speaking there were visitors at Surbiton Cottage, and the new nursery was brought into full use. Mr. and Mrs. Norman of Normansgrove were there with their two children and two maids, and grand-mamma Woodward had her hands quite full in the family nursery line.

It was a beautiful summer evening, and the two young mothers were sitting with Mrs. Woodward and Uncle Bat in the drawing-room, waiting for their lords' return from London. As usual, when they stayed late, the two men were to dine at their club and come down to tea. The nursemaids were walking on the lawn before the window with their charges, and the three ladies were busily employed with some fairly-written manuscript pages, which they were cutting carefully into shape, and arranging in particular form.

'Now, mamma,' said Katie, 'if you laugh once while you are reading it, you 'll spoil it all.'

'I 'll do the best I can, my dear, but I 'm sure I shall break down; you have made it so very abusive,' said Mrs. Woodward.

'Mamma, I think I 'll take out that about official priggism—hadn't I better, Linda?'

'Indeed, I think you had; I 'm sure mamma would break down there,' said Linda. 'Mamma, I 'm sure you would never get over the official priggism.'

'I don't think I should, my dear,' said Mrs. Wood-ward.

'What is it you are all concocting?' said Captain Cuttwater; 'some infernal mischief, I know, craving your pardons.'

'If you tell, Uncle Bat, I 'll never forgive you,' said Katie.

'Oh, you may trust me; I never spoil sport, if I can't make any; but the fun ought to be very good, for you 've been a mortal long time about it.'

And then the two younger ladies again went on clipping and arranging their papers, while Mrs. Woodward re-newed her protest that she would do her best as to reading their production. While they were thus employed the postman's knock was heard, and a letter was brought in from the far-away Australian exiles. The period at which these monthly missives arrived were moments of intense anxiety, and the letter was seized upon with eager avidity. It was from Gertrude to her mother, as all these letters were ; but in such a production they had a joint property, and it was hardly possible to say who first mastered its contents.

It will only be necessary here to give some extracts from the letter, which was by no means a short one. So much must be done in order that our readers may know something of the fate of those who perhaps may be called the hero and heroine of the tale. The author does not so call them ; he professes to do his work without any such appendages to his story—heroism there may be, and he hopes there is—more or less of it there should be in a true picture of most characters ; but heroes and heroines, as so called, are not commonly met with in our daily walks of life.

Before Gertrude's letter had been disposed of, Norman and Charley came in, and it was therefore discussed in full conclave. Alaric's path in the land of his banishment had not been over roses. The upward struggle of men, who have fallen from a high place once gained, that second mounting of the ladder of life, seldom is an easy path. He, and with him Gertrude and his children, had been called on to pay the full price of his backsliding. His history had gone with him to the Antipodes ; and, though the knowledge of what he had done was not there so absolute a clog upon his efforts, so overpowering a burden, as it would have been in London, still it was a burden and a heavy one.

It had been well for Gertrude that she had prepared herself to give up all her luxuries by her six months' residence in that Millbank Paradise of luxuries : for some time she had little enough in the 'good and happy land,' to which she had taught herself and her children to look forward. That land of promise had not flowed with milk and honey when first she put her foot upon its soil ; its produce for her had been gall and bitter herbs for many a weary month after she first landed. But her heart had never sunk within her. She had never forgotten that he, if he were to work well, should have at least one cheerful companion by his side. She had been true to him, then as ever. And yet it is so hard to be true to high principles in little things. The heroism of the Roman, who, for his country's sake, leapt his horse into a bottomless gulf, was as nothing to that of a woman who can keep her temper through poverty, and be cheerful in adversity.

Through poverty, scorn, and bad repute, under the privations of a hard life, separated from so many that she had loved, and from everything that she had liked, Gertrude had still been true to her ideas of her marriage vow ; true, also, to her pure and single love. She had entwined herself with him in sunny weather ; and when the storm came she did her best to shelter the battered stem to which she had trusted herself.

By degrees things mended with them ; and in this letter, which is now passing from eager hand to hand in Katie's drawing-room, Gertrude spoke with better hope of their future prospects.

'Thank God, we are once more all well,' she said ; ' and Alaric's spirits are higher than they were. He has, indeed, had much to try them. They think, I believe, in England, that any kind of work here is sure to command a high price ; of this I am quite sure, that in no employment in England are people so tasked as they are here. Alaric was four months in these men's counting-house, and I am sure another four months would have seen him in his grave. Though I knew not then what other provision might be made for us, I implored him, almost on my knees, to give up that. He was expected to be there for ten, sometimes twelve, hours a day ; and they thought he should always be kept going like a steam-engine. You know Alaric never was afraid of work ; but that would have killed him. And what was it for ? What did they give him for that—for all his talent, all his experience, all his skill ? And he did give them all. His salary was two pounds ten a week ! And then, when he told them of all he was doing for them, they had the baseness to remind him of ——. Dearest mother, is not

the world hard ? It was that that made me insist that
he should leave them.'

Alaric's present path was by no means over roses.
This certainly was a change from those days on which
he had sat, one of a mighty trio, at the Civil Service
Examination Board, striking terror into candidates by
a scratch of his pen, and making happy the desponding
heart by his approving nod. His ambition now was not
to sit among the magnates of Great Britain, and make
his voice thunder through the columns of the *Times* ; it
ranged somewhat lower at this period, and was confined
for the present to a strong desire to see his wife and
bairns sufficiently fed, and not left absolutely without
clothing. He inquired little as to the feeling of the electors
of Strathbogy.

And had he utterly forgotten the stirring motto of his
early days ? Did he ever mutter ' Excelsior ' to himself,
as, with weary steps, he dragged himself home from that
hated counting-house ? Ah ! he had fatally mistaken the
meaning of the word which he had so often used. There
had been the error of his life. ' Excelsior ! ' When he
took such a watchword for his use, he should surely have
taught himself the meaning of it.

He had now learnt that lesson in a school somewhat
of the sternest ; but, as time wore kindly over him, he
did teach himself to accept the lesson with humility.
His spirit had been wellnigh broken as he was carried
from that court-house in the Old Bailey to his prison on
the river-side ; and a broken spirit, like a broken goblet,
can never again become whole. But Nature was a kind
mother to him, and did not permit him to be wholly
crushed. She still left within the plant the germ of life,
which enabled it again to spring up and vivify, though
sorely bruised by the heels of those who had ridden over
it. He still repeated to himself the old watchword,
though now in humbler tone and more bated breath ;
and it may be presumed that he had now a clearer meaning
of its import.

' But his present place,' continued Gertrude, ' is much
—very much more suited to him. He is corresponding
clerk in the first bank here, and though his pay is nearly

double what it was at the other place, his hours of work are not so oppressive. He goes at nine and gets away at five—that is, except on the arrival or dispatch of the English mails.' Here was a place of bliss for a man who had been a commissioner, attending at the office at such hours as best suited himself, and having clerks at his beck to do all that he listed. And yet, as Gertrude said, this was a place of bliss to him. It was a heaven as compared with that other hell.

'Alley is such a noble boy,' said Gertrude, becoming almost joyous as she spoke of her own immediate cares. 'He is most like Katie, I think, of us all; and yet he is very like his papa. He goes to a day-school now, with his books slung over his back in a bag. You never saw such a proud little fellow as he is, and so manly. Charley is just like you—oh! so like. It makes me so happy that he is. He did not talk so early as Alley, but, nevertheless, he is more forward than the other children I see here. The little monkeys! they are neither of them the least like me. But one can always see oneself, and it don't matter if one does not.'

'If ever there was a brick, Gertrude is one,' said Norman.

'A brick!' said Charley—'why you might cut her to pieces, and build another Kensington palace out of the slices. I believe she is a brick.'

'I wonder whether I shall ever see her again?' said Mrs. Woodward, not with dry eyes.

'Oh yes, mamma,' said Katie. 'She shall come home to us some day, and we will endeavour to reward her for it all.'

Dear Katie, who will not love you for such endeavour? But, indeed, the reward for heroism cometh not here.

There was much more in the letter, but enough has been given for our purpose. It will be seen that hope yet remained both for Alaric and his wife; and hope not without a reasonable base. Bad as he had been, it had not been with him as with Undy Scott. The devil had not contrived to put his whole claw upon him. He had not divested himself of human affections and celestial hopes. He had not reduced himself to the present level.

of a beast, with the disadvantages of a soul and of an eternity, as the other man had done. He had not put himself beyond the pale of true brotherhood with his fellow-men. We would have hanged Undy had the law permitted us ; but now we will say farewell to the other, hoping that he may yet achieve exaltation of another kind.

And to thee, Gertrude—how shall we say farewell to thee, excluded as thou art from that dear home, where those who love thee so well are now so happy ? Their only care remaining is now thy absence. Adversity has tried thee in its crucible, and thou art found to be of virgin gold, unalloyed ; hadst thou still been lapped in prosperity, the true ring of thy sterling metal would never have been heard. Farewell to thee, and may those young budding flowerets of thine break forth into golden fruit to gladden thy heart in coming days !

The reading of Gertrude's letter, and the consequent discussion, somewhat put off the execution of the little scheme which had been devised for that evening's amusement ; but, nevertheless, it was still broad daylight when Mrs. Woodward consigned the precious document to her desk ; the drawing-room windows were still open, and the bairns were still being fondled in the room. It was the first week in July, when the night almost loses her dominion, and when those hours which she generally claims as her own, become the pleasantest of the day.

' Oh, Charley,' said Katie, at last, ' we have great news for you, too. Here is another review on " The World's Last Wonder." '

Now ' The World's Last Wonder ' was Charley's third novel ; but he was still sensitive enough on the subject of reviews to look with much anxiety for what was said of him. These notices were habitually sent down to him at Hampton, and his custom was to make his wife or her mother read them, while he sat by in lordly ease in his arm-chair, receiving homage when homage came to him, and criticizing the critics when they were uncivil.

' Have you ? ' said Charley. ' What is it ? Why did you not show it me before ? '

' Why, we were talking of dear Gertrude,' said Katie ;

' and it is not so pleasant but that it will keep. What paper do you think it is ? '

' What paper ? how on earth can I tell ?—show it me.'

' No ; but do guess, Charley ; and then mamma will read it—pray guess now.'

' Oh, bother, I can't guess. *The Literary Censor,* I suppose—I know they have turned against me.'

' No, it 's not that,' said Linda ; ' guess again.'

' The *Guardian Angel,*' said Charley.

' No—that angel has not taken you under his wings as yet,' said Katie.

' I know it 's not the *Times,*' said Charley, ' for I have seen that.'

' O no,' said Katie, seriously ; ' if it was anything of that sort, we would not keep you in suspense.'

' Well, I 'll be shot if I guess any more—there are such thousands of them.'

' But there is only one *Daily Delight,*' said Mrs. Woodward.

' Nonsense ! ' said Charley. ' You don't mean to tell me that my dear old friend and foster-father has fallen foul of me—my old teacher and master, if not spiritual pastor ; well—well—well ! The ingratitude of the age ! I gave him my two beautiful stories, the first-fruits of my vine, all for love ; to think that he should now lay his treacherous axe to the root of the young tree—well, give it here.'

' No—mamma will read it—we want Harry to hear it.'

' O yes—let Mrs. Woodward read it,' said Harry. ' I trust it is severe. I know no man who wants a dragging over the coals more peremptorily than you do.'

' Thankee, sir. Well, grandmamma, go on ; but if there be anything very bad, give me a little notice, for I am nervous.'

And then Mrs. Woodward began to read, Linda sitting with Katie's baby in her arms, and Katie performing a similar office for her sister.

" ' The World's Last Wonder,' by Charles Tudor, Esq.''

' He begins with a lie,' said Charley, ' for I never called myself Esquire.'

' Oh, that was a mistake,' said Katie, forgetting herself.

'Men of that kind shouldn't make such mistakes,' said
Charley. 'When one fellow attempts to cut up another
fellow, he ought to take special care that he does it fairly.'

" By the author of ' Bathos.' "

' I didn't put that in,' said Charley, ' that was the
publisher. I only put Charles Tudor.'

' Don't be so touchy, Charley, and let me go on,' said
Mrs. Woodward.

' Well, fire away—it's good fun to you, I dare say, as
the fly said to the spider.'

' Well, Charley, at any rate we are not the spiders,'
said Linda. Katie said nothing, but she could not help
feeling that she must look rather spiderish.

" Mr. Tudor has acquired some little reputation as a
humorist, but as is so often the case with those who make
us laugh, his very success will prove his ruin."

' Then upon my word the *Daily Delight* is safe,' said
Charley. 'It will never be ruined in that way.'

" There is an elaborate jocosity about him, a determined eternity of most industrious fun, which gives us
the idea of a boy who is being rewarded for having duly
learnt by rote his daily lesson out of Joe Miller."

' Now, I'll bet ten to one he has never read the book
at all—well, never mind—go on.'

" ' The World's Last Wonder ' is the description of
a woman who kept a secret under certain temptations
to reveal it, which, as Mr. Tudor supposes, might have
moved any daughter of Eve to break her faith."

' I haven't supposed anything of the kind,' said Charley.

" This secret, which we shall not disclose, as we would
not wish to be thought less trustworthy than Mr. Tudor's
wonderful woman—— "

' We shall find that he does disclose it, of course ; that
is the way with all of them.'

—" Is presumed to permeate the whole three volumes."

' It is told at full length in the middle of the second,'
said Charley.

" And the effect upon the reader of course is, that he
has ceased to interest himself about it, long before it is
disclosed to him !

" The lady in question is engaged to be married to

a gentleman, a circumstance which in the pages of a novel is not calculated to attract much special attention. She is engaged to be married, but the gentleman who has the honour of being her intended sposo—— ''

'Intended sposo!' said Charley, expressing by his upturned lip a withering amount of scorn—'how well I know the fellow's low attempts at wit! That's the editor himself—that's my literary papa. I know him as well as though I had seen him at it.'

Katie and Mrs. Woodward exchanged furtive glances, but neither of them moved a muscle of her face.

'' But the gentleman who has the honour of being her intended sposo,'' continued Mrs. Woodward.

'What the devil's a sposo?' said Uncle Bat, who was sitting in an arm-chair with a handkerchief over his head.

'Why, you're not a sposo, Uncle Bat,' said Linda; 'but Harry is, and so is Charley.'

'Oh, I see,' said the captain; 'it's a bird with his wings clipped.'

'' But the gentleman who has the honour of being her intended sposo—— '' again read Mrs. Woodward.

'Now I'm sure I'm speaking by the card,' said Charley, 'when I say that there is not another man in London who could have written that line, and who would have used so detestable a word. I think I remember his using it in one of his lectures to me; indeed I'm sure I do. Sposo! I should like to tweak his nose oh!'

'Are you going to let me go on?' said Mrs. Woodward—'' her intended sposo ''—Charley gave a kick with his foot and satisfied himself with that—'' is determined to have nothing to say to her in the matrimonial line till she has revealed to him this secret which he thinks concerns his own honour.''

'There, I knew he'd tell it.'

'He has not told it yet,' said Norman.

'' The lady, however, is obdurate, wonderfully so, of course, seeing that she is the world's last wonder, and so the match is broken off. But the secret is of such a nature that the lady's invincible objection to revealing it is bound up with the fact of her being a promised bride.''

' I wonder he didn't say sposa,' said Charley.

' I never thought of that,' said Katie.

Mrs. Woodward and Linda looked at her, but Charley did not, and her blunder passed by unnoticed.

" Now that she is free from her matrimonial bonds, she is free also to tell the secret ; and indeed the welfare both of the gentleman and of the lady imperiously demands that it should be told. Should he marry her, he is destined to learn it after his marriage ; should he not marry her, he may hear it at any time. She sends for him and tells him, not the first of these facts, by doing which all difficulty would have at once been put an end to—— "

' It is quite clear he has never read the story, quite clear,' said Charley.

" She tells him only the last, viz., that as they are now strangers he may know the secret ; but that when once known it will raise a barrier between them that no years, no penance, no sorrow on his part, no tenderness on hers, can ever break down. She then asks him—will he hear the secret ? "

' She does not ask any such thing,' said Charley ; ' the letter that contains it has been already sent to him. She merely gives him an opportunity of returning it unopened.'

" The gentleman, who is not without a grain of obstinacy in his own composition and many grains of curiosity, declares it to be impossible that he can go to the altar in ignorance of facts which he is bound to know, and the lady, who seems to be of an affectionate disposition, falls in tenderness at his feet. She is indeed in a very winning mood, and quite inclined to use every means allowable to a lady for retaining her lover ; every means that is short of that specially feminine one of telling her secret.

" We will give an extract from this love scene, partly for the sake of its grotesque absurdity—— "

Charley kicked out another foot, as though he thought that the editor of the *Daily Delight* might perhaps be within reach.

" —And partly because it gives a fair example of the manner in which Mr. Tudor endeavours to be droll even in the midst of his most tender passages.

" ' Leonora was at this time seated—— ' "

'Oh, skip the extract,' said Charley; 'I suppose there are three or four pages of it?'

'It goes down to where Leonora says that his fate and her own are in his hands.'

'Yes, about three columns,' said Charley; 'that's an easy way of making an article—eh, Harry?'

'*Aliter non fit, amice, liber,*' said the classical Norman.

'Well, skip the extract, grandmamma.'

"Now, did anyone ever before read such a mixture of the bombastic and the burlesque? We are called upon to cry over every joke, and, for the life of us, we cannot hold our sides when the catastrophes occur. It is a salad in which the pungency of the vinegar has been wholly subdued by the oil, and the fatness of the oil destroyed by the tartness of the vinegar."

'His old simile,' said Charley; 'he was always talking about literary salads.'

"The gentleman, of course, gives way at the last minute," continued Mrs. Woodward. "The scene in which he sits with the unopened letter lying on his table before him has some merit; but this probably arises from the fact that the letter is dumb, and the gentleman equally so."

'D—nation!' said Charley, whose patience could not stand such impudence at this.

"The gentleman, who, as we should have before said, is the eldest son of a man of large reputed fortune——"

'There—I knew he'd tell it.'

'Oh, but he hasn't told it,' said Norman.

'Doesn't the word "reputed" tell it?'

"—The eldest son of a man of large reputed fortune, does at last marry the heroine; and then he discovers—— But what he discovers, those who feel any interest in the matter may learn from the book itself; we must profess that we felt none.

"We will not say there is nothing in the work indicative of talent. The hero's valet, Jacob Brush, and the heroine's lady's-maid, Jacintha Pintail, are both humorous and good in their way. Why it should be so, we do not pretend to say; but it certainly does appear to us that Mr. Tudor is more at home in the servants' hall than in the lady's boudoir."

' Abominable scoundrel ! ' said Charley.

" But what we must chiefly notice," continued the article, " in the furtherance of those views by which we profess that we are governed——"

' Now, I know, we are to have something very grandiloquent and very false,' said Charley.

"—Is this : that no moral purpose can be served by the volumes before us. The hero acts wrongly throughout, but nevertheless he is rewarded at last. There is no Nemesis——"

' No what ? ' said Charley, jumping up from his chair and looking over the table.

' No Nemesis,' said Mrs. Woodward, speaking with only half-sustained voice, and covering with her arms the document which she had been reading.

Charley looked sharply at his wife, then at Linda, then at Mrs. Woodward. Not one of them could keep her face. He made a snatch at the patched-up manuscript, and as he did so, Katie almost threw out of her arms the baby she was holding.

' Take him, Harry, take him,' said she, handing over the child to his father. And then gliding quick as thought through the furniture of the drawing-room, she darted out upon the lawn, to save herself from the coming storm.

Charley was quickly after her ; but as he made his exit, one chair fell to the right of him, and another to the left. Mrs. Woodward followed them, and so did Harry and Linda, each with a baby.

And then Captain Cuttwater, waking from his placid nap, rubbed his eyes in wondering amazement.

' What the devil is all the row about ? ' said he. But there was nobody to answer him.

THE END